LORDS OF THE EARTH

"MONEY, POWER, TEXAS . . . are the forces embodied in Wade Kingslea, whom his grandson suspects not only of involvement in President Kennedy's assassination but of killing his own childhood sweetheart. Mr. Anderson vividly chronicles Wade's wildcatting adventures, as well as the subsequent family disputes that make his grandson turn against him."

—*The New York Times*

"AN AMERICAN CLASSIC . . . larger-than-life . . . skillfully written . . . The book reads as though it were happening rather than recorded."

—*Washington Weekly*

"POWERFUL . . . *Lords of the Earth* paints a detailed picture of Texas mores, celebrates the exhilaration of life in Washington at the cutting edge of the New Frontier, and provides fresh insight into the tragedy of November 22, 1963."

—*Publishers Weekly*

More

LORDS OF THE EARTH

"A KNOCK-OUT OF A NOVEL ... wide-ranging and big as the Texas it so absorbingly depicts, with a roaring plot, a marvelous sense of time and place, and a fascinating range of characters. Superbly constructed, this is a rich and gripping book that never stops moving and never stops surprising. It had me riveted, and I thoroughly enjoyed it."

—Edward Stewart,
author of *Ballerina*

"A GREAT SLICE OF AMERICAN HISTORY ... superb ... strong and gripping ... it moves with roaring leaps and bounds."

—*Nashville Banner*

"EXCITING PEOPLE AND DRAMATIC EVENTS ... Anderson skillfully weaves historical events and true political figures into the story. The action dips and spins in unexpected ways, holding the reader's attention to the last paragraph."

—*Pittsburgh Press*

LORDS OF THE EARTH

"A KING OF A BOOK... various as Texas, rich and surprising as the oil from the Texas gushers that underlie it... One of those hefty, powerful three-generational novels that grip us every decade or so, implacably tearing us away from work, sleep, family, everything!"
                                    —Les Whitten,
                     author of *Conflict of Interest*

"GREAT FUN!... Power, corruption and a Fort Worth connection... Every Fort Worth legend, infamous and otherwise, is here."
                          —*Fort Worth Star-Telegram*

"ANDERSON HAS WRITTEN A COMPELLING STORY!"
                                    —*Library Journal*

PATRICK ANDERSON

LORDS OF THE EARTH

A JOVE BOOK

This Jove book contains the complete
text of the original hardcover edition.
It has been completely reset in a typeface
designed for easy reading, and was printed
from new film.

LORDS OF THE EARTH

A Jove Book / published by arrangement with
Doubleday & Company, Inc.

PRINTING HISTORY
Doubleday & Company edition / April 1984
Jove edition / August 1986

Jove Books are published by The Berkley Publishing Group,
200 Madison Avenue, New York, N.Y. 10016.
The words "A JOVE BOOK" and the "J" with sunburst
are trademarks belonging to Jove Publications, Inc.

*For Larry McMurtry and
Tommy Thompson*

Wade Kingslea and Philip Kingslea

Fort Worth
1964

The richest man in Texas stood accused of a brutal murder, and in the streets of his hometown his fellow Texans hailed him as a hero.

Inside the huge, ornate old Tarrant County courthouse an impassioned young prosecutor declared that Wade Kingslea was a dangerous man who belonged in jail.

But outside, on the courthouse steps, as indifferent to the prosecutor's charges as to the blazing Texas sun, hundreds of the billionaire's admirers rallied to his cause. These were not Kingslea's fellow oilmen but working-class Texans who had savored the Kingslea legend for a lifetime and now unquestioningly supported the old wildcatter in his hour of need.

As they awaited news from the courtroom, these men and women of Fort Worth eagerly swapped Wade Kingslea stories, no longer caring what was fact and what was fiction. They said he had killed three men back in the boomtown where he made his first fortune. They declared he had personally negotiated with Hitler to try to free his son Hoyt from a German POW camp and that he had offered a million dollars to any doctor who could cure his son Coyle's alcoholism. They alleged he had fathered a daughter by a famous movie star who killed herself because he would not marry her and that he once offered his wife Livie a hundred million dollars for a divorce and she laughed in his face.

Some said, not disapprovingly, that Kingslea had masterminded the assassination of President John Kennedy in nearby Dallas a year earlier.

Still, for all the violence of these tales, none of the taletellers suggested that the oilman was guilty of the brutal murder for which he now stood accused.

"Hell, why would Wade Kingslea kill anybody?" demanded a young man who drove a truck for Mrs. Baird's Bakery. "He'd hire somebody to do it for him!"

"It's them Kennedys," declared a hefty woman who sold frosted donuts at Leonard Brothers department store. "That Bobby Kennedy—they're trying to get back at Wade for Dallas!"

"I'll tell you one damn thing for sure—Wade's a great man!" proclaimed an old-timer in a Lone Star beer cap.

Back inside the courtroom the young prosecutor was demanding that Fort Worth's most celebrated citizen be caged like a wild beast. "Your honor," he cried, "a decent woman has been murdered in her own home. This man was seen fleeing the scene. With his money, if you grant him bail, who's to say he won't flee the country?"

The sleepy-eyed old justice of the peace looked amused. "Wade, you don't aim to run off to Timbuktu, do you?" he asked.

"I've never run from anything or anyone in my life," the oilman declared.

"I didn't reckon you would," the JP drawled. "I'm gonna free you on your own recognizance. That means your word is your bond—I'd say that's good enough for most folks here in Cowtown. That's all—you can go."

Moments later Wade Kingslea emerged from the massive sandstone courthouse. His security men held shouting reporters at bay as the tycoon let the cheers and rebel yells of his admirers wash over him. Finally he raised one hand, in a vaguely religious gesture, and the multitude fell silent, transfixed by this proud, erect, tough old man with the silver hair and the glittering hawk's eyes.

"My good friends," he boomed. "In this dark hour I draw my strength from you. Together no power on earth can defeat us. God bless you and God bless our great state of Texas!"

The cheering crowd parted to make way as Kingslea started down the thirteen steps to his waiting Cadillac. Suddenly, out of nowhere, a slender, well-dressed young man leaped out and blocked the oilman's path. They stood frozen, face to face, and some onlookers realized that they shared the same sharp features, the same dark, smoldering eyes.

"You killed her," the young man said furiously.

"No, I didn't kill her," the oilman replied evenly.

"You killed her—and I can prove it!"

The crowd pressed close, savoring this new twist in the Kingslea saga.

"That's his grandson," a woman whispered. "The one who worked for the Kennedys."

"He wrote a book too," a man added. "Made hisself a pile of money."

Wade Kingslea and his grandson Philip, their eyes fixed on one another, were oblivious to the crowd around them. Their lives had been building toward this confrontation for a quarter-century.

"I promise you this," Philip declared. "If the law doesn't make you pay, I will!"

"You're so like me, Philip," the oilman said. "That must be why you hate me so."

"You killed her, you son of a bitch," Philip cried and swung wildly at his grandfather's proud face.

The older man, no stranger to brawls, sidestepped the blow gracefully. Three Kingslea Oil security men rushed forward, knocked Philip to the sidewalk, then melted back into the crowd. Wade Kingslea stepped into his silver-gray Fleetwood and was soon speeding west, into the setting sun. Philip staggered to his feet as the crowd called its farewells to his grandfather.

"God bless you, Wade!"

"We're with you, buddy, all the way!"

Philip fought free of several reporters and pushed his way out of the crowd, whose cheers echoed in his ears, mocking his fury.

To these people, his grandfather was a god, a philosopher, a father, a lover, a hero who had brought excitement and possibility to their drab lives, a champion they would forgive any sin except that of boring them, which was of course the one sin he would never commit.

To these people, Wade Kingslea was, and would always be, a lord of the earth.

Still, Philip vowed, the old man would not kill with impunity. One way or another, he would have his revenge.

_ Book I _

Wade·Kingslea

Goodwill, Texas
1920

CHAPTER ONE

The news of the Goodwill strike lit a fire in Wade Kingslea's guts, a fire that gnawed at him until he thought he might go mad. It had been like that before, with the strikes at Ranger and Desdemona and Vernon. Each time a part of him burned to go seek his fortune in the boomtown, the part that made him different from everyone he knew, the part that believed his should be some grander destiny than a farmer's life in Liberty. Each time he had been tormented by the stories of men as poor and ignorant as himself who'd answered the call of the oil fields and come back rich. Yet each time, finally, habit, caution, and the silken ties of family kept Wade Kingslea home.

This time was different. On a Saturday morning in June, a few months after first word of the Goodwill strike, Kingslea was buying seed in the Liberty general store when there was a commotion in the street. Roy Cooley, the local undertaker's smart-aleck son, came roaring up in a shiny new Model T, honking his horn and yelling his fool head off. He was just back from Goodwill, he told the men who gathered round, where he'd bought an oil lease for one thousand dollars and sold it the next day for twelve thousand, after a gusher came in nearby. Wade Kingslea, hearing the story, slipped away from the crowd and went behind the lumberyard and beat his fist against a wall until it bled. Was he a coward, chained forever to his plow, while other men reaped fortunes? In church the next morning he prayed for guidance, and after Sunday dinner, when his sons had left the table, he told Harriet, "I'm going out to Goodwill to try my luck."

Her eyes widened. "Wade, you don't know nothing about oil." She was a sturdy, fresh-faced woman who wanted nothing more in life than what she had. Sometimes he loved her for her goodness and sometimes he hated her for it.

"I'm leaving this afternoon. I prayed on it."

She began to cry. "When will you come back?"

"When I'm rich," he told her. "Rich as sin."

He wished he could tell her more, could tell her it wasn't just money but freedom he wanted, could make her understand what it was to hate yourself for being ordinary, to dream of worlds you had never seen, but he knew Harriet could not understand. He touched her hand and went to pack his bag. After that he said good-bye to his sons. Coyle, who was eight and plump and gentle like his mother, began to cry. Hoyt, at six, was lean and hard like his father and begged to be taken along. It was only when Wade Kingslea hugged his sons for the last time that his emotions broke through. Trembling, fighting back tears, he left the simple frame farmhouse and began the two-mile walk to the train station. Once he started he never looked back.

Wade Kingslea was not alone in his ambitions. The little crossroads station was packed with would-be millionaires waiting for the train up from Fort Worth. They spent the afternoon drinking, talking, gambling, reading, tossing baseballs, and most of all swapping rumors: the Goodwill field had run dry . . . John D. Rockefeller had bought up the field for a billion dollars . . . the price of oil had plummeted to two cents a barrel . . . the governor had sent in Texas Rangers to put down riots at Goodwill . . . the rumors went on endlessly, but Kingslea ignored them and the men who traded in them. He was a tall, lean, broad-shouldered Texan of twenty-six with sharp, agonized features, dark, burning eyes, and thick, pitch-black hair. In his jeans, suspenders, work boots, flannel shirt, and broad-brimmed hat he looked not unlike the men who surrounded him, but he knew from the start he was different. He watched men nervously making small talk, seeking friends, but he wanted no talk and he wanted no friend. He knew that these men were his competitors, that there were not enough gushers in Goodwill for them all, so he kept to himself, as he had all his life, and the cold glint in his eyes was such that no man challenged his privacy.

The train limped into the station in early evening, already packed with boomtown pilgrims, and the waiting men became an angry, shoving, snarling mob as they fought to get aboard. Kingslea watched as a massive, scar-faced man in a red satin shirt jerked out a blackjack and bashed the head of a skinny farmboy who'd gotten in his way. Kingslea pushed his way onto the last car. It stank of whiskey, piss, and chewing tobacco, and men were packed in like cattle. At first they still snarled and shoved, but as the train moved slowly out of the station, with the sun burning down in the west, a certain peace fell over the travelers. Men settled on their haunches in the aisles or leaned against the walls. They passed whiskey bottles about, or played cards or slept, and two buck-toothed brothers sang a bawdy tune about Alice in a palace in Dallas.

Wade Kingslea stood at the front of the car. Once he saw how many of the men were drunk or armed or both, he felt better standing. One reason for his watchfulness was that the big scar-faced man with the satin shirt and blackjack was sitting in the front row of seats, not ten feet from him; he looked to Kingslea like a rattlesnake coiled to strike. Sitting beside him, in the aisle seat, was a gaunt, white-haired old man with a hacking cough. The old man was wearing a Prince Albert coat that had seen better days, a starched shirt, a Windsor tie, and expensive, hand-stitched cowboy boots. Every few minutes he broke into agonizing fits of coughing, holding a linen handkerchief to his mouth, and when the coughing subsided he would sip from a silver flask.

Kingslea studied this odd pair of seatmates, then his eyes darted down the aisle to a poker game. A moon-faced farmer in overalls and a plaid shirt had raked in three straight pots and was laughing loudly at his good fortune. Kingslea watched the poker players, ready to move fast if trouble broke out, then the trouble erupted right in front of him.

"Shut up that damn coughing, old man!" the scar-faced man roared.

"I beg your pardon, sir," the old man gasped, holding the handkerchief to his mouth.

"Beg my pardon, hell! Get away from me!" The big man, whose scar ran from his left earlobe to the point of his chin, gave the old man a violent shove that sent him sprawling into the aisle. He got to his feet slowly with blood oozing from his nose.

"My bag, if you please," he said, pointing to the purple-flowered carpetbag he'd left beneath his seat.

"Go away, you old fool, or I'll throw your damn bag out the window," the troublemaker roared.

The car had fallen silent, except for the steady clack-clack-clack of wheels on tracks. Even the poker game was suspended as the confrontation played itself out. The old man stood unsteadily in the aisle, holding his dirty handkerchief to his bleeding nose; the troublemaker plopped a muddy boot on the empty seat beside him

What happened next was a turning point in Wade Kingslea's life, and he never fully understood why he did what he did. He became known as a cold, hard, ruthless man, and he had little cause to quarrel with those terms. Yet there was another side to Kingslea in those early days, a side that hated oppression, that ached for the old man being tormented by the bully. It was not that any two-legged bully had ever molested Wade Kingslea; a few had tried and had their profiles permanently altered for their poor judgment. But Kingslea had known other oppressors: barren soil, drought, thin-lipped bankers who could only say no, ignorance and poverty that gripped a man and his family like a bitter, bone-chilling north wind that never stopped blowing. Those were the enemies he was fleeing on this stinking train and it was the misfortune of the scar-faced man to bring them all before Kingslea's eyes in one burning, blinding flash.

"Give the man his bag," Kingslea said.

"Do *what?*" the bully roared.

"You heard me. Give him his bag."

"I'll give you hell," the big man shouted, and he leaped from his seat with his blackjack flying.

Kingslea moved as swiftly as a panther; he might have been waiting all his life for this moment. His left hand shot up and caught the attacker's wrist in an iron grip, and at the same instant he sank his right fist deep into his belly. They struggled in the aisle as other passengers scrambled out of harm's way. The man butted Kingslea's chin with the top of his head, then jerked a knife from his belt and slashed at his ribs. Kingslea howled with pain, kicked the big man in the crotch, seized his knife hand, and sank his teeth into his neck. The knife clattered to the floor and the two of them fell to the aisle. They rolled about for an instant, then Kingslea was atop the scar-faced man, astride his chest, making wild, guttural noises, pounding his head against the floor. The fight was over as suddenly as it had begun, but Kingslea was not finished. He seized the unconscious man by his bloody hair, jerked him to the car's open door, and flung him out into the night.

The car was quiet as a tomb. "Jesus H. Christ," someone whispered. Kingslea stood swaying in the aisle, wild-eyed, gasping for breath, blood soaking his shirt, staring back blindly at the fifty men who were staring at him. The first person to move was the old man with the cough who had sparked the fight. He stood up and asked, "We don't happen to have a doctor in the car, do we?"

No one spoke.

"Well, I'm kind of a half-ass doctor myself," the old man said, "so I guess I'll do the honors."

He gently unbuttoned Kingslea's shirt and stared at the six-inch gash across his ribs.

"If I had the equipment," he said, "I'd say you could use some stitches. But since I don't, my expert opinion is that it'll heal on its own. The best I can do is try to stop any infection. Hold still, son, this will hurt." He dug into his carpetbag and pulled out a clean handkerchief. He soaked the handkerchief with whiskey from his silver flask and washed the wound with it. Kingslea shut his eyes but uttered no cry or protest. Then the old man produced some tape and gauze and bandaged the wound as best he could. When he finished he looked up at Kingslea, who still had not spoken.

"Young man, I've got an empty seat beside me now," he said, "and I'd be honored if you'd join me. It don't look like my former seatmate will be returning."

Kingslea nodded, seeming to come out of his trance, and sat down beside the old man. Up and down the railroad car men relaxed and the poker game started up again.

"Did I kill him?" Kingslea whispered.

The older man shrugged. "Who knows? This car ain't going so fast, and his kind is hard to kill. Here, try some of this—it's better taken internally." He handed over his flask and Kingslea took a long swallow. "Permit me to introduce myself, young man. My name is William V. Festus. Mostly they call me Uncle Billy Festus. Perhaps you've heard of me."

Kingslea shook his head.

"Well, no matter," Festus said. "The main thing is, I appreciate you helping me out."

Kingslea felt himself drawing back, the way he always did when people tried to embrace him, to ensnarl him. "Mister," he said, "I didn't do that to help you out. I didn't like that son of a bitch. I ain't looking to be your bodyguard."

Billy Festus was not offended. "Fair enough," he said. "But you're looking to go to Goodwill and make a bundle in oil—am I right?"

Kingslea ignored the question. Digging into his bag, he came up with a chicken sandwich and began to eat it.

"Well, I'm headed for Goodwill too, and it just so happens that there aren't five men in the world who know more about the oil business than I do. If you want to hook up with me, young man, I'll make you rich!"

Kingslea chewed his sandwich thoughtfully before he replied. "Mister, if you're such a genius of the oil industry, how come you're packed in this cattlecar with the rest of us bums?"

Festus smiled. "A fair question," he said. "Young man ... dammit, what *is* your name?"

"Wade Kingslea."

"Well, Wade Kingslea, to save us some time, kindly do me the honor of looking through some material I have here." He took a large envelope from his bag and handed it over. Kingslea, curious, began to skim through the yellowing old newspaper clippings. There were news stories with headlines like "Local Man Drills Gusher" and "Uncle Billy Does It Again," and there were photographs too, of a younger Billy Festus standing by an oil rig, posing at the wheel of a shiny new automobile, even relaxing in his own private railroad car.

"Where's all them fancy cars now?" Kingslea asked.

The old oilman stared out the window at the moon-swept prairie. "Where are the snows of yesteryear?" he sighed. "Wade, I made my first fortune at Spindletop and I lost it trying to buck Standard Oil. I made more fortunes in California, Louisiana, Oklahoma, and managed to lose them all too. I don't remember all the details. One fortune went to my ex-wife. One went down that sewer they call the stock market. One I just got drunk and when I sobered up it was gone. But the point is, son, that I'm a wildcatter, and I always come back. If there's oil under the ground, Billy Festus will find it. And I'm offering you a chance to be my partner."

"Out of the goodness of your heart?"

Festus coughed and spit noisily into his handkerchief. "No, certainly not, although I fancy there's more goodness in my heart than in most hearts hereabouts. No, I need you because the oil business has changed. The *world* has changed. Back in the Spindletop days there was honor in the oil business. Trust. A handshake was a deal, and that was that. But all that's gone now. The war killed it, killed our idealism. We sent off bright-eyed boys and told 'em they were fighting the war to end war, and we got back a million bitter, dangerous men. I saw it at Ranger and Desdemona. Honor? Hell, every pimp and thief and cutthroat and confidence man in a thousand miles flocked to those little towns like flies to shit. Your life wasn't worth a dime there, and it'll be the same in Goodwill. So, to answer your question, I need you because you're young and strong and can handle yourself in a tight spot. And you need me because I know the oil business!"

Wade Kingslea's eyes narrowed. "I reckon I can learn the oil business on my own," he said. "I figure to get a job on a rig and save my money and when I know enough I'll buy my own rig."

"Oh you will, will you?" the old man said scornfully. "You and ten thousand other dirt farmers who don't know oil from buttermilk! You ever been up on a rig, boy? You got any idea how slick they get? You got any idea how many farm boys fall off 'em and break their backs? You know what's the first thing they do when they hire you for roughnecking? They make you sign the death warrant. You know what that is? It's a document that says if you fall off the rig or stick your hand in the engine or get burnt up in a fire, they don't owe you one damn penny."

"I can take care of myself," Kingslea said stubbornly.

"Maybe you can. So you make ten dollars a day roughnecking and don't get killed. You think you'll save any money living in a boomtown? Even if you did, by the time you knew enough to start out on your own all the decent land'll be leased and most likely the whole damn field'll have gone dry. Listen, Wade, and I'll give you some practical advice. If you want to make some money, go back home and load up your wagon with all the food you can carry. Take it to Goodwill and open you a little lunchroom and if you work hard and serve decent meals you'll make a thousand dollars a week. You won't get *rich*. You won't be an *oilman*. But you could do worse."

Festus doubled up with coughing again, and when he finished his voice was a whisper. "But you don't look to me like somebody who wants to sell sandwiches, Wade. You look to me to have fire in your belly. You look to me like somebody who thinks he's as smart and as tough as any man alive and wants a chance to prove it. Maybe I'm wrong about you. But if I'm right, and you're ready to tackle the world head-on, and maybe make yourself a million dollars in the process, then I'd suggest you join up with me."

Kingslea stared out the window and saw mesquite trees and clumps of sagebrush racing past, bathed in moonlight. He felt as if he was on a ship in the midst of a vast, unknown ocean, sailing toward some unimagined destiny. For the first time in his life he was afraid.

"Who are you, son?" the old wildcatter asked. "Where are you from?"

"I'm nobody. Nobody from nowhere."

Festus waited.

"But I don't intend to stay nobody."

"No reason why you should."

"I left my wife and two sons this morning. Just up and left. I love those boys more than life itself."

"I did the same, Wade, a long time ago."

"Do you still think about them?"

"Every day. A thousand times. But a man has to do what he has to do, and I had to go find oil. There's no right and wrong to it."

"It's not the money. It's . . . it's like you said . . . It's being what you can be. What you have to be. I'm going to be somebody important in this world. It's in me. I've known all my life. Do you understand what I'm saying?"

"I said it myself once upon a time."

"Then you don't think I'm crazy?"

"Hell, I'd bet money that you'll be rich before Christmas if you join up with me. The thing you don't realize is that's when your troubles begin."

Wade Kingslea gazed uncertainly at the old wildcatter. "I guess we could give it a try," he said.

"Good," Billy Festus said. "Now, if you'll excuse me, partner, I'll get a little shut-eye. We've got us a big day ahead tomorrow."

The train's closest stop to Goodwill was the little town of Norway. They pulled into the station there in the middle of the night and found it lit with bonfires and packed with hundreds of men. Many of the men were broken and torn, held together with splints and bloody bandages; they were the wounded, retreating from the oil-field wars. There were men who had shattered their bones in falls from rigs, men who had stuck untrained hands into unfamiliar machinery, men whose heads had been broken or their guts ripped open in barroom brawls and back-alley robberies. As the train jerked to a halt at the station they limped forward, empty-eyed and pale, voyagers who had sought the boomtown's black gold and found only pain and disillusion.

A second group greeted the arriving train. These men bore no wounds, only looks of desperation as they waved scraps of paper and cried out that they had sure-fire oil leases for sale. They were, in fact, doing a brisk business, as the new arrivals, scrambling down from the train, hastened to buy into the oil-field bonanza before it was too late. One of the salesmen seized Billy Festus' arm. "Uncle Billy, I got a lease that'll make you a million," he cried.

"No thank you, my friend, no thank you," Festus said, and he and Kingslea pushed their way through the mob to a line of wagons, cars, and trucks that were bound for Goodwill, five miles to the west.

"How much money you got, Wade?" Festus asked.

"About sixty dollars. How about you?"

"About the same. Got nowhere to go but up, do we?"

Kingslea found a mule skinner who offered them a ride to Goodwill atop a wagonload of potatoes for ten dollars, but Uncle Billy insisted that they ride in a Packard sedan whose driver wanted to charge them twenty.

"Don't we need to save the money?" Kingslea protested.

"Son, in the oil business you've got to think about appearances," Festus said. "Sometimes you spend ten dollars and make a million."

Their driver was a lanky, sad-faced fellow named Grimes who said he'd been Goodwill's town barber for twenty years. His only other passenger was a tiny, bright-eyed young woman with fluffy brown hair and a merry smile. She wore a high-necked, lime-green dress and a flowered hat, and she smiled at them demurely as they climbed into the dusty back seat.

"Howdy, miss," Festus said with a tip of his hat. "You headed for Goodwill?"

"Yes," the girl admitted. "I'm employed there."

"A schoolteacher, I'll wager," Festus said.

"In a manner of speaking," she said and cast a ladylike gaze out the window.

Wade Kingslea stared in awe at the girl's exquisite profile. She looked like someone he'd seen in magazines, one of those ethereal women who drove new cars and wore fine furs in the distant world of the rich. He wanted to ask her name, to make her recognize him, but the words would not emerge. Frustrated, exhausted, he flopped his head back on the seat and was soon asleep.

The five-mile drive took almost two hours. The narrow dirt road was clogged with an endless procession of cars, men on foot, and trucks and mule-drawn wagons loaded with food, lumber, steel pipe, and other boomtown necessities. Cars broke down, horns honked, mule skinners cursed and cracked their whips, mules whinnied their complaints, and men on foot laughed and sang as they trudged along. "Night's the best time to make this trip," Grimes, the driver, declared. "Hot days, mules just keel over and die. And Lordamighty, you oughta see this road when it rains!"

Inevitably, Grimes told his story. Barber or chauffeur, he was a man determined to have a captive audience. "I cut hair in Goodwill fer twenty years and done all right," Grimes began. "Had me forty acres north of town I growed pigs on. Then all this oil craziness began. Right after the first gusher, a man said he'd give me ten thousand dollars fer a lease on my land. I figgered he was crazy and told him I weren't interested, so he came back the next day and offered me twenty thousand and brung the cash with him in a gunny sack. Well hell, I took it, and that's when my troubles began. Things had started getting kinda rough in Goodwill. A bad element was arriving. So me and the wife took the train down to Dallas, looking to have us a good time. I bought me this Packard the first morning and then took the wife to that Neiman-Marcus store, and she spent five thousand dollars on fur coats and diamond rings and such. I begun to see how fast your money went when you was rich. That evening, at the hotel we was staying at, the Adolphus it was called, I met this fine gentleman in a three-piece suit who said he was a stockbroker from New York and I could invest the rest of my money with him and double it overnight. Probably you can guess the rest, mister. The son of a bitch absconded. I barely had enough loose change for gasoline back to Goodwill."

Billy Festus, who had heard thousands of such stories in his time, offered his condolences.

"Hold on," Grimes said. "There's more. We got home and right off a feller offered me fifteen thousand cash for my one-eighth interest in the well they was planning to drill on my land. I didn't want to take it, but the wife had gotten a taste for high living, so I did. Mister, that very night three bandits

with guns broke in my house and stole the fifteen thousand
and my wife's furs and rings and they would have stolen the
Packard too, except it had two flat tires. That made 'em so
mad they beat me up and did some disgusting things to the
wife and told us we was lucky they didn't kill us fer being so
uncooperative."

"Sir, you have suffered unjustly," Festus said.

"That ain't the worst of it!" the man declared. "Damned if
last week they didn't hit a gusher on my land, so that one-
eighth I sold for the fifteen thousand that got stole might have
been worth a million." Grimes shook his head glumly and
eased the Packard around a dead mule. "The way I figure it,
mister, the Lord just didn't intend for me to be rich."

Wade Kingslea missed the driver's tale, for he slept like a
dead man until a half mile outside Goodwill, when the Packard hit a rut and he was jolted awake. He opened his eyes and
looked up into the night sky and saw the fires of hell.

"Sweet Jesus, what's that?" he whispered.

Orange flames shot a hundred feet into the night, a pillar of
fire that bathed the road in pale yellow light.

Billy Festus laughed aloud. "It's the Devil's Candle, son."

"The what?"

"It's just a gusher that caught fire," their driver said. "It's
been burning three days."

"I think it's beautiful," the girl said. It was the first time
she'd spoken.

"You're right, miss," Billy Festus said. "It *is* beautiful.
And expensive and dangerous too." He took a shot from his
ever-present flask. "I remember one time down in Yucatán,
we brought in a gusher and couldn't get her capped and the oil
was shooting two hundred feet into the air and most of it was
flowing into a river, which was fine, except some damn fool
caught the gusher afire, and pretty soon the whole river was
flowing fire for ten miles, all the way to the ocean. Damndest
sight you ever saw—a river of fire."

The sun rose at they neared the boomtown. They passed a
vast settlement where thousands of men lived in old army
tents, Indian tents, shacks, and even wooden crates and boxes.
"Tent City," their driver muttered scornfully. Past the shantytown, off to the north and west, hundreds of oil derricks
stretched as far as the eye could see. It was like a forest of
wooden derricks, eighty feet high and many built so close
together that their bases touched. Soon the Packard was inch-

ing down Goodwill's main street. Even in the early morning it was crowded with cars, wagons, and people. The air was filled with the clamor of honking horns, banging hammers, and the distant din of the oil rigs. A man began trotting alongside their car. "Uncle Billy, got any leases?" he asked. Festus winked at Kingslea. "See what I mean about arriving in style?" he said.

The street was lined with wooden buildings, some old and weathered, some that had sprung up since the boom. There was a bank, jail, livery stable, Gusher Saloon, two pool halls, an oil field supply store, law offices, a lumberyard, doctor, undertaker, auto mechanic, and countless hole-in-the-wall establishments that proclaimed "Leases," "Eats," or "Beds." The Packard got stuck in the traffic and some men with whiskey bottles in their hands stumbled by, followed by a five-piece band playing Dixieland jazz. "Feller in the middle's the local printer," the driver explained. "His well came in last week."

They stopped in front of a big Victorian house at the far end of the main street. The young woman paid the driver and got out. Kingslea jumped out after her. "Can I help you with your bag?" he asked.

"Why, aren't you sweet?" she said. "But it's really not heavy. Thank you anyway, kind sir." She smiled merrily, picked up her bag, and started toward the many-gabled white house.

"Where you gents want to go?" Grimes asked.

"Up there," Billy Festus said. "Where all the activity is."

Grimes drove them to the Excelsior Hotel, a two-story frame establishment with several hundred men milling about in front of it. The hotel's porch had been partitioned off into a dozen small cubicles that had signs proclaiming "Five Star Oil," "Sure Fire Oil," "Pride of Texas Oil," and the like. Inside the cubicles promoters were waving oil leases and negotiating with the shouting, frenzied men before them. Leases and greenbacks constantly changed hands. Kingslea saw one lease sold and resold three times in three minutes.

"They act like they've lost their minds," Kingslea said.

"They have," Festus told him. He was smiling contentedly. "It's called oil fever. It's delirious, contagious, and most often fatal."

A man rushed up to them, wild-eyed and sweaty. "Ain't you Uncle Billy Festus?"

"I am, sir."

"What you got for sale?"

"Nothing at the moment."

"I'll go half on any lease you want to buy, Billy. I got plenty of money too!"

"Perhaps later in the day," Festus told him. "Right now I need a little rest."

"Don't forget me, Billy," the man implored, then plunged back into the mob.

Grimes, the driver of the Packard, had converted his home into a rooming house, and the partners set off in search of it. Along the way, they passed two women standing in a doorway.

"Hey, tall and handsome, come do your drilling here," one called.

"We guaran-dam-tee a gusher," the other added.

"Ladies, ladies, we need our strength," Billy Festus told them.

They found Grimes' house on one of the side streets. He had removed all the furniture from the first floor and painted three-foot-by-six-foot spaces on the floor. These were the "hot beds" that he rented out in eight-hour shifts. A place on the floor cost two dollars and a pillow and blanket cost a dollar more. Grimes had taken a fancy to Festus and Kingslea, however, and he gave them their own private room, an eight-by-ten cubicle that had once been a pantry. The partners thanked him, shut the door to their sleeping quarters, and prepared for bed. Festus stripped to his underwear and folded his coat and pants neatly. He had thin white legs and varicose veins. "Do you by chance have a gun, Wade?" he asked.

"No."

Festus reached into his carpetbag and pulled out a small pistol, a Derringer. "Better take this," he said. He drank some pink medicine from a bottle, then lay down on his side and was soon snoring. Kingslea lay awake for a while, listening to the hammers banging and oil rigs clanging and cars honking outside. The gash across his ribs burned like fire. He was almost asleep when he heard gunfire and shouts nearby. He started to go see what it was, but he was dog-tired, and he decided to mind his own business. Soon he was asleep.

A few minutes before two that afternoon, the partners walked past two scowling men with shotguns and into the

Goodwill National Bank. Pooling their resources, they opened a checking account with a hundred-dollar deposit.

"I understand you close from two until four, then open back up until six," Festus said to the teller. "Is that correct?"

The teller was a burly man with a handlebar mustache and a six-gun on his hip. "That's right, mister. We close up in the afternoons to count the money."

The partners stepped back out into the dazzling afternoon sun.

"Come on, Wade, we got work to do," Festus said.

"What're we gonna do?"

"Get the lay of the land."

Festus marched down the street and led them into the forest of oil derricks that loomed north of Goodwill. Each rig had its own crew of dirty, shirtless, sun-bronzed, shouting men who fired boilers, hauled pipe, changed bits, and otherwise lent their brawn to the search for oil. Other roughnecks slept on the ground or stood sullenly at the edge of their plots of ground with shotguns cradled in their arms. Billy Festus sought out friendly rig operators, peppered them with questions, and scribbled notes on the back of an envelope with a two-inch stub of pencil. He encountered one operator he'd known in Desdemona. This man's rig had a sign saying "Hell or China" nailed to it, and he explained that he was down to three thousand feet and if he didn't strike oil in another five hundred he'd lose his home and his life's savings. Festus gave the man encouragement and in return got permission to climb to the top of his rig. Up there, eighty feet above the ground, he peered in all directions.

"What the hell was that all about?" Kingslea demanded when the old wildcatter had made it safely back to the ground.

"I told you, I'm getting the lay of the land," Festus said. "Hills make a difference. No time to explain it now. Come on—we've got to acquire some capital."

They stopped at the outdoor oil-lease emporium in front of the Excelsior Hotel. The blazing sun had driven the fortune-seekers there to new heights of frenzy. They shouted, shoved, cursed, argued, pleaded, threatened, fought, and sometimes exchanged leases, like creatures possessed, like demons in hell. Festus and Kingslea had been there only minutes when a man rushed up to them, then several more.

"Uncle Billy, you buying or selling?"

"Uncle Billy, what you got?"

"Billy, look at this lease."

"Gentlemen, gentlemen," Festus cried, raising his hands. "I'm interested in acquiring a few properties, and if you'll calm down I'll take a look at what you got."

"Billy, this one's a sure thing!"

"Billy, mine's got a damn river of oil under it!"

The men surrounded Billy Festus. They grabbed at him with sweaty hands; they jumped and stammered in their anxiety. When one impatient fellow jerked at Festus' arm, demanding attention, Wade Kingslea sent him sprawling in the street, and the others were more polite after that.

Festus heard each man out, scribbling more notes on his envelope, and then announced his decisions. "I'll offer you two thousand dollars for your lease, sir," he told a jug-eared dentist from Denton. "And I'll pay three thousand for yours," he told a toothless West Texas farmer.

"Two thousand?" sputtered the dentist. "It's worth ten if it's worth a penny."

"Then keep it, sir," Festus replied. "And I'll offer the two thousand to this gentleman." He indicated a bull of a man with the bulge of a six-shooter under his leather vest.

"Cash?" the man demanded.

"My personal check, sir, drawn on the local bank."

"I want cash," the man insisted.

"You take no risk, sir. The bank reopens in"—Festus pulled a gold watch from his pocket—"in forty-five minutes, and you can cash the check then."

The men started yelling again, and within minutes Festus had written checks totaling seven thousand dollars to buy leases from the dentist, the farmer, and the man with the gun under his coat. He shook hands all around, offered to buy everyone drinks later that evening, and then led Kingslea hurriedly down the street toward the saloon.

Kingslea eyed the old oilman uneasily. "Partner," he said, "if I ain't mistaken, you just deposited one hundred dollars in the bank and then wrote checks for seven thousand dollars, leaving us overdrawn by sixty-nine hundred dollars. And one of those men you gave a rubber check had a gun on his hip. What do we do now?"

"We sell these goddam leases," Festus said grimly.

A crowd had gathered outside the saloon to watch two women brawling. Festus and Kingslea stood across the street and soon a dapper man in a sharkskin suit joined them.

"Billy, you old scoundrel, I might have knowed you'd turn up here. I ain't seen you since the Bowlegs strike."

"I lost my shirt in that one," Festus said. "But I figure to change my luck here."

"You got any good properties?"

"A couple, Henry. A couple."

"Where at?"

"Far end of Gusher Row, mainly."

"I hear they're drilling dusters down there."

"They're not going deep enough. I think this field's like Bowlegs, and if I'd drilled another thousand feet there I'd have made five million dollars."

Henry chewed his lip uncertainly. "You *really* think this field'll keep producing?"

Billy Festus shrugged. "I could be wrong."

Henry made his decision; his eyes gleamed. "By God, Billy, you've been right more'n you been wrong. What you got an old friend can buy?"

Other men had started to gather around. Billy Festus slipped one of the leases from his pocket and held it to his chest like a poker hand. The men strained for a glimpse of it. Kingslea could see their fever rising; they were like dogs in heat.

"Henry, I'd say this here lease is a prime prospect," Festus declared. All around him men fought for a glimpse of the paper. "And I reckon I could sell it to an old friend."

"For how much?" Henry demanded. Sweat was pouring down his face.

Festus scribbled on his envelope for a moment. "Five thousand dollars," he said finally.

When Henry hesitated, another man yelled, "I'll give you six!"

"They brung in another gusher out there this morning," a man declared.

"Billy, will you take my check?" Henry asked.

"Sorry—cash on the barrelhead," Festus said.

"I'll be back with the cash in five minutes," Henry cried. "Wait for me, Billy! Don't sell it!" He tore off down the street, and the other men begged to know what else Billy Festus had for sale. The old wildcatter pulled the two other leases from his pocket and soon a spirited bidding war ensued. By the time Henry returned with his five thousand dollars, Festus had sold the other leases for eight and eleven thousand dollars. In all, he collected twenty-four thousand dollars cash for three leases he'd bought a half hour earlier for seven thousand dollars in worthless checks.

The most amazing thing, Kingslea thought, was how easy it was. Men were begging Festus to take their money.

Cash in hand, Festus pulled his younger partner aside. "Here's twelve thousand," he said, handing over some bills. "The bank opens back up in five minutes. You get over there fast and deposit this and make damn sure you're in line ahead of those men I gave checks to. Particularly that ape with the gun. Meet me at the saloon when you're done."

Kingslea started away, then turned back. "How come you're only putting half the money in the bank?" he asked. "What if somebody robs us?"

"What if somebody robs the bank?" the old man snapped. "Make tracks, boy!"

When Kingslea rejoined his partner in the Gusher Saloon, the old prospector was relaxing with a bottle of Irish whiskey. He grinned a wolfish grin, waved the younger man into a chair, and poured him a drink. "To your wealth and health, Wade," he said. Then he added, under his breath, "And God damn John D. Rockefeller!"

Festus slid ten $100 bills across the table. "Some spending money for you, partner," he said. Kingslea nodded and sipped his drink cautiously.

"I got a question," he said.

"Ask it."

"I just watched you make seventeen thousand dollars for an hour's work, if you call that work. How come you don't do that for a living?"

Festus grinned and poured himself more whiskey. "Two reasons, Wade. One practical. One . . . well, call it philosophical. The practical reason is that eventually some disgruntled customer would kill me. Not that I cheated anybody, mind you. If they're halfway smart, the men I sold those leases will make a profit, either by drilling or reselling them. Still, as a long-term proposition, dealing leases is risky business. I only do it when I'm in serious need of capital."

Festus coughed, then sipped his whiskey.

"What's the other reason?" Kingslea asked.

"The other reason is, by God, I'm an oilman! Trading leases—hell, that's like taking candy from babies. But finding oil in the ground—that's a man's game. It's you against

Mother Nature, and most often she gives you the back of her hand, but, by God, when you win one—when one puny little man, who's like an ant crawling over this huge planet of ours, can drill a hole and find earth's most precious treasure—that's just the greatest thrill there is. I don't mean the money. Money's just green paper, just another tool you need to drill with. I mean the pride of knowing you've done what a million other men set out to do but you were the one who did it. I tell you, Wade, I've gambled in Monte Carlo and I've slept with women who cost a thousand dollars a night and I've hunted for lions in Africa and there's none of it can match the thrill of hearing the earth rumble, feeling it shake under your feet, and seeing a gusher shoot up and turn the sky black."

The old man hawked and spit into his handkerchief. "That's my business, Wade, my business and my pleasure, and I'll be setting out at dawn tomorrow, going courting on old Mother Nature. I'd be pleased if you joined me."

Kingslea stuck out his hand. "Wild horses couldn't keep me away," he said. The partners toasted, then took refuge on the floor when shots broke out up by the bar. They stayed down, like most of the other customers, until the management had subdued a drunken roughneck and tossed him into the street. They were just getting up when Festus's friend Henry, the wildcatter in the sharkskin suit, turned up.

"Join us for dinner, Henry," Festus roared. "My treat!"

Henry stared at his shoes. "Billy, I got a confession to make."

"Make it!"

"You know that lease I bought from you today, for five thousand?"

"A fine piece of property."

"Billy, I hadn't crossed the street before a man offered me ten for it. So I done sold it. But it ain't like I didn't have faith in you."

"Hell, Henry, business is business. Sit down!"

They ordered more whiskey and a dinner of T-bone steaks with French-fries, hot rolls, and corn on the cob, with peach pie for dessert. Henry said he'd heard that Billy Sunday, the celebrated evangelist, had arrived in Goodwill that day, and Uncle Billy said it wouldn't surprise him, as there were plenty of souls in need of saving there. Other oilmen dropped by the table and there were many tales of boomtowns past. After dinner their talk was interrupted when a young Indian girl entered the saloon with an entourage of older men, both white and Indian, and was greeted with cheers and applause.

"Who the hell's that?" Billy Festus demanded. "Poca-hontas?"

"Damn near. That little heathen is only fourteen years old and she's the sole owner of a well that's producing two thousand barrels a day. The newspapers wrote her up, and she's been getting marriage proposals in the mail from all over the world."

"Can she read?"

"Hell, no. But she better marry somebody fast before she wakes up dead," Henry declared.

"How do you mean?" Kingslea asked.

"Young man, you might be surprised how many Injuns and niggers have struck oil in these parts and then died mysterious deaths. Then a couple of weeks later some white man turns up with the document proving that the deceased had deeded over the entire property to him. Curious business."

That set off another round of oil-field tales, as each man tried to top the other. Festus recalled a wildcatter named Ripley who was walking outside Desdemona one night when a robber ordered him to put up his hands. "Ripley put up one hand and the bandit shot him dead," Festus recalled, shaking with laughter. "The thing the robber didn't know was that Ripley was a one-armed man—*he didn't have two hands to put up!*"

Finally Billy Festus' head started to droop. "Better call it a night, gents," he said. "I'm a tired old man who needs some rest." They said good-night to Henry and walked outside. The street was still crowded, and down the block men still bought and sold leases in front of the Excelsior Hotel. "We gonna sleep in that broom closet again?" Kingslea asked.

"No sir," Festus said. "Our fortunes have improved. While you were at the bank, I discovered that an old friend of mine owns a right comfortable house here in Goodwill. Perhaps you'd be good enough to escort me."

They walked down the middle of the street, away from the dark shadows where gunmen might lurk. Festus staggered a bit. Kingslea kept his hand on the gun in his pocket. They passed the brass band, still playing; the printer and his friends and some young women were sitting on the steps outside the livery stable. "Wa-hoo," the printer yelled. "I done spent twelve thousand dollars on this party so far!" One of the women started dancing to the music.

Festus led them to the big Victorian house at the end of the street, the one they had visited briefly that morning. There was a picket fence around its front yard and two men sitting on rocking chairs on its wide porch.

"What is this?" Kingslea asked. "A rooming house?"

Festus laughed, then coughed. "Not to mince words, son, it's a whorehouse. A lady named Helen runs it. Twenty years ago, when she was a whore on Post Office Street in Galveston, and I'd just made a mint at Spindletop, I gave her ten thousand dollars to go in business for herself. Well, needless to say, she's made a fortune. She's got her a fancy house in Dallas, but whenever there's a boom she'll take some girls out there. She figures she owes it to the industry, after all it's done for her. Anyway, we'll be sleeping here tonight, free of charge."

Kingslea was stunned. He remembered the girl in the Packard, with her delicate wrists and her merry smile. He'd been thinking about her all day. "You mean that girl this morning . . . ?" he stammered. "She's a . . . ?"

"You didn't believe she was really a schoolteacher, did you? Come on, let's get to bed."

The two men on the porch had shotguns on their laps, but once Festus gave his name they waved him past. Kingslea hung back. The thought of that tiny, ethereal girl inside this brothel made him sick. "I'm going for a walk," he said.

Festus frowned his disapproval. "Be careful, Wade," he said. "Personally, I'd rather be in a feather bed with some big-titted whore than out on the street with a bunch of drunk roughnecks."

Kingslea stumbled off toward town. The girl's image haunted him; he was dazed to have lost an illusion so quickly. Down by the Excelsior Hotel, he found himself caught up in a tide of men, hundreds of them, who were moving out toward Gusher Row. Kingslea thought at first that a new well had come in, but then a man shouted, "It's Billy Sunday—he's gonna preach!" Kingslea, curious, confused, adrift, let himself be swept along.

The evangelist's followers had erected a huge platform, a kind of altar, ten feet above the ground and directly in front of the still-uncapped, still-burning gusher, so that whoever preached there would be silhouetted against its billowing hundred-foot tower of flame. Two or three thousand men had gathered on the muddy ground before the platform, their upraised faces bathed in the flickering orange glow. When Kingslea arrived, a local Baptist preacher was trying unsuccessfully to capture the crowd's attention, and after him a choir sang "Onward, Christian Soldiers" and was all but drowned out by hoots and catcalls.

Then, suddenly, Billy Sunday stood before them, arms outstretched, a bald, powerfully built man in a frock suit and string tie, who roared in a booming voice: "The Lord be praised! Blessed is the Name of the Lord!"

"Amen," a few men shouted back, but more hooted or tipped up whiskey bottles, and somewhere at the back of the throng a man fired his six-gun into the air.

"Oil!" the preacher roared. "What is oil? Is it the Devil's Brew, seeping up from Hell to ensnare weak pitiful sinners?"

"Damn right, Billy!" someone yelled.

"Is it, brothers? Or is oil the sweet nectar of the Almighty?"

"Don't taste like it!" someone else cried to general laughter.

"I say it is God's Brew, brothers!" Billy Sunday boomed. "I say oil may start in the bowels of Hell, but it can rise to the throne of the All-Powerful! I say oil has been sent to make men free! I say oil can heat our homes and fuel our automobiles! I say oil's blackness can be made as pure as the lilies of the field, even as your sins can be washed away in our Holy Savior's blessed blood! Hallelujah!"

"Hallelujah!" a thousand voices cried.

"I say that those of you who bring the oil forth from the earth are soldiers in the army of the Lord!"

"Amen!" they cried.

Sunday's voice was like a musical instrument, a mighty organ; the boomtown pilgrims were swept along by the power of his words and the fury of his vision.

The evangelist raised a silver bowl above his head.

"I have filled this chalice with oil from this very field," he cried. "Where are the sinners who will come forth and be baptized in the Holy Oil of the Lord?"

A hush fell over the crowd as the preacher held the silver bowl aloft; it sparkled like a star against the curtain of flame. Men began to rush toward the wooden platform, screaming and crying as they scrambled up the ladder. Soon twenty were kneeling on the platform, shoulder to shoulder, tears streaming down their faces. One grizzled roughneck kept moaning. "Forgive my sins, Sweet Jesus!" Billy Sunday marched back and forth before them, preaching like a man possessed.

"You have sinned the sin of greed!"

"Yes, Lord! Amen!"

"You have sinned the sin of lust!"

"I've sinned, Billy, I've sinned!"

"You have sinned the sin of violence!"

"Forgive me, Lord!"

"You are all miserable sinners, come to this hellhole in search of the Devil's coin," Billy Sunday roared. His every utterance now was met with a roar of approval. Men fired their guns into the air, but that seemed not so much an interruption as an affirmation, a part of the ritual. The great evangelist now had them in his palm.

"You are miserable sinners but the Lord will forgive!"

"Hallelujah!"

"The Lord will wash your sins away and give you everlasting life!"

"Praise God!"

"I baptize you now, in the name of the Father and the Son and the Holy Ghost!"

He moved along the line of kneeling, weeping oil-field roughnecks, holding the silver chalice in his left hand and dipping his right index finger into the thick, glistening oil and marking a shimmering black cross on each man's forehead.

"Put away your sins and be born again," he cried. "March forward in the army of the Lord!" The men leaped to their feet, shouting, embracing one another. Some scrambled down the ladder; others leaped to the ground and rolled about as though possessed. The preacher raised his arms to Heaven. "Come forth, sinners, come forth and be saved!"

A hundred men surged forward, toward the wooden altar before the geyser of flame. Wade Kingslea pushed forward with them, tears in his eyes, ready to repent his sins. The preacher's words had pierced his heart. All that he had seen that day was sin and vanity and degradation. Billy Festus with his promise of easy riches was a serpent, a Judas. The girl with her thin wrists and her beguiling smile was a whore, a harlot, a thing of corruption. This entire town, he saw now, was an outpost of Hell, where men suffered and burned for their greed and lust. He could repent and be on the next train out and be reunited with his loved ones by the next afternoon.

He could put away his pride and vanity and return to the life the Lord had meant for him. Sweaty, wild-eyed, Wade Kingslea pushed through the crowd toward the high altar, toward the preacher who could grant forgiveness for his sins.

Then, suddenly, he threw himself face down in the mud and lay there trembling.

"Come forward, sinners!" the evangelist cried, but Wade Kingslea did not move.

He could not move, for a battle was being waged in his soul. If part of him was consumed by guilt, another part could not forget why he had come to this boomtown. That part of him remembered the fire that had burned inside him all of his life, his belief that he was different, that there was greatness in him, that there were mountains he could climb, worlds he could conquer, that the treasures of the earth could be his if he only had the courage to seize them.

"Oh, Lord God, forgive me," he whispered on his knees in the mud, head bowed, as the crowd surged past him. He knew he could not stop now, he knew that he must do what he must do. He had trusted Jesus for a lifetime and never been more than a wretched, penniless dirt farmer; now he would put his trust in oil and Billy Festus, he would embrace the Devil himself if that was the price of freedom.

Wade Kingslea rose slowly to his feet, closing his ears to the preacher's silver-tongued promises, and stumbled away from the altar and the pillar of flame, back toward the little town called Goodwill.

He was exhausted, trembling, his shirt soaked in sweat. On Goodwill's main street he stood in the shadows trying to decide what to do. He was distracted for a moment by the spectacle of a man bleeding to death. It was the big, moon-faced farmer he'd seen playing poker on the train. Minutes before a young roughneck had slashed his gut a dozen times with a razor-sharp knife, but the farmer was too drunk to notice his wounds. He was staggering along the street, with blood soaking his plaid flannel shirt, as men surrounded him and placed bets on how long he could stay on his feet. Kingslea watched the scene, torn between fascination and disgust, and then his blood ran cold as he saw, across the street, next to the livery stable, the big man with the scarred face he had thrown off the train the night before. There were bandages on his forehead and both his hands, but he was very much alive and he was peering at every face in the street.

Kingslea pressed back into the shadows. His enemy seemed not to have seen him. He clutched the Derringer and thought he should kill the man now and be done with him, and yet he knew in the next instant that he hadn't the heart for it, not this night. Instead, he slipped down the street toward the whorehouse that seemed his surest refuge.

The men on the porch let him pass, and a colored maid in a white dress led him to a room on the third floor. The room was small but neat and clean, with flowered wallpaper, a cedar chest, and a brass bed with a white comforter atop it. Kingslea locked the door, checked the window, and then looked into the bathroom. The big old claw-footed tub tempted him, and he started running hot water into it and stripped off his filthy clothing. There was a jar of pink bubble-bath pellets on a shelf by the door, and impulsively he dropped a handful of them into the steaming water. Soon he was soaking, relaxing for the first time in days. He had almost forgotten the preacher and the moon-faced man with the bloody gut and the scar-faced man he thought he would have to kill, when he heard the bedroom door opening. He leaped from the tub and grabbed the Derringer as the girl poked her head into the bathroom.

"My goodness, you *are* a terror!" she said.

Disbelieving, he lowered the gun and snatched a towel to hold before him.

"So modest," she said. "Do you remember me, Mr. Kingslea?"

He nodded dumbly. "You said you were a schoolteacher."

"Well, I *used* to be. And I still do teach gentlemen a thing or two sometimes. Fanny's my name, if I didn't tell you. Your friend Mr. Festus said you might like to see me. Are you finished with your bath? I brought a bottle of quite decent Scotch whiskey with me."

"I'm finished," he said. He took a silk robe from a hook on the wall and slipped it on. As he did, Fanny noticed the gash across his ribs. "Good heavens, what happened to you?" she cried.

"A man cut me," he said. "I should have killed him but I didn't."

"Does it hurt?"

"Don't think about it," he said. "Talk about something else. Tell me whose house this was."

They sat on the edge of the bed. "He was the town

banker," she explained. "He made a pile of money, right at the start of the boom, but then some men beat him half to death, so he moved to Fort Worth and sold his house to Miss Helen quite reasonably. Can I pour you a little Scotch?"

He nodded and sipped gratefully.

"Mr. Kingslea, not to spoil the mood of things, but if you'd like me to stay, there are certain mundane business matters to be concluded."

He stared at her, confused.

"To wit, your room is paid for, but I'm not."

"I . . . I mean . . . how much . . .?"

"One hundred dollars. For all night."

"A hundred dollars?" Until this day, he'd never in his life had a hundred dollars at one time.

Fanny signed. "Mr. Kingslea, if you want a ten-dollar girl, there are various of them to be found in Tent City. But, of course, you'll get what you pay for. And sometimes a little more, in terms of certain unmentionable social diseases."

He hesitated, not because of the money but because part of him wanted her and part of him was deathly afraid of her.

"Of course," she said cheerfully, "if you're short of cash, we might make some other arrangement, if you have any interesting leases."

"Leases?"

She laughed. "They call me Five-percent Fanny, Mr. Kingslea, because I've been known to take a percentage of a lease in lieu of cash."

"Are you serious?" he asked.

"Never more so," she cried. "Look!" She leaped from the bed, slipped a key from somewhere inside her silvery dress, and unlocked a box she took from the cedar chest. She showed him a dozen notarized papers giving her five percent of various oil leases.

"Are any of these producing?" he asked.

"Three dusters so far," she pouted. "But there's one next to a gusher that they start drilling on next week. My hopes are high, Mr. Kingslea!"

"You could get rich," he said incredulously.

"Of *course* I could get rich," she said. "Mr. Kingslea, I am not exactly in Goodwill for the *fun* of it. I'm a gambler, just like you. I *did* teach school, for eighty dollars a month, and there was no future in *that*. Now, the way things are going, I expect in a few months to have five percent of numerous producing wells, whereupon I will return to Dallas and live out my days in extreme comfort and relative chastity."

Kingslea felt reality slipping away from him. There was a killer on the streets looking for him and he was sitting here drinking with a whore who dealt in oil leases. But he liked the way the whiskey burned going down, and he liked the girl's flashing smile too. He reached into his pants and handed her a hundred-dollar bill. She smiled a quick, shy smile and kissed him on the cheek. "I'm glad," she said. "Why don't you warm up the bed while I go anoint myself?"

She disappeared into the bathroom. Kingslea took off the banker's robe and got into the brass bed, under the thick downy comforter. He turned his face to the wall and realized he was trembling. He could hear the girl humming in the bathroom. Quickly he got up and took another long swallow of the Scotch, then got back into the bed just as she returned.

She stood naked in the middle of the room, holding a candlestick. Her body was white and slender and fresh, with small, rose-tipped breasts and a fluffy patch of pubic hair, and her brown hair was loose at her shoulders. He thought of Harriet, whose body was thick and blue-veined and who never wanted him to see her naked. He felt his hands trembling again, whether from fear or passion he did not know.

"Do you want me?" she said.

He nodded, too awed to speak. He thought she was what the women in the magazine advertisements would look like if somehow he could see them naked. It didn't matter that she was a whore; there was magic in her soft, frail body nonetheless.

Fanny blew out the candle and slipped into bed beside him. She pushed him down flat on his back and took his face in both her hands and kissed him on the mouth. He could feel her nipples rubbing against his chest, and he moaned with pleasure. "You're nice," she whispered. "I don't always kiss customers. Only the ones I like."

She stroked his belly with her fingertips. "Such a nice flat belly, Mr. Kingslea," she said. "You can't imagine how many sagging bellies a girl encounters in this line of work."

She kissed his ear and nibbled at his chest and ran her tongue along his belly and then she touched his penis with her fingertips. It was soft, and she took her hand away and kissed him on the mouth again.

"You know what's most beautiful about you, Mr. Kingslea?

Your incredible eyes. I've never seen eyebrows that thick or lashes that long and black. They're absolutely lush, sinful. They make me think of black orchids growing in a deep dark jungle."

She stroked his chest and whispered, "Relax, darling, relax," and she ran her fingertips lightly over his belly and then she took his penis in her hand. "Oh you poor little mouse," she whispered. "Darling, you must relax."

"I'm sorry," he said miserably.

"Don't fret, you lovely man. Tell me, have you ever been outside Texas?"

"No," he confessed.

"Just as I thought! Then it's time for a little trip around the world!" She grinned and rose above him. "All ashore that's going ashore," she cried. "The S.S. *Fanny* is departing for points unknown! Toot-toot-toot!"

He thought she had taken leave of her senses, but she kissed him jauntily, flipped him over onto his stomach, and began to massage his back in a manner most pleasant and relaxing. Next she startled him by taking one of his feet—newly washed, thank God!—into her hands and starting to nibble his toes. Slowly, amazingly, stunningly, her kisses and caresses began to inch upward, until she had explored parts of his body where he had never imagined a woman's lips or tongue or fingers might ever venture. He was dazed, disarmed, helpless, when finally she turned him back over onto his back, whispered "I love your body," and took his half-erect penis into her warm, laughing mouth. She encouraged him gently, then more vigorously, for what seemed an eternity, and still he was soft as a baby.

"You *are* a tough nut to crack," she sighed at last, sad-eyed and out of breath.

"I'm sorry," he groaned.

"Is there something special you like?"

He rolled over to face the wall. "I feel like I'm not a man."

"You're a wonderful man, Mr. Kingslea. Perhaps I was a little too forward."

"It isn't like that with my wife," he said.

"I know, darling."

"That's the trouble," he said. "I have a family. I shouldn't be here."

She stroked his shoulder. "But darling, you *are* here. And we can have such a lovely time."

"I've never been with any woman but Harriet," he said.

Fanny sighed. "Darling, I can't help it about Harriet. I really can't."

He shook with frustration. "I don't know what's right," he cried.

Fanny sat up, fumbled for a glass in the moonlit room, and poured herself some Scotch.

"I'll bet you're a Baptist, aren't you?" she said.

"Yes."

"And all your life the preachers have told you you'd roast in hell for fornicating," she sighed. "Well, Mr. Kingslea, I say the preachers are full of beans. I say making love is more fun than strawberry ice cream. I wouldn't be surprised if it's what people do in Heaven to pass the time, Baptists included. But you'll have to make up your mind for yourself, Mr. Kingslea. They've got your head all stuffed with hellfire and damnation, and you're the only one who can get it unstuffed."

He knew she was right. He had been baptized in guilt, half-drowned in it, the way you drown unwanted kittens the day they're born. The preachers had done this to him, unmanned him, made a fool of him, and he seethed with hate for their guilt-giving tribe.

"Could we just go to sleep?" he asked. "I didn't sleep much last night. Or much the night before."

She touched his eyelids with her fingertips. "Of course, darling," she said. "It's often like this."

By seven the next morning the partners had rented a Model T and were headed out of Goodwill. Billy Festus looked fresh, eager, almost youthful; Kingslea's body ached from the whiskey the night before.

"Boy, you look like hell," Festus said with a grin. "That little schoolteacher give you a hard time?"

Kingslea nodded. "Yeah, she was a handful."

"I had me a big old gal named Ida." Festus started laughing. "I'da fucked her all night if I could."

They drove slowly over the rutted dirt roads, and it was a few minutes before Kingslea paid attention to where they were headed.

"Say, where you taking us?" he demanded "This is south of town, ain't it?"

"That's right," Festus said, his eyes sparkling.

"All the oil's north of town, ain't it?" Kingslea said.

"North and maybe west? Everybody said they got nothing but dusters south of town."

"I got a theory, Wade. I think that field north of town is about to run dry, and the real prospects are out this way."

"But they've drilled out here. Dry holes!"

"What's eight or ten dusters? Maybe they didn't go deep enough."

Kingslea shrugged, too tired to argue, and remembered the bad news he had forgotten to tell his partner. "Billy, you remember the man on the train? The one I threw off?"

"He'd be a hard one to forget."

"I saw him last night."

Billy Festus coughed and spit out the window. "Did he see you?"

"I don't think so."

"Reach in my bag," Festus said. "Look in the brown box."

Kingslea opened the box and found a .38 revolver.

"You better keep that," Festus said "The Derringer is fine for minor disagreements, but we may have some serious disputations ahead."

Kingslea checked the revolver and slipped it into his belt. "You armed?" he asked.

Festus shook his head. "That's your department, son," he said. "But put the Derringer back in my bag for safekeeping."

They passed deserted oil derricks that loomed like giant skeletons above the barren plain. There was little green or growing south of Goodwill; the countryside was sandy, barren, a wasteland punctuated only by mesquite trees and buffalo grass. Kingslea felt terrible. "When does this search begin?" he demanded.

"It already has," Festus told him.

"What're we looking for?"

"Lots of things. Clues on top of the ground that'll tell us what's under the ground."

"You studied geology, Billy?"

"When I was starting out they hadn't invented geology. What I did was learn me some creekology. Come on, I'll show you."

He stopped the Ford and led the way down a long gully to a dry creekbed. Lizards darted about, but Festus ignored them as he moved along the creekbed, examining its pebbles and the rocks imbedded in its clay walls. From time to time he would pop a pebble in his mouth and suck on it or scrape at a rock with his knife. Soon he was soaked in sweat, lost in his work, muttering to himself, and when Kingslea tried to ask questions he would snap, "Watch, Wade, just watch!" Once he pointed to a long flat rock in the side of the gully. "See how it slants," he said. "It's like a road sign. Come on!"

The old man scrambled out of the gully and ran like a rabbit back to the Ford. Soon they were bouncing across the prairie to the southeast. "What is it?" Kingslea demanded.

"Not sure yet," Festus admitted. "But that was sandstone, tilting east to west, and if there's sandstone up top, there might be more down below, soaking up oil like a sponge."

"What does the tilt mean?"

Festus swatted at a yellowjacket. "They call it an anticline," he said. "The earth's like a layer cake, Wade. Layers of rock, sand, salt, shale, oil, and God knows what all down there. But sometimes it shifts, breaks up, so the pieces don't fit, and then traps get formed, places where the oil gets dammed up, like big underground lakes. So one tilting rock up here may mean lots of tilting rocks down there, maybe a trap, maybe a pool of oil. The same way a low round hill, a mound, may mean a salt dome down below and God only knows how much oil underneath it—that's how they found Spindletop!"

They explored five more creeks that day and examined outcroppings of rock on the prairie and marched about low hills that might have been salt domes. They camped beside a tiny creek that night, drinking whiskey and swatting mosquitoes. Kingslea was depressed. He wanted to be back in Goodwill with Fanny, wanted a chance to redeem himself, but his partner was brimming with excitement. "We may be wandering around on top of one big anticline," he said. "The rocks are talking to me. They're leading me by the hand!"

"Leading you where?" Kingslea snapped. "Looks to me like they're leading you away from a producing field and out into a desert."

"Wade, finding oil's an art, like poker, and you've got to follow your instincts."

They were off at dawn the next morning, scrambling like crabs along creekbeds, crawling over rock piles, always moving south and east. The old man sucked on pebbles, pounded rocks together, poked holes in the ground, all the time mumbling to himself; it was as if he had set off on a treasure hunt following clues only he could see. Once, as the wildcatter knelt facedown in a putrid creekbed, Wade Kingslea whispered, "Don't move!"

Billy Festus looked up and saw his partner with the .38 pointed at him. His eyes widened as the gun exploded, then two feet from his head a rattlesnake thrashed about and died.

Billy Festus mopped his face with a dirty silk handkerchief. "You're a hell of a shot, son," he said.

"You ought to be dead, old man."

Festus sighed and got to his feet. "A hazard of the profession," he said. "Let's keep moving."

In early afternoon a blue-black norther moved in, bringing a cooling, soothing wind, and Billy Festus' treasure hunt led them to an unpainted shack in a cedar grove. Chickens scratched in the dirt beside the house. Down the hill lean-bellied hogs rooted in a muddy creek. An ancient black man eyed them from a rickety porch. Behind him, in the doorway, a sullen young woman watched with a squirming baby on her hip.

"Afternoon," Billy Festus said.

The old Negro said nothing.

"Looks like rain," Festus added.

The baby howled and the old Negro continued to stare.

"My name's Festus," the prospector said. "This is Mr. Kingslea, my partner. What's your name, sir?"

"Booker."

"Mr. Booker, my partner and I are prospectors, and . . ."

"Fer what?" the man snapped.

"For oil, sir, and we'd like permission to look about your property."

The old man flashed a toothless, mirthless grin. "Don't matter none to me," he said. *"Woman, hush that chile!"*

"Exactly how much land do you have here, sir?"

"Twenty acre."

"And we're in the center of it now?"

"Jes' about."

"Well, many thanks, Mr. Booker. We'll just take a look around."

Billy Festus led the way down the hill through the cedars and scrub pine to a tiny trickle of a creek. He splashed along in it, like a hound on a scent, until he came to the spot where pigs were rooting in a muddy hole. He sank to his knees in the mud.

"What're you doing?" Kingslea demanded. "This place stinks of pigshit."

"Forget the pigshit. There's sulphur here—can't you smell it?"

Gentle rain began to fall; the old man ignored it. He crawled about, shoving the hogs aside, sniffing the water, peering at the mud, and finally he lifted his hands to the dark sky. "Sweet Mother of God," he cried. "It's oil! Feel this—feel it!"

Wade Kingslea rubbed the muddy water between his thumb and forefinger. It was slick, there was a slight, rainbow-hued film to it, and it gave off the acrid odor of sulphur. The old man had flopped onto his back, face up to the rain, and begun laughing at the sky. "It's down there, Wade," he said. "Don't you see? Mother Nature's been talking to me for two days now and I listened to her and she's brought me to another treasure. Oh, *God*, I love this business!"

"What about the nigger?" Wade Kingslea asked.

Festus coughed and got slowly to his feet. "Ah, Wade, ever the pragmatist. Well, our colored friend, Mr. Booker, is destined to be a wealthy man."

They returned to the house, two filthy white men who'd been grubbing around in a hog pond. The black man eyed their advance as he might that of wild Indians. "What you want now?" he asked.

"Mr. Booker," Festus asked, "have you ever noticed anything unusual in that little creek down there, where the hogs are?"

"Hit's jist a hog wallow. Thar's tar er pitch er somethin' in de crick dat kills fleas. Cures de mange, too. Ain't no good fer drinkin'."

"Mr. Booker," Festus said, "I'd like for you to sign a lease giving me the right to drill for oil on your land."

"Will you pay me?"

"I'll pay you a hundred dollars," Festus said. In the doorway, behind the old man, the woman screamed. "And you'll also have a one-eighth interest in any income from the well," Festus added.

Elijah Booker was not interested in further details. Quickly, clearly fearful that the visitors might change their minds, he marked his X and pocketed the money.

They were a mile outside Goodwill when the storm broke. Their Model T was soon mired to the axle in mud and they

deserted it and slogged into town on foot. The sky was dark
blue and they were soaked by a torrent of rain. Lightning
struck a dead tree near them and it burst into flame. The main
street of Goodwill was a river of mud, with cars and wagons
abandoned in it from one end to the other. Festus led them into
the county registrar's office to register the Booker lease.
While they waited, Kingslea looked at a bulletin board that
was covered with letters from all over the country. Most of
them began, "Son, if you read this, please . . ." or "Reward for
information leading to the whereabouts of . . ."

"They ever find any of those people?" Kingslea asked the
registrar, a thin old man in bifocals.

"They're mostly dead," the man said. "Either in fights or
in accidents. I don't often send word. I figure it's better for
their mamas to think they're somewhere getting rich."

They registered the lease and headed back to the whorehouse, where Festus had been given a room for the duration.
The storm had passed and boys were charging a quarter to
haul well-dressed men across Goodwill's muddy main street
on sleds. Some drunk roughnecks were rolling about in the
mud and flinging it at passersby. Wade Kingslea, trudging
through the ankle-deep muck, was tense and watchful. He
kept his hat pulled down over his face, and his eyes swept the
street ceaselessly. He saw murder in every passing face, and
passersby, if they looked closely, saw the same in his.

It was dark when they reached the whorehouse. They went
to Festus' little room at the back and stripped off their clothes.
Festus had been coughing violently since they were caught in
the downpour and he was soon relaxing in a hot bath. Kingslea put on dry clothes and combed his hair.

"I'll be back in a minute," he called to Festus.

"Where you going?"

"To talk to Fanny."

"Dammit, Wade, we ain't got time for whores tonight. We
got work to do!"

"I'll be right back," Kingslea said and slipped out the door
with Festus calling after him. He hurried down the hallway to
the front parlor. Fanny was there with Ida, the big-breasted
blonde who was Festus' favorite. They were talking to two
middle-aged men. One was tall and had yellow hair that
curled over his ears. The other was short and muscular and
wore a red vest. Kingslea caught Fanny's eye and she excused
herself and met him in the doorway.

"I want you to meet me at midnight," he told her.

"I can't. I'm booked all night."

"Get out of it."

"Helen won't let me. These are two oilmen from St. Louis and they've already paid."

Kingslea flushed with anger. "You're spending the night with me!" he declared and grabbed her wrist.

"Mr. Kingslea, have you gone *mad?*" she said and jerked her arm free. He saw the St. Louis men staring at him. He glared back at them.

"What the hell you doing, Wade?" It was Billy Festus, a robe wrapped around him, still wet from his bath.

"She won't see me tonight," Kingslea said. "One of those drummers there has got her tied up."

"You damn fool, quit worrying about that whore," Festus snapped. "I told you we got work to do."

Seething with anger, Kingslea followed the old wildcatter back to his room. Once the door was locked, Festus turned on him, his eyes flashing. "Listen, Wade, if you're gonna go falling in love with whores, you ain't gonna be any good to me or anybody else. Don't you understand the situation, boy? Right now we can lease land south of town for a dollar an acre, but once word gets out it'll cost a hundred or a thousand. We got to move fast and keep our mouths shut!"

Somewhere Festus had acquired a surveyor's map of the county. Now he spread it out on the floor and began to pore over it, marking the Booker farm, the other farms they had passed, and the creeks they had explored, all with amazing accuracy. He laid out his plan for the next day. They would set out on horseback, because of the mud, with several thousand dollars in cash. Festus figured they had only one day to lease land cheap, then the farmers would see what was happening and raise their prices. His goal was to lease the land for a mile in every direction from the Booker place. When their battle plan was all mapped out, they ate a late supper of sandwiches and beer and went to bed. Festus climbed into the four-poster in his flannel nightshirt and was soon snoring. Kingslea, stretched out on a blanket on the floor, listened to peals of laughter from the parlor, heard gunfire outside, and thought of Fanny in the brass bed on the third floor in the embrace of one of the St. Louis men. He twisted about in anger, imagined charging upstairs to rescue her, and finally fell asleep and dreamed of her white body pressed against his.

When she knocked at the door he thought he was still dreaming. It was Festus who jumped out of bed and let her in. She was wearing a robe and she was crying.

"What is it, girl?" Festus demanded.

"The men from St. Louis know about your lease," she said. "They're on their way out there now, to buy up all the land they can."

"How'd they find out?" Festus demanded. He was already slipping into his pants.

"They saw you coming out of the registrar's office. Then they listened to you talk last night. There's a closet next to this room. One of them snuck in there."

"What'd they do to you?" Kingslea asked. He lit a lamp and saw the bruises on her face.

"They . . . they slapped me around. Told me not to tell you anything."

Festus pulled on his boots. "Dammit, Wade, get your clothes on," he said. "The game has got competitive!"

They ran through the mud to the livery stable in the first soft glow of dawn. A few drunks jeered at them.

"We want two good horses," Kingslea told the livery-stable operator.

"Ain't got no horses," the man sputtered.

"Like hell you don't!"

"Three gentlemen come by here an hour ago and woke me up and rode off with every horse I had."

"The sons of bitches!" Billy Festus cried.

Wade Kingslea pulled the .38 from his belt and pointed it between the man's eyes. "Mister," he said, "if your life depended on it, where would you say we could find two horses?"

The man began to stammer and back away. "I . . . please . . . they said they'd kill . . ."

"I'll kill you right here and now if you don't produce two horses before I count three!" Kingslea vowed. "One—"

"Behind the bank," the man cried. "Two horses tied there." Moments later Festus and Kingslea were galloping south out of Goodwill. They had not ridden far when they passed six dead horses, shot through the head.

After an hour they came to a farmhouse on land they hoped to lease. They stopped a quarter mile away and searched for signs of life.

"We've got to think this through," Festus said. "What those

two have done so far ain't so awful, by oil-field standards. The thing is, we don't know if they're riding hell for leather now trying to sign leases or laying in wait to kill us."

"There's three of 'em," Wade Kingslea said.

"What?"

"The man at the livery stable said three," Kingslea said. "And I figure anybody who'd shoot six horses would shoot us too."

A man emerged from the farmhouse. "Let's be damn careful," Festus said, and they rode slowly forward.

The farmer said three men had ridden by a half hour earlier but had not stopped. He gladly took a hundred dollars for a lease on his eighty acres.

The next house sat in some woods with a windmill beside it and a Model T parked out front. "It's the Weatherbee place," Festus said. "He's got six hundred acres." They approached the house slowly, calling out, "Anybody home?" As they reached the porch a plump, middle-aged woman opened the door. She was wearing a nightgown and robe. Kingslea kept his hand on the .38 inside his coat.

Billy Festus tipped his hat to the woman. "Sorry to trouble you so early, ma'am, but we'd like to talk to your husband about an oil lease."

The woman stared at him blankly. "Come in," she said. "Mr. Weatherbee's in the kitchen."

They stepped into the shadowy parlor. Kingslea felt an itch of concern. Why was the woman so pale? Where was her husband? He was starting to stop Festus when he heard something behind him and he caught a glimpse of the scar-faced man before the blackjack crashed into his head.

When Kingslea awoke he was facedown on the wooden floor. His hands were tied behind him, the .38 was gone, and his head rested in a pool of his own blood. He kept his eyes shut and listened to a man talking. "We're mighty sorry about this, folks," he was saying. "This old coot's a notorious swindler who was out to cheat you and your neighbors out of your oil rights, and that one is a cold-blooded killer from Fort Worth he hired to do his dirty work."

Kingslea opened one eye. The man talking was the yellow-haired one. The Weatherbees were standing before him, the old farmer with his arm around his weeping wife. The other St. Louis man, the short one with the red vest, was in the front doorway. The scar-faced man was standing in the middle of the room with a shotgun pointed at Kingslea's head and with the .38 in his belt. Billy Festus was slumped on a sofa with his head in his hands.

"We want all of you out of our home," the farmer said.

"I understand perfectly," the yellow-haired one said. "We're leaving right away to take these two to the sheriff. But I wish you folks'd reconsider that lease before we go. It's easy money."

"We don't want your money. We want you to leave."

"That one's awake now," the scar-faced man said. "You, get up on your feet."

Kingslea didn't move. He was wondering if somehow he could charge scar-face and kick the shotgun loose, but it seemed hopeless. He strained against the rope.

The scar-faced man kicked him in the mouth. The woman screamed. "Get out of our house," the old farmer shouted. He led his wife into the kitchen and shut the door.

"I said, get up," the one with the scar said.

Kingslea struggled to his feet, spitting blood. The shotgun was pointed at his chest.

Billy Festus coughed, then spoke. "I reckon the two of us ain't likely to survive this ride back to town, are we?"

"That one's gonna get his slow," the scar-faced man said.

"Shut up, Matt," yellow-hair said. "Festus, get on your feet."

Festus coughed again and stayed on the sofa. "Gentlemen, let's talk this over," he said.

"You're in no position to negotiate, old-timer," yellow-hair said. "You and your partner bit off more'n you could chew."

"I'm not talking about my partner," Festus said.

"You old bastard," Kingslea muttered.

"You're a dead man, Wade," Festus said. "The issue right now is me. Gentlemen, allow me to tell you two reasons why you're better off with me alive."

"Make it short, Festus."

"Number one, I'm a wildcatter. I found oil in these parts and I can find more. Why kill the goose that lays the golden eggs?"

"What's your other reason?"

"Nobody'll give a damn if you kill Wade, but I got a lot of friends in Texas. Kill me and there'll be a stink. Go partners with me and we all get rich. How about it, gentlemen?"

The yellow-haired man glanced at his stocky partner, who

shook his head. "We got enough partners," he said.

Billy Festus began coughing again, his frail shoulders jerking and then he was rolling across the floor firing the Derringer at the scar-faced man. The big man dropped the shotgun and sank to his knees with a bullet in his gut. He fumbled for the .38 but Kingslea charged across the room and kicked him in the teeth. The two St. Louis men ran out the front door.

"Untie me," Kingslea screamed. "Damn you, untie me!"

Festus fumbled with the knots until Kingslea was free. Matt, the scar-faced one, was writhing in pain. Kingslea grabbed the .38, jabbed it in his enemy's mouth, and pulled the trigger. The Weatherbees were screaming in the kitchen. Kingslea started for the front door.

"Let 'em go," Billy Festus yelled. The two men were running across a field toward some woods and Kingslea charged after them. Just before they entered the woods he fired and hit the yellow-haired one in the leg. The man shrieked and flopped to the ground. Kingslea ran past him and caught the other man as he mounted one of the horses hidden there. The man raised his hands above his head. "Don't shoot me," he begged.

"So you've got enough partners, you son of a bitch?" Kingslea said. He shot the man in the belly, watched him slide slowly to the ground, then shot him again in the back of the head. He walked back to the field where the tall man was trying to crawl away, despite his shattered leg. Kingslea put the .38 to the man's head and suddenly the man slashed at him with a knife. Kingslea jumped back, howling with rage, then shot the dying man between the eyes.

He rode one of the horses back to the farmhouse. Billy Festus was waiting on the porch.

"You didn't have to kill them," he said.

Kingslea spit blood on the ground. "Where was the Derringer?" he asked.

"In my boot."

"You old bastard, you're mean as a snake."

"Wade, the world won't let a man just look for oil. There's all this other shit they make you slog through."

The partners calmed the Weatherbees, doctored Kingslea's wounds as best they could, and resumed their search for leases. It was not until they stopped beside a brackish creek for lunch that a troublesome question formed in Kingslea's mind. He turned angrily on Billy Festus.

"What if those bastards had said they'd go partners with you?"

The old man stared at him wide-eyed, innocent as a babe. "What do you mean, Wade?"

"I mean you told 'em to kill me and take you as a partner. It wasn't till they said no that you started shooting. What if they'd said yes?"

"Son, I was just stalling for time. I knew those bandits aimed to kill us both."

"Well, you made a damn strong case for just killing me. What if they'd said yes?"

The old oilman's face reddened. "Blast you, is this the thanks I get for saving your miserable life? Good God in heaven, what is this younger generation coming to?"

Kingslea let it drop. He'd never know what Festus had planned; as best he could calculate, the odds were 50–50 either way. By sunset the partners had locked up leases on more than three thousand acres surrounding the Booker property.

Billy Festus figured there was no use keeping his secret any longer. He had all the land he wanted and if others wanted to lease adjoining properties that was fine. They went by the whorehouse and paid Miss Helen a thousand dollars and took Fanny and Ida to the Gusher with them. They found a lawyer, too, and while the champagne flowed they signed the papers that created Festus & Kingslea Petroleum in accordance with the laws of the state of Texas.

"While you got your pen out, Mr. Lawyer," Kingslea said, "I want you to draw up a paper giving five percent of my share to this young lady here."

Fanny hugged Kingslea. The sleeves of her pink silk dress covered the bruises on her arms, but her powder did not quite hide her black eye.

"Wade, you been drinking a good bit," Festus cautioned. "You sure you don't want to think this over?"

"I know what I'm doing!" Kingslea said. "Those drummers from St. Louis would have got the whole damn field if it hadn't been for her."

"Pussy don't have to be so expensive," Festus grumbled, and Fanny stuck out her tongue at him. The lawyer wrote up the document and Kingslea signed it, as Fanny beamed.

A deputy sheriff dropped by their table to congratulate

them on having rid the community of the St. Louis men, who, he said, were notorious swindlers. He added that they might be able to collect a reward for killing Matt, the scar-faced man, who had been wanted for murder in Oklahoma. Festus said they wanted no reward for performing a civic duty and that if one arrived the deputy should give it to the local churches.

Throughout their dinner wildcatters stopped by the table to confirm the rumors of Festus' new leases and to fish for information. Festus was coy. He gladly confessed to having taken the leases south of town, but he said nothing about the traces of sulphur and oil in Elijah Booker's hog pond. "I've just got me a hunch," he would say with a wink, but that was enough to set off a wild stampede. By midnight dozens of men were banging on farmhouse doors all across the southern half of the county, offering ever-increasing amounts of cash in exchange for leases.

When the celebration at the Gusher broke up, Kingslea and Fanny returned to her room for a more intimate celebration. In the next few hours Kingslea learned that what he had been doing with Harriet since their marriage at age sixteen might possibly be called making love or making babies or sexual intercourse, but by no stretch of the imagination could it be called fucking. What he and Harriet had done, generally on Saturday nights, when he was liquored up and she was looking to Sunday morning forgiveness, had been a furtive, joyless act. Harriet endured it passively, as an inexplicable punishment that God had visited upon the female sex, and Kingslea increasingly found that his brief surge of pleasure was more than offset by Harriet's silent shame and his own ever-deepening guilt.

Fanny showed him that fucking could be fun.

They coupled tirelessly, sweatily, proudly, for a considerable period of time and in a variety of configurations previously unknown to him, but a moment came, as he strained toward his fourth orgasm—she was, as best he could divine, in a state of perpetual orgasm—when she urged him to lie still beside her.

"Darling," she whispered, "you're a wonder, but we really must change the pace."

She stroked his belly, nibbled his ear, and otherwise teased him into relaxation, whereupon she began the second phase of his education. In the next hour or so, as they moved this way and that in the moonlight, he began to think of her soft, lithe body as a mighty continent to be explored, and he came to sense dimly the terrible, wonderful truth: a man can spend a lifetime exploring a woman's body and never exhaust all its mysteries and pleasures.

"Is there anything you want me to do?" he whispered in the stillness before dawn.

"I thought you'd never ask," she replied and directed his attentions downward, into the dark, mysterious swamp of her sex.

He began the journey reluctantly, but when the tip of his tongue encountered a small, elusive button of flesh it was as if an electric current had jolted Fanny's body. A tigress moments before, she was suddenly a kitten, whimpering, twisting this way and that. Emboldened, he devoured her eagerly, and as the soft light of dawn filled the bedroom she moaned, she begged for mercy, she whispered that she would die of the tremors that rocked her body one after another, but Kingslea would not stop his explorations until abruptly, with a fearsome cry, she went limp.

Shaking his head in wonder, he poured himself a tumbler of Scotch. Her juices still burned hot and spicy on his tongue. Love's feast was not peaches and cream, he reflected, more like mince pie, but all in all a man could develop a taste for it.

Her eyelids fluttered. "Might I have a sip, good sir?" she whispered.

He held the glass to her lips. "You all right?"

"So all right, sir, that I may expire of sheer happiness."

"Good," he said gruffly, as if it was his habit to drive women to such peaks of ecstasy.

"Mr. Kingslea," she continued, a dreamy smile lighting her face, "if you can locate oil as well as you can locate, shall we say, the wellspring of a lady's pleasure, you will become an extremely wealthy man."

Kingslea grinned proudly, for she had made a connection that was only beginning to stir in his own mind and that would soon become a lifelong conviction: that success in oil and success in bed were justly and inextricably linked.

"Just watch me," he told her.

The next morning, while Kingslea slept late, Festus hired a red-haired Irishman named O'Reilly as their tool pusher, the man who would oversee the drilling of their well. O'Reilly quickly assembled a seven-man crew, hired mules and

wagons, and began hauling in a rusty old steam boiler, a used
rig, lumber for a derrick, thousands of feet of pipe, and crates
of spare parts. Within a week they spudded in; three hundred
men, women, and children cheered as the six-inch bit first
sliced downward into the silent uncomplaining earth. They
called the well Louella Booker #1, in honor of their land-
owner's wife, and at first the crowds kept coming back each
day, hoping to see the miracle that, as they imagined it, would
make millionaires of them all. Women fanned themselves,
men tossed horseshoes, and small boys sold lemonade as they
awaited the gusher of their dreams. But the gusher did not
come. There were, instead, endless delays. The chain that
turned the drilling bit would slip loose. The engine would die,
and O'Reilly would kick and curse and fiddle with it until it
sputtered back to life. After two weeks of frustration, under
the cruel midsummer sun, the cheering crowds and the boys
with lemonade were gone. But the work went on.

At six hundred feet they struck water and sand, and that
cost them a day until they could pour enough mud down the
well to hold back the sand. At twelve hundred feet they drilled
past shale and gumbo mud straight into hard rock that broke
their bit, and had to shut down and change bits. At two thousand feet, well into their third week of drilling, the bit jammed
in rock and wouldn't budge. There was nothing to do but
move the rig fifty feet to the south and start over with Louella
Booker #2. That cost them another week and by then people
were starting to joke about "Festus' Folly."

Wade Kingslea worked a shift on the well every day,
alongside the twenty-dollar-a-day roughnecks, partly because
he wanted to learn every detail of the drilling process, but
more because he was obsessed with the quest for oil. His
fortune was down there, somewhere, perhaps just another
hundred feet, and he wanted it, lusted for it, as he had never
wanted anything else in his life.

For a while he spent his nights with Fanny in Goodwill, but
by the time the drilling entered its second month he was
sleeping in a tent at the site. Fanny drove out one afternoon
and brought him sandwiches and some homemade fudge.
After their picnic, she smiled at him shyly.

"I was wondering," she said, eyes downcast, "if perhaps
you'd like me to take a leave of absence from Miss Helen's."

He looked at her sharply. "What do you mean?"

She blushed. "Well, I didn't know if it bothered you that I

was still . . . working . . . and I could sort of take a vacation—richly deserved, you know—and maybe visit you out here and, oh, see that you had clean clothes and decent food and all."

She touched his hand. "I worry about you, Wade, working so hard in this heat."

He saw it all. Arms reaching to ensnare him, to divert him from his goal. "I don't see any need for that," he told her. "I can see you when I want to."

She nodded quickly. "Of course," she said. "I was hoping you'd feel that way."

He scrambled to his feet. "Thanks for the sandwiches," he said. "I got to get back to the rig."

When he went to the whorehouse the next night he took one of the other girls upstairs. Fanny needed to know she had no claim on him. His infatuation for her was cooling. He'd come to regret giving her five percent of his interest in the field, but his lawyer said the contract would be hard to break, so Kingslea guessed he'd write it off to experience. After that visit to the whorehouse he didn't see Fanny for a week, then she turned up at the well one afternoon and said she was leaving Goodwill.

"One of my wells came in," she explained. "I've got a thousand dollars a week."

"That could dry up overnight."

"True, but I have other wells I expect to produce soon—yours included, Mr. Kingslea—and I'm told there are some excellent real estate opportunities in Dallas these days."

They stood facing one another uncertainly on the hot, windswept Texas prairie, Kingslea tall, grim, oil-soaked, and Fanny tiny, merry, twirling a pink parasol.

"I hear there's lots of fancy stores in Dallas," he said. "You'll have a good time spending that money."

She rose on tiptoes to kiss his cheek. "Good-bye, Wade," she whispered. "Thank you for everything."

He watched as she ran back to her new roadster, waved once, and bounced down the road and out of sight. Her sudden departure left him tormented and confused. The terrible truth was that Wade Kingslea had three women on his mind that autumn, at a time when he wanted nothing at all on his mind except oil.

First of all, there was Fanny, who had taught him so much and given him such pleasure. Fanny was wonderful—and yet she was a whore—and his mind could not reconcile that stunning contradiction.

Moreover, Harriet was still much in his thoughts. Not so much Harriet, as what she represented: the inescapable, indisputable fact of his marriage. Harriet had his sons, Coyle and Hoyt, and to Kingslea that was like having his arms and his legs. He had slipped away from Goodwill twice, driving all night, for quick visits with those two boys. Each time, returning to Goodwill, he thought the dilemma would drive him mad: he could not live without his sons, and yet he could no longer live with their mother. He had seen new worlds now, worlds of possibility, worlds good, decent Harriet could never enter, and he was determined that somehow his sons would make that journey with him.

Finally there was a woman he had never seen in person, only in newspaper photographs, a girl he had loved from afar since boyhood and who still walked in splendor in his dreams. She was Livie Cantrell, the daughter of the richest rancher in Kingslea's corner of Texas, and if he could not bring himself to believe he would ever meet her, she nonetheless remained a symbol of the treasures he would claim when his gusher came in.

The well was down to twenty-five hundred feet and the partners needed money for drilling pipe and wages. Festus sold off fifty acres on the north edge of their property but it brought less than he expected. New wells had come in northwest of Goodwill and that was the hot area now. The railbirds at the Excelsior were saying they'd drink all the oil Billy Festus found south of town. Wade Kingslea was afraid they were right. He was still working on the rig, giving his blood and sweat, listening to the roughnecks complain, always wondering if the old man had led them on a wild-goose chase. At three thousand feet Kingslea wanted to shut down Louella Booker #2 and drill somewhere else. Festus insisted they go down another thousand feet.

"You're throwing good money after bad," Kingslea raged.

"The oil's there," Festus insisted. "I can smell it. Just another thousand feet."

"Five hundred," Kingslea declared. "Five hundred's the limit, or this partnership breaks up!"

Festus reluctantly agreed.

They reached thirty-four hundred feet on a Saturday morning. The crew was grumbling, anxious to knock off for the weekend. Festus was asleep under a tree. Kingslea decided to take another core sample. If nothing showed up, they could close down for the weekend, maybe for good. He was tired and bitter. That morning, high atop the derrick, he had slipped and almost fallen eighty feet to the ground. Why am I doing this, he had wondered. For an old man's dream?

He worked with the crew, pulling the pipe up from the hole, unscrewing each twenty-foot section, and stacking it off to the side of the rig. A section of pipe slipped and bloodied a man's hand. The rest of them replaced the drilling bit with a core barrel, a steel tube whose jagged teeth would scoop up rock or sand and bring it to the surface. When the core barrel was in place, they lowered the pipe into the hole again, piece by piece. A purple sunset had spread across the western sky when they were finally ready to take a core. Kingslea turned on the engine and, far below the earth, steel teeth began to slice into rock and mud.

Finally they had the core barrel. Billy Festus crouched over it, running his fingers through its rock and mud.

"Wade, shine your light closer," he asked.

Kingslea jabbed his flashlight toward the mud. "Looks like the same damn mess to me," he grumbled.

Festus plunged his hands into the mud and began tasting it and holding it close to the light.

"Look at it," the old man whispered.

"Why?" Kingslea said bitterly.

"It's woodbine sand."

"Which means?"

"Which means we're right on top of oil, a lot of it. Tell O'Reilly to keep drilling. All night. This is it, Wade."

"I've heard that before. You can't get that crew to work all night. I say close this well down and try somewhere else."

"We've got to keep drilling."

Kingslea decided he'd humored this old fool too long.

"Billy, we're shutting down."

"We're drilling! O'Reilly, come over here."

O'Reilly hurried over. "What's the plan?"

"The plan is to shut this damn well down," Kingslea said.

"Keep drilling," Festus said. "All night long."

"You gentlemen better decide who's in charge," O'Reilly said.

"I'm in charge," Festus declared. He pulled the Derringer

from his coat pocket and leveled it at his partner. "Wade, stay out of my way."

Kingslea's blood ran hot with anger. There was an old saying in Texas, "Never point a gun at a man unless you're going to shoot him." Kingslea knew he could make the old man eat his damn Derringer. No one would blame him. Instead, he started laughing.

"All right, you old fool," he said. "Drill your damn well. Hell or China. Who cares?"

He sat down with his back to a tree and laughed again as Festus encountered a mutiny among the crew.

"It's Saturday night, Billy!"

"We're tired!"

"There ain't no oil down there!"

"Boys, I'm paying double for this shift," Festus declared. "Forty dollars from now to noon!"

"Let's see the greenbacks!"

Festus began passing out twenty-dollar bills and soon the men were replacing the drilling bit.

At dawn, at thirty-five hundred feet, there was a rumbling in the well. A silver shower filled the sky and the men scattered.

"Is it oil?" a roughneck cried.

"It's water," Festus yelled. "Water and gas, which means the oil ain't far behind."

Kingslea began to feel the excitement. He walked over to the old man. "Are you sure, Billy?"

"I'd bet my life on it," Festus cried.

Word of the all-night drilling had spread and families began to appear soon after dawn. Many were in their Sunday best, ready to go straight to church from the drilling site. A strong, cool wind was bringing rain clouds from the north. They reached thirty-six hundred feet. The wind rocked the derrick and one of the guy wires broke. Kingslea volunteered to climb up the derrick and bolt down a new wire. Rain was falling and he moved carefully up the wet, slick ladder. Eighty feet up he quickly attached the new guy wire. Then he stood for a moment, cooled by the wind and the rain, looking at the people who were gathered around the rig. They were farm families mostly, the sort of people he had grown up with, and seeing them standing there in their Sunday go-to-meeting clothes suddenly took him back to the life he had left behind, and he ached for his wife and his sons and his farm and his friends—

for *himself*, as he once had been. He thought of his sons, solemn Coyle, sturdy Hoyt, growing boys who needed a father, and of Harriet, as decent a woman as ever walked the earth, and tears stung his eyes as the enormity of his sins washed over him. He had turned his back on home, on family, on God, on morality, on all that was decent and holy and deserving of a man's love and labor.

A boy in the crowd was waving at Kingslea. He might have been Coyle or Hoyt. He might have been everything Kingslea had left behind. He raised one hand in recognition but he lacked the spirit to wave to the boy. His sins overwhelmed him. The wind howled and the echoes of a thousand sermons roared in his ears.

Wickedness proceedeth from the wicked.

God will not be mocked.

Vengeance is mine.

Despair filled Wade Kingslea, despair and guilt and hopelessness that gnawed at his bones.

Just then the rumbling began.

At first he thought it was thunder.

The derrick began to shake, the drill pipe to rattle, the very earth to tremble, and he knew it was not thunder but the judgment of God.

The roar was coming from the bowels of the earth, and Kingslea knew that within seconds the swaying derrick would be blown away by thousands of gallons of oil exploding up a narrow hole in the ground, and he would be blown up with it, blown to heaven, blown to hell. He knew there was not time to scramble down the ladder and he knew that if he jumped he would be killed. Below him people were running, screaming, falling to their knees. Kingslea laughed and raised his eyes to the dark sky, awaiting the explosion, awaiting death, awaiting God.

Then, as the pipes clanged madly, as the roar grew deafening, a different instinct seized him. The guy wire he had attached still stretched to the ground. "God, God, God," he screamed and leaped to the wire and began to slide downward. The wire cut through his gloves and sliced his hands like a razor. He screamed in pain, heard the mighty roar of the exploding derrick, felt the blast, felt the wire go slack, felt his body falling, spinning, flying, tossed like a leaf, until he floated into gentle darkness.

The gusher filled the sky and sent the derrick's pipes and

timbers flying like jackstraws. Billy Festus ran about screaming to men to put out their cigarettes. Some of the roughnecks
had stripped to their undershorts and were dancing about in
the falling oil. All around the well, people were laughing,
crying, embracing, praying. A preacher mounted an oil drum
and praised the Lord but no one noticed. Off to the side, a thin
old woman in a sunbonnet lay still and silent in the mud,
crushed by a falling pipe, while her dazed husband knelt beside her whispering, "Sarah Jane, we're rich, we're rich!"

Kingslea lay flat on his back in a pool of mud. He felt the
cool rain on his face, then the pain in his left arm. His eyes
fluttered open and he saw a sky black with oil, his oil. He
groaned and tried to get up, fell back into the mud, and realized that his left arm was broken. His hands were torn and
bleeding. He willed his pain away and stumbled through the
rain and mud and oil and blood until he found Billy Festus,
surrounded by cheering, weeping men and women. Kingslea
pushed them aside until he was face to face with his partner.

"How big is she?" he demanded.

Festus looked puzzled, then began to laugh.

Kingslea, in a rage, seized the old man's collar. "Damn
you, how big is the well? A thousand barrels a day? Five
thousand?"

Festus' eyes narrowed. "You damn fool, what does it matter? This is a *field* of oil. There could be a *million* barrels of
oil down there. You're a rich man, Wade. Let's see you smile.
That's what you wanted, wasn't it?"

Kingslea released the old man and walked away without a
word, away from the gusher, away from the people, walked
blindly until he sank to his knees on a low hill half a mile from
the well. Hundreds of people were arriving now, by car, by
wagon, by foot, joining the throng around the gusher, waving
their arms, embracing, rolling about in the muck. Wade
Kingslea looked at them and they seemed many miles away
from him, like ants scurrying on a distant anthill. He had left
those people now, those ordinary people with ordinary lives.
The earth had yielded up its treasure to him, its black gold.
His doubts were gone now, washed away by the flood of oil.
He had put his life in the hands of God and God had decreed
that he should not die but should live, be rich, powerful, a
lord of the earth. That was his destiny, to do what he wanted
to do, make his own rules, live his life as he chose.

To be free.

Wade Kingslea struggled to his feet. His left arm dangled limp and useless, but he raised his right arm high above his head, and with his torn hand clenched into a bloody fist he saluted the geyser of oil.

"I'll have it all," he promised the distant gusher. "All of it, by God! Everything I want!"

Then the pain overcame him and he pitched forward unconscious onto the soggy ground.

_ *Book II* _

Wade and Livie

Fort Worth
1921

CHAPTER ONE

On the spring day in 1921 when Wade Kingslea arrived in Fort Worth, anxious to assume his place among the Texas oil aristocracy, most people in the city couldn't have cared less about one more newly rich wildcatter. They were all too busy talking about a black man named Fred Rouse who'd managed to get himself killed not once but twice.

Getting yourself killed once in Fort Worth was as easy as falling off a log. But *twice?* That, everyone agreed, took talent.

Fred Rouse's double-barreled departure had come about because the Butchers Union had called a strike at the big packing plants on the city's North Side. The town fathers, unyielding in the face of this homegrown Bolshevism, had called in some free-lance strikebreakers to restore the civic tranquillity. One of the strikebreakers was Fred Rouse, a big, surly black man who made the mistake of firing his gun into a crowd of unarmed pickets. Probably a white man would have gotten by with it, but to be shot at by a gentleman of color was more than the butchers would tolerate. They grabbed Fred Rouse, gave him a beating that was up to their highest professional standards, and left his bloody remains in the street for dead.

Eventually someone came along and tossed the corpse into a wagon, thinking to deposit the late strikebreaker in the Trinity River, but halfway there Rouse sat up, announced there was still life in him, and begged to be taken to a hospital.

That was Fred Rouse's second mistake of the day, for news of his recovery and whereabouts soon spread. That very night a delegation of masked men removed the unlucky Rouse from his hospital bed and soon thereafter left him hanging from a tree on Samuels Avenue.

Fort Worth was like that. Violence was a local tradition. The city had been created seventy-odd years before as a military outpost, from which the U.S. Army could send forth troopers to search out and destroy the Indians who were raping, scalping, kidnapping, and otherwise discomforting settlers in North and West Texas. During the Civil War, with the Army withdrawn, Fort Worth was almost wiped out, by Indians on the one hand and starvation on the other. Still, the city hung on and prospered after the war by becoming the jumping-off point for the great cattle drives to the northern markets.

Thus was born Cowtown, as Fort Worth was affectionately known, a thriving, two-fisted, no-nonsense community on a high bluff overlooking the meandering Trinity River. And central to Cowtown, located just a few blocks from its courthouse, was Hell's Half Acre, as dangerous and degraded a collection of bars, brothels, and gambling houses as could be found east of Hong Kong. For more than half a century, respectable Fort Worth, which increasingly boasted churches, parks, theaters, libraries, debutantes, country clubs, and other harbingers of civilization, coexisted uneasily with the sin, violence, corruption, and degradation of Hell's Half Acre.

The truth was that respectable Fort Worth had a sneaking affection for the desperadoes and gunslingers who made the city their home away from home, from Butch Cassidy and the Sundance Kid at the turn of the century to Bonnie and Clyde and Machine Gun Kelly a few decades later. Decent people were properly outraged when a whore named Sally was found nailed to an outhouse door in Hell's Half Acre, or when a gambler named Luke Short gunned down the town marshal, and ex-gunslinger named Long Hair Jim Courtright, outside the White Elephant Saloon, but those same good people invariably hungered for all the sordid details of the outrage. Over the years decent people in Fort Worth grew somewhat more tolerant of indecent behavior than their counterparts in tamer communities. Fort Worth was wild, dangerous, and crazy, its more thoughtful citizens agreed, but almost never dull.

Such was the city that Wade Kingslea, as an up-and-coming wildcatter, chose for his home. He had visited nearby Dallas and found it a city of simpering clerks and thin-lipped bankers. Fort Worth was Western, wide open, a city with a soft spot for outlaws and renegades, a city where a man could stretch his legs and be what he wanted to be. In the decades ahead Kingslea would roam the wide world over, in search of oil and other pleasures, but Cowtown was always home. The city fit him like a glove.

Before he went to Fort Worth to start his new life, Kingslea made one more trip home to Liberty and his old life there. Harriet and his sons wanted to know when he was coming home to stay, and he could only reply with vague, evasive answers. The truth was that he had been born anew in Goodwill, and he had no intention of staying in Liberty or living with Harriet again, but he was not yet prepared to break that news to her. As soon as decency permitted he pleaded the demands of his new career and once again said good-bye to his family and to the dusty little town that had been his home for twenty-five years.

He arrived in Fort Worth one windswept March day driving a new Pierce-Arrow and with fifty thousand dollars cash in his pocket and two million dollars in the bank, his share of the proceeds of his Goodwill properties. He climbed out of his Pierce-Arrow and stood for a moment staring in unabashed awe at his temporary home, the Westbrook Hotel. He had heard about the Westbrook before, from Fanny, who loved to tell the story of how the dancer Vernon Castle had lived the last months of his life there, before dying in an airplane crash outside Fort Worth during the First World War. Still, for all Fanny's tales, he was not quite prepared for the full glorious reality of the hotel. The Westbrook was an amazing seven stories high, boasted two hundred rooms, each with its own bath, and featured an air-conditioning system that was the talk of Texas.

Grinning proudly, Kingslea marched into this prairie palace, a tall, lean, handsome man, wearing a perfectly tailored pearl-gray suit and carrying a small revolver under his left arm. He stood for a moment, just inside the lobby, surveying the scene there contentedly. The huge lobby had been stripped of furniture, the better to accommodate the several hundred men who were milling about, waving oil leases, peering at maps, dickering over endless deals. Towering above them was a big-breasted, gold-gilded Roman goddess holding aloft a torch. As Kingslea watched, a grizzled old wildcatter, closing a deal, rubbed the goddess's ample behind for luck. Across the lobby a stout man with a walrus mustache slipped a thousand-dollar bill from his pocket, set it afire, and used the

burning greenback to light a companion's cigar. Kingslea felt
at home already.

"Pardon, friend, but would you happen to be Mr. Wade
Kingslea?"

Kingslea whirled about and discovered a short, husky man
of about his own age standing beside him. The man had a
round face, thinning hair, and a shrewd glint to his eyes.

"Who wants to know?"

"Sid Richardson's the name," the stranger said. "I'm in the
oil game myself, Wade, and I heard some good reports on you
out of Goodwill. I wonder if you'd care to join me for a
friendly drink."

Kingslea hesitated. He'd heard of Richardson, as an up-
and-coming wildcatter, but he remained suspicious. "What
for?"

"I was thinking we might do some business together."

"What is your business, Mr. Richardson?"

"Call me Sid, friend. Oh, I buy, I sell, I trade. I'm just an
East Texas horse trader who found out there was more fun and
profit in trading oil leases than in trading horseflesh."

Kingslea shrugged and followed the plump young
wildcatter into the hotel's crowded bar. "How's lady luck been
treating you?" he demanded.

"I can't complain," Richardson said. "Oh, I've been broke
so many times I think it must be habit-forming, but there's
always one more cow pasture with oil under it. I've got my
eye on some properties in West Texas. I was thinking maybe
you'd like to join up with me and my partner, Clint
Murchison, in a few deals out that way."

Kingslea shook his head emphatically. "No hard feelings,
Sid, but I reckon I'm the lone wolf type."

Richardson shrugged good-naturedly. "No hard feelings at
all. Maybe you'd like to join me and a friend for lunch."

Kingslea downed his drink and stood up. "Some other
time," he said.

Just then a woman's voice, rich and regal, burst over them.
"Sidney, I was *expecting* you in the dining room!"

As Sid Richardson scrambled to his feet, Wade Kingslea
turned and to his astonishment saw the woman he had loved
since he was ten years old.

She was almost six feet tall, with milky skin, moss-green
eyes, a full red mouth, and reddish hair piled high atop her
head. To Wade Kingslea she was without question the most

beautiful, desirable woman in the world. And now she was angry, with a cutting edge to her voice.

"Livie, I beg your humble pardon," Richardson was saying. "I got to talking business with this gentleman, and . . ."

The woman looked Kingslea up and down. "Does the gentleman have a name?" she asked coolly.

"The gentleman's name is Wade Kingslea," Richardson said. "Wade, this fine lady, whose bark is substantially worse'n her bite, is Livie Mortimer."

Wade Kingslea stared into the woman's cool green eyes. He felt as if he was dreaming.

"I know you," he said half to himself.

"Have we *met?*" the woman said in a tone that suggested the extreme improbability of such a meeting.

"No," he said. "We haven't met."

There was an awkward pause, then Richardson spoke. "If it ain't being too inquisitive, Wade, how is it you *know* Livie if you haven't *met* her?"

Kingslea regained control of himself. "I grew up in Liberty, Mrs. Mortimer," he said. "When I was a boy, they used to run your picture in the paper."

"Oh, really?" the woman said airily. "Well, Sidney, I believe you invited me for lunch?"

"So I did, Livie. I even invited Mr. Kingslea here to join us. Mr. Kingslea, if you haven't heard, is the Midas of Goodwill. But Mr. Kingslea said he had some urgent business that precluded him from joining us."

The woman glanced at Kingslea again, as if to say, Then why is he still standing there? Kingslea swallowed his considerable pride and said, "Sid, I'd be pleased to join you and Mrs. Mortimer, if the invitation's still good."

"Well, come on, then, and let's see if they've got us a table," Richardson said, and the three of them walked from the bar into the hotel's glittering dining room.

Kingslea was still stunned to be with this woman, who for so many years had been a dream to him, as distant as a star. She was the granddaughter of Earl Cantrell, who owned the biggest ranch in North Texas. Livie Cantrell—the Little Princess of the Panhandle, the papers had called her—was five years younger than Kingslea. Each year on her birthday, starting when she was about five, her grandfather had given her a new pony or carriage, and the newspaper photographers would come and photograph the old Indian fighter and cattle baron with his beautiful granddaughter. And each year the young Wade Kingslea would see her picture, until in time she came to symbolize for him something he could not even define: the idea that there was Something Else beyond the life he had known. Each year he would clip out her picture and hide it in his dresser drawer. Even after he married and had children, she was still in his dreams, a symbol of that other life that in time led him to Goodwill, to Fort Worth, and now to Livie Cantrell herself.

In the dining room Sid Richardson slipped the maître d' a fifty-dollar bill and was rewarded by a large corner table. The two men ordered beer and T-bone steaks; Livie asked for a salad and iced tea.

"I ask Livie out to lunch about once a month," Richardson said. "I'm trying to get her to marry me, or failing that, to let me drill on the Triple Six. The woman's got a half a million acres of land, up north 'n west of here, with nothing on it but dumb old cows and Lord knows how much oil under it, but she's so perverse she won't let me make her a trillionaire."

Livie broke into a wide smile; her eyes gleamed—they reminded Kingslea of foxes' eyes. She was cunning, he thought, and proud and perhaps cruel. And he wanted her, wanted her worse than he had ever wanted anything. He was going crazy trying to remember if she was married. She had married a rich Easterner named Mortimer—that had been in the papers—but Kingslea could not for the life of him remember what had happened to her husband.

"Sidney, I won't marry you because you're not tall enough," she said. "And I won't let you drill the Triple Six, because I don't need any more money and I don't want my land cluttered up with oil rigs."

"The trouble with you, Livie, is you don't appreciate the romance of the oil game," Richardson said. "The adventure of it. Heck, you think adventure is fox hunting or buying a fancy new ball gown from Paris. Livie, if you ever get the oil fever, you'll be worse'n me and Clint. Listen, let me tell you about my friend Peter Red Dog!"

"Peter *Red Dog?*" the young woman said, fascinated.

"My Injun," Richardson said and launched into the tale of a young Indian who was sole owner of two hundred acres of Oklahoma wasteland that Richardson had wanted to lease. The tale went on for some time and involved Murchison and Richardson taking the Indian to Tulsa to sign a lease, whereupon he was kidnapped by two Houston wildcatters and only freed after Murchison blew up a bridge with dynamite. Murchison sounded like quite a boy.

Livie clapped her hands together. "I *love* it, Sid. I just *adore* it."

She had ignored Wade Kingslea throughout the story. But he was studying her, and it came to him, suddenly and absolutely, that she was no more ignoring him than he was her, that she was performing for him, with her perfect profile, her oohs and ahs, her licked lips, her giggles and sighs, as surely as a dancing girl upon a stage, as surely as a whore in his bed. He had never known a woman like this before—rich, bejeweled, famous—but he had learned a lot about women in the past six months, and he thought this one, for all her airs, would be no different. Only the price, that would be different.

"I'll have you, my fine lady," he muttered.

"Beg pardon?" Richardson said.

"I believe Mr. Kingslea is talking to himself," Livie said. "By the way, where is our friend Mr. Murchison?"

"Clint? He's out in West Texas somewhere, most likely in jail."

"I do hope he wins his freedom by the twenty-second of this month, when I'm having a small dinner party at Indian Hill. I want you both there."

"We'll sure try, Livie," Richardson said.

Kingslea, pointedly excluded from the invitation, stood up. "I'd best be going," he said. "The lunch is on me."

Richardson protested, but Kingslea tossed some bills on the table. "A pleasure, Mrs. Mortimer," he added, with an ironic bow.

"Indeed," she said.

"Perhaps we'll meet again."

She battered her long eyelashes. "Perhaps."

He knew damn well they'd meet again.

"Sure you won't change your mind," Sid Richardson said, "and do some business with me 'n Clint?"

Kingslea was coming to like this little man. "I just might," he said. "Let's talk about it."

He turned and sauntered out of the dining room, swaggering a bit, an elegant, formidable-looking man, upon whom were fixed the eyes of most of the women in the room. Olivia Cantrell Mortimer studied him, and there was a certain gleam in her eyes, a certain smug smile on her face, that Sid Richardson had not seen before and that he was pretty sure meant trouble for his new friend Wade Kingslea.

One blistering hot day in the summer of 1853 a seventeen-year-old orphan from Tennessee named Earl Cantrell arrived in Fort Worth with a flea-bitten mule, three dollars, and a vague plan of becoming a cattle rancher. He spent one night in the desolate little fort on the Trinity River, invested two of his three dollars in bacon and beans, and pushed on west. The land was cheap out there, he knew, and he shrugged off the warnings that life was cheap too. Four days out of Fort Worth three Indians set upon Earl Cantrell while he was eating his supper of beans and bacon. Earl survived the melee that followed, if only barely; the Indians survived it not at all. Some cowboys happened to ride by the next morning and found Earl unconscious beside a little creek. His throat was cut, the bowie knife was still clutched in his hand, and three dead Indians were stretched out around him.

While his neck was healing, Cantrell made his home in a Fort Worth saloon and spent most of his time playing poker for small stakes and planning a future that would involve large stakes. He realized that to make a fortune in the cattle business would be wonderfully simple, except for one problem. Land to the north and west of Fort Worth was cheap and plentiful. You needed a lot of it, because it was mostly desert, with precious little growing on it; a rancher had to figure on several acres per cow, but that was no problem because there were millions of unclaimed acres out there.

The problem was the damn Indians.

Past Fort Worth you entered no-man's-land. The Indians roamed free there and robbed and raped and murdered almost at will. Cantrell's advantage, as compared with other would-be ranchers, was that he wasn't afraid of the Indians. He figured that if he'd survived those first three he could survive all the rest of the filthy sons of bitches because from now on he'd take the offensive.

When his neck was healed, Cantrell spied some newcomers to town who looked to have more money than sense. He invited them to join him in a friendly game of five-card, and when it was over he had the thousand dollars that he used to make the down payment on his first ranch, which he called the 666, or Triple Six, in honor of the winning hand that got him started.

For the next few years, Cantrell kept busy raising cattle, buying land, and killing Indians. By the time the Civil War came along he owned about a hundred thousand acres in several counties. That war, a tragedy for so many millions, was a great boon to Cantrell. As the soldiers pulled back from Fort Worth, the Indians became even more bold, and most ranchers feared for their lives and were therefore willing to sell their land cheap. Cantrell bought all the land he could get and in the meantime expanded the small army of well-armed cowboys he had recruited to help him fight his war with the Indians. By the end of the Civil War, he owned something like a half a million acres of land and tens of thousands of longhorns, and in the postwar years, with Americans crying out for beefsteak, he became a very rich man indeed.

Cantrell suffered only one setback in those years: in 1863 Indians carried off his bride of two months to an unknown fate. He was half-crazy for a while, but in time he settled down and married again, this time to the meek, God-fearing daughter of a judge in Dallas. The couple soon produced a son, Earl Bemis Cantrell, Jr., whose misfortune it was to be known all his life as Little Earl Cantrell. Little Earl, raised in his father's long shadow, grew into a shrewd, mean-spirited man who in time took over the management of the Triple Six and made it vastly more profitable than had his cattle-baron father. In time Little Earl married a beautiful, ambitious woman from St. Louis and in the first spring of the new century they produced a daughter, Olivia Regina Cantrell. In the first decade of the century, Little Earl and his wife spent more and more time in Europe and New York, and the raising of their daughter was left to an English governess and, increasingly, to Old Earl himself.

He managed both to spoil the girl rotten and to teach her a great many valuable lessons. Livie learned to ride and shoot, to cook over a campfire, to play a guitar, to mend fences, to shoe horses, to use the stars to navigate the prairie. The lessons he did not teach her were those he had never learned himself: modesty, compassion, patience, a respect for society's rules and regulations. Livie grew up with her grandfather's fiercely independent, frontiersman's view of the world: it was every man for himself and the devil take the hindmost. She was raised as a princess; the Triple Six was her domain, and all who inhabited it were her subjects.

When Livie was twelve there was an incident concerning a

Mexican girl who was a housemaid in Casa Verde, the main house at the Triple Six. Livie one day declared that the sapphire ring her grandfather had given her was missing and that she had seen the Mexican girl leaving her bedroom with the ring in her hand. The girl tearfully denied the accusation, and various friends and priests attested that she was of the highest character. As it happened, Livie's mother tended to believe the Mexican girl, not Livie, because she had been watching the day before when some Yankee visitors had praised the Mexican girl, said she had the prettiest eyes they'd ever seen, and she had watched Livie silently, furiously, leave the room. Still, the mistress of Casa Verde could not take a Mexican's word over that of her own daughter, so the servant girl was banished from the ranch. Not long thereafter, however, Livie too was banished, to Ward-Belmont, a fashionable school for young ladies in far-off Nashville.

Livie soon rebelled against the school's rules and against the idea that she should study anything except those courses she thought of practical value to her. In her senior year her disinclination toward the study of Wordsworth's poetry caused an unfortunate conflict with her earnest young English teacher. Those difficulties climaxed one day that spring when Livie rushed into the headmistress's office, distraught and disheveled, and declared that the English teacher had tried to attack her. The astonished headmistress hurried to the young teacher's office and found him equally distraught. As he told the story, it was Livie who had made advances and vowed revenge when he resisted her.

Livie stuck to her guns.

"How can you do this to me?" cried the young man, who was recently married and highly regarded. "What have I done to you, except behave honorably? Don't you see I can be ruined?"

"Liar!" Livie exclaimed. "Fiend!"

The teacher was dismissed, and Livie graduated and returned to the ranch, only to be met with the news of her grandfather's death. Her genuine grief was only slightly lessened by the realization that she would someday be the sole owner of the Triple Six's half-million acres, a fortune that promised to become even more vast now that oil was being discovered at various locations nearby. Livie announced that she had no further interest in education and that she intended to live at the Triple Six and assist in its management. Her parents were not pleased with her decision. Her father wanted her to make her debut at Fort Worth's new Assembly Ball and then to marry; her mother had cause to suspect that if Livie stayed around the ranch she would become involved with one of the cowboys—a reasonable enough diversion for a married woman but dangerous sport for a young, impressionable girl. Livie's parents were thinking of tempting her with a year in New York, but before that could be arranged she chanced upon the first great love of her life.

Wolf hunts were a popular pastime among wealthy Texans of that era. A few years earlier President Theodore Roosevelt himself had been the honored guest at one celebrated hunt given by a famed cattle baron. Little Earl Cantrell organized a hunt that fall of 1917, and he invited a famous wolf hunter named Tom Rolfe to be his special guest. Livie announced that she would participate, and her father had to agree, for although the hunts were traditionally all-male, he could not deny that Livie could ride and shoot better than most men.

Little Earl had invited a dozen guests, fellow ranchers mostly, and they were accompanied by a small army of cowboys and Mexican servants and by several chuck wagons filled with provisions. On their first afternoon out, Tom Rolfe spotted two gray prairie wolves on a distant rise. He and his famed pony Sidewinder and his carefully trained greyhounds led the chase across the prairie. At the end, it was only Livie, riding her mare Frieda, who kept up with Rolfe and was there when his dogs caught one of the wolves. The wolf lunged at one of the dogs, its fangs at its throat, whereupon Tom Rolfe, who might simply have shot the creature, instead raced up to it and plunged his gloved hand deep into its mouth. Quickly, Rolfe seized the wolf's lower jaw, rendering it quite helpless, and lifted it before him triumphantly. Capturing wolves bare-handed was a feat that Tom Rolfe had perfected and that no other white man in Texas had ever been known to imitate.

The other hunters rode up as the famed wolf hunter held his prey aloft. Seventeen-year-old Livie Cantrell, watching from the edge of the circle, suddenly felt faint. She leaned against a poplar tree, fearful she might fall. Her knees were weak, her heart was pounding; she was ravaged by emotions she had never known before. Tom Rolfe was fifty years old, a bald, stocky, red-faced man, powerfully built, and suddenly Livie realized that she wanted him, wanted to devour him, wanted him to subdue her as boldly and totally as he had that snarling wolf. His strength, his raw physicality, left her breathless. As Tom released the wolf, and the ranchers cheered, Livie stroked Frieda's nose and pondered her next move.

By the third afternoon of the wolf hunt everyone was exhausted. They were camped by a small stream when Tom Rolfe spotted a wolf emerging from some scrub trees. "Who's with me?" he roared. The men groaned, for they were ready for a drink and dinner, but Livie leaped upon Frieda. "I am," she cried, and she and Tom raced for miles across the prairie. Finally the hounds cornered the wolf among some rocks, and again Tom leaped down and seized the creature with his gloved hand.

"Stroke it, my dear," he said when Livie approached. "He's quite harmless now."

Livie reached out cautiously to touch the wolf's soft fur.

"Nothing to fear, child," Tom said. "We'll let this one live." He set the wolf free. They watched it race out of sight, then he extended his canteen to her. "Water?" he asked. She drank deeply from his canteen, savoring the intimacy of the moment.

"I'm not a child," she said.

"Pardon?"

"You called me child. I'm not."

She trembled to be so close to his sweaty, confident masculinity, but she was feeling sure of herself now.

"No, you're not," he agreed. "You're on your way to being one hell of a woman."

"I want us to make love."

He nodded. "I thought you might."

"Will you?"

"I'd be a damn fool not to," Tom said. He led her up a small rise, took off his white Stetson, and spread his buckskin jacket on the ground. "You've done this before, have you?" he asked.

Livie said yes, praying that was the right answer, and he began unbuttoning her blouse. When she was quite naked he kissed her nipples, one after the other, and Livie thought she would faint. She helped him take off his dusty clothes, then she embraced him, pressing her tall, thin body against his short, powerful one. Moaning, she slipped to her knees before him.

"Don't let's rush things," Tom said and stretched her out atop his jacket. "One good turn deserves another." He knelt between her long white legs and touched her with his tongue. "Oh, my love, I'd die for you," she moaned.

"Not necessary, my dear," the wolf hunter said and rose up to enter her.

He was wonderfully skilled, patient, and gentle. The only boy she had made love with before had been as nervous as a rabbit, but Tom had his own easy pace, slow and majestic, like the ocean tides. Soon their bodies moved together—or so it seemed to her in her ecstasy—as surely and triumphantly as he and Sidewinder flew across the prairie after the silver wolves. When she felt her first explosions starting, she begged him to come with her, but Tom kept to his steady pace and it was not until she came a second time, crying out with agonies of delight, that he ejaculated. "My love, my love," she whimpered, swooning into darkness.

When she awoke, Tom was dressed. He was sitting against a cottonwood, smoking his pipe.

"Was I good?" she asked.

"Excellent," Tom said, smiling a bit. He had big, crooked teeth, but wonderful wrinkles fanned out around his eyes when he smiled.

"I want to do it again," she said, reaching out for his hand.

"We haven't time."

"To hell with them."

"No use arousing suspicions."

"I'll meet you tonight, when everyone's asleep."

"Too risky. If your father found out, he'd kill me. Or have me killed."

"Then I'll meet you somewhere. Name the time and place."

Tom Rolfe raised an eyebrow. "You're serious, aren't you?"

"I'm going to be a very rich woman," Livie said, as if that explained everything.

The sun was poised above the western prairie. They would have to ride hard to make it back to the camp before dark. "Put your things on, Livie," he said.

"Don't you care for me at all?" she cried.

Tom Rolfe chewed on his pipe. This girl, he thought, was a hell of a fuck and a hell of a risk. "I'll be in Dallas a week from Monday," he said. "The Clifton Hotel."

"I'll be there," she promised.

Livie concocted an elaborate lie about a dying friend in

Dallas. When she arrived at the hotel room, she found Tom sitting in an easy chair, puffing his pipe, and reading a Zane Grey novel.

"You came," he said.

"I told you I would."

"Would you like some lunch?"

She kissed him. "Put out that smelly pipe and fuck me," she said.

Tom closed his book. "I'll put out my pipe when I'm ready, my dear," he said. "And I'll thank you not to use such language. Talk like a whore and you'll be treated like one."

Livie burned with shame. "I'm sorry," she whispered, possibly the first time in her young life that she had used those words. After a moment Tom stroked her hair.

They stayed in the hotel room for three days and made love more or less nonstop. Tom gave her constant, undreamed-of-pleasure; she wanted, in return, to give him everything, to make him forget every other woman he had ever known. She let her imagination run riot, kissing him here, probing him there, until sometimes he would mutter, "That's a whore's trick," and she would reluctantly break off her explorations. At dawn on their last day together, she wept as she watched him sleeping, placidly snoring, and she realized how utterly she loved him. She imagined herself a slave of love—it was a concept she had encountered in certain forbidden novels that Ward-Belmont girls kept hidden under their mattresses—and she asked nothing more than that this sweet, erotic bondage go on forever. Why should she not have him if she wanted him? With her money she could make Tom one of the lords of Texas.

"You must divorce your wife," she told him that last morning.

"Nonsense. I love my wife."

When she tried to persist, he cut her off. Frustrated, she suggested that they go for a walk. She loved walking with Tom. Men stepped aside when Tom Rolfe passed by. He looked serene, with his pipe and his affable, ruddy face, yet he had an air about him that warned he would be a dangerous man to cross. As they strolled about the shabby neighborhood between their hotel and the train station, they passed a tattoo shop. On impulse, Livie insisted they go inside.

"I want a tattoo," she said. "We both should have one. To remember our precious time together."

"None for me," Rolfe told her.

"Then I will," she declared, and before they left, the tattoo artist, a scrawny old man with one glass eye, had imprinted a tiny pink rosebud on her inner thigh.

"Only you will see it, Tom," she whispered.

"Oh, I doubt that," he said and took her to catch her train.

Her first hint of trouble came when her father picked her up at the train station, instead of one of the cowboys.

"Has your friend's health improved?" Little Earl asked.

"Oh yes," Livie said. She was thinking of Tom. They would marry, she was determined. She was wondering if there was not some way to buy off his wife.

Two miles from Casa Verde, Little Earl turned off the road and drove out onto the dusty, desolate prairie.

"Where are you going?" Livie asked. She hated her father; she always had.

"A lovely sunset, wouldn't you say?"

The sun was a blood-red globe, poised above the distant, table-flat horizon, setting the clouds ablaze. Little Earl stopped the car.

"Let's get out for a minute," he said.

"Why?" She was seized with the idea that he wanted to kill her.

"To have a little talk," he said. She got out and stood beside the car. He opened the trunk. When he approached her, she saw the bullwhip in his hand.

"What are you doing?" she demanded.

"Slut," he shouted. "Whore."

He lashed out and the whip's hard leather thongs cut deep into her arm and back. She screamed in pain and started to run, but the whip sliced her legs, and she fell onto the rocky earth. She lay there, sobbing, bleeding, and her father stood over her, gasping for breath.

"What do you mean, running off with a fifty-year-old man? A man who catches wolves with his hands! Do you want to make me the laughingstock of Texas?'

"I'm going to marry him!"

"You fool! I can run Tom Rolfe out of Texas. He doesn't have a dime."

"I have money."

"No you don't. Not until you're twenty-one."

"I'll do as I please," she sobbed.

"You'll marry a man who is your social equal," her father

shouted. "If you don't, you can go wait tables in Fort Worth for all I care, you little slut!"

He left her there on the prairie.

In the next few days Livie thought seriously of killing her father, but before that could happen her mother arranged for her to go to New York, and it was there that she met her next great love.

The occasion was a charity ball, a benefit for the war orphans of France, at the Waldorf-Astoria. His name was Ralph Preston Mortimer III, and he was one of the steel-mill Mortimers of Pittsburgh and as rich as you could be in America without having oil. Ralph was in his early forties, tall and very thin, with delicate features and hair that was, prematurely, a glistening silver-gray. He called himself an investment banker, but the newspapers called him a "sportsman," which meant that he spent a great deal of his life on yachts and polo fields. Ralph was handsome, witty, charming, and sophisticated: Livie, who was still a few months shy of eighteen, fell in love the first time they danced. As they twirled about the ballroom, with all eyes fixed on them, she thought suddenly of poor, bald, fat, scarred, fifty-year-old, wolf-catching Tom and wondered how she could ever have considered marriage to such a man.

After two weeks Ralph and Livie were secretly engaged. Livie was proceeding to Paris, but it was agreed that Ralph would come to Texas at Christmas to announce the good news to her family and friends. It had been a whirlwind courtship, romantic, dazzling; there was, for Livie, only one slight drawback. She was awed by Ralph's poise and elegance and social grace, but she never felt for him the same passionate physical desire she had known with Tom Rolfe. Nor, for that matter, had Ralph exhibited any sexual interest in her beyond an occasional kiss on the cheek. But she decided that was evidence of his good breeding and of his high morality and deep respect for her. Also, she learned, there had been a great tragedy in Ralph's life. Some years earlier he had married the heiress to one of the great Chicago meat-packing families. Only a few months after the marriage the bride suffered a nervous breakdown. Several years of treatment and confinement had followed, and on one of her visits home the unhappy young woman had flung herself from a bridge. One night Livie whispered to Ralph that she had been told of the tragedy, and he held her hand and wept and said he had vowed never to wed again, so great had been his suffering, but now she had brought him a precious new life. Livie's heart burst with joy at his words.

Ralph's visit to the Triple Six was a glorious success. He charmed Livie's parents, so much so that Little Earl insisted he stay and accompany the family to the annual Fat Stock Show and Rodeo in Fort Worth. Soon all Texas was awed by Livie Cantrell's elegant Yankee millionaire. The women were thrilled by Ralph's looks and manners, and the men were reluctantly impressed by his money, business sense, and horsemanship. After a long talk with Little Earl, Ralph agreed to move to Texas, to direct the operations of the Triple Six there, and to explore the possibilities of oil development. Little Earl also announced plans for construction of a second ranch house, a few miles from Casa Verde, that would be his wedding gift to the young couple.

The wedding was magnificent. Five hundred of the richest people in Texas descended on Casa Verde, many in the private railroad cars that were becoming fashionable, for a week's festivities that included a rodeo, a wolf hunt, fireworks, and what was probably the biggest barbecue in history. Livie was married in a gown that was inlaid with diamonds and pearls, had once belonged to the queen of Spain, and was rumored to have cost seventy-five thousand dollars.

Ralph and Livie had agreed to forgo a wedding trip so they could oversee the construction of their new home. They therefore spent their wedding night in one of the guest cottages at Casa Verde. At midnight, light-headed with champagne, Livie emerged from her bathroom in a sky-blue silk robe. She stood before Ralph, smiling up at him, and then with a toss of her shoulders she let the robe slip to the floor. She offered herself to him, slender and naked, her reddish hair long and loose at her shoulders. "Now, my love," she said. She had decided to pretend she was a virgin. Indeed, in her heart, she knew that nothing before Ralph really mattered.

"You're quite beautiful," Ralph said. He cupped one of her breasts in his hand and examined it rather matter-of-factly. He was still wearing his pajamas and robe.

"Come to bed now," she said and slipped onto the sheets. Ralph kept his robe on but sat beside her on the bed, looking her body up and down, "Excellent," he said. "Excellent."

"I have to explain about . . . this," she said, pointing to the rosebud tattoo on her thigh. "It was a prank, when I was in school."

Ralph smiled for the first time. "It's exquisite," he said. He leaned over and kissed the tattoo and she trembled at his touch. He sat up, sighed, and turned off the lights. Then he sat beside her, kissed her breasts, and stroked her with his middle finger until she began to twist about with painful pleasure. "Come inside me now, my darling," she whispered.

Ralph sat up. "Livie, I have a confession."

"Yes?" A great ache throbbed inside her.

"I have a certain . . . disability."

"What do you mean?"

"Erections are . . . very difficult for me."

"I'll help you," she cried. "I'll make you love me."

"If you wish," he said. She tore open his pajamas and found his tiny limp prick, no larger than her thumb. She kissed and coaxed it for what seemed like hours, but at the end it was still as limp as when she started. By then her neck hurt and she was fighting back tears.

"Perhaps we should sleep awhile," she said.

"Actually, my love, there is a more imaginative solution to the problem," Ralph said. He slipped out of bed and disappeared into the bathroom. When he returned a moment later, crossing the room in the bright moonlight, she saw that he now possessed what seemed to be a huge erection. This sudden, lamb-into-lion transformation left the young bride confused and not a little frightened.

"Ralph, my darling, what . . . ?"

"They strap on," he explained. "Many women prefer them to the real thing."

Then he was above her, menacing, triumphant, and instinctively she reached out to guide the dildo to its mark. "This one's French," Ralph said. "All the best ones are." Then he—it—was inside her.

It hurt at first, but Ralph moved expertly, and in a moment Livie was thinking of that first time they'd danced at the Waldorf ball for the war orphans. Her passion returned, and she began to whisper, "Yes, my darling," and to strain hard against Ralph and his instrument of love. "Are you close?" Ralph asked. "Yes, yes, give me more," she pleaded, and Ralph, whose face was buried in her hair, seemed to laugh and said, "Of course, my sweet!" He slipped his hand beneath her bottom, the better to guide his ever-deepening thrusts, and she felt her orgasm starting, and then, suddenly, he jabbed his middle finger into her. In an instant her ecstasy turned to horror. She was caught, like an animal in some fiendish trap.

"Ralph, stop that," she cried.

"It gives me such pleasure."

"It *hurts*. Take it out."

"The pain will pass, my sweet. You must relax."

"You're insane," she hissed and began to struggle to free herself, but he swiftly had her wrists held tight and he only laughed. "A wife has certain obligations," he whispered and began to move again, taking his perverse pleasure at his leisure. Livie lay stiffly at first, her eyes burning with tears. Even when the pain passed, the physical pain, she felt the even greater pain of humiliation, of submission. Yet amid her mortification, a certain animal cunning emerged. She pretended pleasure. "Oh yes, Ralph darling, you're wonderful," she cried and feigned a mighty orgasm, then went limp beneath him.

Ralph seemed pleased. He extricated himself from her, kissed her on the cheek, got out of bed, and went into the bathroom. She could hear him removing the dildo, washing his hands, and whistling a Sousa march. Livie thought of fleeing, but to where? Across the moonlit prairie in her nightgown to tell her parents she'd married a fiend? No, there was a better solution to the problem, she was sure of that.

"Champagne?" Ralph asked when he emerged from the bathroom.

"Please," she said.

He lifted a bottle from an ice bucket beside the bed and poured two glasses. "To our happiness, my dear," he said.

"I have a certain philosophy, Livie," Ralph said. He had stretched out across the bed, slender and naked in the bright moonlight. "Fate has made it necessary for you and me to pursue money. We can thus give ourselves over to the more challenging—but infinitely more rewarding—pursuit of pleasure, in all its exquisite manifestations. Do you follow me, my child?"

"I think so."

"You are young, but with vast potential. With your beauty, your fierce spirit, your money, with—if I may say so—your basic amorality, with those qualities you are going to be a magnificent partner in my search for pleasure. Have you read de Sade?"

"I . . . I've heard of him," Livie said.

He poured them more champagne, and he was quite charming for a time, as he talked of de Sade and of strange sexual adventures he had sampled in Paris and Buenos Aires and other world capitals; but Livie was not charmed, and later, when finally he was asleep, she lay awake till dawn, trying to decide what on earth she was to do.

The honeymoon was over, literally. Livie's world had become a gilded madhouse. By day, Ralph was charm itself. They rode and swam together, went to teas and balls, and everywhere they were the center of attention. But by night the charming Ralph again became her tormentor. She tried reason, but he only laughed off her arguments for decency and self-respect. She tried tears and pleading, but that only seemed to excite him more. She tried physical resistance, but he was stronger than her, and when once she bit his shoulder, he only bit her back in a way that was most painful and humiliating.

Ralph's desires were, she thought, loathsome. He had some small leather whips—made in China, he said—with which he wished to spank her bottom; she let him do that, although not as hard as he wished. He dressed her in a sailor suit one night, and a schoolgirl's dress another, and she did not mind the costumes, although she thought the entire exercise ridiculous—the goal of sex, after all, was to remove one's clothing, reasoned Livie with her quite logical mind. He was constantly wanting to tie her hands, but she balked at that—God alone knew what he might do if he had her hogtied and helpless.

Most of all, Ralph was obsessed with entering her in that manner that she found most unnatural, painful, and degrading—and that he, therefore, found most desirable. "Your last virginity, my dear," he would jest. She clung to the faint, desperate hope that in time Ralph would come to his senses, would show mercy toward her, but that never came to pass. "You're my wife, Olivia," he would say. "Don't you want to please me?"

She *did* want to please him, that was the problem. She still dreamed of recapturing the magic of their courtship. Finally, one night, she drank a great deal of whiskey and let Ralph do as he wished. The pain was excruciating, even in her stupor, but Ralph was delighted. He kissed her feverishly when he was finished and the next morning filled the bedroom with fresh flowers. Livie no longer cared. She hated him. Most of all, she hated how everybody else loved him: her parents, her friends, the cowboys. It was as if they were all conspirators in her humiliation. She wanted only to be rid of Ralph, but now he seemed quite a permanent fixture at the Triple Six, busy with the construction of their dream house and plans for his horse farm. It was she who seemed the outsider. She knew that if she went to her parents, or to their family lawyer, and said she wanted a divorce, they would all oppose her, say she was hysterical, that she must adjust to marriage. But how could she adjust to this pervert who hurt and humiliated her each night?

In her second month of marriage, Livie knew she must get away or she would go mad. She called the one person she trusted. Then she told Ralph she was going to Dallas on a shopping trip.

They met at the same hotel as before. Had it only been six months? It seemed a lifetime. She threw herself into his arms. "Oh, Tom, for God's sake, make love to me."

He did, as gently and expertly as before, and when they finished she wept with joy and relief. He was a real man, and she had not known what a rare treasure that was.

"Tom, I'm so miserable. My husband is a monster. He forces me to do unspeakable things."

Tom Rolfe puffed on his pipe.

"You've got to help me."

"What did you have in mind?"

"I want you to kill him. No—hear me out. Kill him and then we'll marry. That's what I've always wanted."

"I'm no killer, Livie."

"Don't you want to marry me?" she cried.

Tom Rolfe sighed. "Livie, to be honest, I think marriage to you would be hell on earth."

She began to sob uncontrollably. "You don't love me," she cried.

"I never said I did," Tom Rolfe said and began putting on his pants.

Back at Casa Verde, Livie began to complain of headaches and to submit to Ralph only when he took her by force. She was biding her time now, forming her plan. It was not until she had missed two periods that she was sure. She broke the news one evening when they were having a quiet dinner on the terrace outside the guest cottage.

"I have news, Ralph," she said. "I'm going to have a baby."

He looked at her in astonishment. "That *is* news," he said. "A bloody miracle, in fact."

"I hope you're pleased."

"It was that shopping trip to Dallas, wasn't it?"

"Ralph, you're my husband, and you're the father of my child."

"You little bitch," he said, still smiling.

"And now that we're going to be parents, there are going to be some changes in our relationship," she continued. "We'll have separate bedrooms, for one thing, and there'll be no more . . ."

"Livie," he interrupted, "before you lay down the law, let me give you *my* little surprise. The *Maria* has arrived in Galveston, and I'd like to take you down for a cruise."

She thought about it. Perhaps, in the privacy of his beloved yacht, she could talk sense to him. A divorce, a friendly divorce. It was worth a try. "That sounds very nice, Ralph," she told him.

The *Maria* was eighty feet long and as graceful as a gull. The master bedroom, filled with fresh-cut flowers, French paintings, and iced champagne, was as grand as anything Livie had seen in Europe's finest hotels. The crew of fifteen was Italian and most respectful. But just before they cast off from the dock in Galveston, Ralph had an unsettling surprise for Livie. A broad-shouldered young man with creamy brown skin and sullen eyes came aboard. He was wearing white ducks, a white turtleneck sweater, and a blue blazer. "This is my friend, Carlos, from Buenos Aires," Ralph announced. Carlos bowed and clicked his heels. "Carlos will be our guest on the voyage," Ralph added. Their guest never spoke, nor did his eyes ever leave Livie, who excused herself and went to their cabin, where she tried to take a nap. Once she heard Ralph and Carlos passing by the porthole, laughing and talking in French.

At seven, Ralph joined her. "Come see the sunset, my sweet," he said. "It's quite grand. We'll toast it with champagne and then go in to dinner."

"Ralph, who is Carlos?"

"I told you, he's my friend."

"Why is he here?"

Ralph leered at her. "Because we need him, my dear; because *you* need him."

"What do you mean?"

"Well, if you're so anxious for a stiff prick, Livie dear, then you'll find Carlos most accommodating. No use running off to Dallas for one. We'll all three have a lovely dinner and then adjourn to the bedroom."

"Ralph, are you insane?"

"Not the least. But you're a rather provincial Texas cattle queen who needs to learn how people amuse themselves in the wider world. By the way, have you tried cocaine?"

She saw that Ralph was very high on something, champagne or cocaine or perhaps both, and in that instant she knew what she must do.

"Your plans sound wonderful, Ralph," she said. "Now let's go see the sunset." She smiled and took his arm and led him toward the stern of the yacht. Seagulls squawked overhead, the wind was moist and cool, and Livie was smiling as they leaned against the rail to admire the setting sun.

"How do you feel, Ralph?" she asked.

"A little woozy, but I'll be fine," he said.

Those were Ralph's last words.

Moments later, Livie raced back toward the cabin screaming, "Help, help! My husband has fallen overboard!"

The crew came running, a drunken Carlos appeared, a lifeboat was lowered, but Ralph was never found.

At the official inquest, the newly widowed Mrs. Mortimer testified that her husband had become ill, had leaned over the railing, and had somehow slipped and fallen into the ocean. Investigators found one frightened Italian steward who said he had glimpsed the couple struggling before the man fell overboard, but he later said he had been mistaken. It was officially declared that Ralph had died in a tragic accident. During the inquest a Coast Guard official testified that in all likelihood Mr. Mortimer's body had been devoured by sharks. All eyes were on the elegant young widow as he spoke. Livie, rising to the occasion, sobbed piteously into her lace-trimmed handkerchief. In truth, it was all she could do to keep from laughing. She hoped the sharks had devoured Ralph quite slowly, giving him time to repent his sins at leisure. If there was a just God, Livie thought, Ralph would spend eternity being tormented by demons with flaming dildos.

Thus consoled by religion, and considerably enriched by the addition of Ralph's fortune to her own, Livie went into seclusion at her new home, the grand, ranch-style mansion that was to have been hers and Ralph's. She soon tired of life at Casa Verde, however, and she proceeded to Fort Worth, where she purchased a mansion called Indian Hill, on the city's western bluffs, from the estate of a banker who had inexplicably killed his wife and then himself.

Livie's daughter, Eve Mortimer, was born in the spring of 1920, and Livie, after a period of rest, busied herself redecorating Indian Hill. She was twenty years old, beautiful, widowed, a mother, and very, very rich. All across Texas, the state's elite speculated on when, if ever, Livie Cantrell would meet her match.

Livie was in no hurry. She had learned from her mistakes. She saw now that in the case of Tom she had mistaken sexual attraction for love, and in the case of Ralph she had been too easily awed by social charms. Livie had survived, but she was wiser, and she was bitter. Her greatest mistake, she thought, was having been born a woman in a world inexplicably ruled by men. She enjoyed men, and needed them, but her experience with Ralph had left scars; there was a level at which she would forever hate men. There was one exception, of course, the one great man she had known in her life, her grandfather. Somewhere, someday, she thought, she would find a man who was his equal.

She took lovers from time to time. She preferred men who were rich, physically attractive, and discreet, but she sampled all types—young and middle-aged, intellectual and empty-headed, a policeman, an Englishman, a Jew—on the theory that one should shop about before making a major acquisition. She even once, while having tea with a very wealthy and prominent widow in New York, found herself being seduced by a woman. She let it happen, out of curiosity, and was quite fascinated to discover how much pleasure another woman could give her. She had never known such patient, gentle, loving sex; she doubted that any man could equal it. Still, the fact remained that there was a point in the process when she ached for a stiff prick. Like it or not, that was the way she was made. She began to see that the challenge was to find a stiff prick that came attached to a man who possessed the necessary social, intellectual, and economic standing. After almost a year of widowhood she was starting to despair of finding such a man, when she met Wade Kingslea at the Westbrook Hotel and almost swooned at the sight of those dark, burning eyes, that wide, arrogant mouth, those broad shoulders. She thought he was a man like her grandfather, Earl Cantrell, who would dominate the world around him. She had wanted him, right then, wanted him so urgently that she had no choice but to be rude to him or else she would have fallen at his feet. Livie was glad Wade was an oilman. She thought she might let him drill the Triple Six and make many millions for them both. The idea pleased her. She could make Wade Kingslea a very rich man, if he treated her with the proper respect.

Wade Kingslea and Sid Richardson, back from a month's wildcatting in West Texas, were standing at the curb on Texas Street, staring up at the biggest, most important house that Kingslea had ever seen. It was Indian Hill, the Victorian mansion on Fort Worth's "Silk Stocking Row" that was now Livie Cantrell Mortimer's home. To Kingslea, it seemed more a fortress than a home, and for an instant he feared to launch his invasion.

"Come on, partner, what you so nervous about?" Richardson demanded. "It's just a little ole chili supper."

"I ain't nervous," Kingslea growled. "How many people you suppose will be here?"

"Forty or fifty. Livie's famous for her chili suppers. Among other things."

"What the hell is that supposed to mean?"

"Goodness, Wade, I do believe you've got a yen for the widow Mortimer."

Kingslea squared his shoulders. "Let's get on with it," he said and started toward the mansion. He had, in truth, never been so nervous in his life.

"Good evening, gentlemen."

Kingslea tensed at the butler's greeting. What if he demanded identification, an invitation? Kingslea was ready to kill the man if challenged.

"Evening, Horace," Richardson drawled. "This here's my friend Mr. Kingslea."

"How do you do, sir? Go right on through, gentlemen. Everyone's out back."

They entered a glistening marble foyer and passed beneath a huge, sparkling chandelier. There was a statue of Venus at the bottom of the staircase, and off to the side Kingslea glimpsed a paneled library and more books than he had ever seen before. When they stepped out onto the back porch, a Mexican girl gave them glasses of beer. Several dozen men and women were gathered on the lawn. A mariachi band was playing, flaming torches held back the spring dusk, and in the distance swans glided atop a small lake.

"She *lives* here?" Kingslea muttered.

"Livie's got a whale of a lot of money," Richardson said, "and she's trying to meet the challenge."

As they crossed the lawn, Sid introduced him to several oilmen, bankers, and businessmen. Kingslea kept looking for Livie but she was nowhere in sight. They came upon Clint Murchison telling a group of men about a wildcatter named Hilbert who'd been cheated by a man named Smallwood in one of the Louisiana boomtowns. "Hilbert said he'd get revenge if it took the rest of his life," Clint said. "He tracked Smallwood from town to town, all over the South, for fourteen months and finally caught up with him in a bar in Key West, Florida. He walked up to him and said, 'Smallwood, I'm Hilbert, and you're dead,' and shot him between the eyes. Fourteen months, spent getting even with a man over a ten-thousand-dollar oil deal!" A lively discussion followed as to whether Hilbert was a hero or a fool. Kingslea, who thought he was a fool, sipped his beer and listened to the lively Mexican music and looked for Livie Cantrell. Then, as a quarter-moon rose above the trees, she appeared beside him, wearing a cream-colored silk dress and a pearl choker, her amber hair intricately molded atop her head.

"Mr. Kingslea, what a pleasant surprise," she said.

He searched for irony but found none; she seemed delighted to see him. Suddenly he felt proud and confident.

"Call me Wade," he said. "What shall I call you?"

"Livie," she said. "All my friends do."

"You're very beautiful, Livie."

She blushed demurely. "Thank you, sir. But tell me what you've been doing. Have your explorations with Sid and Clint gone well?"

"We sank a lot of money in some land that could produce some oil. I think it will. But if it doesn't, we'll lose our shirts."

"Goodness, that would be a spectacle."

He still thought she was laughing at him. He had not known women like Livie before, rich, sophisticated women, and something about her confused and frustrated him. She was cordial, she was picture-perfect, but it was as if she was behind glass. How could he reach her?

And still his burgeoning self-confidence welled up inside him; he remembered the one rule he'd learned in Goodwill: if you want it, take it.

"Let's get one thing straight," he said. "I'm not big rich

yet. Not like you and your friends. I will be, but I'm not yet."

Her green eyes searched his face. "Money isn't everything."

"It's most things."

She touched his hand. "I appreciate your honesty. I know a great many men who are rich but not so many who are honest."

"Maybe the richer you get, the harder it is to be honest."

"Perhaps," she said. "Would you like to see my house?"

She took him downstairs and showed him the wine cellar, the billiard room, and an air-conditioning unit that blew air over blocks of ice and then circulated it through the house. She led him through the formal living room with its Persian rugs, French paintings, Italian sofas, and fireplace of green tile from China. The tour was a considerable display of sheer wealth, one that could not have been matched in twenty homes in America, but ultimately it bored Kingslea. He wanted *her*. The rest was just furniture.

"Is there anything else you'd like to see?" she asked after they'd been through the solarium and the library and peeked in the bedroom where her daughter slept. They were standing in the marble foyer, at the bottom of the stairs.

"What's this?" he asked and pointed to a paneled wall beneath the stairway. "There's room for a closet there, but there's no door. Or is there?"

Livie's eyes sparkled. "You're very observant," she said. "That's the vault. The man who built the house kept his cash in there. I use it for my jewelry. Would you like to see it?"

"I wouldn't trouble you."

"No trouble. There are some things I should put away. Excuse me just a moment."

She returned quickly with a key and a jewel box. She slipped the key into the hidden lock, and the almost invisible door swung open. They stepped into the vault and she closed the door behind them. The room was small, perhaps eight by ten feet, with a table in its center and a row of lockboxes built into one wall. Livie had brought some rings in her jewel box; she opened one of the lockboxes and put them inside. Kingslea looked over her shoulder and was shocked at what he saw: hundreds of rings, diamond rings, ruby rings, emerald rings, sapphire rings, crammed into the drawer like trinkets. Livie laughed and began opening other lockboxes. Each contained more jewels: earrings, necklaces, brooches, tiaras; one drawer contained dozens of raw, unset jewels that blazed like fire.

"I think I'm a little crazy about jewelry," she said. "I can't possibly wear it all. But I love having it. Sometimes I want to give a party like this one and throw handfuls of jewels onto the lawn and watch people scramble for them."

"Is that what you want?"

They were standing very close together. His breath was coming irregularly, and he saw hunger in her eyes.

"I don't know what I want," she said. "What do you want?"

"I want you," he said. He cupped her face in his hands and drew her toward him, but she stiffened, held back.

"Me, Wade, or my money?"

"I told you, I'll make my own money, a mountain of it. It's you I want. Everything you are and everything you stand for. I want to bring you down off that pedestal and make you cry and sweat like the rest of us."

"Do it, then."

She opened her mouth to his kiss and he jerked her skirt above her hips. He thrust inside her and she clamped her arms around his neck and moaned so loudly that he thought the people outside must surely hear. She was a big, strong woman who took as well as she gave, and when he had spent himself he clutched her tight, feeling weak, somehow subdued, conquered.

"I wanted you the first time I saw you, at lunch that day with Sid," she whispered. She *was* sweating, the way he wanted her to, and gasping to catch her breath.

"I've wanted you for fifteen years. I wanted you before I knew what it was I wanted."

She dabbed at her face with a handkerchief and smoothed her skirt, all ladylike again. "I've got to get back to the party."

"Meet me tonight, when this is over."

"No."

"Why not?"

"Because you're married. I won't have a sordid backdoor affair. If you want me, you must set your house in order."

Kingslea was livid. "What'd you do?" he demanded. "Give me a free sample? Like somebody opening a candy store?"

Her green eyes sparkled like ice. "Call it that if you like. And come back for more candy. *After* you've removed your disability."

She led them back to the party, and soon she was circulat-

ing gaily among her guests. Kingslea kept to himself, drinking
beer and pondering the new complexities of his life. At midnight, Livie mounted the bandstand and called for attention.

"Dear friends," she cried, "it's been such a memorable
party that I can't bear to see it end. I've arranged for a train to
take us all out to the Triple Six tonight and bring us back
Sunday afternoon. We can ride and swim and have a barbecue
and make a wonderful weekend of it!"

Her guests cheered the invitation. A moment later Livie
sought out Kingslea. "Will you join us?" she asked.

He shook his head. "I have important business."

"Family business?"

"That's right."

"I'm glad," she said. "Please hurry."

He drove home to his wife and children the next morning.

Back in Liberty, Kingslea's old friends and neighbors gave
him a hero's welcome, and he, for his part, could not have
been more gracious toward them. He answered their endless
questions about oil, advised them on business matters, and
obliged many of them with small loans. He spent a good deal
of his time driving around the county, scouting possible drilling sites, and taking leases on several promising pieces of
land.

Whenever Kingslea took out a new lease he brought it
home for his wife Harriet to cosign. She always protested that
she didn't know what she was signing, but he insisted that she
must be a co-owner of his Liberty leases, so that if oil was
found she would have money of her own. That prospect meant
nothing to Harriet. All she wanted was to see her family
united, and now she was filled with joy as that seemed to be
happening. When Kingslea wasn't scouting for oil, he took his
family to church and to square dances and the county fair. He
spent many hours with his sons. Coyle, the older boy, was still
quiet and shy, like his mother. Hoyt was the one who made his
father's heart burst with pride. The boy was fearless. There
was no tree he could not climb, no horse he could not ride.
Soon Kingslea was taking Hoyt on his expeditions around the
county, teaching him about creekbeds and salt domes and
anticlines—the boy had the makings of an oilman.

Kingslea had been home two months when Harriet received
an urgent call from her brother Eddie, who lived in Denver
and was the family black sheep. A housepainter by trade,

Eddie drank and gambled and had been twice divorced. He announced that he had suffered a heart attack and desperately needed Harriet's loving care during his recuperation. Harriet was agonized to have to choose between her ailing brother and her reunited family, but Wade assured her it would be fine if she went to stay with Eddie for a few weeks. He could care for the boys, he assured her, and in fact would take them to Fort Worth for a few days' vacation. Harriet tearfully agreed to this plan.

The next day, Saturday, Wade drove Harriet by his little office to cosign some new leases. She quickly scribbled her name on the pile of documents, anxious to get back home. In church the next morning, the minister proudly announced that Brother Wade Kingslea, who had been so blessed by the Almighty in his oil explorations, had pledged five thousand dollars to pay off the mortgage on the Liberty Baptist Church. As members of the congregation cried, "Hallelujah!" the minister added that Brother Kingslea was providing funds to build a new baseball diamond for the community, to pave the main street, and to provide college scholarships to deserving graduates of the county high school. In bed that night, Harriet wept as she pressed her plump, sweaty body against her husband's and told him how proud and happy he had made her. The next morning she caught the train for Denver and he and the boys drove to Fort Worth.

Upon arrival, Kingslea took the boys to the house he had rented on River Crest Drive and introduced them to their governess.

When he reached Indian Hill, Livie opened the door herself, and it seemed to Kingslea that a whole new world waited for him inside that house. Kingslea gripped his Stetson nervously.

"I've missed you, Wade," she said.

"I've missed you too."

"Come in. I've given the servants the night off."

He shut the door and she threw herself into his arms. Soon she led him into the library. A fire was burning in the fireplace and in seconds they were making love on the bearskin rug. He was amazed and delighted at how strong she was. She was tall and tough and selfish, just as he was. After they had made love, she walked naked to the kitchen and brought them two cold bottles of beer and they sat before the fire and talked.

"I've suffered, Wade," she told him. "I've suffered in

ways you can't imagine. I don't intend to suffer any more in my life."

Her intensity frightened him. "I plan to make you happy," he told her.

"Do. Make me happy, and we'll be so very rich and I'll make you happy. But don't ever make me unhappy or..."

She was stretched out on the bearskin, the bottle of beer cold between her long legs, unable to finish her sentence.

"Or what, Livie?" he demanded.

"Or I'll kill you," she said grimly.

The next day Kingslea had a long talk with his lawyer. They agreed they should give Harriet a week to get settled in Denver before they notified her of the divorce action. Then the lawyer, who was a white-haired, fatherly sort of man, would go to Denver and personally present Harriet with the necessary legal documents. When she protested that she wanted no divorce, the lawyer would remind her that on a Saturday morning two weeks earlier she had signed an agreement wherein she assented to a divorce and to give her husband custody of their sons in exchange for full ownership of various oil properties in the Liberty area. If she protested that she hadn't known what she was signing, that she had thought it was an oil lease, that she hadn't read it, then the lawyer would gently and patiently explain to her that, in the eyes of the law, none of those things mattered. She had signed the agreement.

It was of course possible that Harriet would hire her own lawyer and resist the divorce action, accusing her husband of trickery, not to mention desertion and adultery. But Wade Kingslea was confident. In the first place, his various loans, gifts, and oil leases had made him a hero in Liberty; he would fear no jury there. In the second place, he knew Harriet. Her religion had taught her to suffer in silence, to embrace martyrdom; she would pray and in time decide it was God's will. Finally, Kingslea had reached an understanding with Harriet's quite worthless brother Eddie—whose heart was as sound as a dollar—to pay him one hundred dollars a week as long as Harriet stayed in Denver, so he suspected that Eddie's recuperation would be an exceedingly slow one.

While they waited for the divorce to become final, Wade and Livie maintained separate residences, but all Texas knew of their torrid romance. Kingslea was on the road a lot that year, roaming the Southwest in search of oil, and more often than not finding it. He had boundless faith in himself now, and if some called him a gambler, he thought it was more than that, more like a golden touch. Sometimes he worked in partnership with Sid and Clint, more often on his own, and by the time he and Livie were free to marry he was worth something in excess of ten million dollars. He wasn't big rich, not yet, but he was universally regarded as a man with the character necessary for success in the oil business. His marriage to Livie, at Indian Hill on Christmas Eve, 1922, was Fort Worth's social event of the year.

_ *Book III* _

Coyle and Louise

Fort Worth
1935

CHAPTER ONE

One cloudless autumn afternoon a slender girl of seventeen was crossing the flat, treeless, all-but-deserted campus of Texas Christian University. As she neared the sand-colored university library she heard a great roar go up from the distant football stadium. The girl frowned, for she wanted nothing more than to be at the game, but she had an English exam on Monday morning and she had to study. The distant roar faded and the girl heard another sound, a groan, closer at hand. She turned and saw a nicely dressed young man slumped on the sun-parched earth beside the library. He looked to be in his early twenties, and he was wearing a cream-colored suit, a pale blue shirt, a lemon-colored tie, and saddle shoes. His head hung down loosely on his chest, so that strands of his long black hair fell around his face, and a few drops of blood were trickling from a cut on his chin. The girl hurried to his side.

"What's wrong?" she asked.

"Wha' happen to Slingin' Sammy?" the young man muttered. He did not look up at her.

The girl dropped her schoolbooks and began to dab at his chin with her handkerchief. "Did you fall down?" she asked.

The young man nodded solemnly. "Fell down," he agreed.

Another roar went up from the stadium and the band began to play the TCU fight song.

"Hook 'em, Horned Frogs," the young man bellowed. "Sling 'em, Slingin' Sammy!"

The girl was confused, for she knew that "Hook 'em, Horns" was a cheer for the hated University of Texas Longhorns, not the beloved TCU Horned Frogs. "Have you been drinking?" she asked suddenly.

The young man still had not looked up at her. He seemed to be studying some quite fascinating blade of crabgrass just between his knees. He considered her question for a moment, than he began to laugh. He laughed until he began to cough and to giggle and perhaps to sob a bit. Finally he tried to speak. "Have . . . I . . . been . . . drinking?" he sputtered, and that set off another burst of laughter. "No," he said finally, with great effort, *"I've been thinking!"*

"I think you're crazy," the young woman said indignantly. She began to gather up her books, and as she did the young man flopped over on his back and looked up at her for the first time. That in itself was noteworthy, for this young man had learned early that if you did not look at people, or otherwise admit their existence, it was almost impossible for them to do you harm. But there was something in this girl's voice that made him look up, made him recognize her, and for the rest of his life Coyle Kingslea would treasure that first glimpse of Louise Everett framed against the gentle, boundless Texas sky.

She was of average height, and slender, with small, perfect features, eyes of light blue, a shy, uncertain smile, and long, wavy, golden hair that glowed like a sunrise. She had only recently discovered that she was beautiful, and she carried her beauty uneasily, like a delicate vase that one misstep might shatter. Coyle Kingslea stared at her until he feared his heart might break. She was not young and innocent and beautiful: she was Youth and Innocence and Beauty. He wanted to embrace her, to sing to her, to kiss her fingertips, to spirit her away to some quiet glade, and he might have done all those things, except that he was so drunk he wasn't sure he could stand up.

"I think I'm dead," he said. "I think I drank myself to death and went to Heaven and you're the angel they sent to tell me to go to Hell."

She stared into his eyes. They were the color of smoke and framed by the longest, thickest, blackest eyebrows and eyelashes she had ever seen.

"You are an angel, aren't you?" he asked.

"No, I'm a freshman," she replied. "And I've got to go study."

"Wait," he cried. "Don't leave. Help me up."

She helped him to his feet. He stood unsteadily, one arm around her shoulder, squinting into the late afternoon sun. He was painfully handsome, and she could smell the sharp, unpleasant aroma of gin on his breath.

"I'm Coyle Kingslea," he said.

"I'm Louise Everett."

"I'm gonna buy you a cuppa coffee, Louise Everett."

"No, I really must study. I have an exam and . . ."

"Please have coffee with me," he asked gently, and she could not refuse him. They started across the campus with his arm still around her shoulders. As they neared University Drive a blue Chrysler convertible slid to a stop beside them. A portly black man in a pearl-gray uniform climbed out of the car and tipped his hat to Louise before he turned to the young man.

"Mr. Coyle, where you been?" he asked.

Coyle lowered his voice, as if spies might be about. "Wilson, I was kidnapped by a band of alcoholics on my way to the game. By a miracle, this fair maiden helped me to escape. We're on our way to Doc's for a dose of caffeine."

"Very good, Mr. Coyle." The Negro straightened the young man's coat and brushed some grass from his sleeve, then returned to the Chrysler. Louise and Coyle zigzagged across University Drive just as the first wave of cars poured out of the stadium parking lot. People were honking their horns and waving purple and white banners, for the Horned Frogs had demolished the Baylor Bears. "Drunken Texas Christians everywhere," Coyle muttered as they pushed through the glass doors at Doc's.

The cluttered campus drugstore had a soda fountain at the back. They found an empty booth, and the manager came over and swabbed their already spotless tabletop.

"Howdy, miss. Howdy, Coyle. Well, Slingin' Sammy done it again, didn't he? What'll it be?"

"Two coffees for me, Milt," Coyle said. "And a glass of ice."

"I'd like a cherry Coke, please," Louise added, and the man hurried off to fill their order.

"A cherry Coke," Coyle mused. "Child, you are *evil!*"

"I never got to drink Cokes at home," Louise said. "My mother thought they had drugs in them or something. She's very strict. She wants me to major in religion, but I want to study journalism."

Coyle nodded gravely. "Mothers are like that."

Milt, the manager, brought her cherry Coke, with two straws, and Coyle's two cups of coffee and a glass of ice. Coyle poured cream and sugar into one cup, spooned in some ice, and downed it in one gulp. He whistled, rolled his eyes, and did the same with the second cup. "That'll either sober me up or give me a heart attack," he said. "Or maybe both. Excuse me, angel-face. Be right back." He left the booth, staggering just a bit, stopped at the jukebox, then disappeared into the men's room. In a moment, jazz burst from the jukebox.

Louise watched the kids pouring in from the game. They were loud and happy after the TCU victory, but she felt uncomfortable and depressed. She didn't know who Coyle Kingslea was or what he wanted and she was half-afraid of him. She thought of leaving before he returned. And yet there was something very different and exciting about him, with his beautiful eyes, his expensive clothes, his ironic humor. She watched the boys coming into the drugstore, ordinary Texas boys with ordinary Texas clothes and ordinary Texas faces, the kind of boys she'd known all her life, and she knew she could not leave, not yet. She began to listen to the jazz and she was smiling when he returned. He had washed his face and combed his hair and he looked much better.

"Angel-face, you look *happy!*"

"I love that song! What is it?"

"Benny Goodman. 'Sing, Sing, Sing.'"

"My mother doesn't approve of jazz, either. She thinks it's sinful."

"And here you are, up to your beautiful ears in sin."

She blushed. "If that's sin, then I was born to be a sinner."

He took her hand. "You were born to be an angel. Don't ever forget that. An angel in a world of madness."

There were tears in his eyes and he squeezed her hand so hard it hurt. She was confused, half-afraid of him again, but then a half-dozen laughing, expensively dressed boys and girls burst in the door and raced to their booth.

"We saw your car out front," said a boy with a hip flask protruding from his pocket.

"Who's your friend?"

"Where'd you go after halftime?"

"Don't we get asked to join you?"

"Coyle, you said you'd *call.*" This from a girl with bobbed hair and a red, pouting mouth. Louise glared at her.

"Away, you riffraff," Coyle roared. "Meet me at my old man's party."

Laughing and protesting, the young people raced out again. "Are those your friends?" Louise asked.

"My peers," Coyle said. Bunny Berigan poured from the jukebox, and Coyle sang along. Louise sang with him, delighted, and when the song stopped he pulled out a gold pen and began to sketch on a napkin. When he was finished, he slid his drawing across to her: it showed Louise as an angel, playing jazz on a harp.

"I love it," she exclaimed. "Can I keep it?"

"If you'll go to a party with me."

"A party? When?"

"Tonight. Right now."

"But I've got to go to the library."

'Nonsense, child. I got myself halfway sober just to take you to this party."

"I've got to *study*," she insisted.

"There'll be plenty to study at this party. You can study the madness of the world, face to face."

Despite Louise's protests, Coyle guided her out to the street, where Wilson was waiting with the Chrysler. "I *can't*, Coyle," she insisted, but when he grinned she blushed and smiled back at him.

"Oh, all right," she said. "But if I fail English, *you* face my mother!"

Soon they were moving north on University Drive, through Forest Park, across the Trinity River, past a strip of miniature-golf courses, archery ranges, root-beer stands.

"Whose party is this?" she asked.

"My father's."

"Who is your father?"

"Wade Kingslea." He was watching her face closely, to see how the name would register, but it did not register at all.

"I have to be back at the dorm by eleven," she said. "Or I'll be in all kinds of trouble."

They crossed Camp Bowie Boulevard and turned onto West Seventh Street, into the setting sun. Coyle took her hand and stroked it gently. Louise liked that. Boys had kissed her before, but no one had ever stroked her hand that way.

"Have you ever been in love?" he asked. Coyle felt unsettled. In the past three years he had been pursued by the richest, most celebrated young women in Texas, and none of them had made him feel the way this girl did.

"In love?" she said. "Only with Rudy Vallee. I've had a crush on him since I was thirteen."

"But your mother didn't approve?"

"That's right. I had to sneak over to my girl friend's house to hear him on the radio."

"I think he's going to be here tonight."

"Be where?"

"At my father's party."

"You're teasing me."

"No. A lot of people go to my father's parties. Even I go to my father's parties."

They drove alongside a golf course.

"What course is this?" Louise asked.

"River Crest Country Club. Where the elite meet to eat and cheat."

"Aren't they building a new country club?" she asked. "Over near TCU?"

He nodded with amusement. "Colonial, they're calling it. Strictly for the riffraff."

They turned onto a private road that ran behind the golf course and ended before a vast, peach-colored villa that rose improbably from a grove of towering oaks. Louise's eyes widened. All she could think was, Yes, Rudy Valle *could* be here. "I've never seen a house like this before," she whispered.

Not many people had. In the early 1930s, as if single-handedly to dispel rumors of hard times in America, Wade Kingslea had spent two million dollars to build what was quite possibly the grandest mansion in Texas.

The official opening of Hillcrest, as the Kingslea mansion was known, took place on the Fourth of July, 1933. Actually, there were two opening-day events. First, from eight in the morning until four in the afternoon, the public was permitted to file through the house. Livie Kingslea had bitterly resisted this decision of her husband's. At best, she warned, the visitors would trample the lawns and steal everything they could get their hands on. At worst, she added darkly, the masses might be outraged by the grandeur of the mansion that they would be driven to a Bolshevik outburst of burning and looting.

Kingslea saw the matter differently. In part, his open house was a public-relations gesture, aimed at selling Kingslea gas and oil and at building goodwill for his company. More than that, Kingslea was selling not just his products but himself and his ever-growing legend. Did not the Bible itself say you should not hide your light under a basket? What was the use of having the finest mansion in Texas if no one knew about it? And as for the public being driven to violence by the sight of his fabulous wealth—well, Wade Kingslea knew better than that, for unlike his wife he had been poor. "They won't hate us," he assured her. "Every man who walks through here will think he could have been just as rich—still could, maybe—if he'd just had a break or two. And every woman will think that her son can grow up and have a place like this. And by God, maybe they can—because this is Texas!"

Kingslea understood his fellow Texans perfectly. Twenty thousand of them filed awestruck through his new mansion that day and there was not a dissident or bomb thrower among them. To the contrary, whenever Kingslea stepped into public view, his visitors cheered, applauded, begged for his autograph, and urged him to run for governor of the state.

That evening, with the public's curiosity appeased and the public's debris cleared away, the real housewarming began. It was an outdoor, seated dinner for six hundred guests, who included Charles Lindbergh, Bob Hope, Babe Ruth, Mae West, Will Rogers, Henry Luce, Walter Winchell, Clark Gable, Joseph P. Kennedy, J. Edgar Hoover, Vice President John Nance Garner, two of President Roosevelt's sons, and the Mexican Ambassador to the United States, who, in an unfortunate misunderstanding, was detained at the door when security men took him for a late-arriving waiter.

That had been a major social event, even by Texas standards. By contrast, this party, to which Coyle Kingslea happened to bring Louise Everett, on a crisp October evening in 1935, was only a casual postgame affair for two hundred friends, plus a few celebrities who happened to be passing through and one delegation of New York bankers who were in the state eyeing investment possibilities.

Wilson stopped the Chrysler by the broad front steps and hurried around to get the door for Louise. She and Coyle climbed out and then stood for a moment, hand in hand, looking up at the great Italianate mansion. Coyle began to whistle "Just a Shanty in Old Shantytown" and to dance a soft-shoe shuffle, but Louise, for the first time since they met, paid no attention to him. She was transfixed by his father's mansion. It seemed to stretch on forever until its most distant wings disappeared into oak trees, magnolias, and darkness. She thought of enchanted castles; she had an eerie feeling that if she went inside she would be swallowed up and never seen again.

"Do you want to see the inside?" Coyle asked a bit apologetically.

She shook her head slowly, tempted, uncertain, fearful. She heard music from behind the house and saw a path leading in that direction. "Could we just go around and . . . hear the music?" she asked timidly.

Coyle nodded—he understood the terrors of his father's house—and led her through a tunnel of magnolia trees that emerged onto a flagstone terrace overlooking a green sweep of lawn that seemed to stretch on forever. In the precise center of the lawn, with walkways spreading out from it like spokes on a wheel, was a marble fountain and, rising up from that, a life-size statue of Diana, the Huntress. She stood poised, slender and naked, bow in hand, with a sleek greyhound at her side.

"She's the real thing," Coyle said. "Livie—my stepmother—bought her in Florence. She had to—one of her local rivals had bought a Rembrandt."

"Coyle, Coyle!"

His friends, the same bunch who'd invaded Doc's, raced toward them, faces flushed by gin and excitement.

"Didja hear 'bout Buster?"

"What about him?" Coyle demanded.

"Arrested."

"In *Mexico.*"

"What for?"

"We don't know yet."

"We've called the ambassador."

"Arrested on the International Bridge, we heard."

"The crazy bastard," Coyle sighed and waved to a waiter for champagne. In a moment, their glasses were held high. "To Buster," Coyle said solemnly, "wherever he may be."

Buster's fate quickly forgotten, someone asked, "Hey, Coyle, who's your friend?"

"Louise," he said. "My friend is Louise."

"Louise who?"

"Louise-who-should-be-studying."

"Aren'tcha gonna introduce us?" a girl demanded.

"Reluctantly," Coyle replied. "Louise, this decadent bunch of dipsomaniacs are my oldest and dearest friends." He began rattling off names. The boys mostly had nicknames like Buzz

and Bimbo, Fisheye and Pig (Pig she could remember, for
with his round red face and squinty eyes and look of cheerful
idiocy he *did* look like one), and the girls were named Kay,
Gladys, and Caddy ("Like the car") and Eula and Sweets ("It's
short for Sweetwater, 'cause that's where my Daddy hit his
first well, and I'm just glad it wasn't Yellow Dog or Bowlegs"). The girls encircled Louise, peppering her with questions about her family, her friends at TCU, until Coyle took
her arm and pulled her away.

"Thank you," she said, as he led her across the lawn.
"Your friends are so . . . sophisticated."

He shook his head. "Not sophisticated. Only rich."

"The girls are so beautiful."

"Not as beautiful as you."

"That's not true," she said. "They have . . ."

"They have everything money can buy. You have innocence. They lost that a long time ago, and they can't buy it
back, not with all the money in Texas."

They paused beside the fountain, while the band played
"Poor Butterfly."

"What do you mean, lost their innocence? They all seem so
happy."

Coyle seized two glasses of champagne from a passing
waiter. He nodded toward his friends, who had regrouped on
the terrace. "See Buzz over there? And the blonde with him?"

"She's his wife, isn't she?"

"His fourth wife, to be precise, and he's twenty-three. See
the fellow next to him, with his arm in a sling? He rolled his
car a month ago, coming home drunk from a party. He walked
away and the girl with him was killed. He's forgotten her
name by now. Then there's dear old Pig, who's got two illegitimate sons and is entering a record-breaking fourth year as a
freshman at TCU. And then there's Eula, that virginal-looking
creature next to him, who . . ."

"Please!" Louise cried. Coyle seemed to have changed as
he spoke, to have grown cold and bitter. "Please," she repeated, "just let me enjoy the party. It's so beautiful here."

They watched as a half-dozen young men marched onto the
terrace and were met with applause and whoops. A slender,
dark-haired girl in a clinging pink dress was leading them,
holding hands with two of the biggest boys, who were stars of
the TCU football team that had romped to victory that afternoon. They were lean, muscular, sun-bronzed young men,

their hair cropped short, bruises and cleat marks showing on their faces and arms. They were wearing jeans and boots and sport shirts and purple TCU letter jackets. Louise marveled at how different they looked from Coyle's friends, who tended to be pale and paunchy and long-haired, who wore sport coats and ties and seemed to have drinks and cigarettes permanently affixed to their hands.

"Look at them," Coyle muttered. "The conquering heroes. And every one of them wants to marry an oil millionaire's daughter. The poor dumb bastards."

"Who's the girl in the pink dress?" Louise asked.

"My stepsister, Eve. Little Eve has made the team." He laughed at his own joke.

"She looks so young," Louise said.

"Sweet sixteen and never been missed," he said. "That's my brother, Hoyt, behind her, the one in the blue shirt."

Louise stared at the tall, handsome, uncomplicated-looking boy in the blue shirt and jeans. "He doesn't look like you."

"Doesn't act like me, either," Coyle said. "Hoyt's the all-American boy. His father's pride and joy."

The bitterness was back in his voice. His face was hard and his eyes narrowed as if he was in pain. "Do you hate your father?" she asked.

He laughed. "Not all the time. Come on, you may as well meet him."

He led her up to the terrace where a dozen men were standing in a semicircle around a tall, imposing man whom Louise knew at once to be her host, Wade Kingslea. She knew him by the eyes, for they were dark and deepset and beautiful, like Coyle's, yet they were different, too, for there was hesitation, sadness, vulnerability, in Coyle's glance, but she saw only pride and strength and self-confidence in his father's eyes. Wade Kingslea, in his early forties, was heavier than in his Goodwill days and had a glint of silver at his temples. Louise thought that in his tuxedo, and with his stern good looks, he resembled a movie star more than an oilman.

Kingslea was introducing the New York bankers to three of his closest friends. Two of them, Sid Richardson and Clint Murchison, had been Kingslea's fellow wildcatters for more than a decade, and over the years they had made and lost millions together. At various times, each of them had claimed to be the richest man in Texas, as had their Dallas rival, H. L. Hunt, but Kingslea's fortune, if combined with his wife's, gave him the best claim to that title. His third friend was Amon Carter, the owner of the Fort Worth *Star-Telegram*, a newspaper that tirelessly boosted Fort Worth as "The City Where the West Begins." Carter was a gaunt, balding man who wore, along with his business suit, ostrich-skin cowboy boots and a pearl-handled six-gun in his hand-tooled Western belt.

As Kingslea fell into a heated conversation with a banker named Weissman, Sid Richardson walked over and greeted Coyle and Louise. With a twinkle in his eye, he began telling them the story of three bank robbers in Cisco, Texas, who'd dressed themselves in Santa Claus suits, robbed the local bank, taken some children hostage, and finally been captured and lynched by outraged townspeople. "There was a terrible aftermath to the incident," Richardson said gravely. "The very sight of Santa Claus would drive those poor children into hysterics. As a result, Santa has been banned from Cisco for seven years now. Santa is unknown to a generation of Cisco children—a deprivation unique in the Christian world. What's worse, dissension has now erupted in little Cisco because many parents want to bring Santa back."

Louise never learned the outcome of the controversy in Cisco, because Richardson fell silent, like everyone else on the terrace, when Wade Kingslea suddenly shouted angrily at the banker named Weissman.

"Are you advocating federal control of the oil industry, sir?" Kingslea boomed.

"No, Mr. Kingslea. Only regulation to keep irresponsible operators from depleting the East Texas field."

"Mr. Weissman, I believe in the private ownership of property," Kingslea declared. "I believe that if I own a piece of land, I have an absolute right to drill for oil on that land if I so choose."

"But as a practical matter," the banker continued, "if everyone exercises that absolute right, the price goes down, the field is depleted, and everyone loses."

Louise could see Wade Kingslea's dark eyes flash. "Sir," he said, "as I study the political process, I find that it is invariably socialists and atheists who want to replace private ownership with state control."

"Give 'em hell, Wade!" cried one of the oilmen who had gathered around.

"But, Mr. Kingslea," the New Yorker protested, "we aren't

talking about communism, only about simple regulation for the common good."

"That is enough, sir!" Kingslea snapped. "You are welcome in my home but your views are not."

Suddenly all pretense was stripped away and two hostile forces confronted one another: New York bankers whose interests lay with the huge, Eastern-owned, "major" oil companies, and independent oilmen like Wade Kingslea who fought an endless battle to stay independent of the hated Yankee bankers.

"Excuse me, Mr. Weissman," Kingslea said smoothly, relieving the tension, "I believe my son has a friend he wants me to meet."

As Coyle made the introductions, his father beamed at Louise, took her hands in his own, and insisted that he show her the grounds. She took his arm and crossed the lawn with him, oblivious to the murmured chorus of whispers that followed them, "Who is she? Who is she?" At the bandstand, Kingslea demanded something a man could dance to, and soon he and Louise were twirling gracefully, with hundreds of eyes upon them.

Up on the terrace, Sid Richardson had organized a friendly poker game, to restore good feelings between the Texas oilmen and the New York bankers. He and Amon Carter and Clint Murchison were playing, along with the elderly Weissman, a husky young banker named Coleman, and several other New Yorkers. The visitors dealt hands of draw or stud, civilized poker, but when the deal passed to the Texans they would announce games with complicated rules, numerous wild cards, and unlimited betting. In time, those two old friends, Sid Richardson and Clint Murchison, launched a noisy argument.

"Where'd you get that ace?" Murchison demanded.

"It was dealt me."

"From up your sleeve, you mean!"

"You calling me a cheat!"

"Damn right I am. You been one for thirty years!"

"Gentlemen, gentlemen," chided the banker Weissman.

Richardson leaped to his feet and jerked a small revolver from his pocket. "No man calls me a cheat!" he cried and began to fire pointblank at his old friend and oil-field partner.

Murchison shot up, clutched his chest, rolled his eyes,

spun around twice, and sank to the terrace, moaning, "He done kilt me!"

At the sound of the shots, women began to scream. The poker-playing New Yorkers leaped from their chairs and raced for safety. "These people are insane!" one of them cried.

Out on the dance platform, Louise was startled by the shots. "What is it?" she asked Kingslea.

"It's nothing," her host said with a smile. "Boys will be boys."

But there were more screams, shots, and rebel yells. The band broke off. "You, bandleader," Kingslea called. "Keep playing!"

A plump oilman called Birdy Williamson rushed up. "Wade, you shoulda see'd it. Amon and Sid shot off a coupla rounds and them Yankees like to dropped their drawers. I bet that smartass Weissman is still a-running. Begging your pardon, miss."

"Nobody hurt, was there?" Kingslea asked.

"Just scared silly. They was only shootin' blanks."

The husky young banker named Coleman ran up to them. "Is this your idea of a joke, Kingslea?" he demanded. "An older man like Sidney Weissman could have had a heart attack with those fools shooting off their guns."

"Did he have a heart attack?"

"That's not the point. This is an outrage, and I suspect you put them up to it."

"You are mistaken, Mr. Coleman."

"I doubt that, Kingslea."

"No man comes to my home and calls me a liar, Mr. Coleman."

"I believe I just did."

Kingslea threw a roundhouse right that caught Coleman on the chin and staggered him. Coleman jabbed with his left, jolting Kingslea, and then swung a right that bloodied the oilman's nose. For a moment the two men were toe to toe, both throwing a flurry of rights and lefts, then Coleman staggered backward and dropped to one knee.

A crowd had formed around them. "Get him, Wade, get him!" people cried.

"Get up and fight like a man," Kingslea said scornfully.

The banker lowered his head and charged like a bull. Kingslea stood his ground, and his knee shot upward, perfectly timed, to crash into the younger man's face. Coleman, dazed, stumbled about like a blind man until Kingslea grabbed him by the lapels and threw him into the fountain of Diana. The young banker landed with a great splash and sat there, bloody and defeated, while Kingslea rubbed his bruised knuckles and a crowd of Texans cheered.

Louise Everett, stunned by the sudden violence, stood frozen in the shadows; then Kingslea looked at her and smiled. "Our dance was interrupted," he said. "Mr. Bandleader, let's have some music!"

As the music began again, a tall, stately woman with upswept hair, a dazzling diamond-and-ruby necklace, a royal-blue chiffon dress, and fire in her eye appeared before Wade Kingslea.

"I will not have it, Wade!" she cried. "*I will not have it*. These men are our guests. Several of them are socially prominent. You will apologize to each and every one of them. Now!"

Other guests stepped back from the confrontation; Louise stood motionless, afraid to move.

"Now, Livie . . ."

"Don't 'Now Livie' me! This is my home, Wade, not some Wild West show."

Wade Kingslea sighed, then smiled at Louise, who stood wide-eyed to his right. "Olivia," he said formally, "this is Coyle's friend, Miss Everett."

Livie Kingslea's moss-green eyes flicked in Louise's direction, then shot back to her husband. *"Now,"* she whispered. *"You will apologize now!"*

Kingslea touched a handkerchief to his bloody nose, adjusted his black tie, and bowed to Louise. "Excuse me, my dear," he said. "I seem to be neglecting my duties as a host."

He marched off toward the terrace, and his wife hurried toward the fountain, where some men were helping Coleman to his feet. The band began a Duke Ellington song, and people were laughing and dancing again, but Louise felt immeasurably alone. She wanted to be away from this strange world where people fought and fired guns.

A hand touched her arm and she turned to find Coyle beside her.

"I've got to get back to school," she said.

"Relax, angel," he said. "Night's young."

He grabbed a drink from a waiter and downed it in one gulp.

"Oh, Coyle, why do you drink like that?" she cried.

"Strange phenomenon," he said. "Closer I get to my old man, drunker I get."

She led him to an empty table, trying to persuade him to take her back to school, but his friends, still moving in a pack, raced up to them again.

"We found out 'bout Buster!" the boy called Pig cried.

"They nabbed him with a damn ounce of cocaine!" another boy said.

"Oh, *no!*" Coyle groaned.

"We're going to bail him out," a girl announced. "We've got a lawyer and ten thousand dollars cash."

"And a plane waiting for us," the girl called Caddy added.

"You goin' with us, Coyle?" Pig demanded.

"No, please," Louise said, tugging at his arm.

"Course I'm goin'," Coyle declared, waving his drink. "M' friend Buster's in a filthy stinkin' jail, 'n I'm goin' to get him out!"

Coyle's friends cheered his resolve, then a firm voice cut through the night.

"Coyle, you're drunk, you have a guest, and this is no time for you to fly to Mexico. The rest of you, if you're going, had better get started."

"Yes sir, Mr. Kingslea," the young people shouted and raced off toward their cars.

Coyle and Louise were alone at the table again, with red and yellow Chinese lanterns swaying above their heads.

"Damn him!" Coyle cried and threw his glass into the night.

"Coyle, he was right."

"I'm a grown man," he sobbed. He slumped in his chair, muttering to himself, as Louise fought back tears.

"Mr. Coyle?"

It was Wilson, the chauffeur. "Coffee, Mr. Coyle?"

Coyle lashed out and knocked the cup of coffee to the ground. "Get me a goddam drink!" he commanded.

"Sorry, Mr. Coyle. No more whiskey tonight."

"Listen, you know who I am?" he raged. "You listen, too, sister. I'm Franklin Coyle Kingslea. See this place?" He swung his arm in a vast circle. "All this is gonna be mine!"

Louise was crying. "Won't somebody please take me home?" she asked.

"Take the bitch home," Coyle muttered, and then, suddenly, he slumped forward, unconscious.

"We'll take him up to bed now, Miss Louise," Wilson said. "And then I'll drive you back to the university."

"How could he talk to us like that?"

"It's all right, Miss Louise. He don't mean it. It's just the whiskey talkin'."

Wilson and a young waiter picked Coyle up and carried him toward the mansion. Louise wanted desperately to leave this place. She noticed two of the TCU football players crossing the lawn toward the garage and she thought she might catch a ride back to the campus with them. She hurried after them, along a gravel path that led through some trees. She rounded the corner of the garage, then suddenly she stopped and peered into the darkness beneath a large oak tree. A boy in a letter jacket was leaning with his back to the tree. Someone was kneeling before him. After a moment Louise recognized the girl in the pink dress. It was Eve, Coyle's sister.

"Hey, how 'bout us?" said one of the boys who was watching.

Louise turned and ran blindly back down the path. Bushes and tree limbs tore at her dress, scratched her face. She ran across the lawn, back to the table where she had been before, looking for Wilson. The chauffeur seemed her only hope now, her only way out of this madhouse. But he was nowhere to be found. Up on the bandstand, Rudy Vallee, clutching his famous megaphone, was singing to the Texans.

> "In the morning, in the evening,
>   Ain't we got fun?"

It was one of Louise's favorite songs, yet hearing it now only made her tears flow more freely.

> "There's nothing surer
>   The rich get rich and the poor get—children!"

"Are you ready, Miss Louise?"

She followed Wilson across the lawn. The tinkling music called after her, mocking her as they climbed the steps to the terrace. Suddenly, above the sound of the music, a great roar filled the sky. People stopped dancing and laughing and looked up into the dark heavens. Flashing lights appeared; Louise imagined divine retribution, punishment for the sinners. But it was only a small airplane, circling low above the party—Coyle's friends, waving good-bye, as they began their rescue mission to free Buster from a Mexican jail. The party-goers waved and cheered as the plane circled and disappeared from sight, then they returned to dancing and drinking and laughing and flirting and being rich. Louise Everett stumbled through the darkness with the gentle black man who would take her back to the world she knew.

CHAPTER TWO

A pump girl from Muleshoe, eyes wide with excitement, poked her head in Louise's room. "Phone for you," she cried. "He said it was Coyle *Kingslea!* Is that one of the *Kingslea* Kingsleas?"

Louise, whose head was bowed over her American history textbook, shut her eyes. She had feared this all week.

"Tell him I'm not here," she said. "Please."

"Not *here!* Are you *crazy?* Listen, if you don't like to date millionaires, I sure do!"

"I'm not here," Louise said firmly.

The next afternoon he was waiting outside her dormitory. He smiled nervously.

"I called," he said. "They told me angels don't take calls."

"I'm late for a lab," she lied.

"I'll walk with you."

His smile was gone and his face twitched uncertainly. "Coyle, I don't want to talk to you."

"Just let me tell you why I called."

She didn't want to hurt his feelings. He looked so sad, so pitiful. She wished she'd never met him. "All right."

"Duke Ellington is playing at the Hotel Texas on Saturday night," he said. "A bunch of us are going. I remembered how you like jazz and . . ."

Anger and frustration boiled up inside Louise. She had

been hurt that Saturday night, hurt to see a sweet boy turn into a monster who cursed and insulted her. It still hurt.

"So you thought you'd take me to the party so you could get rip-roaring drunk and call me a lot of nasty names, is that it?" she cried. "Well, no thank you, Mr. Coyle Kingslea! One evening like that was enough."

She pushed past him, but he grabbed her arm.

"Let go of me."

"Just listen to me, please," he pleaded. "I don't even remember what names I called you, but I apologize. I'll be sorry until the day I die. I was crazy drunk. Can't you forgive me?"

She lowered her eyes, remembering how funny he'd been at Doc's that afternoon, when he sang to her and drew her picture.

"Yes, I can forgive you," she told him.

Coyle released her arm. "Then you'll go with me Saturday night?"

She shook her head. "No," she said. "No, I won't."

"Louise, if you'll go, I won't drink. I swear. Just give me another chance. Don't remember me like that."

"I won't," she said. "I'll remember how nice you were . . . before you drank so much."

"Then why won't you . . . ?"

"Don't you understand? We're from two different worlds. I don't belong in your world."

Coyle smiled, despite himself. "Angel, *I* don't belong in my world," he muttered. "Just think about Saturday night, please. I'll call you." He hurried away.

Louise walked to the library and tried to study, but her thoughts were all of Coyle. She stared out over the library, at row after row of students with their noses stuck in books, and it all seemed so immeasurably *dull*. She wanted to see Coyle again, at least the way he had been before he got drunk, and she desperately wanted to see Duke Ellington's band. The boys she knew could barely afford a hot dog, much less a night at the Hotel Texas. That glittering world called to her, danced in her imagination. But not if it meant suffering the pain she had felt the last time. Suddenly, the solution came to her: Coyle had promised not to drink! And as long as he didn't drink, everything would be wonderful. That night Louise dreamed of magical ballrooms, and when Coyle called the next day she said she would accept his invitation, if he promised, cross-my-heart-and-hope-to-die, not to drink.

• • •

Beams of light like dancing, sparkling snowflakes darted through the darkness, bounced off glittering mirrors, skipped across the dance floor, tangled in the hair of laughing girls, shone on bottles and glasses and silver flasks, sparkled on the golden saxophones and trombones of the elegant black men in powder-blue suits who were making music for the young Texans who packed the Crystal Ballroom. Louise had never heard such music. It might have come from the moon, from Mars—or, indeed, from Harlem, which was just as distant from her experience.

Coyle and his friends had a long table beside the dance floor. Pig and Caddy were there, arguing most of the time, and Eve, Coyle's sister, sitting on some football player's lap, and the famous Buster, fresh from the Mexican jail and anxious to tell of his exploits, and a fellow named Willie McNabb, who was trying to drink champagne from his date's slipper, except the slipper leaked and champagne kept spilling on everyone. Louise kept pulling Coyle off to dance, because she loved the music, and all his friends seemed to care about was drinking and laughing and necking and arguing. Coyle looked so handsome, in a light brown suit and yellow shirt and green tie, and he had kept his promise not to drink. When the band took a break, she held his hand and sat close beside him and asked him to tell her about his work.

"I'm a humble scrivener," he said, sipping his Coke.

"A what?"

"A glorified accountant. To be precise, I'm the assistant treasurer of Kingslea Oil. What that means is that my father wants me in the family business and he knows I can count."

"Do you work hard?"

"No."

"Are you happy?"

Coyle shrugged, as if he found the notion of happiness amusing.

"What would you rather do?"

"Angel, if I owned the world, instead of my father owning it, I'd do something in art. Maybe advertising. Maybe art director for a big company."

"Why can't you do that for your father's oil company?"

"Because my father thinks art is for girls. Men are supposed to make money—or count it, in my case."

The band returned and began "Passion Flower." Louise

took Coyle's hand and led him back to the dance floor. She loved dancing with him. There was something courtly about the way he danced, never trying to hold her too close, always moving slowly, gracefully, loving the music as much as she did. She watched Duke Ellington as they danced, a tall, slender, elegant man, and it seemed somehow that he alone was the instrument that made this wondrous music. He seemed a magician, the prince of a fairy kingdom, and seeing him saddened and confused her because she knew how Negroes were treated in Texas and she could not reconcile his elegance, his magic, with what she had heard about colored people all her life.

Back at the table, Pig and Caddy were arguing. "You said this nigger played *jazz,*" Pig declared. "Sumbitch ain't playing jazz—he thinks he's leading the goddam symphony!"

"Oh don't be such a *boor,* Pig," Caddy snapped, and he stormed away from the table.

"I'll go find him," Coyle told her and hurried across the dance floor.

Caddy pulled her chair close to Louise's and lit a Chesterfield with her silver lighter. She was a beautiful girl, with laughing, knowing eyes and long brown hair.

"You're certainly a good influence on Coyle, honey," Caddy said, exhaling smoke through her nose and mouth. "I haven't seen him sober at a party in a coon's age."

"I . . . I told him I wouldn't go out with him if he drank."

"Coyle's a lousy drunk," Caddy agreed. "But at least he's sweet when he's sober. Pig's a disaster either way."

"Then why do you go with him?"

Caddy shrugged. "Who else is there to go with? Pig has mucho dinero. Mucho, mucho, *mucho* dinero, and he's relatively easy to care for and feed." She sipped her gin and giggled. "I just shut my eyes and think of Clark Gable."

Across the table, Buster slumped forward, knocking over a dozen bottles. "Why do they all *drink* so much?" Louise cried. "What's the use of going someplace if all you're going to do is get drunk and pass out?"

Caddy stubbed out her cigarette and studied Louise's face. "Honey, you're awfully young and you'd better be careful about getting involved with Coyle."

"What do you mean?"

"Coyle, Buster, Pig, all these boys have a problem."

"Do you mean being rich?"

"Hey, Caddy, wanta dance?" a boy called.

"Later, honey," Caddy said. "Heap big girl talk."

The boy shrugged and wandered on.

"No, it's more complicated than just being rich," she continued. "The thing is, all those boys have daddys who went to Ranger or Goodwill or Bowlegs or somewhere and made so much money it's ridiculous. Their daddys aren't just rich, they're *legends*. There's no way their sons can compete. So what do they do instead? They get drunk and get laid and wreck cars and spend money like it was going out of fashion. And Louise, it eats them up. They pretend it's big fun, but . . . oh my God, what's *that?*"

The music stopped abruptly. There were shouts over beside the bandstand and men were running that way.

"It's Pig," Caddy cried. "I know it is!"

She jumped up and pushed her way toward the commotion. Louise followed uncertainly.

It *was* Pig, red-faced and snarling. Coyle and another man were holding him as he cursed and struggled to be free. A dozen feet away a policeman gripped the arm of a Negro, one of the band's managers, who had a bloody nose.

The hotel manager, a beefy man named Ford, rushed up. "What the hell's going on here?" he demanded.

"Sumbitch called me a *name,*" Pig exclaimed.

"That's a lie," the Negro said. "That man walked up and hit me for no reason. He ought to be arrested."

The hotel manager looked at Coyle. "Kingslea, are you sober?" he demanded.

"Oddly enough, yes."

"Well, Pig's not. Get him the hell out of here."

Pig raged incoherently, but let Coyle lead him back to the table. Up on the bandstand, Duke Ellington announced an intermission and then hurried down to talk to the Negro with the bloody nose. Louise, surprised at her own audacity, stepped up and asked for his autograph. She groped in her purse for pen and paper.

The bandleader looked amused. "Of course, young lady," he said and scribbled his name.

"I . . . I love your music."

"I enjoy it myself."

"And . . . I'm sorry about what happened."

The bandleader arched an eyebrow. "An occupational hazard, my dear."

At Pig's insistence, they drove out to the Top of the Hill Club, a gambling house perched on a bluff overlooking the Dallas–Fort Worth highway. From its parking lot you could see the Fort Worth skyline to the west, and to the east you had a dazzling view of Pegasus, the Flying Red Horse, soaring above the lights of Dallas. The mighty steed was the world's largest revolving sign, perched atop the Magnolia Oil Building. Pegasus brought so much attention to Dallas that Fort Worth's city fathers in time retaliated by erecting an equally huge red-white-and-blue-neon American flag atop their own Tarrant County courthouse.

Inside, the Top of the Hill was a throwback to the days a half century before when cattle barons, cowboys, and bank robbers drank barbed-wire whiskey side by side in the bars of Fort Worth's infamous Hell's Half Acre. The crowd that packed the Top of the Hill that night included professional gamblers, professional criminals, oilmen, confidence men, off-duty police, college boys, debutantes, and ten-dollar whores, variously drawn there in search of dollars, danger, thrills, sex, or violence.

Still, Louise had a good time at first. The manager, a man named Browning, greeted Coyle warmly. They ordered scrambled eggs, and after they'd eaten, Coyle showed Louise how to play blackjack. Everything was fine until Pig went outside and got in a fight with two Dallas gamblers he said owed him three hundred dollars on a football bet. Coyle tried to help him and got knocked down, and they might have been killed except that a huge man in a camel's hair coat appeared out of nowhere, swinging a blackjack, and soon the gamblers were unconscious on the ground. The man, it developed, was Harley Prendergast, and he worked for Coyle's father. "He used to be my old man's bodyguard, back in the old days," Coyle explained. "Now he's called Chief of Security—but he still swings a mean blackjack."

"Well, honey, how'd you like Cowtown's cafe society?" Caddy demanded from the back seat, as they speeded back to Fort Worth.

"Well, it was *interesting,*" Louise said. "But I think next time I'd like to go to a movie."

They *did* go to a movie on their next date, a Marx Brothers comedy, and Coyle laughed till he cried. He laughed when other people weren't laughing, as if he saw jokes they didn't see. It was almost like hysteria, Louise thought, and yet she was glad to see him so happy.

The next night he took her to a place called the Eighth Avenue Club, a dark, noisy bar that had murals of cartoon characters along its walls. They met Pig and Caddy and some other people there, and Louise was proud because his friends kept pressing drinks on him but he waved them all away.

Coyle asked for her class schedule, and soon he was coming to take her for coffee at Doc's between classes. They would talk about movies and music and books and her studies —about almost everything except his work and his family. You could see him tighten up whenever anyone mentioned his father. It was so strange, Louise thought. All the girls in her dorm were beside themselves because she was dating a Kingslea, yet to Coyle himself, being a Kingslea was like some kind of curse.

One Sunday they drove out to Coyle's parents' lodge on Eagle Mountain Lake. It was too cool to swim, so he took her out in the speedboat, and then they fished with cane poles off the end of the dock.

"I never really liked fishing," Coyle admitted. "I always identified with the worm."

"You're funny," she said.

In the late afternoon they sat on the screened porch and drank Cokes and he sketched the sailboats that were gliding across the lake. She found a magazine with a new poem by Edna St. Vincent Millay and read it aloud and they talked about it. She thought Coyle was so different from his friends. She couldn't imagine Pig or Willie or Buster sketching sailboats or talking about a poem. She tried to remember that terrible night when Coyle had been drunk, but it seemed so unreal, a dream, a nightmare. This, she knew, was the real Coyle.

"You have the most beautiful eyes," she said. "Someday I want a little boy with eyes like yours."

Coyle flipped to a new page in his sketchpad and began to draw rapidly. In a moment he showed her the drawing. It was of a little boy in short pants who looked very much like Coyle. In one hand he held a gin bottle and in the other a pitchfork.

"Careful," he warned. "Your prayers might be answered."

She went over and kissed him and he held her close and they sat on the sofa and watched the sun sink behind the low hills across the lake. On the drive back to town he asked her to go to the Casino with him the next weekend to hear Sammy Kaye's band.

In her English class the next day, a very nice boy asked her to go to a church supper with him the next Sunday, but she said no, because she hoped Coyle would ask her out that day. She thought constantly of Coyle that week. She'd had crushes on boys before, but nothing like this. She was on an emotional roller coaster, up and down, joyful and despondent. What did he want from her? Was he seeing other girls? Where was this leading? Why wasn't he more affectionate? Should she be more aggressive, or would that scare him away? Maybe she should stop seeing him and date boys from school and concentrate on her studies. Wasn't she just riding for a fall? But the next moment she wanted to see him, to kiss him, to tell him something funny she'd heard. Like most girls her age, Louise had thought a lot about love, but she had never imagined it would be such an unsettling condition.

Louise's father, John Everett, set off from Murfreesboro, Tennessee, in 1900, to seek his fortune. He was a big, broad-shouldered, slow-talking, sandy-haired young man, not unacquainted with either bourbon or brawling, but serious-minded and anxious to make his way in the world. In time he settled in Denton, Texas, thirty miles northeast of Fort Worth, and found work as a carpenter's apprentice. He soon learned that he loved wood, loved its smell, its feel, its possibilities: all his life he would believe that a well-made house was as fine a work of art as any poem, and a damn sight more useful.

By the time he was twenty-six, John Everett was in business for himself. He worked hard, and when he wasn't working he played baseball, drank whiskey, argued politics, and kept a sharp eye out for whatever female pulchritude was to be found in Denton County. He was in politics a Populist and in religion a Freethinker, but he sometimes attended the First Baptist Church, in order to qualify for its baseball team, and it was there, in his mid-thirties, still a bachelor, that he chanced to meet Mabel Miller, a petite, fussy milliner from St. Louis who was in Denton visiting her sister. John Everett was attracted by Mabel's bright eyes and strong opinions—it did not seem important, in the first flush of romance, that those opinions were generally the opposite of his own. Mabel, for her part, was not indifferent to his good looks, his broad shoulders, or his success in business. She extended her stay in Texas, and soon the two were married.

With a wife to support, John became all the more industrious. Always popular, he was now one of the most respected men in the community, with a dozen workers in his employ. As John prospered, Mabel devoted herself to the church, the local literary society, and the oil painting that had become her passion, and she was only occasionally heard to grumble about her husband's drinking or that Denton was hopelessly dull for a woman who'd once known the cultural joys of St. Louis.

Their only real regret was that the Almighty had not blessed them with children, and then, quite unexpectedly, as John entered his forties, the Almighty corrected his mistake and sent them a daughter, whom they named Louise after John's mother.

Louise grew into a lively, golden-haired child, destined from the first to be loved and sheltered. She attended, not the public school, but a private academy for young ladies, and after school there were piano and voice lessons, plus frequent communion with the First Baptist Church. The girl might have grown up dull as dishwater, except for a certain native wit, and for the fact that the radio and magazines were bringing the music, fashions, and attitudes of the Jazz Age even to such quiet backwaters as Denton. As she entered her teens, Louise read tales of flappers, frat-houses, and bathtub gin in forbidden copies of *The Saturday Evening Post;* she slipped furtively to a friend's house to hear Paul Whiteman and Rudy Vallee on the radio, and she dreamed of the day when she could escape her mother's high-minded embrace and discover the Real World that she knew awaited her.

When it was time for Louise to enter college her mother wanted her to attend Denton's College of Industrial Arts, an all-girls school which Louise regarded as little more than a prison. Rebelling at last, Louise announced that she wished to enroll in TCU, in Fort Worth, a city that Mabel Everett ranked with Sodom and Gomorrah. But John Everett took his daughter's side, and at length a compromise was reached. John and Mabel would buy a house in Fort Worth and thus be close at hand when Louise entered TCU. So it came to pass that John and Mabel bought a comfortable brick home on Edward Street, overlooking Forest Park, while, less than two miles away, Louise settled into her dormitory and savored the taste of freedom she had dreamed of. She was young, unformed, untested, and her life might have taken any of many directions. As it happened, she chanced to cut across the TCU campus one fall afternoon and meet Coyle Kingslea.

It rained Saturday, plunging Louise into gloom, but in the early evening the clouds cleared, and looking out her dormitory window she saw a rainbow in the west, above the Worth Hills golf course. Louise hummed to herself as she slipped on her new off-the-shoulder gown and waited for Coyle. When he arrived, she kept him waiting for five minutes, so all the other girls could get a good look at him, and then she skipped down the stairs, pirouetted for him, and they hurried out the door hand in hand.

They were almost to his Chrysler when they heard Pig yelling at them.

He came charging through the traffic on University Drive, with cars honking and swerving to miss him, waving his arms, yelling incoherently. When he reached them, he threw his arms around Coyle, sobbing and gasping for breath.

"Pig, what the devil is it?" Coyle demanded.

"They *killed* him," Pig whimpered. "Shot him down like a dog!"

"Who? Killed who?"

Louise gasped, not so much because someone might be dead, as because she knew that, somehow, her evening was ruined.

"Willie! The damn Houston cops *shot* him. Because of a damn *milk truck!*"

Coyle put an arm around Pig and walked him across the campus and slowly got the story from him.

Willie McNabb, Pig's closest friend since sandbox days, had been working for his father's oil company in Houston. Willie was a legendary drinker, famous for his drunken pranks, and the previous night he'd been coming out of an after-hours club in downtown Houston when he'd chanced upon a horse-drawn milk truck. Willie leaped aboard, cried "Hi-yo, Silver" to his friends, cracked the reins, and set off down the street. At that point the milkman appeared, yelled bloody murder, and gave chase. Willie flicked the reins and the horse began to gallop. A policeman, chancing upon the scene, joined the pursuit. Willie began throwing milk bottles out the door to slow his pursuers. One bottle made a car swerve and hit a telephone pole. The policeman, puffing along thirty feet behind the milk wagon, yelled, "Stop or I'll shoot!" Willie responded with more bottles and a dozen eggs. "You'll never take me alive, copper!" he yelled. He was all too right. The policeman fired twice into the air, then stumbled and fired again by accident. It was the third shot which, against all odds, entered the back of Willie's head.

"The sonsabitches killed Willie."

Pig was sobbing uncontrollably. Louise had never imagined him capable of such emotion. "Why the hell would anybody shoot Willie?" Pig sobbed, childlike. He pulled a pint of gin from his pocket and took a long swig and shoved the bottle at Coyle, who gently pushed the bottle away.

"Have you talked to Willie's family?" he asked.

"We're gonna fly to Houston first thing in th' morning. His daddy wants you t'go, too."

"Of course," Coyle said.

"What about tonight?" Louise asked. "Maybe I should go back to the dorm."

"The party goes on," Coyle said. "That's what Willie would have wanted."

"See you later," Pig said and stumbled off toward his car. A few minutes later Coyle and Louise were driving silently out the Jacksboro Highway to the Casino.

The Casino was where the big bands played when they came to Fort Worth. Viewed by day, the nightclub was a big shabby barn overlooking a barren strip of Lake Worth beachfront, but on summer nights it could become an enchanted ballroom. A long balcony overlooked the lake, and when a cool breeze swept in off the water and the moonlight shone down and music filled the night there was no more lovely place in Texas.

Coyle's crowd had their usual long table beside the dance floor. There were endless toasts to Willie, and everyone except Coyle and Louise was soon on the way to oblivion.

Buster was there, drunk, and Buster's girl friend started flirting with Coyle, and finally Louise dragged Coyle out onto the dance floor and let him have it.

"I don't want that girl flirting with you," she cried angrily.

"She's an idiot," he said.

"I'm the idiot," Louise blurted. "I feel out of place with your friends. Coyle, I think about you all the time. I turned down a date this week because of you. But I don't know what you want from me or where we're headed."

He smiled at her. "Did you really turn down a date, angel?"

She nodded.

"For what?"

Louise blushed. "A church supper."

"It's a good thing, too. I'd have gotten my gang together, and we'd have come and torn the place apart."

"Oh, Coyle, you make a joke of everything. I'm serious."

The music stopped, and they stood, holding hands, until the band started another ballad. "Angel, I don't want to make you unhappy," he whispered. "The thing is, I keep losing my friends. One in a car wreck last summer. One in a plane crash the Christmas before. We're all living too fast. I think maybe we're an endangered species."

She held him close. "Then slow down, Coyle. Please. I . . . I'd rather go to movies, or go fishing at the lake, than go to parties and honky-tonks, really."

He kissed her forehead. "Angel, did you really turn down some decent young Christian who wanted to take you to a church supper?"

She nodded.

"Well, if you'll do that, then I'll start turning down all these painted hussies who want to drag me into depravity."

She beamed up at him. "You mean . . . ?"

"Just you and me, angel."

She threw her arms around him. She'd never been so happy in her life. To be going steady with Coyle, she realized, was everything she had dreamed of. She led Coyle back to their table to break the good news to Caddy. But just as they reached the table, so did Pig, wild-eyed and raving. "Gotta talk t'ya, pal," he told Coyle. "Matter'a life 'r death."

Coyle let himself be pulled away. "Oh *no*," Louise said and sat down next to Caddy, who was sipping a gin and ginger.

"Pig's out of his head," Caddy said. "He's got a plan to kidnap the policeman who shot Willie."

Louise tried to rekindle her enthusiasm. "I think Coyle and I are going steady," she said. "At least, he said he wouldn't go out with anybody else, and I won't if he won't. I'm so excited."

Caddy sighed and lit a Chesterfield. "Well, all I can say is good luck, darling."

"You're not very encouraging."

"Louise, I've known Coyle since the third grade, and he's a sweet, beautiful man who's got serious problems."

"You mean his drinking?"

"His drinking. And whatever makes him drink."

"What do you think it is?"

"Part of it is his father. His father and Livie, who is hell on wheels. And part of it is whatever happened to him at M&I."

"At M&I," Louise repeated. "I don't understand."

"Nobody does, really. He started college there, but only stayed a few months. The hazing there is criminal, just out of control. It was after he went there that his drinking got really crazy."

"But he can change," Louise insisted. "He already has."

Caddy shrugged. "Maybe so," she said.

After a while, Coyle and Pig returned, arm in arm. Coyle had loosened his black tie and he was grinning. "Let's dance, angel."

She stiffened when she smelled the gin on his breath.

"Only a nip, my deah," he said in his Cary Grant accent, as Pig shoved a drink at him.

"Coyle, do you have to?" she asked.

He looked at her coldly. "They're shootin' my friends."

"Coyle, *please*."

"Don't tell me what to do, sister," he snapped. "Come on, Pigger, let's go talk things over."

They staggered off again. "Life among the idle rich," Caddy drawled, and she and Louise fended off drunks until Coyle finally returned.

"Pigger's 'sleep in th' car," he announced. He had that pale, wild-eyed look Louise had seen the first night they met.

He insisted that they dance and pulled Louise out to the crowded dance floor, where he muttered and stumbled and banged into other couples until a man shoved him away. "Sumbitch," Coyle cried and swung at the man. He missed and fell down and someone yelled, "Throw the bum out!" Louise pulled Coyle to his feet and Caddy appeared and somehow they got him out to Pig's Cadillac. Pig was passed out in the back seat, and Coyle threw up before he climbed in beside him. Pig woke up long enough to howl, "They killed Willie!" before passing out again. Coyle grabbed at Louise, trying to make her get in the back seat with him, and managed to tear her new dress before he too passed out.

As Caddy guided them along the Jacksboro Highway toward town, Louise slumped down in the seat, weeping help-lessly. Caddy took her hand. "There's none of them worth crying over, honey."

"Why does he *do* it?"

"He doesn't mean it," Caddy said. "Coyle's the sweetest boy in the world when he's not drinking."

"It doesn't matter if he *means* it. He *does* it."

They turned onto University Drive beside the Ringside Club.

"He'll make it up to you," Caddy said. "Coyle can be aw-fully nice when he tries. A couple of years ago he was real sweet on a friend of mine. Then one night, kind of like to-night, he got crazy drunk on her. And she said she'd never see him again."

Louise glanced into the back seat, where Coyle and Pig were slumped together, dead to the world. "What happened?" she asked.

"Coyle started sending her a dozen roses, every day, until her sorority house was knee-deep in roses. So naturally she forgave him. Then a couple of weeks later he got drunk on her again, and that time she *really* gave up on him."

Louise stared out at the early morning traffic as they neared the light at West Seventh Street. She had stopped crying. She felt so very sad and tired and alone. But wiser.

"I wouldn't care if he sent me ten million roses," she vowed. "I never want to see him again."

CHAPTER THREE

A month after the fiasco at the Casino, Louise got a call from Caddy.

"I've missed seeing you," Caddy said.

"I've missed you too," Louise said, wondering if it was true. "How is everybody?"

"Oh, unchanged. Buster got beat and thrown in jail at Willie's funeral. I'm going to London for Christmas. The usual. What've you been up to?"

Louise giggled. "Dating two boys, mainly."

"Sounds like fun."

"It is. I mean, we just go to basketball games and to Doc's for Cokes. Nobody gets in fights or steals milk trucks or anything. One of the boys plays in the band and the other one is on the freshman basketball team. I felt sort of guilty for a while, because the one who plays in the band, Bobby Dean, was getting pretty serious, and I think it hurt his feelings when I started dating Clifton, the one who plays basketball. But then I just decided, what the heck?"

"You're learning," Caddy said. "Tell me, have you talked to Coyle?"

Louise bit her lip. "No. He called once, but I didn't take the call. How is he?"

"Terrible."

"Is he drinking?"

"Well, with Coyle you more or less take that for granted. But he's *down*. So depressed. I don't suppose you're willing to see him again."

"Did he ask you to ask me?"

"No," Caddy lied.

"I can't," Louise cried. "I just can't. It's too painful. I wish I could help him but I don't know how."

"I understand," Caddy said, and they spoke vaguely of having lunch one day.

Louise was busy not only with boys but with her schoolwork. She was making an A in English, and her faculty adviser said she could take an optional journalism course the next semester. Working for a newspaper had become Louise's dream. The very fact of meeting Amon Carter, the *Star-Telegram* publisher, at the Kingslea party had fired her ambitions. Maybe he would give her a job when she graduated. She wanted to write, to travel, to explore that glittering world she had glimpsed at Wade Kingslea's home.

When the envelope arrived in the mail, it did not look like any letter Louise had ever received before. The paper was stiff and creamy white, and the handwriting on the outside looked as if it had been made by a machine. Inside, an engraved invitation announced that Mrs. Wade Kingslea requested the

honor of her presence at a tea honoring Miss Edna St. Vincent
Millay at Hillcrest from 3 to 5 P.M. the following Sunday.
Louise was stunned. She had no idea what the poet was doing
in Texas, much less at the Kingslea home. She smiled and
wondered if the oilmen would come and shoot their guns in
the air. The thought of meeting a famous poet thrilled Louise,
and it also occurred to her that perhaps she could interview her
for the school paper. She was already imagining her interview
when the first doubts crept into her mind.

Why had she received this invitation? Surely not because
Livie Kingslea cared about her or her literary ambitions. No,
clearly Coyle was behind the invitation. If she went to the
tea, would she owe Coyle another date? Then she wouldn't go,
because nothing could be worth another night like the dance
at the Casino. And yet . . . she wanted so badly to meet Millay.
Uncertain, torn by confusion, she called Caddy for advice.

Caddy explained the Millay was lecturing in Dallas, and
she speculated that Livie had arranged the tea as part of her
campaign to be recognized as the unchallenged queen of Texas
hostesses. She agreed, too, that Coyle must have sent Louise
the invitation.

"What do you suppose he *wants?*" Louise asked.

"Maybe he just wants you to have a nice time. He sure
owes you that."

"Do you think Coyle will be there?"

"Probably. His father sure won't attend a tea for a Yankee
poet-lady, so Livie'll probably use Coyle as her official host. I
don't see what your problem is, honey. You've got your
ticket, go to the show. Coyle's not going to attack you."

In fact, Coyle was a perfect gentleman that afternoon. He
was wearing a charcoal-gray suit and a silver tie, and he was
absurdly handsome as he greeted each new arrival. Coyle's
"Aunt Fanny" from Dallas was there, the one he said had been
called "Five-percent Fanny" for some reason, back in the oil-
field days. Livie Kingslea, wearing a blue dress and pearls,
moved majestically among her guests. Coyle greeted Louise
with an uneasy smile. "I hoped you'd come," he said.
"How've you been?"

"Fine," she said, feeling not at all fine. "How about you?"

He shrugged and led her across the room to meet the poet
and Livie Kingslea.

"Miss Everett is a great fan of your work," Coyle told the

poet gravely, without irony. "She can recite most of 'Renascence,' if she's in the mood."

Millay laughed grandly. She was an intense, handsome woman in her forties. "Really?" she said. "I don't believe I could recite it now. I was about your age when I wrote it, my dear."

"I . . . I told my English professor I'd ask you a question."

"Then please do."

"Well, now that I'm here, the question seems silly. But . . . what should someone do who wants to be a poet?"

Millay smiled sadly, experience gazing upon innocence. "To be a poet?" she repeated. "Read. Write. Love. Suffer. And always remember there are more important things than poetry."

"Thank you so much," Louise said, scribbling down Millay's words on a notepad. "That's a beautiful answer."

After tea Millay spoke to the group. One woman asked her if St. Vincent was "an ancestral name." Millay said, "No, not really. I had an uncle who got locked in the hold of a ship and almost died and they took him to St. Vincent's Hospital in New York and saved his life. So my father made that my middle name as a way of saying thank you." She read two of her sonnets, then said, "I want to add a short poem dedicated to Louise Everett, a young woman I met today, as a warning about the passions of youth. I call this one 'Grown-up.'"

> "Was it for this I uttered prayers,
>   And sobbed and cursed and kicked the stairs,
>   That now, domestic as a plate,
>   I should retire at half-past eight?"

The roomful of middle-aged women cheered that sentiment, and soon the tea came to a close. As the guests left, Coyle came over to Louise.

"Miss Millay asked me to give you this," he said. He handed her a volume of "Renascence," inscribed, "Louise, Remember there are more important things than poetry, Edna St. V. Millay."

Louise took the book and hugged it like a baby. "Thank you, Coyle. I know you must have asked her to do it."

"She was glad to," he said. "Do you have a ride?"

"I'll call a cab."

"Wilson will take you. Or I will, if you'll let me."

She stared at him, his beautiful dark eyes so sad and vulnerable, and she wanted nothing more than to be with him. "That would be nice," she said.

She browsed in the library while he spoke to the departing guests. When Coyle returned, he had taken off his tie and put on a blue cashmere coat.

"A nice tea, if you like teas," he said. "Actually, I like teas. It's just tea I don't like."

"It's good for you, though."

"I know. It's what I'm drinking these days."

"I'm glad."

"I wish I'd tried it sooner."

Louise didn't know what to say. She closed her book and stood up. "I guess I should be going."

"I know something else we could do," he said.

"What, Coyle?" she asked nervously. No more disasters, she thought. Please, God, no more disasters.

"We could take a walk, out on the golf course. We could have a picnic. How about it? A walk and a picnic—for old times' sake!"

Her heart melted at his enthusiasm. "All right, Coyle. For old times' sake."

The golf course was deserted and the sky was a dusky pink. Coyle turned up his coat collar and looked incredibly dashing. He led her along the crisp fairways, carrying a blanket and a picnic basket stuffed with leftovers from the tea. She took his arm and walked close beside him. It was so peaceful on the golf course—it was like their own private park. When the sun dropped behind the treetops and the long winter twilight began, he tossed the blanket down on the grass beside a pond.

"Are you cold?" he asked. "You can have my coat."

"I'm fine."

"I used to wade in that pond," he said. "We'd sneak in at night looking for golf balls. Grab 'em with our toes."

"It's so peaceful here."

They feasted on Brie, goose-liver pâté, spiced shrimp, caviar, and stuffed olives and toasted each other with lemonade, and then they sat side by side and listened to the night birds sing. In the last twilight she asked him to read "Renascence" to her and he did, holding the book high to catch the light.

It was almost more than she could bear when he began the last stanza:

> "The world stands out on either side
>   No wider than the heart is wide;
>   Above the world is stretched the sky,—
>   No higher than the soul is high."

She saw the tears in his eyes and she took his hand as he finished:

> "The soul can split the sky in two,
>   And let the face of God shine through.
>   But East and West will pinch the heart
>   That can not keep them pushed apart;
>   And he whose soul is flat—the sky
>   Will cave in on him by and by."

He took her hand and kissed it. "Angel," he whispered. "My soul was flat and you came and made me happy, and now I'm lost again."

The first stars blinked above them. Somewhere in the distance a car honked. He was the only boy she had ever met who would cry over "Renascence," the nicest, gentlest boy she had ever known. She loved him so that she thought her heart might break.

"Coyle, would you tell me something?"

"Of course."

"What makes you drink?"

She saw the pain, the fear, in his eyes. She was afraid of hurting him but she thought she could help.

He looked away.

"Someone said it had something to do with Texas M&I," she said.

"Someone was right."

"Coyle, sometimes it helps to . . . to talk to someone."

He smiled his sad ironic smile. "I've talked to the most expensive shrinks on three continents."

She felt that she was losing him, that he was fading away into the darkness. "You've never talked to me, Coyle," she said. "Please talk to me."

He was leaning back on his elbows, looking up at the

moon. She gazed on his pale, perfect face and thought of Keats, a poem about moonlight and death. Coyle, for his part, was trying to frame an answer, trying to decide whether or not to let her inside the walls he had built around himself. Her question jerked the scab from wounds that would never heal. Why did he drink? He only half knew and he had long since decided that drinking was better than thinking about why he drank. Easier to say he drank because he enjoyed it, because all his friends drank, because they were rich enough to do whatever they pleased. Those were the easy lies; better to repeat them than to look into his soul. And yet he loved this girl, for her goodness and her innocence and her beauty, and sometimes he thought that she could save him, could breathe life into his crushed soul and make it whole again. Coyle shivered and pulled his cashmere coat tighter around his shoulders and told her about the past.

CHAPTER FOUR

In the early years of the twentieth century the Texas legislature created Texas Military and Industrial College, with an eye to providing a sound, inexpensive education for deserving young men who would in time contribute to a greater Texas and a greater America. The new school soon rose up from the flat, dusty farmlands of South Texas, not far from the state prison and a whorehouse that would one day be immortalized in a Broadway musical. Texas M&I was from the first a military college, whose students were required to join the ROTC and who upon graduation were commissioned in the U.S. Army. Over the years, the students, faculty, and alumni of Texas M&I came to see their school as the West Point of the Southwest. Indeed, being Texans, they viewed themselves as superior to West Point in most regards.

Especially in hazing.

Hazing was basic to an M&I education. The freshmen, or Worms, as they were known, were after all civilians who had to be molded into military men, and the freshman year thus became a kind of boot camp. The basic instrument of enlightenment was the paddle, generously applied to the Worms' rear ends, but at times the hazing took more creative forms.

One spring afternoon in the early 1920s, for example, a group of M&I seniors consumed several cases of beer and proceeded to organize the First Annual All-Texas Worm Bounce. They seized a troublesome Worm named Coggins, tied him spread-eagled to his bedsprings, and carried him up to the roof of his three-story dormitory. The idea, they explained to curious onlookers, was to drop Worm Coggins and the bedsprings off the roof and see how high they would bounce. Various engineering students made calculations, based on the height of the building, Coggins' weight, the condition of the bedsprings, wind resistance, and the like, and came up with estimates that Coggins and the bedsprings would bounce anywhere from two to ten feet into the air when they landed on the asphalt parking lot below. A pool was formed and bets placed, and all the while Worm Coggins' howls of protest were scornfully ignored.

As it turned out, Coggins and the bedsprings did not bounce at all. On the way down, the weight of Coggins' body flipped the bedsprings over and they landed on top of him, producing one very flat, dead Worm.

The unfortunate outcome of the Worm Bounce discouraged creative hazing for a few years, but in time Coggins was forgotten, and there then occurred the celebrated railroad-track incident.

This time the Worm was named Gregg, a total malcontent who was rumored to be an atheist and was known for a fact to have spoken derisively of the M&I football team. A group of seniors abducted Gregg from his dormitory one night, drove him far out into the boondock country, and tied him to the railroad tracks, just like in the movies.

"What time's the train come?" one senior demanded.

"'Bout half an hour," another told him.

"Gregg, you chickenshit bastard, you're gonna die—let's see if you can take it like a man!" another urged.

"You fuckers can't scare me," Gregg screamed. "There's no train coming."

"Wait 'n see, Worm."

Gregg cursed them, and they drank more beer. A couple of upperclassmen amused themselves by pissing on Gregg, and one kept calling off the time. Five more minutes. Four. Three.

Then they heard the train whistle.

"Thar she comes!"

"Two minutes left, Gregg!"

"Start praying, fuckhead."

The whistle howled again, closer this time. Gregg couldn't believe it. *There really was a train coming!* He strained against the ropes that held him.

"You bastards, let me up! Hey, come on!"

"Take it like a man, Worm!"

"Aw shit, let's untie him. He ain't worth killing."

The whistle sounded again.

"Please, for God's sake, untie me. Please!"

He could *feel* the train now, feel the ground trembling. He struggled until the ropes cut his flesh.

"Pray, Gregg!"

"Oh, God, please . . ."

"Forget *God*, Gregg. Pray to us. We're the ones who can save your ass."

"Please, Mr. Holmes, Mr. Whipple, Mr. Jennings, please, I pray to you, please, hurry. . ."

He could hear the train's engines now, could see the light.

"PLEASE, HURRY, OH GOD, OH MAMA, DADDY, OH GOD OH GOD . . ."

The upperclassmen leaped back, laughing and spilling their beer, as the huge freight train rattled by. They were overjoyed at how well their prank had worked. For they knew, as Worm Gregg had not, that there were two sets of tracks, side by side, and they had tied the freshman onto the unused track.

The experience, they agreed, would teach Gregg a lesson.

In fact, it did not. A moment later, when they went to untie Worm Gregg and give him a final lecture on manliness, they found to their surprise that he was dead, of a heart attack.

Worm Gregg's unfortunate passing, followed by yet another investigation, caused hazing once again to be toned down at M&I. Even paddling was minimized for a few years. Faculty members would make spot checks in the dormitories —butt checks, they were called—wherein freshmen dropped their drawers so the authorities could see if their rears had been blistered, scarred, or otherwise violated by excessive paddling. But this policy was bitterly resented by the school's alumni, who protested that M&I was turning into a country club, and also by Gregg's own classmates, who as freshmen had suffered the paddle but as upperclassmen were denied the joys of wielding it. Thus by the time Coyle Kingslea entered M&I, the paddle had returned and upperclassmen, long denied the pleasures of "whippin' ass," began to swing their hand-carved paddles with a vengeance.

The fact that Coyle attended M&I at all came about because of an unexpected act of violence that rocked the Kingslea home earlier that summer. Wade and Livie, with Coyle and Hoyt, had been having a quiet dinner. Coyle was just back from visits to the University of Texas and SMU and was agonizing over which university to attend and what fraternity to join. His younger brother listened sullenly. Hoyt didn't see why Coyle could go off to fraternity parties and he couldn't go roughneck in the oil fields that summer. Midway through dinner the front door burst open and four men, swinging chains and howling for blood, invaded the Kingslea home. Their leader was a grizzled, drunken, half-mad wildcatter named Sam Wilkes; the others were his three sons. Sam Wilkes had once been a wealthy man, but now he was broke, and he blamed Wade Kingslea for his misfortune.

Wade Kingslea had barely jumped from his chair when Sam Wilkes' chain flashed across the room and broke his collarbone. For a moment it looked as if Kingslea would be beaten to a pulp, but fifteen-year-old Hoyt, wielding a candelabra, disabled one of the sons, and he and his crippled father, in a wild and bloody brawl, managed to beat the other Wilkeses into unconsciousness. At the end, Kingslea and Hoyt stood arm in arm, victorious. It was only then that Kingslea noticed Coyle, trembling in a corner of the dining room. From the moment the men burst in, Coyle had been frozen with fear. For him, the attack was like a nightmare; this was what he had feared all his life, big, angry, violent men, men like his father. Coyle stood motionless, voiceless, helpless, with tears running down his face. His father stared at him contemptuously, and a few days later announced that in the fall Coyle would attend not SMU or the University of Texas but Texas M&I. "Maybe it'll make a man of him," he said.

On Coyle's first day at M&I, after all the proud parents had left, after the band had played and the commandant had spoken, after the incoming freshmen had eaten hot dogs and beans in a huge mess hall, they were marched out to an athletic field at the western edge of the campus. A light rain had been falling all day and the field was soggy beneath their feet. Bonfires cast an eerie, flickering light over the several hundred young men who milled about, still in civilian clothes, waiting to see what would happen next. Coyle was apprehensive, ill at ease; he didn't know what to expect from M&I. No one he knew had ever gone there. Coyle had been to camp in North Carolina one summer and he had a vague notion that M&I would be like that: lots of sports and exercise.

"Man, I bet they gunna beat our asses!" a boy near him was saying.

"Naw, they stopped that."

"My brother went here and they beat *his* ass."

"Some guy got killed."

"Shit man, I can take it. They can't whup me no worse'n my old man does."

Coyle listened silently, already feeling the outsider among these wiry, hard-muscled farm boys.

"ALL RIGHT YOU FUCKING WORMS, FALL IN!"

A dozen upperclassmen in boots and combat gear were running toward them. They all carried long wooden paddles.

"FALL IN, WORMS, ON THE DOUBLE."

Led by a few boys who had attended military school, the freshmen awkwardly began to form ranks. Coyle did not know enough to hide in the middle of the formation. He wound up on the front row, directly in front of the massive red-faced cadet who seemed to be in charge.

"Ten-hut!"

The freshmen snapped uncertainly to attention. Coyle felt silly. He and his friends had of late affected a prep-school slouch; the idea of throwing one's head back, holding one's chin high, was ridiculous.

"My name's Cadet Captain Hammond," the burly cadet said. "My friends call me Goat, but you ain't my friends. This here is Welcome Night. That means we're welcoming you pigfuckers to Texas M&I. We're gunna teach you some rules tonight, and we're gunna give you some uniforms. The first thing is, line up over by them tents. They'll give you a duffel bag. Put all your clothes and crap in there, put your name on it, and fall in back over here. On the double. Any questions?"

There was a nervous silence. Coyle had a question, but he also had a sense that silence would be golden here. What the hell, he thought, might as well be civilized.

"Ah, Captain Hammond," he said. "Did you mean fall back in *naked?*" he asked.

Hammond looked incredulous. Jaw jutting forward, he advanced on Coyle.

"You got some objection, Worm?"

Coyle could smell whiskey and garlic on Hammond's breath. His stomach began to churn. *Why hadn't he kept quiet?*

"Well, ah, I suppose not . . ." he said, trying to be casual, trying to pull it off.

"Step out here, Worm, and let's have a look at you," Hammond roared. Coyle took a step forward. His hands had started to shake. There was a deathly silence over the field.

"What's your name, Worm?"

"Kingslea. Coyle Kingslea."

"YOU CUNTLICKER, YOUR NAME IS WORM KINGSLEA! LET'S HEAR IT!"

"My name is Worm Kingslea." He could barely get the words out. The awful new reality was settling over him like a shroud. There was no place to hide, no escape. These people were serious.

"YOUR NAME IS WORM KINGSLEA *WHAT?*"

"My name is Worm Kingslea . . . sir."

"LOUDER, FUCKHEAD!"

"MY NAME IS WORM KINGSLEA, SIR!"

"Your name is shit. Assume the position."

Coyle was confused. Behind him someone was laughing. "Sir?"

"Bend over, turdface, and grab your balls, if you've got any!"

Coyle bent over and grabbed his balls. He tensed, awaiting the blow, but none came. Instead, Hammond began gently rubbing his bottom with the paddle.

"That's a sweet little ass on this Worm," he said, still rubbing. "I don't know whether to whip it or fuck it." The ranks howled with laughter. Coyle felt tears of humiliation burning in his eyes. *Why was this happening? What was he doing here?*

Suddenly Hammond swung the paddle, hard, and it exploded across his buttocks and sent him sprawling on the ground. Coyle rolled about, stunned, disbelieving, trying to rub the pain from his burning bottom.

"GET UP, WORM. ASSUME THE POSITION!"

In an instant, Coyle understood everything. He wanted to flee into the night. But he could not. He was here for a reason. All his life he had been soft, spoiled, a coward. Three months before, he had sat frozen by fear while four men tried to beat his father to death. Now, here, he could prove himself. Not to this ape with the paddle but to his father, whose long shadow loomed behind him. He must suffer that he could be strong. He must be a man. With tears burning in his eyes, Coyle got to his feet and bent over again.

"How'd you like that little love pat, Worm?"

"Fine, sir!"

"Want some more?"

"Please, sir."

Goat Hammond was disappointed. Sometimes, on Welcome Night, the Worms wept or begged or fought.

"Kingslea, I think you're a pussy," he snarled. "I ain't got time to fuck with you now. Fall in."

Coyle stepped back into the ranks, his bottom still burning with pain, and soon the Worms had taken off their clothes and were back on the field naked. More upperclassmen appeared, wearing fatigues, carrying paddles and beer bottles; "Wa-hoo, fresh meat!" they cried, and Welcome Night got moving. The upperclassmen moved up and down the line of Worms, asking questions, demanding answers, and whipping ass when they didn't hear what they wanted to hear.

"What's your status, Worm?"

"Sir, I am lower than whale shit at the bottom of the Pacific Ocean, sir. But I am higher than the student-body president at the University of Texas, sir!"

They ran, naked and screaming, around the bonfires. They did push-ups and sit-ups until they groaned and vomited. Hammond began to lead them in "maneuvers." They crawled the length of the field, wallowing in the mud, with upperclassmen whacking their bare asses if they rose up too high. Whenever an upperclassman yelled, "Pile-up," they threw themselves into squirming, twisting piles, and the unlucky ones on the bottom howled that they couldn't breathe, that they were being crushed. After one pile-up a short, wiry boy got up, choking back tears, with his arm dangling at an unnatural angle. An upperclassman came over. "I think it's broke, sir," the boy said. The upperclassman was examining the arm when a tall, skinny boy began to shout at Goat Hammond.

"I've had enough of this shit," he yelled. "I'm here to get an *education!*"

"This is your fucking education, Worm! Assume the position," Hammond yelled.

"Fuck you! I'm leaving!"

"Okay, you cocksucker, go home to your mama. Go to the fucking University of Texas and be a fucking tea-sipper. We don't want you here. Go on, get out of here!"

The tall boy loped off to look for his clothes.

"You Worms, listen up," Hammond yelled. He had the boy with the broken arm beside him. The bone was sticking through the skin just above the elbow. "This Worm here— what's your name, boy?"

"Dickey, sir."

"Worm Dickey here's got a broken arm. You want to go home, Worm?"

"No sir!" the boy said proudly.

"Worm Dickey's got guts. Listen, Worms, someday you may be in a trench somewhere with the fucking Germans or the fucking Russians shooting at your ass, and you're gonna want somebody like Worm Dickey there with you, and not some dicklicker like that one who just left."

Coyle could see tears of pride glistening on Dickey's face.

Hammond announced that Welcome Night was over. They marched down by the gym and hosed the mud off themselves, then they were given blankets and fatigues and assigned to tents down past the football field. Coyle fell on his bunk exhausted. His ass throbbed from the paddlings he had taken, and he was bruised and bleeding from the pile-ups. He was shaken, frightened, yet strangely proud. He had survived.

A few feet away, his tentmates were talking excitedly. They spoke in the sharp, nasal twangs of small-town Texas, and despite their bruises, despite their raw and bleeding buttocks, their enthusiasm was undiminished.

"Man, ain't it fucking *great!*"

"Them whippings ain't *nothing!*"

"I can damn sure take a year of gettin' my ass paddled, long as I get three years of paddlin' somebody else's ass!"

"Right, right!" another boy said, except he pronounced it "Rat, rat!" in the manner of some Texans.

Coyle listened in wonder. He thought he could survive M&I, but he would never understand how so many of these boys could love it.

A Worm could be stopped and paddled at any time, and it was a rare day that passed without at least one paddling. Actually, the paddlings were not the worst of it. After the first few weeks, your ass began to toughen up, until finally it was calloused, hard as leather. Worse than the paddling was the constant verbal abuse, the yelling, the insults, the lack of privacy. Coyle spent those first weeks in a state of shock. He felt like a man who'd been sent to prison by mistake. He withdrew into himself, studying as much as he could, counting the days. His dream was that if he survived the first year, his father would let him transfer. It all came back to his father. Somehow he had to please him, to show him he was a man. That kept him going. It was his father wielding the paddle, his father screaming abuse at him, and he had to prove he could take it, even if it killed him.

He might have, except for Goat Hammond.

In Coyle's second week at M&I, Hammond stopped him outside the Mess Hall.

"What's your name, Worm?"

"Worm Kingslea, sir!"

"Kingslea. You're the Worm who got smart with me on Welcome Night, right?"

"Yes sir!" You never argued. If he had said no, Hammond would have accused him of calling him a liar.

"Your old man's some rich fucking oilman, ain't he?"

"Yes sir!"

"You think you're better'n the rest of us dumb pigfuckers?"

"No sir!"

"Where'd you get them pretty eyes, Worm?"

"I . . . I was born with them, sir."

"I bet your mama thinks you're pretty, Worm."

"Yes sir!"

"Well, I think you're shit, Kingslea. Assume the position!"

Coyle bent over, relieved to get on with the paddling.

WHACK!

The first lick brought tears to his eyes, but he stayed on his feet and did not cry out.

WHACK!

The second lick sent him lurching forward, sent the fire deeper, into his gut, his back, his legs, and he groaned without meaning to.

"What's the matter, Worm?"

"Nothing, sir," he muttered through clenched teeth.

WHACK!

The third lick dropped him to his knees. The buildings were spinning. He tried to get up but fell over onto his back.

"Kingslea, you are one chickenshit Worm. Report to my room at ten o'clock tonight. You understand?"

Coyle struggled to his feet. "Yes sir!" he said, as Goat Hammond marched away.

That night in Goat Hammond's room, while Goat and six of his teammates played poker, Coyle did push-ups. He did two hundred push-ups before his arms gave out, then he did sixty-three sit-ups before his stomach muscles gave out, and then he did ninety-four deep knee bends before his legs collapsed. Then he started over. At three in the morning he was doubled up on Goat's bathroom floor, cramps in his arms and legs, trying to raise himself up to vomit in the toilet instead of on the floor. When he passed out, Hammond sent for some Worms to carry him back to his dorm.

In any army, anonymity is the enlisted man's best friend; to be known by those in command is always a disaster. It was Coyle's misfortune to have been singled out for abuse by an upperclassman who in hazing, as in other areas, was a legend at Texas M&I.

Goat Hammond was a dirt farmer's son from the Rio Grande Valley who was in his fourth agonizing year of being the star player on a losing football team. Football was M&I Achilles' heel. Despite the school's fabled toughness, despite the cadet corps' famous school spirit, the M&I Mules were losers. The unspeakable truth, of course, was that the best football players wanted to attend colleges that offered girls and parties, not go to M&I and have their asses whipped and be told they were lower than whale shit. Goat Hammond, an exception to this rule, was the best football player to attend M&I in a generation. Arriving as a freshman, an aspiring fullback, he joined a team that had gone winless the year before. Grover Hammond and several fellow Worms had vowed not to bathe, shave, brush their teeth, or wipe their asses until the Mules had won a game. By the time the Mules had lost their first four straight, Hammond's English professor had banned him from the classroom, some of his teammates had deserted the athletic dorm for the duration, and one opposing football team had very nearly not come out for the second half of a game it was winning. But then Grover Hammond—now immortalized as Goat—led the Mules to a 13-7 upset over the

Baylor Bears, and a new M&I legend was born.

For all Goat Hammond's legendary achievements, one great prize had eluded him. He had never led the M&I Mules to victory over the hated University of Texas Longhorns. That was his goal, and every Timmie's dream, the fall that Coyle entered Texas M&I. As the big game drew near, there were huge bonfires and pep rallies each night, and for miles the prairie dogs could hear impassioned young men chanting, "Go, Mules, go."

Only two days before the game, Coyle unwittingly aroused the wrath of Goat Hammond. One of Coyle's roommates, a boy from Houston named Snavely, had stolen a bottle of gin the previous weekend when several Worms had sneaked a cow into the room of a senior who was away for the weekend. Snavely decided the sensible thing was to drink the gin before the upperclassmen conducted a room search. Thus, Snavely, Coyle, and another of their roommates set out to dispose of the gin late one night, after the pep rally, while their fourth roommate, a nondrinking Baptist, stood guard. They drank the gin, they laughed, they cried, they sang songs, and just before he passed out Coyle realized it was the first time since he'd arrived at M&I that he'd been happy.

Unfortunately, besides guzzling gin, Coyle drew a picture that night, a cartoon, one that portrayed Goat Hammond as an ape swinging from the limb of a tree. Early the next morning, the sober Baptist roommate, thinking it would be a great joke, pinned the cartoon on the dorm bulletin board. And at 6:30 A.M. as Coyle fell in for the morning roll call, his mouth dry, his head throbbing, he was stunned to see Goat Hammond standing before their formation, waving a cartoon that seemed dimly familiar.

"All right, who's the artist?" Goat roared.

Coyle groaned, disbelieving.

"Okay, we're gonna march with full pack till one of you cocksuckers confesses!"

Groans went up from the ranks. Coyle knew he had no choice.

"I drew it, sir," he said.

Hammond charged forward. "I knew it was you, Kingslea," he roared. "The Worm with the pretty eyes. You want to tell us why you drew this? Was it to piss me off, so I can't play ball on Saturday?"

Coyle hesitated. An honest answer would be, "I did it because I was drunk," but that would get Snavely in trouble, and besides it wasn't the whole truth. The real truth, he thought, the unfortunate truth, was that he had a spark of individuality that had not been extinguished by Texas M&I and perhaps never would be.

"Why'd you draw it, Worm?" Goat Hammond thundered.

"Because I thought it was a good likeness, sir."

The Worms gasped collectively. Even Goat Hammond was stunned.

"You saying I look like a fucking *ape*, Worm?" he asked incredulously.

"That's right, sir."

At the back of the ranks, some Worm began to whistle a funeral dirge.

Goat Hammond's face turned redder than the morning sun. Suddenly he began a mighty howl, an ape call, and began pounding his chest with his two hamlike fists until his jungle chant filled the quadrangle like some echo from the primordial past. Windows opened, passersby froze. It was a moment that would live forever in M&I legend: Goat Hammond's ape call.

Finally he spoke, in a whisper that could be heard for miles: "Worm Kingslea, first I'm gunna take care of them tea-sippers from UT, then I'm gunna show you a fucking ape!"

It was, without question, a magnificent game. The Mules, outweighed, would not be outplayed. Goat Hammond, the star of both offense and defense, was everywhere on the field. In the closing minutes of the first half he carried the ball on eight straight plays, defying the Longhorn defenders to halt him, until he plunged over from the three-yard line to bring the Mules to a 7-7 halftime tie.

Coyle Kingslea watched the game from the grandstand with the other cheering Worms. He had evolved a theory, like the drowning man clutching at a straw, that if the Mules won, Goat Hammond might forgive him. As the second half began, no Worm cheered "Go Mules, go" more eagerly than Coyle.

The Longhorns scored again, but missed the extra point, to lead 13-7. The Mules fought back, but the Longhorn defense stiffened, and it was not until the final moments of the game that the Mules got another chance. Still trailing 13-7, the Mules pushed to the Longhorns' five-yard line. Then a roughness penalty—a Mule fist in a Longhorn face too blatant to be ignored—set them back fifteen yards. With seconds remaining, it was fourth and goal from the twenty. Clearly, the Mules' only hope rested on the Goat's broad shoulders. Somehow, with eleven angry Longhorns keying on him, he would have to bull his way across the goal.

The play began. Goat charged straight into the center of the line. A half-dozen Longhorns piled atop him. A great groan went up. But wait! Suddenly Rabbit Bundy, the Mules' 140-pound quarterback, was scampering around end. *It was a trick. Rabbit had kept the ball!* Two Longhorns had Rabbit trapped at the sideline. Desperately he began to recross the field, now with a swarm of UT defenders stampeding after him. Just as he seemed trapped back at the thirty-yard line, Rabbit did the unexpected, the incredible: he threw the ball, threw the Mules' first pass of the year!

Ten thousand Timmies gasped. Twenty thousand eyes focused on the end zone. And then they understood. For there, all alone in the end zone, waving his arms, with no Longhorn within ten yards of him, was the Goat!

Now, as the football sailed gracefully toward his outstretched hands, ten thousand Timmies began to cheer as they would never cheer again. It was a golden moment, never to be forgotten: the ball dropping gently into the great Goat Hammond's grasp, the tied score, the extra point that would give the M&I Mules a 14-13 upset victory that would live forever in the annals of Texas football.

It was not to be.

The football dropped into Goat Hammond's waiting hands, then dropped out again, bounced off his chest, and fell like a stone to the soft green grass of the end zone. The final gun went off, the University of Texas band began to play "The Eyes of Texas," and the M&I cadets corps stood frozen, disbelieving, in the grandstand. All eyes were on Goat Hammond. For an instant he too was frozen, his eyes heavenward, as if still searching for the phantom pigskin. Then, suddenly, the Goat let out a wild animal cry that filled the stadium. He seized the goalpost in both hands and began beating his head against it. Then his attention turned to the Longhorn players, who were leaping up and down in celebration. He grabbed one of them and threw him to the turf and kicked him in the head. When a second Longhorn came to his teammate's defense, Goat flattened him with one right to the jaw. He was charging two more Longhorns when five of his teammates seized him and carried him struggling off the field and into the locker room.

Fights were breaking out all over the stadium as enraged Timmies, both students and alumni, began to attack University of Texas students and supporters. Down in the locker room, Goat Hammond was out of control. He knocked down four of his teammates, broke wooden benches against the concrete walls, and attacked his coach. Five of his teammates held him down and screamed that the defeat was not his fault, but he howled, kicked, cursed, and bit them. Finally one of them said, "Goat, it's all right, man, let's go get shitfaced, okay?" He seemed to become rational again, and his teammates walked him back to the jock dorm, forming a circle around him, and somebody produced bottles of tequila and Scotch and gin. Goat Hammond seized the tequila bottle and downed it at one long smooth gulp, just glub-glub-glub, like a little boy slurping lemonade, and when he was finished he let out another primordial howl and began to beat the cinderblock wall until his fists were bloody and his friends wrestled him to the floor. He cried like a baby, then he went crazy again and had to be held down, and finally he started in on the bottle of gin. When the gin was half-gone he began to howl, "Get me Worm Kingslea!"

Coyle was waiting in his room. Some of his friends begged him to flee, but he shook off their advice. How could you run from reality, from destiny?

Four members of the football team came to escort him back to the jock dorm. Coyle went with them peacefully, even nonchalantly, whistling a tune. He was a boy of eighteen, five ten in height, one hundred and forty pounds in weight, a good-looking, introspective, somewhat shy young man who liked to dance, to play tennis, to read, to draw, to go to movies—in all, a rather pleasant, unspoiled youth despite his father's wealth. Had he been a freshman at the University of Texas, rather than a Worm at Texas M&I, he would have been pledging one of the top fraternities, dating the prettiest coeds, and becoming known as one of the more popular boys on campus.

As they neared the athletic dorm, Coyle realized that he was whistling "The Eyes of Texas"—the University of Texas song—and began to laugh helplessly. The four young men guarding him shook their heads disgustedly—Worm Kingslea, they had decided, was crazy and deserved whatever he got. They pushed him into Goat's room and then shut the door—

whatever happened, they didn't want to see it.

Goat Hammond was standing in the middle of the room in his shorts with a gin bottle in his hand. His hairy, powerful body was covered with red welts and ugly purple bruises. He squinted as with difficulty he focused on Coyle. His florid face was twisted by pain and anger and alcohol.

"Y' wanted us t'lose, didn't ya, Kingslea?"

"No sir." That was true. He had wanted the Mules to win because it meant so much to so many people who had so little else in their lives to cheer, or even care, about.

"Y' wanted me to drop that pass, din't ya?"

"No sir."

"Y're a fuckin' liar, Kingslea. A fuckin' rich boy an' a fuckin' pretty boy an' a fuckin' liar."

"I can't help being rich, Mr. Hammond, any more than you can help being what you are."

"I don't want your fuckin' philosophy, Kingslea. Assume the position!"

Coyle bent over, smiling despite himself. That was true: Goat Hammond wasn't interested in his philosophy. You could no more reach him, reason with him, than you could reason with the howling north winds that blew down off the Texas plains. Goat Hammond, like his father, Wade Kingslea, was what he was. You could not change them, you could only accept them. Coyle tensed, waiting for the paddling to begin.

"Take off them pants, Worm," Goat muttered.

Coyle hesitated, then slipped off his pants. It was probably best not to anger Goat anymore, he thought. He watched Goat take another swig from his gin bottle and found himself smiling.

"Somethin' funny, Worm?"

Coyle shrugged. "I was just thinking, I'd like a shot of that gin. If you want the truth, I was drunk on gin the other night when I drew that damn picture."

"Y'want some gin, Worm?"

"Sure."

Goat thrust the bottle at him. Coyle tipped it up and took a long swallow. The gin burned all the way down, and almost at once he felt better. What the hell? So he got his ass beat—so what? As the saying went, Goat wouldn't be getting a cherry. He glanced in the mirror on the wall and saw a sight so ridiculous that he never forgot it—himself and Goat Hammond, the skinny Worm and the sturdy Goat, standing there in their olive-drab shorts, passing a bottle of bootleg gin back and forth. Life was strange.

"Assume the position, Worm!"

Coyle bent over. The gin had warmed him; he felt serene as he awaited the first blow. After the first two or three licks, it wouldn't matter. But the sharp slap of the paddle did not come. Instead, after a moment, he felt the smooth hardwood rubbing gently across his bottom, the way it had the first time he'd met Goat, back on Welcome Night.

"That feel good, Worm?"

"Not really."

"You got a sweet li'l ass, Worm. Damn shame to whip it."

Coyle began to feel the danger signals, even before he understood them.

"Think I'd rather fuck it than paddle it," Goat said. He was still rubbing Coyle softly with the paddle.

"That's not in regulations, Goat," Coyle said angrily.

"YOU LITTLE COCKSUCKER, YOU MADE ME DROP THAT PASS!" Goat screamed, and seized Coyle in a bear hug and began tearing at his shorts. Coyle fought loose and ran for the door, but it was locked. Goat grabbed him again and wrestled him toward the bed. Coyle struggled but could not break free. Screaming, he sank his teeth into Goat's neck. Goat began to choke him and Coyle gasped and tried to push and kick, but he was losing consciousness and the last thing he remembered was Goat tearing at his shorts and the pungent smell of gin on the other man's breath as they wrestled on the unmade bed.

Goat's friends, playing poker in the next room, heard the sounds of struggle but kept on with their game. Whatever it took to get Goat quieted down was worth it, they reasoned. Then, after those first screams, there were fifteen minutes or so of silence, perhaps an occasional moan; it was hard to tell because a storm was blowing up outside. Then, just as the storm broke, and as they were finishing a game of seven-card, they heard a scream, a shriek, long and barely human, from Goat's room.

"We better check it out," said Rabbit Bundy, the quarterback.

"Bullshit—play your cards!" said a lineman who had two aces showing.

They started to bet, but then the shriek came again, high-pitched, like a dying animal, and Rabbit Bundy and two other boys ran out of the room and tried Goat's door and when they found it locked and heard a third pitiful howl they kicked the door open.

The room was a shambles. The mattress from Goat's bed had been tossed onto the floor. Coyle, naked and unconscious, was tied to the bedsprings. Goat Hammond, also naked, was sitting beside the bed with a lamp switch in his hand. Rabbit Bundy saw the wires running to the bedsprings and he realized what was happening.

"'S called th' Worm Fry," Goat said. "Y' fuck 'em then y' fry 'em then y' eat 'em for dinner." He began to shake with laughter and he flipped the switch and another jolt of electric current burned through Coyle's torn, broken body. He screamed again, his body jerking upward, and then Rabbit Bundy pulled the wires loose and tackled Goat and after they had gotten him tied down they carried Worm Kingslea to the school hospital.

Coyle regained consciousness the next evening, Sunday evening. A nurse told him that his parents had been notified of his accident and would arrive the next morning. That night, however, Coyle stole some clothing and money from another patient and slipped out of the hospital.

By the next day, Wade Kingslea had a dozen private detectives searching for his missing son. He had by then found out the full story, or most of it, of Coyle's injuries, and he feared that electrical shock might have weakened his son's heart and that indeed he might be dead. Livie Kingslea was curious about Coyle's whereabouts too. She had a private talk with her lawyer to find out exactly when a missing person was declared legally dead. Livie did not care much about Coyle, but she cared a great deal about the Kingslea fortune, and if Coyle was dead her daughter, Eve, stood to inherit equally with Hoyt.

Christmas came and went with no trace of Coyle. It was not until early January that he was heard from and then the first person to get word was not his father but his Aunt Fanny —Frances Todd, she was now—at her home in Dallas.

Fanny O'Brien Todd was one of those rare individuals whose life had followed a plan. As a very young woman she had gone to Goodwill, determined to leave there rich, and in fact, when she left Goodwill, she had five percent of seven producing oil wells that over the years had brought her a half-million dollars. In Dallas she invested shrewdly in real estate, caught on to the 1920s boom, and by the end of the decade was worth something like ten million dollars. It was not a great amount of money, but enough for a single woman to live comfortably in Dallas. She was married once, for strategic purposes, to a widowed judge named Richmond Todd. The marriage was intended to give Fanny respectability, to remove whatever social stigma might have been caused by unkind rumors that sometimes circulated about her early career in Goodwill. To that end the marriage succeeded brilliantly. Fanny nursed Judge Todd lovingly through his final illness, and by the time of his death there was hardly a home in Dallas in which Fanny Todd was not welcome.

Fanny Todd, as the 1930s began, was rich, young, popular, and carefree and might have been one of the happiest women in Texas, except for the inconvenient fact that she was still in love with Wade Kingslea, but that, she had decided, simply could not be helped.

Fanny knew Coyle, and loved him, and worried about him, growing up in the same house with two such powerful figures as Wade and Livie. Throughout Coyle's high school years, whenever Fanny was in Fort Worth, or Coyle could be enticed to Dallas, she would take the boy to a movie or a play. He had not had a mother since Wade snatched him away from his real mother, and Fanny, if she could not be a mother to Coyle, tried at least to be a friend. Thus it was no surprise, that January morning, when Fanny received a collect call from a man in New Orleans who said his name was Jake—"Jes' Jake, ma'am"—and that he was calling for Coyle Kingslea.

"The thing is, ma'am, he din't want me t'call, but I reckon maybe he'll die if he don't see a doc pretty soon."

Fanny got an address, then got Coyle to the phone. "Just stay there, darling," she said. "I'll have a doctor there in an instant."

"I don't want to see my father," Coyle sobbed. "Or Livie. I'll run away if you tell them where I am."

"I want you to stay at my house, till you're well."

"Do you promise not to tell them?"

"Yes, darling. Just do what the doctor says."

The night Coyle fled the M&I hospital, he had caught a ride with a Mexican farmer who was driving a truckload of grapefruit to New Orleans. Once he arrived there, he made friends with some derelicts who lived in the slums west of the

French Quarter. He earned a little money shining shoes in Jackson Square—M&I had at least taught him a skill—and spent it mostly on cheap wine and rotgut whiskey. He was arrested several times for drunkenness, and the enforced sobriety of jail had probably saved his life. The doctor who Fanny sent to treat Coyle found him suffering from malnutrition and pneumonia. He put the boy in the Tulane University Hospital for a week, then Fanny arranged for him to be returned to Dallas in a private railroad car. "The style to which I have grown unaccustomed," he quipped when Fanny greeted him.

He stayed in seclusion at Fanny's home, refusing to let her tell his family of his whereabouts. He did agree to see numerous doctors and psychiatrists, who variously declared that his problem was acute schizophrenia, latent homosexuality, unresolved Oedipal conflicts, and simple dipsomania. "Guilty on all counts," Coyle would joke of their diagnoses. He thought the psychiatrists fools. Who could speak of madness who had not experienced Texas M&I?

When the psychiatrists would ask his goals in life, Coyle would invariably say, "To shine shoes in Jackson Square," and in truth he did not seem to have any grander ambitions. He read a lot, and he and Fanny swam in her indoor pool and read Shakespeare to each other, and she told him the more or less true version of how she had first met his father in Goodwill. Fanny made the mistake, on his second night with her, of offering him a cocktail before dinner. The night ended with Coyle drunk in her arms, sobbing incoherently that he would never be a man, that he could never face his father again. When Fanny got him into bed, she thought seriously of staying and showing him what a fine, desirable young man he was. She didn't do that, but the next weekend she did invite an SMU coed, one of the loveliest girls she knew, to come by and meet Coyle. The encounter was a disaster. Coyle wouldn't go within ten feet of the girl and finally disappeared into his room, where Fanny found him sobbing on his bed.

The next week Wade called. He wouldn't say how he'd learned of Coyle's whereabouts, but for Wade he was quite reasonable, simply asking if he could come see his son. Coyle grimly agreed to the meeting, which took place the next Sunday afternoon in Fanny's library.

Coyle rose nervously to his feet when his father entered the room. Wade hesitated, then extended his hand to his son. Coyle shook his father's hand uneasily.

Fanny thought, *Put your arms around your son, Wade. Embrace him. Love him.*

But Wade Kingslea did not, could not, do those things.

"We've missed you, son," he said.

Coyle nodded solemnly.

"We want you to come home."

Coyle nodded again.

"Coyle, what do you *want* to do?" Kingslea asked with genuine concern.

For an instant, Fanny was afraid Coyle would say he only wanted to shine shoes in Jackson Square, but Coyle only said mildly that he guessed he would go to work for Kingslea Oil. He and his father quickly agreed that he would live at home, take some business courses at TCU, and start work in Kingslea Oil's accounting office. As he left her house, Coyle embraced Fanny, with tears running down his face, and said, "You saved my life."

Back in Fort Worth, Coyle bought a car, played golf at River Crest for a few weeks, and finally started to work. No one asked much about his disappearance. Among the city's rich it was common enough for daughters to disappear for a few months for vaguely defined reasons or for sons to leave town to take the cure for alcoholism or to avoid the aftermath of some scandal or the wrath of an outraged father. Coyle's friends welcomed him back with open arms. Many of them had busted out of college for one reason or another and returned to their father's business, so the same old gang was soon going to parties and country-club dances and football games and weekends at the lake. Coyle drank too much, of course, but so did everyone else. He was rich and handsome and popular, and soon he was dating the most sought-after girls in Texas. It became a joke with his friends: all the girls made their play for Coyle and came away empty-handed. He flattered them, laughed at their jokes, bought them presents, and never showed the slightest interest in marriage. Then, six years after he left M&I, he chanced to meet Louise Everett.

CHAPTER FIVE

Coyle told Louise his story, all of it he could, as they sat on the blanket beside the pond on the golf course that fronted on his father's mansion, and when he finished she took him in her arms and gave him warmth and love until the stars faded and the first milk truck rattled down River Crest Drive. Then, as dawn broke quietly, they walked hand in hand back to Coyle's car. The world seemed soft, serene, improbably sane.

As they crossed the driveway, Livie Kingslea, wrapped in a fire-red robe, appeared on the mansion steps like an avenging angel.

"I'm . . . I'm taking Louise home," Coyle stammered. Louise gripped his hand tightly.

Livie let his words hang in the frosty morning air before she spoke.

"Yes, Coyle," she said disdainfully, "thanks to your father's money, you'll always be taking some girl home at dawn, won't you?"

Coyle turned away, opening the door of his Chrysler for Louise. Louise, huddling beside him in the car, felt as if she'd been lashed with a whip. His father's money? She hated his father's money. She thought his father's money was destroying him. She wished she had the strength to save Coyle from his father's money.

But Livie Kingslea would never believe that.

Nor, she realized with a shudder, would anyone else.

The next day was the most painful of Louise's life. Not because of what they had done; she was glad of that. But the new day brought the old confusions. She was a college freshman, dating two perfectly nice boys, and that was easy, fun, familiar. But Coyle, with his looks and money and friends and problems—Coyle was like an invasion from outer space, tear-

150

ing apart the simple fabric of her life.

He waited two days and then called, polite, nervous, and they met at Doc's for coffee. He was sad and funny and wonderful and Louise thought they were speaking two different languages.

"I won't say I'm sorry..."

"No, don't..."

"If I've done something wrong..."

"You haven't. It's just..."

"...could go to a movie...go straight back to your dorm..."

"I need time to think, Coyle..."

"I need *you*..."

"Please try to understand..."

"...never want to hurt you..."

"Good-bye...please understand..."

She went to a movie with him, then put him off, dated Clifton and Bobby Dean, tried to put him from her mind, failed—it was too confusing, she couldn't study—and finally she resolved that after the Christmas break she would tell Coyle she couldn't see him again. If that didn't work, if it was too painful, she thought she would have to change colleges, go somewhere besides Fort Worth, if that was what it took to get the sweet painful madness of Coyle Kingslea out of her life.

Then she missed her period.

She didn't even notice at first, because she was so busy with exams and dates, and then there could be no doubt at all—she'd been like clockwork since she was thirteen. Louise was thunderstruck. This could not happen, not to her, not because of one sweet sad night that in memory was more dream than flesh-and-blood reality. She had no one to talk to, so she worried, she read maddeningly vague books about pregnancy, and she counted the days, the hours, until her next period was due. When that week too passed, she borrowed a cheap gold ring, went to see a young doctor in the Medical Arts Building, and took the tests that confirmed the shattering truth: she was indeed pregnant.

All this time she had been refusing Coyle's calls. "He was drunk as a skunk," reported the girl who took his third call. Louise felt guilty, but she didn't know what to say to him. She didn't know what she was going to do, but she was determined that she would never bother him, never make demands, never let Livie Kingslea call her a fortune-hunter. Not in a million years.

One morning, as she was trying to summon the courage to call Coyle, she had an unexpected call from Caddy, and they met for coffee.

"I confess—Coyle sent me," Caddy told her. "He's beside himself because you won't take his calls."

Louise stirred her coffee slowly. She had decided she had to talk to someone. "Caddy, if I tell you something, will you swear not to tell a soul?"

"Why, sure, darlin'."

"I mean it. Word of honor!"

Caddy raised her right hand, her gold bracelets jangling. "My lips are sealed," she vowed.

"Caddy, I'm *pregnant,"* Louise blurted, and burst into tears.

Caddy's eyes widened. "Is Coyle . . ."

"Of *course* he is!"

Caddy reached across and took her hands. "Louise, how *wonderful!"*

"Wonderful! I wish I was *dead!"*

"Oh, don't be such a ninny. Now Coyle will marry you and you'll have a beautiful baby and live happily ever after."

"What if he doesn't *want* to marry me? What if I don't want to marry *him?"*

"Louise, if you don't want to marry Coyle, you're crazy. And if he doesn't want to marry you, *he's* crazy—and anyway, he does."

"How do you know?"

"I just *know.* Now he'll have an excuse to."

"What about his parents? I don't even . . ."

"What about them? They can like it or lump it. Louise, *call* him. *Tell* him. *Marry* him. It's going to be wonderful!"

Louise wasn't so sure it would be wonderful, but she called Coyle at his office and he came by her dorm that afternoon and they went for a walk over by the Worth Hills golf course. Louise couldn't get her news out right away, so she let Coyle talk on about the latest gossip, most of which concerned *Star-Telegram* publisher Amon Carter's campaign to persuade President Roosevelt to build a new coliseum-auditorium complex in Fort Worth and name it in honor of Will Rogers.

Finally Louise cried, "Coyle, I'm going to have a baby!"

Coyle's mouth fell open but no words emerged. He looked

so funny that Louise didn't know whether to laugh or cry. "Coyle, I'm not asking you to *do* anything," she told him. "I just thought you ought to know."

He took her hands and finally found his voice. "Angel, marry me," he said. "Please marry me."

She started to sob. "Coyle, you don't *have* to marry me."

"For God's sake, Louise, say you will," he pleaded. "You're all I ever wanted. I'll make you happy, I swear I will."

She stared into his sad, beautiful eyes and then smiled shyly. "All right," she said. "I'll marry you."

He embraced her, twirled her around, laughing and shouting, and then they ran back to get his car. "We'll go to Weatherford this afternoon," he said. "There's a JP there who'll marry us right away—he marries everybody. First we've got to find Pig—I need a best man!"

They found Pig and Caddy at the bar of the Eighth Avenue Club and Pig was not immediately enthusiastic.

"You sure 'bout this, Coyle? No offense, Lu-Lu"—Pig had a habit of calling Louise Lu-Lu, a name she detested—"but a fellow can't run off half-cocked getting married. No pun intended." Pig began to guffaw.

"Of course I'm sure," Coyle declared.

"Hell, let's have a drink and talk it over," Pig declared, and Louise's heart sank.

As it turned out, after two bottles of champagne, Pig was enthusiastic, and the four of them piled into his Cadillac and roared into the setting sun.

When they arrived in Weatherford, the old JP peered out at them dubiously, noting that the groom and his best man were well removed from sobriety, but when Pig solemnly handed him a twenty-dollar bill all doubts and legal formalities miraculously vanished. Within five minutes, Coyle and Louise were, in the eyes of God and the state of Texas, man and wife.

Coyle wanted to drive to Mineral Wells and honeymoon at the Crazy Hotel—"A proper place to start a marriage," he said—but the others convinced him it was too far, and they checked into a two-dollar-a-night motor court outside Weatherford. They finished the champagne and sang "For He's a Jolly Good Fellow" and "Auld Lang Syne" and "The Eyes of Texas" until Caddy cried and they went to their separate rooms.

Coyle yanked off his tie and plopped down on the hand-made bedspread with the huge purple peacock on it, and he muttered that he loved her, that she was his angel forever, and she slipped his shoes off and got in bed beside him and kissed him and held him close and listened to him snore until she fell asleep. She guessed that if you were going to elope to Weatherford and have Pig Powell as your best man, it was about as grand a wedding night as you could expect.

The next morning he groaned and hugged her and whispered, "But what if you're pregnant?" She giggled and they made love and then Pig was pounding on the door. They drove down to a truck stop and ate a huge breakfast of scrambled eggs and country ham and grits and coffee, and then it was time to face reality.

"My parents," he said. "We've got to tell them."

"Just barge right in and break the news," Caddy declared. "They ought to be delirious."

"Somehow I doubt it," Coyle said, and they climbed in the Cadillac for the drive back to Fort Worth.

Wade and Livie were having an argument when Coyle and Louise arrived. Livie wanted to spend the coming summer in Europe—she had developed an interest in royalty—and Wade wanted to spend it looking for oil in South America. Wade had not the slightest interest in the simpering, French-speaking, name-dropping Europeans—all Lord This and Princess That, and not a million dollars in a dozen of them—who so fascinated his wife. Livie, for her part, despised South America, whose inhabitants were all, as she saw it, Mexicans of one stripe or another. Their argument had moved past reason, was exhausting sarcasm, and was nearing the shouting stage when the young couple walked in.

"Dad, Livie, you remember Louise . . ."

"Coyle, if you don't mind, your father and I . . ."

"We have some very important . . ."

"Coyle, we are having a private . . ."

"For God's sake, Livie, let the boy speak."

"Louise and I were married last night."

"You *what?*" Livie cried.

Wade stepped forward with his hands outstretched. "My dear, we're delighted."

"Delighted?" Livie cried. "We don't even know this girl!"

"Livie, *shut up!*" Wade roared, and his wife marched out of the drawing room. "You'll have to excuse Mrs. Kingslea," he explained. "She's a bit upset about another matter. Now, tell me all about this. Coyle, tell them there'll be two more for lunch. By God, son, I always knew you'd bring home a prize!"

Lunch lasted five hours and consisted mostly of Wade Kingslea talking, joking, telling stories about the Goodwill days, and otherwise winning his new daughter-in-law's affections. Coyle, overawed as always by his father, sipped coffee and said very little. In midafternoon Livie joined them and was moderately pleasant to Louise. It was agreed that the young couple would stay in the Kingslea guest house while they looked for a suitable house to rent in Western Heights. Livie spoke of a dinner honoring the newlyweds, and Wade said that his publicity people would handle the newspapers.

In the early evening Louise gasped and said they had to go—she still hadn't told her parents of the marriage.

John and Mabel Everett took the news at first with stunned silence. Soon Mabel began to weep, and her husband turned red in the face and for a moment Louise was afraid he would attack Coyle. But Coyle quickly declared that he knew this was a shock, that he loved their daughter more than anything in the world, that her happiness was his only goal, and that he begged for their understanding and love. Coyle's eloquence, looks, and charm soon swept Louise's mother quite off her feet, but her father was a tougher nut to crack. The old carpenter and Populist was not at all impressed by his new son-in-law's pedigree—as far as John Everett was concerned, men like Wade Kingslea were what was wrong with America. He managed finally to shake Coyle's hand and, grim-faced, give his blessing, and he shuffled off grumbling, "They're not our kind of people."

The newlyweds rented a two-bedroom brick house on El Campo, just off Clover Lane, for forty dollars a month, which was about all they could afford. Coyle, Louise learned, was pretty much on his own financially—which was exactly how he wanted to be. He drew a three-hundred-dollar-a-month salary at Kingslea Oil, he owned the Chrysler, and he had the use of the family membership at River Crest, but he was by no means rich, despite his father's millions.

Louise was terrified at the prospect of confessing her pregnancy to Coyle's parents, but he insisted there was nothing to worry about. "I just wish I had a dollar for every girl in this town who ever eloped and had a baby seven months later," he told her. "It's a tradition, like the Fat Stock Show." It turned out that he was right. They broke the news one evening at the Kingslea house, as the four of them were about to leave for a dance at River Crest, and both Wade and Livie embraced Louise. Then Livie reached behind her head and began to take off the necklace she was wearing. Louise had noticed the necklace when they came in; it featured a ruby the size of a cherry, encircled by diamonds and pearls. Livie smiled her most enigmatic smile and moved toward Louise with the necklace outstretched before her like a talisman.

"This is for you, my dear," she said.

"No, you mustn't," Louise protested.

"For the dear girl who is giving Wade and me our first grandchild," Livie said, and her husband stepped forward to help affix the pendant around Louise's slender neck. By then, even Louise understood that when Livie gave away an expensive necklace, there was some element of calculation, of self-interest, involved. Still, it was pleasant that night as Fort Worth's most imposing matrons gathered round to stare at the jewels that glittered between her breasts. The next morning Coyle said he would put the necklace in their lockbox at the bank, because it was too valuable to keep in the house. After a moment, Louise asked, "How much do you think it's worth?"

Coyle shrugged. "Maybe ten thousand."

Louise put her head down on the dressing table. Was it morning sickness that made her feel so weak or something more complicated?

"Coyle, I don't want it! Why would she give me something so valuable?"

Coyle laughed. "Because once she knew you had a baby in your belly, she figured she'd better get her hooks in you."

"I don't want it!" Louise cried. "Can't we give it back?"

"No we can't," he told her. "That's the point."

But jewels and parties were the exception for Louise and Coyle in that spring of 1936. They spent most evenings at home, listening to the radio, reading, painting the house, or puttering in Louise's garden. Coyle had an old pair of pants that he had cut off above the knees—he would, in time, claim to have been the inventor of Bermuda shorts. Sometimes friends came by for spaghetti and beer. They went out to the Casino once, to see Benny Goodman, and when the weather turned warm they went to the lake on weekends. Coyle wasn't drinking much. Even when Pig or Buster came by, he would only sip a beer. "Honey, I do declare, you have turned Mr. Hyde back into Dr. Jekyll," Caddy quipped one night, as a sober Coyle carried a raving Pig out to his car.

Life was sweet for Louise and Coyle that spring.

Then came Casa Mañana.

CHAPTER SIX

Up on the makeshift stage a girl with a pretty, elfin face was tapdancing her heart out. Down front, Billy Rose was watching her with one eye while he signed papers and barked orders to Coyle Kingslea. It was June, the mercury was in the mid-nineties, and Rose had stripped off his coat and tie.

"That's enough," he yelled. "Honey, we can't use you."

The tap dancer stared at him in disbelief. "I'm a darn good dancer," she said stubbornly.

"What's your name, honey?"' Rose asked.

"Mary Martin," the girl replied.

Rose shrugged. "Mary, you're cute and you can dance, but you're not tall enough."

The girl marched off the stage, fuming, and Billy Rose, the diminutive New York showman whom Amon Carter had imported to stage Casa Mañana, the centerpiece of Fort Worth's Frontier Centennial extravaganza, turned his attention to other matters.

"Coyle, I got some telegrams I want to get off," Rose said. "Make sure the papers hear about 'em. This one here's to that Wallis Simpson broad. I'm offering her twenty-five thousand dollars a week for four weeks at Casa Mañana."

"What you asking the lady to do, Billy?" asked Boatner, the *Star-Telegram*'s tall, bemused reporter.

"Hell, whatever she wants to do. Read poetry or dance the hootchie-kootchie, I don't care. This one, Coyle, it's to Haile Selassie, that half-pint monarch over in Ethiopia. I'm offering him one hundred thousand dollars to appear, but he's got to bring his lions. And this one's to Hitler, that son of a bitch. I want to rent the *Hindenburg*. Got it?"

"Got it," Coyle said and introduced a young reporter from the New York *Herald* who'd just arrived in town.

"Whatta you want to know, boy?" Rose demanded.

"Well, for one thing, how're you going to put on a show with nudity in Texas? And sell booze too? There's laws against those things."

"That's Mr. Amon Carter's department," Rose said. "I run the show, he runs the town. Come on, I'll take you on a tour of the joint."

The showman, with the *Herald* reporter, the *Star-Telegram* reporter, and Coyle Kingslea scurrying in his wake, began a lightning tour of the exposition grounds. More than two thousand workers were busy on the half-finished buildings that in less than a month were supposed to house the greatest, gaudiest show the world had ever seen. The exposition was rising up on a 135-acre tract of land a mile or two west of the downtown bluffs, near the new Will Rogers Memorial Coliseum. Casa Mañana, the House of Tomorrow, complete with Sally Rand and her Nude Ranch, Paul Whiteman and his orchestra, and Florence and her Milk Bath, had come about because some so-called historians had outraged Amon Carter by saying West Texas had no history.

The state of Texas had been laying plans for its 1936 centennial celebration. Amon Carter, whose newspaper never tired of boosting its West Texas circulation region, urged the Centennial Commission to make sure the centennial gave all due attention to the history of West Texas. But a board of historians solemnly declared that West Texas "contains no history to commemorate."

No history in West Texas? What about the fourteen major Spanish explorations there? What about Isleta, the oldest community in the state? What about the great cattle empires and oil fields? What about the skeleton of a prehistoric bison that was found in the Panhandle? The *Star-Telegram* quickly began a yearlong series on the glorious history of West Texas.

Then the Centennial Commission sinned again, unforgivably. It picked Dallas, Fort Worth's great rival to the east, as the site of the Texas Centennial. Dallas? Dallas hadn't even *existed* when Texas won its independence in 1836! Dallas was an eastern city, a city of transplanted Yankees, of bankers and clerks, hardly a Texas city at all! Amon Carter hated Dallas so passionately that when he was occasionally forced to visit there on business, he carried his own lunch and refused to drink the water. He therefore took the choice of Dallas for the centennial site as a personal affront and declared that Fort Worth would put on its own, rival centennial show. "We'll show Dallas how the cow ate the cabbage," the dauntless publisher declared.

In the spring of 1936 the publisher recruited William Samuel Rosenberg, alias Billy Rose, the pint-sized Broadway showman who had produced *Jumbo* and married Fanny Brice, to produce the Fort Worth Frontier Centennial at a salary of one thousand dollars a day. Having done that, the pistol-packing publisher quickly asked his friend Wade Kingslea to host a party at which Rose could meet local oilmen who might be persuaded to underwrite the centennial extravaganza. It was at that party at Hillcrest that Billy Rose, besides collecting pledges of more than two hundred thousand dollars, made a snap decision to hire Coyle to help him with publicity for the show. Thus it happened, in the first months of their marriage, that Coyle and Louise became caught up in the most improbable whirlwind to hit Fort Worth since the days of the cattle drives and Hell's Half Acre.

"That over there's Pioneer Palace," Billy Rose was explaining, as he led Coyle and the reporters across the muddy fair grounds. "An old-time saloon to seat four thousand, with girls dancing on the bar and beer a dime a glass. And over there, that big building going up, that's Casa Mañana. That means House of Tomorrow. Casa's gonna have a revolving stage 130 feet across—bigger than the one in Radio City—and the stage'll be in the middle of a lagoon, and I figure we'll have some gondolas floating around, and . . ."

"Gondolas?" a reporter said. "What the hell do gondolas have to do with Texas?"

"You'll see, you'll see," Rose said impatiently. "Coyle, you got a cigarette?"

Coyle handed the showman a Camel, and he paused briefly for a light.

"Over there, that's Sally Rand's Nude Ranch. She'll dance in Casa Mañana, with those damn fans and balloons and all, but she'll have her own show too. The lady drives a hard bargain."

"What's a Nude Ranch?" the New York *Herald* reporter asked.

Rose shook with laughter. "Son, I'll tell you what it is, it's tits displayed in a tasteful manner."

After a fast lunch of hot dogs and Dr. Peppers, Billy auditioned some Indians for the Wild West show.

"What are you guys, anyway?" he demanded.

"Comanches," declared their leader, a sullen-looking fellow wrapped in a moth-eaten blanket.

"If he's a Comanche, I'm Marie of Rumania," Billy muttered to Coyle. "Okay, let's see your act! Do me a rain dance."

As the Indians began to shuffle about, Amon Carter raced up, waving his Stetson wildly. "Wait'll you hear my news, fellows!" he shouted. Coyle had never seen the publisher so excited. He thought perhaps Dallas had been hit by an earthquake.

"I just talked to J. Frank Norris," the publisher explained. "He's the most powerful Baptist preacher in town, Billy. We'd be in trouble if he was against us, and I knew he wouldn't cotton to those bare-breasted girls of yours."

"You wanted 'em, Mr. Carter," Billy Rose protested.

"I don't deny that. Bare breasts are good for business. Anyway, I called him up and said, 'Frank, you going out of town this summer?'

"And he said, 'I might, Amon. Why do you ask?'

"And I said, 'Frank, we've got this centennial show, and some naked girls, and we're going to sell liquor . . . ,' and I sort of left it hanging, because Frank Norris is not a stupid man. And he thought a minute and he said, 'Amon, I've been intending to hold some revivals, and I reckon I could start 'em a little early.'

"And I said, 'Frank, if you do that, I reckon I could send our religion editor along to see that your revivals got proper coverage.' Hell, he'll be out preaching till Christmas! And if Frank Norris keeps quiet, the mayor and the police won't say a word. Boys, we are home free!"

The three men began shaking hands and pounding each other on the back. "Let's go have a drink, fellows," Amon Carter declared, and as an afterthought he pulled out his sixgun and began firing it into the air. "HOO-RAY FOR FORT WORTH AND WEST TEXAS," he bellowed. "AND HOO-RAY FOR THE FRONTIER CENTENNIAL!"

The days and nights of summer hurried by. Coyle would sleep late, have coffee and juice with Louise, then call the police station to see if any visiting reporters needed bailing out. He'd swing by his office at Kingslea Oil for an hour or two, then drive to the centennial grounds to catch up with Billy Rose. There were always planes to be met, reporters to be shown around, politicians to be flattered, showgirls to be jollied, crises to be juggled.

In the evenings there were endless parties. Wining and dining the visiting newspapermen was part of Coyle's job, and it was exciting for him, too, to meet men his own age who knew the world beyond Texas. Louise went out with them some nights. They might drive out to Lake Como, the Negro neighborhood, to a little tumbledown club called The Humming Bird, where a man named Fats Waller played piano, or perhaps drop by Dante's Inferno, a place on Camp Bowie Boulevard that featured female impersonators and was popular with some of the male dancers who were coming to perform in Casa Mañana.

One Saturday afternoon Coyle took Louise and some reporters to a place called Crystal Springs, out on the White Settlement Road, to hear Bob Wills and his Texas Playboys. The twelve-piece band made music such as Louise had never heard, a mixture of country music and jazz—Western swing, some called it—and strangest of all was Bob Wills himself, who from time to time would punctuate the music with a wild cry that sounded something like "Ah *haaa!*"

"It's just the way· he feels," Coyle said. "The man's a genius."

During an intermission, Bob Wills came over to their table. He was a handsome, dark-haired man with whiskey on his breath. He told Louise, "Miss, you've got eyes the color of bluebonnets," and then he and Coyle went outside for a drink.

Louise enjoyed the parties and nightclubs, but as her belly grew bigger she stopped going out at night, lest the late hours or an accident harm her baby. By midsummer she could sit in the backyard on El Campo and hear Ev Marshall singing "The Night is Young and You're So Beautiful," as the cast rehearsed for Casa Mañana. Sometimes she would hear that song and think of her beautiful baby, alive inside her, and tears would burn her eyes because she knew she would never be happier.

There was only one problem in her life, and that was Coyle's drinking. It was a rare night that summer that he wasn't out until two or three showing some newspapermen the town, and sometimes he would come home too drunk to walk. And yet he was happy. Every morning, even as he groaned about his hangover, he was excited and anxious to get on with the day's work. Louise realized that for the first time in his life Coyle was doing something on his own. Billy Rose might have hired him because he was Wade Kingslea's son, but Coyle was doing a fine job, and all the reporters and musicians liked him just because he was a bright young fellow who enjoyed a good time and knew his way around the town. So Louise guessed it was all right, if Coyle was busy and happy. Still, she wished he could manage to be happy without drinking, the way he had in the first months of their marriage. Casa Mañana was fine, but all she really wanted was her husband and her baby, all to herself.

On the morning of Casa Mañana's opening, Coyle left early. Louise urged him to call her later, because the baby was due any moment. Then Coyle drove out to Meacham Field with Billy Rose to greet a chartered plane that was bringing down a hundred New York columnists and critics. That afternoon a thousand newspapermen and twenty-five thousand ordinary citizens gathered on Sunset Trail for the exposition's opening ceremony. Amon Carter rode in on a Wells Fargo stagecoach, shooting his six-gun into the air for the benefit of the March of Time cameras. Two thousand miles away, on his yacht, off Nova Scotia, President Roosevelt pressed a button that, thanks to miracles of modern science, snipped the ribbon that opened the Frontier Centennial.

A few blocks away, at her home on El Campo Street, Louise Kingslea began to have her first labor pains.

In the early evening they bused the writers out to Amon's estate, Shady Oak, for a champagne and chili dinner. More champagne was consumed than chili. Coyle got a message to call his wife, but in the confusion he never did.

In late afternoon Louise decided it was time to go to the hospital. She called a cab but the man told her all the cabs in town were tied up by the visiting newspapermen. She called Caddy but nobody answered. Her labor pains were getting closer together and she was starting to worry. She decided that if she walked out onto the street, surely someone would come along who could take her to the hospital. She went out onto El Campo but no cars came by. She walked up to Clover Lane and had to sit on the curb when the labor pains started again. She thought she should go home and call the police, call anybody, and then an old black man in a battered Ford truck stopped and asked what the trouble was.

Back at the centennial grounds, Coyle was giving some reporters a sneak preview of Sally Rand's Nude Ranch. "Gentlemen, this is an educational exhibit," he declared. "It will educate the public on the ways of the Old West."

He led the way into a large hall which contained eighteen young women, who were separated from the spectators by a wall of chicken wire. The women were wearing cowboy boots and hats, short skirts, and no shirts. As the astounded reporters gaped, the bare-breasted young women swung on swings, tossed beach balls, shot arrows at targets, and sat astride horses.

"This is education?" a scribe demanded.

"Sally oughta be ashamed of herself!"

"You ain't seen nothing yet," Coyle declared. "Follow me, gentlemen, and we'll visit Miss Florence in her Milk Bath!"

"Bye-bye, girls," the reporters called, but the bare-breasted cowgirls only tossed their beach balls and gazed serenely at the horizon.

Louise and the old Negro were rattling down Clover Lane in his Ford truck when a battered Pontiac filled with white men whizzed past in the other direction. Suddenly the Pontiac squealed to a stop, turned around, and started after them. Louise, preoccupied with her labor pains and with giving the Negro directions to the hospital, did not notice the Pontiac until it pulled alongside them. Then she saw a man in overalls hanging out the window waving a gun.

"What you doin' with that white girl, nigger?" the man shouted.

"Lord, Lord," the Negro said and gunned the truck down a side street.

"Oh, please, get me to the hospital," Louise said, but the Pontiac was roaring after them.

When they left the Nude Ranch, Coyle and the reporters passed the Last Frontier, an outdoor arena where the next day hundreds of latter-day cowboys and Indians would enact an elaborate Wild West show. A poster outside the arena gave the highlights:

THE OLD WEST LIVES AGAIN
See Attack of the Hostile Indians!
Womanhood in Jeopardy!
Thank God for the Rangers!
The Mail Goes Through!

A dress rehearsal of the pageant was in progress and the reporters insisted that they stop to see it. A pioneer family was surrounded by howling Indians. Two girls clutched their hands and looked to the heavens—Womanhood in Jeopardy! A fiendish Indian seized one of the girls by the arms.

"Put it to her, Sitting Bull!" a reporter howled.

"Hey, suppose she's a virgin?" another asked.

"In *this* town?"

"Come on, Injuns, ravish 'em! Wa-hoo!"

Just then, the Texas Rangers galloped in to save the settlers. The reporters booed, and Coyle herded them toward the Casa Mañana pavilion, where the main show was about to begin.

The men in the Pontiac kept yelling and shooting their gun in the air. They tried to curb the Ford but the old Negro, his eyes wide with fear, drove through front yards and then down an alley to escape.

"Please, just let me out," Louise begged, but the Negro was too frightened to stop. The jolting of the truck down the alley was so intense that Louise feared she'd have her baby right there and then. At the end of the alley a garbage truck blocked their path. The Pontiac was roaring up behind them.

"Ah'm sorry, miss," the Negro said. "But Ah think those men aim to kill me."

He jumped out of the truck and scurried away as the Pontiac slid to a halt behind them. Two of the men in overalls raced up to Louise.

"You okay, ma'm?" one asked.

"That nigger kidnap you?"

"Don't let him get away, Homer!"

"Please," Louise said. "I'm going to have a baby. I've got to get to the hospital!"

"Let him go, Homer," the man yelled. "We got to get this lady to the hospital!"

They helped Louise into their Pontiac. "You'll have to give us directions, ma'm," one of them said. "We ain't never been in Fort Worth before. We just come in from Lufkin for this here centennial exhibition."

Up on the revolving stage, Ev Marshall was singing "The Night Is Young and You're So Beautiful" to Faye Cotton, who had been a waitress in Borger before Amon Carter proclaimed her the Sweetheart of Texas. A dancer named Ann Pennington cootchied so passionately in her Little Egypt number that her string of beads snapped; beads bounced into the front row of tables, where Coyle and his party of reporters scrambled for them on their hands and knees. Sally Rand did her famous balloon dance, and one of her five-foot balloons sailed away in the breeze. Coyle kept thinking that he should call Louise, but by then the grand finale had started and to leave was unthinkable. The huge stage was slowly revolving. Five thousand neon lights on a forty-foot replica of the Eiffel Tower were flashing on and off. The entire cast was onstage, including Sally Rand, Paul Whiteman, Little Egypt, the Sweetheart of Texas, and dozens of very tall showgirls in very scanty cowgirl costumes. Eighty-five plastic fountains were spurting pink and blue water into the air and six cowgirls waved the six flags that had flown over Texas and Ev Marshall was singing "Lone Star" as impassive gondoliers paddled their improbable gondolas across the shimmering lagoon. Fireworks went off, Billy Rose wept, Coyle Kingslea passed out, Amon Carter shot his pearl-handled six-guns into the air, and a few miles away, in All Saints Hospital, Louise Everett Kingslea gave birth to a son. When her husband and Billy Rose came staggering into the hospital at dawn to see the baby she did not wake, but later in the day she and Coyle named the boy Philip Everett Kingslea.

CHAPTER SEVEN

Coyle's brother, Hoyt, had announced his engagement that spring to Charlotte (Cissy) Kent, the girl he'd been dating since high school. Coyle and Louise used his work with Casa Mañana and her pregnancy to skip all but the most urgent of the dinners and receptions that preceded the wedding. Coyle had no use at all for his brother and sister-in-law-to-be; he called them Mr. Muscles and Miss Morality. Louise liked Hoyt and Cissy, but she was never really comfortable around them and their friends, for they were terribly earnest young people, the city's establishment-to-be. For all her objections to the way Coyle's friends drank, Louise thought that at least they could be fun, but Hoyt's solemn pronouncements on The Future of Oil and The Sins of Roosevelt gave her a headache.

Still, if Hoyt was dull, Cissy was impressive. Cissy's father was a judge, not wealthy but from one of Fort Worth's founding families. Her mother was an ambitious, clever woman who traded on her husband's status and saw to it from the first that her daughter attended the right camps and dancing classes, invited the right children to her birthday parties, joined the right high school sorority, and in general prepared herself for the right marriage. Fortunately, Cissy had the ambition and talent to live up to her mother's master plan. She was a bright, pretty, outgoing, shrewd girl who was both a cheerleader and class valedictorian at Central High, was a Theta at the University of Texas, made her debut at Fort Worth's Assembly Ball, and was the best tennis player and swimmer of her sex in the city. Once Coyle and Louise were sitting beside the country-club pool when Cissy, slim and graceful, executed a perfect swan dive off the high board.

"She hardly made a splash," Louise sighed.

Coyle rolled his eyes. "And when she tinkles," he said, "little silver bells ring."

To Louise, who tended to blush and stammer around the Kingslea family's rich and famous friends, it seemed that Cissy was everything she was not: poised, articulate, the perfect daughter-in-law. And because she was so awed by her new sister-in-law, she was stunned one day when Caddy said offhandedly, "Well darling, you know it's because of you that Hoyt and Cissy tied the knot."

"Me? What did I have to do with it?"

"You got yourself pregnant, and you got Hoyt and Cissy scared they'd lose the Grandkiddie Sweepstakes."

"Caddy, that's ridiculous."

"Says who? What if Wade and Livie went goo-goo eyes over your baby and rewrote their wills or something? You think Hoyt's gonna let that happen? You just watch little Cissy. She's going from Deb of the Year to Mom of the Year in record time."

"Caddy, you are so cynical!"

"Just experienced, honey."

In fact, it was only two months after the wedding that the newlyweds informed Wade and Livie that they would soon be grandparents a second time. When their child was born, he was christened Wade Kingslea II but was universally known as Skipper or, inevitably, just plain Skip.

There was another society wedding that summer: Pig and Caddy's.

Caddy had pinned down Pig by the most ancient of tactics: she dropped him and began dating other men, including a notorious Houston playboy, old enough to be her father, a rodeo cowboy, and the star quarterback for the University of Texas Longhorns. Pig, soon discovering that other women did not laugh at his jokes or tolerate his binges as good-naturedly as Caddy, saw the error of his ways.

"No, I am not pregnant," Caddy declared when she came to tell Louise of the engagement. "Nor do I intend to be. My God, what if we had children who looked like Pig? Oh, Louise, once I started playing the field I almost lost my resolve—to land the Pigger, I mean. There are some talented men out there, my love. Men who can provide a lady with varied and unexpected delights. Oh, but my heart belonged to Daddy. Pig's so damn *rich,* honey, you just can't get around that. And it's not *just* the bucks. He's sort of sweet in his way. Docile. Pig's kind of a bad habit, like cigarettes or scratching yourself."

Caddy fluttered her pretty eyelashes. "What can I say, darling? It's love."

A moment later, Caddy lowered her voice and asked Louise what she'd heard about the recent events involving Eve Kingslea, Coyle's stepsister. As it happened, Louise had heard nothing. There were bits and pieces of gossip floating about town that hot, busy summer, but precious few people knew the full story, or ever would.

Eve had just graduated from high school, and her preoccupation that summer, besides boys and her suntan, was where she would go to college. Her mother wanted her to go "east" to Sweet Briar, in Virginia, but Eve hadn't the slightest intention of attending a school that excluded boys. The University of Texas was more to Eve's liking. There were plenty of boys there. The trouble was, there was also rules, and curfews, and Eve was not fond of rules. The truth was that Eve didn't want to go to college at all. Why live in some crowded dorm or sorority house when you could live at Hillcrest? Why spend your nights studying when you could be partying and making love? Eve was growing up with the knowledge that she would someday inherit between one and two hundred million dollars, and it seemed to her, logically enough, that she should live her life exactly as she pleased. As it happened, what pleased Eve most was sex, in all its manifestations; that was where the trouble began.

One evening in midsummer Eve attended a party at Shady Oak, Amon Carter's estate, in honor of Casa Mañana performers. Of all the entertainers she met there, the one who interested her most was a rangy, big-breasted blonde named Nellie Potts, who managed Sally Rand's Nude Ranch. It was, as Nellie told it, a demanding job. She had to make sure that eighteen girls were on display every day at the Nude Ranch, and illness, drink, drugs, romance, and other disabilities were forever causing her girls to disappear.

"The truth is, honey, it's no picnic standing there eight hours a day having guys stare at your tits," Nellie declared. "It gets to you after a while."

"I think it'd be neat," Eve said. "To have all those men staring at you and know they couldn't touch you."

"Honey, it's a big, fat bore, believe me," Nellie Potts said.

"I think it'd be neat," Eve repeated and flashed her wide, crooked smile.

Eve had an active imagination, especially where sex was

concerned, and the Nude Ranch fascinated her. A few years earlier, Eve's high school sorority had sponsored a carnival to raise money for charity and among its attractions had been a Kissing Booth. Some of the girls had been embarrassed or reluctant to kiss boys they didn't know for money—even if the money went to feed the needy—but Eve thought it was great. In the aftermath of the Kissing Booth, Eve began to fantasize about a Fucking Booth, at which she and her sorority sisters would sacrifice even more of themselves for the widows and orphans. She would explain her plan to her friends at slumber parties and they would giggle uneasily and tell her she was crazy. Eve didn't think she was crazy, but she did have a dim sense that she was testing the limits of the acceptable. She was already regarded as "wild," but very rich girls could get away with being wild, up to a point. But what were the limits? Were there any limits? Eve didn't know; she was feeling her way.

The Nude Ranch captured Eve's imagination, and a few days later she invited Nellie Potts to Hillcrest for a swim. It was not until Nellie had downed her third gin and tonic that Eve made her proposal.

Nellie threw back her head and laughed. "Honey, you are a real stitch."

"I'm serious, Nellie," Eve said.

"You want to bring down the law on us?"

"That won't happen," Eve said. "Amon Carter and my father run the town. There wouldn't be a Nude Ranch to begin with if they didn't."

Nellie fished the wedge of lime from her glass and licked it thoughtfully. "Honey, what do you want to do such a crazy thing for?"

"Just for fun," Eve said truthfully. "There's nothing to it. Just let me and a couple of my friends slip in and replace three of your girls at the Nude Ranch one afternoon. We think it'd be a kick."

Nellie shook her head. "You crazy kid," she said.

The caper did not go precisely as planned.

Nellie slipped Eve and her two friends into the Nude Ranch dressing room at noon Friday, introduced them as some local girls who would be filling in, and found costumes that fit them. Soon each of them was wearing boots, a short skirt, a bandanna, a cowboy hat—a perfectly fine cowgirl outfit except that they were bare-breasted.

Eve stared at her friends, then at herself in the mirror. "I love it," she whispered. "It's *delicious*."

"Just don't do anything crazy out there," Nellie urged. "Just pretend you're a statue, that's the best way. Eve, you're gonna shoot the bow and arrow, right? And you girls, you toss a beach ball back and forth. But take it slow. You can get awful tired tossin' a beach ball, believe me."

Eve, her two friends, and fifteen other young women took their places in the Nude Ranch. Some girls mounted docile horses or sat on swings. Moments later, the first men started filing past, on the other side of the chicken wire that protected the Nude Ranch from the paying customers. Eve stared back at the gawking men, jiggled her breasts a bit, and shot an arrow at the target. She loved it. Some of the men practically had their tongues hanging out.

Then the problems began.

"Hey, Evie, take it all off!" a boy yelled from behind the wire.

The trouble was that Eve and her friends had gossiped about their scheme, word had spread, and most of the Nude Ranch's customers this afternoon were boys in their crowd. Eve quickly recognized the boys and did a little bump and grind to please them. But as the boys yelled and beat against the wire, instead of filing on through, guards told them to move on. They told the guards to go to hell. Soon police were arriving. Nellie jerked Eve and her friends back to the dressing room and told them to get the hell out, but the damage was done. A *Star-Telegram* reporter was on the scene and word was spreading that something very peculiar had happened at the Nude Ranch.

The reporter went back and told his editor what had happened.

"Those little bitches," the editor sighed.

"I was thinking we might run something."

"Are you crazy?"

"Not with names. Just play it for laughs. Local girls make a debut in show business."

"Listen, son," the editor said, "our publisher, in his wisdom, has chosen to stage that goddam circus, and there's no way in hell we're gonna cover scandal in the Frontier Centennial. Eve Kingslea can fuck Tom Mix's horse in the Wild West show and it ain't news to us. Do me a weather story."

Wade Kingslea heard of Eve's escapade the next morning.
The bearer of the news was Harley Prendergast, Kingslea
Oil's burly director of security. Harley had become Kingslea's
close friend over the years; he prided himself on knowing
Kingslea's moods and needs as well as anyone alive, and one
thing he knew was that Kingslea was sick of his stepdaughter's sexual misbehavior.

Harley had started with Wade back in the boomtown days,
little more than a bodyguard at first, but inevitably his power
had grown. In the "hot oil" wars of the early 1930s, when the
government had tried to limit production in the huge East
Texas oil field, Wade and Harley had gone out night after
night, armed to the teeth, defying National Guard roadblocks
to haul their oil to safe storage in Dallas. Once that war was
won, and Kingslea Oil grew to a mighty empire, there was an
urgent need for inside information on what the rival oil companies were up to, and Harley began to recruit the ex-Texas
Rangers and ex-FBI men who carried out Kingslea Oil's un-
surpassed program of security and intelligence.

Harley spent many of his evenings at places like Ringside
Club and the Top of the Hill, making sure he knew what
gamblers, gangsters, and swindlers were in town, what
women were running around on their husbands, what wildcatters were broke, what college boys were drinking too much,
what cops were on the take. Harley Prendergast, who neither
smoked nor drank, prowled the Texas demimonde like a
hawk, looking for the signs of greed or need or weakness that
could, in the mysterious wheels-within-wheels of the world,
be useful to the boss, Wade Kingslea.

Finally, of course, there were women. Wade slept with
many women, but increasingly he wanted the professionals
who would give him what he wanted without debate. As he
grew older, he wanted his women younger, too, so much so
that Harley lived in constant fear of scandal, for how could
you trust a girl of fourteen or fifteen not to gossip after she'd
slept with a man as famous as Wade Kingslea? Harley handled
all his boss's needs and with such good sense and discretion
that Wade had begun rewarding him with an interest in valuable oil leases. Harley stood to become a rich man, so long as
he kept in Wade Kingslea's favor, and that was one reason he

moved very carefully that morning on the matter of Wade's stepdaughter, Eve.

"I reckon you heard about that business at the centennial grounds yesterday," he said.

"What's that?" Kingslea said suspiciously.

"Oh, nothing much. Your girl, Eve, and one of her pranks."

"Eve? What'd she do?"

"It's all settled now. I talked to the paper. They won't touch it."

"Dammit, what'd the girl *do?*"

Harley fiddled with his coffee spoon. "Just some crazy mischief, Wade," he said. "They talked their way into the Nude Ranch. Joined the show, so to speak."

"The hell you say!" Kingslea thundered.

"Here's proof," Harley said and slid a photograph across the desk. A tourist had taken it, and one of his men had paid one hundred dollars for a copy. It showed Eve, bare-breasted and beaming, posed with her bow and arrow. Wade Kingslea studied the picture, then slammed his fist against the top of his desk.

"Damn her," he raged. *"Damn* her. I gave her my name, Harley. She was Eve Mortimer and I married her mother and adopted her, like my own flesh and blood. I gave her my name and all I get in return is shame and scandal."

"It's hard," Harley said.

"The girl's out of control. Her mother's spoiled her rotten. She thinks she can get away with anything. She's got the morals of an alley cat. I'm scared to death she's gonna cut loose with some escapade that'll make the papers and hurt Kingslea Oil. She could make me a laughingstock."

Kingslea, red-faced, stared out the window at the city, the river, the open prairie to the west. Harley, watching, decided to make his move, a move he hoped would bind him even closer to Kingslea.

"Wade," he said softly, "there's something else Eve's been up to. It's got me worried sick."

"What?"

"I don't like to tell you this," Harley began, and then he told him about Horace Crosby.

It was a simple story. Horace Crosby was a jazz pianist who'd been playing in a Fort Worth nightclub for several months. Eve had met him at the club and begun seeing him.

Several recent nights, after he finished work, they'd spent the
night at the Kingsleas' house on Eagle Mountain Lake. It was
a routine affair, except for one detail.

Horace Crosby was black.

Wade Kingslea, upon hearing that, was beyond anger. His
feelings about Negroes were no secret. He considered them an
inferior race, ignorant at best and depraved at worst.

"She's got to be taught a lesson," he said finally. "For her
own good. A lesson she won't forget."

The next Sunday night, Wade and Olivia Kingslea had a
late dinner at River Crest Country Club. Harley Prendergast
took his wife to dinner at the Cattleman's Cafe, a celebrated
steak house on the North Side, near the stockyards. It was
clear, therefore, that neither man could have been involved
when, just after midnight, five men kicked in the door of the
Kingslea lake house and quickly subdued the black man and
the young white woman who were in bed together.

The Negro, Horace Crosby, was more simply dealt with.
Three men took him outside, battered his face with a lead
pipe, stomped his hands until his future as a pianist was in
doubt, and kicked his testicles until his future as a sexually
active male was also in doubt. Then he was put in the trunk of
a car, driven a dozen miles away, and dumped at the roadside,
to live or die, as he saw fit.

The treatment of Eve Kingslea was more complicated. It
was necessary that she be not just punished but educated. The
man to whom Harley had entrusted this delicate assignment
was a wiry, effeminate ex-convict named Fentress who dyed
his hair orange and had eyes like bullet holes. His two assis-
tants quickly blindfolded Eve and strung her from a rafter
naked, so that her toes barely grazed the floor.

They let her hang there for a while. It was amusing to
watch the stages people went through. At first Eve was defiant, cursing at them, demanding to be released, declaring
that her father would revenge this outrage. But soon enough
she was begging to be let down. After she had cried awhile,
Fentress began to talk to her quite gently, explaining that they
had come to instruct her in the proper behavior of a young
lady.

"Fuck you, you bastard, let me down!" Eve shouted, and
Fentress smiled and reached for an instrument that Eve, had
she not been blindfolded, would immediately have recognized: a twenty-four-inch Gaines Best Heavy Duty Model

Cattle Prod. The steel-shafted prod was powered by eight size C batteries and produced an electrical shock that was sufficient to move a thousand-pound cow in the desired direction or, for that matter, to kill a rat. It would not kill a hundred-pound girl but it would almost certainly move her in the desired direction.

Fentress flipped on the prod, listened to it hum, and then gently asked Eve if in the future she would behave as a proper lady should. When she answered with a curse, he touched the two-pronged tip of the prod between her legs.

One such explosion in the genitals was enough to break the spirit of almost anyone, and indeed when Eve regained consciousness she trembled and wept and swore that she would do anything her captors demanded. But Fentress was not finished. He resumed his questioning, and nothing Eve could say would quite please him. Twice more the cattle prod ravaged her most tender flesh, and when, finally, near dawn, Fentress and his associates left her, curled into a ball on the floor of her father's lodge, she was quite a different person. She could not rise to her feet for several hours, nor could she stop crying, but in time she grasped the realities of the situation: Wade Kingslea had done this to her, and there was nothing she could do about it.

The next day, after a long talk with her mother, Eve agreed to enter Sweet Briar in the fall.

The matter did not rest there.

Livie was outraged. It was not that she condoned Eve's sexual adventures but that Wade's punishment was cruel and excessive. Moreover, Livie thought Wade was trying to use Eve as a pawn in the struggle between husband and wife. Livie had tolerated Wade's own sexual adventures for a long time. They kept him happy and legally vulnerable if she ever wanted to divorce him. Still, she had recently learned of one affair that infuriated her, an affair with a woman whom Livie grudgingly recognized as a threat to her own power over him. That threat, coupled with Wade's vicious treatment of Eve, drove Livie into a fury. Her husband was a brute and a bully and a hypocrite, she reasoned, and it was high time she taught him a lesson.

Wade Kingslea was going to be a father again, and he was delighted. It had for years been a source of anguish that he and

Livie had never had children. He suspected that Livie had years before had an operation to protect her from experiencing the indignities of motherhood a second time. She would not admit that, of course, and when pressed would suggest that his manhood was somehow at fault.

One reason Wade wanted another child was that he was a perfectionist and not satisfied with his two sons by his first wife, Harriet. Coyle, of course, was a coward and a weakling. Hoyt was brave and manly but a bit phlegmatic for his father's tastes. Moreover, as a philosophical matter, Wade felt an obligation to produce as many children as possible. The ignorant masses were breeding like flies, threatening to turn the American republic into a mobocracy, and a man like himself, blessed with superior genes, had a sacred obligation to reproduce.

So he was thrilled to learn that a woman he considered quite superior was going to bear his child. The mother-to-be was none other than his lover from Goodwill days, Fanny O'Brien Todd.

For a long time, Fanny had hated Wade for the way he had rejected her in Goodwill, but as the years passed she found her old affection for him overcoming the hurt. She saw him at parties from time to time, and she thought he was growing more attractive with each year. She thought that at his best there was something godlike about Wade, in his physical presence, in his supreme self-confidence, in the way he dominated everyone around him. She thought Wade had made only one mistake, marrying Livie, and she thought he had finally come to realize that but could see no way out. There was a recurring rumor that Wade had offered Livie a hundred million dollars for a divorce and that she had smiled and said, "But darling, I'd rather sleep with you than have another hundred million."

Fanny and Wade's affair had begun after Coyle had sought refuge with Fanny following his flight from M&I. One evening, a few weeks after Coyle returned home, Wade dropped by Fanny's Turtle Creek home unexpectedly. He paced about, restless, unsettled; she gave him a drink, then another, and he began to talk about Coyle. The gist of what he said was simply that he could not understand the boy's problems, that he had given the boy everything. And Fanny, listening, holding his hand, her heart aching for him, could not speak the unspeakable truth: "You gave him everything but love, Wade; his problem is *you*."

Unable to give him the truth, she gave him herself. They became lovers again that night and it seemed to Fanny that Wade, in his frustration and sorrow for his son, for one night recaptured the fear and vulnerability of the hungry young wildcatter, so desperate for success, that she had loved in Goodwill so many years before. After that night, Wade dropped by her home from time to time, sometimes for a brief visit, sometimes to stay the night.

Kingslea hated contraception, both as a mechanical distraction and as a philosophical concept; it was a woman's responsibility, clearly, and he favored those women who bothered him with it least. One night that summer, as his passions were rising in Fanny's big brass bed, she whispered that they'd have to stop for a moment, and he declared that, by God, he'd just as soon go ahead and have a baby.

"Do you mean that, Wade?"

"You'd have to raise him," he said. "But I'd treat him like my own."

"Wade, are you sure . . . ?"

"Dammit, woman, do you want to argue all night?" he groaned, and they eagerly flung themselves into the business of procreation.

It was a quick decision, but both parties had given it thought. Wade wanted a child, felt that the problem was finding a suitable mother, and had come to think that Fanny was almost certainly the most sensible, reasonable woman he'd ever met. She had, of course, been a whore when he first met her, but upon reflection he had concluded that that was in her favor. Fanny was a fighter, just as he was; she had fought her way up from Goodwill, just as he had, with the tools at her disposal. What, after all, was a whore? There wasn't a bigger whore in Texas than his stepdaughter, Eve, and that winter she would be making her debut in Fort Worth, Dallas, New York, and London.

Fanny, for her part, was in her late thirties and increasingly wanted a child before it was too late. She had thought often of bearing Wade's child; she had considered doing it without even telling him. She could not quite keep herself from speculating that if she bore his child, and if someday he and Livie separated, she and Wade might yet somehow spend their autumnal years together.

Fanny learned that she was pregnant on a Friday morning, and she was overjoyed.

Livie Kingslea learned the news the following Monday, and she was not overjoyed.

Livie had on retainer a former captain of the Texas Rangers named Clarence Doak, who kept her posted on the romantic affairs of her husband and, to a lesser extent, on the activities of her daughter, her two stepsons, and certain of her friends and acquaintances. Wade Kingslea was not an easy man to keep tabs on, for he roamed the world at will, with no fixed schedule, but at length Doak discovered that the oilman was seeing Fanny at her Dallas estate. Livie, learning that, instructed her detective to redouble his surveillance.

The detective knew that Fanny was a creature of habit, and he was therefore alerted when she made an unexpected visit to her doctor. And when she made a second visit a few days later, he was sufficiently curious that he broke into the doctor's office and learned from Fanny's medical records that she was indeed pregnant. When he reported that fact to his employer, Livie Kingslea was beside herself with rage. But she soon composed herself and gave him instructions on how to proceed.

That Wednesday afternoon, as Fanny drove home from her golf game, she was once again pondering the vexing decision she faced: how to *explain* her child. Obviously she could go away, have the child, and then claim to have adopted it—that was the traditional ruse. But it was so cowardly, so hypocritical. Fanny was *proud* of this child, unspeakably so, and a bolder plan tempted her: she would simply *have* the child, and the gossip be damned. She was a rich, popular woman, and why should she worry about what a few unimportant people might say? Indeed, if Wade would give his permission, she wanted to tell her friends that this was, in fact, his child. If she did that, of course, word would reach Livie, but Fanny had decided she didn't care. What, after all, could she do about it?

Fanny was smiling as she pulled her Mercedes-Benz into the four-car garage behind her vast stone mansion. When her butler failed to appear, she shrugged, opened the trunk, and was lifting out her golf clubs when a man seized her from behind. His hand, holding a cloth that was soaked in chloroform, covered her face.

Two men carried Fanny into her home. Her cook and butler had already been overpowered, securely bound, and locked in a closet. Her dining room table had been cleared off, blankets had been draped over it, and several lamps placed around it, to form a makeshift operating table.

"You may place the patient right there," said a kindly-looking white-haired man. "And be gentle about it."

The men did as they were told and then went outside to stand guard, while the kindly-looking doctor went about his business.

The doctor's name was Samuels, and he had been one of the most successful physicians in Houston until he developed a fondness for certain illegal drugs, which in time led the state to remove his license. He still took pride in his work, despite its illegality, and it was with great care and skill that he performed both an abortion and a tubal ligation on Fanny, there on her dining room table.

Fanny would not bear Wade Kingslea's child, or anyone else's, then or thereafter.

When she awoke, Fanny was being watched over by a nurse who had been summoned, anonymously, to her bedside. The intruders, upon their departure, had ransacked her house, so she could, if she wished, tell the servants and the police that the motive of the break-in had been robbery. Fanny, however, did not tell the servants or the police anything. She wept in helpless fury when she realized what had been done to her, then she spoke with her doctor, and soon she chartered a plane to fly her to her home in Palm Springs. She doubted if she would ever come back to Texas. There were lions in the streets, she thought, madness in the hot prairie wind. She didn't think she could stand it any longer.

Wade and Livie never discussed the unpleasant events concerning Eve and Fanny. They had reached that level of wealth and power at which one can employ other people to handle life's unpleasant details; they concerned themselves with ends, not means. Wade and Livie had fought a silent battle, had reached a standoff, and had emerged with increased, if grudging respect for one another. They never spoke of what had happened, because some things were better not discussed. It was simply necessary to reach an understanding.

CHAPTER EIGHT

Billy Rose was headed back to Broadway and Coyle Kingslea wanted to go with him. "Billy and I make a good team," he told Louise excitedly one night that August. "He's always going a mile a minute, and I'm the detail man. And once I learn the ropes, I can produce shows on my own. My God, if you get a hit there's more money in it than oil. All it takes is audacity, angel, and I inherited tons of that from my old man!"

Louise kept her doubts to herself. She couldn't imagine them living in New York, or Coyle as a producer, but it was wonderful to see him so excited about something.

"What does Mr. Rose say?" she asked.

"I'm going to talk to him tomorrow," Coyle explained.

The next morning, as Billy Rose strutted around the centennial grounds, saying his good-byes, Coyle pulled him aside to state his case. Money wasn't the object, he stressed —he wanted to learn the theatrical business. Because of Casa Mañana's huge success, Rose was being deluged with offers to stage other regional extravaganzas, and who was better qualified than Coyle to help him? The little producer's eyes narrowed as he listened.

"You're a bright kid, Coyle," he said finally. "You did a swell job here. New York—I don't know. Give me till tomorrow, okay?"

Coyle didn't sleep much that night. His son, Philip, howled most of the night, and when he wasn't rocking Philip and giving him a bottle he was worrying about what Billy Rose would decide.

Coyle had never wanted anything as much as he wanted this chance to make a career in New York. Never before had he imagined a life for himself outside his father's long shadow.

He cornered Rose in the Worth Hotel lobby the next morning. The showman frowned when he saw him, and said he didn't have time for coffee.

"Did you think about my idea?" Coyle asked.

"Yeah, I thought about it," Rose said glumly.

"So what's the verdict?"

"Coyle, you're a bright kid, but I don't see you in show biz."

"Billy, didn't we make a good team here?"

"Yeah, but this is Texas. Up there, I don't know."

"Give me a reason, Billy. You're beating around the bush."

"Give me a break, kid. What can I say?"

"My father!" Coyle cried. "Did you talk to my father? Did he screw the deal?"

"Kid, use your head. You got a nice life here. A pretty little wife. A baby. A rich daddy. Whatta you want to go to New York for? Jesus, Coyle, Broadway's a jungle!"

All Coyle's bravado was gone. "Billy, please, just tell me one thing," he pleaded. "Did my father tell you not to give me the job?"

The producer started for the hotel's revolving door. "Got to catch a cab, kid."

Coyle kept pace with him. "Did my father blackball me?"

Rose whistled for a Yellow Cab parked down the block, then turned back to Coyle. "Listen, your old man is one rich son of a bitch. There's not many people real anxious to cross him." He shrugged and hopped into the cab. "That's life, kid," he said in farewell. "My love to the wife."

Coyle stood at the curb watching the cab speed away. His last illusions went with it. He saw now that he was trapped, that there was no escape, that if his father wanted him to be assistant treasurer of Kingslea Oil then that was what he would be. A horn honked and he blinked and stepped back from the curb. It was midmorning and there was no place for him to go—not home to face his wife and son, not to the office to face his father, so he went to a pay phone in the hotel and called Pig.

By midnight Louise and Caddy had called a dozen bars but they were always one step behind their husbands. It was four in the morning when Pig called and said Coyle was in jail.

"Can I go get him?" she asked.

"Lu-Lu, I don't think Coyle's going anywhere before

morning, and it may take some doing then. He went after a cop with a barstool."

Louise was at the police station at eight that morning, accompanied by Kingslea Oil's general counsel, but it was mid-afternoon before Coyle was free. When Coyle emerged from the jail and embraced Louise his face was badly bruised and one eye was swollen shut.

"It was a great party, angel," he said. "You should have been there."

"Coyle, are you all right?" she cried.

He winked with his good eye. "Well, angel," he said solemnly, "at least I've learned how a punching bag feels."

Their lawyer was a big, rumpled man with dandruff and a broken nose. "I'll have to tell your father, Coyle," he muttered. "This one cost us some chips with the chief of police."

"We've got plenty of chips," Coyle said and took Louise's arm and led her out to the car.

Coyle went home, took a bath, and spent the rest of the evening playing with Philip. After Philip dropped off to sleep, they listened to *Amos 'n' Andy,* then turned off the radio and got ready for bed. He still hadn't explained why he'd gone on the binge.

"What was it, Coyle?" she said. "Was it something I did?"

"You, angel? No, it was that little jerk Billy Rose. He gave me thumbs down on Broadway."

She took his hand. "It doesn't matter, Coyle."

He shrugged. "Maybe not," he said. "Maybe not."

She hoped that would be the end of it. He'd hardly drunk at all since Philip had been born. With his work at Casa finished, Louise hoped they'd get back to the quiet sort of life they'd led in their first months of marriage. But something had changed. The next afternoon Pig came by to relive their Jacksboro Highway adventures; they consumed a bottle of Scotch in the process. By the time Pig left, Coyle was drunk and belligerent. When she tried to get him to go to bed, he pushed her away. His face was twisted into that terrible grimace that she knew so well now. "Don't tell me what t'do, sister," he snarled. "I'm Franklin Coyle Kingslea, ya unnerstan'?"

His drinking got worse. They went to parties and dances and dinners, and most often they ended with Coyle drunk, maybe passing out peacefully, maybe nasty and insulting to people. The mornings after, when she would try to talk to him, he would shake his head and turn away.

The worst binges were always somehow connected with his father. The winter after Casa Mañana, Coyle asked his father for some money for some oil deals with Pig. After four years as a freshman at TCU, Pig had terminated his academic career and entered the oil business. He had some promising leases and wanted Coyle to help him develop them, but Coyle's father turned him down and that led to a four-day drunk.

Louise didn't understand it. Wade Kingslea had all the money and fame a man could ask, and yet he seemed to take pleasure in dominating his oldest son's life. As far as Louise could see, Coyle's sin was in being different from his father. Hoyt, who was more like his father, was the fair-haired boy; once Hoyt joined Kingslea Oil he was quickly given the money for oil deals that Coyle had been denied. Sometimes Louise thought Coyle's drinking was only his way of crying out to his father, saying, "Pay attention to me, love me!"

Yet the more Louise saw of the oil rich, the more she saw, in one variation or another, the same problems in family after family. The fathers had made their millions young and now were entering middle age, still determined to make all the decisions, to keep their sons in the shadows. Time after time, among the boys of Coyle's generation, she saw alcoholism, drugs, divorces, violence, car wrecks, suicides. Louise began to think that great wealth was not the wonderful blessing that everyone imagined but a curse, an awful cancer that ate away at people's lives. But of course that was not something you could say, or people would think you were crazy.

So they kept on with their lives, taking what pleasure they could, not worrying much about tomorrow. Much of Louise's pleasure came from her son. As she neared two, Philip was a solemn, brown-haired boy with his mother's fine-boned face and his father's dark, watchful eyes. On his second birthday, Coyle and Louise took Philip to a Sunday matinee of the Ringling Brothers Circus at the new Will Rogers Coliseum. Soon Coyle was nipping from his ever-present gin bottle. There was something about crowds that frightened Coyle, terrified him, so while everyone else was laughing at the clowns and cheering the acrobats, Coyle was getting drunker and drunker, until finally the man sitting next to them told him to put the bottle away.

Coyle leaped to his feet. "Listen, you horse-faced son of a bitch," he roared, "you shut your mouth or I'll knock your block off, unnerstan'?"

The man pushed Coyle over backward. Coyle struggled to his feet and threw his gin bottle at him. People were screaming and scrambling out of the way. The police were about to arrest Coyle when Louise, holding Philip in her arms, pleaded with them to let her take him home.

A red-nosed Irish police sergeant reluctantly agreed, and Louise drove them home. She kept her temper until she had calmed Philip and put him to bed. Then she turned furiously to her husband. "I've never been so humiliated in my life," she cried. "Coyle, we can't even go to the *circus!* I can't go on like this. You've got to stop drinking. If you don't . . ." She started to cry. "If you don't, I don't know what I'll do."

Coyle was sitting on the edge of the bed, trying without success to get his shoes off. He looked up at her with that awful leer, his lips pulled back across his teeth in a grimace of rage and pain.

"You shut t'fuck up," he snarled.

She went and knelt beside him. "Coyle, don't *talk* to me like that, *please.*"

He muttered something incomprehensible and slapped her with the back of his hand. The blow caught her by surprise and sent her tumbling to the floor. "Coyle!" she screamed, but he stared at her blankly, then dropped back on the bed unconscious. Louise got unsteadily to her feet and went into the bathroom. Her cheek was red and puffy and it ached with a throbbing pain. She washed her face and sat down on the edge of the tub and tried to think. Finally she called Caddy and asked her to come get her and Philip.

Pig was prospering in the oil business, and he had bought a big stone house on Crestline Drive, across from the River Crest golf course. At breakfast the next morning, he shuffled around in a purple robe, pouring orange juice, himself bleary-eyed from the previous night's party, and tried to play the peacemaker.

"Lu-Lu, you got to give the fellow another chance," he insisted.

"I've given him another chance twenty times," Louise protested.

"Hell, everybody has fights."

"Pig, look at her *face,*" Caddy cried. "He *hit* her."

"Well, hell, you get drunk and somebody says something to you and you swing at 'em and you don't even know what you're doin'," Pig said.

"Pig, get *out* of here," Caddy said. "Just kindly leave the room so Louise and I can talk."

Pig grumbled and shuffled out to the sun porch.

Caddy poured more coffee. "What're you going to do?"

"Go stay with my parents, I guess."

"Will you go back to him?"

"I don't know. Not unless he stops drinking. Really *stops.*"

Caddy nodded and lit a Chesterfield. "Make it stick," she said. "If you give in again, it'll be like this forever."

Louise stared into her coffee cup. For the first time she was thinking the unthinkable: she might have to divorce Coyle.

Louise's parents took her in gladly. Her father had never approved of Coyle, and even her mother had become disillusioned by his drinking.

Louise and Philip moved into her old room on the second floor. From the window you could see the treetops of Forest Park and in the evenings you could hear the lions roaring down in the zoo. John Everett built his grandson a sandbox under a tree in the back yard and hung a tire swing from its limbs. During the days Everett sat in his easy chair, chain-smoking Camels and listening to the news from Europe. His wife was busy teaching Philip his ABCs. In the evenings they would sit in the back yard and drink iced tea and push Philip on the tire swing and listen for the lions. Louise missed Coyle and worried about him, but it was a relief to live without the constant fear of what he might do.

It was ten days before she heard from him. Caddy drove over one evening and handed her an envelope. The note inside was written in Coyle' elegant, old-fashioned handwriting. It said, "I wish that, before you do anything definite, you would talk to me. Please don't let anything I might have said or done during a crazy delirium break up a relationship that to me, at least, was beautiful. Do whatever you think best for your own happiness but if possible give me a little break, for God knows I'm sorry. If it ends, please be consoled that it was all my fault, as looking back I can't recall your having done anything wrong. Can't I hear from you?"

Caddy watched as Louise read the note twice, then folded it and put it in her pocket. "Will you see him?" she asked.

"I don't know."

"For what it's worth, he really has quit. He's been at our house the last three nights and not touched a drop."

"He's quit before. So many times." Louise hesitated. "How is he?"

"Subdued. Sad. Louise, I *do* think Coyle wants to change."

"It's Philip I worry about. Which is worse for him, no father or a father who's stumbling around drunk half the time?" '

"Could he see a psychiatrist or something?" Caddy asked.

"He's done all that. I hate to say it, but I think if anybody can help him, it's me."

Philip came out and climbed into the tire swing. Louise's father stepped out on the porch, said hello to Caddy, muttered something about Hitler, and went inside to pour some tea.

"He said you could meet at our place," Caddy said. "Sort of neutral ground. Pig and I can discreetly hide in the attic."

Louise gave Philip a big push. He laughed with joy as the rope twisted and whirled him in dizzying circles.

"Tomorrow evening," Louise said. "I'll come by at six after Philip's had his dinner."

Coyle was waiting on the porch when they arrived. Philip yelled, "Daddy, Daddy," and ran to him. Coyle embraced the boy and lifted him into the air. His eyes glistened as Louise approached him. Coyle looked wonderful; even a week without drinking would take the puffiness from his face. He smiled nervously.

"I'm glad you came," he said.

"How are you?" she asked.

"Better."

There was an awkward pause, then Caddy came out and they all went to the back yard for tea—even Pig had a glass of tea—but soon Caddy and Pig excused themselves and went into the house. Louise and Coyle sat face to face, in two wrought-iron chairs, with Philip nestled in Coyle's lap.

"I've missed you," he said. "Both of you."

"Philip's missed you," she said.

"But not you?"

"I have to be honest, Coyle. I've . . . I've had mixed feelings."

"You should. I'm only glad they're mixed. You should hate me."

Her eyes stung with sudden tears. "I could never hate you, not ever. But I have to think about Philip and . . . and his life."

Coyle stroked the boy's hair. "Of course you do. Louise, there's no use my telling you I love you and I'm sorry. You know that. All I can say that matters is that I haven't had a drink since the night you left and I'll never have another one if you come back. You and the boy have brought me all the happiness I've ever known."

Philip slid from his father's lap and began to poke a stick in the goldfish pond at the back of the yard.

"Louise, I'm sick," he said. "I've had to admit that to myself, since you left. I don't understand it. Part of it was that mess at M&I and part of it is my father. All my life I've felt like people were staring at me, criticizing me, comparing me with my father. At a party, or wherever I'm surrounded by people, I feel all those eyes on me and I think I'm not good enough, not man enough, so I drink."

He flashed a tight, ironic smile. "Usually there's a point, around the sixth drink, when I think I'm just as tough a character as my old man. Unfortunately, that's when I either pass out or take a swing at somebody."

"You can't drink, Coyle. You just *can't.*"

He nodded ruefully. "I know. You kid yourself for so long. You say, 'Tonight I'll stop at two and be Mr. Charm.' But it doesn't work. I can't take that first drink, Louise, not today, not tomorrow, not ever. And if you'll help me, I won't."

She took his hand. "You know I'll help you."

"I won't be the life of the party anymore. Pig may never speak to me again. But, *God,* we could be so happy." Suddenly he was enthusiastic. "Even these last ten days, even without you, it's been so damn good just to be sober, to be in control, not to be hiding in the bottom of a gin bottle. And it can be that way forever, angel, forever and ever."

She loved his enthusiasm, his resolve, but she had seen it before. "I hope so, Coyle," she said. "But you understand, if we come back, there won't be any more chances."

"I understand."

Philip ran over with a squirming goldfish in his hand. "Put him back, darling," Louise said.

"Go'fish."

"That's right, darling, goldfish. But we have to leave them in the water or they die. Put it back now."

"Go'fish," the child said and started reluctantly back to the pond.

"Then you'll come back?" Coyle asked.

She nodded, a bit uncertainly.

"When?"

"Tonight, I guess," she said, and he put his arms around her. Over by the pond their son, seeing his parents preoccupied, slipped the goldfish into his pocket.

The next few months were the happiest of Louise's life.

They spent most evenings at home, just the three of them. Louise puttered in her garden and Coyle cooked chicken or hamburgers on the back grill. After dinner they might stroll down Clover Lane to check the progress of the new South Hi-Mount Elementary School that was being built or sit on the back porch and listen to Fibber McGee or Fred Allen on the radio. They took Philip to see *Snow White* and Louise got around to reading *Gone with the Wind*. When friends came by they listened to the new records, songs like "The Dipsy Doodle" and "The Very Thought of You," and Coyle would wheel out his portable bar, which boasted every known soft drink. "Try my pop, you'll never stop," was his motto, and even Pig sipped a Dr. Pepper when he came to visit.

Their good fortune increased when a young baseball player named Dusty Rhodes came to town to play for the Fort Worth Cats and moved in next door with his wife, June, and daughter, Jenny, who was about Philip's age. Dusty and June were nondrinking Baptists and delightful people, and dark-eyed, laughing Jenny was just about the most beautiful child the world had ever seen. She and Philip played together endlessly, conspiring happily in the private world of two-year-olds, and it wasn't long before Louise concocted a fantasy wherein, some two decades later, the two of them would fall in love and wed and live happily ever after—as happy as Louise herself was that glorious summer when Coyle Kingslea stayed sober.

Coyle and Louise declined most invitations, and when they went out they tried to avoid places where Coyle would be under pressure to drink. Louise thought Coyle passed his most severe test one Sunday afternoon when they went to visit with his parents at Hillcrest. Several West Texas oilmen were also visiting that afternoon, and while Philip frolicked on the playground that Wade had installed for his two grandsons the oilmen sat on the long flagstone terrace and talked oil and politics. Soon the talk turned to Franklin Roosevelt, and the oilmen could barely contain themselves:

"... worse than Stalin ..."

"... really a Jew, I heard ..."

". . . can't spend your way out of a Depression . . ."

". . . ones on welfare are all foreigners anyway. . ."

". . . way I hear it, his brain's rottin' away, because he caught—beggin' your pardon, ladies—a serious social disease from Eleanor. . ."

Louise, who was innocent of politics, kept her eyes on her husband. She knew how violently he disagreed with everything these men were saying. But Coyle sipped his iced tea and listened politely, a faint smile on his face. Louise, watching him, suddenly got up and walked past his chair and kissed him, then hurried out to see Philip.

After the oilmen left, Wade Kingslea was in an expansive mood. "A lot of nice houses going up west of here," he said. "You ought to think of buying, Coyle. That boy of yours needs some room to run."

"Can't afford it," Coyle said.

"I imagine we could work something out," his father said.

Coyle sipped his tea. "We're happy where we are."

His father's face darkened. Coyle loved to spurn his father's money. "It's the only weapon you have against the rich," he would say. "It drives them batty."

But Wade Kingslea soon found a way to seize his son's attention. "Did I tell you Bailey Shroup was retiring?" he asked. Shroup was Coyle's boss, Kingslea Oil's secretary-treasurer.

"No you didn't," Coyle said.

"He just told me. Damn fool wants to retire to Mexico."

Kingslea called for another bourbon, then changed the subject, leaving the question of Bailey Shroup's replacement hanging in the air. Coyle watched his father nervously but nothing more was said about the job he so desperately wanted.

The next afternoon, as soon as Coyle came home from work, Louise knew something was wrong. Instead of kissing her, he avoided her eyes, wandered around the back yard for a moment, then slumped down at the picnic table with his head in his hands. She put her hand on his shoulder and asked him what was the matter.

"My father's interviewing people for that job. He hasn't said a word to me."

Louise sat down beside him. She wanted so much to help him. But how? "Coyle, you . . . you'll just have to ask him to interview you."

"To hell with him."

"No, Coyle. You've got to show him you're the most qualified man. That's fair."

He turned to her with a stricken look. "Don't you see?" he said. "If he turns me down, I'll have to leave."

"Then leave," she said. "There are other things you can do."

Philip ran over with an old tennis ball in his hand. "Play catch, Daddy?"

"In a minute, son," Coyle said. "Louise, don't you see? I don't know what else I *could* do. At Kingslea Oil, I'm the boss's son. Anyplace else, I'm just a local playboy. The town drunk, some would say."

She put her arms around him. "Coyle, listen to me. People love you. You could go anywhere and do anything. Don't . . . don't *hate* yourself so. Just go to your father and tell him you want that job."

"Daddy, throw ball," Philip cried.

Coyle got up slowly. "I guess I'll have to." Then he turned to his son. "Okay, Dizzy Dean, let's see you fling one."

The week after Labor Day Coyle went to see his father in his tenth-floor office overlooking the west side of Fort Worth. After a minimum of pleasantry, he got to the matter at hand.

"Father, I want to talk to you about the treasurer's job. I want you to consider me for it. I think I've got the experience. And with all respect to Bailey, I think we could make some improvements in our procurement system, and there are some diversifications we should consider. I'm not asking for any special treatment, just to be considered the same as anybody else."

He stopped, hoping his father would ask him about his ideas for procurement and diversification. But Wade Kingslea only fiddled with his cigar. Despite the air conditioning Coyle felt himself start to sweat.

"Coyle," his father said, "it's your attitude that concerns me."

"My attitude?" Coyle repeated, disbelieving.

"The oil business isn't just a job to me, Coyle. Isn't just a way to make a dollar. No sir, I'm in the oil business because I love this country and I want to keep it strong and free."

Oh God, Coyle thought, for he saw what was coming.

"In my view, Coyle, the oil industry is a brotherhood of like-minded men, pulling together, for their country's good. Now when I say I'm concerned about your attitude, I mean that you seem to have ideas that aren't shared by we who are leaders of the industry."

He stared at his son accusingly.

"What ideas do you mean?" Coyle asked as politely as he could.

"For one thing, I mean you saying that regulation would be good for the industry," Wade Kingslea snapped.

"Father, there are plenty of oilmen who think that if we don't police ourselves, we're only inviting government regulation," Coyle protested.

"Then they're damn fools!" his father shouted. "Give those damn Reds in Washington the first inch, and they'll take a mile."

The conversation was out of control; Coyle wondered if he could possibly get it back on the track. "We may disagree on some issues," he said. "But I care about the country and I care about Kingslea Oil. You've made it a great company, and I want to help keep it great."

"Son, I hope and pray that in time you'll take a major role in Kingslea Oil. But I'm not sure that time is here yet."

"Father, I've been with the company for six years. I've done everything I've been asked to do. Hoyt's only been here for two years and already he's . . ."

"Coyle," his father said sternly. "It would be difficult to imagine two young men more dissimilar than you and Hoyt. Dammit, boy, that the *point!* Your stability. Your damn drinking."

"I haven't had a drink in nearly three months," Coyle said.

"Fine, but I'll be more impressed when it's three years," his father shot back. "Show me a year or two of sobriety and hard work and responsible conduct, *then* we'll discuss a larger role for you."

Coyle felt it all slipping away, everything. "I can't deny my drinking," he said. "I'm trying to change. If you'll give me a chance, Father, I won't let you down."

"Won't let me down?" his father snapped. "By God, it wasn't long ago that you wanted to run off with some little Jew and be a Broadway hustler. Is that the kind of loyalty you'll give Kingslea Oil?"

Wade Kingslea stood up, framed against the looming Texas sky. "Show me some work, son, then we'll talk about a promotion."

Coyle got to his feet. "That's final?" he said.

"I found a fellow in Oklahoma City I'm putting in the treasurer's job," his father said. "A good man. You can learn from him."

Coyle stared at his father's lean, hard, cold face as if he'd never seen it before. He seemed to see a glint of pleasure in the dark, piercing eyes. He had a sudden, stunning thought: *This man hates me. But why? Because I'm not like him? Because I am like my mother? Because I remind him of his past? Because I am younger, and will outlive him, and will inherit his treasure? For all those reasons, and others I cannot imagine? Or does it matter? He hates me and he has made me hate myself.*

"Thank you for your time, Father," he said and quietly left the office.

He drove home and found a note from Louise saying she'd taken Philip shopping. He paced about the house, trying to decide what to do. Should he quit his job? Would any other oil company hire him? Or would he have to swallow his pride and stay at Kingslea Oil under the new man? He heard someone at the front door. He rushed to open it, hoping it was Louise. He felt giddy, like a man who is about to stumble and fall, and he thought she could steady him, could bind up his wounds, could give him the love that would help him survive. Coyle threw open the front door, but it was Pig, not Louise. He'd just closed a big deal, he said, and a bunch of them were going to celebrate.

Louise smelled the gin the moment she opened the door. She put down the sack of groceries and saw Coyle sprawled on the sofa. "Where the hell you been?" he muttered.

She shoved Philip through the kitchen door and told him to go play in his sandbox. "What's the matter, Coyle?" she asked.

"Din't get th' job."

He fumbled for the gin bottle on the floor.

"Coyle, you promised you wouldn't drink."

"Fuck 'em all!" he snarled. His hair was in his eyes and his face was that ugly, anguished mask she knew so well now.

"I told you I'd leave, Coyle."

"Asked him for t'job. Begged 'im. Told me t'go t'hell. Been telling me that my whole damn life." He lowered his head and began to sob. How could she leave him, she asked herself. How could she leave him when he needed her so desperately?

"Coyle, the job doesn't *matter*," she said. "If you'll just go to sleep."

Philip came in and studied his father.

"What's matter with Daddy?"

"Daddy's sick," Louise said. "Go outside and play."

"Daddy sick?" the boy said. He put his hand on Coyle's shoulder. "Daddy get well?"

Coyle looked up, trying to focus on the child. "G'way, kid," he muttered.

"Daddy sick?"

"Philip, come *on*," Louise cried and reached down to pick him up, but before she could the boy threw his arms around Coyle's neck and began to cry. Coyle pushed him away and Louise tried to pick him up and Philip grabbed for his father again and Coyle screamed, "Leave me *alone!*" and slapped the child hard across the face and fell back sobbing on the sofa. Philip tumbled to the floor and Louise lifted him into her arms.

"I'm leaving, Coyle," she cried. "Do you hear? You'll never hit my baby again."

She ran toward the front door, dragging Philip along with her. Coyle stumbled to his feet and grabbed her arm. They struggled for a moment, then she pushed him away and got the door open and ran out into the yard. Philip was crying, and Coyle caught her again at the curb. "Won't let you go," he said. Louise screamed and he slapped her with his free hand and then Dusty Rhodes ran out of his house and pushed Coyle aside.

"Sonuvabitch," Coyle yelled and swung at the baseball player. He missed and fell down in the grass and lay there sobbing.

"You can come to our house," Dusty said. "Do you want me to call the police?"

"No," Louise said. "I just want to get away from here. Please don't let him follow me." She took Philip's hand and pulled him down El Campo toward Montgomery Street. Her purse and her money and the car keys were all in the house and she wasn't going back there. All she knew to do was to walk to her parents' house, so that was what they did, the two of them.

• • •

When he was older, Philip Kingslea believed that everything that ever happened to you was recorded in your memory, buried deep but always there, and there were moments when you could remember it all. He always remembered that afternoon that he walked with his mother to his grandparents' house. He remembered how dark the living room had been and the sharp smell of gin on his father's breath just before he hit him and the way his mother's golden hair swirled around her shoulders as she struggled with his father. He remembered Dusty's striped shirt and his father stretched out on the grass and the terrible heat as they walked along the side of the road because there were no sidewalks. Many years later he drove a car over that route and found it was only four miles, but in memory it was a journey that had no end. He remembered the heat, the burning sun that had melted the tar in the blacktop roads so they were soft and sticky under his feet. He remembered how he walked until he was too tired to go on, and then his mother carried him, and when she was too tired to carry him he walked again. He remembered men offering them rides and his mother saying no. He remembered how they had to get off the road when cars passed and the weeds beside the road were as tall as he was and they scratched his face and felt rough and sticky when he pushed them away. He remembered walking along West Vickery, beside the railroad tracks, and stopping for a drink of water at a gas station where colored men were sitting in the shade smoking corncob pipes. He remembered when they reached University Drive and stopped beside the river to rest. He remembered the place in Forest Park where a huge tree limb stretched out horizontally across the road, and they passed under it, and after that for many years he had a dream in which he was marching in a parade of children and he was the smallest child, marching at the rear by himself, and just as he passed under that limb a madman with a hideous, snarling face swooped down and pulled him up into the tree to some horrible fate while the parade passed on without him. He remembered walking up the steep hill by the Forest Park Apartments and coming to his grandparents' house and his grandmother crying and making lemonade and his grandfather switching off his radio and pacing about in his slippers and shouting that he would kill Coyle Kingslea, and finally he remembered falling asleep in his mother's arms while the lions roared down in the zoo. Those were things that he remembered from that September day, and also that he did not see his father again for a long time.

CHAPTER NINE

Everyone agreed she could not return to him, and yet there were times when Louise let herself think of it. There was always the dream that someday, somehow, Coyle would stop his drinking and become all that she knew he could be. But the reality was that he was an alcoholic who had hit her, hit their son, and she could not live with him and cling to any self-respect.

This time he made no effort at reconciliation. In fact, when Caddy took Louise to lunch one day that fall at the new Colonial Country Club, she reported that Coyle had vanished.

"No one knows *where* he is," she exclaimed. "You haven't heard from him, have you?"

Louise shook her head. "Maybe he's in a hospital."

"That's what I thought," Caddy said. "He's drying out somewhere. Or maybe he just took off. He could be on Skid Row somewhere."

"Oh God," Louise gasped. "He did that once, when he left M&I."

"You still love him, don't you?"

"That doesn't matter. I'll never live with him again."

They talked about the "War of the Worlds" radio show the week before, the one that had everyone thinking the Martians had landed, and about the war in Europe, and then Caddy swore Louise to secrecy and told her about her affair. "I can't feel guilty," she said. "I mean, I *know* what Pig does on his trips to Houston and New York. I want my fun too."

"Who *is* he?"

Caddy giggled. "It's such a cliché—he's my tennis coach. He's only twenty. And so gorgeous."

Caddy poked at her crabmeat cocktail. "How about you, darlin'? I know some fellows who'd love to take you out, if you say the word."

Louise shook her head. "I wouldn't go out with any of Coyle's friends, or any of that crowd. Once was enough. Besides, I'm still married."

"Haven't you filed for divorce?"

"I don't want to think about it."

"Louise, you've *got* to do something. You son is one of the two—knock on wood—heirs to maybe five hundred million dollars. Certain understandings must be reached."

"I don't want any understandings. I just want my son."

"Honey, you've *got* him, that's the point. Let Wade Kingslea pay through the nose if he ever wants to see his grandson again. That's how the game is played."

Louise shook her head stubbornly. "I don't *want* their money. All it's ever done is make people miserable."

Two days later Wade Kingslea's secretary called Louise and asked if she would be so good as to come by the oilman's office for a talk.

"A talk about what?" Louise asked.

"About . . . about some legal matters, I believe," the secretary said. Few people questioned her employer's invitations.

"There's nothing I want to talk about, Mrs. Garrett."

"Just a minute, please," the woman said, and in a moment Louise's father-in-law came on the line.

"Louise? How are you, my dear? I do think we should talk. Suppose I drop by your parents' house? How would tonight at seven be?"

She hesitated, overwhelmed. "I . . . I don't know what there is to talk about, Mr. Kingslea."

"We have to think about Philip's future."

"I do think about it, all the time."

"Louise, I'm the boy's grandfather. You won't refuse to see me, will you?"

She saw that it was inevitable. "Seven tonight will be fine," she told him.

The Everett home on Edward Street had a big front porch with comfortable wicker chairs and a sofa. The four of them waited there, watching the first stars appear, until Wade Kingslea's Fleetwood glided to a stop at the curb. Louise's parents went inside, and she took Philip by the hand and led him out to meet his grandfather in the front yard, under the big fir tree. Kingslea shook the boy's hand solemnly and produced some gumdrops from his pocket.

"With his mother's permission, of course," he said.

Louise nodded. "Take the candy and go inside, Philip. Grandmother will read you a story."

The boy went in and Louise and her father-in-law took chairs on the porch. "Do you mind if I smoke?" he asked.

"No."

Kingslea lit a cigar and dropped the match into a big clay ashtray, one Louise's father had brought back from Mexico.

"Louise, let me say at the outset, I don't blame you for a thing. Not a thing. Except perhaps for marrying Coyle in the first place. But I guess not many girls would turn down a young man with his money. The sad truth is that Coyle has serious emotional problems, and he should never have married. You did your best, I give you full credit for that. The way he treated you, you had no choice but to leave him."

Louise marveled at Wade Kingslea, so handsome, so self-confident, so wrong about everything.

"I didn't leave him because of the way he treated me, Mr. Kingslea," she said. "I left him because he hit our son."

"Of course, my dear, of course. Now. . ."

"Do you know where he is?"

"Coyle? No, but I have people looking for him. He'll turn up. The real question is, when he does return, do you want a reconciliation?"

"No, I don't."

"Then you'll file for divorce?"

"I suppose so."

"Who's your lawyer?"

"I don't know. I think my father has a lawyer."

"Of course. Louise, the point I want to make is, I care about you and Philip; I care about his education. I want him to have every advantage. I have high hopes for the boy. He's bright—you can see that already—and he won't necessarily inherit his father's weaknesses. Outstanding genetic traits often skip a generation. I've been reading a book about it."

Louise was aghast. "I have high hopes for him, too, Mr. Kingslea."

"But what are your plans, Louise? To remarry?"

She smiled for the first time that evening. "I wouldn't say I was in a hurry to remarry. I suppose I'll get a job."

"Then who will raise Philip?"

"I don't know. My parents will help."

"Louise, it shouldn't be necessary for you to work. I'm prepared to contribute generously to Philip's upbringing."

She had known it was coming. She'd been thinking about it ever since her talk with Caddy. And her answer always had to be the same. "I don't want your money, Mr. Kingslea."

The oilman rolled his cigar between his thumb and middle finger, as if deep in contemplation. "In a sense, it's his money," he said. "He was born to it—he's a Kingslea. We're only talking . . . technicalities."

"I'm not talking technicalities, Mr. Kingslea."

The oilman sighed and crossed his legs. He was wearing a pinstripe suit and hand-tooled cowboy boots, and the light from the streetlight glistened on his silver hair. "How old are you, Louise?"

"Twenty-one."

"Twenty-one. And very lovely. And very intelligent. But perhaps not old enough to understand what it means to turn down a great deal of money."

"I'm old enough to know what I've seen in the last three years. I've seen Coyle and his friends drinking themselves to death, destroying themselves and other people too—that's what all that wonderful money has done for them."

"Louise, you know as well as I do there are many people who manage to reconcile wealth with sensible, productive lives."

"Unfortunately, your son and his friends are not among them," she said bitterly.

"Let's get back to the point. You're an attractive young woman. Whether or not you remarry, you'll want an active social life. Boys, parties. Perhaps you'll want to return to college. All of this will be hard to reconcile with motherhood."

"I think I can . . ."

"Let me finish, please. There's a war coming. The young men your age are going to have to fight it."

Louise couldn't see what he was driving at but she sensed it was ominous.

"Let me suggest a course of action that may not have occurred to you. It may even offend you—but I urge you to give it serious consideration. Mrs. Kingslea and I are, as you know, relatively young people. And yet we're old enough that we won't be uprooted by this war that's coming. We're Philip's grandparents, but we love him as if he were our own child. What I'm proposing is that Livie and I legally adopt Philip. We would . . ."

"Adopt him?"

"That's right. He would live with us, and we'd have a nurse and all the necessary help, and you wouldn't be tied down by the obligations of motherhood. Still, you would have very generous privileges of visitation, and . . ."

"Adopt him?"

"Yes. It's hardly unprecedented. I could name you . . ."

"Mr. Kingslea." Lousie felt something snap inside her. "You must be out of your mind," she said, suddenly enjoying herself. "After what you did to your *own* son, do you really think I'd let you raise *my* son? Oh, that's wonderful, Mr. Kingslea. That's priceless."

"Hear me out, please."

"I'd give Philip to a band of Gypsies before I'd give him to *you,* Wade Kingslea. What would you do if he wasn't man enough for you? Beat him with a razor strap? Send him to Texas M&I?"

"Listen to me! I may not make this offer again. Give me Philip for adoption, and I'll do two things. First, I'll immediately settle one million dollars on you. Second . . ."

"You *are* insane."

"Second, I'll establish a ten-million-dollar trust fund for the boy, to pass to him when he's twenty-one, and of course he would stand to inherit a great deal more when I die."

"You want to buy my son," she whispered.

"You're letting yourself be ruled by your emotions, Louise."

"That's right, I am," she cried. "It's a pity you never tried it, Mr. Kingslea. All you talk about is money, money, money. How you'll give Philip ten million dollars. Have you ever thought about what you *can't* give him?"

He stared at her in honest confusion. "What can't I give him?" he asked incredulously.

"Love, Mr. Kingslea. L-o-v-e, love. You can't give it because you don't have it and it's not for sale anywhere."

Wade Kingslea stood up. "You're acting like a damn fool," he snapped.

The front door banged open and John Everett stepped out. The old carpenter was sixty, but he was still formidable. "No, sir, it's you who's acting the fool," he said. "Now get off my property or, by God, I'll thrash you within an inch of your life!"

Kingslea dropped his cigar into the Mexican ashtray. "Louise," he said, "my lawyers will see to it that you and your son never see a penny of my money."

"That's fine, Mr. Kingslea."

"You and your son will cease to exist, so far as the Kingslea family is concerned."

"Off my property," John Everett repeated, stepping forward, and Wade Kingslea retreated to his Fleetwood and was gone.

The lawyers worked out a simple, uncontested divorce agreement. Louise received custody of her son but neither asked for nor received any alimony or child support. The question of Coyle's visitation rights was left open, until such time as he might reappear. The only point of dispute arose when Wade Kingslea's lawyer demanded that Louise return the ruby necklace that Livie had given her; it had only been a loan, the lawyer said. Louise was willing to give the necklace back, but her lawyer insisted that it had been a gift and she should keep it. Wade Kingslea's lawyer did not press the point, since he knew how much more Louise could have gotten if she had tried.

Louise's parents were happy for her to live with them, but after a few months Louise realized that she was bored, that her mother was starting to treat her like a child, and it was time for her to find a job. Her old dream of journalism returned. She had often met Amon Carter at parties with the Kingsleas, and she decided to ask him for a job in his paper's society department—she *did* have a certain hard-won knowledge of Fort Worth society.

So one morning she caught the bus downtown to the *Star-Telegram*'s office on West Seventh Street. Amon Carter's secretary peered at her suspiciously. "I'll see if he's in," she said enigmatically—didn't she *know?*—and disappeared.

Louise didn't mind waiting, for it was exciting to watch the city room, as telephones rang and Teletype machines clattered and reporters yelled and argued and banged out their stories. One short, red-haired reporter caught her eye and winked; Louise blushed and looked away. The walls outside Carter's office were covered with pictures of the publisher with famous people: Roosevelt, Churchill, Will Rogers, Vice President Garner, Babe Ruth. The publisher had dedicated himself to making Fort Worth famous, and in the process he had made himself famous. It was said that the first time he entered Buckingham Palace he waved his six-gun and yelled, "Hooray for Fort Worth and West Texas!"

After a while, Carter emerged from his office and she stood to greet him.

"Mr. Carter?" she said uncertainly.

"Yes, miss? What can I do for you?"

"I'm . . . I'm Louise Kingslea."

He peered at her as if he had not met her twenty times at parties. "Oh yes," he said absently. "Coyle's wife."

"Mr. Carter, we talked once . . . I mean, I told you how I'd always wanted to be a reporter, and now that Coyle and I are separated, I'm . . . I'm looking for a job, and I wondered . . . maybe in the society department?"

The publisher seemed to be examining her from a great height. "You dropped out of TCU, didn't you?" he said suddenly.

"Yes sir," she whispered. "When we got married."

"A young person needs an education," he said gravely. "We're only hiring reporters with college degrees. Come back if you get yours. Good luck." And then he was marching briskly through the city room, as reporters snapped to right and left.

"*Well, hoo-ray for Fort Worth and West Texas,*" Louise thought. Then she lifted her chin high and left the newspaper office.

She found a job, finally, as a receptionist in one of the downtown law firms. The office manager told her that if she would work on her typing she might in time become a legal secretary. The pay was only thirty dollars a week, but since she was still living with her parents she could manage. The people at the law firm were nice. Some of the young lawyers flirted with her, but most of them were married, and the single ones lost interest when she said she was divorced and had a son. But she wasn't much interested in dating. When she wasn't working she wanted to spend all the time she could with Philip. He was growing and changing so quickly. Louise's mother had taken the boy's education in hand. She sat him down before a blackboard every morning to learn the

ABCs, and by his fourth birthday he was reading the comic strips in the *Star-Telegram*. There were no other children Philip's age on the block, so he spent a lot of time playing by himself. There was a toolshed in the back yard where he spent many happy hours with his invisible friend, Roger. Louise's mother was worried that for him to have an invisible friend was a sign of abnormality, but Louise convinced her it was normal enough. In fact, a quarter century later Philip Kingslea would still spend his days in a small room playing with invisible friends, but then it would be called writing fiction and it would bring him a certain celebrity.

Louise and Caddy still met for lunch once in a while, but it had stopped being much fun. Caddy drank too much and gossiped about her lovers and joked about how she hoped the Army would take Pig so she could have some real fun. She had heard a report that Coyle was in a hospital for alcoholics in New Jersey, but she wasn't sure if it was true. She did know for a fact, everyone knew, that Eve had eloped with a football player and Livie had gotten the marriage annulled, whereupon Eve proceeded to London where she was studying art and having an affair with a married member of Parliament. Hoyt was taking flying lessons, in anticipation of being a pilot when the war started.

All of their lives were caught up in the coming war—the fall of France, the bombing of London—and yet Louise paid precious little attention to those far-off events. Her thoughts were mostly on her job, her child, and her social life. She was starting to be caught up in a new Fort Worth, one she had not known before, a city filled with young secretaries and salesmen and engineers and accountants who were flocking to town as the wartime boom began. Before, Louise had known only TCU, and then Coyle's country-club world, but now she met young people who didn't know River Crest Country Club from the stockyards, young men and women who embraced an eat-drink-and-be-merry philosophy as the distant thunder of war swept nearer. They went for hamburgers at the Triple XXX on West Seventh or to dance at the Ringside Club, and when there wasn't money for that there was always a party at somebody's apartment. Louise went to parties every weekend, met dozens of boys, consoled the ones who feared the war, cautioned those who were eager for battle, danced with this one, kissed that one, took a few home to meet her family, and in the spring of 1941 surprised everyone, herself included, by marrying a good-looking, Alabama-born car salesman named Al Henderson.

Years later, when her son asked why she had married Al, Louise replied, with a certain hard-won irony, "Because he was the first one who asked me." There was some truth to that, for most of the men she met in those frenetic prewar years were looking for something other than marriage, but it was not the whole story. Louise was concerned that Philip needed a father, and among Al's virtues was his skill at hunting, fishing, golf, baseball, tinkering with cars, and other manly pursuits. Finally, Al was fun; with his jokes and his South Alabama drawl he was the life of any party. When Louise had gone to parties with Coyle she had rarely enjoyed herself, for she was always worrying about how soon he would get drunk and how she would get him home. Drinking never fazed Al. He was always busy meeting people and telling stories and making deals. Louise had no illusions about Al. He was a small-town boy who'd lasted only one semester in college. His ties were too loud and his jokes were too blue. He would never impress Caddy or the kind of people the Kingsleas knew. But Louise didn't care about that. She'd known enough millionaires for one lifetime. Al was fun, he was respectful toward her, he was affectionate toward Philip, and when he very solemnly asked her to marry him she thought it over for a day and said yes.

Al was selling used cars, but that, he assured her, was only temporary, until the right thing came along. The right thing was variously portrayed as his own new-car dealership, a Mexican restaurant, a sporting goods store, a catfish farm, or a dude ranch. Al was the original optimist. The war would bring boom times to Texas, he declared, and he intended to prosper with them. He would escape military service, he confided, because of an ailment variously described as a trick knee, flat feet, or a bum ticker. Their first home was a garage apartment on Clover Lane, only a few blocks from where Louise and Coyle had lived. Al encouraged Louise to keep her job at the law firm, and they found a colored woman to babysit with Philip for seventy-five cents a day. Louise and Al were on a fishing trip to Possom Kingdom when they heard the news of Pearl Harbor, and Al whooped with joy at the prospect of boom times ahead. Indeed, as the huge Consolidated-Vultee plant west of town began to turn out

B-24s and Fort Worth was packed with soldiers and assembly-line workers, Al was selling used cars as fast as he could get his hands on them. With the help of one thousand dollars from Louise's father, they bought a house on Valentine Street, on one of the blocks of two-bedroom frame houses that were sprouting like weeds in the cow pastures around Western Heights High School. Only two blocks north of the T&P railroad tracks, it was by no means a fashionable neighborhood; most of their neighbors worked for the railroad or on the assembly line out at Consolidated, but they were decent, hardworking people, and Louise was content.

In the summer of 1942 Louise gave birth to a daughter, Alice. That fall Philip entered the first grade at the South Hi-Mount Elementary School, but his first-grade career ended abruptly when the teacher discovered he could already read and promoted him to the second grade. There, to his inexpressible delight, he was reunited with his sweetheart from sandbox days, Jenny Rhodes.

Jenny's dad, Dusty Rhodes, was coaching an army baseball team at Fort Sam Houston, and Jenny and her mother had settled down in Fort Worth for the duration. Jenny was the prettiest girl in the second grade (and in the entire world, Philip was sure) and the best student and the best athlete, too, able to run and pitch and bat as well as any boy. She was, in truth, mature beyond her years, self-confident, and a natural leader. Jenny had grown up on baseball diamonds, hearing the adoring crowds cheer her father, and she grew up believing that the cheers would last forever.

Philip was neither the athlete nor the leader that Jenny was, but they shared a love of books and movies and the popular songs of the day. In the years ahead, they swapped funny books and chased lightning bugs, they held hands in Saturday matinees and shared Cokes afterward, and one summer night, for a lark, she gave him his first kiss, a memory that would not fade. Jenny was special in his life, and a lot of other lives, for many years to come.

For Louise, the war years were a busy and not unpleasant time. She got Philip off to school in the morning, then spent her day playing with Alice, cleaning house, shopping, and trying to find time to read the new *Saturday Evening Post* and *Collier's* when they came in. One night a week she played bridge with some other women from the neighborhood, and Al had his poker club one night. On Friday and Saturday nights they usually went for beer and hamburgers to whatever tavern Al was frequenting that month. The honky-tonks were Al's natural habitat. He'd walk in as if he owned the place, with his easy grin, his Hawaiian shirt, his hat pushed back on his head, and soon he would be kidding with the waitresses, dropping quarters in the jukebox, making friends with whoever was on the next stool or at the next table. Al never met a stranger. He would circulate about the room, making friends, making deals, while Louise gave Alice her bottle and Philip would wander over to stand beside the jukebox. Philip loved the jukeboxes and soon he knew the words to Hank Snow's "I'm Moving On" and to Roy Acuff's "Great Speckled Bird" and other country classics by heart. He didn't exactly understand the songs, except that grown-ups worried a lot about love and whiskey and car wrecks, but there was an intensity to the music that captivated him. Standing there in front of the jukeboxes, letting the music wash over him, he could for a time leave behind the world of Al Henderson and honky-tonks and strangers with questions and compliments he didn't want to hear.

On weekends, if the weather was good, Al usually got in a round of golf, and sometimes Louise and Philip went with him. Al was a fair country golfer, who could break seventy-five if a good-sized bet depended on it. He made the rounds of the local municipal courses, putting together foursomes, suggesting friendly bets, blowing shots on the front nine, doubling his bets, and then usually managing enough clutch shots on the back nine to bring him home twenty or thirty dollars ahead. There was an ugly scene one Saturday afternoon, on the last green at the Rockwood course, when a man who'd lost twenty dollars to Al accused him of kicking his ball out of the rough. Louise pleaded with Al to give the man his money back, but Al, a putter in his hand, called the man a lying son of a bitch, and the man grumbled and backed down.

Philip, for his part, hated golf. He hated the heat and the flies and the endless walking and the silly way the men cheered their good shots and cursed their bad ones. Mostly, he hated golf because he associated it with Al, and he could never understand why Al had come into his life in the first place. It wasn't that his stepfather hadn't tried to be nice to him, but Philip didn't want Al to be nice to him or to teach him golf or fishing or baseball or anything else. Sometimes, as they were trailing Al around a golf course, Philip would think about his father and carry on imaginary conversations with him. He would ask his father why he had gone away and Coyle would whisper that President Roosevelt had assigned him to a secret mission in Europe, to blow up Hitler and end the war. That would make Philip feel better, for it was clear that Al was an aberration that would soon be removed from his life.

All in all, Louise thought hers was not a bad life. It was a long way from her life with Coyle, or from her girlish dreams of journalism, but it was a pleasant enough existence with a man she liked (she could not say loved; she guessed she would never love another man as she had loved Coyle) and with two wonderful children. Al annoyed her sometimes, by coming home late or by his haphazard way with money, but they rarely argued. About their only serious disagreement came when she told him about the necklace she had stored in a lockbox in the bank. Al wanted that necklace. In his imagination it would underwrite the new-car dealership he dreamed of. But Louise insisted that the necklace—her only legacy of her marriage to Coyle—was for Philip's education, and she made it stick, although sometimes Al would joke, "My princess has a buried treasure," and she knew the necklace was still very much on his mind.

One morning a few days before Christmas of 1944, Louise was listening to Don MacNeil's *Breakfast Club* when the phone rang. She answered it cheerfully, thinking it was a friend calling about bridge club, only to find that the caller was Coyle.

The sound of his voice made her dizzy. How many years had it been? She managed to stammer a hello and to ask where he was living.

"I'm down in Houston," he said. "I've opened an office there for my father. I'm home for Christmas. Louise, I was hoping I could see Philip."

Louise was close to tears. How could he make such a request, out of the blue?

"Coyle . . . he hardly knows you. It would be such a shock. I . . . I just don't know."

"It can be any way you want it," he said. "At your house. At my father's house. With you present, of course. And Louise, I've been on the wagon for ten months."

He was pleading, and she could not resist. But not at her house. And not at Hillcrest either—she'd see her son in hell first. She told Coyle to meet them at Horne's, a drugstore on Camp Bowie Boulevard, at five that afternoon.

Louise had no sooner stopped her Ford coupe in front of the drugstore than Coyle was hurrying toward them. He was wearing a brown tweed suit, a snap-brim hat, and a camel's hair overcoat. His face was fuller than she remembered, and there was more gray in his hair, but if anything he was more handsome than when she had met him.

He smiled at Louise, then stared past her at his son. "Hi there," he said. "Remember me?"

Philip stared back at his father. "Sort of."

"How about a Coke?" Coyle said, and they went into the drugstore. The conversation went haltingly at first, but then Coyle asked Philip if he liked to read. As it happened, reading was almost all Philip did like in those days. He rode the bus downtown to the public library each Saturday morning, returned the five books he'd checked out the Saturday before, and checked out five more to read that week. Given his father's encouragement, he began to talk excitedly of his favorite books, and suddenly it was six-thirty and they had to go.

Outside, a light snow was falling. Coyle shook Philip's hand, then said good-bye to Louise.

"We didn't have time to talk," she said.

"I know. You look wonderful."

"You too."

"The boy's a delight. You've done such a splendid job."

"He's a lot like you."

"God forbid."

"In nice ways."

"Louise, I'll only be here through New Year's Day. Can I call again? To see Philip, I mean?"

"Of course," she said. "Good-bye, Coyle."

"Good-bye. Thank you."

"Take care of yourself," she added and backed out onto Camp Bowie Boulevard. "Did you enjoy the visit?" Louise asked her son.

"If you hadn't told me, I would have known he was my father."

"How? Because he looks like you?"

"No," he said. "Because he *is* like me."

They drove in silence the rest of the way home. Louise began to realize that the visit had meant as much to her as to her son. Seeing Coyle, on his best behavior, had stirred up long-buried memories. Her marriage to Al was in trouble. Louise had begun to tire of Al's beloved beer joints, and when she would refuse to go with him to the taverns Al would snap, "Maybe you're too good for a country boy like me!" He had opened his own used-car lot, but it folded amid a storm of recriminations and unpaid bills. He was drinking more, staying out later, and forever bringing up her "buried treasure." She wondered if the marriage was yet another mistake. But she had to ask herself if the fault was not hers, if she was not too critical or demanding. No marriage was perfect. And there were the children to think of. It was all so painful and confusing, and seeing Coyle only made it worse, conjuring up the world of might-have-beens.

He called again on the morning of New Year's Eve and she agreed that she and Philip would meet him again, same time and same place. Louise hoped this time she and Coyle would have time to talk. She wanted to know what he'd been doing in the years since they separated. Caddy had heard a wild story about Coyle marrying a Colorado cattle heiress and then leaving her after a shootout with the ranch foreman.

When she parked in front of the drugstore, Coyle's car was already there. She took Philip inside and spotted Coyle hunched over a cup of coffee at the far end of the counter. She walked up smiling and said, "We're here."

He turned toward them, knocking over a glass of water.

Once she saw him, the bleary eyes, the twisted smile, she remembered everything.

"'appy N'Year," he mumbled.

"Oh, *Coyle!*"

Louise grabbed Philip's arm. The boy was staring wide-eyed at his father. "Come on, Philip, we've got to go."

They started down the aisle and Coyle stumbled after them. "Jus' a damn minute. Wantta see m'son."

She shoved Philip out the door and into the Ford. As she was fumbling with the key, Coyle pulled the door open, snatched the key out of the ignition, leered drunkenly, and put it in his pocket. "Y'not goin' noplace," he declared.

Louise, clutching Philip by the hand, ran back into the drugstore. Coyle stumbled after her. "Wantta see m'boy," he yelled. The store manager, a frail man with bifocals, told Coyle to leave, but Coyle pushed him aside and started down the aisle toward Louise and Philip.

"I'll call the police," the manager cried.

Coyle cornered them in the back of the store. "Don't run 'way from me. Y'know who I am? I'm Franklin Coyle Kingslea, that's who." He dropped to one knee and put his face close to Philip's. "You're too good-lookin', kid. It'll get ya in a lotta trouble, like it did your old man."

The manager was yelling into the phone. Louise grabbed Coyle's arm. "Coyle, he's calling the *police!* Do you want Philip to see them take you away?"

He glared at her with wild eyes, then plunged his hand into the pocket of his coat. She remembered the story that he'd shot someone in Wyoming, and for an instant she thought he might be reaching for a gun, but when his hand emerged he was only holding her car keys. As he held them out to her, the madness went from his face and he began to sob. "'m sorry, Louise. Sorry, kid. I love ya . . . both of ya."

He turned and brushed past the half-dozen people who were staring at them. The store manager rushed up to Louise. "The police are on the way, lady."

Louise took Philip's hand and led him outside to the car. Coyle's car was gone. She and Philip climbed into the Ford coupe. The manager and some people were standing at the front door watching her. Louise fought back tears; she didn't want Philip to see her cry. The boy sat there, huddled against the door, showing no sign of his emotions. "I'm sorry," she told him. "Your father . . . your father was sick."

"He was drunk, wasn't he?" Philip said.

"Yes," she said. "But it was because he's sick."

"Will he come to see me again?"

"Do you want him to?"

"I don't know," Philip said.

The next week a box arrived addressed to Master Philip Kingslea. It contained a set of twenty leather-bound, handsomely illustrated children's books. Philip was stunned by the gift; he hardly left his room for a month. Louise thought of trying to write Coyle, but she decided to let well enough alone.

A few weeks later Louise had lunch with Caddy and caught up on all the gossip. Pig was an army captain working on oil allocations at the Pentagon; the latest news was that he'd gotten in a fight with some Australian officers in the Mayflower bar and gotten his nose broken and was trying to parlay the injury into a Purple Heart. Eve Kingslea was still in London, working for the Red Cross, and was engaged to a handsome, titled Frenchman on de Gaulle's staff. Caddy also talked about the local scandal caused when Jim Phillips, a boy Louise had met a few times at parties, published a novel called *The Inheritors, a roman à clef* about rich young people in Fort Worth. Louise had read the novel, thought it amazingly accurate, and didn't understand what all the fuss was about.

But the most important news involved Hoyt Kingslea. He had led a B-29 squadron on more than twenty missions over Germany, but finally his plane had been shot down and he was taken prisoner. Louise thought of Hoyt, the brother-in-law she had hardly known, big, bullheaded, outgoing, opinionated, the Kingslea son who seemed destined to follow in his father's footsteps, and the thought of him imprisoned, perhaps hungry and suffering, was almost more than she could bear.

After newspaper stories of Hoyt's capture appeared, there were rumors that Wade Kingslea had offered the Germans millions of dollars for his son's freedom. According to one popular rumor, the fighting had stopped all along one bloody battlefield while a certain Texas-born general met with German generals under a flag of truce to negotiate, unsuccessfully, for Hoyt Kingslea's release.

The true end to Hoyt's story exploded on the front page of the *Star-Telegram* one morning and was more heroic and more tragic. Major Kingslea had led his men in a daring escape from a prison camp in Poland. When the Germans gave pursuit, Hoyt had taken the one rifle they had and stayed behind to delay the Germans. The other men escaped; Hoyt was killed.

Louise wept when she read the news. She had never been close to Hoyt's wife, Cissy, but now her heart went out to her as a wife and mother. She sent Cissy a handwritten note, but she never heard back from her. She guessed she'd received so many letters of condolence that she couldn't answer them all.

Philip, at the age of eight, didn't think much about the war. The war meant you couldn't buy bubble gum or tires for your bike and that the Japs and the Jerries were the villains in the funny books. The war meant that gas was rationed, although Al Henderson always managed to have a full tank. The war meant that his mother grew a victory garden and that Al raised chickens and rabbits in the back yard. Of course, everyone knew that if the Japs or the Jerries ever bombed America, Fort Worth was a prime target, because Consolidated was mass-producing the mighty B-36s, but Philip and his friends didn't worry much about being blown up. They went shoeless and shirtless in the summers and rode their bikes up and down Clover Lane and Alamo and Valentine and Lisbon streets. They joined the Cub Scouts and went exploring in the fields to the west and followed creeks under T&P railroad viaducts and sometimes on the walls of the viaducts they saw crude pictures of men and women joining their bodies in ways that seemed quite unimaginable. They watched the older boys play war in vacant lots with their niggershooters, wooden guns with clothespin triggers that fired long, knotted strips of inner tube. The more elaborate niggershooters could raise a welt at thirty feet, and it was a neighborhood legend that one had once put a boy's eye out, but no one knew for sure because he had moved away.

On Saturday mornings Philip rode the bus downtown to the public library, and there, a few months after Hoyt Kingslea's death, he had an unexpected confrontation.

The top floor of the public library was not open to the public in those days. The huge reading room stood empty, with a gallery of local pioneers gazing down from oil paintings on the walls.

Philip loved it up there. He went out of curiosity the first time, slipping past the "Closed" sign on the stairs, and after that he went back because something drew him to the stillness of those huge rooms and to the dark, brooding portraits on their walls. It was the most private place he knew.

One morning, as he wandered there, savoring the space and solitude, a tall, silver-haired man appeared out of nowhere.

"Hello, Philip," the man said.

"Hello."

"Do you know who I am?"

"Yes."

"We haven't seen each other in several years."

"I've seen your picture in the newspaper."

"That's quite a load of books you have there. You must be quite a reader."

The boy nodded. "I'm in the fourth grade," he said. "I skipped a grade."

"And do you like school?"

"Pretty much. It's boring sometimes."

"What are your favorite books?"

"*Huckleberry Finn* is my very favorite. I liked *Toby Tyler*

and *Black Beauty* too. I read a lot of books about baseball
players and cowboys and soldiers and things like that."

"You must read books about great men."

"Like who?"

The older man thought a moment. "General MacArthur,"
he said. "I would call him a great man."

"I like him," the boy said enthusiastically. "He said, 'I
shall return,' and wears sunglasses and smokes a pipe. He's
. . . sort of *mysterious,* like somebody in a book. I like him
better than Ike. All Ike does is grin all the time."

The older man smiled. "Your instincts are sound," he said.
"Tell me, did you hear about your uncle Hoyt?"

Philip nodded solemnly. "Was he a great man?"

"He was a brave man. He might have become a great
man."

The boy brushed his dark hair back from his eyes and
blurted, "Do you know where my father is?"

"In Houston, I believe. Would you like to see him?"

"Yes."

"I understand you go from here to a matinee movie at the
Bowie Theater."

"That's right. I get an allowance. Eleven cents for the
movie and a nickel for a candy bar, and ten cents for a stamp
for my savings-bond book and ten cents to ride the bus to the
library and back. That's thirty-six cents a week."

"That's a strict budget."

"Sometimes I earn extra money."

"Would you like for me to give you a ride to the movie?
That would save you a nickel. Or you could skip the movie
and come by my house for a soda pop."

Philip considered the offer carefully. "No," he said finally.
"I'd better not."

"Why not? Are you afraid of me?"

"No. But I don't think my mother would like it."

"Has she told you things about me?"

"She said you're mean and selfish."

"Do you believe that?"

"I guess so."

"Tell me, do you suppose someone can be mean and selfish
sometimes and kind and unselfish other times?"

"I guess so."

"I don't feel mean or selfish toward you, Philip. I want us
to be friends."

The boy stared back at his grandfather and did not reply. Wade Kingslea, in a strange way, was pleased. He thought the boy had shown poise in this encounter, maturity beyond his years. He was intelligent and cautious, and those were qualities the older man approved.

"Are you sure I can't give you a ride, Philip? Your mother wouldn't have to know."

Philip shook his head. "I better not."

"Is there anything I can do for you?"

For the first time, the boy showed emotion. He blinked back tears. "Tell my father I miss him," he whispered and turned and walked rapidly away.

Watching him go, Wade Kingslea felt a stab of pain, the same kind of heartache he had known when Hoyt died. This boy, his flesh and blood, was being denied him, and he hated it. He had another grandson, of course, Skipper, who was smart and strong and athletic, but this boy was different. Philip was growing up the way Kingslea himself had grown up, a half century before, watchful, an outsider, a dreamer, and Kingslea understood his pain and his loneliness and he loved him for it.

_ *Book IV* _

Philip Kingslea

Fort Worth
1952–53

CHAPTER ONE

"HEIGHTS FIGHT HEIGHTS FIGHT YEA HEIGHTS FIGHT!"

The Western Heights High School auditorium throbbed with the shouts and chants of five hundred frenzied teenagers, determined by their mighty din to inspire their team to victory.

"HEIGHTS FIGHT HEIGHTS FIGHT YEA HEIGHTS FIGHT!"

Up on the stage, the thirty-odd members of the Scorpion football team stood in a line, burly, crew-cut boys in jeans and T-shirts, their arms folded across their chests, their faces set in grim resolve.

"HEIGHTS FIGHT HEIGHTS FIGHT YEA HEIGHTS FIGHT!"

At the front of the stage, leaping and twirling, whipping the student body to ever-greater peaks of passion, were the cheerleaders, five girls and a token male. The boy and four of the girls might have saved their energy, for all eyes were fixed on the head cheerleader, Jennifer Rhodes. The incomparable Jenny Rhodes, with her olive skin, her dazzling smile, her flashing brown eyes, her lithe, lovely body, was the most admired, most lusted-for girl in the school. Jenny Rhodes, who stood now, her gorgeous face bejeweled with sweat, one hand resting on her cocked hip, her head thrown back, trying to catch her breath.

"Come on, y'all," she implored. "Let's *hear* it!"

"HEIGHTS FIGHT HEIGHTS FIGHT YEA HEIGHTS FIGHT!"

"Bullshit," muttered Philip Kingslea.

Philip was watching Jenny Rhodes from the back row of the auditorium. He had been in love with her since sandbox days, but now they were bitter antagonists. Jenny was the head cheerleader, the very embodiment of school spirit, and Philip was a rebel, a dissident, an infidel, a leader of other sullen lads who lacked school spirit. On either side of him were his two closest friends, Fearless Festus and Pancho Hernandez. Fearless was a tall, gangling boy with unruly straw-colored hair, granny glasses, and a mad gleam in his eye; he was the grandson of Uncle Billy Festus, the one-time oil-field partner of Philip's own grandfather. Pancho Hernandez was a handsome, olive-skinned youth with elaborate, glistening ducktails—Pancho was, so far as anyone could recall, the only Mexican ever to attend WHHS.

Philip and his friends were obliged to attend the pep rallies, and most often they endured them in stony silence. Today, however, they were poised to strike a blow against the empire.

"Ready?" whispered Fearless during the lull between cheers.

"Ready," Philip replied, and at his signal the boys on the back row began a cheer of their own:

> "BLOOD,
>   GUTS,
>   KICK 'EM IN THE NUTS!"

As the new cheer spread, the powers-that-be realized they were being challenged, indeed satirized. Rupert Glasscock, the school's weak-chinned, bug-eyed principal, quickly dispatched two assistant coaches, Homer (Burpin') Turpin and Claude Odum, to seek out the troublemakers. The two coaches raced to the back of the auditorium.

"You, Kingslea, Festus, Gonzales, cut out that crap!" the coaches roared.

Philip raised his hands in innocence. "Me, coach?" he said, and indeed his cheer had taken on a life of its own. The two coaches raced about, waving their arms helplessly, and it fell to Jenny Rhodes to quell the insurrection.

"HEIGHTS FIGHT HEIGHTS FIGHT," she shouted into the microphone, and soon the loyalists in the front of the auditorium were locked in a shouting match with the rebels in the rear. For a moment "HEIGHTS FIGHT" thundered against "BLOOD, GUTS, KICK 'EM IN THE NUTS!" then school spirit carried the day. The assistant coaches patrolled the aisles and the rebellion was quashed.

"Most of us have got school spirit," Jenny Rhodes raged

into the microphone. "But there's still that ten percent that doesn't care if our Scorpions win."

For an instant, across the vast auditorium, Philip and Jenny were eye to eye. He flashed her the finger and said very distinctly, "FUCK YOU!"

Students turned to jeer and shake their fists at the loathsome ten-percenters at the back of the auditorium: Philip Kingslea, a slender, dark-haired boy who stared back defiantly at his adversaries; Fearless Festus, who grinned and tipped the Mouseketeers beanie he always wore to pep rallies; Pancho Hernandez, who combed his elegant ducktails; and their dozens or so partners in crime. They were a motley crew: thin boys with acne, fat boys with thick glasses, solemn boys with slide rules on their belts, wild-eyed boys who read Melville or Mencken or *Mad* magazine, a fringe of misfits and malcontents.

"Come on," Jenny Rhodes cried, "let's show the ten-percenters what real school spirit is!"

"HEIGHTS FIGHT HEIGHTS FIGHT YEA HEIGHTS FIGHT!"

"Damn sheep," Philip muttered.

"I thought she was gonna sic the mob on us," Pancho said.

"I could plant a bomb under the stage," mused Fearless, who was given to bomb fantasies.

Up on the stage, the members of the Scorpion football squad were stepping forward to deliver short speeches. Their comments were mostly brief and ungrammatical; to be inarticulate was considered *prima facie* evidence of manliness. A mountainous linebacker called Tank Tomkins grunted, "Gunna killem!" into the microphone, and his fellow students went wild with joy.

The last of the gladiators to speak was a strikingly handsome young man, who, as he stepped forward, received the day's loudest ovation.

"Your distinguished cousin," Pancho said.

"The bastard," Philip added.

Skip Kingslea looked like a young Greek god or some Texas version thereof. He was six two, broad-shouldered, narrow-hipped, lithe, graceful, a natural athlete. Skip had high cheekbones, a long jaw, and the deepset Kingslea eyes, but he was blond and blue-eyed like his mother, Cissy Kingslea, the widow of the martyred Hoyt Kingslea. Skip did not wear a crew cut like most of the football players; rather, he let his dark-blond hair grow long and brushed it straight back, so that it gave his face a dashing, leonine look. Nor was he clad in jeans and a T-shirt, like most of the boys. Skip was given to the Eastern, Ivy League styles: he wore penny loafers, argyle socks, well-pressed khaki pants, a pale-blue button-down shirt, and a maroon cashmere sweater. Skip could afford to be different for he was a precocious athlete, a letterman in five sports; already, as a junior, he was a likely All-State quarterback, and there was talk that he would be a high school All-American in his senior year.

"We can win this game," Skip declared, and his fellow students cheered deliriously.

"We can win it despite the ten percent that's not behind us!"

More frenzy and many fists shaken toward the back row.

As Skip continued his pep talk, many of the students let their eyes move back and forth between him and Jenny Rhodes, who was beaming at him from the edge of the stage. Word of their romance had electrified the school that week. Both had recently broken up with other people, and they had attended the team picnic together the previous Sunday. It seemed, to their dazzled classmates, to be destiny, a true mating of immortals, for Skip and Jenny were mythical figures, the Best Athlete and the Most Beautiful Girl, and scores of plump girls and pimply boys lived vicariously through their trials and triumphs.

As his fellow students cheered, Skip rambled on about school spirit and how lucky they were to go to the greatest school in the greatest city in the greatest state in the greatest country in the world.

Finally, mercifully, the speeches ended, heads were bowed, and the Alma Mater was sung, with tears in many eyes:

> "Our dear school has taught us what to be
> Our dear school has shown us victory
> So where e'er we roam on land or sea
> Western Heights is home to you and me!"

"Bullshit," Philip Kingslea muttered in the back row.

"Blow the mother up," Fearless Festus whispered.

The doors to the auditorium flew open, and Philip and his friends quickly made their escape.

"You coming over?" Fearless called.

"Yeah, in a few minutes," Philip said. He turned and pushed his way through the school's crowded corridors to his locker on the second floor, where he stashed his books and grabbed his blue windbreaker. Just as he slammed his locker shut, Jenny Rhodes ran up to him, eyes blazing.

"I'm really mad at you, P.K.," she announced. She had called him P.K. as long as he could remember.

"I'm pretty hacked at you, if you want the truth," he said. "What is this ten-percenter crap? You trying to get me killed?"

"What is this 'Blood, guts, kick 'em in the nuts!' crap?" Jenny shot back.

"It's a great cheer. I wrote it. It kinda gets to the heart of things, don't you think?"

"P.K., you are going too far. Some people are really mad."

"They can like it or lump it."

"It's not just your cheer," Jenny said. "It's that column you wrote. Coach Moran blew his top. Some alumni have been calling in, asking why the school paper is criticizing the coach."

Philip grinned with pleasure. That fall, for no good reason, he had been made sports editor of the school paper, the *Scorpion*. And in his sports column that week he had committed a crime unprecedented in the history of Texas high school journalism: he had Criticized the Coach. In particular, he had noted that while the WHHS Scorpions clung to Coach Duff Moran's beloved double-wing formation and had lost three games already, the winningest teams in the state had all switched over to the T formation. "There must be a moral to this, if anyone is interested in morals," he had concluded.

"If they don't like my column, that's tough," he declared.

Jenny looked pained. "P.K., I'm telling you, the guys on the team are foaming at the mouth. For your own sake, watch out."

He looked at her angry, lovely face, and all he could think was that he loved her, he'd loved her for years, and for her to be going with his cousin Skip was like a knife in his guts.

"Yeah, I guess you're an expert on what the football team thinks, aren't you?" he snapped. "What the hell are you going with Skip for? Did you need it to be elected Homecoming Queen?"

The sudden flash of anger in her face told him that he'd struck home.

"I wouldn't mind being Homecoming Queen," she told

him. "But I happen to like Skip a lot. He's not perfect, but neither am I and neither are you. And I think it's crazy for you two to hate each other so much. Whatever happened happened a long time ago, P.K., and it didn't involve you two."

He didn't know what to say to her. How could he explain why he hated his cousin so? He could barely understand it himself. Skip was a symbol to him, of wealth, of football mania, of arrogance, of everything he hated about Texas. And for Skip to have *her* was more than he could bear.

"I've got to go," he stammered.

Quickly he was down the stairs and out the door into the bright October afternoon. He walked through the school parking lot, still half-filled with students' cars: Ford Victorias, Olds 88s, Chevy Bel Airs, a few Cadillacs. There was a saying that in the WHHS parking lot the only old cars belonged to the teachers.

As soon as he was off school property, Philip lit a Lucky. His car, a battered 1939 Plymouth, was down the street. He thought he'd go by Fearless' house for a beer, then to the Stevenson rally, then maybe on to the game that night, mainly in hopes of seeing the Scorpions get their butts stomped.

He was almost to his car when he noticed the three boys standing beside it. One was Skip Kingslea. The others were Tank Tomkins and Mickey Capps, the Scorpions' 130-pound safety man.

"What's this, a convention?" Philip asked. He remembered Jenny's warning, but there was nothing to do but bluff it through. That or run, and he wasn't running.

"We want to talk to you," Mickey said.

"I'm busy," Philip said.

"Shuduhfuckup," Tank Tomkins growled.

"Get out of my *way*," Philip said and tried to push Mickey aside, but the wiry young athlete sank his fist into the pit of Philip's stomach. He fell to his knees in the street, trying not to be sick.

"Brave bastards, aren't you?" he whispered.

"You're as big as he is," Skip said. "Get up and fight."

Blind with rage, Philip scrambled to his feet and charged Mickey, swinging his fists wildly. Mickey sidestepped and let fly a left jab that caught Philip in the mouth and sent him sprawling. He tasted blood and his head was spinning.

"Had enough, Mr. Sports Editor?" It was Skip.

"Go to hell," Philip muttered.

"We're fed up with you sniping at the coach," Skip said.

"Up yours, Skipper," Philip said. He was on his hands and knees, spitting blood. Part of him wanted to get up and take a swing at Skip, and part of him didn't want to be hit in the face again.

"You think you're hot stuff," Skip said. "You're nothing."

"I'll write what I want to write," Philip muttered.

"You better watch it," Skip said, and then he and his companions climbed into Skip's two-tone Ford Victoria and sped away.

Philip got up and leaned against his car. His lip was starting to swell. A half block away, back on the school parking lot, he saw Coach Turpin watching him. Philip spit blood on the ground and got into his Plymouth and headed for Fearless' house on River Crest Drive. Tears burned his eyes. He felt humiliated, violated. It had been like this as long as he could remember. In the fourth grade the biggest boys in the class— Tank Tomkins had been the ringleader—had set out to give all the other boys the Royal Flush. Some of the boys took it as a joke, an honor even, but Philip resisted. He stayed out of the rest room for a week, but one day he had to go, and he slipped into the rest room, hoping no one would notice. Suddenly Tank and some other boys were lifting him into the air, holding his head down in one of the toilets, flushing it over and over, laughing as he screamed and sputtered, half-afraid he would drown. Finally they raced away and left him wet and sobbing on the cold tile floor.

He was different from them and they couldn't stand that.

He pulled into Fearless' driveway and stopped behind the Batmobile, an old Fleetwood that Fearless had customized. It had a police radio and a small refrigerator and a device that shot cherry bombs at other cars. Once Fearless had installed seat belts and rigged the front seat so it would flop back at the punch of a button and any unsuspecting passenger would be held captive flat on her back. The Love Seat, Fearless dubbed it. Unfortunately, the first girl he tried the Love Seat on was an utterly humorless debutante who yelled rape so loud that Fearless was shipped off to a military school. But he came back. Fearless always came back. He was like one of those criminals who boasts that no jail can hold him. Fearless' parents had been exiling him to military schools since he was ten, but few would take him now, because the schools that Fearless attended were invariably struck by mysterious fires.

Philip sat in his car for a minute, smoking a cigarette, groping for a plan to avenge himself on Skip Kingslea. Finally he went to look for his friends. Fearless had an apartment behind his parents' house; that way he and his parents could go weeks without speaking. Philip found Fearless and Pancho drinking beer and listening to Fearless' new tapes of his parents' telephone conversations. Both his parents had lovers and Fearless was taping them with an eye to future blackmail.

"What happened to your lip?" Pancho asked. "You better put some ice on that."

"The jocks didn't like my column," Philip said. "They sent a delegation to protest. Skipper and Tank and Mickey."

Fearless brought him a beer and some ice cubes for his lip. "Let's blow up their cars," he said.

A few years earlier some rival Fort Worth gamblers had settled a territorial dispute by a rash of car bombings, and those blasts had captured the imagination of the young Fearless Festus.

"Bombing cars isn't the answer," Pancho said. "They'd put your ass in prison."

"They'd have to prove it first," Fearless declared. When he got that wild gleam in his eyes it was hard to tell exactly how serious he was. There was a portrait of his grandfather, the legendary Uncle Billy Festus, on the wall, and Philip thought they looked a lot alike. Probably Uncle Billy had been crazy, too, except his madness had been focused on finding oil.

"Let's give 'em what they gave you," Pancho said. "I could handle Mickey and Skip. Oh, would I like to pop that blue-eyed gringo Skip. Tank I'd use a tire tool on, but I could manage."

Philip knew Pancho was dead serious. Pancho had arrived in Fort Worth two years earlier when his father, a Mexican biologist, had come to TCU for a research project. His father had rented a house in Western Heights, not realizing that Mexicans did not rent houses in Western Heights and Mexican teenagers did not attend Western Heights High School. The principal, Rupert Glasscock, made a personal call on Dr. Hernandez to suggest that his son would be happier at Technical High, where Mexican boys traditionally went to learn a trade. Dr. Hernandez insisted that his son would attend WHHS, which was nearer their home. His first day at WHHS Pancho was beaten up. His second day too. On his third day he arrived with his hands taped and a roll of dimes in each fist, and he took on all comers until people left him alone.

"Fighting them isn't the answer," Philip said. "There's too many of them. The whole damn football team." He began to pace about the room. "Maybe I could write something. Maybe a column about how they beat me up."

"Could you get that published?" Pancho asked.

"I don't know," Philip admitted. "I'd have to talk to Mrs. Ritter."

"Mrs. Ritter?" Fearless said. "Is she the journalism teacher with the big boobs?" He cupped his hands before him to suggest the enormity of Mrs. Ritter's chest.

"She's okay," Philip said impatiently. "Listen, Pancho, there's something else I'm thinking about. Skip is running for student-body president and . . . I guess I was thinking maybe we could run somebody against him."

"How're you gonna beat the All-American boy?" Pancho demanded. "He's rich, he's handsome, he's captain of the football team, and he's balling Jenny Rhodes."

"You don't *know* that," Philip protested.

"Come on, man, face reality."

Philip didn't argue the point. "The thing is, he's an arrogant bastard, and I say we can beat him."

Pancho was not convinced. "Look, the school is filled with sheep. Skip's a big jock and he drives a Cadillac, so they think he's God."

"We can beat him," Philip insisted.

"So who's your candidate?" Pancho demanded.

"I was thinking about Fearless."

"Me?" Fearless cried. "Never!"

"The thing is," Philip said, "with Fearless, you sort of make a joke of it. I mean, your average guy isn't a football hero and a millionaire, so why should he vote for a guy who is? Your average guy is a scrawny nincompoop, just like Fearless . . ."

"I am not a nincompoop," Fearless protested. "I'm a genius."

"It might work," Pancho conceded.

"This is insane," Fearless cried.

"Festus is bestus!" Philip shouted. "How's that for a slogan?"

"Not bad," Pancho said.

"I will not run!" Fearless said.

"You're being drafted, Fearless," Philip told him. "Like

Ike. The people need you."

"No," Fearless yelled. "A thousand times no!"

"Democracy in action," Pancho mused.

They finished their beers, and Pancho left to meet his girl friend. Fearless decided to tinker with the Batmobile. Philip drove over to the Will Rogers Coliseum. Adlai Stevenson, the Democratic candidate for president, was to speak there at six. Philip was going to the rally partly in hopes of getting an item for a current events column he was writing for the *Scorpion*. But there was another, more elusive reason that Philip was going to hear Adlai Stevenson that October evening. All his life he had known nothing but Texas. All his life teachers and preachers and newspapers and politicians had told him how lucky he was to live in the biggest state, the state with the most oil and the prettiest women and the best football teams, the state that had produced Neiman-Marcus and H.L. Hunt and Doak Walker and Sam Rayburn and the Alamo and the Texas Rangers and J. Frank Dobie and countless other wonders. And it seemed to Philip that almost all his class-mates agreed and were profoundly grateful to have been born and bred in this best of all possible states.

Philip did not agree.

He was sick of Texas. He thought Texas was a vast prison from which someday he would escape. Until then he was part of an underground, with others like Fearless and Pancho, who shared his heresies, who scorned the local gods. He was grop-ing for an alternative he could not define, an Other that was not Texas or Texan. In the past year or two he had begun to glimpse that Other, like a radio operator picking up faint sig-nals from a distant transmitter. He had begun to find it in books by writers like Sinclair Lewis and H.L. Mencken, whose views were decidedly non-Texan. He sensed an Other in the Negro music he and his friends listened to, outlaw music by the Clovers, Joe Turner, Ruth Brown, and Lloyd Price, songs that hinted at pleasures unknown in the prim and proper jingles of the Hit Parade. He sensed an Other in the local bars he and his friends were starting to frequent, bars that harked back to the Hell's Half Acre of an earlier Fort Worth, bars where a young buckaroo with a fake ID could guz-zle his Lone Star and laugh at the official pieties of the God-fearing, Bible-thumping, flag-waving Texas establishment.

Philip didn't know much about politics, but he sensed that there, too, there must be an Other, and it was that belief which drew him to the Stevenson rally. All he really knew about Stevenson was that his grandfather and all the oilmen were bitterly opposed to him, over the tidelands-oil issue, and that the *Star-Telegram* and other Texas papers were attacking him mercilessly. That was enough to convince Philip that Stevenson must be worth listening to.

The local Democrats—the few who were supporting the national ticket that year—had erected a rickety platform on the grass in front of the statue of Will Rogers. It had a red-white-and-blue TEXANS FOR STEVENSON banner hanging above it, and there were a few hundred blue-collar workers, college students, and curiosity seekers scattered around. Over at the side a five-man brass band in tan cowboy suits and red string ties was warming up.

A three-car motorcade arrived and the band began to play "Happy Days Are Here Again" and Stevenson got out and waved and mounted the platform.

Philip scanned the crowd and noticed a black Fleetwood parked across West Lancaster. Its driver was Harley Prendergast, the director of security for Kingslea Oil, chomping on a cigar and gazing impassively at the speechmaking. As Philip watched, two men in green windbreakers got out of a Pontiac parked behind the Fleetwood and spoke to Harley. Then they ran across the street toward the rally. Both men were carrying paper sacks, as if they'd brought their dinners. Then, as the men slipped into the crowd, Philip's attention was drawn back to the speaker's stand.

"What about our schoolkids?" a man was yelling.

"My friend," Stevenson said, "the tidelands oil can benefit all the schoolchildren of America."

"Like hell—it's ours!"

"Don't be misled by the oil companies' rhetoric," Stevenson declared, and then the first egg whizzed past his head. "My good friends," he said, but then he had to duck two more eggs.

"Go home, you queer," someone yelled. The band struck up "Happy Days Are Here Again," and some men hustled Stevenson to safety. Philip saw the two men in green windbreakers running back toward their Pontiac. He raced after them but they jumped in the car and sped away. Harley Prendergast was already gone.

Philip saw a man with a notebook and ran over to him. "Are you a reporter for the *Star-Telegram?*"

" 'Fraid so," the man said. He smelled of beer.

"I know who threw the eggs," Philip declared. "Two guys in green windbreakers. They were in a white Pontiac."

"You get the license number?"

Philip's mouth fell open. He hadn't even thought of that. "No. But listen, just before they threw the eggs, they talked to Harley Prendergast. He works for Kingslea Oil."

"So?"

"So Wade Kingslea is giving big money to Eisenhower, and now he's got his goons out throwing eggs at Stevenson."

The reporter put his notebook away. "An interesting theory."

"Aren't you going to print it?"

The older man lit a Camel with a Zippo lighter. "Print what? You can't prove anything. And if you could, my paper wouldn't print it, us being Democrats for Ike this year. Listen, kid, Stevenson was lucky they threw eggs and not bricks."

Philip and Fearless and Pancho went to the game that night. The rest of the student body was standing down by the forty-yard line, yelling their heads off, but Philip and his friends sat high up in Farrington Field stadium, with a blanket wrapped around their shoulders, drinking a bottle of twenty-year-old Napoleon brandy that Fearless had stolen from his father. Down on the field, the Scorpions were trouncing the North Side Steers. Philip and his friends yelled, "Blood, guts, kick 'em in the nuts!" a few times, but nobody paid any attention.

When the game was over, they stayed in the stands awhile, finishing the brandy and letting the crowd thin out. If past experience was any guide, some North Side guys would be roaming around outside the stadium looking for Western Heights guys to beat up. They talked about what they'd do that night. Fearless was going to drive Pancho out to the Wagon Wheel, a club on the Jacksboro Highway where Pancho played saxophone sometimes. Philip had to work the next morning, so he said good-night to his friends and drove on home.

They still lived in the house on Valentine Street. Al, his stepfather, was asleep in his chair in the living room when Philip went in. He was in his shorts and a T-shirt and there were a couple of cans of Pearl on the table beside him. Philip walked on past him into the dining room, where his mother was sitting at the table reading a book. Louise was still a beautiful woman, but time had etched lines around her mouth, and there was a mist of sadness in her sky-blue eyes. She looked up and smiled.

"How was the game?"

He shrugged. "The good guys won. Skip was a hero."

His mother peered at his face. "What happened to your lip?"

"I had an accident," he said. "What're you reading?"

Louise held up a library copy of Edna Ferber's *Giant*.

"How is it?" he asked.

Louise laughed mirthlessly. "Well, she finds the Texas rich to be more lovable than I ever did, but perhaps my experience wasn't typical."

Philip winced. He hated it when she was bitter, because there was nothing he could do to help her.

"There's something I want to ask you about," she said.

"What?"

"I'm thinking about getting a job. But I'd need some help from you. If I was working, I'd worry about Alice getting home from school with nobody here."

"What kind of a job?" He didn't like the idea of her working. He didn't know why, except that somehow women weren't supposed to work.

"I don't know," she said. "I guess I'd brush up on my typing. I feel like I have to do something. We've got your college coming up."

"That's no problem," he said. "I can work, and we've got the necklace."

The famous necklace, so central to their family mythology, the diamond and ruby necklace that Livie Kingslea had given Louise and that Louise had kept, safe in her lockbox, for more than a decade.

They were counting on the necklace all the more so because when Louise's parents had died the previous year, nothing was left of the modest fortune that John Everett had built up in the first third of the century. He had invested heavily in real estate in the 1920s and seen his holdings wiped out in the 1930s. Much of what was left was spent on the doctors and nurses who tended his wife in her long final illness.

"I know we have the necklace," Louise said. "But we don't

know yet how much it's worth, or how much college will cost, or whether Al will be working, and . . . and I'd just *feel* better if I had a job."

Philip stared at her, confused. He had worked at one job or another since he was ten, but he didn't want her working. And yet she was right. She couldn't count on Al.

"Sure, I'll help any way I can," he said.

He kissed her good-night and went to bed, and Louise stayed at the dining room table reading *Giant*.

CHAPTER TWO

Philip worked Saturdays and Sundays at Mrs. Baird's Bakery, loading trucks and making "hotshot" deliveries to stores and restaurants around the city. He was paid $1.25 an hour, about $20 a weekend, enough to keep him in gasoline, beer, and cigarettes. That weekend, as he loaded the bread trucks, he was still kicking around his plan to run Fearless against Skip for student-body president. More urgently, he was trying to decide what to do about Harley Prendergast and the two thugs who'd thrown eggs at Adlai Stevenson. By the time he got to school on Monday morning he'd made up his mind.

Journalism was his first-period class. He nodded to Mrs. Ritter, his plump young teacher, and went straight to his type-writer. It took him only a few minutes to bang out a new item for his "In the News" column:

When Democrat Adlai Stevenson spoke in Fort Worth last week he was pelted with eggs and forced to beat a hasty retreat. This reporter saw the two egg-throwers emerge from a white Pontiac, toss their missiles, and escape while police looked the other way. Who were the culprits? Disgruntled Democrats? Rowdy Republicans? Here's a clue. Soon before they tossed their eggs, the pair conferred with Harley Prendergast, the brawny chief of security for Kingslea Oil. Prendergast's boss, of course, is oil tycoon Wade Kingslea, one of the biggest financial backers of Republican candidate Dwight D. Eisenhower. A question for today: Did Wade Kingslea decide that giving Petrobucks to Ike wasn't enough, and he'd contribute a few eggs to the nation's most celebrated Egghead as well?

He read over the column, penciled in a few changes, and dropped it on Mrs. Ritter's desk.

"My column," he announced.

She looked up at him and smiled. Clara Ritter was a round-faced young woman who wore her thick brown hair trimmer short and had a sunny smile. Philip thought she would really be pretty if she would lose some weight. She was from Tennessee—she said that Tex Ritter was her husband's cousin—and she spoke with that state's soft twang.

"What's it about?" she asked.

Philip shrugged. "The Stevenson rally Friday," he said. He was hoping she'd be so busy she wouldn't read the column. He had an idea it might cause trouble and he figured Mrs. Ritter would be better off if she wasn't involved.

"Are you still for Stevenson?" she asked.

"Madly for Adlai," he said.

"Because of the tidelands issue?" she asked.

Philip laughed. "No, because everyone else is against him."

He went back to his typewriter and tried to concoct a sports column that would amuse him without outraging the rest of the school. The whole thing of him being sports editor was crazy. He should have been editor of the paper. He was their best writer; the year before he'd won a first prize in a state-wide contest with a feature on one of the WHHS janitors. But Mr. Glasscock had intervened to make sure that a rich girl named Ellen Campbell got to be editor. It was like that a lot at their school. Glasscock and the teachers sucked up to the rich kids, the ones whose parents were big shots. So Philip got to be sports editor as his consolation prize. The trouble was that the *Scorpion*'s sports editors had always been journalistic cheerleaders, and he didn't see his job that way.

His English class got into a discussion of the novel *Giant* that afternoon. Just about everybody hated the book.

"I didn't *read* it," declared a cattle heiress named Minnie Keene, "but my mama says it's an *outrage!*"

"It's supposed to be about the King Ranch," someone added.

"And Glen McCarthy."

"Why don't they sue?"

"What does some *Yankee* know about *Texas?*"

The teacher, Miss Abbott, a three-hundred-pound spinster, glanced at Philip. He liked her well enough. She was always telling him that if he'd only make an effort he could make A's in English. But that was the thing she couldn't understand, that he wasn't going to make an effort. It wasn't anything personal, it was just the way he felt about school.

"You, Philip, have you read it?"

"Read what, Miss Abbott?"

"Read *Giant,* you impudent pup!"

"Oh, *Giant.* Yeah, I read it."

"And what did you think of it?"

"I thought it was hilarious."

His reply set off an angry reaction from his classmates.

". . . funny . . . ?"

". . . an outrage!"

". . . must hate Texas . . ."

"Quiet!" Miss Abbott roared. "Philip, defend your position. Why did you like this book?"

"I liked it because I thought it was true." He enjoyed this. Books were his turf. He would debate books with these idiots all day. "It glamorized the Benedicts, the ranching family, but it showed a lot of other rich Texans as dumb, tasteless clods, and . . ."

"Stop him!" cried Minnie, the cattle heiress. "He's insulting Texas!" She was a gorgeous, empty-headed girl with red hair that glowed like a prairie sunset.

"Your problem, Minnie, is that you think everybody in Texas is rich," Philip said.

"Your problem," she shot back, "is you're some kind of a . . . *Communist!*"

"Because I read books, you jerk?" he snapped, and suddenly half the room was shouting.

"Quiet!" Miss Abbott roared, as a young woman entered the classroom and handed the teacher a note.

"Philip, you're wanted in Mr. Glasscock's office," Miss Abbott announced.

Philip gathered up his books. *"Communist!"* Minnie hissed after him.

Clara Ritter was sitting on the bench outside Mr. Glasscock's office.

"What's going on?" he asked her.

"I don't know," she said.

"Probably we've won a prize or something," Philip said. After a few minutes Mr. Glasscock's secretary escorted them into the great man's office.

Rupert Glasscock's family owned Fort Worth's leading funeral home. Back in the 1880s his grandfather, a hard-drinking carpenter, had realized that at the rate cowboys and gamblers were killing each other in Hell's Half Acre there was money to be made in the casket business. From there it was a short step to opening the city's first funeral home. Rupert Glasscock was the first of his family not to follow the mortician's trade; he had chosen to bury the brains of the young rather than the bones of the old, as Philip had once put it.

Mr. Glasscock rose as they entered his office, which was lined with photographs of the principal with such notables as Amon Carter, Ben Hogan, and Wade Kingslea. He was a pale, obsequious man, of middle years, with wavy brown hair that looked suspiciously like a wig.

"Please sit down, both of you," the principal said in funereal tones. "I want to talk about the *Scorpion.*" He lit his pipe, and sweet-smelling smoke began to fill the small office. Philip considered coughing but decided not to press his luck.

"I was a journalist myself, in my college days," Mr. Glasscock continued, puffing contentedly. "Chief editorial writer for the Abilene Christian *Messenger.* A challenging experience. I remember the controversy over mixed bathing, my junior year..."

He rambled on about the glories of journalism and listed the various WHHS graduates who'd advanced to the University of Texas or TCU papers, or even to the *Star-Telegram,* which he clearly viewed as the pinnacle of American journalism. "We take great pride in their achievements," he declared. "And, Philip, you have the potential to join their ranks. You have a definite way with words, a real gift."

He smiled his tight-lipped mortician's smile. There was an awkward pause.

"He certainly does have a talent," Mrs. Ritter said.

"Well, thank you," Philip said warily. Was it possible that

old shit-for-brains had some taste after all?

Suddenly Mr. Glasscock reached into a drawer, yanked out a copy of the *Scorpion,* and slapped it down on his desk. "But you have abused your talent, Philip," he declared. "And you have caused very serious problems for us all!"

Mrs. Ritter gasped. Philip leaned forward to see the paper. It was folded open to one of his sports columns, and the column was circled in red.

"I was *astounded* by this column," the principal declared. His eyes seemed to pop from his head. "As were several of our alumni who have contacted me about it. This column is nothing less than an attack on the professional abilities of a highly successful football coach, Duff Moran, and by a young man who, to my knowledge, has never stepped onto a grid-iron."

"The column is true," Philip shot back. "I never mentioned Coach Moran's name."

"Oh, you were very clever, I grant you that," the principal replied. "You insinuate that if Coach Moran would simply use the formation of *your* preference, we would win all our games."

Clara Ritter spoke for the first time. "Mr. Glasscock," she said. "I think Philip was only stating his opinion, as we en-courage all our columnists to do."

"Opinion!" the principal cried. "His *opinion* was a blatant insult to a man who was coaching before he was born!"

"Well," Mrs. Ritter said in her soft Tennessee drawl, "we do teach the students to believe in freedom of the press."

Philip stared at the young teacher's profile. Her chin was raised high, her lips trembled a bit, and for all her plumpness she suddenly seemed quite beautiful.

"Don't talk to me about freedom of the press!" Mr. Glasscock roared. "The *Scorpion* is a school publication, in-tended to support our school and our team!"

"Leave her alone," Philip snapped. "I can't believe you're so shook up about one item in a sports column."

"I am not 'shook up,'" Mr. Glasscock replied. "I am out-raged. And it's not just 'one item.' We also have *this.*"

He dug into his drawer again and brought forth the "In the News" column Philip had written that morning.

"You must be very pleased with yourself, Philip," the prin-cipal said with frigid irony. "Having accused Coach Moran of incompetence, you now accuse one of Fort Worth's most distinguished citizens of a conspiracy to disrupt a political rally."

"That column's true," Philip declared. "Harley Prendergast *was* there, and he *did* talk to the men who threw the eggs, and he *does* work for Wade Kingslea, and Kingslea *did* give a lot of money to Eisenhower."

"All of which does not prove—as you insinuate—that Mr. Kingslea had the slightest connection with this incident."

"He was behind it," Philip said. "I can't prove it, but I know it. Let people make up their own minds."

"Philip, it is no secret that you are estranged from the Kingslea family," the principal said. "That is no concern of mine. But it *is* my concern when you try to use the school paper to carry on a personal vendetta."

"Your concern is that Wade Kingslea owns half this town and you want to bow and scrape for him like everybody else."

Mr. Glasscock shot to his feet. "Young man, you're very close to suspension!"

Philip was on his feet too. "You can't suspend me for what I write."

"I can when what you write is malicious and libelous and detrimental to the school system. I've already spoken to the school board attorney."

"Do it!" Philip said. "Suspend me. It'll make a great story for the *Star-Telegram*."

He thought he had the principal there. Mr. Glasscock didn't want a scandal; that might hurt his chances of being superintendent of schools.

"Sit down, Philip," the principal said gently and sank into his own chair. Philip remained standing until Mrs. Ritter touched his arm.

"It isn't my wish to suspend you. Only to stop this abuse of the student newspaper. Henceforth, Mrs. Ritter, all of Philip's copy is to be read and approved by me prior to publication."

"I'll quit the paper," Philip said.

"That would be foolish," the principal said. "You must learn to accept authority in this world, Philip."

"Only the authority I want to accept."

"It doesn't work that way, young man. You must decide. Either I approve your articles, or they are not published."

Philip sat on the edge of the chair. Every atom of his being wanted to tell Rupert Glasscock exactly where to go and what to do. And yet he hesitated. He hesitated because up until this instant, this scene had been like a play, like a story he was reading. He had viewed it from a distance, detached from it, enjoying it. Now they had reached a moment of truth. If he pushed this fool too far, no doubt he would be suspended. And what would that mean? That he would not graduate in June? That he wouldn't get into college the next fall? He didn't know. He only knew that these bastards had power over his life and he hated it.

"I'll think about it," he said.

"Fine, Philip, you do that," the principal said. "And in the meantime, Mrs. Ritter, I will hold you responsible."

"I understand," she whispered.

"Good," the principal said. "And now that we understand one another, you are excused."

Philip and Mrs. Ritter walked back to the journalism classroom in silence. When they entered the empty room, she turned to the wall and began to sob.

"Damn him," she whispered.

Philip stared at her in confusion. "Hey, it's okay, Mrs. Ritter."

"No, it's *not*," she said. "You have as much right to print your opinions as . . . as Amon Carter or . . . Or Arthur Krock or *anybody*."

"Well, I probably went too far."

"No," she said. "I should have said more. It was just that . . . that I can't afford to get fired from this job."

She started crying again, leaning against the blackboard, her shoulders shaking. It made Philip feel terrible. He hadn't minded the scene with Mr. Glasscock; he thought it had worked out pretty well, all things considered. But he hated to see Mrs. Ritter cry after the way she'd stuck up for him. It reminded him of a time he'd seen his mother cry, when Al had lost his job and they didn't have any money or anything to eat in the house. He didn't know much about Mrs. Ritter. He'd heard that her husband was in Korea. Without really thinking it through, he put his hand on her arm.

"Hey, don't cry," he said. "It's okay."

She turned, without ever looking up, and suddenly she was in his arms. It just happened. He could feel her tears, warm and wet against his shirt, and her thick brown hair, smelling good, fresh and sweet, like pine needles, tickling his nose. He could feel her breasts, too, warm and heavy against his chest, and as she wept they rubbed against him in a way that felt wonderful. He felt more confused than ever. He wanted her to stop crying but he didn't want her to leave his embrace. He held her very gently, his hands meeting in the small of her back, fearful of doing something wrong.

"Hey, no sweat," he whispered. "Glasscock's an idiot. Everybody knows that. Don't let him scare you."

"I just *can't* lose this job."

When she spoke her breath was warm and moist against his neck. He felt weak inside.

"You're a sweet boy, Philip," she said. "You . . ."

The door flew open and a girl walked in. Philip jumped back. Mrs. Ritter flushed and began examining papers on her desk. Philip wished he could strangle the girl.

As it happened, the girl hadn't notice their embrace. "I can't find my history book," she mumbled, and after poking around for a moment she left.

Philip and Clara stood staring at one another. He had no idea what to say. Her eyes were red from crying, but she had the hint of a smile on her round, pretty face. The bell rang, announcing the end of school, and somehow it spurred Philip into action.

"I'll see you later," he said. "Thanks for . . . for sticking up for me."

He gave her a nervous grin and started for the door.

"Thank *you*, Philip," she said, but he was out the door, out of the building, crossing the parking lot toward his Plymouth, lighting a Lucky, trying to sort out the mad jumble of his thoughts. He wasn't thinking about Rupert Glasscock and all that crap. Who gave a damn about Rupert Glasscock? He was thinking, rather, about Clara Ritter and how soft and warm her breasts had been against his chest and how her eyes had sparkled through her tears and about her gentle, enigmatic "Thank *you*, Philip," when they parted.

It was crazy, of course, but he was thinking that somehow he would hold her in his arms again.

CHAPTER THREE

Richard Nixon, whom the Republican Party in its wisdom had nominated to be vice president of the United States, stood smiling on Wade Kingslea's well-manicured lawn, surrounded by a sea of Cadillacs.

The Cadillacs came gliding down Kingslea's private roadway, a sparkling flotilla of jet back, royal blue, sunset pink, burnished gold. There were Cadillacs, of jade, lavender, emerald, canary yellow, creamy white, desert tan, a great glimmering body-by-Fisher cornucopia of Cadillacs—sleek Coupe de Villes, fishtailed Fleetwoods, Cadillacs with police radios, with silver Longhorns and gold oil derricks as hood ornaments. Cadillacs monogrammed with their owner's initials, Cadillacs with wet bars inside, with one-way glass windows, with suede and mohair and calfskin and mink interiors. Scores of these mighty chariots overflowed Wade Kingslea's private drive and spilled over onto the thick Bermuda grass of his lawn. Their owners leaped out, clutching checkbooks, waving ten-gallon hats, letting fly rebel yells, vying for the attention of the young California politician with the sly smile, the five o'clock shadow, the ski-jump nose.

"Hey, Senator, how much you need?"

"Is ten thousand enough?"

"Hell, Wilber, I'd pay ten thousand to watch flies fuck—make it twenty!"

"Hey, Dick, you tell old Ike that Clyde McNabb said howdy—you hear?"

"You better do right on that offshore oil, Senator!"

"Wa-hoo, we gonna beat them Commie sonsabitches!"

Richard Nixon stood in the center of the circle of shouting, jostling oilmen. His darted this way and that, and he was sweating despite the chill of the late October evening.

Wade Kingslea, the host of this Democrats-for-Eisenhower fundraiser, stood off to the side, smiling benignly. Someone unfamiliar with American politics might have thought that the elegant, imposing Wade Kingslea was a candidate for president or vice president and that Richard Nixon was his valet or chauffeur. But that was not the case, nor would Kingslea have wished it so. He bet on politicians the way he bet on racehorses. Sometimes he bought politicians, when he could find one who was likely to stay bought. But he'd never wanted to be one, because politicians were not free men.

Wade Kingslea glanced at his watch and then said, "Gentlemen, if you'll kindly settle down, Senator Nixon will say a few words before he has to catch his plane."

A hundred feet away, flat on his belly behind some bushes where the golf course met Wade Kingslea's property, Philip peered out intently at the oilmen and the ski-jumped-nosed politician. He had crept as close as he dared, close enough to see and hear, and he had a pencil and notebook clutched in his hands.

As soon as he had heard gossip at school of this private reception, he had known he would be an uninvited guest. Perhaps he could get a story out of it, for the school paper. Perhaps his grandfather would make some jest or boast that would incriminate him in the egg-throwing incident—to make *that* stick would be sweet revenge.

But he was there for other reasons too.

He had been there before, lurking in the bushes, spying on his grandfather's world. Part of him hated his grandfather, yet part of him, in his most private mythology, saw this mansion as the palace of a great king and himself as a royal prince, cheated of his birthright. He had been only twelve when he had started coming here on summer nights, to sit in the darkness and stare at his grandfather's palace with its music and laughter, its glittering fountains and sparkling princesses; sometimes he dreamed of stepping forward to claim all that should be his, and sometimes he dreamed of burning it all to the ground.

Who was he? Was he Wade Kingslea's grandson? Or Coyle Kingslea's son? Or Al Henderson's stepson? Or all of these? Or none? Or could he, somehow, someday, be only himself? All his life, as far back as he could remember, he had heard the gossip, the whispers. He was a Kingslea and not a Kingslea. It hadn't mattered in grade school, but when he'd entered high school, with the rich kids, with his cousin Skip, he'd heard more of it. He was a distant cousin. He was some sort of usurper, a fraud. He had once been told to his face by a scornful classmate that he was an illegitimate son, a bastard Kingslea. And he had not answered back, even then. Instead he turned inward, to his own world, to an isolation where nothing hurt him.

Who was he? That was the question that gnawed at him. He might hate his grandfather, but all that mattered was finding out who he was, what he could be, and his grandfather, somehow, was central to that quest, that mystery.

Down in front of the mansion, Richard Nixon was telling the oilmen that Texas was like a second home to him, that Texans loved freedom as much as he did, and Philip was scribbling it down when suddenly someone flipped him over on his back. He looked up and saw a man kneeling above him and another man standing over him with a gun.

"What the hell?" Philip said.

"Shut up," the kneeling man said and slipped Philip's billfold from his pocket. "What're you doing here?"

"Who wants to know?"

"We're Secret Service. What're you doing here?"

"I write for my school paper. I wanted a story."

One of the agents studied Philip's driver's license. "You related to Mr. Kingslea?" he said.

"His grandson."

The agent put his gun away, looking disappointed. "I'll check it out," he said and trotted off toward the mansion. The other agent stood up. "You could get killed with a stunt like this."

Philip sat up and the agent gave him back his billfold. Down by the house Nixon was pounding his fist into his palm and yelling about Communists in government. The other agent returned with Harley Prendergast beside him.

"You know him?" he asked Prendergast.

Harley spit on the ground. He was wearing a ten-gallon hat and a camel's hair overcoat. "I know him," he said. "He's got no business here."

"Listen, if you guys are Secret Service, ask this character who threw the eggs at Adlai Stevenson," Philip said, but the agents laughed and walked back toward the mansion.

"You stay put," Prendergast said. Philip shrugged and sat against a tree. It was a cloudy evening; the sunset was a pink smear across the western sky. Nixon finished his speech and the oilmen sang out their rebel yells. Nixon, waving both arms, stepped into a limousine and was gone. As dusk settled over the lawn, the oilmen climbed into their Cadillacs and began to glide away.

"Let's go," Prendergast said. Philip got up and followed him toward the house. He no longer wanted to escape. This could be his story; whatever happened was his story.

They entered the mansion, crossed the marble foyer, and stepped into a big, dimly lit room. It was lined with books, ceiling to floor; a fire crackled in the fireplace, and a lion's head glared from above the mantel. Philip felt giddy; he remembered the room, the lion's head, from a dozen years before, a Christmas when he and his father had played on the floor with his new electric train.

"Hello, Philip."

He fought back to the present and for the first time noticed his grandfather in a high-backed chair before the fire.

"That'll be all, Harley," Wade Kingslea said, and the big man disappeared.

"Sit down, Philip," his grandfather said. "I was just having a drink." Kingslea had taken off his coat and loosened his tie. There was an ice bucket and a bottle of Glenlivet Scotch on the table beside his chair.

"Can I leave?" Philip asked. "Or am I under arrest?"

"Of course you can leave. But that would be foolish, wouldn't it? We have a lot of catching up to do. Have a sandwich. Have something to drink."

Philip sat down in a chair opposite his grandfather. "I wouldn't mind a beer," he said.

Kingslea raised his eyebrows in mild disapproval, but he called out in Spanish and a slender Mexican girl in a pale blue dress soon appeared with a ham sandwich and a cold bottle of Carta Blanca. Philip took a long swallow.

"Go easy on that stuff," his grandfather said. "It caused your father a lot of grief."

"I'm not my father."

"True," the older man said. "And how is your mother?"

"She's fine."

"She was a sweet and beautiful girl but far too young to deal with Coyle's problems. Tell me, do you see your father?"

"I see him," Philip said tersely.

Kingslea frowned and sipped his drink. "Well, tell me

about yourself," he said. "I understand you write for the school paper."

"That's right."

Kingslea laughed. "I also understand you wanted to blame me because someone threw eggs at Adlai Stevenson."

"You were behind it, weren't you?"

"Why would I do a damn fool thing like that? Stevenson hasn't got a prayer of carrying Texas."

"He was a good governor and he'd be a good president," Philip declared.

"What was so good about him?" his grandfather demanded. "Give me an example."

Philip hesitated. In truth, he didn't know much about Stevenson. "He . . . he's for civil rights," he said. "He's helped the Negroes."

"Helped them with pretty words," Kingslea said scornfully. "I've given the Negro race more real help than Stevenson ever has."

"You? How? I read an interview in the *Star-Telegram* where you supported segregation."

"I oppose race-mixing, certainly," Kingslea said. "Separate education is best for both races."

"It's supposed to be separate but *equal,*" Philip said.

"True. And to that end I donated ten thousand dollars last month to the United Negro College Fund of Texas."

"To continue segregation," Philip snapped.

"The Negro college president who came to my office was glad enough to accept my check. Would you say he was mistaken?"

Philip hesitated. He didn't know much about the civil-rights issue. He'd read about it in *The New Republic,* a magazine he'd discovered that held views on Negroes that were very different from those he'd read in the *Star-Telegram* all his life. He'd never known any Negroes. They were just people who sat on the back of the buses and worked for rich people as maids and yardmen. They lived out in Lake Como, and sometimes white kids drove through there and threw cherry bombs at them.

"I don't guess anybody's ever mistaken to take ten thousand dollars," he said to his grandfather. "You said you had the college president to your office. Would you have had him in your home?"

"No, I wouldn't. And I doubt seriously that he'd care to

visit my home. But I submit to you that my donation will do more for Negro education in Texas than all your Mr. Stevenson's pretty words."

"You had Richard Nixon in your home," Philip said. "Is *he* your idea of a great statesman?"

Kingslea chuckled and finished his glass of Scotch. "Touché, young man, touché," he said. "No, Dick Nixon is trash, but in this campaign he is a necessary evil."

"What does that mean?"

"It means that General Eisenhower wishes to take the high road, so we need a Nixon to do the dirty work."

Kingslea fished two ice cubes from the silver bucket, dropped them into his glass, and filled it with Scotch. Philip watched him silently, then turned quickly when he heard footsteps in the foyer. Livie Kingslea stood in the doorway. She looked tall and proud and cold and deadly, like an elegant black widow spider.

"Wade, I'm going to the club for dinner."

"Very well, my dear."

Livie narrowed her eyes, focusing on Philip, and stepped into the room. She stopped ten feet from the boy, staring at him intently, angrily. He didn't move.

"Is this who I think it is?" she asked her husband.

"Can't you tell by looking?"

Livie sighed bitterly. Philip could see reflected firelight burning in her eyes. "Yes, I can tell," she said. "Exactly what is this?"

"Just a friendly chat, my dear," Kingslea said.

"Don't do anything foolish, Wade," she snapped. "We don't owe this boy a thing."

"No one has suggested that we do, Livie," Kingslea said. His wife shot Philip a last angry glance and marched out of the library to her waiting limousine. Kingslea swirled the ice cubes in his Scotch.

"You'll have to excuse Mrs. Kingslea," he said. "She isn't always the soul of courtesy."

Philip swigged his beer. "We just read *Macbeth* in English class," he said. "She reminds me of Lady Macbeth."

Wade Kingslea threw back his head and roared. "My God, boy, you do have a sharp tongue. I'll give you that. Well, where were we? We were talking about your school paper. Is journalism your interest?"

"Maybe. I want to go to college. Then I want to write."

"Write what?"

"I don't know yet."

"What do you read?"

"Different things. H. L. Mencken. Sinclair Lewis. Somerset Maugham. Scott Fitzgerald."

Kingslea laughed.

"What's so funny?" Philip demanded.

"I wouldn't take those men as my heroes," his grandfather said. "I happen to have met them all. Lewis and Fitzgerald were drunks. Maugham's a queer, and Mencken's a pompous ass."

"They're great writers," Philip said angrily.

"Perhaps so, but not great men."

"What do you call a great man? Someone who makes a million dollars?"

Kingslea looked amused. "No, not a million," he said. "Any damn fool can make a million these days. But to make a hundred million is generally a sign of character."

"You dug a hole in the ground," Philip said.

"I beg your pardon?"

"You dug a hole in the ground and oil came out and made you rich. It was blind luck, like winning a bingo game, but you think it makes you a great man."

Kingslea's eyes narrowed. "If you believe that, young man, you're less intelligent than I'd assumed."

"Why shouldn't I believe it?"

"Philip, something drew me to Goodwill in 1920. Call it fate or destiny or God's will or whatever you like, but it wasn't luck, I can assure you. When I arrived there, I found thousands of men struggling to find oil, men who would have killed to bring in one well. And out of those thousands, many were found dead in some ditch, most went home emptyhanded, and only a very, very few made their fortunes. What I did was no more luck than Colonel Lindbergh flying across the Atlantic Ocean was luck. Think what you please, but in each generation a few men dream great dreams and have the will and the strength and the vision to make those dreams come true."

There was something urgent in his voice, something that cried out for belief. Philip was suddenly amused: it wasn't enough for him to have a billion dollars, you had to believe he was a man of destiny as well.

"I think you're crazy as hell," he said, savoring each word.

To Philip's surprise, his grandfather began to laugh again. It dawned on Philip that his grandfather was drunk. The idea startled him; he had never thought of the old man as subject to the lesser vices.

"If I'm crazy, young man, then America is crazy," Kingslea said. "Because I'm what America wants to be."

"Rich, you mean?"

"Not just rich. Free. My own man. A ruler of men. The world is a jungle, Philip, and most men are poor frightened creatures, lurking in the shadows, hiding under rocks. Only a very few of us are lions, leaders, men of destiny, lords of the earth. That's what I set out to be, back in Goodwill, when I didn't have two dimes to rub together, and that's what I became. And so can you, young man. You're a Kingslea! You don't have the money, but that doesn't matter. You've got the blood, *my* blood, and that's what counts!"

The old man peered at Philip defiantly, as if challenging him to disagree, but Philip did not want to argue. They *did* have the same blood; that was why he was here.

"Where did it come from?" he asked. "This blood. This greatness. This . . . this being different?"

Kingslea smiled proudly. "My people were Quakers on my mother's side, or did you know that?"

Philip knew it. He'd read everything there was to read about his grandfather in the Fort Worth Public Library.

"Quakers are pacifists, aren't they?"

His grandfather ignored the question. "They were strong people, brave people—wouldn't take their hats off to the king of England himself. They were pioneers, too. Came over to America in the 1650s and settled in Pennsylvania. My people, the Pridemores, moved on down to Virginia in the 1750s and settled in the wilderness, the Indian country. Then in 1866, after the Civil War, my grandmother and her husband came to Texas. That's the kind of people you come from, Philip, that's the kind of blood you have inside you. You and your cousin Skip too, both of you."

"Skip's an arrogant . . ." Philip began.

"Skip is intelligent, a brilliant athlete, and a natural leader. I intend for him to go to law school and then into politics. Skip could be governor of Texas. By God, he could be president of the United States!"

"Heaven help us then," Philip said.

"Don't be cynical. Your father was cynical and it ruined his life."

Philip stiffened. His grandfather fascinated him, but he couldn't take any more. *"You* ruined my father's life," he said.

"I gave him everything," Wade Kingslea snapped. "Coyle had inherent flaws in his nature, and he turned to alcohol."

"You gave him everything but a chance."

Kingslea poked the fire; sparks flew like tiny meteors around his head. "You talk a lot of nonsense, Philip, but I like your spirit. You're a fighter, and you got that from me. We should be friends."

"You're crazy."

"Oh, you're young and you think you've got to rebel against me, but you're like me. You've got my blood."

Philip shot out of his chair. "I'm not anything like you!"

"Hate me if you please, but you're my flesh and blood. If you ever want anything all you have to do is ask. You talk about college. That costs plenty. If . . ."

"I don't want a dime from you," Philip shouted. "You ruined my father's life and you ruined my mother's life and . . ." He was sobbing, shouting.

"All that was a long time ago," Kingslea said softly. "None of it matters now. What matters is that you're strong like me."

Philip ran blindly out of the library, through the marble foyer, down the front steps. As he raced across the golf course he screamed into the night, "I'm not anything like you, not anything at all!"

Back in the library, Wade Kingslea watched as the young Mexican girl gathered up the dishes. She had creamy skin and hard little breasts. He said in Spanish that she should await him in her room. She blushed and whispered, *"Sí,* Señor Kingslea." When she had gone he stood before the fire finishing his drink. Wade Kingslea was pleased. He liked this unknown grandson of his. He was a hothead, of course, and filled with half-baked ideas, but the boy had spirit, had fire in his belly, and those were qualities a man needed, in this jungle of a world.

CHAPTER FOUR

The week after they were chewed out by Mr. Glasscock, Philip and Mrs. Ritter had a long talk. He threatened to quit the paper rather than have the principal approve everything he wrote, but she said he must stay because he was the best writer they had. Philip was starting to realize that just about anything he wanted to write for the paper would offend Mr. Glasscock. It wasn't just Coach Moran: Philip thought Ike was a jerk, and Doris Day, and Lawrence Welk, and Amon Carter with his stupid six-guns, and John Wayne, and whoever wrote *Silas Marner*, and Billy Graham, and the local state senator, who claimed the Communists were poisoning America's toothpaste, and the rich Texans who dressed up like Neiman-Marcus cowboys for the annual Fat Stock Show—the sad fact was that just about everything and everybody Rupert Glasscock admired, Philip thought was full of crap. Philip planned to spell out FUCK YOU RUPE in his next sports column, by starting the first paragraph with an *F*, the next with a *U*, and so forth, but beyond that sort of subterfuge he didn't think he was likely to express his deeper feelings in the *Scorpion*.

But he didn't quit the paper. One reason was that he dreamed of attending a good college and he wanted it on his record that he'd been an editor of his high school paper. His grades weren't much, and he'd never joined any clubs or been elected to anything, so about all he had going for him was writing for the paper and winning some prizes for it. The other reason he didn't quit was Mrs. Ritter. He liked having her tell him how talented he was, liked having her to talk to, liked the memory of his arms around her and the pine-needle sweetness of her hair and the warmth of her breasts. Mr. Glasscock had made them conspirators. He'd come to think of teachers as enemies, guards in the prison, but Clara Ritter was an ally, a friend. He couldn't give that up, not even if it meant letting Rupert Glasscock approve his copy.

On the Saturday morning before the student-body elections Philip stopped by the TCU library before going to work. That summer he'd gotten interested in the Scopes trial, the great Monkey Trial in Tennessee, and he'd gotten permission to go into the library stacks to look up books and articles about it. He loved it back there. You could wander among the books, and there were desks where you could sit and read and not be bothered. One of the things he'd discovered in the stacks was a shelf with catalogues from hundreds of American colleges.

He devoured the catalogues of far-off, exotic-sounding colleges—Stanford, Sewanee, Northwestern, Tulane, Washington and Lee, Harvard, Columbia, Reed, Williams; he gobbled up lore about their faculties, courses, fraternities, traditions. His own college career was less than a year off, and he wanted most of all to go far from Texas. The wonderful part was that he could, thanks to the necklace that his mother had kept for a dozen years in a lockbox at the First National Bank. He would have the money and he had decided, finally, what college he wanted most urgently to attend.

Princeton.

He had fallen in love with Princeton that summer when he first read F. Scott Fitzgerald's *This Side of Paradise*. He could close his eyes and see its ivy-covered towers. To follow in Fitzgerald's footsteps, to attend Princeton, to join the Cottage Club, to write for the *Tiger* and the *Nassau Lit,* to compose songs for Triangle, perhaps to write his own *This Side of Paradise*—to do those things seemed to Philip to be as far from Texas and as close to paradise as he could imagine.

So he dropped by the TCU library that Saturday morning and sat reading the Princeton catalogue, and at a quarter to twelve he drove over to Mrs. Baird's Bakery and spent the next eight hours loading cartons of bread into big trucks bound for West Texas.

When he got off work he drove to the nearest 7-Eleven to buy a six-pack. The clerk was a crusty old fellow who demanded to see his ID. Philip feigned annoyance but handed over his driver's license, which proclaimed him to be age twenty-one. The clerk muttered his disbelief but took Philip's dollar and surrendered a six-pack of Falstaff. The ID was

Fearless' handiwork; forgery was among his talents, and for ten dollars he would make you any age you pleased.

Philip cracked a beer and drove west, out to Western Heights. In addition to thinking about Princeton, he'd been thinking about Clara Ritter. He knew where she lived, in a garage apartment behind a mustard-colored brick house on El Campo. He even knew the woman who owned the house, because when he was twelve he'd thrown a shopper's guide called the *West Side News* in that neighborhood. Her name was Eula Hanratty, and she was a dentist's widow, a nasty old bitch who complained about everything.

Clara Ritter's eyes widened when she opened the door. She was barefoot and wearing jeans and a University of Tennessee T-shirt.

"I . . . I was just passing by," he said, "and there was something I wanted to ask you about."

Her eyes shot to Mrs. Hanratty's house, to the rear bedroom where the old woman spent most of her time watching television. "Why . . . why, sure, Philip," she stammered. "Come on in. The place is kind of a mess."

The apartment was nothing to brag about, just one room with a battered old sofa that made into a bed, and a kitchenette off in one corner.

"Would you like a Coke?" she asked.

He held up the paper sack he'd carried in. "Actually, I've got some beer," he said. "I just got off work. You could have one with me."

She frowned, then laughed. "Okay," she said, and he opened two beers and she brought out a bag of Fritos. They sat down on the sofa and he raised his beer can high.

"F.O.T.P.," he said.

"What?"

"Freedom of the press," he explained. "Cheers."

She clanked her beer against his and they drank the toast. Then there was an awkward pause. "The reason I came by," he said quickly, "was that I'm about to apply to a college and I wanted to ask you to write a letter for me." He told her about Princeton, and about his grades not being much, and how he thought a good recommendation from her might be important. She promised to write a letter the next day. They talked about college for a while, and she told him about the University of Tennessee and the football games and fraternity parties there. When he got up to get himself a second beer she turned on her radio and a Billy May song came on and it didn't seem like she was his teacher at all.

"It's Saturday night," she said. "Why doesn't a good-looking guy like you have a date?"

Philip shrugged. "There's nobody who interests me."

"There are lots of pretty girls at Heights," she said.

"There are lots of bird-brained girls at Heights."

"There must be *someone* who meets your high standards," she teased.

"Jenny Rhodes," he said. "She meets my high standards."

"She *is* nice," Clara agreed. "And so pretty."

"Jenny was my first love," he said. "Many years ago."

"When?"

"Sixth grade. We'd go to the Saturday afternoon shoot-'em-ups together and then to the drugstore for Cokes afterward."

"What happened to this great romance?"

Philip made a sour face. "What happened was, we went on to junior high next year, with a whole new bunch of kids, the River Crest crowd, and she discovered high society. But I don't blame her. That's the way things are. She's the neatest girl in the school, so she goes with the hotshot guys. Rich guys and jocks."

"Jenny's going with Skip Kingslea now, isn't she?" Clara asked.

"Yeah," he said. "She's going with Skip."

"Are you related to him?"

"Distantly."

"How distantly?"

"About a hundred million dollars distant."

"Philip, I don't understand WHHS, I really don't. When I went to high school, back in Tennessee, everybody was about the same. I mean, the doctor's son got to drive his dad's Buick on dates, and some kids didn't have much, but we were pretty much all one big crowd. It's so *different* here. You've got all these cliques, all these kids driving expensive cars, all that . . . that . . ."

"All that money," he said. "Kids whose parents have ranches and oil fields and five-Cadillac garages. Formal dances starting in the seventh grade. All the people who belong to the country clubs—I love that, they 'belong to it,' like it owned them, which maybe it does. Oh boy, Mrs. Ritter, I could write you a great article about the social structure of our school, but I don't think Mr. Glasscock would let us print it."

"Tell me about it," she said. "Maybe someday you can write it."

"It's pretty complicated," he said. "I went to this elementary school, South Hi-Mount—the one down on Clover Lane—that was for the kids who lived south of Camp Bowie Boulevard. It was pretty much like your school—everybody was about the same. But there was this other elementary school, North Hi-Mount, for the kids north of Camp Bowie, and that was a different world. Those were the kids whose families drive Cadillacs and who belong to the country club and go off to fancy camps in the summer and have braces on their teeth. Both bunches of kids met in the seventh grade, in junior high, and the rich kids just sort of took over. The teachers all knew them, and they got be the editors of the school paper and all, and they were elected to all the class offices, and they had their sororities and their dances and everything."

He killed his can of Falstaff. "It was like the rest of us were a bunch of peasants. It's kind of a caste system, like in India. I think it's probably hardest on the girls. Your average guy doesn't care about formal dances and sororities, but if you're a girl you either make Musette, the hotshot sorority, or you don't, and if you don't you're pretty much of a second-class citizen."

"Jenny Rhodes is a Musette, isn't she?" Clara asked.

"Yeah, and she's not rich, but she's so popular they had to take her. Mostly, the rich girls join Musettes and the rest have to settle for the consolation prize, which is being a Teen or a Belle. The Teens are the goody-goody girls, the ones who are always telling you how they just *love* being a Teen and how they gathered more old clothes for the Lena Pope Home than the Musettes did. Did you ever read *Brave New World*, where the Deltas, the real peons of society, are taught to say, 'I'm glad I'm a Delta'? Well that's how the Teens are, pretending they never even *wanted* to be Musettes."

He swigged his beer. "Then there's the Belles, who're the sexy sorority. No social pretensions whatsoever. They wear their hair in ducks and French-inhale their cigarettes and dance the dirty bop. I love the Belles," he said. "They're the only ones who invite me to their dances."

"Do you care?" she asked. "About the dances, I mean."

He shrugged. "Not anymore. Maybe I did back when I was a sophomore."

He propped his feet up on her rickety coffee table. The crazy thing was he liked talking about this stuff; if you talked about it it couldn't hurt you. "Actually, the Mussettes did invite me to one of their formals," he said. "It was the summer before the seventh grade, and out of nowhere I get this invitation to a formal at River Crest. My mother was all excited, and we went out and bought me this white suit to wear, and the night of the great event she dropped me off at the country-club door and I go inside thinking, Wow, I have arrived! Well, there are these two old crones sitting at a table by the door, and one of them gives me a big sloppy smile and says, 'And who might *you* be, young man?' I tell her I'm Philip Kingslea and her smile wilts and she says, '*Philip* Kingslea?' and whispers to the other crone, and the other crone—she had a gardenia in her hair—whispers back, '*Louise's* son,' Louise being my mother, who once had the rare good fortune to be married to a Kingslea. Anyway, the first crone giggles and says, 'Goodness, there's been a silly mix-up,' and the one with the gardenia says, 'Well, you stay anyway, sonny, and have a nice time,' which is not exactly the warmest welcome a fellow ever received, but I go on into the ballroom and get me a glass of punch and check things out. Well, the truth is the party was a fiasco. These kids are about thirteen years old and they don't know what the hell they're supposed to do. Most of the guys are over in one corner, horsing around. Somebody discovered that if you shuffled your feet on the rug and touched somebody, it'd make a spark, so that was mainly what they were doing. The girls were over in the other corner, in their pastel pink and blue formals, with lots of lace and corsages taped to their shoulders, giggling and wondering what the hell to do. It was pitiful, really; I mean, most of these girls didn't have any, you know, chest, but they're wearing these low-cut gowns that were all the rage. And there was this band, all these old bald-headed guys who started playing Jan Garber's greatest hits and finally a couple of girls started dancing together. Well, that was the scene, the guys in their tuxes making sparks and the flat-chested girls in their formals dancing with each other, and I'm over at the side guzzling pineapple punch when who walks up to me but my long-lost cousin Skip.

"'What're *you* doing here?' asks the Skipper, not being one to mince words.

"'Just watching the shcw,' says I.

"'You don't belong here,' he says, all charm.

"'Skip, for once I think you're right,' I say and walk out. At the door the crone with the gardenia gives me this crocodile smile and says, 'Did you have a nice time, sonny?' I give her a big smile back and say, 'Lady, it's the best time I've had since Grandma caught her tit in the wringer,' and got the hell out of there."

Clara shook with laughter. He kept sneaking glances at her breasts. He didn't think she was wearing a brassiere.

"Did you really say that to the woman?" she said.

"Listen, that's not the worst thing I ever said to anybody," he told her. "You want to hear the worst thing I ever said to anybody?"

"Yes, please," she said. "I absolutely do."

He opened two more beers. When he returned to the sofa he sat sideways, facing her, with one arm stretched out on the back of the sofa so that his hand was only inches from her shoulder. She didn't seem to notice but in a moment he pretended to scratch his ear and pulled his hand back.

"The worst thing I ever said," he told her, "was when I was a sophomore and I decided I wanted to be popular. That's what every American kid wants, right? So I read all the 'Tips to Teens' columns and they all said that the way to be popular was to be friendly. Smile a lot. Love your neighbor. So I decided to launch a friendliness offensive. Probably you've noticed how in the halls at school, between classes, all the hotshots spend all their time flashing big grins and yelling, 'Hi!' at each other. Right down the line, like a recorded announcement, 'Hi! Hi! Hi!' So I figure I'll play their silly game. I start grinning like a madman and yelling, 'Hi!' at everybody I see, and you know what? *I'm invisible!* The rich girls all look right through me. There is this one girl who really hacks me off. Minnie Keene, the Cattle Queen—her old man owns about a trillion acres west of here. Minnie sat next to me in Spanish class last year, and since she can barely speak English, much less Spanish, she's always copying my homework. Which is fine with me, because whenever she wants to borrow my homework she always comes and rubs up against me, whereupon I turn to jelly. Well, when I start my friendliness offensive, it happens that I pass Minnie every day outside the library, so I give her my big 'Hi!' and I am met with total silence. I mean, the year before she was rubbing her boobs against my arm in exchange for copying my homework, which is a form of prostitution if you stop and think about it, but now she doesn't know I'm alive. For a week I yell, 'Hi!' at Minnie and she ignores me, and finally I go berserk. I stop Minnie, and I won't let her past. All the while I'm yelling, 'HI! HI, MINNIE!' Minnie's eyes get big as saucers; she figures this pervert is going to attack her. And I keep yelling like a madman, 'HI, MINNIE! HI, YOU STUCK-UP BITCH! HI, IT'S ME, PHILIP, THE ONE YOU USED TO RUB YOUR TITS AGAINST!'

"Well, logically enough, Minnie started running down the corridor like King Kong was after her, and I'm in hot pursuit, still yelling, 'HI! HI! HI!' and finally Coach Turpin tackled me and dragged me to the principal's office. Anyway, that's the worst thing I ever did, so far."

She looked at him with an enigmatic smile on her lips. Her eyes were gentle blue-green and she wasn't wearing any makeup. Her skin looked wonderfully soft and white.

"You probably think I'm nutty as a fruitcake," he said.

Clara shook her head. "No," she said. "I think you're a writer."

"Huh?"

"You feel things," she said. "And you remember them, with all those wonderful details."

Philip frowned uncertainly. He'd never thought of it that way. All he knew was that certain scenes were there, etched in his memory, part of the permanent record.

He noticed a photograph of a pugnacious-looking fellow in a PFC's uniform. "Is that your husband?" he asked.

She nodded. "Yes, that's Donny. I took it just before he left for Korea."

"When's he coming back?"

She stared at the floor. "I don't know," she said. "It's all a big mess."

She looked so depressed that he didn't know what to say. The radio started playing, "How Much Is That Doggie in the Window?"

"Jesus Christ," Philip said and began to fiddle with the dial. He found his favorite Negro station; it was playing

"Lawdy Miss Clawdy." That made him feel better, but Clara was still staring gloomily at the floor.

"Hey, you want to dance?" he said. "I'm not much good—kind of left-footed—but it'll take your mind off your troubles."

Clara looked at him for a moment and then grinned. "Sure. Why not?"

They danced a kind of slow bop. She was pretty good, better than he was. They were laughing and having a good time when someone started banging on the door. "Clara?" a woman yelled.

"Oh my God, it's Mrs. Hanratty," Clara cried. "Hide the beer. Turn off the radio."

Philip put the cans behind the sofa and Clara was trying to fan away the smell of beer when the landlady let herself in. Her hair was in curlers and she was wearing a ratty-looking pink robe.

"I heard screaming," she said.

"It . . . it must have been the radio," Clara stammered.

Hanratty's eyes scanned the apartment, as if for a body or a bloody knife. "Well, let's do remember the neighbors," she said. "You and your guest, too."

"We will," Clara promised, and the landlady backed out the door.

"Nosy old bitch," Philip said and retrieved their beers. He settled back onto the sofa, still feeling fine, not bothered by Mrs. Hanratty; in his experience the world was filled with Mrs. Hanrattys and you learned to ignore them.

But Clara was staring straight ahead, her lips trembling. "I hate her," she said.

He didn't know what to say.

"We were having a good time and she had to come and spoil it. I can't even have one guest without her snooping on me." She buried her face in her hands. "I hate her and I hate my job and I hate this city and . . ."

She started to sob.

"Hey, it's okay," he said.

"No, it's *not* okay," she insisted. "Oh, Philip, I got a letter from Donny today. He says he's going to reenlist. I don't know when I'll see him again. I came to Texas to be close to him when he was in basic training and now he's gone and I'm stuck in this awful place. I don't have any friends and Mr.

Glasscock hates me and my landlady spies on me . . ."

"Couldn't . . . couldn't you go back to Tennessee?" he asked.

"My parents *told* me not to get married. I can't go crawling back to them. I've got to finish out this year at least. Oh, Philip, we've both got to finish this year somehow."

He touched her hair. It was soft, mysterious. He let his fingers slide down until they rested on her neck. "Don't cry," he said.

She stared into his face. She wasn't crying, wasn't smiling, wasn't doing anything but looking at him, as if she'd never seen him before. She reached out and touched his face and then pulled him toward her and kissed him on the mouth. It was all happening so fast that it was like a dream and he wasn't sure what he was supposed to do. She kept on kissing him and making little whimpering sounds, and he kissed her back, and after a while he began to rub her arm. She seemed to like it, so he thought, what the hell, and let his hand slide lightly across one of her breasts. He did it quickly, so it would seem like a mistake, just an accident, if she got mad, but she moaned and put her tongue in his mouth so he did it again and this time he let his hand stay on her breast. She *wasn't* wearing a bra, and her breast felt huge and warm and wonderful, and he just held his hand against it while she kissed him and then she put her hand on his and he knew she was going to jerk his hand away but instead she sort of moved his hand up and down and he got the idea that she wanted him to rub her breasts. He did, both of them, and she moaned so loud he was afraid Hanratty might hear, and suddenly she sat up straight and he guessed he'd gone too far and she would tell him to leave but instead she said, "You make me feel so good," and pulled off her T-shirt. The next thing he knew he was kissing her breasts and sucking her nipples and she was saying, "Yes, yes," and suddenly she stood up, her hair all disheveled, her face pale, her eyes blurry and unfocused, and began to slip off her jeans. When he hesitated, she began to unbutton his shirt, and then he got the idea and slipped out of his jeans. "Help me with the sofa," she said, and they yanked out the sofa so that it made into a bed.

In bed he thought of a poem he had read that year, Andrew Marvell's "To His Coy Mistress," when the poet says he will take two hundred years to admire each breast and "thirty thousand to the rest." Clara was not exactly coy, and he was no poet, but he felt as if he could spend hours just staring at her glorious breasts, her white, round, wonderful belly, her big, strong thighs. He realized suddenly that her body was not plump, as he had thought, but was perfection, the absolute Platonic ideal of what a woman's body should be; her breasts were not overlarge but Rubenesque, wonders of nature; her bottom was not unduly broad but the best of all possible bottoms, beside which the once-admired bottoms of beauty queens and cheerleaders would now seem bony, niggardly, pathetic.

But if Philip was content to gaze upon Clara, Clara was not content to be gazed upon. She put her arms around him and quickly, without him quite realizing what was happening, he was atop and inside her. She was miraculously warm and wet, like honey; he moved slowly at first, uncertainly, and whispered, "Do you like that?" and she answered, "I like everything you do," and after that it all was easy. The only thing wrong was that her fold-out bed sagged at the bottom and he kept sliding down and having to sort of screw his way back uphill, until after a while his knees were raw and his back hurt, but he ignored it and he came three times and the way she was moaning he guessed she'd come twenty times. Finally they slowed down and stopped, sweaty and exhausted, wrapped in each other's arms. He still couldn't believe what had happened.

After a while she said, "Was it the first time for you?"

It wasn't as easy a question as it sounded. He had gone with Fearless a few times to the Rosebud Motel, a whorehouse out on the Jacksboro Highway, but what happened there was nothing like this. The girls there took your five dollars, the price of a no-frills quickie, fended off your biographical inquiries, flopped down half-dressed on the bed, did the deed quickly and without enthusiasm, complaining bitterly if you took more than a minute or two, hobbled into the bathroom with a towel between their legs, then dashed out to greet the next customer, leaving you naked and unsated on the sagging motel bed, wishing you had your five dollars back.

"Not exactly," he said. He wasn't sure which was more shameful: to be a virgin or to be a whoremonger.

After a while, Clara began to laugh. "I wonder what they would do if they found out I had slept with a student?"

"Make you Teacher of the Year!"

"You're wonderful," she said and he felt himself stirring.

"Oh God, you're too much," she said.

"Just once more," he pleaded.

"No," she said. "I can't make the landlady mad. Tomorrow."

He was still in a daze as he went down the steps and out to his car. He thought Mrs. Hanratty was probably peering out her window at him but he didn't care. He drove around for a while trying to sort out what had happened. He wasn't sure if he had seduced Clara or she had seduced him. He wasn't sure what this meant or where it would lead. He was poised somewhere between arrogance and affection, between wanting to yell, *Hey, I screwed one of my teachers,* and thinking that he really liked her, really wanted them to be friends. He'd never felt that way about any girl except Jenny. He suddenly asked himself, *What the hell am I doing?* and of course he didn't have the foggiest notion what he was doing. But he liked the uncertainty. He guessed that not knowing what came next was what made life interesting.

CHAPTER FIVE

It took Philip and Pancho a few days to persuade Fearless to run for student-body president against Skip Kingslea, but once Fearless grasped the sheer perversity of the idea he threw himself into the campaign with all his considerable energy. He started coming to school in outlandish costumes, the better to draw attention to himself. He would be Buffalo Bill one day, Sitting Bull the next, and Santa Claus the day after that. Money was no object, of course, and they had printed hundreds of "Fetus Is Bestus" buttons and bumper stickers to pass out at school. Every afternoon when school let out Fearless would sit out in the parking lot in the Batmobile and yell to passersby, "Hi, I'm Fearless, take me for your leader!" Naturally, all the respectable kids in school ignored the Festus campaign, but the rank and file was increasingly intrigued.

Every day Fearless would invite four or five guys to join him in the Batmobile and they would listen to his police radio and Fearless would pass around a chilled bottle of Everclear gin. Everclear was 180-proof gin that retailed for $1.39 a quart, and if you were lucky it would only immobilze you temporarily and not blind you permanently. Nobody in his right mind would drink Everclear gin, but Fearless figured that the average high school kid wasn't in his right mind where free booze was concerned. As the good fellowship spread, there in the Batmobile, Fearless would produce his legendary collection of fuck books, or Eight Page Bibles, as they were sometimes known. Most kids had seen a few of them, passed around in the school yards over the years, but Fearless had dozens of them, in mint condition—"a priceless collection," he boasted, "invaluable to scholars of Texas culture." The Eight Page Bibles, so called because they were always exactly eight pages, were crude cartoon books, said to be drawn by some sex fiends down in Mexico, that featured famous people screwing. Sometimes the famous people were movie stars and sometimes they were cartoon characters like Blondie and Dagwood or Superman and Lois Lane. When the gin and the fuck books had everybody feeling mellow, Fearless would take his new friends for a spin in the Batmobile, whizzing around town at twice the speed limit, sometimes slowing down to take potshots at road signs with one of his antique guns. Politics, Fearless declared, was the most fun he'd ever had.

Out of these afternoon orgies Fearless was building a hard core of campaign workers, most of whom had the mistaken impression that if he was elected, the gin and the fuck books would flow forever. This hard core, possibly demented by too much Everclear (any Everclear being by definition too much), had taken to following Fearless down the corridors between classes, chanting, "We want Fearless, we want Fearless!" Festus Fever was sweeping the school.

The Friday before the election Philip and Pancho organized a rally during the lunch hour. It was a fine Indian summer day. Kids were sitting out on the grass talking, or shooting baskets, or sneaking off to their cars to smoke and listen to the radio, when suddenly a three-piece band appeared, tuba, trumpet, and trombone, and began honking out, "Happy Days Are Here Again." That racket, plus the spectacle of Fearless dancing around in a Superman suit, drew a crowd of fifty or sixty kids, and Pancho jumped up on the steps outside the gym and began a campaign speech.

"What'd Skipper Kingslea ever do for any of you?" he demanded.

"He's a great football player," a girl yelled.

"Absolutely," Pancho agreed. "So he's captain of the football team, that's cool. But why make him student-body president?"

Philip saw Tank Tomkins, Mickey Capps, and Jo-Jo Tomlinson coming before Pancho did.

"You, Hernandez, shut your face," Jo-Jo yelled. "You're running down the team. That Festus, he ain't nothing but a fruit."

"You apes think you're running the school," Pancho yelled back. "Let the voters decide!"

"Sumbitch," Tank Tomkins roared, all patience exhausted; he tackled Pancho and sent him tumbling to the ground. Pancho came up swinging, and he was holding his own until Mickey tripped him up from behind. Philip jumped on Mickey's back and they wrestled while Pancho tried to hold off Tank and Jo-Jo at the same time. Fearless was yelling, "Somebody stop those beasts!" but it looked as though his campaign managers were about to get clobbered.

Then the miracle occurred.

A sullen hot-rodder named Gillespie darted out of the crowd and clipped Jo-Jo on the chin. A funny-looking little guy named Neff, who'd worked with Philip at Mrs. Baird's Bakery one summer, ran over and slugged Mickey Capps. The football players were fighting for their lives when Coach Turpin charged up, blowing his whistle.

"Who started it?" he demanded. "Hernandez, did you start it?"

"Go to hell," Pancho snarled. His nose was bleeding and one eye was shut, but he grinned triumphantly. He raced back up the steps and resumed his speech. "Listen to me," Pancho yelled. "Don't let the jocks push you around. Screw the bastards. Elect your own man for student-body president. Here he is, the people's choice, Fearless Festus!"

Fearless, a straw-haired scarecrow in a Superman suit, danced up the steps, waving his arms like a madman.

"We want Festus, we want Festus!" the multitude cried.

"You've got me, you've got me," the candidate promised.

Off to the side, Pancho threw his arms around Philip. "Man, we're gonna win," he cried. "It's the revolution! I feel like Pancho Villa!"

Philip, whose ears still rang from a punch he'd taken, tried to look enthused. The way he remembered it, Pancho Villa came to a bad end.

In fact, the Festus campaign met its Waterloo a few days later in Texas History class.

There was no escape from Texas History. The legislature had decreed that no one could graduate without endless study of the glories of the Lone Star State. Philip, Pancho, and Fearless had for their Texas History teacher one Jubal Muldoon, a palsied old geezer whose eyes glowed with perfect joy as he recalled the wisdom of Sam Houston, the victory of San Jacinto, and all the other majestic moments of yesteryear. Fearless had outraged Muldoon earlier in the year with a brilliantly documented paper that proved that the battle of the Alamo was a fiasco, brought about by bickering among the Texas generals. "Lies, filthy lies!" Muldoon had raged.

On this day, everyone was to report on some aspect of Fort Worth history. Philip had come across the tale of Sally, the whore who'd been crucified on an outhouse door in Hell's Half Acre some seventy years before. The incident had fired his imagination as had little else in his hometown's history, so much that he wrote a poem about it. He showed his poem to Pancho and Fearless, then forgot about it. Fearless, of course, never forgot.

That drowsy afternoon they listened to a girl named Coretta Mott deliver a report on the history of the Fat Stock Show. "The livestock industry has been the heart and soul of Cowtown for nearly a hundred years," Coretta concluded, all misty-eyed. "Long may it grow and prosper!"

Philip groaned. All the livestock industry meant to him was that WHHS had its idiot Ranch Week every year, when the rich kids dressed up in cowboy outfits, and that on certain days of the year, when the wind blew just right, the stench from the stockyards made the whole damn town smell like a sewer.

"We have a few minutes remaining," Mr. Muldoon announced. "Would anyone else care to give their report?"

The room was quiet as a tomb, except for one boy who was snoring.

"Oh come now, no volunteers?" the ancient scholar chided.

"I have my report ready," Fearless announced. He was wearing a Confederate uniform.

"Well, let's hear it then, by all means," the teacher said.

Fearless strode to the front of the room. "My report relates to a terrible tragedy in frontier Fort Worth," Fearless declared. He had a weakness for alliteration.

"Excellent," Muldoon said, teetering forward dangerously.

"I hope you don't mind that I've written it in verse form."

"I'm sure we'll be delighted."

Fearless adjusted his glasses and cleared his throat, making the most of his moment. In the back of the room Philip felt the first pangs of alarm. What was the crazy bastard up to?

"What follows is a true-life tale," Fearless announced to his sleepy classmates. "I call it 'The Ballard of Sally, A Soiled Dove.'"

"Oh no," Philip groaned, but by then Fearless had started to declaim:

> "Oh he nailed the poor whore
>   To the outhouse door
>   And he left her there to die . . ."

Fearless paused for dramatic effect. Everyone was awake by then. Mr. Muldoon was sputtering. Several young virgins gasped. Fearless, undaunted, continued:

> "The last words she spoke
>   Before her heart broke
>   Were, 'He seemed like such a swell guy!'"

Mr. Muldoon was on his feet, croaking, "Stop this outrage!" Fearless was dancing around like the queen of the May while various of his hard-core followers chanted, "We want Festus!" Soon one of the coaches came to drag him away.

"He blew it," Pancho groaned. "The crazy bastard blew it."

Blown it he had. Mr. Glasscock had been looking for an excuse to put down the Festus revolution, and by raving about a crucified whore in front of innocent young women in Texas History class Fearless had given the principal all he needed. Fearless was ruled ineligible for election, and the next day

Skip Kingslea was elected student-body president without opposition.

And yet, the spirit of rebellion lived on. That evening, as Philip and Fearless cruised about in the Batmobile, killing the last of the Everclear, the ousted candidate vowed, "Those pigfuckers haven't heard the last of Fearless Festus!"

Nor had they.

CHAPTER SIX

After the first time he made love with Clara Ritter, Philip stayed awake until dawn, tormented. He told himself that he had committed a dastardly deed, that his sins would be found out, that he would bring down disaster upon Clara and himself. He imagined Clara refusing to speak to him again, Clara leaving Fort Worth forever, Clara killing herself in shame and remorse. Although he had counted himself an atheist since discovering Schopenhauer the previous summer, Philip could not in this crisis shake off a lifetime of Sunday-school-induced morality: clearly, by bedding his journalism teacher, he had sinned against God, Man, and the Fort Worth Public School System. How, he asked himself, could he have been so cold, so calculating? He had gone there with seduction in his heart, he had played upon the poor woman's loneliness; he clouded her mind with drink (although, in truth, he could not recall her having finished her second beer). When Philip pulled himself from bed on Sunday morning and began to dress for work, it was all he could do to keep from calling Clara to beg forgiveness. The only reason he didn't was his realization that the manly thing to do was to confront her face to face. That evening, after he had loaded his last bread truck, he drove grimly to her apartment, the proverbial criminal returning to the scene of the crime. He mounted the stairs to her garage apartment like a condemned man ascending the gallows. He knocked twice on the door. After an eternity it opened and her round face rose up like the moon. She wore a small, shy smile. He stepped inside, his heart pounding, and leaned against the door. He was about to start his speech, the one that began, "Mrs. Ritter, I've been thinking about it all day," but before he could speak she put her arms around him. "I've missed you so," she said and within seconds they were back in her sagging fold-out bed, making love as wantonly as before. This time, all his guilt and good intentions seemed banished forever.

Philip's knowledge of sex, pre-Clara, had been minimal. Besides his visits to the Rosebud Motel, he had engaged in some inconclusive groping on dates with "nice" girls, and he had read Fearless' Eight Page Bibles, plus such sex primers of the era as *I, the Jury, God's Little Acre,* and *The Sexual Side of Marriage.* All of which had left him not only profoundly ignorant but hopelessly confused.

Clara, in time, changed all that.

The first time or two they made love he performed with all the subtlety of a man fleeing an angry bear. What he was really fleeing was this fear that Clara would come to her senses and banish him from this carnal Eden. Only slowly did it dawn upon him that Clara did not want to escape his clutches, that indeed she wanted to be in his clutches far more than was possible. When that stunning realization came to him, he slowed the pace. Slow, he found, was good. You kissed, touched, tasted, licked, stroked, sucked, nibbled, bit, laughed, teased, explored, and saved the best for last, whereupon the best miraculously became better. When in doubt, he decided, go slow.

Their every round of lovemaking became an adventure, a further exploration of the vast, unknown continent of sexuality. Clara led him on this delicious exploration with such subtlety that he believed himself the guide. One night, in their second week together, as he was rising up to enter her, she rolled toward him and to his amazement he found that they were making love side by side, rocking as contentedly as two babes in a single cradle. The next night, as they rolled about the bed, he suddenly found that he was flat on his back and she had mounted *him.* He was stunned. The world was topsy-turvy. He was upended, like a wrestler pinned, like a helpless turtle, like a man unmanned. He knew in his heart this was wrong, perverse, unnatural. Or was it? It *felt* good, and Clara looked quite wonderful as she bobbed above him, her eyes closed, a Mona Lisa smile upon her lips, her breasts dangling like twin moons above his awestruck face. He began to rethink what was natural and what was not.

He found, most of all, that he could lose himself in her big, warm, enveloping body. Everything he wanted to forget could be forgotten there. It was like getting drunk, except you felt good the next day.

All was not sex, of course.

They talked. They talked about school, sex, journalism, religion, poetry, Texas, Tennessee, college, cars, records, cats, Bob and Ray, H. Allen Smith, Cole Porter, E. E. Cummings, *Elmer Gantry, The Rubaiyat,* dancing, disc jockeys, Negroes, Harry Truman, *Citizen Kane,* Oscar Wilde, teaching, museums, *Cyrano de Bergerac,* God, the oil business, and each other. He told her about his dream of Princeton and she told him about the little Methodist college in Tennessee where her brother taught English. She introduced him to her favorite books and authors, to Emily Dickinson and *Animal Farm* and *The Catcher in the Rye,* to bluegrass and Jimmie Rogers and the Carter Family. Talking with Clara, he decided, was almost as much fun as making love with her.

One night he asked her the most basic, bedeviling question: "Why are you doing this?" She propped herself on one elbow, a sheet wrapped around her, and said, "I shouldn't be, of course. This is against everything I've ever learned or believed. Because I'm married. Because I'm older. Because I'm a teacher. This drove me crazy for a while, when I first thought of it, and then when we first did it. But Philip, I've been so lonely. I felt like I'd been dropped into the bottom of a well. I married Donny and I thought that was True Love, and then I finally realized wanted mostly to beat the draft and didn't care about me. Still, there was excitement, and moving around the country, and doing things together. And sex. I won't say sex with Donny was wonderful, but when he went away I missed it. You get used to it and then when it's gone you sort of ache. You start staring at men on the street, their bottoms and their crotches and the muscles in their arms and the way they walk, until sometimes you think you're going to grab some poor man and drag him into the bushes and attack him. God, it's awful to do without, once you know what you're missing. That's where I was, hating Texas and my job and hating Donny and my life, wondering how I could have gotten so screwed up, and then I met you, with those beautiful eyes, and you were my secret fantasy right away, and then that awful Mr. Glasscock jumped on us, and you put your arms around me when I cried and I wanted you so badly. Then that Saturday night you knocked on my door and I almost fell over I was so excited. Then we started talking and I got worried that you'd just come to talk, that you had no idea how I wanted you."

"I was scared," he told her. "I thought you thought I was just some horny kid."

"You didn't *know* how I felt? You couldn't *guess?*"

"I sort of hoped. I mean, *something* made me come here. But I was scared to death."

"After we started dancing I knew I couldn't let you get away. If you hadn't touched me the way you did, I was going to kiss you anyway. There was no way I was going to let you out that door."

"I'm glad," he said, quite confused. He had not dreamed that women thought like that. Nor had he known precisely what had brought him to her bed. Instinct, he thought, something beyond understanding, like the movement of the planets. He wondered if somewhere there were other women who could make him as happy as Clara had. No, he thought, surely not.

Despite good sex and good talk, life was not perfect for the lovers.

They lived in fear of discovery. Her garage apartment, facing directly onto the windows of the hated Hanratty, was a source of constant frustration. Clara, hoping to disarm the landlady, had slyly mentioned that her students might drop by from time to time, for work on the school paper, but the old crone had decreed that no teenagers were to darken her driveway after sundown, when it would be impossible to tell them from prowlers. Tearfully, Clara told Philip he must visit her only in the daytime, and with a profusion of books under his arm, so as to seem an innocent schoolboy. That rule was soon broken, but each nighttime visit became an agonizing drama, a raid upon the enemy camp, as Philip strained to slip unseen past Hanratty's windows.

His schemes proliferated. He proposed to come and go via a rope ladder, dropped from her kitchen window to the alley.

Only with difficulty did Clara persuade him that some neighbor would take him for a cat burglar and summon the police. Another of his schemes was to enter in disguise: as a deliveryman, a plumber, a soldier, even in one flight of fancy, as a coed in a skirt and wig. Reason prevailed only when Clara warned that the police might stop him on the street and take him for a burglar, if not a pervert. He thought of taking her to a motel but feared that some motel manager, noting their ages (could they claim to be brother and sister?), might summon the vice squad. He thought of asking Fearless for the use of his apartment, but he was afraid that Fearless would somehow install a tape recorder under the bed. They spoke of Clara moving to a more private apartment, but if she broke her lease who could say what revenge Hanratty might inflict on the all-too-vulnerable lovers.

Then the answer came to him. It was so simple, as plain as the nose on his face. As did countless other lovers each night, all across Fort Worth, and indeed all across the civilized world, they would go make love in a parked car!

Thus, one cool Wednesday evening, Clara slipped away from her apartment, met Philip down the block, and climbed into his Plymouth for the drive to Forest Park. The first crisis arose at a traffic light on University Drive, in the form of an Olds 88 driven by a classmate of Philip's. "Get down!" he cried, and Clara made the rest of the trip with her head in his lap, giggling and fiddling with the radio dial. They reached the park, found a secluded spot, and were kissing passionately when they heard the beat of a drum and the honk of a trombone nearby. "My God, what's that?" Clara said. It proved to be some drunk TCU students, out in search of Pete the Python, who had escaped from the Forest Park Zoo some weeks before. Even after the drunken safari passed by, Clara declared that she could not make love in a park that had an eighteen-foot python slithering around loose, so Philip drove to the Worth Hills golf course. There, beneath some trees on the seventh fairway, they found the privacy they sought and were just starting to make love when suddenly lights flashed, voices cried out, and the car began to rock violently. "Sons of bitches," Philip cried at the five guys who were jumping up and down on his running board. Fortunately he had locked the doors, and the hecklers had not slashed his tires. He got the Plymouth started and roared away, only to have the hecklers pursue him in a Lincoln. By the time he eluded them, Clara was in hysterics. "They should be put in jail," she cried. "They should be horsewhipped!" Philip didn't have the heart to tell her that he and his friends had done their share of heckling, that it was just something that teenage boys did, like window-peeping or beating off, when they didn't have anything better to do. That night, for once, Clara was glad to be home. Despite Hanratty, the neighbors, and the exposed stairway, her little garage apartment seemed their safest sanctuary.

In time, the combination of sex, talk, and adversity led to an inevitable result:

Love.

"I . . . I . . . I love you," he whispered to her one night.

They had lain quietly for half an hour, and he had rehearsed his three-word speech for all that time. A hundred times he had almost spoken, then drawn back from the fateful admission. To what might love lead? To marriage, fatherhood, scandal, tragedy? No matter, he must speak his heart!

"Mmmmm," Clara said contentedly.

Had she not heard? Not understood? Could she have been asleep?

Panicked, he spoke again, louder, "Clara, I *love* you."

She pressed against him sleepily. "You're such a sweet boy," she whispered.

Panic turned to fury. She was toying with his emotions.

"Don't you care?" he demanded. "Doesn't it mean anything to you if I say that?"

She propped herself up on one elbow and stared at him. Her eyes were huge, heartbreaking. He was suspended between love and anger.

"Philip, that's the nicest, most wonderful thing anybody ever said to me," she said and kissed him wetly on the mouth.

He was relieved but not satisfied. He gazed into her sweet, sleepy eyes, waiting for her to say what she should say, but she only snuggled against him.

Finally he could wait no longer.

"Don't you love *me?*" he asked.

She stared at him with wise, sad eyes. Clara had learned the word's essential emptiness. Love, she knew, was what people did, not what they said.

"I do love you, Philip," she said, very distinctly, as if to a child. "I'll always love you."

Victorious, he fell asleep.

With love, of course, came problems.

One problem, to his amazement, concerned sex.

It had not escaped Philip's attention, in their endless search for privacy, that Western Heights High School was usually empty after 4 P.M. Once or twice, when they had lingered in the journalism classroom after school, he had kissed her before she laughed and broke away. She laughed, but he brooded, and soon the idea of sex in the deserted classroom grew to an obsession with him. He could see it all: he would have her, on her very desk, as a phantom journalism class watched in astonishment. The idea was insane, of course, monstrous, a fantasy from an Eight Page Bible, but he could not put it from his mind.

Philip was rational enough to know he could not simply propose this madness to Clara, for she would surely be outraged. No, the need was to act, trusting fiery passion to overcome dull reason. Thus, one cloudy afternoon, as Clara stood at her desk reading copy for the next *Scorpion,* Philip stepped close behind her. They could hear, in the distance, the shouts of the football squad in practice. Otherwise, the school was silent. Philip kissed Clara wetly behind her left ear.

"Ummmm," she said and kept reading.

"Ummmm yourself," he said and cupped her breasts.

*"Phil-*ip!" she whispered.

"Ummm, you feel good." He rubbed his erection against her.

"Philip, stop!"

"Let's make love!"

She slipped free of his embrace and turned to face him. "Here?"

"I can lock the door."

"Philip, we *can't.*"

He put his arms around her. "I want to," he declared, as if that settled the issue. "And you do too. You've thought about it, haven't you?"

"Well, maybe I have, but I'm not going to *do* it."

He kissed her roughly, thinking that brute force was the answer. That was what all women lusted for, according to teenagers' folklore. He had slipped one hand under her dress when she slapped him.

"Philip, are you *insane?* You stop this!"

He jerked back. His cheek hurt and his pride hurt worse. "Damn you," he cried and rushed from the classroom.

He would have visited her that night. They had learned that

the hated Hanratty played canasta away from home every other Wednesday, giving them an evening free of her snooping. But Philip, rejected, did not go to Clara; he would make her suffer as he was suffering. He went instead to Fearless' apartment and drank tequila and listened to Fearless' insane plan for blowing up Farrington Field that Friday night, during the Scorpions' last football game of the season. Near midnight, drunk and homeward bound, he detoured past Clara's apartment and chanced upon Eula Hanratty, home from canasta, climbing out of her battered Hudson. "You old bag of bones," he howled and in his rage narrowly missed colliding with a parked car.

The next morning he awoke, remembered his sins, and groaned. Could Hanratty have recognized him? Would Clara forgive him? How could he have been so insane? He must be demented, a pervert, to even dream of having sex with Clara *on her desk in her classroom!* He cut school that day, pondered suicide or running off to California; instead, that evening, he made his way to Clara's door to beg forgiveness.

Her eyes were red with weeping.

Is this what I have done to her?

"I'm sorry," he said. "I was crazy. Forgive me."

She turned away. "It's all right, Philip," she said.

"It was crazy," he said. *"Crazy!"*

Sad-faced Clara summoned a smile. "No crazier than the rest of this," she said. "I sort of wish we had. It might have been fun."

He was speechless. Her mind changed more swiftly than the Texas weather. Were all women like this?

"You're not mad?" he asked.

She threw herself onto the sofa. "It doesn't matter, Philip," she said. "I'm sorry I slapped you. There was something else on my mind."

"What is it?" he cried. "What's wrong?"

"I got a letter from Donny," she said. "He wants a divorce."

Tears welled in her eyes. Confused, Philip took her hand. "Great," he said. "That's great, isn't it?"

"I feel like such a failure."

"No," he insisted. "You're lucky to be rid of him."

She seemed not to hear. "My husband wants to divorce me and I can't go home and face my parents and I'm in Texas with a job I hate and I'm taking advantage of a sweet boy who . . ."

She broke off and ran into the kitchen to fetch a paper towel to blow her nose. Philip's heart went out to her. More than ever he wanted to comfort her, to protect her. This was the woman he loved, the only woman who understood him. When she returned, he put his arms around her. His emotions raged inside him. Suddenly the future was clear to him; the words came tumbling out.

"We'll get married," he announced. "You get your divorce and I'll go to Princeton and we'll get an apartment and you can teach until I get my degree!"

Her body, safe in the circle of his arms, began to shake. For an awful instant he thought she was laughing at him, then he realized she was crying again, harder than ever. He felt a tremor of annoyance. Why should she be crying when he had just proposed to her?

"What's wrong?" he asked. "Don't you want to marry me?"

"Oh, Philip, thank you," she said. "But I can't marry you."

"Why not?" he demanded.

"What would your mother say if you married a woman seven years older than you are?"

"Seven years isn't so much," he protested.

"It's not just our ages," she added.

"Then what *is* it?"

"Can't you see? I'm a dumpy little schoolteacher from Tennessee. You're somebody special. You'll be somebody, a writer or a newspaperman. And ten years from now you won't want to be married to a fat little schoolteacher."

"Yes I will," he vowed.

"We were lonely, Philip. We helped each other. But you have to understand, it can't last."

Her words crushed him. Their love not last? Oh fickle, faithless woman!

And yet, in part of his mind, Philip knew Clara was dead right.

"You've got to leave," she said. "Mrs. Hanratty complained again today. But before you go there's something I have to tell you. Please listen to me and please don't argue. This has to stop. It's too painful and too dangerous. I don't want you to come back, ever again."

"No," he protested.

"A clean break," she said. "It's best."

"No," he repeated. "You can't just throw me out."

"I'm sorry, Philip. Really."

"Let me come once more," he pleaded. "Just to talk."

"No, no."

"Dammit, I insist!" he said. "You owe me that much!"

"All right, Philip," she said. "Sunday afternoon. And just to talk."

He put his arms around her. He thought he might persuade her to go to bed, but she broke away and opened the door for him. Outside, he lit a Lucky and stood for a moment on the landing. He could see the glow of the TV set in Mrs. Hanratty's bedroom and, floating above her house, an orange harvest moon. Part of him wanted to be back in Clara's arms and part of him would have been relieved never to see her again. *How do I get into these messes?* he asked himself. He sighed and flipped his half-smoked Lucky into Hanratty's back yard.

Eula Hanratty, her nose pressed against the window, watched him descend the stairs. His cigarette, so insolently flipped into her yard, was the last straw. She was sick of seeing this boy come and go at all hours. It was an outrage against all decency, more than a Christian woman could tolerate. Mrs. Hanratty, her hands trembling with anger, reached for the telephone book. It was time to put a stop to this.

CHAPTER SEVEN

Fearless Festus' career as a prankster, which reached a climax that weekend when he blew up Farrington Field, had started modestly enough, back in the seventh grade, with a stink-bomb offensive. In the eighth grade he perfected an underwear demolition device—essentially a waterproofed cherry bomb

—that he used to blow up most of the toilets in their school one chaotic afternoon. By the ninth grade, newly obsessed with sex, Fearless daringly set loose a dozen mice in the girls' locker room, sending thirty nubile coeds, most of them naked, racing hysterically into the school's corridors.

By then, Fearless was a folk hero to his fellow students, but he was less popular with school administrators. Whenever some new outrage occurred, the powers-that-be had a good idea who the culprit was but they could never prove it. Fearless, although possibly mad, was not stupid. Despite periodic raids on his person, his locker, and his car, evidence of his guilt was never found. When the authorities would threaten to expel him anyway, as a precautionary measure, Fearless would summon his lawyer to protect the good name of Festus.

By his junior year at WHHS, Fearless had become quite sophisticated in the art of wiretapping. He bugged the faculty lounge that spring and thus obtained two memorable tapes. On one of them, several women teachers revealed their true opinion of Mr. Glasscock. On the other, two coaches, Homer ("Burpin'") Turpin and Elwood Beane, discussed in sordid detail the outrages they would be pleased to perpetrate on the school's most choice coeds.

Unfortunately, after Fearless played the tapes for a few friends, someone shot off his mouth, and the coaches learned what was afoot. Seeing their good names and careers endangered, the two desperate men seized Fearless after school one day, dragged him to the roof of the school building, and dangled him over the edge by one ankle, vowing to drop him to the concrete below unless he produced the dreaded tape. Fearless, finding himself in no position to bargain, confessed that the tape was under the front seat of the Batmobile. Coach Turpin raced off to fetch it while Coach Beane kept Fearless dangling. Even when Coach Turpin returned with the tape, Fearless was not released.

"You've got the tape, let me go," he pleaded, hanging upside down thirty feet above some concrete steps.

"How do we know there ain't no copy?" Burpin' Turpin demanded.

"There's not, I swear," Fearless cried. His face was beet-red and his granny glasses had already crashed to the steps below.

"I say drop the little fart, Homer," Coach Beane said.

"Hell, Elwood, it'd probably kill him."

"Might not. Might knock some sense in his head. Anyhow, if it kilt him, he couldn't aggravate us no more."

"Lord knows that's true," Coach Turpin conceded. "And the little turd probably *does* have a copy."

"No I don't, I swear," Fearless screamed.

"Can't trust the little prick, Homer," Coach Beane warned.

"I swear," Fearless wailed. "On my mother's honor."

The coaches, not being acquainted with Fearless' mother, took that as a binding oath and at length released their captive, but with a solemn vow: "You ever mess with us agin, boy, and we'll cut off your balls with a rusty knife!"

The experience left Fearless subdued. It was only after Mr. Glasscock disqualified him from the race for student-body president that the old Fearless returned.

"They'll pay," he vowed to Philip one day not long after the Festus campaign was terminated. "I've got a plan to blow up Farrington Field!"

"Fearless, you can't *kill* people," Philip protested.

"Well, not blow it up with dynamite," Fearless conceded. "More of a symbolic blowing. Let me think. It's coming . . . it's coming!"

He began to pace the floor, a tall, skinny, wild-eyed youth in hand-tooled boots, jeans and a lime-green cowboy shirt, waving a bottle of tequila as he spun out his mad plot. "The white lines around the football field . . . chalk lines . . . you could mix potassium nitrate with the chalk . . ." He swigged more tequila, summoning his muse. "And the goalposts . . . blow them up . . . cut the lights . . . take over the PA system . . ."

"Fearless, they'd know it was you! They'd expel you. They'd prosecute."

"Let them expel me! I'm sick of their Mickey Mouse school."

He could afford his bravado. The Festus Foundation, to which his father gave great sums of money rather than pay taxes, had recently awarded three million dollars to Cal Tech for a Department of Petroleum Science; Fearless could throttle Mr. Glasscock on the courthouse steps and still be admitted to Cal Tech the following September.

"We'll need an iron-clad alibi," Fearless added.

"What is this *we* crap?" Philip demanded. *"I'm* not blowing up Farrington Field!"

"The grandeur of it, Philip!" Fearless cried. "It'd be like Guy Fawkes!"

"No, Fearless, no. I'm a literary man. Bombings aren't my line."

Fearless muttered about fair-weather friends and springtime patriots, but he found himself another conspirator.

On the fateful Friday night, Philip and Pancho and Pancho's date huddled under a blanket high up in the Farrington Field stadium, nipping from a fifth of Cutty Sark and howling like madmen every few minutes. Their howls were not madness, however; if the bombing occurred, they wanted the world to know they'd been harmlessly getting drunk.

Down on the field the Scorpions were romping past the Technical High School Bulldogs, or the "hapless Tech Bulldogs" as they were known in the sports pages. The Bulldogs were hapless because Tech was the school to which Mexicans and poor whites went to learn a trade, and its students were not much interested in gridiron glory. When the first half ended, with the Scorpions ahead by 34–6, the WHHS kids were yelling themselves silly but the Tech fans were mostly heading home.

The Tech band wandered onto the field. There were only about a dozen of them, wearing ratty old green and white uniforms, and they mostly looked to be drunk as they stumbled through their fight song. Philip, high in the stadium, was not too drunk to note that Billy Bulldog, Tech's six-foot mascot, stayed behind after the band raced off the field.

"Where's Fearless?" Pancho demanded. "Has he chickened out?"

"Timing," Philip said gravely. "Timing is the key. Ripeness is all."

The Scorpion band marched proudly onto the field and began a complicated "Salute to Freedom" extravaganza. First, the band formed itself into the outline of a B-36, complete with propellers that spun and bombs that dropped. Then, as the band played "Deep in the Heart of Texas," Mr. Glasscock, narrating over the public-address system, rambled on about the Land of the Free and Godless Communism. Finally, after the B-36 had dropped its bombs, the band formed an outline of Texas and played the fight song and everyone cheered while the Scorpions trotted back onto the field.

Just then, the madman struck.

First, the stadium lights went off.

There were screams, then laughter and cheers, as the shivering fans assumed the darkness was somehow part of the halftime show.

Then flames raced across the football field.

They began at opposite ends of the field and shot along the sidelines so that in seconds the Scorpion team and band were imprisoned by a wall of flames. The flames shot five feet into the darkness, casting an eerie orange light. You could see the football players standing about openmouthed and the band members starting to run around and hug each other.

"The lunatic strikes," Pancho whispered.

"Billy Bulldog," Philip said. "That was Fearless. Or one of his partners. He set the chalk lines on fire."

"ON YOUR KNEES, SINNERS!"

The voice that boomed over the PA system was loud and majestic and angry. People screamed in terror, and some dropped to their knees.

"ON YOUR KNEES, I SAY. THIS IS YOUR HEAVENLY FATHER TALKING."

There were four mighty explosions, and multicolored skyrockets shot up from both goalposts. More people were sinking to their knees. Down on the field Philip could see Mr. Glasscock yelling at some cops and pointing toward the booth that housed the PA system.

"It's the Judgment Day!" a man cried.

"It's the Commies!" another insisted.

"Ah, hell, it's just that damn Fearless Festus," a student said.

"YOU'LL ALL ROAST IN EVERLASTING FLAME," the voice of God announced. "YOU'VE TURNED YOUR BACKS ON THE LITTLE LORD JESUS. YOU CARE MORE ABOUT YOUR CADILLACS THAN ABOUT THE STARVING ARMENIANS. I SAY TO HELL WITH YOU!"

"Sweet Lord, forgive us," a woman cried.

"WHAT KIND OF PERVERTS HAVE YOU LET EDUCATE YOUR DEAR CHILDREN?" God demanded. "LISTEN TO THIS, YOU WRETCHED SONS OF BITCHES!"

The PA system crackled for a moment, then a woman's angry voice filled the stadium.

"I SAY RUPERT GLASSCOCK'S NOTHING BUT AN OLD FAG!"

"WELL, IF HE'S SUCH A FAG," another woman said,

"HOW COME HE'S ALWAYS FEELING ME UP EVERY TIME I GO TO HIS OFFICE?"

The voices of the two young teachers were all too familiar, and shouts of disbelief filled the stadium.

"He had copies," Philip said. "Fearless had copies of the tapes."

The PA system crackled again and a man's gruff voice filled the night.

"HOMER, HOW'D YOU LIKE TO FUCK THAT TRIXIE CLATTERBUCK?"

"FUCK HER, ELWOOD? AH WOULDN'T FUCK THAT DEAR CHILD. SHE'S TABLE PUSSY."

Down on the field, coaches Turpin and Beane, howling like wolves, vaulted the wall of fire and leaped into the stands, crying, "Where's Festus? We'll kill the little bastard!"

Even as the two coaches raced about, their voices could be heard for miles debating the relative merits of oral and anal sex with a certain drum majorette. Then, suddenly, their voices stopped, the stadium lights went on, and a new voice filled the night:

"THIS IS RUPERT GLASSCOCK SPEAKING!"

Philip sighed, killed the last of the Cutty Sark, and surveyed what Fearless had wrought. Across the stadium people were screaming, crying, fighting, praying, running for exits; he hoped Fearless had planned his getaway well.

"I KNOW WHO IS RESPONSIBLE FOR THIS OUTRAGE," Mr. Glasscock declared, "AND I GIVE YOU MY WORD HE WILL BE BROUGHT TO JUSTICE!"

He never was.

CHAPTER EIGHT

Philip awoke when he heard his mother and Alice leaving for Sunday school. He slipped on some jeans and a shirt and went out to say good-bye to them. It was a windy morning with something uneasy in the air. Philip leaned in the car window and kissed Alice on the ear and told her she was beautiful. She did, in fact, have her mother's good looks as well as Al's happy-go-lucky nature. She made average grades in school, never opened a book unless she had to, and was the most popular kid on the block. The only thing unusual about Alice was that she was crazy about golf. She had gotten it from Al. He didn't play much any more, but she was always out in a vacant lot, with a rusty eight-iron and hacked-up golf ball, swinging away.

Philip walked around and kissed his mother. "Pray for me," he told her.

"You could come pray for yourself," she said good-naturedly and waved as they drove away.

Back inside, Al was sitting on the sofa in his boxer shorts reading the Sunday comics. Dick Tracy was about as deep as Al delved into the world of affairs. *You son of a bitch, you ought to read the want ads,* Philip thought, but he didn't say it. He and Al didn't speak except in emergencies. Instead he poured himself some coffee, called in sick to the bakery, and settled down to read the paper.

When the phone rang, Philip hesitated, then answered it, thinking it might be Clara, or even Fearless, who had vanished after the outrage at Farrington Field. The police had surrounded his house, but all they'd found were his parents, who were delighted to learn that their son was a fugitive. Philip figured Fearless was probably in California, lying low until he could enter Cal Tech in the fall.

The caller turned out to be the manager of a grocery store demanding payment on one of Al's bad checks.

"It's for you," Philip called.

"Tell 'em I'm not here," Al said.

"He says he's not here," Philip told the store manager.

"Then tell him I'm calling the district attorney," the manager declared.

"He's calling the DA," Philip said.

"Damn you," Al snapped, but he took the call. When Philip left the house Al was giving the man a song and dance about his little girl needing an operation. Philip started to drive around. It was too early to go see Clara but he had to get away from the house. He didn't hate Al anymore: he was past that. He just didn't want to think about him.

After a while he decided to go see his father.

Coyle had moved back to Fort Worth five years earlier. His

father had finally made him secretary-treasurer of Kingslea Oil, although he continued to control the purse strings himself. Coyle bought a small brick house on Birchman, just off Camp Bowie Boulevard. Coyle had been married when he came back to Fort Worth. Philip met the woman, whose name was Adrian, one time. She told him how she loved his father and she was going to change him and make his life wonderful. A month later Coyle got drunk and slapped her around and she had him thrown in jail. Then Adrian took his Buick and drove to Reno. Since then, Philip saw Coyle's name in the society pages now and then, taking this or that rich widow to this or that charity ball, but Coyle's romances never lasted very long.

Philip knocked on Coyle's door at noon. There wasn't any answer so he took the key from under the mat and let himself in. The place was a mess, with a couple of empty gin bottles on the floor. Philip straightened the house up and then went back out to his Plymouth. He had a pretty good idea where Coyle was. He drove east on West Lancaster, ascending the high western bluff where the cattle barons had built their homes at the turn of the century. He passed the Victorian mansion where Wade Kingslea, more than thirty years before, had courted Livie Cantrell. The old mansions were fading now, as the city's rich moved west to River Crest and Westover Hills; some had become rooming houses, and the Cantrell place was a home for unwed mothers. Philip stood in front of an elegant old mansion that was one of the most expensive places in Texas to sober up.

A plump nurse with robin's-egg eyes sat at a desk in the hallway.

"Is Mr. Kingslea here?" Philip asked.

"Why, yes," the woman said. "He was just . . ."

Just then Coyle walked in. He was wearing a rumpled salt-and-pepper tweed suit, a blue shirt and no tie, and handsome English shoes without socks. "Hi kid," he said, summoning a ghost of a grin. "I was about to call a cab."

"I can drive you home," Philip said.

Coyle signed some papers with a trembling hand, and they went outside. The wind was blowing hard. The sky had been bright blue that morning, but now a brownish haze blotted out the sun.

"Sandstorm," Coyle said as he eased himself into the Plymouth.

"A bad night?" Philip asked.

Coyle sighed and lit a Lucky on the third match. "It all started at lunch on Friday," he said. "A wildcatter of my acquaintance had just got divorced for the third time from the same woman and he said by God we ought to celebrate. The last thing I remember, we were arguing over a blonde and a check. He got the blonde and I got the check."

There was a lot of traffic, mostly families headed home from church. The sandstorm kept turning the sky a darker brown.

Back at Coyle's house, Philip made coffee while his father showered. He came out wearing lemon-colored silk pajamas and a monogrammed royal-blue robe. As he sipped his coffee, some color returned to his face.

"Your grandfather tells me he had an interesting conversation with you," Coyle said.

"It was all right."

"He was quite taken with you."

"His trouble is he thinks he's God," Philip said.

Coyle stirred his coffee. "How's school?"

"Same old garbage."

"You dating anybody?"

Philip hesitated. He thought he'd better talk to Coyle about his mess with Clara; if he didn't talk to somebody, he might go crazy.

"Sort of," he said.

"What does that mean?"

"I'm involved with a woman. It's complicated."

Coyle's eyes narrowed. Complicated involvements with women were something he knew a great deal about.

"Married?"

Philip nodded.

"Where's the husband?"

"In Korea."

"Thank God for that. Who is she?"

"One of my teachers. She's twenty-three."

"Good Lord, boy," Coyle said. He poured himself more coffee. "Philip, I want you to listen to me. I know I'm not much of a father. Mostly I'm a horrible example. But I've learned a lot about women in my life, most of it the hard way, and rule number one is you don't get involved with married women. The reason for that isn't morality, it's pure self-interest. We have something in Texas called the Unwritten Law. That means no jury will convict a man for shooting his wife's lover. What it really means is it's open season on young Romeos who get caught in the wrong bed. Just don't do it, son. There are plenty of single women out there, millions of them, more than you can imagine."

Coyle used the stub of one cigarette to light another.

"Philip, if this got out, she could be fired and God knows what they'd do to you. Where does this woman live?"

"In a garage apartment over on El Campo. We've been careful."

"Careful! How many times do you think a teenage boy can visit his teacher's garage apartment before the whole town knows?"

"I love her," Philip said stubbornly. "I've thought about marrying her."

"*Marrying* her? What in the world do you know about marriage? You think you get married and screw the rest of your life, but that's not how it is. You get married and work the rest of your life. You're a good-looking boy, Philip, and a lot of women will throw themselves at you, but . . ."

"It wasn't like that. I . . . I seduced her."

"Listen to me, son. You've got to stop seeing this woman."

"I know," Philip said.

After a while, Coyle took a nap, and Philip drove over for his farewell visit with Clara. The sky was an ominous brown haze, with only a rosy blur where the sun shone through.

Clara and Philip tried to have a sensible talk, but it didn't work. Soon they had unfolded the sofa and were making love. "This is the last time," she reminded him.

"I hate it," he said. "Why shouldn't we do what we want to do?"

"The world has rules, Philip."

"Stupid rules."

"They're still the rules."

"Not for me. Not for my life."

She hugged him. "Maybe not," she said. "Promise me you'll keep on with your writing."

"I will." She stroked his chest and soon he was daydreaming, not of Clara but of Princeton, the fairy-tale Princeton he knew from three readings of *This Side of Paradise*.

"You've got to go," she said.

"I know." But instead they began to make love again. "Oh, Philip, Philip," she whispered. They rocked gently and he heard her moans and the sandstorm howling in the trees and then he heard an unexpected sound. A car door slammed, then two more. It wasn't right. He knew the sounds of this street. He had lain many hours in her sagging bed, and he knew the dogs that barked, the hot-rodder down the block, the buses that groaned by every half hour. The car doors slamming were alien, an intrusion, and some deep, protective instinct made him leave Clara's embrace and peer out the window.

The sandstorm raged above the rooftops. Four figures, eerie in the brownish glow, were frozen in the driveway. Mrs. Hanratty, a Medusa in hair-curlers, pointed at the garage apartment. Beside her, bug-eyed and vengeful, was Rupert Glasscock, and behind them were two men in crew cuts and cheap suits.

"Get your clothes on!" Philip yelled.

"What is it?"

"Police."

Clara ran into the bathroom. Philip yanked on his jeans and his shirt and was looking for his socks when the men started banging on the door.

"Open up!"

"Go away," Philip yelled back. He had one sock on when the men kicked the door open and charged in. "Get out of here," Philip cried.

"Where's the woman?" Rupert Glasscock demanded. One of the cops was banging on the bathroom door and Clara was screaming inside. Philip grabbed the cop who was beating on the door. The other cop pushed him, and Philip swung at him. Then he was flat on his back, with both cops atop him; he saw a blackjack flash through the air and that was all he knew until he woke up in the back seat of a squad car. His head throbbed and his hands were handcuffed behind his back. One of the cops was driving and Mr. Glasscock was beside him.

"What the hell?" Philip said. "Get these things off me."

"Well, Rocky Marciano's woke up," the cop said.

"What is this? I haven't done anything."

"You assaulted a police officer, sonny," the cop said.

"The hell I did. You characters broke in without a warrant. You could have been gangsters."

Rupert Glasscock's eyes bulged ferociously. "Young man, you and Mrs. Ritter stand accused of lewd and immoral conduct!"

"We were working on the yearbook," Philip snapped.

The cop laughed. "Some yearbook."

The car stopped behind the police station. Philip saw Clara getting out of a car in front of him. "Don't say anything," Philip yelled to her. "Get a lawyer."

"You're a real live wire," the cop said. After Clara disappeared into the police station, the cop took Philip inside, to a small windowless room. The cop took the handcuffs off. "Wait here," he said and left Philip alone in the room. Philip rubbed his wrists, then tried the door. It was locked. A desk and two chairs just about filled the room. Philip sat down on one of the chairs and tried to come up with a plan to get them out of this mess.

The door opened and a man of about thirty came in. He was wearing boots with his tan suit and he had a grizzled, cowboy look.

"I'm L. T. Sykes, the assistant district attorney," he said.

"Good," Philip said. "I want to sue the cops who beat me up."

"Sonny, let's cut the crap," L. T. Sykes said. "We've got witnesses who've seen you coming and going from the Ritter woman's apartment all hours of the day and night. Today we found you both there half-naked. She faces charges of contributing to the delinquency of a minor, i.e., you. You assaulted a police officer."

"They kicked down the door. They never showed a warrant. They knocked me out with a blackjack. I'm gonna sue the bastards."

"Fellow, you're about one smartass remark away from the reform school," Sykes snapped.

"Bullshit!" Philip shot back. "I'm not some Mexican you can push around. I want to see a lawyer."

"You'll see one when I'm finished with you. First, I'll take your statement. The whole thing, about you and the Ritter woman. Tell the truth and make it easy on yourself."

"The truth is that she's a great teacher and I went to see her a few times to talk about journalism and college."

"That's all you've got to say?"

"Sometimes we talked about poetry."

Sykes stood up. "You're gonna be sorry, son."

Philip stood up and faced him. "Show me the warrant," he said.

Sykes slammed the door behind him. Philip felt better. He thought he was onto something about the warrant. Maybe the cops had screwed up.

Sykes came back in with Mr. Glasscock. "We have Mrs. Ritter's confession, Philip," the principal said, "Now we want yours."

"Let's have *your* confession, Mr. Glasscock," Philip said. "Tell us how you sent those apes in there with no warrant to beat me up with a blackjack. That'll make a great story for the newspapers."

"Young man, you're in serious trouble," the principal said.

"I want a lawyer."

Sykes nodded to the principal and they left the room again. Philip thought he had them worried but he couldn't be sure. The question was how far he should push it. He didn't know, but his head ached and he wanted to make the bastards sweat if he could.

Sykes came back in alone. "I'm gonna give you a break, fellow," he said and pushed a piece of paper across the desk at him. "Sign this and you won't have to go to jail."

The paper said that in exchange for the two plainclothesmen dropping assault charges against him, Philip waived all claims in connection with his arrest. He shoved it back at Sykes.

"Forget it," Philip said.

Sykes stood up again. "There's somebody to see you." He opened the door. Philip expected Clara but instead it was his mother.

"I'll leave you alone," the prosecutor said. Philip put his arms around his mother. "Don't cry," he told her.

She kept on crying anyway, and for the first time he felt bad.

"What are they going to do to you?" she asked.

"Nothing. I just need a lawyer."

"Philip, why did you get involved with that woman?"

He was stunned. "She's a good person. I . . . I love her."

"Philip, she's a married woman seven years older than you. She only used you."

"You don't understand," he protested. How could the whole world be so crazy? He hadn't killed anybody. All he'd done was make love to a nice woman. Was even his *mother* against him?

"Sign the paper," she said. "The waiver. Mr. Sykes said they'd let the whole thing drop if you do."

Her words infuriated him. Sykes was some dumb Texas hillbilly. It drove him crazy to see his mother call him Mister.

"I'm not signing. I'm going to sue the sons of bitches."

"Philip, if you don't sign, they'll keep you in jail."

"Great. I'll sue them for an extra million."

She turned away. "Philip, don't you understand? I can't stand to see them keep you here, like a criminal."

"Please don't cry." He put his hands on her waist and she turned and faced him. How could he make her understand?

"They kicked down the door. They knocked me out with a blackjack. They treated Clara like . . . like a whore."

"Philip, what does it matter? The woman has agreed to leave Fort Worth. All that matters is you and your education and your future. Why won't you sign the paper?"

He turned away. Why couldn't she understand? That he couldn't surrender. That you had to stand up to the bastards or they'd run over you for the rest of your life. "Because . . . because to sign it would be compromising."

Louise took his hand. "Philip, let me tell you something I've learned. Everyone has to compromise with life at some point. I didn't know that when I married your father. I thought we'd live in a rose-covered cottage and be happy forever after. But it wasn't like that. I loved him but I divorced him, because he hit you. That was a compromise and marrying Al was, too. He was someone to help raise you. And staying married to him is a compromise but I don't know anything better to do right now. So sometimes you have to compromise. You can't always have everything just the way you'd like it."

"I know, but . . ."

"I don't blame you if you fell in love with . . . with Clara. God knows you need love; we all do. After I've given you an alcoholic father and a worthless stepfather, I really can't blame you for much, can I? But I don't think I can stand it if they keep you here in jail. Ever since you were born I've counted on so much from you, expected so much . . ."

He put his arms around her. He still thought he was right, but as he held her he knew that being right didn't matter. He signed the papers and they went home.

CHAPTER NINE

Philip made peace with his high school that spring. Princeton's dean of admissions had written that his prospects would be brighter if his grades improved, so he stopped making trouble and started studying. Pretty soon he had As in everything but PE, and he figured the coaches wouldn't give him an A in PE if he ran the four-minute mile.

Mostly he spent a lot of time waiting for the mailman that spring, looking for the letter from Princeton. On the Saturday before Easter, he worked till five, then drove home to check the mail. Nothing had come, so he drove on down to the Parklane to catch up with his new friends, the Duke and Sherry. The Parklane was a dingy bar down by the Trinity River in Forest Park. The Duke and Sherry were sitting in their big corner booth with two girls and another man. The girls were Gail, the Duke's girl, and Candy, whom Philip dated when her regular boyfriend was out on the rodeo circuit. The other man in the booth was Roger, Sherry's queer friend from Dallas.

Sherry was a jet jockey who was stationed out at Carswell Air Force Base. He was a small, wiry, baby-faced fellow with an angelic smile and a honey-colored flat-top haircut. When Philip arrived, Sherry was telling how he'd tried to smuggle a whore back across the border that weekend by hiding her under the hood of his car. "We'd of made it, too, except the dumb bunny burned her tit on the engine block and started yelling her head off just as we were crossing the border. The last I saw, the *Federales* were dragging the poor naked mutilated child off to God knows what unspeakable fate!"

"Sherry, you are evil!" Roger said. Roger was a plump, cheerful fellow who decorated windows for Neiman-Marcus.

"He's not evil," the Duke snarled. "He's just a nasty little jet jockey who likes to screw billygoats and small boys." The Duke was a burly, dark-visaged man who was celebrated both as a barfighter and an intellectual. He was in a very nasty mood, because his partner had trumped his ace in a bridge tournament that morning. Philip had met the Duke at a chess tournament at TCU. The Duke had been impressed that Philip had read Schopenhauer and Nietzsche, his two favorite philosophers, and Philip had started hanging out with the Duke and his friend Sherry. They were his best friends, now that Fearless was a fugitive and Pancho had gone off to play in a band.

A kid from North Texas State came over from the bar and told them the world might blow up that night. "See, there's this atomic-bomb test scheduled today, out in the Pacific," the fellow explained. "We heard that Einstein said there'd be a chain reaction that'd blow up the world. We don't know if it's true, but everybody figured it was a good excuse for a party."

Candy turned to Philip. "Who's Einstein?"

"He discovered the theory of relativity."

Candy wrinkled her pretty brow, then seized Sherry's hand. "Let's dance," she said, and they slipped out of the booth. Philip followed and went to the men's room. Somebody had scratched on the rubber machine: "Don't buy this bubblegum —it tastes like rubber!"

When he came out, a crowd had formed around Candy and Sherry as they bopped to "One Mint Julep." Candy was one of the world's great boppers.

Philip went back to the booth. The Duke was still pissed about the guy who'd trumped his ace. "I should have broke his fucking fingers," he muttered. Philip hoped the Duke would cheer up, because he had an exceedingly nasty temper when his dark moods came upon him. Most bars in town gave him free drinks, to stay on his good side.

Tommie Sue, who owned the Parklane with her husband, Woodie, hobbled over to say hello. Woodie was blind, and drunk most of the time, and Tommie Sue ran the place. She'd messed up her foot in a motorcycle accident, but she hobbled around on crutches yelling, "Let's do it to it!" and trying to keep the peace. That wasn't easy, because three distinct groups patronized the Parklane: college kids, cowboys, and queers. The queers were segregated into the booths on the far side of the bar, from whence they would periodically emerge to play Eddie Fisher's "Keep It Gay" on the jukebox. They were trying to persuade people to call them gay, but no one did, queer being the universally accepted term for their condition.

Sherry and Candy came back to the booth. "Hey, I got a new shipment of weed up from the border," Sherry announced. "You better try some, Junior."

"No way," Philip said.

"It'll free your mind."

"Man, I read an article about what that stuff does to you," Philip insisted.

"Yeah, yeah, the one about the honor student in Florida who smoked one reefer and killed his mama. You *believe* that crap?"

"Well, hell, it was in *The Saturday Evening Post*."

"Big deal," Sherry said. "Look, I smoke the weed, and have I killed my mother?"

"I give up, have you?"

"Funny, I can't remember."

"Do you *grow* the stuff?" Gail asked. She was a tall redhead who worked as a hostess at the Hotel Texas coffee shop.

"Mexicans grow it. I consume it."

"I want to learn how to grow stuff," Candy said. She had dark eyes and pouty lips and a magnificent chest, and she wore her shiny black hair brushed back in ducktails. Candy was built for speed.

"You want to grow some weed?" Sherry demanded.

"No way, José," Candy declared. "I mean legal stuff."

"I can help you," Roger cried. "I'm a dedicated gardener."

"Would you?" Candy asked. "My back yard's like a damn desert."

"I've got this wonderful gardening book out in my car," Roger said. "I'll go get it right this minute!" He hurried away with his funny lard-ass walk.

The rest of them watched the couples bopping and listened to the Duke grumble about President Eisenhower, and after a while Gail asked what had happened to Roger. Philip said he'd go check.

It was dusk. Philip walked down to the river to pee, then he heard someone yell. He ran back up and saw Roger on his knees in the parking lot with blood spurting from his nose. Two cowboys were standing over him. One had a bushy beard and the other one's belt said "Chester" on the back.

"Come on, chubby, do your stuff," Chester taunted.

"Please, leave me alone," Roger begged.

The bearded one kicked Roger in the gut and he pitched forward on his face, still clutching his gardening book.

"Hey, cut it out," Philip yelled. He ran forward, not having much of a plan, and Chester threw him down beside Roger.

"What's this, another tootie-fruity?"

"Ah, hell, let's have a beer," Chester drawled. He spit tobacco juice at Roger, then the two of them marched off, their boot heels click-clacking on the pavement. Philip helped Roger up and wiped the blood off his face. Roger had a bloody nose and a split lip but nothing was broken. When he quit sobbing he handed the gardening book to Philip. "Give this to Candy," he said. "With my love."

"You give it to her," Philip said.

"No, I'm going home," Roger said. "Tell Sherry I'll call him tomorrow. Fort Worth is such a rough town. I don't know why I come here at all." He sighed. "Except for Sherry."

Philip helped Roger into his green DeSoto. "Good-bye, Philip," he said, clutching his hand. "You're such a *kind* boy. You don't seem like a Texan at all."

"Thanks," Philip said. He watched as Roger guided the DeSoto onto University Drive and back toward the relative safety of Dallas. Philip was in no hurry to return to the bar. He knew what would happen when he did, unless the two cowboys had the good sense to flee the Parklane immediately. Philip walked down to the riverbank. The river was olive-green and peaceful in the twilight. He guessed it still looked pretty much as it had when Ripley Arnold had founded Fort Worth a hundred years before. He knew all that from Texas history. Buffalo and deer had come to this river for uncounted centuries to drink, and Indians had come to hunt them. In 1690 a Spanish priest had passed through here and, noting the river's three forks, he had christened it "Rio de la Santisima Trinidad," river of the sacred trinity. Later the Texans shortened that to Trinity River. The first settlers rejoiced at all the wildlife to be found in and around the river: wild turkeys, eagles, ducks, geese, antelope, white-tail deer, panthers, wolves, bobcats, foxes, raccoons, beavers, an abundance of fish, even an occasional alligator. The birds and animals were mostly gone. What you found now, on the road that ran beside the river, were root-beer stands and beer joints and used-car lots and miniature-golf courses, and if you ventured down to the riverbank, just beer cans and rubbers and old tires and an occasional corpse.

Philip watched the last light fade across the slow-moving river and he thought of poor Roger, driving back to Dallas with blood all over his Neiman-Marcus shirt. Then he shrugged and went back inside and told his friends about Roger's mishap.

"Someone *hit* my friend Roger?" Sherry said. "Spilt his innocent blood? Ruint his visit to Cowtown?"

Philip nodded.

"Which ones?" the Duke demanded. His scowl had been replaced by a tight little smile.

"The two at the end of the bar," Philip said.

The Duke looked at Sherry, Sherry looked at the Duke, and the two of them stood up. It was all formal now, a ritual. "Pardon us, dearly beloved," Sherry said. "Duty calls."

Candy clapped her hands. "I love it," she cried, "I just *love* it!"

Philip watched his friends cross the dance floor. If you didn't know them, you wouldn't have thought much about them. Sherry stood five six in his boots and didn't weigh one thirty dripping wet. The Duke was five ten and one seventy, but all his weight was in his upper body, in his barrel chest and massive forearms. Philip knew that both of them carried switchblade knives in their right-hand pants pockets; he'd seen them practicing their draws, like gunfighters of yesteryear. But it wasn't likely they'd use the knives, not unless someone came at them with a beer bottle. Serious barfighting wasn't like in the movies, where people swung chairs and threw each other out windows. A man could get hurt doing that. Real bar-fighting was speed and efficiency. No muss, no fuss.

The two cowboys were swigging Lone Star at the end of the bar. Probably they'd forgotten all about Roger. Sherry slipped in between them, as if reaching for some peanuts, all the while smiling his mad angelic smile and proceeded to knock over Chester's beer. Chester scowled and grabbed for his glass, whereupon Sherry, still smiling, sank a vicious left jab into the lower reaches of his gut. As Chester doubled up in agony, Sherry added a karate chop to his Adam's apple, at which point Chester flopped to the floor, clutching his throat.

Chester's bearded friend turned to help him, but he only turned an inch or two before the Duke threw a left to his gut, a

right to his heart, a left to his mouth, and a right to his ear—
all bam-bam-bam-bam, in one unbroken motion—whereupon
the bearded cowboy was unconscious on the floor. The fight,
if you could call it that, had lasted something less than five
seconds. It was followed by a momentary hush, as people
tried to figure what the two cowboys were doing moaning and
bleeding on the floor.

"What's going on?" yelled Woodie, the owner, who being
blind missed a lot.

"We are instructing a couple of shitkickers in human brotherhood," the Duke explained.

Chester made an unwise attempt to rise to his knees.
Sherry kicked him in the heart with his pointy-toed boot, returning Chester to the horizontal.

"Maybe you could help these boys out to their car," the
Duke said to a couple of inoffensive cowboys who were
standing nearby, and the pair quickly grabbed Chester and his
friend by their boots and dragged them out.

They all went out and watched as the two battered cowboys
lurched away in a red Ford pickup with a "Made in Texas by
Texans" bumper sticker. The Duke was in a good mood now,
his trumped ace forgotten, and they went back inside and
Sherry told stories about his kills in Korea and Roger's com-
patriots sent over a lot of free drinks. Up at the bar, the kids
from North Texas State were singing "So Long, It's Been
Good to Know You," in anticipation of the world blowing up
in a few hours, if Einstein was right. After a while the Duke
said he wanted a change of scenery, so they climbed into
Sherry's souped-up Olds 88 and headed for the Oui, up on
Bluebonnet Circle. They were always piling into Sherry's 88
or the Duke's Bel Air that spring and roaring off to somewhere, to the Parklane or the Oui or the 216 or over to the
Bayou for Dixieland or out to Jack's for dancing on Saturday
night or to the little clubs on East Rosedale where old Negroes
sang the blues, or out to the Wagon Wheel or the Silver Slipper on the Jacksboro Highway if Sherry and the Duke were
looking for trouble, or down to Carlson's for a chiliburger, or
out to the Casino when Billy May or Ray Anthony or Stan
Kenton came to town or over to LuAnne's in Dallas, where
the SMU kids went to dance, or north to the Duke's favorite
steakhouse in Ponder, or south to Mexico for the bullfights, or
west to a ranch outside Weatherford where they had cockfights
on Sunday nights. There was always some louder band, some

wilder party, some hotter chili, some more menacing bar to send them speeding through the Texas night. Sometimes when they were racing along half-drunk in the darkness Philip thought it was not just the money that made Texas what it was but the distances too, that unreachable horizon that lured you on, always promising more more more but in the end mocking you, laughing at you, humbling you.

When they stopped outside the Oui, Sherry passed around some weed. Philip thought about the honor student in Florida who reputedly took one puff and dispatched his mother with an axe, but everyone else was smoking the stuff so he said what the hell and tried it.

The Oui was a relatively quiet place, a neighborhood bar frequented by TCU students of past and present. They got a table in the back room and Philip played "Night Train" and "Blue Tango" so he and Candy could dance close. Candy did hair someplace downtown and didn't care about much except dancing and making love. Philip had been spending some nights at her apartment. If her bronco-buster boyfriend returned unexpectedly he'd probably be killed, but he'd decided it was worth the risk. After they danced a while Philip realized that everyone else in the room had disappeared and the jukebox was inside his head and his body and Candy's had melted together. She stuck her tongue in his ear and it burned like fire and she rubbed herself against him and the fire spread until he thought he'd scream. There was no one else anywhere and he thought they'd make love right there, floating in the music, adrift in the universe, and then a distant voice told him that the reason the world was so strange and serene was Sherry's weed. Philip started laughing and Candy did too.

"What are we laughing about?" she asked after a while.

"I'm not going to kill my mother," he said.

"She'll be glad."

They went back to the table, at peace with the world, but then Sherry bit the waitress on the ass and they had to beat a hasty retreat. Philip could see it was going to be one of those nights, but he was past caring. They smoked some more weed and drove to a little Mexican restaurant down by the courthouse. You could see the big red-white-and-blue neon flag atop the courthouse dome. Their Mexican dinner was fine, until the Duke threw an enchilada in the face of an air force sergeant at the next table, and some cooks charged out of the kitchen, waving butcher knives, and they had to leave there too. They drove around for a while, drinking tequila and listening to the Grand Ole Opry—the girls protested, but the Duke called it their cultural heritage. Gail started to cry. She was crazy about the Duke but she couldn't handle Sherry. The thing was, Sherry was crazy as a loon, but he was also one hell of a jet jockey, with medals and certified kills to prove it, and the Duke admired the hell out of that. What Sherry did on the ground didn't matter.

They kept charging from bar to bar, not exactly looking for trouble, just looking. Philip had a theory that on any given night there were ten or twenty bands of madmen like them bouncing around the local bars, and trouble came when two or three of the groups happened to collide. At midnight they drove back to the Parklane to hear the POWs. The place was packed; it always was when the POWs played.

The POWs had all been to Korea that year. Shades, the piano player, had been blinded there, and they were all pretty strange. They wore old fatigues and let their hair grow long and made music that wasn't like anybody else's music. Their most famous song was called "Korea." They closed the Parklane with it most Saturday nights.

It started very softly, just Shades toying with the piano and a whisper of the saxophone, so that if you shut your eyes you might think of waves or flowers or falling leaves. After a while Shades began to say, "Korea, Korea," so gently that it sounded like a girl's name. One couple started dancing, thinking this was a ballad like "Tenderly" or "Stardust," but soon they noticed they were alone and stopped. Philip was standing behind Candy, with his arms around her, holding her as tight as he could, half afraid of what was coming.

The music kept getting louder. Shades was yelling "Korea" now, and the saxophone was howling and the drummer was crying "Good-bye Mama, good-bye Daddy." The song changed from week to week and nobody ever knew how long it would last. It got more wild and intense. Shades was banging the piano and yelling, "Korea, Korea," at the top of his lungs, and the horns wailed and the music ripped and tore like shrapnel and all the POWs were yelling, "Korea, Korea," like lost souls in hell and the drummer was crying "Good-bye Mama, good-bye Sally," and people in the bar were yelling with them and some were crying and some left because they couldn't take it. Philip, holding Candy close, his face buried in her hair, felt the pain in the music and he thought the musicians were describing the war but he also thought they were saying that everyone had his Korea, that Korea was whatever tore your flesh and broke your heart, that Korea could be Texas, could be your father's drinking, could be your mother marrying Al Henderson. He squeezed Candy and told her he loved her because he knew she hated this; then the music stopped and the Parklane was deathly quiet until Tommie Sue started hobbling around yelling, "Last call for alcohol!"

They stumbled out into the night. Gail begged to go home but Sherry wanted to drive. They headed south out of town and soon Sherry cut the lights and navigated by moonlight. When a car came toward them he would hog the middle of the road and wait until the two cars were a few hundred feet apart and then cut his lights on, whereupon life became vivid for a few seconds. Texas Roulette, Sherry called it. Gail was crying but nobody cared. The third car they challenged was a state trooper. Sherry ran him into a ditch, howled with joy, and made a U-turn. The trooper took a brave stand in the middle of the highway, fumbling for his revolver. Sherry went straight at him and the poor bastard got off one shot and then dived back into the ditch. The girls were screaming bloody murder, and even the Duke was grumbling, but Sherry was as happy as a jet jockey could be, on the ground. Six patrol cars chased them, and Sherry toyed with them for an hour, never quite losing them, until he was low on gas and cut through a corn-field and headed back north to Cowtown while all the cops were speeding south.

"King of the road!" he cried, washing down bennies with the last of the tequila.

"Lords of the earth," Philip whispered in the back seat.

Speeding along University Drive at dawn, they passed carloads of starched, smiling families. "It's Easter," Gail explained. "They're going to a sunrise service."

Candy said she wanted to sing a hymn. They settled on "Jesus Loves Me." They all knew it, every last verse. "Old J.C.," Sherry mused. "World wouldn't be so crappy, if folks'd listen to old J.C."

They stopped at the Parklane, where Philip had left his Plymouth. He led Candy down by the river to hear the birds sing.

After a while she tugged at his arm. "Let's go ball."

He kept watching the river, dappled in the morning light.

"Come *on*, Philip," Candy said. "You're thinking about that school again, aren't you? Whatta you call it?"

"Princeton," he said. "It's called Princeton."

CHAPTER TEN

Philip was sitting on the front steps the next Saturday, waiting for the mail, when Alice asked him for a ride over to the Worth Hills golf course.

"You got a big match, slugger?"

Alice shrugged. She was eleven, with reddish hair and freckles. "I'll probably just hit some."

When they got to the course, over behind TCU, he watched her for a while. She had a canvas golf bag, a three-wood, some rusty, cast-off irons, and a sack full of balls she'd fished out of the pond. She started swinging her eight-iron and most of her shots landed within ten feet of the hat she'd put on the fairway for a target. Alice didn't have the strength to do much with a driver yet, but she was a wonder with irons. A few months earlier, when Al realized what she could do, he'd taken her out to the Ridglea course and tried to make some money off her, betting people that she could outshoot them.

Once Alice started swinging a golf club, she never looked up. People yelled hello and cars honked and she just kept stroking away. Philip, watching her, thought she was about golf the way he'd been about books at her age. It was her private world, her escape.

"Hey, L.B., L.B., come whack some with us!"

Four guys were running down the ninth fairway, yelling and waving their arms. Two of them were slapping golf balls along, hockey style. One of them ran up to Alice. "Come on, L.B.," he wheezed. "We're gonna play down to Colonial."

The guy was wearing a red baseball cap and swigging a beer.

"I dunno, Magoo," Alice said. "I gotta practice."

"Come on, L.B.," Magoo said. "You'll bring me good luck. I gotta win forty bucks today or I lose my car. Look, I'll buy you a cheeseburger and a chocolate malt if I win."

"You're on," Alice said and started gathering up her balls. The guy in the red hat ran to catch up with his friends.

"What's that all about?" Philip demanded.

"Oh, just some crazy guys I met here," Alice said. "They do weird stuff like, oh, playing the course backwards."

"Why'd he call you 'L.B.'?"

Alice blushed. "They call me Little Babe, for . . . you know." Babe Zaharias, the Texas-born Olympic medalist turned golf pro, was Alice's number-one hero. As far as Philip knew, the only book Alice had ever read voluntarily was a teenager's biography of the Babe.

"So what does your friend mean they'll play down to Colonial?"

Alice laughed. "Those guys—Magoo and Cecil the Parachute and Dirty Dan—sometimes, just for the heck of it, they play down the street from here to Colonial."

"Down the street?"

"Yeah, you get some great rolls. You've just got to keep moving, 'cause people get mad when you play through their yards."

The next thing he knew, his eleven-year-old sister and four madmen had teed off from the hood of someone's car and were banging their way down Alton Drive toward Colonial Country Club.

Philip walked back to his Plymouth, shaking his head and muttering. As best he could see, the whole damn city was insane.

When Philip pulled into the driveway, his mother was waving from the porch. He saw the letter in her hand and he jumped out of the car and raced to her side. His hands were trembling as he tore the letter open. All he could think was, What if they say no?

But the letter said yes, and the next thing Philip knew he was yelling at the top of his lungs. "They let me in Princeton," he kept saying. "I can't believe it." He and Louise were both crying.

After a while he kissed his mother and drove over to Dusty

Rhodes' Texaco on West Seventh Street, where Jenny spent her Saturdays pumping gas.

When Dusty Rhodes returned from his army duty in World War II, he was for several years a crowd-pleasing second baseman for the Fort Worth Cats, who were the Brooklyn Dodgers farm team in the Class AA Texas League. Jenny, in those days, was the team's first and only batgirl, and she became famous throughout the state as she chased after foul balls in her scaled-down Cats uniform with her black pigtails flying. When Jenny was twelve, she had her first crush, on a lanky, tobacco-chewing, home-run-hitting center fielder for the Cats named Eddie Snider, who soon would be called up to the Dodgers and become the immortal Duke Snider. Dusty Rhodes, a hustling infielder who could never hit a curve ball, didn't get the call to Brooklyn and in 1950 decided to hang up his spikes. He might have coached in the Dodger organization —Branch Rickey himself had promised him that—but Dusty was tired of life on the road. Instead, he opened his Texaco station, and he soon made it the most successful station in the city. Dusty had a standing offer that if anyone waited more than thirty seconds at his station without being served, his tank of gas was free, and he had yet to give away his first tank.

Philip found her leaning against the Coke machine. She was wearing jeans and a sweatshirt and had a smudge of grease on her cheek.

"Hey, why don't you get to work?" Philip yelled.

Jenny tossed him her most heart-stopping smile. "Hey, P.K., what's up?"

"Nothing much. Just thought I'd buy you a Coke."

"Do it, don't talk about it."

He dropped a dime in the machine and pulled out two Cokes. "Cheers," he said. Jenny glanced at the bottom of her bottle. "Local," she said. "I had one from Los Angeles last week. So what's new? You still running around with those fly-boys?"

"Yeah, some."

"I hear you're going with a sexy lady who does the dirty bop. Candy, is that her name?"

"That's right. Candy is dandy."

"And liquor is quicker. So what is it with you and this sexy lady?"

"You're the only sexy lady for me."

"I'm not sexy. I'm just an old broken-down cheerleader."

A Cadillac pulled into the station and Jenny filled it with gas while Philip sipped his Coke. When she came back, he said, "I guess there is one thing new with me."

"What's that?"

"Read this," he said. She read the letter and then threw her arms around him. "P.K., that's tremendous," she cried. "God, you must be so happy. From Cowtown to Princeton."

"Yeah, I'm pretty pleased."

"What'll you major in?" she asked.

"English, probably. I want to write for the literary magazine."

"Old P.K., the man of letters," she said. "I wonder if you'll criticize the coach at Princeton."

"At Princeton they'll have a coach who knows what the hell he's doing."

She hugged him again. "You're such a cynic. You really are."

"What about you, Jen? You going to the University of Texas?"

"You bet."

"And major in what?"

"I don't know yet. Major in partying, maybe. I went down to some rush parties last weekend and it was a ball. We went to a dance at the Phi Gam house and they had a Dixieland band and champagne."

"Dammit, Jen, with your brains you ought to major in law or business or something. You don't want to just party for four years and marry some rich jerk and eat bonbons the rest of your life."

"Oh, I know, P.K., but I want to have a little *fun*, too. Don't you?"

Just then, Skip Kingslea's Ford Victoria skidded to a stop beside them. "Well, the All-American boy," Philip said.

Skip came over wearing tennis clothes and a cocky smile.

"Look who's here," he said.

"Guess what?" Jenny said. "Philip's going to Princeton. He got the letter today."

"Big deal," Skip said.

"Come on, Skip," Jenny said. "It's pretty darn impressive."

"No it's not," Skip said. "It just means he can't make it in

Texas so he's got to run off someplace where they don't know him."

"Skip, if you don't . . ." Jenny protested.

"And I'll tell you something else. It won't take them long up there to figure out what a jerk he is. He'll be against Princeton just like he's against Texas. That's all he knows how to do, be against everything."

"Go fuck yourself, Skipper," Philip snapped.

"What is the *matter* with you two?" Jenny cried.

"Watch your mouth, fellow," Skip warned.

"Watch yours," Philip said.

Skip pushed him up against the Coke machine. Jenny yelled, "Stop it!" and suddenly a third man pushed them apart.

"You want to fight, join the Army," Dusty Rhodes snapped. "I'm running a business here. Both of you, get going."

"Okay, Mr. Rhodes," Skip said. "See you tonight, Jenny."

Philip started back to his car. That was the worst part, knowing she would be with Skip that night. There was a lot of talk that they were sleeping together. That kind of talk would ruin most girls' reputations, but Jenny was so popular that she could get away with it. She was a goddess to the younger girls at Western Heights; they all imitated the way Jenny Rhodes walked and smiled and did her hair. But Philip hated to think about her with Skip.

He started home and heard the Clovers sing "Ting-a-ling" and thought about Candy and began to feel better. Pretty soon he'd leave for Princeton and wouldn't have to worry about Skip Kingslea for a long time. Like forever.

Louise had taken a job as the office manager for a tire company. It paid seventy dollars a week, enough to keep a roof over their heads when Al was out of work. On the day Philip was to graduate from high school, she got off work early and met Philip at the First National Bank. They were going to get her necklace out of the lockbox and take it to Haltom's Jewelers to be appraised.

Louise arrived a few minutes late and smiled nervously and took Philip's hand. They approached a desk where a young man with shiny, slicked-back hair was talking on the phone. The young man reluctantly got off the phone and led them deep into the bowels of the bank to a room lined with lockboxes. Louise gave him her key and he slid her lockbox out of the wall and set it on a table in the center of the room. "I'll wait outside," the young man announced.

Louise's hands were trembling as she fumbled with the lid of the box, and Philip felt his own heart beating hard. The famous family jewels. The diamond and ruby necklace that Livie Kingslea had taken from her own neck and put around Louise's when she learned Louise was pregnant. The necklace that Louise had kept locked away, all these years, and that now would be her son's passport to Princeton. Philip leaned forward, tense, expectant. He'd seen this necklace in his dreams.

He watched his mother's face in profile as she raised the lid. She was aglow. It was as if some radiant light from the treasure trove had washed away the sorrows of a decade.

Louise gazed into the box.

Then she screamed.

"It's not here!"

Philip grabbed the box, looked inside it, turned it upside down, and finally banged it furiously against the table.

The lockbox was empty.

The young banker with the Brylcream hair peered in at them. "Is something the matter?" he asked.

"I . . . this must be the wrong box," Louise gasped.

The young man examined the lockbox and her key. "This is your box," he said. "You can see, the numbers are the same."

"But my necklace isn't here," she protested. "Someone must have stolen it."

"That's quite impossible," the young man said icily.

For an instant, Philip thought he was going to cry. This one hurt. The pain was white-hot and then he gritted his teeth and banished it. He felt irony returning, a grim amusement, something like peace. Of *course* the lockbox was empty. What else would it be? His mistake had been getting his hopes up, counting on something besides himself. No one was going to look out for Philip Kingslea but Philip Kingslea. How foolish to have thought some magical necklace was going to waft him off to Princeton.

Princeton! That was a joke. What business did he have at Princeton? He didn't even know where Princeton was.

The slick-haired young banker had gone in search of his superior. Philip stood in the tomblike vault with his arm around Louise. "Where can it be?" she sobbed.

"Don't worry," he told her. "It doesn't matter." He meant

it. He didn't need Livie Kingslea's necklace. He didn't need anything or anybody. He felt hard, cold, like a diamond.

A bank vice president hurried in, all white hair and solicitude. "There must be an explanation," he said and started thumbing through a ledger.

"Ah, here we are," the banker said. "You see, Mrs. Henderson, you entered the box in April of 1950."

"No, I didn't."

"But here's your signature."

"No, it's *not* my signature!"

"Not your . . . ?"

"It's my husband's signature," Louise said and broke into tears again. Philip put his arm around her. "Come on," he said. "Let's get out of here." Suddenly this all made sense.

"Oh, I remember now," the banker said.

"Remember what?" Philip snapped.

"When Mr. Henderson came in. I dealt with him myself. Very pleasant fellow. He said you were seriously ill, Mrs. Henderson, and he needed access to the lockbox."

"No, no, no," Louise said.

The banker licked his lips uncomfortably. "He brought me an affidavit, signed by you, giving him access."

"I didn't sign anything," Louise whispered.

"The filling station," Philip said.

"Beg pardon?" the banker said.

Louise nodded; she understood. A few years earlier Al had bought a run-down Humble station. Just where he'd gotten the money had been a mystery; he'd talked vaguely of a silent partner. Philip worked in the station that summer, along with a Negro named Burbage who was supposed to do wax jobs. Al didn't care much for pumping gas, and the whole thing fell apart in a couple of months. Al sold the station at a loss; he somehow came out of the deal with a two-year-old Pontiac, but it was repossessed on Labor Day.

"What will we do?" Louise asked as they started home.

"We could send him to prison."

Louise began to sob. Philip took her hand. "Don't worry about it," he told her. "Princeton was just a dream."

"Maybe you could get a scholarship."

"It's too late for that. There's no way to swing it now. It'd cost three thousand a year, and I can't save more than five or six hundred in the summers."

"Maybe if you talked to Coyle . . ."

"I don't want their money," he snapped. "Look, it'll work out. I can go to TCU."

"It isn't fair," she sobbed. "You wanted to go to Princeton."

"It'll work out," he repeated stubbornly.

Al was there when they got home, nursing a can of Pearl and watching a Western on television. He got up when he saw Louise crying. "What's the matter, honey?" he asked.

"How much did you get for the necklace?" Philip asked.

Al stared at him openmouthed. "Do what?" he said.

"The necklace, damn it. The one you stole from her lockbox on April 10, 1950. How much did you get for it?"

"Just hold on there," Al said indignantly.

"Oh, Al, don't lie," Louise said. "We talked to the man at the bank. The one you gave the affidavit that you'd forged my signature on."

Al sagged as if he'd been hit. He was in his mid-forties now, a wiry man with thinning hair and nervous eyes.

"Honey, I wanted to tell you," Al said. "That station was such a good opportunity..."

"Yeah, it was a gold mine," Philip said. "How much did you get for the necklace?"

Al turned away. "What does it matter?"

"It matters because it was my college education," Philip yelled.

"Ten thousand," Al said.

Philip started to laugh. It was that or cry. "Four years at Princeton," he said, "and you blew it on a crummy filling station and a secondhand Pontiac. You're a wizard, Al."

Louise sank into a chair. Al knelt beside her. "I'll make it up to you, honey," he whispered.

Philip exploded. "Out!" he yelled.

They both looked at him in astonishment. For a dozen years, whatever happened, Al had sweet-talked Louise and she had forgiven him.

"Get out," he said coldly. "Just leave and don't come back."

Al drew himself up. "Hold on, young man," he said.

"If you're not out of here in five minutes," Philip said, "I'll call the DA and have you arrested for stealing that necklace."

Al looked at Louise. "Honey?" he said, imploring.

Louise's face was etched with pain. "You should go," she whispered.

Al went into the bedroom. Soon he returned with a suitcase in his hand. He stood there for a moment, red-eyed and trembling. "Louise, I always did the best I could," he said.

Louise didn't look up. "I know you did, Al."

Philip stared at Al and felt a new pain inside. It was true enough; Al had always done his best. His best just wasn't worth a damn.

"Philip, I tried to be a daddy to you."

Philip guessed that was true too. He could remember when Al had tried to teach him to play baseball and fish. It hadn't worked, that was all.

Al stuck out his hand. "So long, Philip," he said. "Good luck."

Philip shook his hand. "Good luck, Al," he muttered and then his stepfather was gone.

Out in the yard, Al called to Alice, who was across the street hitting golf balls. She came over and he put his arm around her and whispered to her and then she was crying and he was hugging her.

"I can't do it to her," Louise said.

"You've got to," Philip told her. After a moment Louise went outside and Alice ran to her and Al got into his old Ford and was gone.

Philip wanted to skip his graduation ceremony that night. They could mail him their stupid diploma. But it was important to his mother so he agreed to go. Louise had invited Caddy to attend the graduation with her. Philip didn't know Caddy well, only that she and Louise had lunch occasionally. Caddy picked them up in her jade-green El Dorado and took them to Colonial for dinner. When Philip got in she kissed him on the mouth and said, "My God, Louise, he's the very *image* of Coyle!" She was a flashy woman with platinum hair, plucked eyebrows, and a lot of jewelry. When Louise complimented her jade ring and asked if she'd bought it to go with the El Dorado, Caddy laughed and said, "To tell you the awful truth, dear, I bought the car to go with the ring."

They got the best table at the country club, one that overlooked the big eighteenth green, and Caddy ordered champagne and was soon regaling them with tales of her husbands and lovers. She said that one of her lovers, a Houston oilman, had a hook instead of a right hand because of a mishap involving the pet lion he kept in his back yard. She insisted that her first husband, Pig Powell, was now married to twin sisters, one in Midland and one in Longview. Philip laughed at the stories and studied Caddy, with her jewels and her El Dorado and her winters in Palm Springs, and he thought that the difference between her life and his mother's life had nothing to do with beauty or brains or decency but only with toughness, calculation. Caddy had been careful to marry only rich men and to squeeze everything out of them she could. His mother had married a Kingslea and divorced him and not gotten a dime.

You had to be tough, he thought, tough as nails.

After dinner, Louise went off to the ladies' room and Caddy stayed at the table, studying Philip with cold green eyes, puffing on an English cigarette.

"I can't get over how much you look like Coyle."

"How well did you know my father?' he asked.

Caddy shrugged. "Well enough. We had an affair once. For four days I was madly in love with him and then he got drunk and knocked me down a flight of stairs and called me names I'd never heard before and passed out in a pool of his own vomit."

Philip kept staring at her. He guessed if someone bought you dinner at the country club you had to hear her out.

"You look like him," Caddy said. "I hope you don't drink like him."

"I don't," Philip said.

"Good," she said. "Sometime we'll talk about your father."

"I'd like that," he said.

He went outside and smoked some of Sherry's weed. He thought it would make the commencement speeches easier to take. He'd smoked in school a few times that spring. The weed made the pep rallies and Texas History class and Rupert Glasscock all seem quite hilarious. When he smoked, he imagined himself a traveler from some distant planet, briefly examining this strange earthling institution, *high school,* this strange place, *Texas,* before zooming on to some more rational world.

Caddy drove them to the TCU auditorium. Philip's classmates were milling around in their caps and gowns, waiting to march inside. Philip saw Jenny standing with Skip and some other kids. He went over and spoke to her and ignored the others.

"Hi, beautiful," he said.

"Hi, P.K."

"Let me take you away from all this."

She laughed and he took her hand and they walked to the edge of the crowd. "You all set for Princeton?" she asked.

"Oh, who knows? Who knows what evil lurks? How about you? You all set for UT and Kappa Alpha Theta?"

"Raring to go," she said. "Listen, what about Princeton? Is anything wrong?"

"Wrong? What could be wrong? I'm going to buzz up in my Stutz Bearcat, with my racoon coat and my silver hip-flask, and I'll join the Triangle Club and write for the *Tiger* and you're going to come up on party weekends and be my date and you'll take the Ivy League by storm and meanwhile I'll write my novel and when it's published we'll meet at the Plaza and ride a carriage through Central Park and jump in the fountain with our clothes on and then we'll go up to our suite overlooking the park and take off our wet clothes and . . ."

She was laughing and hugging him and people were staring and they didn't care. "I love you," he said. "I've loved you since the goddam second grade."

The band was playing "Pomp and Circumstance" and everyone was lining up to march inside.

"Do you remember when we'd go to the Saturday matinees and hold hands?" he asked. "Do you remember *The Purple Heart* about the fiendish Japs torturing our boys? Saddest movie I ever saw. Do you remember how you liked Gene Autry and I liked Roy Rogers? And how we'd go to the drugstore afterward for cherry Cokes?" He guessed he sounded like an idiot, but it was all there in his head. It always would be.

Everyone else was in line but he couldn't leave her. Then someone grabbed his arm. "Come on, Jenny," Skip said. "It's time to go in. Can't you leave this jerk alone?"

"We're coming," Jenny said.

"Has he told you he won't be going to Princeton?" Skip asked.

"Shut up, you bastard," Philip snapped.

"What do you mean?' Jenny asked. "What happened?"

"What happened was, a long time ago his mother conned my grandmother out of a necklace. Now his stepfather has conned *her* out of it, which is pretty funny."

What followed was so natural, so effortless, so absolutely perfect, that Philip would remember it with pride the rest of his life. Without thinking, with Sherry's mad little grin on his face, he unleashed the methodical left-to-the-gut, right-to-the-head combination the Duke had taught him, and then Skip was on his knees with blood spurting from his aquiline nose. "Oh God, P.K.," Jenny sighed. Philip savored his triumph for a moment, then he raced into the night, leaving his classmates to their pomp and circumstance, bellowing "Wahoo!" and laughing his fool head off.

CHAPTER ELEVEN

Philip hit the bars with the Duke that night and was dead to the world when the phone started ringing the next morning. Groaning, he answered it.

"Philip? It's me!"

"Huh? Who the—"

"Me, Philip! Clara. Congratulations!"

"Jesus, Clara; hang on while I make coffee."

"Oh, I didn't wake you, did I?"

When he came back, she said, "So how *are* you?"

"Me? Oh, I'm fine. Great. How about you?"

"Fine, too," Clara said. "My divorce is going through, and I've got a teaching job for the fall, and . . . well, there's a fellow I'm pretty serious about."

"I'm glad," he said. "Really."

"Did you hear from Princeton?"

Philip lit a Lucky. "Yeah, they accepted me. The thing is, a problem came up."

"What kind of a problem?"

"A money problem. I thought I had some I didn't have."

"What about a scholarship?"

"It's too late. Listen, don't worry about it. Maybe I'll go to TCU for a year. Disguise myself as a Texas Christian. Hold on again, will you. My water's boiling."

He went back to the kitchen and fixed instant coffee. After a few sips he thought he might live. When he got back on the phone, Clara said he ought to talk to her brother.

"Your brother? Why?"

"Don't you remember? He teaches at Page College, in Tennessee. It's a nice little school, Philip, and they've got some scholarship money. Frank's up there this summer, painting the dorms and all. You ought to call him, and . . ."

Someone started banging on the front door. Philip tried to ignore it but it got louder and made his head hurt. "Hold a minute," he told Clara, and he went and cracked the door. Two men were on the porch. One of them flashed a badge. Philip thought they must be looking for Al, one of his bad checks.

"Are you Philip Kingslea?"

"That's right."

"You're under arrest."

"For what?"

"Assault with a deadly weapon. Get some clothes on."

"You're out of your mind."

"Get some clothes on, boy, unless you want to go like you are."

The detectives pushed their way into the house. Philip told Clara he had to go and put on some jeans and a shirt.

"Why'd you slug that fellow?" one of the detectives asked on the ride downtown. "Some kind of family feud?" They were on West Seventh, passing Montgomery Ward. You could still see the dark stain, a dozen feet up the side of the building, left by the big flood of 1949. He'd been a Boy Scout then, and they'd spent a weekend cleaning a few tons of muck and slime out of some Pentecostal church.

"No comment, mister," said the ex-Boy Scout. "Not until I talk to my lawyer."

At the jail, they photographed and fingerprinted him and finally let him make a phone call. He caught his mother just as she was returning from the Safeway. "Don't worry, it's all crazy," he told her. "Just get me a lawyer."

They took him to a cell on the top floor of the jail with a fine view of the stockyards. He threw up and felt a little better.

"Hey, buddy, you okay?" someone called.

A very fat young man was peering through the bars of another cell. He had two black eyes, one arm in a sling, and a bandage around his head.

"I'm more okay than you are," Philip said. "You got a cigarette?"

"You bet," the fellow said. "Catch."

He tossed a pack of Pall Malls across. Philip caught the pack, took a few cigarettes, lit one, and tossed the pack back. A lifetime of Jimmy Cagney movies had prepared him for jail.

"What they got you for?" the fellow asked.

"Rape and murder."

The fat fellow's eyes lit up. "No shit?" He looked as if he'd just met Al Capone.

"How about you?" Philip said.

"Ah, hell, I just got drunk and tried to outrun the highway patrol. I'da done it, too, but the bastards shot my tires out."

Philip shot the bull with the fellow for a while, until they'd smoked up all his Pall Malls, and then he took a nap. It was midafternoon when a deputy led Philip to a small conference room where a man with thick glasses and a pockmarked face was waiting.

"Philip, I'm Milton McBee," the man said. "Your mother and I attend church together and she has asked me to represent you."

"Glad to meet you," Philip said. "You wouldn't have a cigarette, would you?"

"I'm afraid I don't smoke," the lawyer said.

"Mr. McBee, I don't understand what's going on. Last night I slugged a guy. A thousand guys get slugged in this town every night. So what am I doing in jail?"

Milton McBee fiddled with his wedding band. "I believe the heart of the problem is the mother of the boy you hit, Mrs. Kingslea . . ."

"Cissy."

"Yes. She seems to be furious that you broke her son's nose and caused him to miss his graduation ceremony. I understand she told the district attorney that she intends to pursue this matter to the utmost."

"What is this about assault with a deadly weapon? I hit the guy with my fist."

"The boy told police he thought you had brass knuckles or a piece of pipe or something in your hand."

"I wish I had, but I didn't. Look, how do I get out of here?"

"We're going to a bond hearing now," the lawyer said.

The hearing was downstairs in a JP's dusty office. The JP was an old fellow named Mullins, who looked mad as hell at being called in on a Saturday afternoon. L. T. Sykes, the assistant district attorney whom Philip had tangled with before, was standing in front of the JP's desk. Louise, looking pale and frightened, waited at the side; Philip winked at her.

"What's this all about?" the JP demanded. "I never got so many phone calls about one bloody nose in my whole life."

"Your honor," L. T. Sykes said, "last night, at the Western Heights graduation ceremony, this boy struck another boy in the face and broke his nose. There's some indication that the defendant may have had brass knuckles or a piece of pipe in his hand."

"That's a lie," Philip said.

"Just hold your horses, young fellow," the JP said. "Mr. McBee, what do you have to say?"

McBee stepped forward. "Your honor, the other boy was larger. He sought out my client, seized his arm, and threatened him. My client was acting in self-defense. He doesn't deny hitting the other boy—who, incidentally, was his cousin—but he had no weapon and there is no evidence of one. My client is a young man with no prior record, and I submit that these charges should be dropped here and now."

The JP laughed. "I'm not going to do that, Mr. McBee."

"In that case, I request that my client be released on his own recognizance."

"Just a minute, your honor," Sykes said. "This same young man was brought in last fall for assault on a police officer, and . . ."

"That was dropped and you know it!" Philip snapped.

"The fact remains," Sykes said, "that this is a violence-prone juvenile who is a menace to the community. I happen to know that he's been running around with an older crowd, a bunch of hoodlums. I think he should be incarcerated until we find out more about this matter."

The JP frowned. "Mr. McBee?"

"Your honor, all that about an older crowd is hearsay. As

for an earlier charge, apparently it was dropped. We ask that Philip be released immediately."

The JP frowned unhappily. "I'm worried about this young man. I reckon we'd better set his bond at five thousand dollars. That's all."

Philip heard his mother cry out. A deputy started pulling at his arm. "Hey, I'm being railroaded," he protested, but the deputy was leading him out the door. "What's happening?" Philip asked his lawyer. They were standing by the elevator.

"I'm afraid you'll have to stay here unless you can make five thousand dollars bond," the lawyer said. "If you don't, I'll try on Monday to get the bond reduced."

"Monday?" Philip said. Then he started to laugh. He couldn't help it.

"Is something funny?" McBee said.

"Yeah," Philip said. "If I had five thousand dollars I'd be on my way to Princeton."

It wasn't funny back in the cell. He didn't know where his mother could get five hundred dollars, much less five thousand. And if he didn't make bail, the question was how long he could stand it in jail.

"Mr. Philip, what you doin' in dere?"

A gnarled, rheumy-eyed old Negro in a frock coat was leaning on a broom outside his cell. "Popeye, you old reprobate, how are you?" Philip called.

"I'se okay, Mr. Philip. You still drivin' dat bread truck?"

"Not this weekend."

"What dey got you fer?"

Popeye was a courthouse character who cleaned out the jail, sold newspapers out on Main Street, and did some bootlegging when he felt like it. The last Christmas Eve they'd sat in Philip's bread truck outside the jail and celebrated with a half-pint of Popeye's finest rotgut.

"I did a terrible thing. I broke a rich boy's nose."

Popeye shook his head sadly. "Dem rich folks, Mr. Philip, dey thinks dey owns de world. How long you in fer?"

"I don't know," Philip admitted. "Listen, have you got any cigarettes?"

Popeye dug into his frock coat and produced a pack of Picayunes. "Take dese, Mr. Philip. How 'bout money? You got any money?"

"Not really."

Popeye shoved a wadded-up five-dollar bill through the bars. "Take dis," he said. Philip pushed the bill back. "No, you keep it," he said.

"Hell, boy, you in de jail, not me. You need de money for cigarettes an' stuff."

"Don't you need it?"

"De Lord, he'll take care of ole Popeye. You pay me back when you git out, okay?"

"Okay, pal," Philip said. "Thanks." He reached through the bars and shook the old Negro's hand. Popeye winked and moved on down the corridor.

Philip was starting to panic. He'd heard stories of what happened to young guys in jail. He'd worked one summer with a half-crazy ex-con who was always winking and saying, "Baby, dey'd love ya in duh joint!" He thought he might go crazy if he had to spend the night in this place. Already he could feel the walls starting to close in. He wondered if he ought to call Coyle and borrow the money for bail. He'd sworn a long time back never to take a dime from Coyle, because it was really Wade Kingslea's money, and he'd hated Wade Kingslea as long as he could remember, hated him for what he'd done to his father and to his mother. But now he wasn't so sure. Maybe anybody's money was all right as long as it got him out of this terrible place. He sat staring at the wall, agonizing, trying to weigh his old hatred against his present fears. The hell of it was, he couldn't even think that his imprisonment was wrong. In this town, how could you clobber somebody as rich as Skip without Cissy getting her pound of flesh?

A deputy came to his door. "I've got to use the phone," Philip yelled.

"Relax, kid," the deputy said. He had a potbelly and a "God Is Love" tattoo. He rattled a big ring of keys and opened the door of the cell.

"What's happening?" Philip demanded.

"Hell, you didn't think anybody named Kingslea was gonna spend the night in the Tarrant County jail, did you?" the deputy growled.

He led Philip back to the conference room and again McBee was waiting.

"What's going on?" Philip said.

"Somebody made your bond," the lawyer said.

"What do you mean, 'somebody'?"

"It wasn't me or your mother. Look, I told her I'd give you a ride home."

"I don't need a ride." Philip stuck out his hand. "Thanks for everything."

"You're sure? About the ride?"

"I've got a couple of things to do."

"Well, good luck, Philip. Come see us in church sometime."

Philip smiled. "Maybe I will."

Five minutes later, Philip stepped out into the gentle June twilight. Freedom stunned him, even more than confinement had. It was so simple. Someone signed a paper, someone turned a key, and you were free.

As he started down the steps to the street, a gleaming black Fleetwood eased to a stop at the curb and Wade Kingslea got out. He was wearing a three-piece, charcoal-gray suit that had been hand-tailored for him in London and carrying a silver-handled walking stick. His neatly trimmed hair was silver, too, but his thick eyebrows were still black as sin.

A new, more subtle, more elegant Wade Kingslea had been evolving over the past dozen years. In the 1920s and 1930s he had been obsessed by oil, oil and money. Now he was obsessed with power. The turning point had been the Second World War, when Franklin Roosevelt asked him to serve on the Petroleum War Advisory Council. In the 1930s Kingslea had bitterly resented government power; in Washington, in the 1940s, he began to understand that power. He also began to understand Roosevelt himself, whom he grudgingly respected; the need was to find a president with Roosevelt's guile who would serve the cause of conservatism.

World War II, Kingslea soon learned, was really World Oil War I, the first war fought both on and for oil. For the United States, the war began when Roosevelt cut off Japan's oil, and it ended when the Germans were not so much defeated as denied the oil they needed to keep fighting. It was oil that had sent the Japanese into Indochina and sent Rommel racing toward the rich fields of the Middle East. It was oil finally that had led to a bitter war-within-a-war in Washington, as oilmen like Kingslea bitterly resisted the efforts of New Deal liberals to use the war as an excuse to nationalize the oil industry. The experience left Kingslea with a simple realization: oil and government were natural enemies; eventually, either oil would control government or government would control oil.

Harry Truman, Roosevelt's successor, was a disaster, as far as Kingslea was concerned, and he spent several years studying the crop of national politicians, looking for one he could help to the White House in 1952.

When talk of Eisenhower began, Kingslea was electrified —of course the man could be elected, but what did he stand for?

Kingslea had met Eisenhower during the war, so he called him in Paris, where he was commander of the NATO forces, and said he'd like to come over for a chat. Ike had sounded delighted. Kingslea and Sid Richardson flew over together and promised Eisenhower that if he chose to run as a Republican, they would put up a million dollars to help him build a political organization, and there would be more money later as it was needed.

Ike didn't say yes and he didn't say no. He smiled, nodded, asked a few questions, told a few stories, and sent them on their way. "That is the first man I've ever seen turn down a million dollars," Richardson complained as they left. "He's either a genius or a fool, and I'm afraid he's no fool."

Eisenhower eventually took their money, lots of it, but it was mixed in with other people's money so no one group could boast that it owned him. It was hard to get your hooks in Ike. He respected money, but he never forgot that he was the hero and that you needed him more than he needed you.

Ike won, of course. Kingslea had been to Washington to see him that very week. They lunched at the White House, then went for a round of golf at Burning Tree. It was most pleasant, but somehow the things that Kingslea wanted commitments on—the depletion allowance, exemptions for natural gas, import quotas—never got pinned down. Ike was slick as glass. Nor did Kingslea want to push him too hard. Kingslea was starting to see a long-term role for himself as presidential adviser and political kingmaker. He had another goal, too, that was more and more on his mind. He had been watching as Joe Kennedy masterminded his son Jack's political career; clearly Joe intended to have the boy in the White House by 1960 or 1964. Kingslea had been grooming his grandson Skip since the boy's father was killed in the war, and he saw no reason that Skip should not enter politics and go just as far as Joe Kennedy's playboy son.

But if he was to reach his goals, Kingslea understood that

his own reputation must be spotless. He had begun to cut back on his more questionable oil deals, and on his women, too, lest any hint of scandal ruin his standing in Washington.

That was one reason Wade Kingslea was waiting outside the Tarrant County jail when his grandson Philip emerged that June evening. The Kingslea family did not need a silly public feud that could make him a laughingstock. Besides, Kingslea remained interested in Philip. Despite everything, he thought the boy had potential.

"Good evening, Philip," he said, as his grandson stopped before him on the sidewalk.

"Hello," Philip said. He wanted to keep going, but that seemed stupid. His grandfather was here for a reason. Maybe both of them were.

"Congratulations on your graduation."

"Thanks."

"You must have had quite a celebration."

Philip shrugged. "Not really."

"I'm told you punched your cousin Skip in the nose."

"You want to know something?"

"What?"

"I'd do it again."

Wade Kingslea smiled indulgently. People were stopping to stare at him but they kept a respectful distance.

"Tell me, why do you dislike Skip so?"

"Because he thinks he's better than I am."

"And you disagree?"

"He's richer. And a better athlete. But not better."

"You're making distinctions that Skip doesn't make. He thinks richer is better, because he's never been poor. I'm afraid you're wiser than he. Never underestimate the uses of adversity, young man. I was poor for a long time, twenty-five years, but it made me strong, just as your life has made you strong, if somewhat hotheaded."

"Did you make my bail?" Philip asked. He had to ask. He owed the old man that. Sometimes he wasn't even sure why he hated his grandfather so. Maybe it was just another habit.

"Yes, I posted it."

"Why?"

"Skip's mother has reached an age at which women often behave illogically. Your punching Skip is not a matter for the courts."

Philip wondered if that was the real reason. "You could

lose your money, you know, if I leave town."

"I'm aware of the risk."

"Well, thanks," Philip said. The words did not come easily. He waited awkwardly. He saw Popeye peddling the *Star-Telegram* down the street. He wondered if his exploits had made the news.

"I heard about your mother's necklace," Kingslea said.

Philip stared at the sidewalk. "Yeah. Well, don't worry about it."

"That man should be prosecuted. The necklace was yours by right."

Philip shrugged. What was there to say? His grandfather pulled an envelope from his pocket. "This is for you."

Philip hesitated. "What is it?"

"Call it a graduation present." Kingslea jabbed the envelope at him like a knife. Reluctantly, Philip took it. "Go ahead, open it," Kingslea said.

He tore open the envelope. It was stuffed with thousand-dollar bills. "It's for your education," Kingslea said. "To make up for the necklace."

It hurt just to look at the money. Little green pieces of paper that meant so much. "No," he said, "I don't want it."

He pushed the envelope back at his grandfather, but Kingslea wouldn't accept it.

"Philip, the money means nothing to me and it means a great deal to you."

"Maybe that's the point."

"I don't understand."

"Look, I was your grandson once, and . . ."

"You still are . . ."

". . . and you tried to buy me from my mother and she wouldn't sell so you cut us off. That was your decision. I was three years old and didn't have a hell of a lot to do with it."

"That was a long time ago, Philip. Passions were high at the time. Your mother . . ."

"Don't say anything about my mother. Not a word."

"It was a long time ago. Perhaps I acted impulsively. You can look upon this money as a kind of reparation. It's little enough."

"I can't take it."

"No one would even know."

"You'd know. I'd know. Don't you see?"

"No, I don't see. I don't see at all."

"Listen, I'm going to make it in the world, just like you made it. And I'm going to make it on my own, just like you did. If there's one thing I've learned in my life, it's to take care of myself. If I take a handout from you, I lose that, and if I lose it, I'm nothing."

Kingslea stared at him for a long time. "Take the money, Philip," he said abruptly, and he stepped into his Fleetwood and was gone.

Philip stood with the envelope burning his hand. The Princeton that he had banished from his mind, had burned to the ground, rose up suddenly, ivory towers shimmering before his eyes. "Damn you," he said.

He walked to the corner where Popeye was selling papers.

"Dey done let you out, Mr. Philip," the Negro said. He had a strong smell of rotgut about him. His frock coat looked like it'd been slept in for a decade or two, and he'd sliced open the toes of his old patent-leather shoes to make life more tolerable for his corns.

"You got anything to drink, Popeye?"

Popeye glanced up and down the street with watery eyes, then produced a half-pint of Four Roses. Philip took a long swig. "I owe you some money," he said.

"No hurry, Mr. Philip. I trusts you."

Philip stuck the envelope in the Negro's hand. "Keep the change," he said and ran down the street. He hadn't gone far when he heard the old man cry out, "De Lawd be praised!"

Popeye had fallen to his knees. His hands, clutching the thousand-dollar bills, stretched toward the heavens. "Sweet Jesus," he kept howling.

The next morning, while his mother was at church, Philip called Clara's brother in Tennessee. Then he drove to a filling station on West Seventh and sold the Plymouth for fifty dollars. "So long, Old Paint," he said, patting the Plymouth on its battered hood before he started home.

When his mother got back from church he told her what he was going to do.

"I don't understand," she said. "When will you be back?"

"I don't know. Maybe Thanksgiving. The thing is, if I go up now and work all summer on the dorms, they'll give me a scholarship."

"I've never even heard of Page College," Louise said.

"It's a great place," he told her. "The Princeton of East Tennessee."

She put her arms around him. "I don't want to lose you."

He held her close. "I've got to go," he said. "I'd better pack and get started."

Dazed, Louise fixed him some sandwiches while he packed. He stuffed his duffel bag with clothing and squeezed in two paperback books, *This Side of Paradise* and Jim Phillips' Fort Worth novel, *The Inheritors*. He thought about calling his father, and Jenny, but he decided he'd write them, or see them at Christmas, or something. He didn't want to talk to anybody. He just wanted to leave.

When he was packed he went out to the back yard, where Alice was putting away. The week before, she'd won a trophy in the Park Department's pitch-and-putt tournament for kids, and she was convinced the U.S. Open was next.

"So long, slugger," he said. "I'm taking off for college."

She eased in a six-footer, then brushed back her reddish hair and stared at him. "Where to?"

"A place in Tennessee."

"When'll you be back?"

"I don't know. Listen, take care of your mom, okay?"

"Sure." Tears were welling in her eyes.

"And don't spend all your time hitting golf balls. Hit the books once in a while."

Alice bit her lip but tears splashed down her cheeks. Philip handed her a twenty-dollar bill. "Buy yourself a decent putter," he said. She threw her arms around him and sobbed and he talked to her awhile, gave her a lot of dumb big-brother advice, and then finally said his good-bye and went to get his bag.

As they drove out to the east side of town, Louise said, "But what if you aren't here for your trial? Won't your grandfather lose his five thousand dollars?"

"The way I figure it, he doesn't want me here. The last thing he needs is one Kingslea taking another Kingslea to court. It'd make him look like an idiot when he's trying to be a great statesman."

It was past two when they stopped at the edge of the highway that stretched east to Dallas and beyond. The temperature was in the upper nineties. Trucks stirred great clouds of dust as they rumbled past. Louise was fighting back tears. He put his arms around her. "I feel terrible," he said. "I feel like I'm running off and leaving you. Maybe I should stay here and get a job and . . ."

"No. It's all right. Your college comes . . ."

"The thing is, I've got to get out of this town. I've been fighting it all my life and it's starting to win. Sometimes I think I'll go crazy here. Sometimes I think I'll kill somebody."

Now she was crying. "Philip, Philip," she sobbed.

"Somewhere out there there's a world where I belong. A world where people care about books and music and movies and . . . people. Where they care about something besides their stupid Cadillacs and their stupid country clubs and their stupid football games and . . ."

"If only I'd been able to give you . . ."

"No, no, don't say that. You've been wonderful. You've been an angel, all my life."

Louise wiped her eyes with a Kleenex. "I'm not an angel. I'm just a woman living her life and making her share of mistakes."

A truck roared past and shook their car. Dust mingled with their sweat and tears. "What will you do for spending money?" she asked. "Maybe I can send you some."

"No, don't worry about it. I'll find a job."

"Coyle wants to help you. He called me. He's upset."

"I don't want his money. I'll write him."

"He does care about you. He loves you."

"I know that. Listen, I'm no broker than Wade Kingslea was when he went off to Goodwill. Someday I'll come back to this town and I'll show those sons of bitches."

"Philip, they aren't important. All that matters is for you to be happy. I don't care if you sell shoes, if you're happy."

"I won't sell shoes. I'll be somebody important."

Louise put her arms around him. "Just be the best that you can," she said. "You've always made me so proud."

He held her close for a long time, then he got out and waved as she started back home. When she was out of sight, Philip stuck out his thumb.

It wasn't long until an old Dodge pickup stopped. The driver was a young fellow wearing boots and jeans and a Hawaiian shirt. "Where ya headed?"

"Tennessee."

"I'm going to Little Rock. Hop in."

The driver's name was Leon Purvis and he was going to Little Rock to get his gun collection back from his ex-wife. Or maybe to kill her; it wasn't clear. They bought a couple of six-packs and started trading dirty jokes. Philip knew hundreds of dirty jokes. He hadn't learned much in school, and he guessed that all those dirty jokes, plus his knowledge of bopping and bar-fighting and Western swing, were the cultural heritage he took with him from Texas as he went forth to confront the larger world.

Everything was fine until they passed through a little East Texas town that had a banner over its main street warning, "Don't Let the Sun Set on You Here, Nigger!" That set Leon off on Negroes and Communists and the Supreme Court. Philip sank down in the seat. He'd listened to that crap all his life and he'd be damned if he'd listen to it all the way to Little Rock. He peered up the road until he saw what he was looking for.

"Let me out," he said. "Just this side of that sign."

"Man, this is only Texarkana," Leon protested.

"I know."

Leon grumbled and stopped the truck. "No hard feelings," Philip said. "I've got something on my mind."

Leon Purvis shrugged and the Dodge rattled away. Philip looked back toward Texas. The flat land stretched on forever toward a raging orange sunset. He thought of his Quaker ancestors, moving west through here, nearly a century before. He wondered if they'd found whatever they were seeking. Then he turned and walked to the big roadside sign that said, "YOU ARE NOW LEAVING THE GREAT STATE OF TEXAS!"

He stared at the sign until he began to shake with laughter. He imagined an invisible line that ran past the sign, separating Texas from the rest of the world. He'd never in his life been outside of Texas. Still laughing, he backed up, took a running start, and vaulted over the invisible line, into Arkansas. He started to walk east, then turned back. He stopped beside the sign, undid his fly, and peed back into Texas. Then he buttoned his jeans, put his hands to his mouth, and yelled at the top of his lungs *"Adiós, motherfuckers!"* With a last glance at the blazing sunset, he started running east as fast as he could, toward Tennessee, toward college, toward the future, toward the good, free, sane, unencumbered life he knew was waiting for him, somewhere up the road.

_ *Book V* _

Philip and Jenny

Washington
1961–63

CHAPTER ONE

Shortly after noon on January 20, 1961, as a youthful, vigorous John F. Kennedy, newly inaugurated as president of the United States, poked the frigid air with his forefinger and exhorted Americans to ask what they could do for their country, Philip Kingslea was watching from a nearby VIP grandstand and thinking he was the luckiest son of a bitch alive.

Lucky to have blundered into the Kennedy campaign and made himself useful. Lucky to be headed for a job in Kennedy's White House. Lucky, most of all, at the still-tender age of twenty-five, to have found something to believe in. When Kennedy, closing his speech, implored "Let us go forth to lead the land we love," Philip Kingslea, who considered himself one of the most cynical men alive, burst into tears of joy.

Looking back, he thought his good luck had begun the day he arrived, dusty and broke after three days' hitchhiking, at Page College in Tennessee. After Texas, Page had been a new world. In the world he had fled, young men had been admired for money and athletic skill, and he had ranked poorly in both departments. At Page College, no one had much money, and athletic events were valued mainly as an excuse for beer-drinking. At Page, young men became popular if they appreciated the right books, records, and fashions, if they did well but not excessively well in the classroom, if they brandished a scathing wit, if they dated "sharp" coeds, and if they possessed the proper ivory-tower disdain for the forces of materialism that reportedly lurked off-campus.

In all of this, Philip excelled. He wrote satirical verse and caustic movie reviews for the school paper, squired some of the more celebrated coeds in that corner of Tennessee, dressed (thanks to furtive visits to thrift shops in Nashville, Dallas, and Atlanta) in the approved Ivy League style, revered the writings of Hemingway, Wolfe, and Fitzgerald, and the music

321

of Dave Brubeck, Stan Kenton, and the Modern Jazz Quartet, and was willing, when the occasion demanded, to get famously drunk. He was, in sum, the very model of a cool, buttoned-down collegian of the silent fifties, and it came as a distinct jolt to him when, one June morning in 1957, he was handed a diploma and told to go forth, with a clear head and a pure heart, to conquer the waiting world.

In truth, he went forth with a brutal hangover, and only as far as Nashville, where through a second burst of good fortune he landed a job as a sixty-five-dollar-a-week reporter for the Nashville *Sun*.

Journalism had not been his goal. If he had a goal, in those days, it was to write a novel, but his novels all seemed to start off very much like *The Great Gatsby* and to bog down at about the fourth page. He therefore considered law school as a practical alternative and had gone to Nashville to investigate scholarship possibilities at Vanderbilt's school of law. He never made it to the law school, however, because on that visit he happened to look up a Sweet Briar coed of his acquaintance, Hillary Pickett, and thus to meet her father, Wellman Pickett, the editor of the Nashville *Sun*.

Wellman Pickett was a bald, ramrod-straight, no-nonsense gentleman who was considered by the best people in Nashville to be a traitor to his class. He was, on the one hand, a fourth-generation Nashvillian, a Vanderbilt alumnus, the husband of a much-admired and socially impeccable wife, the father of three debutantes, and a resident of Belle Meade, the city's most exclusive enclave. He was, on the other hand, the editor of a newspaper that vigorously advocated equal rights for Negroes, a nuclear test ban, an increased and expanded minimum wage, and the reelection of Estes Kefauver, all of which had caused more than a few crosses to be burned on his well-manicured lawn.

For some reason, Wellman Pickett took a liking to the rather aimless young man who turned up on his doorstep that summer, and having an opening in his newsroom, offered him a job. Philip jumped at it. The salary was less than princely, but had not Hemingway started as a reporter? Within days he had mastered the art of obituary writing, and after only two weeks he won his first by-line with a dozen deft paragraphs about an irate hillbilly singer who attacked a smart-mouthed disc jockey with an icepick and tossed his well-ventilated remains into the Cumberland River.

Philip soon proved his worth as a reporter. He wrote well and quickly. Perhaps more importantly, he viewed the world with a certain detachment, a certain lack of emotional involvement, that might have made him a less than perfect friend or lover but helped make him an effective journalist. He understood instinctively that, to a reporter, people were always a means to an end, and the end was the story he was writing that day.

By the summer of 1960, after three good years with the *Sun,* he longed for new worlds to conquer. He was planning a trip to New York, to confront the editors of the mighty *Times,* when Senator John F. Kennedy's campaign for president unexpectedly beckoned.

One morning in late summer, a few hours before Kennedy was to arrive in Nashville for a rally, Wellman Pickett summoned Philip to his small, spartan office at the front of the newsroom. A blond, compact, good-looking man of forty was pacing like a caged tiger. He was wearing gray pleatless pants, a brown tweed coat, a regimental tie, and a worried look.

"Phil Kingslea, Harry Flynn," the editor said. The man glanced briefly at Philip and kept on pacing. 'Harry is with the Kennedy campaign."

"We're about to blow this damned election, Wellman," Harry Flynn declared. He had a sharp, nasal Boston accent, much like John Kennedy's. "You've read the stories about the well-oiled Kennedy juggernaut? Well, I've seen campaigns for dogcatcher run better. We're down five points in two weeks and now nobody knows how to handle this Houston thing."

The editor nodded sympathetically. "Phil's a Texan, Harry," he said. "Let's see how he feels about the Houston invitation."

Philip eyed the editor and the politician suspiciously. He didn't know what the hell his being from Texas had to do with anything.

"Philip, as you know, the religious issue is hurting Senator Kennedy, especially in the South," the editor said. "All the more so since some influential ministers have expressed fears that the senator, as president, might owe his first allegiance to the pope. The senator has to counterattack; the question is how and when. He has an invitation to appear before the Houston Ministerial Association, to answer their questions about his religious views, but . . ."

"We've got to spike this thing, once and for all," Flynn

said impatiently. "But is Houston the place? I talked to Bob last night. He's been to Texas and he thinks they're all crazy as bedbugs down there. He wants to do it, but then he says how can we let the whole damn campaign swing on what some loony Baptist preacher in Texas may say to Jack on TV."

Philip studied Flynn. There were a dozen facts he would need to know before he could form an intelligent opinion. But he understood that in politics you rarely had all the facts you needed. That was the art of it, you flew blind, on instinct and guts.

"Do it," Philip said.

"Why?" Harry Flynn demanded.

"Because your man's got class," Philip said. "Because in a confrontation with those people he can't help but come out ahead."

"That's what I think," Flynn said. "But, dammit, what if there's a disaster down there?"

Philip shrugged; his was the certitude of the uninvolved. "Do it," he repeated.

Harry Flynn jammed his fists deeper into his Brooks Brothers trousers. "What about that local stuff, Wellman?" he asked.

Once again, Philip didn't know what Harry Flynn was talking about, but his editor did. "Phil, Senator Kennedy needs a bit of local color for his speech here today, and Harry wondered if you could help him out."

"What kind of local color?" Philip asked.

"Anything that'll make it sound like he knows where the hell he is," Flynn snapped.

Philip understood. "There are four or five bases to touch," he said. "Andy Jackson. The Volunteer spirit. FDR. TVA. Music City, U.S.A."

"Put it on paper, Tex," Flynn said. "Three hundred words, maximum."

Philip glanced uncertainly at his boss, until the editor gave him a quiet nod.

"When do you need it?"

"Yesterday," Flynn snapped.

Ten minutes later Philip returned to the editor's office with two pages of copy. Flynn read it anxiously. "Not bad," he muttered. "Come on, Tex, we've got a plane to meet."

"What plane?" Philip said. He had begun to actively dislike Flynn the first time he called him "Tex."

"The candidate's plane," Flynn said. "After the rally here, you go to Memphis, then Birmingham and Atlanta and God-knows-where."

"What the hell are you talking about?" Philip demanded.

"You're joining the campaign," the visitor said. "We need a guy who can write. Come on, shake a leg."

Philip looked at the editor. "You've got first call on me, Mr. Pickett," he said.

Wellman Pickett smiled wistfully. "Oh, we'd be losing you soon enough in any event, Phil. You've got too much talent and ambition to stay much longer. You might as well join the campaign. It'll be a priceless experience, and you might wind up in the White House."

Philip was moved. Wellman Pickett had hardly spoken ten kind words to him in three years, yet he was perhaps the man in the world Philip most admired. Pickett had hired him, taught him most of what he knew about reporting, and now was giving him a boost toward that larger world that he still dreamed of.

Philip stuck out his hand. "Thank you, sir, for everything."

"Good luck to you, Phil," the editor said. "Keep in touch."

An hour later, Philip climbed into a limousine with Jack Kennedy.

Outside the Nashville airport, while passersby cheered and photographers danced about, Harry Flynn shoved Philip into the front seat and climbed in the back himself with the candidate. Kennedy waved at a few last potential voters on the sidewalk, then as the limo eased onto the highway he sank back in the seat and shut his eyes. Flynn began giving the candidate an expert summary of the political situation in Tennessee. Kennedy, his eyes still closed, seemed to have fallen asleep, but suddenly he said, "Rollins, the county clerk, is he a big buck-toothed character who believes in flying saucers?"

Flynn looked sharply at Philip, who nodded.

"That's him," Flynn said.

"I thought so," the candidate said. "I talked to him at a fundraiser here in fifty-eight."

As they neared the city, Flynn said, "Jack, I've got some local color for you."

The candidate sighed, opened his eyes, skimmed the two pages, and put them in his coat pocket. Philip sat tensely in the front seat, awaiting some word of thanks or praise. None came.

"This is Phil Kingslea, who wrote that for us," Flynn said. "Phil's from Texas. He thinks you ought to go to Houston."

Kennedy glanced at Philip. "Any relation to Wade Kingslea?"

Philip hesitated. His relationship to Wade Kingslea was too complicated to explain now. In any event, he was annoyed at Kennedy. A simple "Hello" or "Thank you" wouldn't have broken his jaw.

"Not politically," Philip said.

Kennedy seemed satisfied. A moment later, when the first crowds appeared on the sidewalks, he sat up and began to wave and suddenly looked five years younger.

Twenty minutes later, Kennedy delivered Philip's "local stuff" from a flag-bedecked platform outside the War Memorial Auditorium with such wit and self-assurance that any listener might have thought Nashville his second home. Philip could not help feeling a tremor of pride as this shrewd, sophisticated politician, who might well be the next president, spoke *his* words, cracked *his* jokes. And yet, even as he savored the pride, he resisted it. He had seen the young political aides who spoke meekly of "the Boss" or "the Chief" they served. Philip wanted no Boss. Something deep inside him hated authority. Authority was Rupert Glasscock, authority was Wade Kingslea, authority was Texas, authority was all the self-satisfied sons of bitches who had ever tried to tell him what to do and be and think.

What, then, was he doing attaching himself to a rich, arrogant young politician who hadn't bothered to say hello or good-bye to him that afternoon? Shouldn't he forget this political madness and hurry back to the *Sun?* He asked himself that as the band played and Kennedy waved to the cheering crowd and Harry Flynn pulled him back toward the motorcade. By the time they reached the airport he had made up his mind. With no clean clothes, no toothbrush, no money, and not much idea of what he was doing, he boarded a plane for the candidate's next stop, leaving behind a job he loved and a girl he thought he wanted to marry.

What the hell am I doing?

As the plane started down the runway, Philip shut his eyes and thought of the time, seven years before, when he'd hitchhiked to Tennessee to enroll in a college he'd never seen. Sometimes you had to trust to luck and call it destiny. Then he was in the air, winging west, toward some new frontier.

• • •

The main thing that Philip learned from the Kennedy campaign was that in any presidential campaign, at any given moment, the overwhelming majority of the participants haven't the slightest idea what they are doing. Philip was lucky: he knew exactly what he was doing. He was flying into strange cities, gathering information, and writing speech introductions for the candidate. All around him, day after day, he saw people screwing up: microphones didn't work, halls were too large or too small, politicians who should have been flattered were ignored. Sometimes, when he saw a catastrophe brewing, he would call Harry Flynn and the screw-up would be averted. "Good work, Tex," Flynn would growl, and Philip knew his stock was rising.

He learned a little about Flynn that fall, from newspaper stories and from others in the campaign, particularly women, who were not loath to gossip about such a dashing and mysterious figure. He learned that Flynn went back to prep school days with the Kennedys; that he was between Jack and Bob in age and was a friend of both; that at Harvard he had been an Ivy League tennis champion, that he had been a much-decorated paratrooper in Europe in World War II; that he was a lawyer who represented the Kennedy family in some matters; that he had a wife and several children back in Boston; and that, if one young woman was to be believed, he was having an affair with a well-known movie actress in Los Angeles.

All of which mattered very little to Philip; what mattered was that in the chaos of the campaign, Harry knew what he was doing.

One morning that fall, Philip was in the Denver airport, talking to Harry on the phone.

"Did you hear about Houston?" Harry yelled.

Philip was immediately defensive. Houston? What had gone wrong in Houston? He had in fact been out of touch with the world for the past ten hours, busy with a leggy University of Colorado coed whose extraordinary fantasy life seemed to center exclusively on Senator Kennedy. The fact that Philip was an intimate adviser of the handsome senator (for so she imagined, and he did not disillusion her) had quickly won him an invitation to a long and memorable night.

"What about Houston?" he yelled back at Harry. The coed, pink-cheeked and languid, was plucking at his arm. "Is it Senator *Kennedy?*" she implored.

"The fucking *ministers,* Tex," Harry yelled halfway across the continent. "Jack spoke to them last night. It went like a charm."

"That's great," Philip said.

"Is he *there?*" the girl whispered. "Can I *speak* to him?"

"Listen, Harry, there's a young lady here who's been, ah, very hospitable to me, and I wondered if the senator could say hello." Philip knew, as the coed did not, that Harry was in Washington and Senator Kennedy was in Los Angeles, but he thought he would at least play out the string. To his surprise, Harry went a step further.

"Sure, Tex, put the dear child on."

Philip handed the girl the phone. It was only when her eyes widened and her lips began to tremble that he understood Harry's game—for Harry's Boston accent and crisp delivery were near-identical to his friend Jack Kennedy's.

"Oh, I will, Senator, I will," the coed cried into the phone. Tears welled in her eyes. "Oh God, yes, yes, good-bye!"

The girl hung up the phone and threw her arms around Philip. "Oh thank you," she sobbed. "Promise me you'll come back again."

"I will," Philip vowed and raced off to catch his plane.

Philip's greatest contribution to the campaign came abruptly, at a rally in St. Louis. To get to the speaker's platform, Kennedy and his entourage had to walk through a long line of cheering spectators, held back by ropes and sawhorses. Philip tagged along behind the candidate, confused and frightened by the roar of the crowd. The strange thing about a campaign was how isolated you became. You lived in airplanes and buses and hotels and strangers' homes and you focused on your one little piece of the campaign, whatever it was. You ate too much and drank too much and slept too little and told too many lies and what had once seemed a crusade became an ordeal. It was always a shock to go to the rallies and hear the cheers and realize there were millions of decent people out there who were counting on you to save America from Richard Nixon.

Philip was thinking about a blonde he'd met at the airport rally that afternoon, wondering if she'd be at the VIP reception that night, when he noticed the tall man in the pea jacket, leaning against a tree. He wasn't cheering like everyone else; that was what caught Philip's eye. Philip was walking along, thinking of the girl, watching the tall man in the pea jacket, when he saw the gun.

There was no time to think. Kennedy was abreast of the man. Philip flew forward, moving as he'd never moved before, and crashed into the man and they were rolling over and over on the ground. Philip smelled whiskey and sweat and felt the gun between them and then he heard an explosion and felt a terrible pain and he heard people screaming and he saw Harry Flynn's face and the man was gone. He lay on his back looking up, seeing frightened faces and black sky, wondering if his pain would go away, and then he turned and saw Harry atop the man in the pea jacket, pounding him in the face until the police pulled him off. Then Harry, white with rage, crawled over to Philip.

"You okay, kid?"

Philip was laughing and crying at the same time. He couldn't help it. He'd never thought about being dead before. "Yeah, I'm okay," he said. "The bastard kneed me in the balls."

"Your lip's cut," Harry said. He took out a handkerchief and gently wiped blood off Philip's face. They heard a distant cheer as Kennedy mounted the platform.

"You're A-1 okay, Tex," Harry said. "I keep a book and your name goes in there in gold letters."

Philip sat up. His balls ached but he would survive. It started to seem funny. The Speechwriter's Moment of Glory.

"Harry, there's just one thing I want you to do for me."

"Name it, kid."

"Stop calling me Tex."

On election night Philip got drunk with a lot of other Democrats in a Washington ballroom. The next afternoon, he caught a plane to Nashville to see the girl who not many months before he'd wanted to marry. Her name was Meg and their romance had been a case of opposites attracting. Meg was the beloved, sheltered daughter of a prosperous lawyer in a small Tennessee town. She had pale blue eyes and a timid smile, and she was teaching the second grade in a Nashville school. She didn't smoke or drink, she was a devout Methodist, and she was a virgin. She was also the gentlest, most loving person he'd ever known. He wanted to love and protect her, to take warmth and goodness from her. Yet throughout their romance they both had feared that it could not last, that opposites, in the end, were opposites. He feared that Meg was a delicate wildflower, indigenous to Tennessee, who could not be transplanted to whatever frontiers awaited him. That, finally, was what Meg feared. They spent a final night in one another's arms, talking of what might have been. Then Philip caught a plane to Washington to see where his luck would carry him next.

CHAPTER TWO

After President Kennedy delivered his Inaugural Address, Philip fought his way through the snow and the crowd to the White House. What he found when he reached that hallowed building was the same thing he had endured for four months of the campaign: chaos.

The chaos in the opening hours of the Kennedy administration had to do with who got what offices. In a reasonable world, where lines of authority were neatly drawn, all that would have been decided in advance, but this was not a reasonable world, and there was a mad scramble for the offices that were biggest and/or closest to the Oval Office. Philip wandered the elegant, unfamiliar corridors, watching with amusement as various of Kennedy's "band of brothers" yelled, argued, and in one case came to blows over who got what.

Philip stayed out of the struggle. And eventually he was assigned a tiny, windowless cubicle in the White House basement. You could hear the toilets flush next door in the men's room, but Philip was content. The important question was what he would be doing in his new office.

In a reasonable world, Philip would have been assigned to Ted Sorensen, the chief speechwriter, or Pierre Salinger, the press secretary, but the Kennedy world, as Philip had learned, was a series of competing fiefdoms, and chance had put him in Harry Flynn's domain. That was fine, except that Flynn had nothing to do with writing. In fact, just what he did do was something of a mystery. He occupied a good-sized office on the second floor of the White House, overlooking Pennsylvania Avenue, and he had been designated a Special Assistant to the President, but his duties were nowhere defined.

For weeks Philip kept after Harry: What the hell was he supposed to be doing? "Patience, Tex, patience," Harry would say, and finally one snowy morning, he received a fateful call from Faddle.

Faddle was one of Pierre Salinger's two secretaries. The other was called fiddle. Philip could never remember which was Fiddle and which was Faddle.

"Pierre wants to see you right away," Faddle announced. Philip raced upstairs and found the press secretary in his office, a fat cigar in his mouth and a thick pile of documents in his hand.

"Flynn said you could help me out, Pete," Salinger barked. "Take this crap and boil it down to a thousand words the president can work from."

"What is it?"

"I dunno," Salinger said. "Youth unemployment, I think. Have me something by noon."

Philip grabbed the documents and raced back to his cubbyhole. The president was meeting with some labor leaders that afternoon, he found, and the Labor Department had sent over a "suggested presidential statement" that was unreadable. Philip attacked it gleefully and quickly handed Salinger a thousand words that made sense. Two hours later he watched in the East Room as Kennedy spoke of youth unemployment; he was crisp, factual, and eloquent, and the tough old labor skates gave him a standing ovation.

Thus was born Philip's new career. He became the man in charge of writing what was often called "the Rose Garden crap" or "the East Room crap," those being the two locations in which the president most often addressed visitors to the White House. It was dog work, work that no one else wanted, but Philip seized it eagerly. There was a new assignment almost daily; juvenile delinquency, senior citizens, cancer research, foreign aid, an endless succession of problems to be deplored and challenges to be welcomed. Word soon spread that Philip was a fellow who got the job done. Most of the senior White House figures learned his name, although Salinger persisted in calling him Pete. He worked until eight or nine every night. It was only in the late evenings, when the phones stopped ringing, that he could sometimes have a drink and a chat with Harry Flynn or Larry O'Brien or some of the other top men. He began to grasp the subtleties of the Kennedy world. He learned who were Jack's men and who were Bobby's men and to appreciate the rivalries between them. He began to see that, there in the elegant White House world of antiques and Oriental rugs, tough, ambitious men wielded long knives. He watched one brilliant, too-ambitious young writer try to bypass Sorensen and get himself exiled to the Siberia of the State Department. Philip had decorated his little basement cubbyhole with Picasso prints and a W. C. Fields poster, and he didn't want to be exiled. His strategy for survival was simple: work hard, lie low, and be a friend to all.

He had almost no social life that winter. The White House world was self-contained; even sex was an afterthought in those first heady months.

He did, that spring, begin an off-and-on affair with a White House secretary named Mandy. She was a self-described tough Mick, a plain, flat-chested Irish girl from South Boston who'd finished one year at Boston College before she was caught up in the Kennedy campaign. Mandy had few illusions about the Kennedys, of whom she said, "They think women are good for two things; one you do with a typewriter and the other you do on your back." Still, she had risen to become the secretary of a powerful man, and she was, among other things, a phenomenal source of gossip.

There were, Philip learned, no secrets from the White House secretarial staff. Mandy knew who was sleeping with whom, who was up and who was down in the presidential favor, and just about everything else worth knowing. She passed on a few tidbits about Philip's boss, Harry Flynn. She said his wife, who was still up in Boston, was expecting their sixth child, that his campaign affair with the actress in Los Angeles was definitely over, and that another affair—details still murky—seemed to be unfolding. She said that her boss claimed that Harry's power came from his intimacy with the president's father—"old Joe's spy in the White House," her boss called Harry. Mandy also revealed that the White House secretaries had compiled a list of the ten most attractive men in the administration and that Harry had placed a solid third behind the president and the attorney general. Philip found that hard to grasp. Harry was a pretty good-looking guy, and in good shape, but at twenty-five it was hard for Philip to believe that young women would get excited about a man who was forty and thus had one foot practically in the grave.

One April morning Philip got a call from Harry. It was the week of the disastrous U.S.-sponsored invasion at Cuba's Bay of Pigs.

"What're you doing for lunch, Tex?"

"Not a hell of a lot."

"Come up at one. I'll take you to Sans Souci."

"What's the occasion?"

"We need to show our smiling faces. We don't want people to think we're hiding out just because Jack took some lumps."

They rated the best table in the house. Harry was wearing a new, two-button suit, the kind the president wore, and his PT-109 tie clasp, not the bronze-plated kind that Philip and the other peons wore but one of the silver ones the president had given to his earliest supporters. Harry ordered a dry martini with a twist and Philip asked for a Heineken. He'd read somewhere that the president's favorite drinks were daiquiris and Heineken beer. He downed his first glass of beer and then he couldn't keep quiet any longer.

"Harry, why the hell did he *do* it?"

"Why did who do what?" Harry sipped the martini and let his eyes play around the room; a gunfighter checking out the saloon.

"Why did the president invade Cuba?"

"Some people gave him bad information." Harry finished his martini and waved for another. "See, we got him elected because we ignored the experts—they all said he was too young and too liberal and too Catholic—but then he got in the Oval Office and he made the mistake of listening to the so-called experts."

"It was so damn *dumb*," Philip said.

"Jack'll learn from it."

"Harry, it isn't just that the invasion was a fiasco. Even if it had worked, it would have been *wrong*. We've got no business invading Cuba."

Harry's eyes narrowed. "Can it, Tex," he said.

"What do you mean, can it?"

"I mean what's done is done. The president needs our loyalty now."

"I'm loyal," Philip said, "but . . ."

"If you're loyal, there aren't any buts."

"Oh bullshit, Harry."

"How old are you, Tex?" Harry demanded. His eyes had narrowed and he pointed his forefinger, Kennedy-style.

"Twenty-five," Philip said. "And quit calling me Tex."

"Twenty-five and got an office in the White House and a job writing for the president. Not bad. Got any idea why it happened?"

"Because I'm a hell of a writer."

Harry laughed. "Writers are a dime a dozen."

"Thanks."

"You're there because one night last October you were ready to take a bullet for Jack."

"That was instinct."

"It was guts. Guts and loyalty. The Kennedys want that. And when they find it they don't forget it."

"Oh hell, Harry. The president doesn't know I'm alive."

"Don't be a dope. Do you think I'd put you in the White House without Jack's okay?"

The waiter brought their food—Veal Marengo for Harry, pepper steak for Philip—and out of the blue Harry said, "Whatta you know about the John Birch Society?"

"Not much. A guy named Robert Welch started it. He wrote a book that said Eisenhower was part of the Communist conspiracy."

"Right. So you can imagine what he thinks of our guy," Harry said. "The thing is, the Birch Society is spreading; they've got cells all over the country and they've got money and they put out these scandal-sheet publications."

Philip's mind was racing ahead. What was Harry getting at? Did he want the president to make a speech denouncing extremist groups? Philip did not immediately find out, for a syndicated columnist named Wallace Leeds appeared at their table and asked if he could join them.

For the next twenty minutes the columnist quizzed Harry about the Bay of Pigs. Harry was unflappable. The president had been given bad advice. The president would learn from the mistake. Harry spoke with such certitude that soon Philip could see the columnist starting to buy the argument. Philip wondered what Harry really thought about the Bay of Pigs. But that, of course, was something neither he, nor the columnist, nor anyone except Harry and the president would ever know.

When the columnist left, Harry paid the bill and stood up. "It's too pretty to be indoors," he said.

They walked over to Lafayette Park, where Harry steered them to a park bench. Across the avenue the White House glistened, postcard-pretty, in the spring sunshine. Harry took some newspaper clippings from his pocket. "Seen these?" he asked.

The clippings were from a right-wing rag called *The Defender*. One front-page story purported to tell the facts about Kennedy's secret marriage, at age twenty, to a Florida divorcée who had, it claimed, been given a million dollars for an annulment. Another story purported to reveal that Kennedy was secretly dying of a rare blood disease and plans were afoot to change the Constitution so Bobby could succeed him as president.

"I saw some of these during the campaign," Philip said. "I thought maybe they'd given up."

Harry shook his head, then spoke fervently. "Phil, these next few weeks are crucial for the president. This Cuba thing can make or break him. Jerks like these"—he waved the clippings—"will be out to put the knife to him now. We can't let 'em get started. We've got to nail these bastards."

Philip was fascinated but he didn't see what this had to do with him.

"You know where this rag is printed?" Harry demanded.

"Birmingham?"

"It used to be. Right now it's coming out of Fort Worth. That's your old hometown, isn't it?"

Philip felt the first stab of apprehension. "Yeah."

"Fort Worth," Harry said, as if the words were strange, exotic. "Jesus, it sounds like a John Wayne movie. How far is it to Fort Appache?"

"Not far."

"What I want to know is who's behind this rag. Who writes it? Who prints it? Who pays for it? Who distributes it?"

"What would you do if you knew?"

"That's my department, pal. Maybe the IRS would want to talk to them. Maybe Justice would. All I want you to do is get me some names."

"*Me* get you names? Wait a minute, Harry. That's crazy."

"Why is it crazy?"

"For one thing, I haven't lived there for years. I'd be going in cold. Get the FBI to check it. Get somebody from Johnson's staff to check it."

"Offhand, Tex, I can't think of two people in the world I trust less than J. Edgar Hoover and Lyndon B. Johnson. Look, you're a reporter, right?"

"Right," Philip said glumly.

"Okay, and it's your old hometown, so you've got an excuse to go down there. You're just going home to see Mom. You've got a mom, haven't you?"

"The last time I looked."

"Okay, so you go visit her and you do a little nosing around on the side."

Philip stared up at a dappled sky. The first green buds blurred the chestnut trees. He wondered why he was resisting this so. He only knew that he hated to go back, that a nameless terror seized him whenever he returned. Sometimes he thought of Texas as a vast prison from which he had somehow escaped, and every time he went back he had a chilling fear that they would lock the gates behind him.

"I don't like it, Harry."

"Listen, Phil, you're a bright boy. Jack's gonna be president for eight years, and you could go a long way. You don't want to stay down in that broom closet writing manifestos about senior citizens, do you?"

Philip shrugged. In truth, he *didn't* want to stay in his broom closet forever, but he hadn't figured a way out of it. There were three first-rate writers ahead of him in the pecking order.

"I'm no gumshoe, Harry."

"Listen, there's a little office down the hall from me I think I can open up. A view of the park. You wouldn't be interested, would you?"

Philip started to laugh. Every man had his price. His was getting out of that damn closet in the basement with the toilets flushing next door. "I'll go to Texas, Harry."

Harry grinned. "Terrific," he said.

Terrific was a big Kennedy word. Everything was terrific. The president used it all the time, so now everybody else was using it. The White House secretaries were always saying everything was terrific. Philip had taken a vow never to use the damn word.

"I guess I ought to get back to my broom closet," he said. "You coming?"

"I'm meeting somebody here," Harry said. "Relax. Enjoy the sun."

Philip shut his eyes. The sun was gentle, soothing, on his face. He heard children laughing across the park.

"Well, look who's here," Harry said.

Philip opened his eyes. For a moment the world was green and golden, and then she seemed to step out of the sun. He saw that unforgettable smile and thought he was dreaming and then leaped to his feet.

"My God, is it *you?*"

"P.K., it's *you!*"

He swung her in joyous circles, burying his face in her soft, thick, intoxicating hair.

"Where did you come from?" he demanded. "What are you doing? What's going on?"

"I'm a lawyer," Jenny Rhodes said. "At the Justice Department."

They stood in the middle of a walkway, holding hands, oblivious to the tourists who streamed by. Philip could not digest this new reality all at once. He thought he'd heard, years before, that Jenny had gone to law school, but the fact of her standing there stunned him. All he could think was that she was as beautiful as ever, that he loved her as much as ever.

Harry watched them with a crooked smile. "I take it that you two are acquainted," he said.

"I have been in love with this woman since the age of three," Philip said.

"We went to the Saturday afternoon shoot-'em-ups together," Jenny said. "We held hands and cheered for Roy Rogers."

"And Gabby Hayes," Philip added. "And Don Winslow of the Navy."

"Miss Rhodes has been advising me on the subtleties of the campaign-financing laws," Harry said, although no one had asked.

Jenny beamed. "I hope to keep Mr. Flynn out of prison."

Philip kept shaking his head. "Harry, I haven't seen this woman in *eight years,*" he said. "Since the night we graduated from high school. My God, there's so much I want to know." He hesitated. "But I guess you two have work to do."

Harry winked. "Nothing that can't wait. You kids do your catching up; I'll go buy some cigars." He started toward the Hay-Adams; Philip and Jenny settled onto the park bench. He took her hands and gazed at her in wonder.

"Tell me everything," he said. "From graduation night on."

"The infamous night you slugged your cousin Skip."

"I'd do it again. So what happened? The last time I saw you, you were about to go to the University of Texas and pledge Theta and be a cheerleader and marry a millionaire. What went wrong?"

Jenny smiled wistfully. "I don't know. I changed, I guess. I'd done all that in high school and I just . . . got tired of it. I got serious about school, and then I got interested in law."

"How was law school?"

"A little rough," she said. "I was the only woman in my class—the only one who made it through—and the professors gave me a hard time. But I survived. I made the *Law Review,* if you want the truth. Then I got a chance to come with Justice. But tell me about *you,* P.K."

He had been watching her closely as she spoke, enthralled by her beauty, as always, but seeing something in her eyes, in her smile, something in *her* that he did not remember. He could not have chosen a word to describe this quality: a shadow, a hesitation, a depth, a sadness, an uncertainty, something that had not existed in the girl he had known. He told himself that this shadow, this change, was only maturity; Jenny was a woman now, not the girl of his memories.

"Me? Oh, I was a reporter in Nashville, and I stumbled into the campaign, and now I'm a mole in the bowels of the White House. What I really do is grind out all the stuff for the president that nobody else wants to write."

"It sounds exciting."

He shrugged. "It has its moments."

"Old P.K., always the cynic. Do you remember the time you wrote the sports column denouncing Coach Moran?"

"I remember the time a certain politically ambitious cheerleader denounced me before the whole school as a subversive ten-percenter."

She squeezed his hands. "Will you ever forgive me?"

He touched her hair. She still wore it short, brushed straight back, and it shone like ebony. "You're so damn beautiful. Did I ever tell you?"

"Maybe once, a long time ago," she said. "How's your mother?"

"She's great. She got married again, and..." He saw Harry Flynn returning, puffing on a long cigar. "Look, we've got to have dinner. Where can I call you?"

"At Justice. The solicitor general's office."

"It may be a week or so. Harry's sending me on this idiot trip to Texas."

"Anytime, P.K."

Harry grinned at them. "You lovebirds all caught up?"

"For the moment," Philip said.

"Then I'll borrow Miss Rhodes back."

Philip hugged her again, then hurried toward Pennsylvania Avenue. Halfway there he turned back and waved. Harry and Jenny watched in silence until he disappeared behind the West Wing gates.

"Jesus, I didn't know you knew him," Harry said finally.

"There's a lot you don't know."

"I'm learning."

Jenny worried an invisible flaw on the sleeve of her sweater. "What about the weekend?" she asked.

Harry squinted into the sun. He had a perpetual squint, from a lifetime of outdoor sports. She thought it saved him from prettiness.

"Ruth's coming down. She just called. Sorry."

"Don't be sorry," she said. "I don't own you. You don't own me. We're just two people who met in a taxicab on a rainy night."

"Hey, don't be gloomy. It's spring."

Jenny stood up. "Spring has sprung, the grass has riz, I wonder where the flowers is."

"Jesus, what's that?"

"Just a fragment of my youth."

"I want to see you tonight."

"I want to see you tonight, too."

He flashed his cocky, world-conquering New Frontier grin. "That's more like it," he said. "That's terrific."

CHAPTER THREE

On the flight to Texas, visions of Jenny danced in his head. He saw her at eight, racing across a playground, pigtails flying, and at sixteen, in her cheerleader's costume, leaping and twirling. He remembered puppy love and then the high school years when he had lost her to football heroes. But they were grown now, peers in the quicksilver world of Kennedy's Washington, and he longed for her. He thought of the change he had seen, or imagined, in her, the sadness, and he half-remembered something someone had said about her, in a bar, when he was home from college one Christmas, that she had changed, that something had happened to her, but he could remember no more, nor did he really care. All that mattered was that he had found her again.

When he arrived in Fort Worth he checked into the Hotel Texas and in the early evening was driving his rented car west on Camp Bowie Boulevard. Once this brick-paved street had been the center of his universe. Now as he passed its endless neon-bright bedlam of root-beer stands, used-car lots, and hamburger joints, all he could think was how stupendously tacky it was and that he had grown up thinking the whole world looked like this.

Louise and her new husband lived in a new neighborhood out past the Weatherford traffic circle, in what had been open prairie when Philip was a boy. Louise had surprised Philip a few months earlier by calling to say she was about to be married. Philip had flown down for the ceremony but barely met her new husband, a dentist named Asa Matlock. He knew only that Asa was a tall, lanky widower with a big nose and an easy grin and that he and Louise had met in church.

It was dusk when he found their meandering house on a cul-de-sac called Laramie Trail. "Come in, boy, come in,"

Asa cried at the door. Philip embraced his mother and followed them out to the patio. "How about a beer, son?" Asa asked. "I quit the hard stuff—it got too darn hard on *me!*" The three of them sat in the twilight, drinking beer and talking, mostly about Philip's job and about Alice's growing success as an amateur golfer. Asa had a solemn look about him, but he was given to unpredictable bursts of humor. At one point he exclaimed, quite out of nowhere, "Boy oh boy, Philip's in the White House and I'm in the doghouse." On their second beer, Philip told his only dentist joke, Ben Hecht's story about the headline he sneaked into a Chicago paper after a dentist raped a patient: DENTIST FILLS WRONG CAVITY. Asa loved that, and Philip was coming to like Asa, particularly as he realized that the man was entirely devoted to Louise. He rushed around in his "Praise the Lord and Pass the Chili Peppers" apron, opening beers, mixing the salad, and wouldn't let Louise lift a finger.

After dinner, as they were having coffee, Alice stormed in, still wearing her golf shoes, and threw her arms around Philip. "The Prodigal has returned," she cried.

"How'd the tournament go?" Louise asked.

"I took second," Alice said. She was a good-looking girl of nineteen now, rangy and tanned, and still with her tomboy's freckles and red hair. "I blew it on the last hole. And it was all Philip's fault!"

"My fault?"

"Yeah—on that last green I got to thinking about my famous big brother coming home and it got me all flustered and I three-putted."

"Don't blame me if you can't putt," Philip said. "How's North Texas?"

"Aw, it's *there*. I mean, it's a good school, if what you want is to be a teacher or something."

"Didn't you pledge Zeta?" he asked.

"I did but then I depledged. They were always wanting me to go to teas or study the Greek alphabet or something, and I wanted to be out playing golf. I don't think I'm the sorority type."

"Philip, you ought to see this little lady play," Asa said. "She can hit the ball a country mile."

Alice poured herself a beer. "Well, as long as we're having this family reunion, I might as well make an announcement."

"Oh, Lord, she's gonna get married," Asa declared.

"Worse'n that," Alice said. "I'm gonna turn pro!"

"Turn pro?" Louise cried. "But what about school?"

"Mom, let's face it, I'm not the world's leading scholar."

"Sis, it's a big jump from amateur golf in Texas to professional golf," Philip said.

"Sure it is," Alice said. "Just like it was a big jump for you when you ran off and joined the Kennedy campaign. But you thought you had the stuff, and so do I."

"What's it like on the women's tour?" Philip asked.

"Well, if you really want to know, it's a traveling circus. It's all disorganized, and the money's not so great, unless you really start winning, and most of the girls drive to tournaments together, and double up in motel rooms, and you get to play on all the ratty courses where they can't afford to put on a men's tournament—but Philip, it's competing against the best players in the world. And if you're really good, like the Babe, or Patty Berg, or Kathy Whitworth, you can win fifteen or twenty thousand dollars a year."

"Are you that good?" Philip asked.

"Let me show you her trophies," Louise said.

"Oh, Mom, for cripe's sake," Alice protested, but Louise had left the room. "Listen, I didn't used to be that good," Alice said, deadly serious. "But I've got this coach now—the man's a genius—and it's like I'm playing a whole new game. Since I started with him, I won in Odessa and Beaumont and Tulsa. I mean I'm *good*. Give me a couple of years of competition and I'll be ready for *anybody!*"

Louise returned with an armload of trophies, and Alice squirmed as her mother recited the particulars of each victory. Philip was impressed but not yet convinced.

"How do you support yourself out there on the tour?"

Alice made a face. "That is a tiny little problem."

"I reckon I can make her an advance," Asa said.

"No you can't," Alice said. "When you married Mom, you didn't take me to raise." She unfolded herself from the chair. "Listen, I don't mean to be the party-pooper, but I've got a match at eight in the morning."

Philip got up. "I've got to be up early too," he said.

"I reckon the old folks'll have to carry on the party alone, then," Asa said and grinned and put his arm around Louise. She smiled back at him and Philip thought she looked as young and lovely as Alice. He shook Asa's hand, and then his mother walked him out to the car. The full moon bathed the street in light; you could have read a book by it. Philip held his mother's hand. "He's a diamond in the rough," he said.

"He's a wonderful man," Louise said. "I haven't been so happy since . . ." She smiled ". . . since twenty-odd years ago, when your father gave up drinking for two months."

Philip had breakfast in his hotel room the next morning and pondered his strategy. He had copies of *The Defender,* and he had Harry's assurance that it was printed in Fort Worth, that the Birch Society was behind it, and that Wade Kingslea was probably behind the Birch Society. Beyond that, it was up to him to prove who was doing what. He sighed and reached for the Yellow Pages.

There were twenty-odd printing shops listed. He tore out the page with their addresses and started making the rounds. The first shop he tried was the one that printed his high school paper. He remembered the manager, a sour, wizened old fellow with a glass eye. Philip told him he wanted to get some political pamphlets printed, then pulled out a copy of *The Defender.* "These look right nice," he drawled. "Know who prints 'em?"

"Nope," the fellow replied, and that was that.

The next printer he asked about *The Defender* said, "Could be anybody." The one after that snapped, "Who wants to know?" Philip decided to rethink his strategy. Checking every print shop in town could take forever and could also alert the Birchers that someone was snooping around. He stopped at a phone booth out in River Oaks; the temperature was already in the mid-nineties and he was sweating by the time he reached his father at Kingslea Oil.

"How in the world are you, boy?" Coyle demanded. "How long are you in town?"

"A couple of days," Philip said.

"I've got a few surprises for you," Coyle said. "Can you come for dinner?"

"That'd be great," Philip said, and Coyle gave him the address of his new home in Westover Hills.

Philip put down the phone unhappily. He figured that if he pumped Coyle he could find out plenty about the local Birch Society. Coyle knew every rich right-winger in Fort Worth. He hated to use him like that, but it looked like his best shot.

He tried a couple more print shops, then stopped at An-

gelo's for lunch. Angelo's was a ramshackle joint on White
Settlement Road that served what was possibly the best barbecue in the world.

A barbecue sandwich and a mug of beer lifted his spirits,
but then he struck out at two more print shops. He was driving
west on Camp Bowie Boulevard, when he noticed a blue neon
sign that proclaimed Chez Duke. Philip wheeled into the
parking lot. Could it be?

Chez Duke was a big, dark lounge, elegant by the local
standard. His old friend was hunched over a chessboard at the
end of the bar.

The Duke looked up, their eyes met, and he gazed back
down at the chessboard. "Checkmate," he said and pocketed
two ten-dollar bills that were lying on the bar, while his oppo-
nent, an air force captain, grumbled and ordered another beer.

"What the hell do ya say, kid?" the Duke roared and advanced on Philip with his hand outstretched. He had put on
weight, but he still moved as gracefully as a middleweight. He
was wearing a flashy blue suit, a Countess Mara tie, and pearl
cufflinks.

"You're still the champ, Duke," Philip said, shaking his
surprisingly small, soft hand. "Nice place you got here. Not
like those bucket-of-blood joints we used to drink in."

"Sit down, have a drink," the Duke said. "Millie, bring the
good stuff. What the hell you doin' now, kid? I lost track of
you up in Tennessee somewhere."

"I'm still a reporter in Nashville," he lied. "I'm in town to
see my mother. She got married again."

"Tell her to come in," the Duke said. "Drinks are on the
house. Your cousin Skip, he comes by sometimes."

"How is he?"

"Obnoxious. He had a brawl with his date the last time he
was in. If he wasn't so damn rich I'da kicked his ass from
here to Mineral Wells."

"I thought Skip was married."

"He was, but it didn't take. I hear he's carrying a torch for
that cheerleader you were so hot for. What's her name?"

"Jenny."

"Yeah. There was a story about him and her getting in
trouble together, a long time ago. Down in Mexico."

"Mexico? What kind of trouble?"

"I forget," the Duke said. "Or maybe I never knew."

Philip frowned, perplexed by the rumor. "Hear anything from Sherry?" he asked.

"Sherry cashed in."

"Plane?"

"Car. The crazy bastard."

The Duke chronicled the lives and fortunes of their drinking companions of yesteryear: a musician imprisoned on a drug charge, a waitress married to a newly rich wildcatter, a gay artist turned fashionable interior decorator. The monologue brought back all those mad nights they'd spent drinking and brawling and racing about Texas in search of . . . what? Excitement? Escape? He couldn't remember.

Chez Duke was filling up with the happy-hour crowd. Philip thought he'd better make his move. "I'm doing a piece on Texas politics," he said. "What's going on?"

The Duke scowled disdainfully. "Texas politics is a bunch of jerkoffs yelling about who hates which Kennedy the most."

"What do you hear about the John Birch Society?"

The Duke shrugged. His eyes shone black, and he had a quarter-moon scar on his chin that Philip didn't remember. "Some of my best customers are certified Birch Society crazies," he said.

Philip pulled out a copy of *The Defender* and laid it on the table. "Ever seen one of these?"

"Yeah, I've seen 'em."

"Wouldn't know who prints 'em, would you?"

The Duke gave him a long, cold stare. "Maybe I do," he said. "And maybe I wouldn't want any trouble with 'em."

"No trouble. Point me in the right direction and I'll forget I ever knew you."

The Duke bit off the end of a cigar and spit it into the ashtray. "It's a place called Four Star Printing, out White Settlement Road. They print our football cards. I was out there last winter and I saw that *Defender* rag. I remember the story about Kennedy being married before. You think there's anything to it?"

Philip shrugged. "Who knows?"

"The thing is, the people at Four Star do jobs that aren't always on the Q-T. You don't want to mess with 'em is my advice."

"I understand."

The Duke walked Philip out to his car. A blazing late-afternoon sun greeted them; the Duke slipped on a pair of military-style sunglasses. He put his foot up on the bumper of a maroon-and-cream Coupe de Ville. "Mine," he explained. "How long you in town, kid?"

"Maybe two or three days."

"Come by one night, I'll show you around town. Lot more action than in the old days. I know a couple of girls could join us."

"I'll try to."

As they spoke, a wiry young man approached them. He wore dirty jeans and a sweat shirt; he had a narrow, angry face and sullen eyes.

"Hey, Duke, you got anything for me?" he asked.

The Duke scowled behind his dark glasses. "Fuck off, kid."

"Aw, come on, Duke," the young man whined.

"I *said*, fuck off," the Duke repeated and gave the boy a shove that sent him reeling.

"Watch it," the boy snarled. He climbed into a rusty Nash Rambler and rattled away.

"Who was that?" Philip asked.

"Just a punk."

"He looked familiar."

The Duke shrugged impatiently. "Name's Lee Harvey Oswald. Lives over on Collinwood. Had a brother named Robert who was at Heights about the time you were."

Philip put out his hand. "Thanks for everything, Duke. I'm glad to see you prospering."

The Duke laughed. "This is just the start. I got plans for a supper club that'll knock your eyes out. Listen, if a man knows his way around, the sky's the limit in this town."

Driving away, Philip wondered who the Duke was in with. There had been organized gambling in Fort Worth as far back as anyone could remember. From time to time the gamblers made news when they settled their disputes with bombs or bullets. Philip thought of the Duke and his Coupe de Ville and laughed. The Duke could take care of himself, if anyone could.

Philip hadn't talked to his father since Christmas, and when he arrived at Coyle's elegant new glass-and-sandstone house in Westover Hills he was greeted by two major surprises: Coyle was married, and he'd quit drinking. The two

facts, it turned out, were not unrelated. His wife was a handsome, serene Indian woman named Imelda; she had been a
nurse in a sanitarium near Las Cruces when they'd met. "Let's
face it," Coyle joked, "a nurse was always what I needed, not
a wife." Coyle was in high spirits, and at fifty he looked better
than Philip had ever seen him. He had even taken up golf:
"You know that pond at River Crest? They've named it after
me, I've lost so many balls there." The three of them sat in the
high-ceilinged living room and sipped apple juice and talked
about Coyle's life. His father, pleased by his marriage, had
finally made him treasurer and vice president of Kingslea Oil,
and he had been named to the board of directors of two banks
and the local symphony. Coyle joked of his newfound sobriety: "I was like a Cactus Jack Garner; when the old bandit
turned ninety he announced, 'I reckon I've had enough,' and
never touched another drop. I managed to reach that point at
fifty."

They talked, too, of the president. When Philip recited
Kennedy's achievements, Coyle warned, "You don't understand what you're up against down here. It's not Kennedy's
politics they hate. It's *him*. His style, his taste, his pretty wife,
his religion. They can forgive a man his politics, but they
can't forgive him for being young and handsome and witty
and elegant and everything they're not."

Imelda went to start dinner, and Philip admired their collection of Indian art. "Imelda got me interested," Coyle said.
"Art collecting is the new rage: Cowtown is infected with
culture. People compete with Rembrandts now instead of Cadillacs. You should see your grandfather's collection."

Philip left Coyle's house at eleven, never having brought
up the John Birch Society. He couldn't do it. Coyle was too
happy to involve him in a lot of political garbage.

He drove out White Settlement Road, past the site of the
old Crystal Springs ballroom, where Bob Wills had once told
Louise she had eyes like bluebonnets, until he came to Four
Star Printing. It was a dingy place, dark and deserted now, but
next door a tavern called Maud's was going strong. Philip
found a stool at the bar and ordered a Lone Star. Marty Rob-
bins' "El Paso" was playing on the jukebox, but you couldn't
hear the words. He nursed his beer and thought about Jenny.
He had to get out of this damn town and back to her. But how?
The more he thought about it, the more he knew what he had
to do.

Just before closing time, when everyone else in Maud's was howling for a last round, Philip went outside and peed in the shadows beside the honky-tonk. When he was convinced that no one was watching, he raced across a patch of weeds to the back door of Four Star Printing. He tried the door but it was locked. A man and a woman came out of Maud's and embraced in the shadows. Some drunks stumbled out after them. Philip hugged the wall and waited.

"Wa-hoo," a man bellowed. "Ah'm a curly-haired wolf an' it's mah night to howl!"

"You're a drunk peckerwood is what you is," a woman declared.

"What you doin' heah with mah wife?"

"Wife hell!"

"Leave him be, Clovis—he's sick!"

There were sounds of combat: a grunt of pain, the scrape of boots on gravel, someone falling down, someone throwing up, women crying for help. Philip, taking advantage of the din, broke a windowpane, and entered the printing shop.

Keeping low, he found a storeroom and lit matches to get a look at Four Star's work: a community newspaper, a church bulletin, some old football cards, some Dallas nightclub owner's card that featured a bare-breasted girl dancing the cancan. But no *Defender*. He slipped into the front room where one wall was lined with file cabinets. Lighting another match, he checked the file under *D* for Defender.

Nothing.

He tried *B* for Birch Society.

Nothing.

He tired *J* for John Birch Society.

Nothing.

A police siren wailed out on White Settlement Road, then skidded to a halt in the honky-tonk parking lot. Philip threw himself flat on the floor, his heart pounding. But the police, after arresting one of the victims of the brawl, raced away, in search of the others.

Philip got up from the dusty floor, lit another match, and opened the file cabinet one more time, this time to *K*.

He found what he was after, a fat folder containing a dozen invoices made out to Kingslea Oil. Some were marked "political literature" and some added "Per *The Defender*." Philip stuffed the invoices into his pocket, scrambled to his feet, and slipped out of the back door. All was quiet in the honky-tonk parking lot, except for one battered Packard that rocked gently, powered by a couple in its back seat.

By the time he reached his hotel he was laughing aloud. He was damn good at this. To hell with speechwriting; he'd go to the Riviera and be a cat burglar. He had a nightcap and went to bed, pretty pleased with himself.

The phone awoke him at nine. A man's voice boomed out at him:

"Philip? It's Wade Kingslea!"

Philip muttered a hello.

"Why didn't you call me? The latch is always out, boy."

"That's . . . good of you."

"I'll tell you what: come have breakfast with me. My office is only three blocks away."

"I've . . . I've got a plane to catch."

"Nonsense. The next flight to Washington doesn't leave till noon and I'll guarantee you it won't leave without you."

"I . . . I've got some calls . . ."

"Nonsense, my boy. A man needs a good breakfast to start the day. I'll send a car for you."

Philip was starting to smile. He'd got what he came for; why not have breakfast with the old bastard?

"I'll walk," he said.

Wade Kingslea came around from behind his desk to greet Philip. "Come in, my boy, come in," he cried, pumping Philip's hand. "Wonderful to see you. Sit down, have some coffee. How do you like your eggs? Scrambled all right?"

"Scrambled is fine," Philip said. He lowered himself into a low-slung, modern chair as a pretty secretary poured coffee. His grandfather's office, on the top floor of the Kingslea Oil Tower, the skyscraper he had built for himself, had two glass walls that provided a panoramic view to the north and west. You could see two forks of the greenish-brown Trinity River merge and twist off to the east. To the north were the stockyards, and to the west, the tower of the Will Rogers Coliseum, Farrington Field, the East-West Freeway, and the far-flung western subdivisions. Far to the northwest, Philip saw a plane rising from Carswell Air Force Base. Past that, the endless prairie glowed with morning mist; he imagined Indians astride fleet ponies, circling on the horizon.

"You're looking well, Philip," Kingslea said.

"So are you." The old man looked lean and tough, ageless.

"I understand you're doing well, up there in Washington,"

Kingslea said. "By God, boy, I hope you're a good politician, because you're one hell of an incompetent burglar!"

Kingslea threw back his head and roared, and Philip stared at him in dismay.

"Drink your coffee while it's hot, boy," the old man commanded. "You see, Philip, printers are a tight-knit fraternity. Once an outsider starts poking around, they sound the alarm. My people had heard all about you by noon yesterday—one of my men was at the next table when you had lunch. At Angelo's, wasn't it?"

Philip sipped his coffee.

"Fine place, Angelo's," Kingslea said. "Although I urge you to try Sammy's, out on East Belknap—I do believe their sauce may be better. In any event, my people checked the car-rental agency and found out who you were, and a good thing, too, or you might have been arrested last night. But I couldn't let that happen, could I?"

A Negro served scrambled eggs, country ham, grits, buttered toast, and more coffee. When he had gone, Kingslea continued, "I would appreciate it if you would return those invoices to me. The people at Four Star feel strongly about it—they need their records, you see."

Philip couldn't afford to argue. Any publicity and he'd be ruined—and his grandfather damn well knew it. He reached into his pocket and tossed the invoices onto Kingslea's desk.

"I must say, Philip, I don't understand why you went to so much trouble. I'd gladly have told you I was supporting that little newspaper. You tell Harry Flynn to call me anytime he wants to discuss my political opinions."

"Harry didn't know about this," Philip said. "I was just in town and curious about who was publishing that rag."

Kingslea chuckled indulgently. "Really now, do you take me for a fool? Harry Flynn is Joe Kennedy's hatchet man—has been for years. You tell Flynn I said the First Amendment applies to oilmen, too, as well as to agitators and race mixers."

"I'll tell him," Philip promised. "Now let me ask you something."

"Anything, my boy."

"Do you really believe all that Birch Society garbage about Eisenhower being a Communist?"

Kingslea broke out laughing. "No, no, no, my boy. That's political hyperbole, of course. Ike was a fool, not a Red. But it is not my intention to sit by silently while the Kennedys tax me into the poorhouse to perpetuate their own political dynasty."

"I think you must be some distance from the poorhouse," Philip said. He nodded toward the wall to his right. "Is that part of the art collection I've been hearing about?"

Kingslea stood up, beaming. "Oh, did you notice? Come have a look." He took Philip's arm and guided him toward the paintings. "Most of my collection is at home, of course, or on loan to museums, but I bring a few things into brighten up the office. That's my Dufy—lovely, isn't it?—those are the jockeys exercising their horses at the racetrack at Deauville. And that's my Matisse, and my Paul Klee, and the one Picasso I've allowed myself, despite the man's politics. And notice the little Rembrandt by the door." He turned on Philip with narrowed eyes. "Do you know what these paintings mean to me?"

"What?"

"They mean America! They're a constant reminder that in our free republic a man can start out as penniless as I was and one day have the priceless treasures of European art hanging on his walls. That's a way of life worth preserving, my boy!"

Philip nodded with due gravity.

"Why don't you come back to Texas?" Kingslea demanded. "It's a land of opportunity still, despite the federal bureaucrats. A young man with your brains could write his own ticket."

Philip was stunned. "What would I do in Texas?"

"Come to work for Kingslea Oil. I'll put you in charge of my public relations. Or you can run some radio stations for me. Of course, what you should do is learn the oil business. Exploration—that's where the fun is. Your cousin Skip is over in Libya right now, looking over some possibilities. What do you say?"

Philip was quite speechless.

"I know we've had our differences," the old man continued, "but that's ancient history now. I understand you saw your father last night—you see how well he's doing. Oh, local society hasn't quite forgiven Coyle for marrying an Indian, but I certainly don't care. Fort Worth is a lively spot! We've got that new Van Cliburn piano festival, and the Amon Carter museum. What do you say, Philip? Those Kennedys are cynical people—they only want to use you. Back here in

Texas there are people who care about you!"

Philip stared out at the distant western horizon and for an instant the fantasy unfurled before him, like a magic carpet, as endless as the Texas prairie: Kingslea Oil, white-coated servants, cool drinks at poolside, private planes, weekends in Acapulco, languid, empty-headed women, a fleet of Cadillacs, the works. He savored the image, then almost laughed aloud.

"Thanks," he said. "But I think I'll stay where I am."

His grandfather stiffened. "I think the problem is that you have some sort of grudge against Texas."

"Perhaps so."

"Then you'd best get over it," Kingslea said, "because Texas is America. Texas is reality. Texas is what all the world wants to be."

Philip stared at his grandfather. There was nothing to say, except the unspeakable truth that he thought the old man was crazy. After a moment he pointed toward a wall that was covered with photographs of his grandfather with famous men. One of the biggest pictures showed Kingslea arm in arm with a grinning Lyndon Johnson. "I didn't know you and LBJ were so intimate."

Kingslea, scowling, returned to his desk. "Lyndon may well be president one day, so I'd be a damn fool not to be civil to him."

"President?" Philip said. "If he serves two terms as vice president he'll be in his sixties." He was startled at the suggestion. Everyone knew how unhappy and isolated Johnson was as Kennedy's vice president. Harry Flynn, who loathed Johnson, was always making jokes about sending Lyndon on another fact-finding mission to Korea.

"Lyndon could be president two minutes from now," Kingslea said. "He's only a heartbeat away."

Something in his grandfather's voice chilled Philip to the bone. "I'd better be going. Thanks for breakfast."

His grandfather took his arm. "Tell me one thing," he said, his face close to Philip's. "Doesn't it trouble you to work for a Catholic president? How do we know what the pope may tell him to do?"

Philip stared back into his grandfather's huge, burning eyes and thought the man was quite mad. The pope? What did the pope have to do with anything?

"In my experience," Philip said, "if a man gets to be president, he's probably got his religion pretty well under control."

Kingslea guffawed. "By God, boy, you are a cynic. But you've got good blood inside you. Think about what I've said."

"I will," Philip said, truthfully enough. Five minutes later, he was headed for Amon Carter Field in his grandfather's chauffeured limousine. As the city slipped away behind him, Philip told himself that his visit had not gone so badly. He'd found out what he'd come to find out, and he could give Harry an abridged version of his adventures.

Philip shut his eyes, sank back, exhausted, in black-leather upholstery as soft as dreams, and soon, once again, his thoughts were on Jenny Rhodes.

CHAPTER FOUR

The devils danced around her, howling, cavorting in the flames, and Jenny screamed and begged and the beast loomed against the dark sky like some monstrous deity and she fought and cried for salvation and then Harry was rocking her, whispering it was only the dream.

She clung to him, trembling, the old pajama top she wore soaked with cold sweat. Harry held her close but the dream held her too, pulling her back. "Talk to me," she said.

"About what?"

"Anything. When we talk it goes away."

He pushed hair back from her damp forehead. "Let me get a beer," he said.

She wanted to say, *No, don't leave me, not even for a minute,* but he had snapped on the light and started toward the kitchen, naked and gorgeous, with his trim, hard body, the body of a man half his age. When he was gone she curled into a ball and shut her eyes and the devils howled again and the beast lunged and darkness sucked like quicksand and then Harry was shaking her. "Come on," he said. "We'll talk about

Texas. Was your old man really called Dusty Rhodes?"

She seized his question like a lifeline, tossed down into her darkness from the world of light and reason. "All ballplayers named Rhodes are called Dusty," she said. "It's like Muddy Waters or Slim Pickens."

"And old Dusty could hit the ball, huh?"

"Listen, the summer of forty-one he hit .357 for the Cats. The next year, forty-two, should have been his year with the Dodgers, but instead he went into the Army. After the war was too late, so he stayed with the Cats until he retired."

Harry sipped his beer. "And you were the bat girl for the Cats."

Jenny nodded. "It was wonderful. I can still shut my eyes and hear the crack of a bat against the ball and the crowds cheering, and see the green grass and the white lines and the red clay of the infield, and smell that mustard and beer and popcorn and chewing tobacco and the oil the players used on their gloves. I grew up thinking the world was a big baseball park, a place where people cheered if you did something good and the umpires threw out people who did anything bad."

"Is that why you went to law school? Because you wanted a world with white lines and umpires?" He stroked her hair; she was starting to relax.

"Maybe. I love the law. You can lose yourself in the law."

"So you went from bat girl to cheerleader to lawyer?"

"A steady progression, up into the light."

"Cheerleaders don't go to law school," he said. "Something changed you."

"That's true."

"And you won't tell me what?"

"You have to give people their privacy," she said. "I don't ask you about your wife. Or the president. Or your job."

"They don't make me wake up screaming."

"Just talk to me," she said. "Please. Until it goes away."

"So how was law school?" he said. "Were you the only girl in your class?"

She touched his hand gratefully. "My class consisted of two hundred white males, one black male, one black female, and me. I was considered a bigger freak than the blacks, because at least there'd been a Supreme Court decision, forcing the law school to admit the blacks, but the guys couldn't figure why *I* was there, except maybe to find a husband. I felt so sorry for the two Negroes. They'd been handpicked, to integrate the University of Texas law school, and there was such pressure on them, but they just weren't prepared."

The phone rang, and Harry swung his legs off the side of the bed and answered it. Jenny clung to his other hand.

"Yeah, Jack," Harry said. "No, I was up. Yeah, what happened? No! The hell she did."

It was the third time the president had called while Jenny was at Harry's apartment. The first time, Jenny had expected something momentous, but all they had done was laugh about a girl named Elsie. This call was also about a girl, and Harry kept saying, "The *hell* she did," and he and the president gossiped like fraternity brothers while Jenny clutched Harry's hand. She made herself think about the time she'd met Harry, on a rainy night in March. She'd climbed into a cab outside of Justice and there was Harry, grinning at her. It was his grin that had won her, right then and there, before even Harry knew of his conquest. It had been one of those days when the past clawed at the present, ripping her mind apart, and there was Harry, beautiful, cocky, world-conquering Harry, with that wide, wonderful grin that brought you in from the cold and gave you something warm to drink and made you laugh and promised you that everything would come up roses. "Where to?" the cabbie had demanded, and Harry said "Georgetown" and Jenny hesitated only an instant and said, "Yes, Georgetown." He asked if she'd like a drink, and he was quite presentable in his tweed coat and penny loafers, and he wasn't wearing a ring so she said yes, and they found a little bar near Thirty-first and M and he said he was Harry Mumble and he was a lawyer in Boston. That didn't explain his PT-109 tie clasp but by then she didn't care, and after dinner he asked if she wanted to go back to his place for a nightcap and she went gladly because in three hours with the mysterious Harry Mumble she had not once slipped into the past. The next morning when she looked around his apartment and saw the photograph of him and the president and the other one of him and his children, it hadn't seemed to matter.

"Sleepy?" Harry said when he finally put down the phone.

"Not really."

"I meant to tell you, there's a party at Bob's house on Sunday. You ought to come."

"I haven't been invited."

"I'm inviting you."

"It's not your party."

"Jesus, Jen, do you want an engraved invitation? I'll have Bob's secretary call you, okay?"

"Harry, number one, I am a lowly GS-11 lawyer and he's the attorney general and . . ."

"He's an attorney general who likes to have GS-11's at his parties, as long as they're pretty girls . . ."

"And number two, I don't have a date."

"I'll tell Phil Kingslea to ask you."

"No! Keep him out of this."

"The kid's crazy about you."

"I *know* he's crazy about me. I don't *want* him to be."

"He's a nice kid. A little wet behind the ears, but you could do worse."

Her dark eyes flashed with anger. "You don't understand, do you, Harry? You don't understand at all."

"Understand what?"

"I'm not good enough for him." She was losing control; Harry had seen it before. "He's a sweet, decent boy, a boy I knew when I was in pigtails, a boy who still thinks I'm like that"—she was spitting out the words now, entranced, unreachable—"He doesn't know I'm a cheap whore who's . . ."

He shook her like a rag doll. "Cut out that crazy talk," he snapped.

"I'm not good enough for him," she cried. "I'm not . . ."

He slapped her hard, then took her in his arms. "Tell me what it is."

"No," she sobbed, "I can't."

"Maybe I could help."

"You do help me. You're my beautiful, sensible, married lover who talks to me and holds me and makes the darkness go away. You don't know how much you help me."

"You've got to trust somebody, sometime," he told her.

"Make love to me," she said.

He turned off the light and she rubbed his back with the palm of her hands until his skin was hot. He unbuttoned her pajamas and kissed her breasts. She liked for him to bite her nipples, hard, until it hurt, but instead he kissed them gently, until they were as hard and shiny as marbles. They tasted salty, like tears.

Hickory Hill, Robert Kennedy's Virginia estate, was ablaze with life and color. Children raced up and down its hills, pursued by dogs and an occasional parent. Frisbees and footballs flew through the sweet spring air. Couples gathered on the big stone terrace behind the house, overlooking the pool, or out by the tennis court. Most of the men were in their thirties or early forties. A year before they had been lawyers and reporters and stockbrokers in places like Denver and Nashville and Portland, but they had rallied around John Kennedy's campaign for president and now they ruled Washington like an occupying army.

Philip Kingslea, walking down the hill with Jenny Rhodes, was floating a few inches off the ground. "You know what?" he said.

"What?"

"You're the prettiest girl here."

She squeezed his hand. Dogwoods and spring flowers dotted the rich Virginia countryside. "There's Harry Flynn, down by the tennis court," Philip said. "Let's go say hello."

She didn't want to say hello to Harry. She hated this duplicity. But she'd agreed to come and there was no escape.

Harry and some other people were sitting on a blanket beside the tennis court. Harry stood up, wearing a tennis outfit, and grinned at them. "Phil Kingslea, Jenny Rhodes, this is my wife, Ruth."

A pretty, very pregnant woman with short, tawny hair smiled up at them. "Forgive me if I don't get up," she said. "I'm huge."

Jenny wanted to scream. His *wife?* What was his wife doing here? But she had no choice but to drop down on the grass beside Philip.

"Ethel called me about this picnic," Ruth Flynn was explaining. "I thought it'd be fun to surprise Harry. He hasn't seen the children in ages."

Harry beamed. "See that mob over there?" he said, pointing to twenty-odd children chasing after a soccer ball. "Well, half of those are Bob's and the other half are mine."

"I've heard all about you, Philip," Ruth Flynn said. "Harry says you're doing a wonderful job."

Philip shrugged. "I keep busy."

"Hey, come on, Tex, don't be modest," Harry said. "Tell everybody what happened yesterday."

"Oh hell, Harry," Philip said.

"Come on," Harry pressed. "It's not every day the president of the United States praises a fellow. Tell us."

"Well," Philip said, "the president had spoken to some farmers in the Rose Garden, and after he finished he came over to me and said, 'I hear you're doing a terrific job.'"

"Fabulous," Ruth Flynn said.

"Tell us what you said," Harry insisted.

Philip grinned. "Well, I sort of went blank, and then I said, 'Mr. President, *you're* doing a terrific job.'"

"And then what'd *he* say?" Harry demanded. He loved being the ringmaster.

"He said, 'Spread the word.'"

Everyone laughed at that. "I'm glad Jack has kept his sense of humor," Ruth Flynn said. Philip noted how casually she tossed out "Jack" and "Ethel"; no one was likely to forget that the Flynns went back with the Kennedys far before 1960.

"What do you do, Jenny?" Ruth asked. It was more of the status game; Ruth Flynn did not have to explain what *she* did.

"I'm a lawyer at the Justice Department," Jenny said. "Right now I'm working on the reapportionment case."

"Goodness, what does *that* mean?"

Jenny choked back her anger at Harry for bringing her here and tried to explain her job to his very proper wife. The case she was working on, *Baker v. Carr,* was an attempt to force the Tennessee legislature to reapportion itself.

"What it comes down to is one man, one vote," Harry injected, when Jenny bogged down in legalese. "Right now, if you're some Tennessee moonshiner or Georgia cracker, it's one man, ten votes. If the court makes them reapportion, it'll turn politics upside down."

A golden-haired child raced up to Harry. Jenny knew at once it was his daughter; she had his green eyes, his high cheekbones, his wide, sensual mouth. *Damned to beauty,* Jenny thought.

"Fell down," the child announced, pointing to a skinned knee. Harry spit on his handkerchief and wiped the dirt from the wound. The child bit her lip, trying to be brave, but tears began to slide down her rosy cheeks.

"Stop that," Harry growled. "Flynns don't cry."

The girl wiped her eyes, straightened her shoulders, and charged back into the mob of children.

Flynns don't cry, Jenny thought. That was Harry.

"Here comes Bob," someone cried.

Faces were upturned, hands raised. Bob Kennedy emerged

from his home and moved slowly down the hillside, squinting into the sun. He wore tennis whites, but he could have been a mighty prelate, berobed, bestowing benedictions: a handshake here, a grin there, his fingers tousling a child's hair. Suddenly he stood above them.

"Come on, Harry, I'm going to whip your butt."

"You and who else," Harry said. "Listen, Bob, you remember Phil Kingslea? And Jenny Rhodes?"

Kennedy nodded at Philip, then tossed Jenny a boyish grin. He pointed his forefinger at her, thumb bent, like a toy revolver. "Don't tell me," he said. "*Baker v. Carr*, right?"

"Right," Jenny said. She was beaming, which delighted Philip, because she'd seemed depressed all afternoon. He watched for her smiles, troubled by the sadness that seemed now to live in her eyes.

The people who had been playing vacated the court without being asked, and Harry and Kennedy began to warm up. Philip wondered if Harry, with his cigars and martinis, would be a match for Kennedy. It was soon clear that he was. Harry played a stylish, classic game; Kennedy was, by contrast, a scrambler.

Philip thought that Harry, with his blond hair, his classic serve, his baggy tennis shorts, looked like someone out of the twenties, out of a country club scene in a Fitzgerald tale. "Your husband plays a beautiful game of tennis," he said to Ruth Flynn.

Ruth cocked an eyebrow. "Oh yes, he's very much the Golden Boy," she said. "Would you excuse me? I think I'll go find Ethel."

Jenny relaxed as Ruth Flynn moved up toward the house. Soon she was caught up in the match. Harry was so damned graceful, so damned gorgeous. For a while she forgot about her anger and just wanted him, wanted all that energy to envelop her, to electrify her, to bring her peace.

Forty or fifty people were applauding when Kennedy finally won the match. He had given himself a couple of disputed line calls, and Philip thought Harry had blown the last game, but no one cared.

The men began to organize a game of touch football. Philip begged out of the game, wisely, because it proved to be a very tough game of touch. Some of the men wore cleats. Several of them had played college football and one had played professionally. Before the game ended there were several scuffles and bloody noses. Jenny and Philip sat on the hillside, drinking beer and watching the melee.

"Lords of the earth," Philip muttered.

"What?" she said.

"A long time ago, my grandfather told me he was a lord of the earth, because he struck oil and that made him a man of destiny. You know what? He's full of it. These people right here today, they're the ones with the power that matters. See that guy down there in the green T-shirt? He's going to change how black and white people live in the South, how they educate their children. The guy who just caught the pass—he's going to put Jimmy Hoffa's ass in jail. The fellow over there with the bloody nose—he made the Peace Corps happen, no matter who claims the credit now. These are the real lords of the earth—they're going to change this country, change the world!"

She looked at him in wonder; she'd never known him so serious before. "I hope so," she said. "Sometimes it's so hard to change anything."

As Jenny looked out over the playing fields of Hickory Hill, she saw something quite different. She saw young, virile, assertive men, preening for her and the other women. Something quite new had happened in American politics. The Kennedys had brought it a glamour that was part money, part sex, part celebrity, and part power. Suddenly, incredibly, the sexiest man in America wasn't an actor or singer: he was the president. These young men playing touch football were part of a royal court; Hickory Hill was their Versailles. Sex was everywhere, an electric current that united them all; she had felt it in a hundred glances and inquiries she'd gotten that day. Jenny hated it. She wanted to escape from sex. All she wanted was her work, her sanity, her privacy, and Harry when she needed him.

And Philip; what in God's name was she going to do about Philip?

People began to leave around five-thirty. Harry and Ruth Flynn rounded up their brood—beautiful blond children, stairsteps from two up to ten—and made a boisterous exit. Philip and Jenny sat on the hillside and watched a final tennis match.

"That must have been exciting," Jenny said. "When the president said you were doing a good job."

Philip shrugged and sipped his beer. "It was," he said. "But . . ."

"But what?"

He frowned. It was so hard to explain. "But I just hate this whole idea that if the president or Bobby gives you his blessing you're supposed to fall down and die of happiness."

"It's their party, Philip."

"I know, I know, but . . . Listen, let me tell you about the first time I ever saw Bobby. It was last November, just after the election. I was down by Lafayette Square and he came driving by in a powder-blue Cadillac convertible, with the top down, and wearing a powder-blue cashmere sweater to match, and he had that rich, arrogant look on his face, and I thought, Oh, God, it's Texas all over again. I mean, he could have been Skip Kingslea driving down River Crest Drive."

"You can't get away from it, can you?"

"Nobody can," he said. "Don't you remember the song? 'The eyes of Texas are upon you, you cannot get away.' The past dies hard."

"Yes," she said. "Yes it does."

"Do you ever think about going back? To Texas, I mean."

"Sometimes," Jenny said. "It can be a nice life—the richer you are, the nicer it gets. But you have to play by their rules."

"I couldn't live there again. Too many terrible things happen."

"Those things happen everywhere," she said. "It's the human condition."

He shook his head stubbornly. "No. It's worse there. All that money makes it worse."

Long shadows swept across the lawn. The last tennis game was ending. Philip helped Jenny to her feet and they walked to his car—a cream-colored TR-3, his only extravagance. As they crossed the Chain Bridge, he said, "How about dinner?"

Her answer came too quickly: "I'm sorry, Philip—I have to work on my brief tonight."

They drove in silence back to the carriage house she rented near the Washington Cathedral. He stopped in the heavy darkness of her driveway. Neither of them moved.

"What is it?" he said. "Is it me? Is it some other guy?"

"It's not you. You're wonderful. It's not anything. I just . . . I just have to work tonight."

"How about tomorrow night?"

"I'm sorry. I have to work then, too."

"Next weekend?"

"I . . . maybe. Call me."

"Who is he? The other guy?"

"There isn't anybody," she said. "I just . . . this case is so important and it takes up so much time and . . ."

"I work hard too, Jen, but I can make time for you. What *is* it?"

She lowered her head. "Philip, you're an old, old friend, but this just isn't a time when I can get involved with anyone."

"You can't pick those times," he said.

"Don't be angry."

"You've changed, Jenny. Can't you tell me what it is?"

"Perhaps it's the human condition," she whispered. She kissed his cheek. "Thanks for a wonderful day."

She ran into her house. Philip drove to a Georgetown bar and picked up a nurse and, as far as he could recall the next day, had a rousing good time. He made himself wait until Tuesday afternoon before he called Jenny about the weekend.

CHAPTER FIVE

It was a good time to be young in Washington, perhaps the best time ever.

The young men and women who had flocked to Kennedy's Washington found there was more to the city than politics and monuments. They went to A.V.'s Ristorante Italiano for spaghetti and clam sauce, to the Calvert Cafe for moussaka and thick Turkish coffee, to Chez Odette for *coq au vin*, to the China Doll for dim sum, to the Shamrock for bluegrass music, to the Circle Theater for the best old movies and to the Arena Stage for the best new plays, to Georgetown for Sunday brunches and out into the Virginia countryside for Sunday drives, to Rehoboth Beach for lazy, boozy summer weekends.

Philip wanted to share this rich, unfolding world with Jenny, but she danced beyond his grasp. They went out every week or two that summer, and she was sweet and sad and distant. When he kissed her goodnight she was like a sister. It made him feel awful, naked.

Still, there was his work. Always more work to take his mind off Jenny.

By the late summer, more and more was being heard of the war in Vietnam. A silent struggle was raging within the administration over the U.S. commitment there. President Kennedy had begun to praise President Diem, and the few hundred American military "advisers" there had become several thousand. To Philip and most people he knew, the whole process was a mystery. Why were thousands of American troops going there? Why was Vietnam important? Why was the reclusive Diem indispensable? Only the generals and the CIA seemed to know.

One day there was a briefing for the White House senior staff on Vietnam, and Harry asked Philip to go in his place. The briefing was in the White House theater. Philip arrived late and took a seat in the back row. There were twenty or so staff people there and some generals and CIA officials up at the front with maps and charts and pointers.

Philip dutifully took notes as the generals spoke of "the national interest" and "counterinsurgency" and "tactical mobility" and countries that would fall like "dominoes" and Asians whose "hearts and minds" could be won with "psychological warfare." Finally, with the air of a man showing his ace in the hole, the most bestarred of the generals declared, "To address the technological aspects of the conflict, I want to call upon one of our nation's most brilliant young scientists, Dr. Clayton Festus." Philip gasped as a skinny, straw-haired, all-too-familiar apparition rose up before them. He was wearing tweeds and an egg-stained foulard now, instead of boots and jeans, but the same mad, myopic gleam still shone in Fearless Festus' eyes.

"Gentlemen, we stand at the dawn of a new era in modern warfare," Fearless declared in his shrill voice. He proceeded to outline the military miracles that would be wrought in Vietnam: electronic sensors and laser beams that would punish the primitive foe; rifles with ultraviolet telescopes that could "see" in the dark; antipersonnel missiles that would be drawn to the enemy's body heat; miraculous cameras that could spot a skinny Vietnamese on a jungle path from two miles up; supersonic jet bombers that could blast North Vietnam back into the Stone Age; even, he confided, eyes ablaze, an electronic "wall" to be built across Vietnam to keep out the Communist hordes.

As the meeting broke up, Philip seized his old friend's bony arm. "Fearless, you crazy bastard, it's good to see you!"

Fearless paled; his eyes grew large behind his granny glasses. "I heard you were here," he muttered.

"Tell me one thing," Philip said. "Do you really believe that stuff about electronic walls?"

Fearless glanced about nervously. "It's no joke. It's all on the drawing board. Vietnam can be the greatest technological proving-ground in history."

The generals and CIA officials were starting to leave. "Call me," Philip said. "We've got some catching up to do. I haven't seen you since you blew up Farrington Field."

Fearless shook his head grimly. "I'm going back to Saigon tonight. We've got a war to win!"

He hurried after the general with long, ostrichlike strides. Philip shook with laughter. He couldn't help it. The last time he'd seen Fearless Festus, he'd blown up a football field. Now he had a whole country to blow up.

"Did you get that ABA speech written, Tex?"

"Does a dog have fleas?"

"Mine don't," Harry said. "Come on in. You seen this one?" He waved a tabloid newspaper. It was called *The Militant* and it featured a front-page cartoon of John Kennedy embracing a fat Negro woman and Bob Kennedy ripping pages out of the Constitution.

"Your grandfather's latest contribution to public enlightenment," Harry said. "He's started himself a nice little tax-exempt foundation to finance his crusade, and he's buying radio stations too."

"What're we gonna do about it?"

"I don't know yet," Harry admitted. "Come on, let's go see if the president does justice to that speech of yours."

"At the end you could yell, 'Author, author.'"

Harry frowned. "Tex, that sense of humor will get you in trouble yet."

They walked down to the Rose Garden; there, to Philip's amazement, he found Jenny standing amid a lot of lawyers in dark suits, like a flower in an ash heap. "What're you doing here?" he asked.

"I invited her," Harry said. "Thought she might like to hear your oratory."

The president came out, slender and tanned, and began his remarks to this American Bar Association delegation. Philip, who had drafted the president's speech, listened carefully, to hear what worked or didn't work.

Jenny, too, listened for a while, but then she stopped hearing Kennedy's words and just stared at him. He was so damn perfect. His hair was right and his suit was right and his gestures were right; there wasn't anything about him she would have changed. She wanted him; she guessed that every woman who saw him wanted him.

Suddenly the ceremony was over. The lawyers applauded and the president disappeared into the Oval Office.

"What'd you think?" Harry asked.

"He was wonderful," Jenny said.

"He was better last week, with the Peace Corps volunteers," Philip said.

The lawyers were starting to leave. "I'd better go," Jenny said.

"Actually, I've got a problem I need your help on," Harry told her. "If you can stay a few minutes."

"Of course." Who was ever too busy too linger in the White House?

From Harry's office window, she could see red and yellow tulips in the park and Andy Jackson astride his horse. Harry locked his door and leaned against it, grinning his most cocky grin.

"So what's your problem?" she asked.

"You. You're my problem."

He kissed her until she was breathless, then eased her down onto the rug. "No," she protested, but he took her quickly, hungrily. Soon she was close, wanting him, but suddenly he spent himself and their coupling ended as abruptly as it had begun. Harry was buckling his belt, lighting a Viceroy, and she still lay on the rug, breathless, unfinished.

"Want a drink?" he asked.

Jenny tried not to be angry. Harry was like that sometimes. He took his pleasure greedily and seemed not to know or care about her needs. But that was the way men were, she knew.

They took your body and used it . . . tormented you . . . She felt the darkness pulling at her and she stood up quickly, smoothing her dress. "Yes, a drink, please." She stared out the window at the bright flowers until he handed her a tumbler of Scotch.

"Was that spontaneous, Harry, or premeditated?"

He grinned. "Maybe a little of both."

"I wonder what stories these walls could tell."

"Let's hope they don't."

She tasted her drink. She could still feel him warm inside her and her own restless, unsatisfied itch.

"Did we solve your problem?" she said.

"Only partially. Perhaps we could discuss my problem again tonight."

She gazed across the avenue at the people and the flowers in the park. "That's an excellent idea."

Philip, knowing that Jenny's birthday fell at the end of the summer, insisted on taking her to dinner. They went to Rive Gauche, the city's best French restaurant. Her beauty won them a choice table, and soon they were drinking champagne and talking of many things. He told her of his trips to Harlem and Chicago, visiting juvenile-delinquency projects to gather material for a possible presidential speech. He tried to describe the numbing horror of Harlem with block after block, mile after mile, of tenements and women and children whose lives seemed hopeless. But the subject did not blend well with their champagne and crabmeat cocktails, so he told her of his sister Alice's successes on the pro-golf circuit. Jenny, when she could slip a word in, spoke of the efforts, unsuccessful so far, to draft her father, Dusty Rhodes, to run for mayor of Fort Worth and of her own continuing labors on the *Baker v. Carr* reapportionment case.

After coffee and brandy, they walked to his apartment, on the top floor of a P Street town house. He put on a Billie Holiday album and poured Cutty Sark. They sat on the floor, their backs against the sofa, and listened to the music. *Love, oh love, oh careless love*. After a while he kissed her. It was the same as always.

"Happy birthday," he said.

"It was a wonderful dinner."

She stroked his hand, and he knew the easy thing would be just to let it drift away, the way he had so many other nights.

But he had promised himself to settle it tonight, one way or the other.

"What is it, Jenny? Why can't I get through to you?"

She kept on gently stroking his fingers. "It's me," she said. "My work. Not knowing what I want to do. Not . . . not wanting to be involved."

"You don't give me a chance."

"I'm sorry. I haven't been fair. I thought we could go out sometimes and . . ."

"And just be friends," he said bitterly.

She lowered her eyes. "It wasn't fair."

"I've wanted to be patient," he said. "I've tried to understand. But dammit, I've been in love with you for so long . . ."

"Don't make me special, Philip. Don't waste your time waiting for me. You could make some girl so happy, someone who deserves you."

"I don't want some girl. I want you."

"Keep looking. Fall in love. Then you'll forget about me."

"Thanks," he said. "Thanks a million."

She lowered her eyes. He splashed more Cutty Sark into his glass. Out on the street, a girl was laughing.

"There's somebody else, isn't there?" he demanded.

She shook her head stubbornly.

"Dammit, there's *got* to be. Don't *lie* to me! That's the worst part of it."

Jenny bit her lip. "Yes, there's someore," she whispered.

"Who?"

"I can't say."

"Who, dammit, who?"

"Philip, what does it matter?"

"Someone in Texas?"

She shook her head.

"Skip? Is it Skip? I heard he was divorced."

"He calls me sometimes. That's all."

"Someone at Justice?"

"No."

"Someone who's married?"

"No, no, no!"

He grabbed her shoulders and shook her. "Quit lying to me," he yelled.

Jenny started to sob.

"Just tell me the truth," he pleaded. "For Christ's sake, Jenny, we've known each other for twenty years. Just tell me the *truth*. You owe me that much."

She looked at him for a long time. She thought of Harry. His wife had brought the new baby and the other children to Washington; they were spending the weekend house-hunting. She thought Philip was right; she owed him the truth.

"It's Harry," she whispered.

"What?"

"I'm having an affair with Harry."

"Harry *Flynn?*"

"Yes."

"For Christ's sake, he's forty years old and married."

She finished her drink. "I know that."

"That dirty son of a bitch."

"Don't blame Harry. He's what I need right now."

"Why? Why is he what you need? Why can't I be what you need? Do you think he's going to leave his wife and marry you?"

"No. I don't think that."

"Then why Harry? He's just using you."

"We use each other. Harry's not the problem."

"Then what is the problem?"

"I'm the problem, Philip. I can't explain. Can't we just be friends? Please?"

"No, we can't be friends," he yelled. "You don't need a friend. You need a patsy. Someone to hold your hand and take you to movies while you sneak around with Harry Flynn."

He lowered his head and began to cry. She knelt beside him, touching his arm. "Don't hate me."

"I don't. I couldn't. It just hurts so damn much. I've wanted you for so long. In high school I couldn't have you because I was a nobody and you went with the rich guys and the jocks. Okay, I survived that. But now I'm somebody. I've worked like hell to be somebody and I still want you and I still can't have you. I don't understand it and it hurts. I don't know what I've done wrong."

She put her arms around him. "You haven't done anything wrong. It's me. I'm . . . something happened to me, a long time ago. I haven't gotten over it. Maybe I never will."

"What was it? What happened?"

"I can't explain."

"Maybe I could help."

"No."

What could it have been? What could have changed her

so? He tried to think, tried to understand. Something half-remembered floated in the twilight of his memory. He blurted out the word:

"Mexico."

She stared at him with wide, frightened eyes. "What did you hear?"

He couldn't lie. "Nothing. Just a scrap of gossip. But what was it? What happened in Mexico?"

"I can't tell you. Maybe someday, but not now."

"Please," he begged. "I want to help."

"Philip, aren't there things in your life that hurt you, things you don't want to talk about, things you have to work out on your own?"

"Yes," he admitted.

She got up. "I'm going now. I don't think we should see each other again."

Jenny went to the door, then turned back. He was still sitting on the floor, head down. She couldn't leave him like that.

She went back to him, holding out her hand. "Philip?"

He looked up at her numbly.

"Aren't you leaving?"

"No," she said. "I want us to make love."

He got up, and she kissed him, the passionate kiss he had wanted for so long. He put his hands on her waist and pulled her close and felt himself stirring, hurting. The warmth of her mouth amazed him. He slid his hands up from her waist, feeling her ribs, the wonder of her breasts. She whispered his name, then stepped back.

"Dear Philip," she said. She loosened a button and her dress dropped to the floor. She stood before him in a bra and half-slip, and then, with a sudden, graceful motion, the bra was gone. He buried his face in her breasts. "Oh God oh God oh God," he whispered. "You're so perfect."

She took his hand and led him toward the bedroom.

Suddenly he stopped, gasping for breath, leaning against the doorway. His hair curled into his face, and she thought he looked beautiful and half-mad. "What's the matter?"

"I can't."

"Can't what?"

"I don't want your charity."

"Philip . . ."

"That's what it's called, you know. A charity fuck. You

screw the poor cripple to cheer him up. Well, keep it! I don't want it."

She drew back from his fury. "I only wanted . . ."

"I've got a little pride left, Jenny. I don't take charity. No sloppy seconds. Save it for Harry Flynn."

"Philip, please."

"GET OUT OF MY FUCKING LIFE, WILL YOU?"

He pushed past her and threw himself onto his bed.

She stood in the doorway. "I'm sorry," she whispered. "I'm sorry for everything." She dressed quickly and left him there, sobbing into a pillow.

CHAPTER SIX

Alice's first round in the Miami Open was a disaster. She three-putted three of the last four holes, to finish with a 79, and when she and Cricket got back to the Flamingo Motel she threw herself across her bed in despair.

"I'm all bloated," she cried. "It was like I was putting with gloves on—no feel in my hands at all. Oh, God, why did it have to start today?"

"Take some aspirin," Cricket advised. "Haven't you ever had a period before?"

Cricket, a tall, laconic Californian, was Alice's best friend on the tour. They drove to most of the tournaments together in Cricket's old Hudson.

"Yeah, several," Alice said. "But not on the first day of the most important tournament I ever played."

Cricket stepped on a cockroach that was skittering across the floor, then opened two beers. "You want to send out for pizza?" she asked.

"Cricket, I am serious! This is it. Custer's last stand. I am down to my last fifty bucks and if I don't win some money here the party is over, and I go back to Fort Worth and wait tables."

"Relax," Cricket said. "You'll probably break the course record tomorrow."

"Indubitably," Alice giggled, and they settled back to watch a cowboy movie.

Things were better for Alice the next morning. Her cramps weren't so bad, and she had some feel in her hands. She shot a solid 74 to finish the day in fourth place, five strokes back of Mickey Wright. That meant she had a shot at a decent payday, if she could manage one more good round.

There was a cocktail party at the club that evening, and Alice and Cricket decided to grab some free food. Cricket was gloomy because she'd shot an 80, plus she hadn't heard from her boyfriend. Some red-faced sport in a yellow coat cornered them and kept talking about how terrible Kennedy was. Alice didn't know anything about politics. She figured the most exciting thing that had happened that year was Elvis getting out of the Army.

"You know who elected Kennedy, don't you?" the guy demanded. "The three Cs—the Coons, the Catholics, and Cook County!"

"That's four," Cricket said. "Cs, I mean."

"I'm getting a headache," Alice said. "We better get back to the motel."

"Hey, are you gals roomies?" the man demanded.

"That's right," Alice said. She saw what was coming and it made her mad. Guys like this always thought that either you were a tramp or you went for other women. They couldn't believe you could be a professional athlete and a normal woman, too.

"Hey," the guy said. "I heard that a lot of you women golfers . . ."

"Sir, I am not a thespian," Cricket declared, and they grabbed a handful of shrimp and retreated to the Flamingo.

Alice lay awake a long time, thinking about all the money she didn't have. She'd been doing okay, until she'd gone into a slump a month earlier. She knew the exact moment her slump began. It was the last day of the Mobile Open, and she was in contention, but who showed up on the first tee but her long-lost father, Al. She'd known he was back in Alabama somewhere, but it wasn't the perfect moment for a reunion.

He insisted on going around with her and offering helpful tips
on her game, and naturally she went to pieces and shot an 84.
On top of everything else, Al asked her to loan him fifty
dollars. Which she did, just to be rid of him. Then she went
back to her motel room and bawled like a baby. She hadn't
won a dime in the four weeks since then. Which was how she
came to Miami, broke, depressed, and resolved either to win
some money or to pack it in.

The next morning, the third and last of the Miami tournament, it was raining cats and dogs. Alice didn't mind. Golf
balls became notoriously unpredictable on wet grass, so most
players eased up, went for the safe shot. That was Alice's
game to begin with, safe and sane, down the middle, so she
figured the long-ball hitters were hurting more than she was.

She got her par on the first hole and plodded on through the
rain, ignoring the gallery, ignoring the other players, oblivious
to everything except the hole she was playing. That was the
wonderful thing about golf: every hole was a world unto itself,
every hole had its own cast of characters, its own plot, its own
comedy and tragedy, its own meaning. She could spend hours
replaying in her mind holes that she'd played months before
—they were that real to her, that important, just as books or
movies were real and important to someone like Philip. When
you were on your game, when you had your concentration,
there was nothing in the world except you and the ball and the
club and the hole, and those moments were the purest ecstasy
she had ever known.

The rain settled her, helped isolate her. She played the
front nine in even par and discovered that she was in second
place, three strokes behind Mickey Wright. Everyone else had
faded, wilted in the rain.

She hooked her drive on the tenth hole and scrambled for a
bogey. She left the green cursing herself. She'd lost her concentration; she started thinking about the prize money instead
of thinking about her game. *Settle down,* she kept telling herself, *settle down and play your game.* Grim-faced, soaked to
the skin, she ran off another string of pars, and as she stepped
up to the seventeenth tee the word came that Mickey had
bogied eighteen.

The seventeenth was a long, 180-yard par three. The rain
had finally stopped, and as Alice gazed down the fairway, the
sun came out, blindingly, beautifully, an omen. Alice was
reaching for her five-wood when she heard a man cry, in a

familiar West Texas drawl, "Go get 'em, Alice honey!"

She turned and saw Asa, in a fire-engine red shirt, and her mother beside him. She ran over and hugged them. "We meant to surprise you," Louise said.

"Your mom's never been to Florida before," Asa added with his big grin.

Alice stepped up to the tee in a daze. Louise had never seen her play on the pro tour and she wanted to make her proud. All those years growing up, knowing that Philip was the favorite, the special one, while she was always about to flunk out of school, she'd dreamed that someday she would do something to make her mother proud.

Now was her chance.

If she didn't blow it.

She teed off and it felt right, all the way. She saw the ball falling onto the green, pin high, and she heard the people cheering. For an instant she thought she'd holed out, and she ran forward, only to see that her ball had stopped inches from the pin. People were yelling, and Asa hugged her, but Alice strode down the fairway, isolated again, telling herself over and over, *Concentrate, concentrate*.

She tapped in her birdie putt and then marched to the eighteenth tee, one stroke behind one of the real legends of women's golf.

The eighteenth was a long par-five dogleg right that played to a big green protected by water on one side and bunkers on the other. Alice needed a birdie to force a playoff. Trying for a long drive, she tried too hard and sliced into the rough. Her ball stopped behind a huge live oak that blocked her way to the green. She saw only two choices: she could go over the tree or around it. Over looked impossible: the tree was too tall, the air too damp and heavy. Her caddy urged her to chip out, around the tree, and lay up for her par. That was the safe shot, a par still gave her second place. But second place wasn't good enough, not with her mother watching. Alice thought of all those years when Louise had worked at that stupid tire company, always seeing that her daughter had new clothes, never buying anything for herself.

Second place sucked.

There was another way to play the shot: *under* the tree. Its branches drooped near the ground, festooned with Spanish moss, but a low shot could slide beneath the branches and have clear sailing to the green. If she hit the tree, of course, she was dead, but she didn't think about that. She jerked out her trusty five-wood and rifled a gambler's shot knee high— quail high, they called it in Texas—and it sailed inches below the wet fingers of moss, skittered across a rain-soaked bunker, and stopped on the high edge of the green, fifty feet above the hole.

The gallery cheered as Alice walked grimly to the green, then prowled about, lining up her eagle putt. All the while, unknown to the gallery, she was fighting to stop her heart from pounding, her hands from shaking, her stomach from churning. She didn't dare look at Louise and Asa. She felt tears burning her eyes—for a moment she thought she would break down, right there on the green. But she gritted her teeth and the concentration came back and the people were gone and there wasn't anything in the world except her and that long, downhill putt, breaking slowly left on a soggy green.

If you don't get up, you can't get in.

All alone in the universe, she bent over her ball, studied it for an eternity, then stroked it with all the hope and guts and precision that were in her. She watched the ball slide across the wet grass, on its own now, like a child, prey to the temptations of an imperfect world. It left a bright ripple of water in its wake as it curved toward the tiny, distant hole.

Was it too soft, too high?

No, no, no, her ball sailed smoothly, surely, bravely to the hole and plopped in for her eagle three. The crowd went crazy, and Alice, her arms raised high, danced about the green, laughing, crying, embracing her mother and Asa and Cricket. Alice Henderson, a lanky, pigtailed girl from Fort Worth, not yet twenty years old, had won her first professional golf tournament. She walked off the green feeling proud, strong, reborn. She had served notice on the world there was a new girl in town, and that the world, if it was halfway smart, had better give her room.

CHAPTER SEVEN

In the fall of 1961 a U.S. army commander in Europe, one David Baxter, was found to be indoctrinating his troops with his own right-wing political views, which included some highly unflattering opinions about his commander-in-chief, President Kennedy. The White House suggested that the general button his lip, whereupon the general resigned in protest, which led his supporters on the far right to protest that the Kennedys were trying to "muzzle" the military.

An isolated event, it would seem, a minor flap. Yet such is the Rube Goldberg process by which great events unfold that, very soon, that controversy over a general in Europe would result in Philip's meeting a woman who became important in his life, and in time the process moved on to inspire violence at the University of Mississippi and a bitter vendetta between the Kennedy White House and Wade Kingslea.

In the aftermath of the "muzzling the military" controversy, the White House made a halfhearted attempt to "clear" speeches by all top government officials. The problem was that nobody in the White House wanted to actually *read* all the deadly-dull pronouncements that the various officials were delivering each day. Inevitably, many of the speeches filtered down to Philip, the low man on the totem pole, for his glassy-eyed perusal.

Thus it happened, one autumn night, that Philip sent a speech back to the secretary of labor with a note attached saying it was a nice piece of work. And thus again, the next morning his phone rang.

"Hello?" he groaned.

"Phil Kingslea?"

"You got him."

"This is Chrissie Cohen. I work at the Labor Department.

Listen, I heard you liked the secretary's speech."

"It was okay."

"Okay? It was terrific—I wrote it!"

Philip smiled indulgently. The girl sounded young, and every speechwriter needed a few crumbs of praise now and then.

"It was a nice speech, Chrissie," he said. "It was short, lucid, factual, and funny. You done good."

"You is a man of taste."

"It comes and goes."

"So how about me buying you a drink after work?"

Philip sighed. What could a girl named Chrissie Cohen look like? He imagined her squat, dumpy, an eager beaver, with ink on her fingers and statistics on her mind.

"Listen, meet me at Chez When at seven," she said. "Then, if we don't hate each other, maybe we'll up the ante to dinner. Okay?"

"Okay," he sighed. What the hell; he hadn't taken a girl out for a month. "How will I know you?"

"You won't," Chrissie said. "I'll know you."

Chez When was across Lafayette Park, over by the AFL-CIO building. Philip had no sooner taken a stool at the bar when she grabbed his sleeve, announced, "Hi! I'm Chrissie," and gave him a peck on the cheek. She wasn't dumpy, as he'd imagined, but tall, five nine or so, with a peasant's sturdy shoulders, big breasts, broad hips. She had large, dark eyes, a formidable nose, olive skin, and a wide, mobile mouth that broke into a happy, goofy grin at every opportunity. They knocked down a few Scotches and then went over to Chez François for dinner. Chrissie, it developed, was from Chicago and had graduated from Northwestern. He thought she said her father owned a grocery store; he liked her for that; he imagined her a scholarship student, come to Washington to fight for social justice.

"I know all about you," she announced, over after-dinner cognac.

"How?"

"Oh, I've got my sources."

"Whatta your sources say?"

"That you're this great-looking guy who's single and a terrific writer and really going places."

"I'm the White House garbage man."

"Listen, Charlie, you come over to the Labor Department

if you want to see garbage. You know what else I heard?"

"What?"

"This is gossip, you understand. What the girls say. They say you've had a velly, velly sad love affair."

Philip twirled his Courvoisier and wondered how much could have gotten out about him and Jenny. Those damn White House secretaries. They knew everything.

"Confirm or deny?" Chrissie asked.

Philip shook his head. "Ain't nobody's business but my own."

She touched his hand. "You mad at me?"

"No."

"Then let's go to Georgetown—I know this great place to dance."

It was not until they were outside that she told him about Amelia. Amelia was her motorcycle—named for the aviatrix —which was conveniently chained to a tree outside. Philip climbed on behind Chrissie and held on for dear life while they roared to Georgetown. They danced in some dive until it closed, whereupon they made their way back to his bed.

"You sure you want to do this?" he asked. She seemed so damn young.

"Absolutely," she said. She tossed her silver Hopi bracelet onto his bureau and slipped out of her bright Mexican skirt.

"Why?" he said, although his protest was growing weaker.

"Because you've got the prettiest eyes I've ever seen," Chrissie said, casting aside her peasant blouse.

"Suppose you figure out tomorrow I'm a real bastard?"

"That's tomorrow."

An hour or so later, when they seemed to have made enough love for one Thursday night, she whispered, "Goodnight, sweet prince," and they drifted off to sleep.

The next morning she lured him into the shower, shampooed him, and then fixed breakfast, straightened up his kitchen, and gave him a ride to work on Amelia. By the weekend she had moved in, although she kept her apartment on Capitol Hill "in case my folks come to town."

It would be fair to say that in the next few months Chrissie took Philip in hand. She shamed him into picking up his dirty clothes, for example, and she persuaded him that if one partner to a relationship does the cooking, simple justice demands that the other do the dishes. She introduced him to the "new wave" movies arriving from France, persuaded him to wear his hair longer, and bought him some new shirts and ties that were, she insisted, more suitable for a man of his station than those he had been wearing since his newspaper days.

Chrissie even shaped a social life for him. He hadn't gone out much in Washington, aside from his dates with Jenny, and he didn't know many people except the ones he worked with. Chrissie, however, was part of a network of young people who toiled at Labor and State and Justice and the Peace Corps. They had endless beer busts and softball games and beach parties and spaghetti dinners where everyone sat on the floor and drank jugs of Mountain Red and argued about whether Kennedy was bold enough and whether things would be better in his second term. Philip didn't often join in the political debates. He liked to sit quietly, drinking his wine, studying people's faces and gestures and slang; Chrissie, who in her wilder moments seemed to be some sort of socialist, had opinions enough for both of them.

At Chrissie's urging, they took a train to New York one weekend, stayed at the Algonquin, saw *The Fantasticks,* and went to a noisy club in the Village to hear a folksinger named Bob Dylan; "Jesus, *I* can sing better than that guy," Philip groused, but Chrissie proclaimed the lad a genius. Philip was coming to learn that Chrissie had a few quirks to her generally sterling character. Her favorite drink was Dubonnet laced with gin. She thought Chuck Berry was the greatest living American. She had a truly perverse habit of reading the last chapter of a novel first, then, if she liked the ending, starting at the beginning. But these were forgivable flaws. All in all, he had never known a woman who was more fun or more eager to please. As winter became spring, Philip knew that he liked her, he respected her, he admired her, he enjoyed her. There was only one problem.

He didn't love her.

One spring day they walked in the park at Dumbarton Oaks. Chrissie ran ahead, twirling her arms. "Feel that air— it's champagne!" she cried. She raced across the grass and suddenly, gracefully, turned three cartwheels, her brown legs flashing in the sun. She plopped down on the ground, grinning at him. "You try it," she said.

"Not on your life."

"Come on, Gloomy Gus, cut loose. Have some fun."

"Chrissie, some of us manage to have fun without turning cartwheels."

He sat down beside her, staring at some distant trees.

"What's eating you?" she demanded.

"Nothing."

"You thinking about Miss Texas again?"

"What?"

"You know, the Sweetheart of the Rodeo. Jenny Jet-Set."

"Look, what brought her up?"

"I brought her up. You know why? Because sometimes I'm with you and you get that faraway look in your eye and I think you're really with her."

He took her hand. "I'm with you, Chrissie," he said and tried to believe it was true.

They stayed up late that night listening to the Everly Brothers, drinking too much brandy, trying to talk. There was a lot he wanted to tell her, but he didn't know how. It wasn't easy as writing a speech.

He refilled her glass. The Everlys were singing that it was so sad to watch good love go bad. "You know what I admire most about you?"

"My brilliant mind? My gorgeous, insatiable body?"

"The way you're so goddam cheerful all the time. The way you turned those cartwheels today. Fantastic!"

"Nothing to it. See, the air was champagne and it made me drunk."

"It's not that easy, Chris. People are different. You're so open, to people, to life, to everything. I'm not that way. I've got walls around me."

"Why? Why not tear 'em down?"

"It's not that easy. A lot of crap happened to me when I was a kid."

"A lot of crap happened to everybody when they were a kid."

He sloshed more brandy into their glasses. "Maybe so. I learned to tune things out. Don't let people too close. Work's easy—I'm great at work—but people hurt you. What you don't feel can't hurt you."

"But that's *wrong*, Philip. It's *not* feeling that hurts you. You've got to open up. You've got to learn to love. You've got to love stupid people and winos and bag ladies and dirty old men, because they're people, they're life, and that's the greatest thing in the universe. It's beautiful and it's sacred and it's free—it's all around us. Dig it! Wallow in it!"

He squeezed her hand. "You're so damn great, Chrissie."

"I don't understand you," she cried. "I really don't. I don't understand this thing with you and your grandfather. Why can't you just forget the old fart? It's like you had a family curse."

"I can't explain my grandfather. My grandfather is Texas. My grandfather thinks he can buy anything he wants. He tried to buy me once. What he can't buy he wants to destroy. Does that make sense to you?"

"I don't think so."

"He destroyed my father. No. Crippled him. You can't ignore Wade. You've got to love him or hate him."

"What about Jenny Cheerleader? Can't you forget her?"

"Jenny's special. If I never see her again, she's still special."

"Look, she dumped all over you. Quit mooning about her."

"There was a time when Jenny and my mother were the only people I cared about. I can't forget that."

"To hell with Jenny—what about *me?*"

"I'm sorry, Chrissie. You're wonderful."

She wiped her eyes and stood up. "Come to bed, Charlie. Maybe some good healthy sex will bring you to your senses."

But he never quite came to his senses. The next week he read in the paper that the Supreme Court had ruled for the government in *Baker v. Carr.* He thought of Jenny and how proud she must be. He reached for the telephone to call her before he realized that was crazy. She knew where he was. The moment passed, but her memory still haunted him, still hurt like hell.

Harry Flynn called Philip to his office one day that month. They'd never spoken about Harry's affair with Jenny. Philip had choked back his anger and admitted that he had no right to tell Jenny who to sleep with, or who to love.

Harry was on the phone when he entered the office, his feet up on his desk and a nasty grin on his face.

"Jesus, Walter, I don't see why Lyndon can't fly commercial," he was saying. "He's a great man of the people, isn't he? He'd be lonely in *Air Force One,* with no flesh to press."

He hung up and winked at Philip. "Poor Lyndon, he doesn't think he's vice president," he said. "He thinks he's the king of Siam."

"What's up?" Philip said, all business.

"You want to go to Cleveland with the president tomorrow?"

"Is the pope a Catholic?"

"Talk to Sorensen. He can't go, and we need a writer on the plane."

"I thought I was the fifth-string speechwriter."

"You might be up to third string, Tex. You might even make second string. Look, we've got the congressional elections staring us in the face, and Jack's gonna be traveling a lot this year. I want to get you on the plane as much as I can, but you've got to do your part."

"Who do I have to kill?"

"In Cleveland, the mayor will want Jack to add some stuff to his speech about air pollution. I don't want that crap in the speech, because it'll screw up my fund-raising. You got it?"

"Sure. Our friends the polluters."

"Don't add one word to that speech without my okay—mine or Jack's."

"I got you," Philip agreed.

On the flight to Cleveland, Philip fended off questions from reporters about who he was and what he did. "Just research," was all he would say. When they landed in Cleveland, the mayor's policy guy grabbed Philip and started a song and dance about the mayor's anti-pollution crusade.

"Whatta you think?" Salinger asked, when they got to the hotel.

"Harry said don't touch it."

"We've gotta give the poor bastard something."

"He's got one of those juvenile delinquency grants," Philip said. "You know, Bob's program."

"Gimme a couple of graphs on it," Salinger said. "Lay it on thick."

Philip commandeered a typewriter, banged out some fulsome praise of the mayor's dedication to law-abiding youth, and hurried up to the president's suite. Salinger was on the phone when he went in. The president was standing by the window, looking over his speech. The amazing thing was how quiet it was. Elsewhere in the hotel, reporters and photographers and cops and local Democrats and the mayor's people and assorted crazies were all pushing and shoving, shouting and scheming, trying to get a few inches closer to the throne of power, but the space around the president remained majestically still, the eye of the storm.

"Here's the insert Pierre asked for, Mr. President," Philip said.

Kennedy glanced at the paper and gave Philip a wry smile. "Harry said don't knock the smokestacks, did he?"

"Yes sir."

Kennedy looked amused. "Okay, Phil, this looks good," he said. He returned to his speech, and Philip eased himself out of the suite. A half-hour later, he watched from the back of a packed ballroom as Kennedy delivered his speech. He called Harry from the airport to report what had happened. "Terrific, Tex," Harry declared.

In the months ahead, Philip made several more campaign trips with the president. On one he spent a hectic half-hour rewriting an incomprehensible text that the State Department had provided—and he did the job so well that Salinger bought him a drink at the end of the day. Philip realized that somewhere along the line he had passed a test, for you did not get into the president's presence unless he wanted you there. He began to have a new goal: to win a place on the campaign plane in 1964. He thought it could happen. Harry trusted him, Salinger liked him, Sorensen tolerated him, and the president knew his name—great political careers had been built on less.

Then Harry Flynn went to Mississippi.

A week after he got back, Harry spent a long night with Jenny at her apartment, trying to explain what he had seen. The telling wasn't easy. Harry had survived five months of combat in Europe, but that one night at the school called Ole Miss was the worst thing he had ever seen.

He went by accident. A federal judge had ordered the enrollment of a Negro named James Meredith at the previously all-white University of Mississippi at Oxford. The governor dragged his feet, claiming that he could not guarantee Meredith's safety. Finally a force of federal marshals was sent in to enforce the court order. Harry Flynn dropped by Bob Kennedy's office one Sunday morning that September, as Bob and his top lieutenants were making plans for the confrontation. Several of them were about to leave for Mississippi. "Why don't you go along, Harry?" Bob tossed out, and the next thing Harry knew he was on a plane flying south.

He spent the longest night of his life there, trapped in the university's administration building, the Lyceum they called it, where a few hundred marshals were trying to hold off a mob of several thousand howling, brick-throwing Southerners. The president went on national television at nine o'clock, pleading for reason, but by then snipers had started firing on the marshals from out of the darkness. Two men died, and scores were torn and bloodied by flying rocks and bottles and by the sniper fire. It was Americans firing at other Americans—that was the worst of it—and before the night was over Harry Flynn knew it hadn't happened by accident.

"At midnight, Dean and I slipped out the back, to see if we could find the snipers. Do you know Dean?"

"No," she admitted. "I've heard you talk about him."

"Dean Markham. Played ball with Bob at Harvard. A good man. Tough as nails. See, we had to take out the snipers. They were forcing the marshals back inside the building. And that meant that eventually the mob would try to overrun the building. We'd been holding them off with tear gas, but if they overran us we'd have to use guns and there'd have been a bloodbath."

"Where were the troops?"

"If there was any way in hell, we wanted to settle this without troops. Anyway, Dean and I took off through the dark. And we found two snipers, over in the woods. A couple of peckerwoods with a rifle and a jar of moonshine, having themselves a fine old time."

"What'd you do?"

"We took 'em out. They never knew what hit 'em. Maybe they woke up and thought it was the moonshine. Then we scouted around the campus. There were still a few dear little coeds out, chanting, 'Fuck the Kennedys,' but mainly it was some very tough boys out there. I started noticing the license plates on all those pickup trucks. Tennessee. Alabama. Louisiana. I counted twenty of them from out of state. That doesn't just happen. I've organized rallies. You don't get that many people to travel that far that fast unless somebody is organizing them. So, the next thing I see is Baxter."

"General Baxter?"

"Yeah, *General* Baxter. There's a statue of Johnny Reb there across from the Lyceum, and he was standing on the pedestal, waving a Confederate flag, telling his troops to charge. *Do you understand what I'm saying? This man was a general in the United States Army and he's telling a gang of rednecks to attack U.S. marshals who are trying to enforce a federal court order*. That's anarchy, Jenny. That's lynch law."

"I know." She'd never seen him like this before.

"Baxter's just the front man. There's someone behind him. And I know who it is."

"Who?"

"Your friend Wade Kingslea."

"How do you know?"

"I know," he said. His smile was as sharp as a knife. "Baxter is Kingslea's boy now. He's playing him up in those right-wing rags he publishes. He's running him for governor of Texas. And he sent him to Mississippi to do his dirty work."

"Why? What does Wade Kingslea care if one Negro attends Ole Miss?"

"He doesn't. But he cares about the 1964 election. We may have lost half the South when we sent those troops into Oxford. *That's* what Kingslea wants."

Harry crumpled his empty beer can and tossed it across the room into a wicker wastebasket. "But he went too far. There's a line you don't cross in politics. You don't stir up lynch mobs. You don't get people killed."

"If you can prove it, indict him," Jenny said.

"I don't want to indict him," Harry said angrily. "I want to teach the son of a bitch a lesson. A lesson in what is known as hardball."

Harry's campaign against Wade Kingslea began to unfold in the early months of 1963.

Harry had men from the campaign who were personally loyal to him stationed in all the key agencies. These men were his eyes and ears throughout the vast empire of government, and when he called them to his office and urged them to look very closely at Kingslea Oil's far-flung operations, they were eager to oblige. Soon a hostile army was advancing, from a great many directions, on Kingslea Oil and its founder. Harry received weekly reports from the lawyers and regulators who were tightening the screws on his enemy, and he savored them. There were, Harry believed, two kinds of revenge. In the first, a man knew what you were doing to him but was helpless to prevent it. In the second, a man knew he was being punished but could not be sure why or by whom. That uncertainty caused the sharper pain, gave the sweeter revenge, and Harry intended to inflict it on Wade Kingslea for a long, long time.

By the spring, Kingslea was feeling the pain.

At first, he and his lawyers could not be sure that the Kennedys were waging all-out war against them. It was in the nature of things that Kingslea Oil would fight countless legal skirmishes with the federal government; its lawyers won more battles than they lost. But, as the months passed, it was clear that something unprecedented, something sinister, was afoot. One of Kingslea's lobbyists was under indictment for bribing a congressman. The IRS, reversing an earlier decision, was demanding seven million dollars in back taxes. The FCC had revoked the licenses for two of Kingslea's radio stations. The Justice Department had charged two Kingslea Oil officials with bribing certain Saudi princes to obtain oil concessions. The list went on, until Kingslea was sure the Kennedys had launched a major campaign against him. But who was behind it? Was its goal harassment or total destruction?

It was urgent that Wade Kingslea know the answers to those questions, and thus one Sunday afternoon he flew to Washington, to meet with the one man in America he knew could give him answers.

Kingslea spent Sunday night at the suite he maintained at the Mayflower Hotel. On Monday morning, at precisely ten o'clock, he was ushered into the dark, cluttered office of his old friend J. Edgar Hoover, the director of the Federal Bureau of Investigation.

"You're looking well, Edgar," Kingslea said. That was not precisely true. Hoover, in his late sixties, was a heap of jowls, wattles, liver spots, and sagging flesh—he looked like a huge, malevolent frog. Still, as Kingslea knew, flattery was never wasted on the director. He was surrounded by men who were fond of telling him to his uncomplaining face that he was the greatest man of the century. Of all time, some of them said.

"It's a hard time, Wade, a hard time," Hoover said, as he sank heavily back into his chair. "The government is in the hands of incompetent fools, and the Reds and race-mixers are trying to take over."

Hoover launched an hour-long monologue that at various times touched upon the sex life of the president's father, the capture of John Dillinger, the rape of a young girl by a black man in Chicago, the spread of radicalism in American universities, and the alleged homosexuality and/or communism of

endless senators and congressmen. The monologue was difficult to follow, in part because Hoover had recently become
obsessed by an American pacifist named David Dellinger and
it was often difficult to tell if he was denouncing Dillinger, the
gangster, or Dellinger, the pacifist.

In time Kingslea's mind began to wander and he let his
eyes explore the hundreds of odds and ends that cluttered
Hoover's office. He saw a portrait of Shirley Temple in a
ballerina costume, Oriental rugs and jade carvings, a lock of
hair supposedly from the head of Adolf Hitler, a carved
wooden stallion, a Ming incense burner, a pair of Colt re-
volvers made into bookends, several bullwhips, an oil painting of a young bullfighter in tight black pants, a bronze figure
of a gladiator, a porcelain mermaid, a variety of carved and
sculptured dogs, an elephant-foot ashtray, and an amazing
number of small statues of nude children.

The monologue ended abruptly. "Well, Wade, how are
things in Texas?" the director asked.

"Tolerable, Edgar, considering the political climate,"
Kingslea said. "In fact, I have some good news for you." He
reached into his pocket and passed a sheet of paper across the
desk.

Hoover studied the paper gravely. It reported that in the
first three months of the year he had earned about six thousand
dollars from his oil holdings in Texas. These earnings were the
result of a unique secret arrangement between Hoover and his
friend Kingslea. A dozen years before, Kingslea had organized a thousand-dollar-a-plate Patriot's Dinner in Fort Worth,
at which Hoover and Senator Joseph McCarthy had been
given gold plaques and checks for ten thousand dollars in recognition of their service to the cause of freedom. Newspaper
accounts gave the impression that Hoover's ten thousand
would be donated to charity, but in fact it went back to Kingslea with the understanding that he would invest it in oil leases
as he saw fit. Over the years, Hoover's income from oil had
generally exceeded his modest government salary.

Hoover folded the paper and put it in his coat pocket.
"You're a brilliant man, Wade," he said.

Kingslea waved away the compliment. "God put the oil
there, Edgar, to reward men who work hard and love their
country. Finding it isn't difficult. The hard part is beating back
the bureaucrats and regulators and radicals who want to take
away everything we've worked for. And, by God, it's never

been worse than it is this very day!"

Hoover nodded knowingly. He knew exactly why Kingslea was here. One of Kingslea Oil's top security officers was a former FBI agent in Texas. After a moment, Hoover pulled a paper from his desk drawer. "Look at this, Wade," he said. "I think it will interest you."

Kingslea read the paper with mounting outrage. It was a long memo, addressed to Harry Flynn, in which a young lawyer at the Justice Department outlined plans for a legal attack on Kingslea Oil. The memo was quite brilliant in its analysis. It was also quite foolish in that its ideas had ever been committed to paper. Most of Harry's people knew better, but this young lawyer, carried away by zeal, had typed his plan and kept a copy for himself, locked in his desk drawer. That was his mistake, for just as Harry Flynn had his men posted throughout the government, so did J. Edgar Hoover, and Hoover's men rarely made mistakes.

"Flynn," Kingslea said bitterly. "I thought so."

"He was in Mississippi," Hoover said. "He is responsible for the treatment of David Baxter as well."

Their friend General Baxter, as a result of his activities at Ole Miss, had been charged with sedition and had for a time been held in a federal psychiatric hospital.

"Do you know Flynn?" Kingslea asked.

"He came to see me, not long after his crowd took over," Hoover said. "A courtesy call, he said. What he wanted, of course, was for me to turn over Bureau files to him to use in his political vendettas. Oh, Mr. Harry Flynn is a fourteen-carat son of a bitch, Wade, I'll promise you that. But charming, very charming."

"I can't take this lying down. He's got half the government after me. He and his kind are trying to destroy freedom and decency, and to set up their own dynasty. Give me your advice, Edgar. Flynn must have a chink in his armor."

Hoover nodded, staring off into space, an inscrutable Buddha, who seemed if anything to be contemplating a statue of three nude children of uncertain gender.

Kingslea waited. Hoover could make him wait, just a bit. Hoover never let you forget that while you might be immensely rich, he was immensely powerful, that while you might be a lord of the earth, he was hailed by millions as something close to a god.

"Oh, he's got his chink," Hoover said finally. "All that

Kennedy crowd does. They're all the same. Degenerates. Weak, pampered, hypocritical degenerates."

He scowled at the nude children awhile, lost in his thoughts, and then absentmindedly pulled a slip of paper from his desk. He glanced at it a moment, shrugged his heavy shoulders, and slid it across the desk to Kingslea.

Only two words were written on the paper:

Jenny Rhodes.

CHAPTER EIGHT

Chrissie called Philip at his office one day and announced that her father was in town. "He wants to take us to dinner. There's no way out."

"No problem," Philip said.

"Says you," Chrissie said. "Look, he doesn't know we're like, living together, so he'll pick me up at my old place and then we'll come get you."

Philip thought it was all pretty funny. He didn't know anything about Chrissie's family, but he thought she'd said her father owned a grocery store. He was therefore prepared to meet a humble Jewish shopkeeper who would be awed by his daughter's dashing boyfriend.

It wasn't like that.

Sid Cohen arrived in Georgetown, with a subdued Chrissie in tow, driving the longest, most ostentatious automobile Philip had ever seen outside of Texas. It was a customized Lincoln Continental that featured a telephone, a wet bar, two TV sets, and license plates that proclaimed BIG SID. Sid was, as promised, a big, bald, scowling fellow who sported a silver-gray Italian suit, a two-carat pinkie ring, and a platinum lapel pin that informed the political world that he had contributed ten thousand dollars to the Democratic National Committee.

"So this hick cop stopped me for speeding out in Virginia,"

Sid said, by way of greeting. "'Where ya from, mister?' he asks me. 'Chicago,' I tell him. 'Hey, you can't fool me,' he says back. 'I seen your Illinois license plates!'"

Sid roared, slapped Philip on the knee, and announced that their destination was Duke Zeibert's. When they stopped in front of the restaurant, he gave a young black man a twenty-dollar bill to park the Continental and warned that he'd break both his legs if he scratched it. Then Sid led them inside, where he rated an embrace from Duke Zeibert and the best table in the house.

It developed that Sid's *father* had been the humble Jewish grocer. Sid owned a chain of supermarkets and divided his time between building shopping centers and playing politics. Throughout dinner a steady stream of congressmen filed past their table, hands outstretched, seeking Sid's blessing and, it was clear, his dollars.

Finally, as the brandy arrived, Sid told his daughter, "Sweetheart, go powder your nose, and don't be quick about it."

"I get the hint," Chrissie said glumly and wandered off.

"Now, young man, let's talk turkey!" Sid declared. "You're living with my little girl without benefit of matrimony, and I want to know your intentions."

Philip gulped, took a puff on the cigar Sid had forced upon him, broke into a fit of coughing. "I . . . I . . ." he sputtered.

"Oh, I know she keeps that dump on Capital Hill," Sid added. "But I also know where she spends her nights. I wasn't born the day before yesterday. So when are you going to marry her?"

"We never talked about it," Philip said, although that was not precisely true.

"So let's talk about it," Sid declared. "I don't know what you young people are coming to. When I was your age I had a wife, two kids and half a million dollars in the bank. A man who's shacked up don't get ahead in the world, boy!"

"Washington's kind of a temporary place, Sid," Philip said. "Chrissie might go back to Chicago. I might work in the campaign next year. It's hard to make plans."

"You're a writer, right?"

"Right."

"Well, there's no money in writing. I checked it out. You're a bright boy—I checked that out too—but you need a new line of work. Come out to Chicago and I'll set you up in real estate. You can make big bucks, boy, or my name's not Sidney I. Cohen!"

"I don't know anything about real estate," Philip protested.

"So I'll teach you. What's the matter—you don't want to be rich?"

"I don't even know if Chrissie wants to marry me."

"Then what's she doing cohabitating with you?" Sid demanded. "You think my baby's some kind of tramp?"

"I think she's wonderful. I truly do. But I don't know if she wants to marry anybody right now."

Sid chewed his cigar ferociously. "Young man, you're giving me heartburn," he growled, just as Chrissie returned.

"I'm sleepy," she announced.

"So sleep," Sid declared. He stood up, tossed a wad of bills on the table, and hustled them out. Driving home, he aimed straight for Georgetown.

"I'll . . . I'll go to my place," Chrissie protested.

"Oh hell, you think the old man's a dummy?" Sid demanded. "Me 'n this fellow see eyeball to eyeball—right, Phil? Capitol Hill's no place for a decent girl—too many Ubangis prowling the streets."

He pumped Philip's hand in parting. "Think Chicago," he commanded. "The city of broad shoulders!"

Inside Philip's apartment, Chrissie flopped into a chair. "So now you know my secret," she declared.

Philip opened two beers. "He could be worse."

"You should meet my mom. My mom's a dear. My mom's got a master's in psychology."

"Your mom needs a master's in psychology."

"So what did Sid tell you?"

"That if I'd make an honest woman of you he'd make a real estate tycoon of me."

"To which you replied?"

"Vaguely."

"I'll bet."

"What was I supposed to say? I don't know what I'm going to do. Or what you're going to do. Or anything. But I don't think I'm going to be a Chicago real estate tycoon."

"Then what do you want, Philip? Seriously."

He sat down beside her. "Chrissie, I don't know what I want except maybe to work on the campaign next year. The terrible truth is, I'm sick of my job. I mean, Kennedy's great —he's doing the best anyone could—but my job is to write fairy tales. 'Sir Lancelot emerged from his castle this morning, slew the dragon of Intolerance, saved the fair princess, and rode off smiling.' How many years can I keep writing fairy tales before it rots my brain?"

"So what's your alternative?"

"I could go back to reporting. What I'd really like to do is write a book."

"A book," Chrissie said glumly.

"That's right. Maybe something about politics. Maybe even a novel. Jesus, when I look at what McMurtry and Brammer had done—I *know* those guys! McMurtry worked at Mrs. Baird's Bakery, in Fort Worth, one summer when I was there. He was just this scrawny kid from Archer City. Now he's written a novel, a hell of a good novel. It's called *Horseman, Pass By*. They're making a movie out of it—*Hud*, they're calling the movie. See, the thing about Texas is, it *creates* writers. You can't just *live* there, the way you can in Oregon or Maine or somewhere. They won't let you. You've got to love it or hate it. You've got to either be a true believer or a rebel. It's monolithic, like Russia. Someday, Pampa or Uvalde or Nacogdoches will turn out a Dostoevski—he'll hate that damn state so much it'll make him a genius."

"So that's your fantasy?" Chrissie said. "To write a novel?"

"Yeah. I think that'd be the greatest thing in the world."

"It never entered your mind that maybe the greatest thing in the world would be to marry some nice lady and make babies?"

Philip, not knowing what to say, put on Erroll Garner's *Concert by the Sea*. As the music filled the night, he tried for the umpteenth time to define his feelings for Chrissie. She was special, wonderful, but did he love her? He wasn't sure what love was. He knew that thinking about Jenny hurt him—literally, gave him a physical pain, somewhere in the region of his heart—and that thinking about Chrissie made him smile. Which was love and what was the other one? He thought that perhaps his strongest emotion was a hunger for freedom, to be able to travel or write or whatever he pleased. *That* was his one true love.

"A guy I knew at Labor went to be the Peace Corps director in Peru," Chrissie said. "I got a letter from him today. He wants me to come be his deputy. It might be fun."

"It might be," Philip said. "What do you want to do?"

"I want to marry you, you bastard."

He put his arms around her, trying to figure out what was right. He didn't get far. Perhaps he did love Chrissie, in a way, but he loved his ambitions, his freedom, more, and he wasn't ready to give them up. If he did that, he didn't see how he could make her happy, or himself, or anyone else.

On a windy morning in late April, Ruth Flynn returned home from her car-pooling duties and began to check the mail. There were the usual bills and invitations and also a manila envelope with no return address, addressed to her. Puzzled, she tore it open.

She found a four-page, single-spaced memorandum headed "MEETINGS BETWEEN MR. HARRY FLYNN AND MISS JENNIFER (JENNY) RHODES 1961–1963." A typical entry read: "11-3-61, Mr. Flynn and Miss Rhodes met for dinner, Calvert Cafe, returned to Miss Rhodes' home; Mr. Flynn departed 1 A.M." There were dozens of entries like that.

Halfway through the memo, Ruth threw it down on the kitchen table and lit a cigarette. She found her hands shaking. Her mind rejected these sudden, terrible allegations. She told herself it was some cruel hoax. But then she began to study the memo again, with growing fury. Certain of the dates had meaning to her. Their oldest son's birthday party the previous year, which Harry had missed, calling at the last moment to say he had to work late. A Fourth of July weekend when he failed to join them at the Cape. Seizing her calendar, she found a dozen dates when Harry had not been with his family because, it seemed, he had been with someone named Jenny Rhodes.

Ruth paced her big, bright kitchen. She was a wealthy woman, a timber heiress, who might have married any of the richest, most eligible men of her time. Instead, she had married the dashing but penniless Harry Flynn, and because of his ties to the Kennedys, she had been caught up in a political world that was not entirely to her liking. In her own world, Boston, Ruth was a social figure of the highest magnitude, but in the Kennedy world you were inevitably, no matter who you were, a lady-in-waiting to the women of the royal family. Ruth had too much money and too much pride to think she had to stay married to Harry forever. She seized the phone, savoring the luxury of recklessness.

Harry's secretary said he was "with someone."

"Miss Davis, I want to speak to my husband within ten seconds," Ruth said quite fiercely.

"Yes ma'm," the secretary said, and Harry quickly came on the line.

"Harry, who is Jenny Rhodes?"

"What?"

"Where were you last Wednesday night?"

"Hey..."

"Or on Benjy's birthday?"

"Listen, Ruth..."

"Or the Fourth of July?"

"What's got into you? Jenny is Phil Kingslea's girl. You met her at Hickory Hill, remember?"

She did remember: a quite stunning young woman, with dark eyes and a gorgeous figure.

"You're lying, Harry."

"Look, I took her out a couple of times, to talk about her and Phil."

"A couple of times? Harry, I've got a list of fifty times you were with her."

"A list?" Harry was beginning to grasp the urgency of the problem.

"That's right, Harry. Names and times and places."

"Wait there," he said. "I'll be right home. We'll get to the bottom of this."

"You bastard," she said. "You gold-plated bastard."

Ruth put down the phone and began to cry. She saw what was coming. He would put his arms around her, sweet-talk a little, lie a little, promise a lot, and she would forgive him. That was the pattern, the role she was supposed to play: husbands strayed, wives forgave. Ruth washed her face, spoke to her housekeeper, and went out to her Buick station wagon. She didn't think she'd forgive Harry just yet.

Harry, driving out Massachusetts Avenue, tried desperately to sort out the problem. He had to find out who had done this to him. He had to do something about Jenny. He had to talk to Phil Kingslea, to make sure he'd back him up. But first he had to talk to Ruth, before she did anything crazy.

As it happened, Harry was speeding out Massachusetts Avenue as Ruth was driving in; they passed each other somewhere around the National Cathedral. Thus, as Harry arrived at their home, to find Ruth gone, she was arriving at the Justice Department, to seek justice in the highest available tribunal. She hurried to the Attorney General's fifth-floor office and, because she was Ruth Flynn, she was quickly admitted. Bob Kennedy greeted her in his shirtsleeves, looking small and boyish in the huge, somber office. He guided her to a sofa and asked what the trouble was.

"This," she said dramatically and thrust the mysterious memo to him.

Soon Kennedy was only pretending to read the memo, because he understood the problem and needed time to think. The more he thought, the more furious he became with Harry Flynn. A man had to keep his affairs under control—if a man couldn't do that, how the hell could he help run a country? You damn sure couldn't let the FBI or the Birch Society or whoever this was keep lists of when you met your girlfriend. How dumb could you get? Harry understood the stakes they were playing for. This mess could explode and hurt Jack. That was the unforgivable sin.

"I thought you should know," Ruth said. "She works in your department." She was nervous, afraid she'd gone too far.

"You were right to tell me," Bob said. He stood up and Ruth had no choice but to do the same.

"What should I do?" she asked, fighting back tears.

"Don't do anything," Bob said. "Leave everything to me."

She drove home and found Harry waiting for her. "I want to make love," was all she said.

When Jenny arrived at the office the next morning, her boss was waiting to see her. She thought she knew why. A dozen reapportionment cases were rising toward the Supreme Court and it was urgent that Justice define its policy on them.

But reapportionment wasn't what her boss, a big Irishman named Leo Hardesty, wanted to talk about.

"I'm afraid I've got bad news, Jenny," he said.

Bad news? Was she being taken off the case? "What?"

Leo didn't look at her. "There's been a reorganization. We're losing a slot. I'm afraid it's yours."

"Losing a slot?"

"It was a budget cutback. We just got word."

Jenny was confused. "Do I have to move to another division?"

"No. Your job is just . . . gone."

"Gone? Am I being fired?"

"Officially, it's a reduction in force. Happens all the . . ."

"Leo, are other jobs being lost?"

"I don't know, Jenny, I don't know." He looked like he was about to break down.

"Who can I talk to? Who can explain it?"

Leo stared at the floor. "Maybe the administrative office. They got word from the Budget Bureau, I think."

Suddenly Jenny realized it would be pointless to seek an explanation. The bureaucrats could give you a runaround forever; it was what they were best at.

"You've got thirty days," Leo said. "We'll give you the highest possible recommendation. Maybe some other agency. . ."

He walked her to the door, then put his arms around her. "It's rotten, Jenny," he said. "I don't understand it. I've never seen anything like it."

Jenny hurried to the women's restroom. It was one of the more private places at the Justice Department; she could cry in peace.

Back at her office, she called Harry. Surely he could get to the bottom of this. But Harry's secretary said he and his family had left on a vacation. She wouldn't say where. Slowly, Jenny began to understand. Something had gone terribly wrong.

She walked up Pennsylvania Avenue toward the White House, trying to decide what to do. The flowers were out along the avenue and people were smiling, whistling, holding hands, celebrating spring's return. Jenny wanted to scream, to flee. It had been ten years since the night in Mexico that changed her life. She had come to Washington to escape and now she had messed up her life here too. Would she spend the next ten years fleeing?

Suddenly she knew what she must do.

She went into a Dart drugstore and called Fort Worth.

Skip said he'd fly up that evening.

Philip and Chrissie were expecting their guests any minute when the phone call came. The guests were to be Millie, Chrissie's college roommate, and her new husband, a medical student. Chrissie had spent most of the afternoon in the kitchen working on her celebrated veal stew and cherry tart.

Just before eight, Philip went into the kitchen and mixed her a gin-and-Dubonnet. "Relax," he said. "It'll be great."

She gulped at her drink. "I burned the tart."

Philip examined the tart, which looked perfect. "Relax," he said again. He went back to the living room and, in the spirit of the occasion, put on an album of Ella Fitzgerald and Louis Armstrong. Then the phone rang.

"Oh God, I'll bet they're lost," Chrissie cried. But it wasn't the honeymooners. "For you," she said.

It was a fellow Philip knew at Justice, a fellow he'd done some favors for.

"Listen, Philip, you know Jenny Rhodes, right?" the fellow said.

"Right."

"Well something's happened. She got canned this morning —don't ask me why, nobody understands it—and she left the building and never came back."

"Jenny? Fired?"

"Yeah, that's right. And there's this other thing. Don't quote me, but yesterday afternoon Harry Flynn's wife went barging into the AG's office in a huff. Don't ask me why. But it's two strange happenings in two days—Harry's wife storms in yesterday and Jenny's fired today. So, I thought you'd want to know."

"Yeah, thanks," Philip said and put down the phone. Ella and Louie were singing "Cheek to Cheek." Chrissie was staring at him.

"What is it?" she asked.

"Nothing."

"Philip, what *is* it?"

"Nothing, I said."

He turned away from her and dialed Jenny's number.

She answered on the first ring.

"It's me," he said. "Is something wrong?"

"Who? Oh, P.K., *you.* No, nothing's wrong."

"I heard you got fired."

"It doesn't matter."

"What the hell is going on?"

"There's nothing you can do. I've got to go now. I'm . . . I'm going somewhere."

"Where?"

"For God's sake, stop asking me questions! I'm going back to Texas. Back where I belong. Back to Cowtown. Back to my glorious golden girlhood. Back to reality. Back to . . ."

"Look, I'll be right over."

"Don't," she said. "I won't be here." She hung up.

Philip grabbed his car keys. Chrissie was staring at him. "I'll be right back," he said. "A friend of mine is—in trouble."

"Jenny," Chrissie said flatly.

"That's right. She lost her job. She's upset. She . . ."

"So Sir Galahad gallops to the rescue," Chrissie said.

"Look, Chrissie . . ."

"What has that bitch done for you lately? Has she cooked your dinner lately? Has she ironed your stupid shirts? Has she screwed you lately?"

"This is someone I've known for twenty years, someone who . . ."

"I don't *care* about that crap," Chrissie raged. "Look, Charlie, if you go out that door, don't come back."

"Don't yell at me."

"I'll yell if I please. We've got guests coming and you can't just walk out because some crazy Texas bitch calls and . . ."

"I'll be back as soon as I can," he said.

Jenny opened her door and looked surprised.

"I . . . I thought you were Skip," she said.

He pushed past her into the house.

"What happened about your job?" he asked.

"I don't really know."

"I heard that Harry's wife barged into Bob Kennedy's office yesterday."

Jenny sat down and lit a cigarette. "That makes sense," she said.

"How do you think she found out?"

"It doesn't really matter, does it?"

Philip paced about. "It might," he said. "You might have got caught in one hell of a crossfire."

"Well, I'm out of it now."

He knelt before her and took her hands. "Why?" he demanded. "Why Skip? Why Texas? Can't you take some time, think this over?"

She shook her head defiantly. "It's all settled. He'll be here soon. We're flying back tonight."

"There aren't any flights this late."

"Skip's flying us, in his plane."

"I didn't know the All-American boy flew," he said bitterly.

"Can't you stop it?" she said. "You aren't sixteen anymore. None of us is."

She was wrong. There was a part of him that would always be sixteen, lying in the street with his mouth bleeding while Skip and his football buddies laughed at him.

"He's an interesting man," she said. "There's no one his age in Texas who's been more successful in oil."

"He started the game with a few chips, you know."

She ignored him. "Skip's shrewd. He plans to run for office. Maybe next year. There's a new congressional district."

"Yeah, I know. His grandfather wants to make him president. The Joe Kennedy syndrome. All over America nasty old millionaires are scheming to get their progeny into the White House."

"Don't underestimate them."

"Look, why are you running back to Texas? Stay here. Go with a private firm."

"I was wrong about the law," she said. "I thought you could bury yourself in the law."

"But why do you want to bury yourself? And what has Skip got to do with anything? What is it between you two?"

"I'm going to marry Skip," she said, as if it was the most obvious thing in the world.

"Marry him?"

"We were almost married in college. Skip and I understand each other."

Philip stared at her as if he'd never seen her before. "I don't understand you. Why marry Skip? For his money?"

"Money isn't so terrible, P.K. Money buys peace and privacy and solitude. Money builds big, beautiful walls. Money. . ."

"You think you can bury yourself in money, like you tried to bury yourself in the law. Why, Jenny? That isn't the girl I knew, the girl . . ."

"The girl in pigtails at the baseball games," she cried. "The cheerleader, shaking her ass for the crowd. The Homecoming Queen. That girl is gone, P.K., dead and buried, R.I.P."

"What happened, Jenny?"

"I can't explain."

He grabbed her arms, shook her. "Was it Mexico?"

"I can't . . ."

"Tell me," he yelled. Her eyes were wild and terrible, like an animal's in a trap.

"Have you ever been turned inside out, P.K.? Have you ever been a fly on a pin? Have you ever been dragged through slime? Have you ever. . ."

"Jenny!"

". . . prayed to die? Have you ever seen fire and hell and monsters? Have you ever been a monster yourself and done things that God can't forgive?"

She broke loose from him and ran into the kitchen. After a moment he heard the back door slam. He ran after her, but from her porch he could only see darkness.

"Jenny, where are you?" he called, but the only reply was the wind.

He heard someone behind him. It was Skip Kingslea, framed in the kitchen door. He was heavier than Philip remembered him, but still a tall, graceful, broad-shouldered man, whose high cheekbones and thick, golden hair gave him a leonine look.

"What's going on?" Skip demanded.

"Jenny's . . . she ran outside."

Skip pushed past him, plunging into the darkness. He crossed the dark yard as if confident that some force would lead him to her. Philip followed uncertainly in his wake. In a moment they heard her sobbing. Skip found her huddled beneath a lilac bush. He put his arms around her and whispered, "It's all right now," and helped her back into the house.

"Do you want to stay here tonight?" Skip asked her.

Jenny pushed her hair back from her eyes; her face was pink and splotchy. "No. To fly at night . . . it should be lovely."

"It will be," Skip said. "Everything will be fine now." He stood with his arm around her. She seemed to take strength from him.

"You two . . ." Jenny said. "I guess it's been a long time."

The cousins stared at each other, then Skip put out his hand and Philip reluctantly shook it. "This is no time to talk," Skip said. "But I want to, some other time."

Philip didn't reply.

"We'd better start," Jenny said.

"Do you have bags?" Skip asked.

"They're in the bedroom."

"I'll get them," Philip said.

"No, I will," Skip said. "You walk Jen to the car."

Philip took Jenny's arm and led her outside. A limousine waited at the curb. "I don't understand any of this."

"I don't either," she said. "Not really. I just do what I have to do."

"I want you to be happy."

"I'm going to try, P.K. I'm going to try so hard."

"Sometime, I'm coming to see you."

"I know. And I'll explain everything. It'll be easier then."

Skip came out of the house, carrying three bags. The chauffeur jumped out to help him. A thin slice of moon floated high above the street. Jenny hugged Philip, then slid into the back seat. Skip stood before Philip.

"I'm going to make her happy," he said.

"I hope you can."

"I want you to come see us," Skip added. "I know we've had our differences, but that was kid stuff. I respect what you've done up here. I'd like to talk to you about politics. I'm no big fan of the Kennedys, but they know how to play the game."

"I'll call when I'm in Texas," Philip promised. They shook hands, then Skip got into the limousine with Jenny, and in a moment they were gone.

Philip drove aimlessly around Northwest Washington, trying to make sense of what he had seen. All he knew was that something terrible had happened to Jennie in Mexico, that she had promised to explain it to him someday, and that somehow Skip could help her. Beyond that, it was all a mystery.

It was nearly eleven when he got back to his apartment. Chrissie's note was on the kitchen table:

Dear Philip: I'm heading for Peru, via Chicago. I guess I'll write you somewhere along the way. Try to love somebody, even if it's not me. It was fun. Love, Chrissie.

    PS. Write that novel—I promise not to read it backwards.

• • •

He sat staring at the note for a long time, thinking that he'd managed to lose two women in one night, some sort of record. The strange thing was, when he fell into bed, it was Chrissie he missed, for the first time.

CHAPTER NINE

The president was going to Texas, and no one was happy about it.

Most of all, no one was happy about the stop in Dallas. Philip kept getting calls from people warning him that Dallas had become the hate capital of America, that Dallas was where both Lyndon Johnson and Adlai Stevenson had been cursed and shoved and spat upon by angry mobs, that it was insane for the president to go there.

Philip agreed, but it was not his job to tell the president where to go; so he kept quiet, until one day in early November when he received an unexpected telephone call.

His secretary, Ginny, a saucy wench, stuck her pretty, impudent face in his door, giggling giddily. "Do you know a duke?" she demanded. "Not a king, not an earl, but a duke?"

"What's the joke?" Philip asked.

"No joke, sahib. He's calling from a pay phone in Texas. Won't give his name. Talks like Humphrey Bogart. Says, 'Tell him it de duke.'"

"Oh, hell. I'll talk to him."

As Ginny retreated, convulsed by the absurdity of the opposite sex, he barked a hello.

"Whatta ya say, kid?" his old friend growled.

"Hello, Duke. What's up?"

"When you were down here that time, you didn't tell me you were working for the Kennedys."

"I couldn't, then. So how's Chez Duke?"

"I tell you, nobody ever went broke selling booze and beefsteak in Texas. I'm gonna open a bigger place next year."

"That's great."

"Your old girl friend, the one who married Skipper Kingslea, was in last week."

"Jenny? How'd she look?"

"She looked like a million bucks. And drank like a fish."

Philip was annoyed. There had been a time when the Duke was amusing, but that time was long past. "What's on your mind?"

"Hang on," the Duke commanded, and there was a distant clanging of bells as he dropped quarters into the phone. "Listen, kid, in my business I keep my mouth shut and my ears open, because my average customer makes Attila the Hun look liberal. But me personally, I think Kennedy's fine—you understand?"

"Sure."

'Okay, listen up. If you repeat what I say, you're a liar. But you better keep your man out of Dallas."

"Why? What have you heard?"

"That if Kennedy goes to Dallas there's liable to be big trouble."

"What kind of trouble, Duke? Be specific." But the Duke was gone.

Philip stared out his window at Lafayette Park. It was a chill, blustery day; red and yellow leaves were cascading down from the trees, to lie limp and shiny on the wet, dying grass. After a while he sighed and walked down to Harry Flynn's office.

"What's on your mind?" Harry asked.

"Dallas," Philip said. "I keep getting calls from people who say the president shouldn't go there."

"Welcome to the club. Who've you talked to?"

"A guy in Senator Fulbright's office—he said the senator begged the president not to go there. And a Dallas lawyer I know. He talked for a half-hour about all the violence there, about the anti-Kennedy jokes, about the 'K.O. the Kennedy' bumper stickers, and H. L. Hunt and the Birchers and all the crap they're putting out—Harry, the man was begging me, saying for God's sake don't let Kennedy come here."

Harry nodded. "Look at this," he said and tossed a letter across his desk. It was from the National Committeeman from

Texas, who said he feared for the president's safety if he went to Dallas.

"He's been up here," Harry said, "trying to get Dallas canceled. He's a good man, too, not some nervous Nellie."

"Then for God's sake, Harry, why don't you talk to the president? Drop Dallas from the schedule."

Harry frowned and fiddled with his PT-109 tie clasp.

"I'll tell you why we're not going to cancel Dallas. It looks like the Republicans will nominate Goldwater, which means Jack has a chance to win big next year. To get a mandate, to get the Congress we need."

"Harry, you won't get your mandate in Dallas."

"I know that," Harry shot back. "But we've got to carry Texas to win big. Last time, we won it by less than fifty thousand votes out of a million cast. Today, we'd lose it. The party is split wide open. We've got a Democratic senator and governor, Yarborough and Connally, who hate each other's guts."

"So send Lyndon down to patch things up."

"Lyndon," Harry said scornfully. "Lyndon's a eunuch down there. The only one who can get unity is the president. If he goes down, and draws big crowds, shows he's strong, the others will fall in line."

"Okay," Philip said. "Go to Austin, it's a nice little college town; they've even got a few liberals there. Go to San Antonio, where there are lots of Mexican-Americans to cheer him. Go to Houston or Fort Worth, where labor is strong enough to turn out a crowd. But Dallas is *poison!*"

"That's right," Harry said with his cocky grin. "That's why Jack's going there."

"That's crazy," Philip protested.

"Do you know why Jack is president? Because he's got guts. All through his life, he's come to turning points, where he could go the easy way or the hard way. In the war. When he ran for the Senate in '52. When he had his back operation. When he decided to run in '60. The smart boys always said to wait for a sure thing. But you don't get to be president waiting for a sure thing."

"But Dallas, Harry . . ."

"Listen, Jack's not president of forty-nine states. He's not president of all of Texas except Dallas. He's president of all the country, all the people, and he can't let a few right-wing kooks keep him out of Dallas. He's got to serve notice that they're in for a fight and they're gonna get their butts whipped."

"Harry, so many people think there'll be trouble."

"Okay, you get some boos. You get some nasty signs waved at you. Maybe you get some eggs thrown. We can live with that."

Philip ached with frustration. "Harry, it could be worse than eggs. Look, I admit I'm a little crazy on the subject of Texas. But I grew up in the place, and it's not like Boston or wherever you grew up. There's a *tradition* of violence. They're *proud* of it. When I look back, half of what I remember is violence. Fights at school. Fights in bars. Fights at football games. Gamblers blowing up each other's cars. Guys driving through the Negro district shooting out windows. A girl's father drew a gun on me once because I brought her in a half-hour late. Harry, it's a crazy, dangerous place, and Dallas is the very worst of it. He just shouldn't *go* there."

Harry sighed. "I'm not real happy about it. But he's going and that's that. Do you want to make the trip? Maybe you can help out."

"Sure," Philip said. "Sure, I'll go." But when he got back to his office he stared out into the rain for a long time. It had always been exciting to go on a presidential trip, but this time he was scared to death.

Two days before the Texas trip, Philip was in Pierre Salinger's office when the president summoned the press secretary. Salinger waved for Philip to come with him; "He won't bite you, kid," he growled.

Kennedy was at his desk signing a pile of letters. He was wearing his glasses; the White House grapevine said his farsightedness was getting worse. The grapevine also said he had been depressed all week, perhaps lingering sadness from the death of his newborn son, two months earlier.

Kennedy bantered with Salinger about his upcoming trip to Japan. Salinger complained that it would cause him problems with his wife. "Courage, Pierre," Kennedy said. "Marriage is what we have instead of war."

Philip drank it all in. Moments like this were precious. Everytime he was around Kennedy he liked him more. He thought Kennedy walked the razor's edge between irony and idealism; he understood the madness of the world, and he had chosen to confront it nonetheless.

As they were about to leave, Kennedy took off his glasses and rubbed his eyes. "I wish I weren't going to Texas," he said.

"It'll be a great trip," Salinger said, waving his cigar. "You'll draw the biggest crowds ever."

Kennedy looked unconvinced. "What do you say, Phil? You're a Texan, aren't you?"

Philip hesitated. This was his chance, to air his fears, to plead for cancellation.

But of course he couldn't do that. He couldn't trouble this tired, depressed, lonely man when it was too late to change anything. He would only make himself look foolish.

"It'll be great," he said. "They'll love you."

Kennedy managed a skeptical smile. "Let's hope so."

The president flew to Texas aboard *Air Force One* on a Thursday afternoon. Philip caught a ride on a backup plane filled with unhappy congressmen. The congressmen, if you listened to their tales, had a lot of specific complaints, about this and that indignity they had suffered, but in general they were simply complaining that a cruel and inscrutable fate had made them lowly congressmen, when clearly, in a just world, they would be United States senators, if not president.

They landed in San Antonio in midafternoon. It was hot, and the crowd cheered wildly, particularly for Mrs. Kennedy. The unhappy congressmen were soon muttering that Jackie would save the trip. A brief battle ensued when Ralph Yarborough, the state's liberal senator, refused to get into the same car with Vice President Johnson; absurdly, the main goal of the trip seemed to be to get these two mush-mouthed, big-eared Texans into the same automobile, in the name of party unity.

The local politicians were whispering about a handbill that had been passed out on the streets of Dallas that morning. It featured police-style mug shots of the president, full-face and profile, with the caption "WANTED FOR TREASON."

Philip dropped off from the presidential party in San Antonio. Kennedy would spent an hour there, then fly to Houston for a dinner, then to Fort Worth for the night. Philip flew commercial straight to Fort Worth.

It was early evening when he stopped his rented Impala outside Chez Duke. "Is the Duke here?" he asked a hostess with plucked eyebrows and platinum hair.

The woman eyed him coolly. "Nope," she replied.

"Where is he? I'm an old friend of his."

"Florida."

"Where in Florida?"

The woman made a face. "Miami? Key West? Who the hell cares?"

His mother and Asa greeted him warmly on their front porch.

"By golly, boy, where's the president?" Asa demanded. "I thought you were bringing him to dinner."

"He'll be along," Philip said. "He had to stop in Houston first."

"I hope so," Asa declared. "I aim to give him a piece of my mind."

Philip wondered if Asa was serious. "What did you aim to tell him?" Could it be that this otherwise sterling man was a right-wing nut?

"I've got a plan for the president," Asa said gravely. "I know some folks think a tax cut is what we need. And some folks want a new trade policy. But you see, Philip, what we really need is a henway. The way I see it . . ."

"A *what*, Asa?"

"A henway. The way the darn economy is today. . ."

"Asa, what the hell's a henway?"

His homely stepfather gave him a look of perfect innocence. "Oh, two or three pounds," he said.

Louise rolled her eyes, Asa shook with laughter, and they led Philip to the kitchen, where he was given a beer and a copy of the new *Sports Illustrated*. The magazine featured a story on Alice, as one of the new stars of the LPGA tour. "It's so crazy," Louise said. "The thing she got the most publicity for was when they fined her because her skirt was too short."

"She's been playing great," Asa said. "That girl will earn fifteen thousand dollars this year."

"What are your plans?" Louise asked. "Can you stay for dinner? If only you'd given us some notice . . ."

"They've got me a room at the Hotel Texas. I've got to get back there and do some work." That was not precisely true, but he didn't want to be tied down.

"The president lands at Carswell about eleven," he added, "and goes to the Hotel Texas to spend the night."

"We know," Louise said. "They printed his schedule in the

Star-Telegram. We thought we might go wave to him when he drives by."

Philip gaped at his mother, quite amazed. Louise's hair was mostly gray now and cut short, and she was well tanned after a summer's flirtation with golf. He'd never thought of her or Asa as political. "That'd be terrific," he said.

"We're *proud* of the president," Louise added. "Not everyone in Texas is H. L. Hunt or Wade Kingslea, my dear."

"It just seems that way," Philip said.

He soon made his excuses and left. He drove around aimlessly for a while. To call or not to call? He found himself in a pay phone.

"Jenny? It's me."

"P.K.? Where are you?" She didn't sound surprised.

"I'm in town."

"Oh, with the president?"

"Sort of. Look, is this a good time to call?"

"A fine time. Skip's in Mexico City, and I'm watching TV."

"I'd like to see you."

"Then do," she said. "Just give me a little time."

A light rain was falling. He drove down Crestline Drive, then onto River Crest Drive. He parked under some trees and crossed the golf course until he could see his grandfather's mansion.

The porch light went on and three men came out. One was his grandfather, resplendent in a smoking jacket. One was a wiry, sandy-haired man wearing sunglasses and a cheap suit. The third man was dark-skinned, Mexican perhaps, and powerfully built; he wore his hair in a shiny pompadour, and diamond rings flashed on both his hands. The three men huddled head to head; the dark-skinned man gestured excitedly, Wade Kingslea nodded gravely, as if settling some crucial point, and then the visitors hurried to a waiting Mercury.

Philip raced forward, wanting the Mercury's license number, but he was too late. Angry, troubled, he returned to his car and drove west to Jenny's house.

She was Jenny Kingslea now. His mother had sent him the clippings when she and Skip married. There had been a lot of clippings, for Skip and Jenny were mythical figures in their hometown: he the football hero turned dashing oil tycoon; she the baseball-team mascot and cheerleader who had gone off to

Washington, then returned in triumph to claim her prince. The Sweetheart of Cowtown, one overwrought society columnist had dubbed her.

She met him at the door of her and Skip's white-columned house near Ridglea Country Club.

"I call on the Sweetheart of Cowtown," he said.

"You could be kicked in the shins by the Sweetheart of Cowtown." She was wearing black satin pants, a shimmering silver blouse, pearl earrings, and more makeup than she needed. He stepped past her into a glistening marble foyer. "It's a nice place," he said, for want of anything better to say.

"Skip has a *real* mansion he wants to build," Jenny said. "A Texas Taj Mahal. He's got the blueprints and everything. But he's afraid to build it because they might use it against him when he runs for Congress."

"Tell him to build it. Tell him log cabins are out. Ostentatious wealth is what America wants in its leaders now."

"Old P.K., the eternal cynic." She led him into a Chinese-red study with a bar and two walls of leather-bound books, the kind rich Texans bought by the yard to show their devotion to culture.

"Is it for sure that he'll run?"

"Absolutely. His grandfather has it all planned."

"How do you feel about it?"

"I like it. At least I could help in politics. I can't help him find oil. Would you like a martini? My latest vice."

"Gin is the only vice I ever overcame," he said. "I'd settle for a beer."

She poured herself a martini from an icy crystal pitcher and pointed him to a refrigerator packed with Lone Star and Carta Blanca. Her wrist, as it passed before him, was breathtakingly delicate; he ached to touch it.

"So what have you been doing?" he asked.

Jenny smiled wistfully. "I swim, I play tennis. I have thus far resisted the Junior League, leading to rumors that I'm a snob and/or a subversive. Most of my friends have two or three children now. *Mucho* peer pressure to join the sisterhood."

"Are you?"

She sipped her martini. "I suppose so. If I stay with Skip."

He let that pass. Now that he was here with her, he realized that he didn't know what he felt for her or what he wanted from her.

"How is Harry?" she asked. "And the girl you were going with?"

"The girl escaped my clutches. She's in Peru with the Peace Corps. Harry's okay. He's worried about this trip."

Jenny grimaced. "He ought to be. The political climate here—it's unreal."

"Do you know any reason that a man who's...I don't know, Mexican or Spanish or Cuban, would have been leaving Wade's house tonight?"

"Oil?" she said with a tiny shrug, as if that small word could explain anything. They settled at either end of a velvet-covered sofa and were soon talking about people they had known in school, their marriages and divorces and affairs, the unlikely setbacks and successes that emerged in people's lives. A boy who'd been two years ahead of them, the editor of *The Scorpion*, was a writer for *Life* now. A handsome football star was in Hollywood and had been in a movie. Through it all, despite her easy laughter, he sensed an undercurrent of despair.

"Jenny, are you happy?" he asked suddenly.

She poured herself another martini, then faced him on the rose-colored sofa.

"Happy?" she repeated. "I'm not sure I know what that means. I know I've learned a lot. It's very strange to be married to a man as rich as Skip. I can have anything I want but it all comes from him. It's not like the mythology, of the young couple struggling to make ends meet. Skip, in his world, is like a god. He's smart and he's lucky and he works hard, and he makes millions of dollars. And while he's out making millions, I'm here playing tennis and buying clothes and being beautiful. Which is fine with Skip—he's not the problem. The problem is that you start feeling guilty and dependent. I let all the servants go—I couldn't stand having them around. Why can't I take care of my house and my husband? You start to get obsessed. About four o'clock in the afternoon you start to think. How do I look? How do I smell? How does the house look? What about dinner? You think, this man works hard, he gives me everything, and he deserves a clean house and fresh flowers and whatever dinner he wants, and, yes, good sex, and children too if he wants them. You have a couple of drinks and start racing around getting everything perfect, for the big moment when he marches in the door. You're like a kid with her report card, wanting Daddy's approval. You start sinking into a slave mentality. You start to lose your *self*, P.K. It's so terribly unequal."

He took her hand. "Aren't I ridiculous?" she asked. "Complaining about the agonies of being rich? But it's not easy, P.K. It's so hard to keep your self-respect."

"Jenny, he's lucky to have you."

"No, he's not. That's the point."

He looked at his watch. "The president's landing about now," he said. "Want to drive over and see the motorcade?"

"I want to get out of this house."

They got some beer and drove to the high school parking lot. It was strange to be there. Down the street, he could see the spot where Skip Kingslea and his buddies had beat him up, ten years before. This parking lot too was the place where Fearless Festus had sat in the Batmobile, sharing his Eight Page Bibles and Everclear gin in his quixotic campaign for student-body president. Those memories all seemed quite unreal, yet no more unreal than to be sitting here with Jenny, ten years later, waiting for the president of the United States to pass by.

People lined the edge of the freeway. "There he comes," someone yelled, and motorcycles and limousines sped past in the rain; everyone cheered and then it was over and they started back to their cars. They could tell their grandchildren that they had seen a president, even if all they had really seen was a dark car speeding through a rainy night.

Philip and Jenny went back to the car and he opened a beer.

"Do you want me to take you home?"

"Could we just sit here for a while?" she asked.

"Sure," he said.

"I have to get out of the house sometimes," she said. "It's *his* house. Everything is his. I'm his. Sometimes I just want to be alone, anonymous. Does that make sense?"

"I like to be alone," he said. "It's my natural condition."

She took his hand. The rain was falling harder. "Dear P.K. You always understood everything."

"Not really. Sometimes I think I don't understand anything, except how to write someone else's speeches."

She kissed his fingers, one at a time. "Do you want me to tell you about Mexico?" she asked.

CHAPTER TEN

"There were four of us," Jenny began, "Skip and I, and Ellen Campbell and Mike Slaughter. Ellen had been dating Mike that summer, and in August Mike asked us all down to his parents' ranch in South Texas for one final blast before we went off to college.

"I know you didn't like Ellen, because she got to be editor of the paper instead of you, but she was really a smart, sweet, wonderful girl. She was going to Wellesley to study premed and be a doctor, like her father. And you know Mike: just a big, happy-go-lucky boy who was heading off to Texas Tech to play football.

"We drove down in Skip's car, drinking beer and telling Little Moron jokes and acting silly—I guess we all knew it was the end of something, that no matter how good college was it'd never be as wonderful as high school. We drove down on Friday afternoon and had dinner with Mike's parents and later on we swam, and there was a great burst of shooting stars, and at midnight Skip and I slipped off to make love while Ellen and Mike sat by the pool and talked.

"The next day we rode around the ranch on horseback and in the afternoon Mike took us up in his Beechcraft. We flew down along the Rio Grande and you could see the Mexican towns across the river, all brown and beige and pastel, and Mike buzzed some Mexicans who were walking their goats along a dirt road. I remember that night, talking to Ellen. She was so perplexed, because she was a virgin and determined to stay one until she married, but she knew that if she went to medical school she might not marry for years. She kept asking me if it was *normal* to wait that long. I remember telling her, 'Ellie, I promise you, it'll all work out.'

"The next day, Sunday, was cloudy and cool, like rain was

411

coming, and Mike and Skip said they wanted to go to the bullfights in Reynosa. Well, Ellen and I didn't give a hoot about the bullfights. I'd always hated Mexico, at least the border towns, because they're so poor and ugly and depressing. But we got in the car and headed south. And it was exciting after a while, when you began to see the palm trees and the orange groves, because it's another world down there.

"You know how it is in the border towns, with people selling beer and trinkets and tacos and that sticky pink candy that always has flies all over it, and people yelling in Spanish, and bands playing—it's fun, it's like a fiesta when it's good. I'll never forget how Skip and Mike looked. They were wearing their jeans, of course, and T-shirts and boots and baseball caps and their letter jackets, because it was cool. On the way to the bullring they bought a couple of huge sombreros, and they gave me and Ellen their baseball caps to wear. We were in jeans, too, and windbreakers and I remember Skip saying that with my short hair and the baseball cap and my jeans I looked like a boy.

"I remember the way the Mexican men stared at me and Ellen, but I felt safe, because I knew that no one could ever bother us while we were with Mike and Skip. They were so beautiful—these two tall, narrow-hipped, broad-shouldered boys in their boots and tight jeans and sombreros, strutting along, towering over the Mexicans, as we walked down the street to the bullring.

"The bullring was pretty seedy. We had seats on the sunny side, up with the Mexicans, not down in the shade with all the American tourists. The bulls and the bullfighters were pretty third-rate too, but we kept drinking tequila and chasing it with beer and after a while it all seemed glorious and we were cheering our heads off. Then something strange happened. The last bull of the day was a really beautiful animal. He came in and ran around the ring a few times and then charged straight for the wall, the first wall, the one about five feet high that people stand behind, and he jumped and somehow he pivoted on that wall with his front feet and sailed up over the second wall and landed in the front row of tourists. It was horrible. People were screaming and running, and for an instant you thought the bull would charge around and kill everybody. But before the bull could even get up, all these Mexican men jumped on him and started hacking at him with their pocketknives and finally a policeman came and shot him in the head and they dragged him away. The matador was standing in the middle of the ring with no bull to fight.

"That was the end of the bullfights, so we started back to town. It was dusk, with one of those violet skies you get in the Valley, and there were colored lights hanging over the main street and people yelling and trying to sell you things. Skip and Mike were pretty high by then, and I wasn't so far behind them. Ellen wanted to start back, but Mike and Skip wanted to stay in Reynosa.

"'What can you *do* here?' Ellen asked.

"'Lotsa things,' Mike said. 'Nightclubs. Cockfights. Shows. Real special shows.'

"'What kind of shows?' Ellen asked.

"'Ever seen a girl pick up a Coke bottle?' Mike asked.

"'What's so special about that?' Ellen said.

"'Without using her hands?' Mike said and he and Skip howled. Even I had to laugh because Ellen was so innocent. I knew a little more—boys had told me about Mexico.

"We went to a bar and had more tequila and beer, and that was when either Skip or Mike, I honestly can't remember, said that we should take a tour of Boys Town."

"No," Philip cried. "You never take a white woman to Boys Town. Anybody knows that."

"Ellen didn't even understand what Boys Town was. I whispered to her that it was the red-light district, and she said she certainly wasn't going there. But the boys wouldn't drop it. Skip kept saying that with our jeans and windbreakers and the baseball caps we'd pass for boys. By then they'd won me over, so we found a decent-looking cafe and left her there and told her we'd be back in an hour."

"No," Philip groaned. "No, no, no."

"Why did I do it? Because of the tequila, partly. And because it seemed like a lark, before I went off to college and Rush Week and all that. Or maybe I just have a death wish; who knows? Anyway, we set off down the street, me with my baseball cap and my fists stuck in the pockets of my windbreaker to try to conceal my chest. The boys called me Little Joe, our big joke.

"The road to Boys Town was crowded with American soldiers and college boys, and after a couple of blocks you started coming to these tiny one-room houses, just cribs, really, with women sitting in the doorways. Some of the boys would stop and talk to them, but not many, because they were the old women. The young women were all farther on.

"We could see the neon lights up ahead. The main part of Boys Town was two blocks that were all bars and cantinas, with music blaring out of them, and men in the doorways yelling that they had the coldest drinks and the hottest girls. We went all the way to the end of the street, to a place called Pepe's, that Mike said was the best bar there. We looked in the window, and it seemed harmless enough, just a bar and a jukebox and tables, and people dancing and drinking and talking. So we went on in. I sort of stayed behind Skip and Mike, hoping no one would notice me. We got a table and a waitress brought us beer and a photographer came and took our picture. The girls sat in chairs against the wall, until you went and asked them to come to your table. I remember thinking how young and pretty they were—somehow, it reminded me of rush parties I'd been to.

"Then this man, this Mexican, came to our table.

"He was about thirty or thirty-five. He looked fat, at first, but he wasn't. He was a powerful man, with huge arms and a cold, ugly face, but he acted very friendly. He said, 'Hey, how you fellows doin'?' and of course Skip said we were doing fine and called him *amigo* and asked his name. He said his name was Tony, and Skip told him our names were Skip and Mike and Joe—Little Joe, he said. I just sat there trying to be invisible. Out on the street it had been all right, because it was dark and crowded and no one paid any attention to me, but in here I felt like everyone was staring at me, and I was sure Tony knew I was a girl.

"Tony was wearing black pants and the kind of shirt that policemen wear, with funny pockets and epaulets and all, and Mike started calling him the Sheriff. He asked if we'd like some tequila and of course Skip said sure we'd like some tequila, and he brought over a bottle and joined us and everybody started to drink tequila. Except Tony wasn't drinking any. He said he used to live in San Antonio. Skip asked him if he liked it there and Tony grinned—he had awful teeth—and said, 'No, too damn many Texans there,' and everyone had a big laugh. I kept whispering to Skip that it was time to go, that Ellen was waiting for us, but Skip was drunk and enjoying himself and Tony said maybe we wanted some girls, said he knew where they put on some great shows, not far away, and it was then that Skip got deathly pale, and his head started dropping down. I knew right away that he wasn't drunk, he was sick, or drugged.

" *'Skip, we've got to go!'* I told him, but he said, 'Feel dizzy—need some air,' and slumped down.

" 'Hey, my friend, he sick, he need air,' Tony said, and a couple of Mexican men came over and helped Skip up, but instead of taking him outside they took him through the door beside the jukebox, where the whores had been taking the American boys, the door that led inside the building. Then Mike passed out—one moment he was talking and the next moment he was gone. The Mexicans carried him away too. No one else in the bar seemed to notice. It was just a couple of drunk Americans. Tony and I were alone at the table. I should have gotten up and run, right then, out the door, but I was confused and scared and half-drunk and afraid to go out onto the street, with all those people, in the dark. I kept thinking that if only Skip would come back everything would be all right.

"Tony kept staring at me and saying, 'Hey, Little Joe, you don't say much, eh? You want a girl? You come to Mexico to go bang-bang, eh?' I just kept shaking my head and after a while the other men came back. One of them was a boy of sixteen or so, very thin, with huge, sad eyes, but the other two were dirty and mean looking. They and Tony talked back and forth in Spanish, and I was about to cry, and finally I said, 'Please, I've got to see my friends.'

" 'Hey, you want to see your friends? No sweat!' Tony said, 'Come on, we see your friends.'

"He took my arm and started to lead me to the door and part of me wanted to scream but part of me kept thinking that we would find Skip and everything would be all right again. We kept going down this long hallway, turning this way and that way, and he was squeezing my arm until it hurt, and we passed girls in their slips and bras, and we went out a door and across an alley and into another building, and Tony said, 'Here's where your friends are,' and he kicked open a door and pushed me into a room. There wasn't much light. There was a brass bed and a kind of alcove beside it with a painted plaster statue of the Virgin Mary and candles burning. Then I saw Skip and Mike. They were on the floor, unconscious, tied up with ropes.

"I tried to push past Tony, but he knocked me down. I got

up and tried to fight him but he knocked me down again, and this time he pulled a knife.

"'You come to Mexico to go bang-bang, eh?' he said, and I begged him to let me go, but he jabbed at me with the knife until I was in a corner, on my knees, trembling, afraid he was going to kill me.

"'My friend is rich,' I told him. 'He will pay you a lot of money to let us go.'

"But Tony only laughed and said, 'We go bang-bang first, then he pay money.'

"He told me to take off my clothes. I begged some more, but he put the knife to my neck and I knew I had to do what he said. I took off my clothes, and he pushed me onto the bed, and I was crying, but at the same time I told myself, I can survive this, it's only sex. But it wasn't only sex. He got into bed, with the knife in one hand, and it wasn't pleasure he wanted. He wanted to hurt me, to punish me. He did awful things, and the more I cried and begged for mercy the more he hurt me. I tried to block it all out. I thought of high school, being Homecoming Queen, people cheering me, Skip giving me the roses, and all the while this man kept hurting me, terribly. When he finished, the last thing he did was to spit in my face.

"I lay there, looking at the candles, the Virgin in the alcove, and I hurt terribly, but I thought at least it's over. I was wrong, of course.

"He opened the door and his friends came in and they stood around the bed and laughed at me and grabbed at me and I . . . I guess I was like an animal, then, when you poke at it with sharp sticks, and it tries to draw back into its hole, but there was no escape, and they began to do things to me . . ."

"No, please," Philip said.

"Let me finish," Jenny said. "I've never told this to a friend before. To doctors and psychiatrists but not to a friend. There's a reason I'm doing this. It's not just for fun."

"I know," he said.

"The three of them raped me, over and over until I lost all sense of time or place or self. The worst part of it isn't the pain. The worst is the degradation, the nothingness, the realization that you'd once been a person, that in another world people loved you, but now you were a thing that was hated. This was your world now, and you were garbage, nothing at all. Your other world was forgotten, and there was only darkness and pain and horror and hate. One of them—the boy with the sad eyes—whipped me with his belt and I hardly knew it. One of them made me say, 'I am a whore,' over and over until I believed it. That one dark room was the only world that mattered and there I was a whore. That was the reality. All I wanted was to die.

"I don't know how long it lasted. At some point Skip and Mike began to stir and they kicked them and dragged them into another room, and I was too weak to even get up and see if there was any way to escape. I thought my only hope was Ellen. I kept thinking that she would go to the police and tell them we were at Pepe's and that any minute the police would break down the door and save me. That was my dream, while the men were raping me, and after a while the door opened and I thought it must be the police, but it was Tony. He had Ellen by the arm and he pushed her onto the bed beside me.

"That hurt worse than anything else. They had Ellen too, poor, innocent Ellen.

"'Jenny, what have they done to you?' she cried.

"'Run, Ellie, run,' I told her. 'Don't let them hurt you.'

"She tried, but Tony grabbed her and threw her on the bed beside me. 'Your friend want to see you,' he said. 'I think she come to Mexico to go bang-bang too, eh?'

"Ellen was so brave. She stood up and said, 'My friend needs a doctor. Get out of my way or I'll have you arrested.'

"He laughed at her, and she slashed at his face with her fingernails, and he yelled and the other men ran into the room and grabbed her and started to tear off her clothes. I tried to help her but they knocked me down and in a minute she was naked and Tony was standing there with his face bleeding and his knife in her face. 'Oh, you another big Texas girl, you gonna bang-bang good,' he said, and he began to touch her while the others held her. 'No, please,' she kept saying, but the men just laughed and began to joke about who would go first.

"I couldn't stand it. I said, 'Tony, you must have some decency. You must have a mother or a sister...' and he said, 'Yeah, the gringos make them whores like I make you.'

"I said, 'It doesn't matter what you do to me. But this girl is a virgin. Do whatever you want to me, but for God's sake leave her alone.'

"Tony pointed to his face, where she'd scratched it. 'My face, it a virgin too, eh?' he said.

" 'Just leave her alone,' I said.

"He leered at me, and he said, 'Sure, we take real good care of the virgin, eh?' He spoke to the others and they went out and left us there in the room.

"I put my arms around Ellen. We lay there on the bed and I tried to comfort her. I told her, 'Just remember I love you. Everyone loves you. This isn't you and it isn't real and soon it'll be gone like a bad dream.'

" 'Why are we here?' she asked me. 'Why do they want to hurt us?'

" 'They're monsters. They're evil. But you're stronger than they are because good is stronger than evil.'

"I got out of the bed and tried the doors and the windows but they were locked. I went back to Ellen and we held each other and she kissed my cuts and welts and it was then that the hammering started outside. Ellen started saying the Lord's Prayer. I tried to pray with her but I kept hearing this banging outside our window. All I could think of was those scenes in Western movies when they build a scaffold to hang someone. Finally I looked out the window. The shutters were closed but there was a crack and I could see a small courtyard and some men milling around in the dark. I saw Tony, giving the orders. And then I saw this thing they were hammering on, sort of a frame, pitched at an angle. My eyes were getting used to the dark and I saw something big move on the other side of the courtyard, and finally I saw that it was an animal. A donkey.

"I screamed. I couldn't believe it. And yet I could believe it, too, because boys had told me things they'd seen in the border towns.

" 'What is it?' Ellen asked me, and I went back to the bed and put my arms around her but I couldn't tell her what I thought it was, I couldn't speak the words, and we lay there with our arms around each other until Tony came back.

" 'Hey, we got a fellow out here, he like virgins,' he said. 'Which one of you virgins want to come see him, eh?'

" 'Take me,' I said. 'Whatever it is, do it to me. Leave her alone.'

" 'Good deal,' Tony said. 'You come on, your friend can watch.'

"He dragged me outside. The moon had come out, and someone lit a torch, and you could hear mariachi music in the distance. They dragged me over to this . . . this wooden frame and tied me to it. It was like a narrow bed, except it was slanted and had cushions on it. They brought the donkey over beside me and the men watched and laughed. I started praying then, really praying. I hadn't meant it before, but now I did. It was like you were about to die and there was nothing else to do. There was a woman who led the creature around. She was fat and she looked simple-minded. She kept smiling at me and talking to me in Spanish. She was the woman who . . . who had sex with the animal in one of their shows, and she kept talking to me, but I wasn't listening. I was praying, asking God if I had done something to make me deserve this, if I'd been given too much, if I'd been cruel to other people without knowing it, if there was some reason for this. The woman kept talking and rubbing the donkey's nose—I think she was very proud of her donkey and wanted to tell me what a fine donkey he was, and finally Tony said something and the woman brought the donkey around and he began to climb up this frame, this ramp, that was over me. Then he was above me, this beast looming against the black sky, groaning and snorting, and I saw that the woman was rubbing his . . . his penis with oil and, my God, it was huge, so huge, and I knew that this would kill me, and I began to beg. I thought I was past that but I started to beg again, with this huge beast over me, me naked and cold—I was having spasms—and Tony said something and two men began to raise my legs up and I cried, 'No, please don't do this to me.'

"Tony put his face next to mine. 'You be good show, huh?' he said.

"'Please,' I said. 'I'll do anything.'

"'You rather he bang your friend, huh?' he said.

"'Please, let us go.'

"'Who it be? You or your virgin friend, eh?'

"'No, please,' I said, and Tony laughed and they raised me up and the woman guided the donkey's . . . guided it toward me and it touched me and I screamed, 'Do it to her, do it to her, for God's sake don't do this to me!' and the men all laughed and they led the donkey back and let me down and brought Ellen out. I was so ashamed that I couldn't look at her. I . . ."

"No," Philip said. "No, you mustn't . . ."

"I'd tried to be brave and loyal. That was the way I was raised. But you have a breaking point, Philip, everyone has a breaking point. Ellen was screaming and I tried to look away but they made me watch—Tony held a knife to my neck—

and they put her on the frame and the donkey climbed up the ramp and they lifted up her beautiful long legs and the fat woman was smiling and holding the donkey and the creature lunged and Ellen was screaming and the men were laughing and the music was playing in the distance and it was then that Skip and Mike burst in.

"They'd gotten free somehow, and they came charging out like the wrath of God. Skip was swinging a bed slat, and Mike had a broken beer bottle in each hand. They were howling and knocking men down and slashing and kicking them, and men were screaming and running and I remember thinking. Yes, kill them all, make them suffer too. The torch got put out, and the donkey was braying, and the fat woman was howling and some of the Mexicans tried to fight back and there were some shots and someone knocked me down and Skip put a blanket around me and the police came. Five or six Mexicans were on the ground, bleeding terribly, and the police wanted to take me to a doctor, and Skip wouldn't let me go without him, and finally I asked where Ellen was.

"That was when we realized that somehow Tony had gotten away and had taken Ellen with him."

Jenny sipped her beer. It was nearly two, early in the morning of November 22, and the moon had broken through the clouds. Philip clutched her hand; he thought he would never let her go again.

"When Skip called his grandfather and told him what had happened, it was like a war had broken out along the border. Wade didn't trust the Mexicans, so he sent his own army down there, hundreds of men, and he offered a fifty-thousand-dollar reward for whoever caught Tony. His men swept along the border, village to village, house to house, looking for Tony and Ellen. It turned out that he was a bandit who preyed on tourists on the road to Monterrey.

"It took them ten days to find him. He was in a cabin in the mountains and there was a shoot-out and they killed him.

"They found Ellen, chained inside the cabin. She was like a child, a child who has been abused and is afraid of everyone. She's still in a mental hospital, a place outside Houston. Wade pays for everything. I go see her every few months. The last time I was there she said, 'Jenny, I have a wonderful new doctor I want you to meet. He's helped me so. I'm going to Wellesley, you know, and study medicine and help people.'"

Jenny lowered her head. "But the truth is that she'll probably never leave there. It's strange, bodies heal so much more easily than minds do.

"I healed, more or less. I started at the university, but I was a different person. I kept to myself and began to read and study, seriously for the first time in my life. Eventually I got interested in law. I'd seen evil, pure evil, and it was human, human hate and ignorance and cruelty, and I thought the only force we have to challenge evil with is the law. So I went to law school.

"I function, Philip. I put on a good performance. In some ways I'm one of the sanest people you'll ever know. But in other ways I'm a little mad."

"No," he protested.

"I have my nightmares and my little phobias. Do you remember the time you wanted to take me to a Mexican restaurant, and I wouldn't go? There are movies I can't watch. Rape isn't an academic issue to me. I tried to read a book about the Holocaust once, and I broke down, because I'd seen one tiny little corner of the Holocaust and I couldn't stand to gaze upon the real thing. There's a part of me that will never really trust a man, or love a man, the way I'd like to. And I hate myself sometimes, for what I did to Ellen, for the way I betrayed her. If I'd just been braver, just held on a little longer, then Ellen would be well today and . . ."

"Jenny, for God's sake stop it!" he pleaded. "You couldn't help what happened."

"I know. That's what doctors have told me for ten years."

"Is it getting better?"

"I don't know. Perhaps. I've tried so hard to escape from it. Into the law. Into the affair with Harry. Into marriage with Skip. I loved the Justice Department so much. It was like a huge womb. The law is so vast, and I could be a cog in the machine, be safe in that fortress. But of course it's not that easy. I met Harry and had my affair with him, because I knew Harry was no threat to me. He didn't want to marry me, or to understand me, only to make love to me, and that was fine. You were the threat. I wanted us to be friends, but I was afraid you'd fall in love with me, or even that I'd fall in love with you, and I couldn't do that, because I'd only hurt you . . ."

"No, no . . ."

"I'm a cracked plate, P.K. I'll never be whole again. I've got too much guilt and too much fear."

"Jenny, please . . ."

"When I was fired at Justice, it was like the sky had fallen. It felt so safe there. I didn't know where to hide. Skip wanted to marry me, even before Mexico. In some ways, what happened hurt him worse than it did me. He blamed himself. He wanted to make it up to me, and marrying me was the only way he knew. I know you hated him in high school, but he's changed. He's vain, God knows, but he's strong and thoughtful, in his way. So I married him, because I hoped he'd take care of me. That's my story, P.K. It's why I treated you so terribly in Washington. It wasn't that I didn't care for you."

They sat in silence, watching dark clouds slide across the moon. He thought of a dozen things to say, but they all, before he spoke them, seemed pointless. What could he tell her that she didn't already know?

"Do you want me to take you home?" he said finally.

"No," she said. "I don't want to go there."

He touched her face. "I want to do whatever you want to do. But I don't want to leave you."

"I don't want you to," she said.

"I don't mean that I want to . . . that I'm trying to . . . it isn't that."

"I'm not afraid of you."

"We could go to my hotel. Nobody would notice us this late."

"All right," she said.

The hotel lobby was deserted, except for one drunk reporter who winked at Jenny as they got into the elevator. Philip felt awkward once they entered his tiny, sixth-floor room. Jenny took a shower, whistling to herself, then slipped in beside him in the dark.

He put his arms around her. "I just want to hold you." He couldn't believe how warm she was or how rough his hands felt against her skin. Her hair was wet on his face. "You're wonderful," he whispered. "You're beautiful and wonderful and good and you're going to be happy. Nothing can keep you from being happy."

"Dear P.K.," she said. Her hands were light as feathers.

"We'll always be friends," he told her. "Don't think about hurting me. You couldn't hurt me."

He trembled, clinging to her, and she whispered, "Don't cry for me."

"It's just that . . . such awful things happen."

"Good things too. We have to love, all we can."

She kissed his eyes. He wanted her but he wanted more not to hurt her. He was almost asleep when she touched him a certain way. Her fingers burned like fire. "You won't hurt me," she promised. He took her slowly, cautiously, riding her heartbeat like a gentle wave, and her sex was a small blind animal that gnawed at him until he cried out in pain and sorrow and joy and surrender.

He was more asleep than awake when she whispered, "Where are the Kennedys?"

"Two floors above us."

"Do you suppose they're like us tonight?"

"I hope so," he told her, and they slept, tangled together like children.

CHAPTER ELEVEN

Morning surprised them. He buried his face in the strong hot beat of her heart.

"I don't want to leave you," he said.

"Don't then. Please don't."

He went to the window. People were gathering in a parking lot across the street. "I'm sorry," he said. "We go to Dallas after this. They may need fixes in his speech. That's what they think I'm here for."

"What do they know?"

He started to dress. She sat up in bed and watched him. "When you were a little boy, you were so serious about doing your work and pleasing the teacher," she said. "You're still that way, you know."

He sat on the edge of the bed and gripped her hand. His clothing was like a wall between them. Why was he leaving her?

"What are we going to do?" he asked.

"What do you want us to do?"

"I don't know."

"I think we should give it some time," she said. "Call me . . . at Christmas."

He calculated the weeks, the days. "At Christmas," he repeated. A roar rose up from the street: the president had emerged from the hotel.

"I hate good-byes," he said. "I guess this was the best night of my life."

She clung to him, lovely with her tousled hair. "I do love you, P.K., in my own erratic way."

"Christmas," he said again and kissed her one last time and hurried out the door.

Once he walked out of the hotel he forced her from his mind. He stepped into his other world, the make-believe world of politics, and focused on John Kennedy, who was across the street, standing on the back of a flatbed truck, speaking to a few hundred workingmen in a light rain.

Philip walked to the edge of the crowd, where Ken O'Donnell and Larry O'Brien were staring gravely at the overcast sky. If it rained all day, fewer Texans would venture out to see the motorcade, and those who did would not really see Kennedy, because a bubbletop would be placed atop his convertible. A hard rain would undo months of planning, would spoil the day's politics.

A reporter showed Philip the front page of the Dallas *Morning News*. "YARBOROUGH SNUBS LBJ," it proclaimed.

"Damn," Philip muttered. "I thought they got that fool into the car with Johnson."

"That was last night, in the dark," the reporter said. "Take a look at this." He turned to an inside page, where a full-page advertisement was headed, "WELCOME MR. KENNEDY TO DALLAS," and proceeded to charge the president with various acts of treason and appeasement.

"The sons of bitches," Philip said. "What kind of a rag would print crap like that?"

"Dallas could be nasty," the reporter said. "I hope you wore your bulletproof vest."

"That's not real funny," Philip said. He walked into the hotel and found the ballroom where the huge Chamber of Commerce breakfast was being held. Two thousand Texans were listening to a choir sing "The Eyes of Texas." The president was at the head table but his wife, the star of the trip, was nowhere to be seen. Philip joined Harry at the back of the room.

"Did you see the Dallas paper?" he asked.

"Yeah," Harry said grimly.

"Who's behind it?"

Harry shrugged. "Hunt? The Birchers? Your grandfather?"

A great roar filled the ballroom. Heads turned toward a distant door. Soon, hundreds of well-dressed men and women were leaping atop their chairs, cheering, waving their arms. Mrs. Kennedy, radiant in a raspberry-pink suit, was making her entrance. She inched forward shyly, with klieg lights blazing upon her and the Texans howling like a lynch mob.

Philip went back outside. O'Brien and O'Donnell were still watching the sky. The two Irishmen's names were often linked, but they were vastly different: O'Donnell was grim, withdrawn, unknowable, black Irish; O'Brien was redheaded, freckled, stocky, genial, a politician's politician. Suddenly, as they watched, the sun broke through the clouds. O'Brien grinned. "Kennedy weather," he quipped—no rain, no bubbletop, big crowds, the luck of the Irish. Even the Texas sun came out on cue.

The motorcade was ready. Philip watched as the determined O'Brien muscled Senator Yarborough into a car with Lyndon Johnson.

The motorcade began to move. Philip tried to nap. He felt terrible. From too much beer and too little sleep. From his confusion over Jenny. From his anger and sorrow over her story of Mexico. Everything about this trip was starting to depress him. Who gave a damn if Yarborough rode in a car with Johnson? What was Mrs. Kennedy doing in the Hotel Texas ballroom with two thousand Yahoos howling at her?

He was sick of politics. Even this motorcade was more political madness. They wanted to move the president thirty miles east to Dallas. So naturally they were going to drive west to Carswell Air Force Base, put everybody into planes, fly east to Love Field, and drive the rest of the way. It was idiotic, unless you happened to be a politician. Politicians loved airports. They loved to descend from the skies, like gods, there to accept the acclaim of the earthbound multitudes. Even Kennedy, who knew better, played the game.

A tumultuous reception greeted Kennedy at Carswell Air Force Base. Scores of enlisted men surrounded him, cheering, snapping pictures, jostling for a handshake. "They can't all be from Massachusetts," O'Brien joked. Philip watched, feeling proud of Kennedy, proud to work for him.

As the plane rose up from Carswell, tipping sideways in a long circle around the city, Philip glimpsed Jenny's house. He let himself think about her, and the questions came tumbling out. What did she want? What did he want? He had the habit of loving her, but what did that mean? Did he love the laughing girl in his memory or the troubled woman of the night before? How "cracked" was she? His mind spun madly: he could imagine stealing her from Skip, and he could imagine never seeing her again. He was relieved when Love Field rose up to meet them. Another diversion: the circus came to Dallas.

It was as if there were two rival receptions at the airport. The local liberals cheered and waved signs that said, "WE LOVE JACK AND JACKIE" and "ALL THE WAY WITH JFK." But they were outnumbered by an array of hostile signs, signs that said things like "BURY KING JOHN" and "GOLDWATER IN '64." Kennedy headed for the friendly faces. He greeted an old woman in a wheelchair; his wife walked beside him, cradling a bunch of roses. They moved along a fence together, touching outstretched hands. There were cheers and catcalls. Reporters followed, coldly studying the crowd like creatures in a zoo. There was tension in the air such as Philip had never seen in dozens of campaign swings. Everyone was waiting for something to happen. The "WANTED FOR TREASON" leaflets, the full-page ad that morning, the attacks on Johnson and Stevenson, it was as if all of those had been warnings to Kennedy to keep out of this city. Kennedy knew all of that, but he lingered at the airport, waving and shaking hands, beyond the call of duty. It was as if he meant to show the haters that others in Dallas welcomed him or simply that he was not afraid.

The motorcade started up. Philip had lost his car; then Harry was yelling, "Come on, Tex, shake a leg," and he jumped into a car with Harry and two congressmen, three or four cars behind the president's Lincoln convertible. It was noon, on a hot, muggy Texas day.

They moved along Mockingbird Lane, past warehouses and vacant lots and pastel-colored bungalows, with only a few curiosity seekers out to gaze at them. "The president's really pissed," Harry said. "The Pentagon predicted cool weather in

Texas, so Jackie brought winter clothes, and now it's in the eighties."

"They should have called my mother," Philip said. "She'd have told them the temperature."

"The Pentagon hasn't got brains enough to call your mother," Harry said.

They were passing little knots of people. The two congressmen began to smile and wave. A few of the people waved back, a few held hostile signs, but most just stared at the passing limousines, sullen, mute. Philip wanted to yell at them, *You don't have to be sheep, you can be more than that*. One of the congressmen started talking about Dallas, even as he grinned and waved.

"Worse damn place in the world. There's no labor to speak of, no liberals, no opposition. The oil gang and the corporate big shots have molded an entire city in their own image. Right-wing craziness is the local religion. It trickles down from the top until you get junior executives and clerks who talk like millionaires. People who won't have a dime when they retire but tell you Social Security is socialism. Even the kids are brainwashed—it's the only city in America with reactionary ten-year-olds."

"The crowds haven't been bad," said Harry, the pragmatist.

Downtown, people were four or five deep on the sidewalks, and most of the signs were friendly. People were yelling, "Jackie, Jackie!" They entered a canyon of sleek skyscrapers, monuments to money. Here the sidewalks were ten deep with waving, cheering office workers; the mood was frenzied, electric. "My God, it's like Broadway," Harry muttered.

They passed Neiman-Marcus. Philip remembered going there when he was a teenager, just to look; the mood was always that of a museum, or a church, not a clothing store.

The president's car reached the Mercantile Building, headquarters for H. L. Hunt's empire. Philip wondered if Hunt was up there, gazing down on this president he hated. He hoped so; he hoped Wade Kingslea was watching, too, for he thought that these thousands of cheering people were nothing less than a political revolution. Despite the oilmen, despite the Dallas *Morning News*, despite the Birchers, despite the corporate orthodoxy, tens of thousands of ordinary people had turned out to cheer Jack Kennedy.

"He's won, Harry, he's won," Philip yelled. "He challenged the sons of bitches and he's won!"

Harry grinned. He was waving back at the crowds on the sidewalk now, like the congressmen. Philip laughed and began to wave too.

They left the shining canyon and began to pass through a wasteland of bars, loan companies, and pawn shops. The courthouse was up ahead. A clock outside a chili parlor said twelve-thirty. They were turning a corner. Up front, he could see the president and Jackie waving to people in a kind of park. She was wearing one of those pillbox hats she had popularized; even Chrissie had bought one. There was an underpass ahead. Philip thought of the Duke, and his warning, and all the other warnings. They'd been wrong, all of them. Dallas was no problem.

When Philip heard the first sharp explosion, he took it for a firecracker.

But Harry, the combat veteran, was on his feet, yelling, "Down, get down," not to them but to the president up ahead.

More shots, echoing between the buildings, and Harry yelling, "Get down, Jack, get down." The two congressmen dived to the floor. The cars ahead of them began to speed away.

"Keep up with them," Harry told their driver. They were passing some sort of park or plaza. People were running up a hillside. A screaming man held his daughter in his arms. A policeman waved his gun. A dark-skinned man with a pompadour and glittering rings was walking rapidly up the hill.

They roared onto a freeway but lost the president's car. "Turn on your radio," Harry yelled.

"What's happened?" one of the congressmen asked.

"Somebody's hit," Harry said.

"Who?"

"How the hell do I know?" Harry snapped.

The trooper took them to the Trade Mart, their official destination, but they found only confusion there. Harry persuaded the trooper to take them to the nearest hospital, Parkland Hospital. Philip kept thinking, *They can't have shot him, they can't have shot him. Why had they come to this damn city in the first place? Why hadn't it rained? Why hadn't he warned Kennedy when he had the chance? Oh God, don't let him be dead.*

They pulled into the circular driveway outside the hospital and they saw the crowd bunched around the president's car.

Harry leaped from the car and raced toward the scene. Philip, uncertain, followed. In his mind, *They've killed him* wrestled with *It will only be a wound, he can't be dead.*

The crowd around the Lincoln parted, and some men carried Governor Connally away on a stretcher. His shirt was soaked with blood but he was conscious. *It was Connally they shot,* Philip told himself, and he wanted to shout with joy.

Then he saw Harry.

He came out of the crowd and took two or three steps, stiff-legged, like a sleepwalker, then doubled over as if someone had kicked him in the gut. His face was contorted, drained of color, and his shoulders shook, but he did not speak or shed tears. *Flynns don't cry.* He only looked broken, ruined. Philip wanted to speak to him but he couldn't; one could only respect his privacy. Instead he pushed forward until he, too, could glimpse whatever horror waited in the Lincoln convertible.

Mrs. Kennedy, her pink suit soaked with blood, was huddled in the back seat, oblivious to the onlookers. Her husband's shattered head rested in her lap. She was whispering to him.

A Secret Service man touched her arm. "Please, Mrs. Kennedy," he said.

She didn't move.

"Please," the agent said again. "We've got to get him to a doctor."

"I'm not going to let him go," she said.

It was all frozen in time, indelible: the blood-soaked dress, the stricken president, her ravaged face, the helpless gawkers.

"We've got to take him in, Mrs. Kennedy."

"No. You know he's dead. Let me alone."

The agent, understanding, slipped off his coat and handed it to her, and she wrapped it around her husband's mutilated head. His privacy protected, she let the men carry his limp, bleeding body away.

Harry and Ken O'Donnell helped her out of the Lincoln and they fell in behind the men who were carrying Kennedy into the hospital. Some Secret Service men followed, and Philip joined them. It was his instinct, a reporter's instinct to go where the story was, to see his thing through to the end. The police let them pass, and a nurse guided them through a maze of corridors to a small operating room. Mrs. Kennedy and the others stopped in the corridor as her husband was laid out on an operating table and quickly surrounded by doctors. The corridor was a scene of bedlam. Phones rang, doctors and nurses raced by, and policemen came and went, muttering of conspiracies. The sight of the doctors around Kennedy gave them a spark of hope. Perhaps they could make a miracle. Someone found a folding chair for Mrs. Kennedy. The men stood around her protectively. O'Donnell was mute, devastated. O'Brien arrived and tried to speak, but words would not come.

Events flowed past them. Until the shots rang out, they had been men of vast authority; now they were passive, helpless, as the bizarre drama unfolded.

A Secret Service man knocked down an intruder who claimed he was an FBI agent.

The mayor of Dallas wandered by, muttering, "It didn't happen."

Senator Yarborough passed by, declaring, "Excalibur has sunk beneath the waves."

A frenzied priest appeared, brandishing what he said was a Relic of the True Cross; he prayed over the president's wife until the Irishmen eased him away.

"What's the president's blood type?" a nurse cried.

The doctors worked on.

Policemen raced past, muttering, cursing, confused. The Kennedy men eyed them coldly. Where were they when the president was gunned down? Philip wondered, perhaps they all wondered, if the Dallas police might not be part of whatever conspiracy had struck down the president. They all felt surrounded, trapped, in a hostile, murderous land. Philip hoped no one would remember he was a Texan. All Texans were suspect now.

A slender young doctor came out of the operating room. Mrs. Kennedy looked up at him expectantly. "I'm sorry, ma'm," was all he could say.

"I'm going in there," she said, rising up, starting toward the small room where doctors still surrounded her husband.

A large, determined nurse blocked the door. "You can't come in here," she said.

Mrs. Kennedy tried to push past the nurse.

The nurse, larger and stronger, pushed back.

The men watched, frozen, disbelieving.

"I want to be there when he dies," she pleaded.

A doctor came and eased the president's wife past the

nurse. But even inside the operating room, she could only wait in a corner while the doctors worked on.

Eternities inched by. A tall, blue-eyed doctor, tears streaming down his face, told her "The president is dead."

A nurse asked about disposition of the body.

Kilduff, the press officer, asked permission to announce the president's death. "Don't say anything," O'Donnell commanded. He could not admit it yet. An announcement would make it true.

A huge bronze casket was wheeled in. Mrs. Kennedy put her wedding ring on her husband's finger. O'Donnell urged that she return to the airport, to the security of *Air Force One*. She said she would not leave the hospital until her husband did.

Laughter rang down the corridor. At them? At her? Philip ran down the hallway until he found two smirking nurses. "Shut your stupid mouths," he said, and they fled.

A black man was mopping the floor where John Kennedy had died. "Why can't we leave?" his widow asked.

Philip thought of Jenny, Mexico; was there no end to horror?

A pudgy man with glittery eyes confronted them. "I am T. P. Wise, the county coroner," he announced. "There's been a homicide here. The body can't be moved until I perform my autopsy."

A Secret Service man stepped up. "My friend," the agent said, "this is the body of the president of the United States, and we're going to take it back to Washington."

"No," the coroner declared, "not until there is an autopsy."

"My friend," the agent persisted, "we're taking the president back to Washington."

"You aren't taking the *body* anywhere."

The Kennedy men stared furiously at the coroner.

The priest with the True Cross returned, praying and chanting in Latin.

A doctor tried to reason with T. P. Wise. "The widow says she will stay until the body is removed," he said. "We can't have that."

"Procedures must be followed," the coroner said.

"This is the president of the United States."

"We can't lose the chain of evidence."

They searched for a Justice of the Peace to overrule the coroner. The widow sat motionless. Philip confronted the coroner, fists clenched. "Listen, you idiot," he began, but Harry pulled him back. "Not yet," Harry said.

A young JP rushed in, shaken, stammering. After a flurry of telephone calls he said he was sorry, but the law was clear; there must be an autopsy.

"How long will it take?" a Secret Service man asked.

The JP shrugged. "Maybe three hours," he said.

That was the breaking point. "We're not staying here three hours," O'Donnell said. "We're not staying here another three minutes."

The coffin, with Kennedy inside it, rested on a large rolling cart. Nearly a dozen of them surrounded it: O'Brien, O'Donnell, Flynn, Dave Powers, Philip, Congressman Henry Gonzales, the Secret Service men. The widow stood at the rear, one hand resting lightly on the coffin's cover.

T. P. Wise, eyes ablaze, one hand upraised, blocked their passage.

"The laws of the state of Texas must be obeyed," he cried.

"He's right," the JP said.

Behind them a nervous young policeman fingered his revolver.

"We're leaving," O'Donnell said.

The two sides confronted one another. What the Kennedy force proposed to do was quite insane. They were courting disaster, more tragedy, more bloodshed. The world of reason was forgotten; there was only this corridor, this coroner, this coffin, this widow. Against all odds, they must make one last show of devotion to the man inside the coffin.

"Let's go," O'Brien said.

The coffin began to inch forward.

The young policeman came toward them. He looked uncertain, frightened. "Those guys say you can't go," he warned.

"One side," commanded O'Brien, his face red and furious.

"Stop them!" T. P. Wise shouted.

Suddenly, twenty men were caught up in the struggle. Shouts and curses rang out. The Kennedy men were pushing the coffin, other men were trying to stop it, and still others were trying to get out of the way.

Somehow, they were out the door, moving down long, unfamiliar corridors. People watched them from doorways. Behind them, T. P. Wise's voice echoed: "I'll have you all arrested."

"Keep going," Harry Flynn said.

"Are they coming?" one of the Secret Service men asked.

Philip told Harry, "Don't wait for me," and raced back down the hall.

He saw T. P. Wise slip into a small office, and he went in after him. The coroner was yelling into a telephone, "Dammit to hell, operator, get me an outside line."

Philip knocked the phone out of his hands.

"Damn you," the coroner roared. "You Washington big shots think you can . . ."

Philip executed the old one-two, his left deep into the man's soft belly, his right clipping the point of his chin, and as the coroner sank unconscious to the floor Philip went out of control. Choking back a scream, he kicked the coroner in the ribs, then dropped to his knees and raised his fist high, poised to pound the man's face to mush. He was an animal, lusting for gore, death, revenge. Then, somehow, he fought free of the madness and fell face down beside his victim, sobbing over and over, *"Oh God, don't let me be like them."*

He eased back into the corridor, to make his escape, and came face to face with one of the doctors who had worked on Kennedy. C. J. Carrico, his nameplate said. He was a wiry, dark-haired man about Philip's age—Philip thought perhaps they'd met somewhere, years before, at some party. "We're sorry about Wise," the doctor said. "We're not all like that down here."

"I know," Philip said. "I know."

He ran down the corridor until he burst into the blinding afternoon sunlight. The others were lifting the coffin into a white Cadillac hearse. A knot of reporters was watching; some were crying. The priest was back, still waving the True Cross.

"Who's going to pay me?" the owner of the hearse demanded.

Philip squeezed into the hearse beside Harry. "Are they coming?" Harry asked.

"I don't know," Philip said.

"Let's get out of here," Harry told the driver.

Soon they were speeding toward the airport. Philip kept looking back, expecting to see police cars, a posse led by T. P. Wise.

"The president is waiting in *Air Force One*," one of the agents said.

What the hell did he mean? Philip wondered. The president

waiting? The president was dead in this hearse. Then it hit him like lightning. *Lyndon is president now!* It seemed quite preposterous.

They skidded to a stop beside *Air Force One*. The Irishmen began wrestling the heavy coffin onto the plane. Philip watched, uncertain. A taxi squealed to a halt beside them, and a young Texan, a fellow Philip had met in Washington, leaped out and shouted to the police that it was urgent that he see the president. The new administration was taking shape.

Harry came over. "Time to get aboard," he said.

Philip shook his head. "I'm staying here."

Harry, his face drawn, ravaged, did not protest.

"What will you do?" Philip asked. "Stay with Johnson?"

Harry almost smiled. "All Lyndon Johnson's got for me is a locked room and a loaded gun," he said. "But you should stay. He could use you."

Air Force One's great engines began to roar; Philip stuck out his hand. "Harry, I'm sorry about . . . about everything."

"It wasn't your fault," Harry said.

Philip watched from the terminal until the plane was off the ground. Then he went outside and found a cab to take him to Fort Worth.

Only when they pulled away from the airport did he relax. Ever since they'd left the hospital, he'd been sure the police would come and get him for slugging Wise. He tried to laugh at his paranoia and instead he started to cry. At first he hoped the driver wouldn't notice, then he didn't care.

"A bad day, huh?" the driver said finally.

"Yeah, a bad day."

Philip's hand ached from hitting Wise. He had the driver stop at a tavern. Some workmen were drinking and playing shuffleboard. Only the old woman behind the counter was watching Walter Cronkite. "My heart's plumb broke," she said and sold him a six-pack. Back in the cab, he offered the driver a beer. "Why the hell not?" the driver said. Philip wasn't sure why he was going to Fort Worth except that he couldn't imagine going to Washington and working for Lyndon Johnson. Washington was over now; the book was closed. He thought of Chrissie, getting the news in Peru, and grieved for her.

The Fort Worth skyline loomed ahead, glittering, indifferent, when a radio report said the man charged with killing Kennedy was named Lee Harvey Oswald.

The name jarred Philip's memory. He knew that name, but

from where? He tried to think. Oswald: a Shakespearean name, fit for a villain. Then he remembered. Lee Harvey Oswald was the ratty-looking kid who'd come up to him and the Duke, outside the Duke's bar two years before.

Facts began to lurch about in his mind.

The Duke knew Oswald.

The Duke had warned him about Dallas.

The radio began to spit out more facts on Oswald. He had served in the Army. He had gone to Russia. He had been arrested in a pro-Castro demonstration.

Castro.

Cuba.

The swarthy man outside Wade Kingslea's house the night before, the one with rings and a pompadour, might he not have been Cuban?

Had he not seen that same man, running up a grassy slope, in the little park, moments after the shooting?

He had read intelligence reports on the Cuban exiles. There were thousands of them in Miami, armed, angry, trained to kill, convinced Kennedy had betrayed them at the Bay of Pigs.

The woman had said the Duke was in Florida, perhaps in Miami.

He saw the Kingslea Tower, his grandfather's skyscraper, shining in the distance. He thought of their talk, two years before. Lyndon is a man you can deal with, his grandfather had said. Lyndon is only a heartbeat away from being president.

Now Kennedy was dead, and Harry Flynn's vendetta against Kingslea Oil had died with him.

One lone malcontent, one punk like Oswald, could not have killed the president. There had to be others behind him. The more Philip thought of it, the more sure he was. The realization stunned him.

Wade Kingslea had plotted John Kennedy's death.

He could not doubt it. The old man had the motive, the money, the hate, the cunning, the audacity, the madness to plot a crime of that immensity. Even now, he must be gloating in his mansion or his skyscraper.

Now Philip knew why he had stayed in Texas.

To prove what his grandfather had done.

Book VI

Philip and Wade

Fort Worth
1963–65

CHAPTER ONE

Philip spent the long weekend at his mother and Asa's house, watching the dark saga unfold on television. He saw the smirking, defiant Lee Harvey Oswald deny his guilt, saw the improbable Jack Ruby glide from the shadows to gun down Oswald, saw the black-clad Kennedy clan march down Pennsylvania Avenue behind the caisson that bore the dead president. Monday evening, after the funeral, he went to his room, got out his old portable typewriter, and began to put down his memories of John Kennedy. He wrote feverishly, fueled by grief and Cutty Sark, and at dawn thirty pages of manuscript were scattered around him like November's leaves. Exhausted, he threw himself on the bed and slept until late afternoon. Then he drank coffee and gathered up his pages, curious to see what had resulted from his fit of creativity.

He found that he had written a series of brief glimpses of John Kennedy, Robert Kennedy, Harry Flynn, Larry O'Brien, and others of the Kennedy circle. It was a highly personal account of what he had seen and felt, pro and con; in truth, the memoir was more about him than the Kennedys. He began, "From the moment I joined the Kennedy Administration I was determined to cling to my objectivity—to work long and hard but deep within me to remain a neutral on the New Frontier."

He described his annoyance the first time he met Kennedy, in a limousine in Nashville, and the candidate barely spoke to him. He recalled his disdain the first time he saw Bob Kennedy drive by in his baby-blue Cadillac convertible and his outrage when Harry Flynn persisted in calling him Tex. He pictured the touch-football mania at Hickory Hill and a time he'd seen Bob Kennedy chew out a foolish, helpless bureaucrat. But there were admiring glimpses, too. He tried to capture the moment, at dusk on a summer evening, when he'd seen President Kennedy romping on the White House lawn with his children. His last scenes were of the Texas trip: a weary Kennedy saying he didn't want to go to Texas; a radiant Jackie Kennedy entering the Hotel Texas ballroom; their arrival in Dallas, with Kennedy plunging proudly into the crowd, as if to defy the hostile demonstrators. His last image was of Kennedy in the canyon of skyscrapers, the sun on his face, smiling and waving to the wildly cheering Texans, triumphant, and of himself a few cars back, realizing that somewhere along the way, in those thousand days, he had stopped being a neutral and had become a partisan, proud to work for this brave, iridescent, irreplaceable man.

He didn't write of the gunshots that rang out a few moments later, or of Harry screaming, "Get down, Jack, get down!" or of what he had seen outside the hospital or inside its corridors. Enough people would write of that.

He read over his memoir with mixed, uncertain feelings. He could not begin to judge its value; it was too personal. He wanted to show it to someone but he didn't know who. He wished Chrissie were there; she would have understood. Finally he thought of a New York *Times* reporter he knew named Curtis, a Mississippian who shared his fascination with Kennedy. On impulse, he put his article into an envelope and mailed it to Curtis in Washington, with a note that said, "See what you think of this." He'd no sooner mailed it than he was kicking himself, sure that Curtis would find his writing maudlin or self-serving or amateurish. Or perhaps it was that he had exposed a part of himself, an open wound, that he was not sure he wanted anyone to see. Then he forgot about the memoir, because the time for mourning was past; he had work to do.

Philip took the murder of John Kennedy personally. Because he had seen the horror firsthand. Because he was a Texan. Because he felt a gnawing guilt that somehow, back in Washington, he should have stopped Kennedy from going to Texas. Most of all, because he believed his grandfather, Wade Kingslea, was somehow responsible.

He was not alone in that suspicion. All over America the finger-pointing had begun, as the political right blamed Castro or Khrushchev for the tragedy and the political left blamed the CIA or anti-Castro Cubans or such Texas oilmen as H. L. Hunt and Wade Kingslea. Unlike the others who suspected

Wade Kingslea, however, Philip had evidence to back up his suspicions. He knew of Harry Flynn's costly vendetta against Kingslea Oil. He knew, if his eyes had not deceived him, of the Cuban (as he now imagined him) who had been on Kingslea's front porch one night and in Dealey Plaza the next noon. And he knew, from the Duke's phone call, that there had been talk of a murder in Dallas three weeks before the shots rang out.

The Duke was the key. He had known Oswald, had known something was afoot, had tried by his phone call to sound the alarm. But the Duke was nowhere to be found.

Chez Duke stayed closed that entire weekend. Philip called the Duke's home number and got no answer.

Then, Thursday afternoon, he drove by Chez Duke again and found it open.

He took a stool at the end of the bar. His friend was nowhere to be seen. Neither was the blonde who'd said he was in Florida. The bartender was a beefy guy with a wad of gum in his jaw. The only waitress on duty was a skinny, big-eyed girl with bangs. Some of the men at the bar were talking about the assassination. One said it was "a dirty damn shame" and another said, "the son of a bitch had it coming." Their consensus was that Castro was responsible, although one man, a lawyer, insisted with a certain civic pride that Wade Kingslea had been the mastermind.

When Philip saw the waitress standing alone at the jukebox, a quarter in her hand, a blissful smile on her face, he went to her.

"Whatcha playing?" he asked.

She pointed to Roy Orbison's "Pretty Woman."

"I met him one time," she explained. "He grew up in Wink. He's as plain as an ole mud fence, but he sure can sing."

She had an indelible East Texas accent; Wink and sing came out Wank and sang.

"He's good," Philip agreed. "Say, you don't know where I could find the Duke, do you?"

The girl's dark eyes grew enormous and she skittered away without another word. Philip went into the men's room, cursing his stupidity. He should have gone slower, sweet-talked her, asked her out. When he went back to the bar, the girl was whispering to the bartender. In a moment the fellow came over to Philip. He was polishing a glass, his hands high, so the glass was only a couple of feet from Philip's face.

"Something I can help you with, mister?"

"Yeah, I'm looking for the Duke. He's an old friend of mine."

"He's not here."

"Know where he is?"

"Nope."

"I was here last Thursday and a blond woman said he was in Florida."

"Maybe he is."

"Look, he must call in. Will you give him a message?"

"He don't call in."

"You mean he's just vanished?"

The bartender chewed his gum thoughtfully. "Could be."

"What's the blonde's name?"

"I'm tired of your questions, mister."

"Look, I'm a friend of the Duke's and there's no reason for you to stonewall me like this."

"The blonde's name is Doris Jones," the bartender said. "She lives out by the lake. Now how about you getting the hell out of here?"

Philip went to his car, trembling with anger and frustration. He thought about coming back when the bar closed and grabbing the girl and trying to scare the truth out of her. He thought of trying to track down the blonde, but there must be a hundred Joneses "out by the lake." Then he remembered he had another lead and he drove toward Westover Hills.

Imelda, Coyle's wife, answered the door, and she was not glad to see him.

"Is Coyle here?" Philip asked, after she stared at him wordlessly for a long moment.

She nodded and took his arm. "Yes, he's here. But Philip, don't excite him. He . . . he hasn't been well."

Coyle appeared behind her and Philip understood.

He was wearing a robe, and he had that pale, shrunken look Philip remembered all too well.

"Well, look who's here," Coyle said, but his smile was forced, pained. He looked as if he'd been whipped.

"Coffee, Philip?" Imelda asked.

"Please."

She brought the coffee, glanced at Coyle nervously, then left them alone.

Coyle spooned sugar into his coffee with trembling hands. "As you might have guessed, I went off the wagon this weekend," he said. "First time in three years. It was the Kennedy thing, of course, not that that's an excuse. But, my God, it shook me. You live in a place all your life, you think perhaps it's getting more decent, more civilized, then—bang!—something like that happens. Jack Kennedy, a good president, a good man, gets his brains blown out in Dealey Plaza."

Coyle put down his coffee cup, lit a cigarette, and stuck it into the ivory filter he used. He was ten or fifteen pounds overweight, soft around the middle, but still strikingly handsome. Philip wondered if something more than the Kennedy assassination, something closer to home, had knocked his father off the wagon.

"I've got to ask you something."

Coyle nodded. "I think I know what it is."

"I think Wade had something to do with the Kennedy assassination."

His father stared at him for a long time, while ash from his cigarette tumbled unnoticed onto his robe. "Quite a few people think that," Coyle said finally. "Do you have evidence?"

"The night before the assassination, Thursday night, about seven o'clock, two men went to see him at Hillcrest. One was a wiry, sandy-haired American in a cheap suit. The other might have been Mexican or Cuban. He was husky, about five eight, and had a big pompadour, and wore four or five diamond rings. The one with the rings was in Dealey Plaza the next day."

"It could have been a coincidence," Coyle said.

"It could be a conspiracy."

"Do you want my honest opinion?"

"Sure."

"I won't say I think Wade is incapable of plotting to kill Kennedy. It was the first thing I thought, when I heard the news. That it was him or Hunt, and Wade is a more dangerous man than Hunt. But I think that if Wade was going to kill a president, he'd probably be in New York or London when it happened, not at lunch at the Fort Worth Club. And I'm almost positive that he wouldn't invite his gunmen, if that's what you're suggesting, to come to his home the night before the killing."

Philip said, "On the other hand, if you're Wade Kingslea, and you think you're God, and you're forced to delegate something very important, you might have a hard time letting go."

Coyle noticed the ashes on his robe and brushed them onto the floor. "What do you propose to do with this information?"

"I could take it to the FBI."

"Why don't you?"

"Because I don't trust them. And because I hate to go off half-cocked if there's some reasonable explanation."

"Therefore?"

"Ask him what those men were doing at his house that night. Ask him if he'll sit down with me and explain it."

"And if he won't?"

"Then I'll make public what I saw."

"He won't like this, you know."

"I don't give a damn what he likes."

The next morning he drove to Dallas.

He didn't want to go to Dealey Plaza, or even to Dallas, ever again, but he was drawn, irresistibly, on a dark pilgrimage. If you wanted to confront the horror and mystery of Kennedy's murder, you had to start there, at the scene of the crime.

Many others were in that dismal park, or plaza, that windy, chill morning in late November. Some were snapping pictures; some wandered about aimlessly, shaking their heads in disbelief; some wept; others yelled to friends and gawked at points of interest: the sixth-floor window where Oswald supposedly perched, the "grassy knoll" where many witnesses thought the shots had come from, and the spot on Elm where Kennedy was hit, as his motorcade moved toward an underpass.

Philip climbed the knoll and studied the places where a sniper might have hidden. After a while he noticed a man with a notebook moving around the park, asking people questions. Curious, Philip posted himself in the man's path, and soon enough the fellow approached him.

"Howdy, friend," he began. "My name's Hob Wilkes, and I wonder if I could ask you a question or two."

The man was in his forties, heavyset and homely, with a knobby, acne-scarred face and small, suspicious eyes. He wore a tan sport coat, a yellow shirt, a porkpie hat, and a garish, hand-painted necktie, and he spoke with a Deep South drawl.

"Sure," Philip said, "ask away."

"Did you happen to be here when the president got shot?"

"No," Philip said untruthfully.

"Do you have any friends or neighbors who were?"

Philip shook his head. "Sorry," he said.

"That's okay, friend," Wilkes said.

Before he could get away, Philip said, "Why do you ask? Are you a policeman?"

Wilkes grinned, showing crooked teeth. "No, sir, I'm just a private citizen who thinks the so-called 'official' version of the shooting just flat don't make sense. Hell's bells, if Oswald was the only sniper, how come so many folks say they heard shots from up the top of that hill?" Wilkes' face reddened and his voice rose as he pointed up the knoll. "How come the damn *doctors* at Parkland Hospital said he was shot in the front of the neck and then, after the Secret Service got to 'em, said they were wrong and it was an exit wound? Answer me that!"

"I can't answer it, Mr. Wilkes," Philip said. "But I'd like to know what you think."

"Call me Hob. What I think, mister, is we can't let 'em kill our president and then lie to us about it. The American people have got to know the truth about this damn thing!"

"What exactly are you doing?" Philip asked. He was studying the Southerner closely, trying to decide if he was a crank.

"You got a minute, friend?"

They sat down on a park bench and Wilkes took a hand-drawn map from his pocket. The map showed the witnesses he had interviewed, where they had been standing and where they thought the shots had come from. "You see, I done talked to twenty-two witnesses so far, and most of 'em haven't been talked to by the police. Out of that twenty-two, fifteen said they thought the shots came from somewhere up the top of this hill. Only three people thought the shots came from up where Oswald was. That's a right interesting statistic, wouldn't you say?"

"I sure would," Philip said. "How come you're here, Hob? What do you do for a living?"

"I'm in the lumber business." He handed Philip a card that said, "Hob Wilkes Lumber, Everything for Your Building Needs, Dothan, Alabama."

"The reason I'm here," he continued, "is that it didn't take me long, just from watching TV, to figure out that something stank. So I decided I'd come check things out for myself. I ain't the only one, either. Well, I reckon I better get back to asking folks questions."

"Would you mind if I came along?"

Wilkes eyed him suspiciously. "What'd you say your name was, friend?"

"Phil King," Philip said. "I'm a reporter." He showed Wilkes an old *Sun* ID with that name on it. You never knew when a fake press card would come in handy.

Wilkes examined the card and grinned. "I mighta knowed it," he said. "The way you learned all about me and never even told me who you was. Sure, Phil, be my guest."

In the next hour Wilkes expertly questioned a dozen people. Most were curiosity seekers, on their first visit to the scene, but one woman said her sister had witnessed the shooting, from not more than twenty feet away, then had hurried home to bed and hadn't talked to anyone. Wilkes winked at Philip as he wrote down the woman's name and phone number.

At a little past noon Wilkes snapped his notebook shut. "There's a bunch of us been meeting for lunch to talk things over," he said. "Maybe you'd like to join in."

"Sure," Philip said.

Wilkes led him across Houston Street to a hole-in-the-wall called the Do-Rite Diner. They got coffee and bowls of watery beef stew at the counter, then joined some men at a table by the front window.

Wilkes began the introductions—a retired lawyer named Love, and an engineer named Poteet—and then a gangling young man in thick horn-rimmed glasses burst through the door.

"You won't believe what I just found out!" he declared.

"What's that, Bradley?" Hob Wilkes asked.

The young man, who wore an old tweed coat and looked like a graduate student, hunched over the table. "I found a security guard who saw Ruby in the Mercantile Building, H. L. Hunt's building, the day before the assassination!"

"I knew it," one man exclaimed. "They killed him for control of the international oil market."

"Hold your horses," Wilkes said. "Bradley, what was Ruby doing there?"

"I don't know," the young man admitted.

"It's a big building," Wilkes said. "Ruby could have gone

there for a lot of reasons besides to see H. L. Hunt. Hadn't you better try to find out if he had any business there? What about that stripper, would she know?"

The young man jumped up. "I'll find out," he promised, and rushed out the door.

"Well now," Wilkes said, "I was trying to introduce Phil King here, who's a reporter for the Nashville *Sun*. Phil, why don't you tell us just what it is you're interested in."

"I'm like you," Philip said. "Just trying to figure out what happened. I wish you'd tell me what you think."

They responded eagerly, one after another. Love, the lawyer, explained the extreme improbability of the FBI's "single bullet" theory, which held that one bullet had passed through Kennedy and gone on to inflict Governor Connally's wounds. Poteet, the engineer, outlined what was known of Kennedy's wounds and argued passionately that one sniper, firing from above and behind, could not have inflicted those wounds.

Philip, obsessed with finding the Duke, had not paid much attention to the growing controversy over the number of shots and where they had come from. Some of what these men said was impressive. Some of it was wildly speculative. Yet Philip found it hard to write these men off as cranks. In a mad world, who were the cranks? A month earlier, it was the cranks who had said Kennedy should stay out of Dallas.

He asked questions for an hour, until Bradley rejoined them. "I talked to the stripper," he said. "She thinks Ruby gave some girl a ride to Hunt's building. She'll try to find her tonight."

Bradley shrugged. "So all I've really got new is some souvenirs from Ruby's club." He reached into his pocket and tossed onto the table some matchbooks and business cards, a swizzle stick, and a snapshot of Ruby with two brawny strippers.

Philip glanced at one of the cards. It said, "Admit One, Carousel Club, Compliments of Your Friend Jack Ruby" and beside that was a sketch of a bare-breasted girl doing a cancan kick in a champagne glass. He tossed back the card and studied the picture of Ruby and the strippers. Ever since he'd seen Ruby's picture in the papers he'd been gripped by the idea that somewhere, sometime, he'd met Jack Ruby.

He looked at the men around the table. Some were serious, intelligent, concerned. But he had a terrible sense that nothing they did was going to matter, that forces were at work that were bigger than all of them. The sensible thing was to forget this mess, to get on with his life.

He stood up. "Thanks for your help, fellows."

Some of the men said good-bye, and as Philip turned to go his eye fell again on Jack Ruby's business card.

The dancing girl.

He'd seen her before, and in a flash he knew where.

"Son of a bitch," he muttered. He was weak in the knees. He saw Hob Wilkes staring at him with cool, curious eyes.

Philip went to the pay phone, and called the number on Hob's business card. "Wilkes Lumber," a man said in a South Alabama drawl.

"Hob there?" Philip asked.

"Nawsir, he done gone off to Texas fer a coupla weeks."

Philip nodded to Hob Wilkes, and they went outside together.

"Let's talk," Philip said.

They walked back over to the plaza. A tall woman in a long white gown was walking up the grassy knoll with her arms outstretched. "That's Annie," Hob said. "She's a psychic. She thinks the spirits of the assassins are still there, and she's doing her damndest to sniff 'em out. Now, what's on your mind?"

"Two things," Philip said. "Number one, that card from Ruby's club was printed at a place called Four Star Printing on White Settlement Road in Fort Worth. They used to print a right-wing newspaper called *The Defender* for Wade Kingslea. Maybe that doesn't prove a thing, but it's a link between them."

Wilkes lit a Tiparillo. "It sure as hell is."

"Number two, I've got a source who saw a brown-skinned man, maybe Cuban, running up the grassy knoll just after the shots were fired. I'm wondering if any of your witnesses have mentioned him."

"Got any more description?"

"Maybe thirty-five. Husky. Long, shiny black hair, in a pompadour. And rings. Diamond rings, two or three on each hand."

"Show me where he was."

Philip led him to the spot, halfway up the hill. The psychic was still wandering about, eyes closed, arms outstretched, white gown flowing. .

"He was about here," Philip said. "Headed up that way."

"You didn't see a weapon, did you? Your source, I mean."

"No," Philip said. "Look, here's the kicker. This same Cuban was at Wade Kingslea's house the night before. He talked to Kingslea. My source saw them."

"He's sure it's the same man?"

Philip hesitated. Could he be sure? One sighting was at dusk, in a drizzle, from fifty feet away; the other only an instant, from a speeding car.

"He's sure."

Wilkes chewed on his Tiparillo. "You told anybody this? The police? The FBI? Your editor?"

Philip shook his head. "Not yet. I thought you and I might work on it together."

A woman pointed her camera in their direction and Hob turned his back on her. "I tell you, Phil," he said. "There's several brown-skinned gentlemen floating around the edges of this thing. Suppose I poke around and see what I come up with."

"Good."

"You'll be back, then?"

"I'll be back," Philip said.

Two calls awaited him in Fort Worth: one from Ginny, his secretary at the White House, the other from Coyle.

He called Ginny first. "Hello, stranger," she said. "Where have *you* been?"

"Out in the real world. What's up?"

"Well don't bite my head off. I just wanted to know where you wanted your check sent."

"My *check?*"

"You know—they're green and you starve without them."

"I figured I was off the payroll once I didn't come back to Washington."

"Nope," Ginny said. "They're being real nice to all the Kennedy people. I mean, a lot of them have just sort of disappeared, like you. Philip, what *are* you going to do?"

"I don't know," he said and hung up.

Next he called Coyle, who said Wade Kingslea would see them that night.

"Oh, I know what they're saying—that I had Kennedy killed," Wade Kingslea declared. The three of them were sitting around the fire in his study, with the lion's head gazing down serenely. Philip and his grandfather were drinking Scotch, while Coyle sipped coffee.

"Perhaps I should be flattered," the oilman continued, "to be viewed as such a master criminal. But why would I kill Kennedy? It was my intention, by my support of Senator Goldwater, to defeat Kennedy, quite legally, in next year's election."

"Who do you think did kill him?" Philip asked.

"Oswald killed him!" Kingslea roared. "It's time for you liberals to face facts, young man."

Philip believed almost nothing that his grandfather was saying. He didn't think Goldwater could have defeated Kennedy. Even if he could have, that still would have given Harry Flynn another year to beat up on Kingslea Oil. Moreover, the more his grandfather waved Oswald at him—dead, defecting, Castro-loving Oswald—the more Philip saw him as the perfect cover for a right-wing plot. If there had not been an Oswald, the right-wing would have had to invent one. Maybe they had.

"I guess Coyle told you, there are a couple of specific questions I want to ask you."

"He did, and you may."

"First, the night before the assassination, two men came here, to your home. One was dark-skinned, maybe Mexican or Cuban. Who were they?"

Kingslea's eyes flashed. "Who says these men came to my home?"

Philip shook his head. "I'm not going to answer that. But you know they were here and so do I."

"Even if they were, what does it matter?"

"It matters because at least one of them was in Dealey Plaza the next day, when Kennedy was shot."

"They were a pair of cheap hustlers who fast-talked their way past my security people. I had my butler show them out."

"What were their names?"

"The Mexican said his name was Gomez. The other one was called Samuels."

"Where were they from?"

"Blast it, I didn't spend two minutes with them."

"Did you notice what kind of car they were in?"

"I never saw the damn car!" the old man declared.

That was two lies: he had seen the men out himself, not a

butler, and he'd been within twenty feet of their car. Philip decided to try a shot in the dark.

"Did you know that, besides yourself, Four Star Printing had Jack Ruby for a customer?"

Kingslea rose to his feet. "I fail to see the significance of that fact, if it is a fact."

"It could be a coincidence," Philip said.

"Young man, I have been extremely tolerant of you for a great many years," Kingslea continued, "but when you accuse me of murder, you are testing my patience to the limit."

"I haven't accused you of anything," Philip said. He had risen too.

"All my life men have tried to stand in my way, to destroy me," Kingslea raged, "and without exception they lived to regret that mistake. I suggest you consider that, young man, and that you return to Washington, D.C., or wherever you make your home, and do not stay here causing trouble and running a grave risk . . ."

"Wade, stop it," Coyle cried.

"Running a grave risk of serious consequences for poking your nose into matters that are not your concern."

"Thanks for the advice," Philip said, and made his exit.

Philip was often back at the Do-Rite Diner in the weeks ahead, exchanging theories and scraps of information with Hob Wilkes and the other assassination buffs who gathered there. They were a mixed bag, some cranks, some not, but united by a fierce belief that Oswald had not acted alone. They jokingly called themselves the PBI, the People's Bureau of Investigation, or the Do-Rite Diner Irregulars. People came and went, the phone rang constantly, and hardly a day passed that they didn't find some new lead, some new possibility.

One fringe member of the group was a tall, doleful fellow named Harold Kranz, whom the others called Digger O'Dell, after the friendly undertaker on Fred Allen's radio show. Kranz approached Philip on his second visit to the Do-Rite, pulling his chair close, glancing about furtively, and whispering, "You know they're killing the witnesses, don't you?"

Philip asked what he meant, and Kranz eagerly outlined his theory. Key figures in the case, he said, were dying mysterious deaths. A stripper in Ruby's nightclub, one of his closest friends, was found hanged the week after the assassination. "They *said* it was suicide," Kranz muttered darkly. And the cab driver who had driven Oswald back to his rooming house had died that week when his cab supposedly crashed into a tree. "Very odd, wouldn't you say?" Kranz demanded. "He's been driving a cab for twenty years, and he suddenly runs into a tree."

Philip was noncommittal. He had covered the police beat, in his reporting days, and he knew how many people died bizarre deaths every day. Cab drivers had accidents. Strippers became depressed and hanged themselves. Two deaths didn't make a conspiracy. But Digger O'Dell saw these deaths spreading like a cancer, like a tidal wave that could engulf them all. "There'll be more," he warned, eyes blazing. "No one who knows anything is safe."

Philip kept searching for the Duke. He went to see two of the Chez Duke waitresses in their homes. One slammed the door in his face, screaming, "I don't want no part of it!" The other, the Roy Orbison fan, let him in, gave him a beer, and soon collapsed in his arms, sobbing that she believed the Duke was dead. Finally, one night in mid-December, Philip broke into the Duke's house, out past Bluebonnet Circle, but all he found was that someone had been there before him. The place was a wreck, with papers thrown everywhere, and no clues to the Duke's whereabouts.

Over coffee one morning, Hob Wilkes asked Philip if he had a few hours to spare. "Sure," Philip said. "What's up?"

"I got me a Cuban lady I want you to meet."

"Let's go," Philip told him.

They drove in Hob's old pickup to the northern outskirts of Dallas, where the city began to spill out onto the prairie, and stopped finally before a dreary trailer park. Hob lit a Tiparillo and led Philip to a small trailer perched on cinder blocks.

"This woman came out of Cuba in the spring of '59," Hob said as he knocked on the door. "She's had a right hard time of it."

The woman who opened the door had bright, angry eyes, and might once have been pretty.

"Mrs. Ortiz, this here's Mr. King, the reporter I told you about," Hob began. The woman looked at Philip suspiciously. "I don't want my name in no paper," she said.

"He understands that," Hob said. "We just want to talk."

They stood in the trailer's tiny kitchen. A baby was asleep in the next room and the place stank of dirty diapers.

"Now, Mrs. Ortiz, tell us about the three men who came to see you."

"I only knew one of them," the woman said.

"I understand," Hob said. "Just tell us what happened."

"This man, I'd known him back in Havana. He worked with my husband. But I hadn't seen him since then, until he came here in September. He said he was looking for my husband. I said my husband had left me. He asked where he went. I said maybe back to Miami. That was all. I never seen them again."

"Tell us about the other two men."

"One of them looked like Oswald. I'm not sure. He was wearing a hat. But when I seen Oswald on TV, I said, 'That's him.'"

"And what about the other man?"

The woman shrugged. "He looked Cuban."

"How old?"

"Thirty—thirty-five. Not as tall as you. A strong man. *Un toro.*"

"Was he wearing rings, Mrs. Ortiz?" Philip asked.

"I don't remember no rings," the woman said.

"Did he have a pompadour? Did his hair curl up like this?" He tried to show, with his hands, how the man's hair had looked.

"Just regular hair," the woman said. "Black. Long, maybe."

"Was there anything else about him?" Hob asked. "Scars. A moustache? A gold tooth. Tattoos? Anything unusual?"

"I don't remember nothing."

Hob thanked the woman and handed her a twenty-dollar bill, then they walked back to his pickup.

"The way I heard it, her husband was a real tough *hombre,*" Hob said. "One of the boys who pulled out fingernails for Batista."

"It's all so damn vague," Philip said dejectedly. "It's like we're grabbing at straws. She *might* have seen my Cuban. She *might* have seen Oswald."

Hob puffed contentedly on his cigar. "Sure we're grabbing at straws. My theory is that this case'll never be easy. The easy answer is what the FBI is saying, that Oswald did it alone. That's nice and tidy, but you and I don't believe it. I don't expect us to find a smoking gun, Phil. We're gonna have to build us a circumstantial case. We've got to find us a thread here and a thread there, till it all starts to make sense. Hell, I'd say we found us a pretty interesting little thread today. You've got you a brown-skinned fellow you say was at Kingslea's house one night and at Dealey Plaza the next day, and now we find out that same fellow might have been running around Dallas with Oswald and one of Batista's thugs. If that's true, I'd call it a good day's work."

"If," Philip said bitterly. "If, if, if."

"Let's just keep finding them threads," Hob Wilkes said. "Then maybe one day we'll weave us a rope big enough to hang some son of a bitch."

Jenny phoned that night. Christmas was at hand, but he hadn't called her, because he wasn't sure what he wanted to say.

She said she and Skip were leaving town the next day, and she asked if he wanted to come to lunch. Troubled, uncertain, he said yes, if only because, for twenty years, he'd never imagined saying no to her.

He knocked on her door not knowing what he wanted to happen. She opened the door herself, radiant in pearls and a pea-green wool dress, and gave him a careful peck on the cheek. They went to the Chinese-red library for a drink, then to the huge dining room where a nervous Negro girl served Montrachet and crabmeat salads. Their talk was halting, uncertain. He thought it was because they had been lovers; somehow, that made them start anew, strangers. She explained that she and Skip were leaving for London that evening. Soon after their return, she added, Skip would announce he was running for Congress.

When Philip said that it all sounded very exciting, Jenny shrugged absently and rang a little silver bell for more wine. That was the thing that struck him most about Jenny, how distanced she seemed from everything around her. Skip and London and Congress might all have been incidents in a book she was reading. He wondered if she would ever come out of her shell. Perhaps she wouldn't have to, for with her beauty and Skip's money she could glide effortlessly through life, untouched and untouching, like a hawk making slow, graceful circles in a desert sky.

After lunch the girl brought coffee and Jenny lit a cigarette. Philip had quit smoking a few months earlier, and her cigarette annoyed him. After knowing Jenny for twenty years, he was starting to see her with critical eyes.

"I may have a baby," she said. "I think I owe Skip that."

He didn't know what to say, except the unspeakable truth that no one should have a child unless they were absolutely sure they wanted it.

"Are you sorry about what we did?" he asked her.

She stared at him with her sad, gorgeous brown eyes, a half-smile playing on her lips. "No. But when I got home I realized it was the end of something, not the beginning."

"We're still friends," he said.

"I know. But once I went to bed with you I lost the magic that had made you love me." Jenny laughed and rubbed out her cigarette. "You entered paradise and found it was just another amusement park."

"That should be my line," he said. "I'm the cynic."

Jenny smiled her old, dazzling smile. "No, P.K. You try to be a cynic, but you're really an idealist. You're sad because the world won't live up to your high standards."

She walked him to the front door and she gave him a long, urgent kiss. "Do you want to stay?" When he hesitated, she added, "I'll send the girl home."

His face was buried in her hair, hair so gloriously warm and thick and soft. He had a sudden, crazy notion that she wanted to have his baby, and he knew he didn't want his child raised in whatever chaos lay ahead for Skip and Jenny.

"No," he said. "I love you, but no."

She frowned, holding his hands. "I thought of marrying you, you know. When I wanted to leave Washington, I thought of calling you instead of Skip."

"Why didn't you? Because he's rich?"

"That was one reason. But the main reason was that I think I'll make Skip less unhappy than I would you."

Everything about her confused him. "I'll call you," he said.

"Good," Jenny said, and she watched from her doorway as he hurried away.

Philip was back at the Do-Rite two mornings before Christmas. He was looking for Hob, wondering if one of them should fly to Miami and look for the Cuban, but Hob wasn't at the diner, only Bradley and Kranz. Kranz pulled his chair close to Philip's and began to tell him about the new addition to his ever-lengthening death list. The latest victim was a re-porter for a West Texas paper, Kranz said. He had phoned his editor, excited about a new lead on the Kennedy assassination, and that night he'd been found dead in his hotel room, his neck broken by a karate chop.

"What do you think of *that?*" Kranz demanded.

Philip didn't know what to think of it. Either Kranz was crazy or a monstrous, murderous conspiracy was in progress. It was easier to think Kranz was crazy.

Kranz had other sinister events to relate, and to escape him Philip asked Bradly what he'd been doing. Bradley was just back from a meeting with Jack Ruby's sister and eager to report.

"There were six of them, growing up in Chicago," he said. "Jack, his brother, Earl, and four sisters. It was a tough neighborhood, and anybody who got smart with those sisters had to answer to Jack. Well, Eva, the sister I talked to, was a pretty tough cookie herself. She came to Dallas after the war and bought into a place called the Singapore Club, in South Dallas. Jack came down to help her run it. The first thing they did was change the name of the place to the Silver Spur and turn it into a hillbilly joint. A real bucket-of-blood. Ruby was the bouncer. One time he got into a fight where . . ."

"They called it what?" Philip demanded.

"The Silver Spur," Bradley said. "A hillbilly joint. A real shit-kicker. Ruby got into this one fight where a guy bit off his . . ."

"Where was it?"

"South Ervay Street. What's wrong?"

"Have you got a map of Dallas?"

"Yeah, yeah," Bradley said impatiently and yanked a map out of his briefcase. Philip studied it a moment, then started for the door.

"Where you going?" Bradley demanded. They had a rule that they told each other where they would be. Kranz had them all edgy about mysterious disappearances.

"To the Silver Spur," Philip called over his shoulder.

"The guy bit off his *finger,*" Bradley yelled after him.

The Silver Spur was the Club Caribe now, but it was still a dingy roadhouse with a Lone Star sign over the door and a parking lot that could hold thirty or forty cars and four or five brawls. It was the kind of place where beer costs two bits and the broken noses and black eyes were on the house. It was the kind of bottom-rung dive you only patronized if you were a loser and knew you were a loser and hungered for the company of other losers.

Philip remembered what he'd said the first time he laid eyes on this place: "We drove to Dallas for *this?*" What he'd meant was that Fort Worth was overflowing with dumps like the Silver Spur, Fort Worth practically held the patent on them, and you went to Dallas because it had pretensions toward elegance, because in Dallas there were bars with piped-in classical music and fancy pink drinks and waitresses who could add up your check without moving their lips.

But he'd come here, to the Silver Spur, on one of those aimless nights with Sherry and the Duke, a decade before.

He shook his head and went up and banged on the door of the Club Caribe. It was only noon but there was an ancient Buick Roadmaster parked out back. He kept banging on the door until it opened. The guy who greeted him was maybe fifty, bald and dried-up, with a cigarette drooping from his lips and a blackjack in his hand.

"We ain't open," he announced.

"I need some information."

"Try the library."

"I'll pay for it."

The man looked him up and down. "You a cop?"

"No."

The man stepped back and Philip followed him inside.

The interior of the Club Caribe looked like a million other dumps that were no more meant to be seen at noon than were the women you found in them. Still, that distant night came back to him. They'd come here looking for the Duke's cousin. He remembered talking to Ruby when they arrived, asking about the cousin. He had been thinner then, with more hair, but it was Ruby, an eager, fast-talking guy who wanted to be your pal.

Eventually the Duke's cousin had showed up. A big guy, six three or more. A cop. No, an ex-cop. Maybe Sherry had brought him some weed. That part was hazy. But he remembered how close the Duke had been to his cousin, how much he'd admired him. They'd talked about opening a bar together someday. What the hell had the cousin's name been? They'd joked about his name—it had been the same as somebody famous.

"What're you after, fellow?" the bald man asked. They'd settled in a booth by the door.

"This was Jack Ruby's place," Philip said.

"You asking me or telling me?"

"Asking."

"It was Ruby's. Before he moved uptown. That's no secret."

"I'm looking for a guy I met here, eight or ten years ago, when Ruby was still here. A big guy. Dark hair. Six three, maybe six four. He was maybe twenty-five then. He'd been a cop, but he got in some trouble. He might have been a gambler when I met him."

The man shrugged. "Could be a lot of people," he said.

"He had a name like somebody famous," Philip said. He was trying desperately to remember. Who was it? Names exploded in his mind. Had they kidded the guy? Called him Senator?

"Eisenhower!" Philip exclaimed. "His name was something like Eisenhower. Does that mean anything?"

"Mister, I got work to do."

"Eidenberg! That was his name. Sherry kept calling him Ike. Do you know a big guy named Eidenberg?"

"What if I do?"

Philip put a twenty on the table. The fellow pocketed it.

"Marty Eidenberg," he said. "Try the phone book."

Philip knocked on the door of a small brick house not far from the Club Caribe until a big scowling man in pajamas opened it.

"Look, you want a place to bet, catch me later," the man said.

"That's not it," Philip said. "We met a long time ago. I was a friend of the Duke's."

The man studied him unhappily. "Well, hell, come on in," he said. "It's cold standing here."

They stepped inside. There was a plastic Christmas tree atop the TV, and a lot of beer cans strewn about.

"Marty? Who is it?" a woman called.

"Nobody," Marty said.

"I'm looking for the Duke," Philip said. "Do you know where he is?"

Marty shrugged. "He comes and goes."

"Do you hear from him?"

"I might."

"Listen, it's urgent. He left his bar a month ago and no-body knows where he is."

"The Duke can take care of himself," Marty said.

"Here are my phone numbers. Will you have him call me if you hear from him?"

"Sure," Marty said. "Why not?"

"Marty," the woman called. "Come back to bed."

He went back to the Do-Rite and choked down a greasy hamburger. Bradley had heard that a woman had told the FBI she saw a second, brown-coated man in Oswald's window. A second rifleman would change everything, and there was in-tense debate about whether her story was part of the cover-up.

At four the pay phone rang. Freddy, the Do-Rite's owner, answered it. He had long since made it clear that he thought the assassination buffs were all nutty as fruitcakes, but they were cash customers, so he tolerated them.

"For you, Phil," he called.

Philip hurried to the phone.

"It's Marty," a man said. "I talked to the Duke. He wants to see you."

"Where is he?"

"A place out at the lake. You got a pencil?"

"Yeah," Philip said and took down the directions. "Look, can I call him?"

"There's no phone," Marty said. "It's just a cabin. He said to hurry, 'cause he'll be leaving tonight. And to come alone."

Philip went back to the table. The talk had turned to a man named Holland who said he had stood on the railroad overpass and had seen a puff of smoke from atop the grassy knoll.

"Where's Hob?" Philip asked.

"Out pounding on doors, I guess," Bradley said.

Philip agonized for a moment. "Tell him to meet me here later."

"Where're you going?" Bradley asked.

"To meet a guy, out at Lake Dallas."

"Be more specific," Kranz demanded.

"I haven't got time," Philip said.

A few flakes of snow were falling when he turned at a red mailbox and drove between tall pines to a cabin overlooking the lake. A cream and blue Coupe de Ville was parked out front; Philip guessed the Duke was still riding in style.

He beat on the cabin door. "Duke? You in there?"

There was no answer, only the whine of a motorboat echoing across the silver, shimmering lake.

"Duke?" He tried the door, pushed it open, and stepped inside. The windows were shuttered, and he could barely see the cot across the room, with someone lying atop it.

"Duke? You son of a bitch, wake up!"

Grinning, he crossed to the cot.

It was the Duke, but he didn't wake up and never would.

"Oh my God," Philip yelled and ran for the door.

Incredibly, the door was locked. He felt himself starting to panic as he jerked and twisted the knob and the door didn't budge.

He tried to calm himself. Could the door have blown shut and locked by accident? But what about the dead man behind him? He was trapped in a dark cabin with a corpse. "Hey, is anybody out there?" he yelled.

He thought he heard footsteps, but no answer came.

He checked the cabin's four windows. Each was covered by wooden shutters and nailed tight from the outside. He grabbed a chair and banged against the shutters but they didn't give.

Then he smelled the smoke.

He smelled it and then he saw it, curling up from the floorboards. He ran to the spot and felt the heat and heard the crackle of fire under the cabin. He backed away, thinking, No, this can't be happening. He let himself think it was a dream, that it would all vanish soon, but then he knew that it was real, that he was locked in a burning cabin and he was going to die unless he found a way out.

The smoke was billowing up, thick and black; he choked and tried to hide from it. He beat on the shutters again but they held firm. He threw himself against the locked door, again and again until his shoulder throbbed with pain.

The hot, vile smoke seared his lungs. He clawed at the door until his hands were torn and bleeding. He fell to the floor trying to suck air from the crack under the door. Images flashed through his mind: Louise, young and golden-haired; Coyle, shyly handing him a present; pigtailed Alice sinking a putt; Jenny, leaping and twirling; John Kennedy waving into the Texas sun.

He was breathing the smoke now, gagging and twisting on the floor. All he could think was that he didn't want to die, not here, not yet. His last thought was a profound sadness, a disbelief that such a thing could happen.

He didn't hear the cars outside the cabin or the shot that blasted the lock off the door.

He was only dimly aware of the man dragging him outside as flames shot up to the cabin's roof.

A mouth pressed against his own, forcing fresh air into his burning lungs. In a moment he was gagging, gasping, sobbing, but breathing in the sweet pure night air. He got to his knees and vomited into the sandy earth. Finally he looked up at the man who stood over him, puffing a cheap cigar.

"Well, brother Kingslea, you gonna live?" Hob Wilkes drawled.

Philip tried to speak but he couldn't.

"Is your thug friend in there?" Wilkes demanded, nodding at the burning cabin.

"Yes," Philip whispered, and his body began to tremble as he realized that he had almost died in that inferno.

"Who are you?" he asked. Wilkes flashed a badge. Philip, recognizing it, almost laughed. "You, FBI?"

"We ain't all part of some damn conspiracy," Wilkes said. "When I drove up here, a car was leaving and the cabin was burning. And like a damn fool I saved your miserable life and let the car get away."

"Thanks anyway."

"I should have let your ass fry. Digger O'Dell would've loved that. Another fatal coincidence."

"How'd you know I was here?"

Wilkes showed his crooked teeth. "You'll never know, sonny."

Philip knew that Wilkes was right, he'd never know. And he realized, too, with a surge of relief, that he didn't give a damn.

"I'm gonna give you some good advice, my young friend," Wilkes drawled. "Number one, you're gonna tell me every damn thing you know about this case. Everything. Got it?"

"What's number two?"

"Number two is tomorrow morning you pack your bag and kiss your mama good-bye and get your sweet ass out of Texas and leave this mess to us folks who get paid for it."

It was, Philip decided, the best advice he'd ever received in his life.

He followed it.

CHAPTER TWO

Philip returned to his Georgetown apartment on a raw January afternoon, built a fire, and began to dig through an enormous pile of mail. Amid the unread magazines, unpaid bills, and unwanted advertisements, a dull yellow telegram caught his eye. He ripped it open, fearing disaster, only to find a quite meaningless message: "Call me collect. Urgent. Harold Hayes. Esquire."

Who the hell was Harold Hayes, Esquire? Yet another of the world's unnumbered millions of cranks? Philip had humored his last crank. He tossed the telegram aside and dipped into the pile again.

This time he fished out three fat letters from Chrissie in Peru. The first reported her excitement as she arrived in the mountain village where she was to live for several months. In the second she was deeply depressed by the endless poverty and suffering she had encountered: "What we're doing is the smallest possible drop in the biggest possible bucket. It's good for Sarge Shriver's image, and it may be good for our souls, but it can't begin to change the reality of these people's lives. God may help these people, or Marx may, but when I cry all night because I've held another dead baby in my arms I can't convince myself that the Peace Corps ever will." In her third letter, written after the assassination, Chrissie vowed to stay on in Peru, as a tribute to the dead president: "I don't believe that politics is all cynicism and manipulation. I don't believe he died for nothing. I believe his death can have meaning if those of us who share his ideals can take inspiration from his life and will go forth and try to make the world a better place."

Her letter concluded: "I think of you a lot. You're headed somewhere, maybe somewhere you have to go alone. You have so much talent. Don't waste it writing speeches for someone else. Go out and write for yourself. You can do it. And write me, too. Love, Chrissie."

Philip tossed her letters aside and stared into the crackling fire. If he hadn't acted like a fool one night, racing off to save Jenny from the man she wanted to marry, Chrissie would be here with him now. How he wished she were. She was so damned sensible. What *was* he going to do? He didn't have the slightest idea, so he plunged into his pile of mail again, as if an answer might be hidden there. His next discovery was a letter on New York *Times* stationery.

It proved to be a note from his friend Curtis: "Phil, thought your Kennedy piece was first-rate. I took the liberty of sending it to Harold Hayes at *Esquire*. Call me and we'll hoist a few. Regards, Curtis."

Holy shit! Harold Hayes was the editor of *Esquire!*

He seized the telegram and read it again. "Call me collect. Urgent." The telegram was dated two weeks earlier.

Could they possibly have *liked* his memoir? Could they want to *publish* it?

Philip grabbed his phone, got the magazine's office, stammered to Hayes' secretary about the telegram, and by some miracle found himself talking to the editor of *Esquire*.

"We loved your piece," said Hayes in gentle North Carolina tones. "But I do think you should come up for a chat. Let's see . . . how about lunch, the day after tomorrow? At one?"

Philip was flabbergasted. "I . . . but . . . I mean, what do want want to talk about?"

"Just a few editorial queries. Plus, we'd like to meet you."

"But do you want to *print* my article?"

"Of course," the editor said. "Didn't I say so?"

Philip returned to the White House the next morning, for the first time since he'd left on the fateful trip to Texas. To go back was strange, eerie. From the outside, the grand old mansion was unchanged, but within its walls vast empires had toppled. Yesterday's scorned vice president was today's larger-than-life president. The Kennedy men were scattered now, mere mortals again, replaced by Texans with mysterious names like Moyers, Jenkins, Valenti. Bill Moyers' secretary had awakened Philip that morning, asking if he could come see her boss. Philip had no idea what Moyers wanted, unless it was to tell him he was finally off the payroll.

Moyers was enshrined in the big corner office that had been Sorensen's. *Sic transit gloria.* He greeted Philip warmly and told his secretary to hold his calls, a nice touch. They'd met once or twice before, when Moyers was a bright young man at the Peace Corps. He was solemn, painfully sincere, not yet thirty, an ex-divinity student who, some said, invoked powers not of this world to manage the unmanageable Lyndon Johnson.

Moyers served tea and spoke of Fort Worth, where he'd once attended the Baptist Seminary. Unfortunately, Philip was as innocent of the Baptist Seminary as Moyers was of the bars and whorehouses that were Philip's most enduring memory of Cowtown. Undaunted, Moyers guided the talk to the new president, his high hopes for the nation, his dedication to the Kennedy legacy.

"I hope you'll stay and help us," he declared. "We need you."

Philip savored the flattery, even as he disbelieved it. *They* needed *him?*

"Doing what?"

"I'm starting to pull together our legislative program," Moyers explained. "You've been dealing with the agencies for three years, writing about them. Everyone speaks highly of you. I want you to get into the substance. Help me put our program together."

Philip thought Moyers was talking on two levels. On one level he was offering him a better job than the Kennedys had ever offered him. On another, the unspoken, political level, he was saying, "We're afraid Bob Kennedy will challenge us for the nomination this summer, and we're out to lock up all the Kennedy people we can, even minor players like yourself."

He liked Moyers. The guy was bright, smooth, decent. But he was playing the game. That was the question Philip had to decide. Did he want to keep playing the game, to keep on being a pawn on the political chessboard?

"I don't know what I'm going to do," he said. "I may try some writing, on my own. I'll call you."

Moyers walked him to the door. "That would be nice," he mused as they shook hands. "To be your own man."

Harold Hayes was a tall, auburn-haired North Carolinian who, over lunch in his office, proposed a few minor cuts in Philip's article. Philip, still fearful that the editor would change his mind, quickly agreed to the deletions. But Hayes spoke with enthusiasm about his work: "People have sent us pieces saying they love the Kennedys, or hate them, but yours is the first to suggest ambiguity about them. I hope we'll be publishing more of your work."

It slowly dawned on Philip that this charming man, the editor of one of America's great magazines, was wooing him. "You'll hear from the other magazines, once this piece is published," Hayes declared. "They'll offer you assignments and a lot of money. But money isn't all you should consider. *Life* or the *Post* may pay two or three thousand dollars for an article, but that's for what *they* want. We may pay less, but we want what *you* want to write. And in the long run your reputation will depend on whether you write your best."

As Philip was leaving, Hayes said, "I showed your piece to two editors at publishing houses, and they'd both like to see you today, if you have time. Here are their names."

He handed Philip a scrap of paper, which proclaimed that an editor named Stanford Price hoped to see him at three and that one Julian Swann might be available at five.

"What do they want?" he demanded of Hayes.

The editor waved a hand indifferently, as if such miracles were commonplace. "Well, I imagine Stan Price wants you to expand your piece into a book," he said. "And Julian Swann . . . well, heaven knows *what* he'll want, but you'll enjoy meeting him. Stan and Julian are really the alpha and omega of American publishing right now."

With that enigmatic aside, the editor of *Esquire* shook Philip's hand and left him to wander unaided down Madison Avenue in a state of dire, if nonalcoholic, intoxication. Skyscrapers spun giddily and the heavens burned with fire.

Most incredibly of all, he was on his way to an appointment with a famed editor who might ask him to write a book.

A book!

The idea left him dizzy, delirious. He saw that book in his mind's eye, and he lusted for it as his grandfather, four decades before, had lusted for black gold. Dazed, disbelieving, Philip stumbled into a building, up an elevator, into an office, to confront one of the men who made dreams come true.

Stanford Price, editor in chief of Livesay and Miller, Publishers, was a short, erect man in his sixties, with close-cropped white hair, a military bearing, and a no-nonsense manner. His small office was overflowing with books, and his walls were decorated with photographs of himself with a gallery of celebrated American writers. He shook Philip's hand and got right to the point.

"That was a fine, sensitive piece you wrote on the Kennedys. The tone was perfect and the ending was quite moving. Have you thought of writing more on the same subject?"

"I . . . I've thought about expanding the piece into a short book," Philip said.

"That's precisely what you should do," the editor answered approvingly. " 'Short' is the operative word. The *Esquire* piece runs—what?—four thousand words, and there's not a false note in it. Can you sustain that over, say, fifty thousand words?"

"I don't know," Philip admitted. It was an issue that, in his euphoria, he had not confronted.

Price lit his pipe and puffed thoughtfully. "Tell me, how did you happen to write the piece?"

"The night they buried Kennedy, I stayed up until dawn and drank Scotch and wrote down everything I could remember about him. That was the article."

"Well, my suggestion is that you drink some more Scotch and decide if you've got enough material for a book. If you think you do, bring me an outline and I'd like to publish it."

Philip stared at the man dumbly.

"I could advance you three thousand dollars," Price said. "This may not be a big book, but it could be a good, solid start to your career. What do you say?"

Say? Philip wanted to shout, "Yes!" and race out the door before the man came to his senses. That they would give him money to write a book was beyond belief.

And yet he hesitated.

"I think it's a good idea," he said. "But I guess I should think it over."

"By all means," the editor agreed.

It was with some impatience that Philip headed for his next

appointment. He didn't want to meet another editor. He only wanted to get to his typewriter and start working on his book, which in his imagination was already a front-runner for the next year's Pulitzer Prize.

Still, some instinct made him keep his appointment with Julian Swann.

Stanford Price's small, cluttered office had been on the third floor of an old building, overlooking a noisy, dirty river of midtown traffic. Julian Swann's spacious, stylish office at Wide World Books was on the thirty-third floor of a glittering skyscraper that looked west on all America.

Swann's pony-tailed secretary pointed Philip into the editor's office, where he was met by a towering, orange-haired apparition who was hopping about to the beat of a tune that had filled the airwaves of late. A harmonica howled, drums pounded, guitars twanged, and Julian Swann was singing along in ecstasy: "Love Me Do."

Seeing Philip, he broke off his vocal. "Oh hello," he said cheerfully. "You must be the lad who wrote the Kennedy piece."

With a final howl or two, the record cut itself off. "Aren't they wonderful?" Swann demanded.

"I . . . I read something about them," Philip said.

"Beatlemania!" the editor declared. "You wouldn't care to write a book about them, would you?"

Philip shook his head. "I don't think so."

"Well, what book *would* you like to write?"

Julian Swann might have been in his midthirties, although it was hard to say, just as it was hard to say if his reddish-orange hair was dyed or not. He was wearing a tan, Italian-cut suit, an orchid-hued shirt, and a flowered ascot. With his tall, gawky frame, his narrow face, his darting eyes, his beak of a nose, and his sudden, jerky movements, he resembled some huge, possibly dangerous jungle bird.

"You . . . you read my *Esquire* piece?"

"Of course. That's why you're here."

"Well, I may expand it into a book."

Swann flopped into his reclining chair, scowling ferociously. "That would be a *serious* mistake," he said firmly.

"Why?" Philip demanded, furious to hear his book—his baby—so curtly dismissed.

"My dear boy, it's an absolutely first-rate magazine piece,

but—don't you see—it's a *magazine piece*. Stretch it to ten times its natural length and you'll destroy it. The magic would be gone."

Philip glared at the editor, but even as he did he realized that what he said made sense. He'd put his heart and soul into the four thousand words of the *Esquire* piece, and he couldn't imagine where another forty thousand words would come from.

"Of course," Swann said. "If you absolutely *insist,* I'll publish it. But if I do, I'll lose money and you'll lose far more than I will."

"I don't understand," Philip admitted.

"Of course you don't, because you don't know the book business. You've written a brilliant magazine piece, and you've come to New York and all you see are people who want to wine and dine you and wave money at you. Naturally, it all seems quite heavenly. But that's because you're a beautiful young virgin whom everyone wants to deflower. It won't be the same, if you come back a year from now, after you've written a nice little memoir that sells four thousand copies. Then you'd be ready to write a big book, but you'd find that people weren't quite so interested. Why? Because your first book would have established you, in the eyes of editors, critics, and book salesmen as someone who writes nice, *small* books. *This* is your moment, Philip. The *Esquire* piece has opened doors. Don't waste your opportunity. Think of a big book, one that will put the world at your feet."

Philip slumped in his chair. "I haven't thought of anything except my Kennedy piece."

"Well, let's put our thinking caps on," the editor said. "Tell me, have you ever considered writing a novel?"

"Sure. But I don't know if I could."

"Of course you could. Any fool can write a novel—thousands do. And anyone who can write something as sensitive as your piece—which you must realize was utterly novelistic— might even write a *good* novel. So the question is, what should your novel be *about?* Tell me more about yourself. Where are you from?"

Philip strained to keep up as Julian Swann's thoughts bounced this way and that. "Texas," he said. "I'm from Texas."

"Oh, of course!" the editor cried. "You're the grandson of that terrible Wade Kingslea. That man is the very *embodiment* of evil. In another age, he would have been Tamburlaine or Attila."

"That's him," Philip said.

Swann peered at Philip with rising interest. "If you don't mind my asking," he said, "do you think he was involved in the Kennedy assassination?"

Philip shrugged. "I don't know. It's possible."

Julian Swann's small, amber eyes began to gleam. "How do you and your grandfather get along?" he asked.

"We don't."

"Not at all?"

"Look, I loathe the bastard," Philip said impatiently.

"My God, my God, I feel the lightning about to strike," the editor cried.

He leaped from his chair and began to pace about his office like a man possessed. "That's it, my boy," he said. "Don't you see?"

"See what?"

Swann's reply came slowly, solemnly, like a judge pronouncing the most horrific of sentences:

"You will write me a novel about a Texas oil tycoon who conspires to murder the president of the United States!"

With a triumphant smile lighting his face, Swann poked a bony finger at Philip's nose.

"That, my young friend, is a book that will make you rich and famous!"

Philip was stunned. "Or notorious," he muttered.

"The difference matters only to the obscure," the editor declared. "What do you say?"

"I don't know what to say," Philip admitted. "I wouldn't know where to begin."

"You've already begun, by talking to me," Swann said. "The question is, do you want to talk seriously about it?"

Philip's mind was spinning. The idea was quite mad. And yet, even as he hesitated, he felt doors opening in his mind, doors opening and memories pouring out—of Texas, of high school, of his grandfather, of Kennedy, of Dallas. What was fact and what was fiction? He didn't know or care; he only knew that those memories were overpowering, that he wanted to be swept along by them, wherever they might lead.

"Yes," he said, "I would like to talk about it."

Swann grabbed his phone and told his secretary to call Sardi's and leave word for Princess somebody—her name was unclear, perhaps Italian—that he would be late. That done, he turned back to Philip, rubbing his hands together gleefully.

"Well, we know how your novel ends," he said. "But how does it begin? Why does this oilman want to kill this president?"

"Politics?" Philip ventured.

"Well, yes, but it should be more than that, don't you think? Don't our truly interesting obsessions tend to reach far into the past?"

Philip nodded slowly. Swann was right: our most true, most terrible obsessions go far, far back. He shut his eyes and began to see, dimly, into the past. "They met in the oilfields," he said. It was as if someone else was speaking. "In East Texas, in the 1930s, when they were young men."

"Why? What were they doing there?"

"The oilman . . . the one who becomes an oilman . . . was a young, hungry, ambitious farmer . . . He left his wife and son to go to the oil fields and make his fortune. He had to. He couldn't help it."

"And the other one? The future president? Why is he there? Is he young and hungry too?"

Philip gestured impatiently. "No, no. He's rich. A college student—at Princeton. He's gone to work in the oil fields during his summer vacation."

"Why?"

"To get away from his father. To prove he's man enough. To see Texas. And one day he arrives in a little East Texas boomtown and he meets the other fellow."

"Let's give them names," Swann said.

"Brad. The oilman's name is Brad. The college student's name is . . . oh, hell, Frank. So they meet and . . . and have a fight."

"No," the editor said. "That's too obvious. They become friends first."

"Okay. Brad gets Frank a job on the rig with him."

"So why do they fall out?" Swann demanded.

Philip hesitated. His crystal ball was suddenly dark. Why the hell *did* they fall out?

"Over a girl!"

"And what is a decent woman doing in this grubby little boomtown?" Swann demanded.

"Her father owns the rig they're working on," Philip said.

"She comes for a visit. They both flirt with her. But the father encourages the Princeton boy and tells the roughneck to get lost. So Frank takes her on a date. But when he comes out of her house, Brad is waiting for him. They have a fight. A real knock-down, drag-out."

"Who wins the fight?"

"Frank knocks Brad out. It's the first time anybody's ever whipped Brad at anything. And when he comes to, he swears that he'll get even with Frank some day."

Julian Swann abruptly stood up. "Well, there it is," he said. "The first chapter of your novel. Now, alas, I must join a lady—a princess, indeed—for a drink."

Philip was still in the oilfields. "Wait a minute—what happens next?"

"Oh, I dare say you'll think of something," Swann said. "Brad obviously makes his fortune in oil. Frank goes back to Princeton, off to war, and then into politics. Eventually he becomes president, and Brad still hates him, and there's some final confrontation. Brad loses, so he plots the assassination."

"It's so strange," Philip said. "It's like plucking it out of the air."

"The art of fiction, my boy. Now here's what I propose. You write the first chapter of your novel—the meeting, the fight, just as we've discussed it—and a short outline of the book. I need that to satisfy my corporate masters. Then I'll give you a ten-thousand-dollar advance to write the book. Plus a five-thousand-dollar bonus if you finish by the first of July. I'd like to hurry it out for the fall, you see—in November we'll have both the presidential election and the first anniversary of the Kennedy assassination, which would make your novel rather timely. So, are we in agreement?"

Philip threw up his hands. "I don't *know*," he cried. "Harold Hayes wants me to write for *Esquire*. Stanford Price wants me to write a Kennedy memoir. You want me to write this novel. It's all happened in one day. How do I know what's right?"

Swann smiled benignly. "You're learning an important lesson, Philip," he said. "The hard part of being a writer isn't writing. The hard part is deciding what to write."

Philip nodded glumly.

"And do you know why that is?"

"Why?"

"Because to decide what to write, you must first decide

who you are—*that* is the hard part!"

Swann slipped on a camel's hair topcoat. "Why don't you join my friend and me for a drink?" he said. "You look like you could use one."

A beaming maître d' greeted them at Sardi's. "Ah, Mr. Swann, the princess awaits you," he announced and led them to a table where a slender woman in her forties smiled up at them. Julian made introductions, but Philip, his mind still in Texas, did not catch her name. She had bright, nervous eyes, a wide mouth, and thick, unruly black hair, and she gave Philip an odd smile before plunging deep into conversation with Julian Swann. She seemed to be urging him to cosponsor a dinner to benefit the civil-rights movement; Philip threw down two Scotches and tried to imagine himself writing a novel.

Soon their little party was breaking up. Julian urged Philip to come to a book-publication party later in the evening. Why not, Philip thought. But the editor had another engagement first. "Then why don't you come with me?" the princess exclaimed. "We can meet Julian later!"

Philip had no better plan, and soon he was riding through Central Park in a taxicab with a princess whose name he didn't know, trying to decide whether to accept ten thousand dollars to write a novel that would, for all practical purposes, accuse his grandfather of murdering President Kennedy. A novel that, but for a mad genius named Julian Swann, would never have entered his mind.

"Life is strange," he murmured.

Beside him, wrapped in sable, seemingly lost in her own thoughts, the princess—he thought Julian had called her Eve —smiled mysteriously and murmured in reply, "It certainly is."

He looked at her with interest. She seemed eccentric but pleasant enough. Not unattractive in her nervous way. He wanted to know more about her, and that was the highest compliment at his disposal.

An Irish doorman leaped up, tipped his hat, and held the door with a flourish as they entered her building on the west side of Central Park. "Titles are so helpful with . . . you know . . . doormen and restaurants," she whispered as the elevator lifted them smoothly up to the twenty-first floor.

Princess Whazit, as he had come to think of her, threw

open the door on a vast, two-level apartment with French impressionists on the walls and a spectacular view of Central Park. "Anyone home?" she cried.

"Just me, ma'am," a dumpy woman in a white uniform called from the kitchen door.

"Oh, Mrs. Riley, thank goodness. Fix us something to eat, please. Ham sandwiches. Fruit. Caviar. Whatever we have. I'm absolutely famished!"

She led Philip past a Matisse and into a small library. She helped him out of his coat and then, quite unexpectedly, kissed him. He leaned against the door, amused, and let her greedy kiss go on, thinking that perhaps this was how princesses welcomed handsome commoners to their West Side palaces, thinking that the day's wonders were not yet quite ended.

After a moment she stepped back, one bejeweled hand on his chest, breathing with difficulty.

"I *shouldn't* have done that!" she declared. "It was simply an irresistible impulse." She sighed and fumbled in her pocket for a cigarette. He lit it for her.

"Thank you," she said. "You see, I've always believed that a woman should have the courage of her compulsions. Still, the fact remains that I'm *deeply* in love with a *wonderful* man and I must *restrain* myself. Oh, you dear boy, you don't know who I am, do you?"

"Princess somebody."

"Oh, forget that. I'm Eve. Eve Kingslea. I'm sort of your aunt."

"Good God," he muttered.

"Not *exactly* your aunt. Let's see. My mother, Livie, married your grandfather, Wade, which made your father, poor dear Coyle, my stepbrother. So I guess I'm your stepaunt."

Philip strained to recall the intricacies of Kingslea family history. "Wade . . . he wasn't your father, was he?"

"No, no. My father . . . well, let's put it this way: Livie was *married* to an awful man named Mortimer, at least until he was eaten by sharks under the most *mysterious* circumstances, but I think my *real* father was a wonderful man who caught wolves with his bare hands. It's all very sordid and complicated and *Texan*, don't you think?"

She paced about the room. "Anyway, I'd call us kissing cousins, at the very least. I remember seeing you at Hillcrest a time or two, when you were just a toddler—I am a *few* years older than you. Do you go back to Texas? I don't. Wade and I had the most *gruesome* falling out, when I was just a girl. He didn't approve of a . . . a *fellow* I was seeing. A piano player. He had his henchmen *torture* me and exiled me to Sweet Briar, and later on, when I persisted in marching to a different drummer, he gave me twenty million dollars on the understanding that I would stay out of Texas, which was the most *amazing* bargain, because I would have gladly stayed out of Texas for *nothing*. Wouldn't you?"

"How'd you get to be a princess?" Philip asked.

"Oh, my third husband was an Italian prince. Quite penniless, of course, but with exquisite manners. At the moment I'm in love with the most wonderful Frenchman, who unfortunately is in Paris tonight. Well, my dear kinsman, we must make a decision. We *can* meet Julian at the book party, but I warn you the book is yet another biography of Virginia Wolf. Wouldn't you rather *die* than go listen to a roomful of tweedy people babble about Bloomsbury?"

"I would definitely rather stay here and drink."

"Spoken like a true Kingslea!" Eve cried and hurried off to see about dinner.

They dined quite grandly on leftovers, washed down with Perrier-Jouet, and then they sat, talking and drinking cognac, on a sofa that overlooked the lights and shadows of Central Park. Eve told him many tales of Texas, including a report on her mother's newfound passion for Art: "Livie was deep into religion for a time, you see, but the problem with religion is that it's so disgustingly *democratic*. I mean, you can have the bishop to tea and all that, but ultimately you must share God with the unwashed masses. Well, Livie breaks out in a cold sweat at the very *thought* of the masses, so in time she turned from God to Art. The advantage of Art, of course, is that you needn't *share*. If you buy a Turner or a Remington or whatever, it's by damn *yours*. Well, soon Hillcrest was lousy with Art—it looked like a *warehouse*—and that's when Livie dreamed up her museum. A shrine to her own inimitable good taste. She put up ten million and badgered Wade into doing the same, and I understand the groundbreaking is imminent. The Wade and Olivia Kingslea Museum of World Art, it will modestly be called. Of course, there are *other* museums being built in Fort Worth, so naturally the Kingslea must be the biggest and best. Don't you just *love* it?"

He told Eve about the decision he faced: to work in the

White House, to write the small book based on his *Esquire* article, or to write the big novel that Julian Swann wanted.

"Darling, it's clear to me that you should cast your lot with Julian," Eve said. "The man is a genius. He can make you rich."

"I'm not sure I'd like being rich," Philip confessed.

"What a silly thing to say! Of course you would. *Everyone* likes being rich. It's like cocaine. Even the people who don't like it *like* it—what they don't like is how *much* they like it."

Philip sipped his cognac. He was quite drunk and hadn't felt better in months. "I think part of my problem is that I was poor so long I convinced myself there was virtue in it. Besides which, I went to a little ivory-tower college where they taught you to believe in Art for Art's Sake and to scorn writers who Sold Out for filthy lucre."

"Oh, my dear Philip," Eve said. "You really must rise above romanticism and face the world as it is. Money is freedom."

He smiled out at the city's lights and abruptly yawned.

"Oh dear, I'm boring you," Eve said.

"No, but it's late. I'd better find a hotel."

"Nonsense! You'll stay in my guest room. It's upstairs, last door on the left. The bed's made. Agreed?"

Philip hesitated.

"I absolutely *promise* not to attack you," Eve added. "Not even if you *beg* me to. Will you stay?"

"Sure," he said, and she grinned and took his arm and walked him to the stairs. She seemed very small and vulnerable.

"May I ask you something?" Eve said.

"Of course."

"Do you like me?"

Her eyes were moss-green, like Livie's but without the malice. She seemed delicately poised, as if his reply meant the world to her. He thought that he did like her, in a way he was too tired and drunk to explain. He thought they had rebelled against the same thing, in different ways, that somehow they were both exiles.

"Yes," he said. "You seem . . . very sensible."

Eve looked truly grateful. "I am, you know. As sensible as anyone could be, with so much money."

He awoke at dawn and went for a walk in Central Park. In the cold morning light he kept coming back to the White

House job. The sensible thing. A good job, good salary, good contacts, good future. The only trouble was that he had tried it already, and he was sick of it, sick of working for other men, sick of writing meaningless speeches, sick of playing his piano in a whorehouse. He knew exactly what he wanted to do: to write a book. But which book? The nice little book or the not so nice big book? The novel that Julian Swann wanted was a gamble. It was swinging for the fences: you hit your home run or you struck out. You made your million or you got run out of town. Maybe laughed out of town. That novel, any novel, would be a leap into the darkness. How much easier to work in the White House, to play the game a few years, and then go write for the *Times* or *Newsweek*. Of course, everyone he knew who wrote for the *Times* or *Newsweek* was miserable and after a few drinks would tell you about the novel he would write someday, except he never wrote it because he was hooked by the security and prestige that went with being miserable. As Philip plodded along, ignoring early-morning joggers and horseback riders, he wanted to bellow out his frustration. He felt poised between the known and the unknown, the safe and the scandalous, and he thought that must have been how his grandfather felt, so many years before, when he left his farm and family to risk everything in the oil fields.

That thought would not leave him. Should he cling to shabby security when a world waited to be conquered? Could Wade Kingslea have stayed and rotted on his farm? Could he keep grinding out speeches forever? What the hell was the point of a half-life like that? In an instant his decision was made, and once it was made he knew it could not have been otherwise.

By noon he was at work on his novel.

Eve insisted that he stay and work in her guest room, and he saw no reason to return to Washington. Washington was in his mind now. Eve's guest room was small, about the size of the tool shed where he'd played with his invisible friend Roger a quarter-century before.

How to begin?

A single, virgin sheet of snow-white paper stared back at him from his typewriter, looking as cold and vast and unconquerable as the Russian steppes.

He had to get his future president to East Texas and into a

confrontation with the tycoon-to-be. But how?

He tried setting the stage. He described East Texas, the flat, arid land, the pine forests and cottonfields, the farmed-out scrub country that, by the miracle of oil, had become the richest land in the world. He spent the afternoon writing pretty words, then he cried, "Damn, damn!" and threw it all into the wastebasket. It was dull, flat. He was lousy at descriptive writing—a rose was a rose was a rose in Philip's book and a tree was a tree was a tree—and anyway, people weren't going to buy this book for the scenery.

He started over.

This time he began with his hero, now called Frank Morgan, riding the train to Texas and reflecting on his life, his conflicts with his father, his success at Princeton, his determination to prove himself in the rough-and-tumble oil fields.

Darkness had fallen over Manhattan when Philip finally got Frank into the little boomtown called Red Dog. He read over what he had written and almost wept.

It was awful.

He'd written two thousand words and nothing had *happened*. Just some college kid mulling over his life. Where was the action, the conflict, the suspense? He pitched this latest disaster into the wastebasket. Maybe he wasn't cut out to write novels. They looked so damn *easy* when you read them.

A new idea hit him like a bullet.

He imagined himself a reporter, invisible, standing on Red Dog's dusty main street one hot afternoon. A bus rattled up and a dozen passengers climbed out. Some roughnecks, loitering in front of the local hotel, eyed them. Philip stared into the darkness outside his window and the scene came into focus. Grinning, he began to write:

> The first person Frank Morgan saw when he climbed down from the bus in the boomtown called Red Dog was a swaggering young roughneck who spit tobacco juice at his feet. "Ain't he a dandy?" Brad Wilkes declared, to the vast amusement of three other grubby roustabouts. "You lost, buddy? You lookin' for Neiman-Marcus, maybe?"

Philip reread that opening three times, made a few minor changes and decided it would do. No, it wouldn't make anyone forget the opening of *Gatsby* or *A Farewell to Arms*. Yes, it echoed a thousand Western movies from his youth.

Still, it would do.

In a few sentences he had put his antagonists into conflict, and he didn't think many people would stop reading until they learned how Frank got out of this jam. And then he'd hook them with something else.

Frank cracked a joke that got him out of danger and offered Brad and his friends a drink from the bottle in his suitcase. The pragmatic Brad, thinking it useful to have a rich, educated friend, got Frank a job on his rig. On payday they got roaring drunk together. Frank taught Brad the Princeton fight song, and they sat at the rig telling each other their life stories.

Enter the girl.

What the hell was her name? Philip thought names might drive him crazy. Brad was Brad because it was short, and not entirely unlike Wade, and he was named Wilkes as homage to Hob Wilkes, who not so long before, in another world, had saved Philip's life.

Becky. The girl's name was Becky. For Becky Thatcher. Homage to the author of *Huckleberry Finn*.

But who was Becky? Was she fair or dark, shy or brazen? How did she walk and talk and laugh and kiss and do her hair?

Philip might have pondered those imponderables for hours, but instead the answer came to him in a flash.

Becky was Jenny. The vivacious, irrepressible, unforgettable Jenny of their school days. Jenny before tragedy darkened her life.

Becky visited the rig. Frank and Brad, like Huck and Tom, went a-courtin', but her wildcatter father chased Brad away and it was Frank who got the date. Brad vowed revenge.

As dawn broke over Manhattan, Frank and Brad were brawling in the main street of Red Dog. Only after Frank was bloody but triumphant did Philip sleep.

He awoke in midafternoon and went downstairs, where Eve introduced him to a suave French investment banker named Jean-Pierre, who greeted Philip warmly, clearly unconcerned that a young man had moved into his lover's apartment. They had tea and Eve asked about the novel.

"It's going great," Philip declared, and Eve insisted that they all go out to dinner to celebrate. But when Philip went upstairs to dress he made the mistake of rereading what he had written, and he was plunged into gloom.

When Eve knocked at his door and said they were ready to

go, he told her he was sorry, but he must work instead. Eve said she understood, she'd lived with a writer once.

He worked all night again, and when dawn came Sunday he'd shortened his opening chapter by half. He thought it was better but he couldn't be sure. The more he read it the more uncertain he became. Someone else might find drama and illusion in what he had written, but all he saw were choices he had made, descriptions that didn't satisfy him, characters that seemed in his gloom to be not flesh and blood but only black words on white paper.

He slept a few hours, then joined Eve and Jean-Pierre for brunch. Eve's two children were home from school for the day. Gillian, the girl, was fourteen, plump and lively, a freshman at Madeira. Andy, the boy, was tall and solemn and polite, a star of the Choate basketball team. It had snowed overnight—Philip, staring out his window into the blizzard, had seen only Texas—and Eve organized a romp in the park. It became a merry afternoon of snowmen and snowballs, followed by hot chocolate and songs around the piano. Philip stood a bit apart from the others, watching, smiling, but not singing, enjoying their happiness but mainly wondering if he could fit the afternoon into his novel.

That night, convinced he could breathe no more life into his first chapter, he began to write his outline. What had happened to Frank and Brad after their bloody brawl? How had rich, spoiled Frank become a liberal president, and penniless, tough Brad a reactionary oil tycoon? Soon, with a gusher here, a congressional campaign there, their lives began to take shape.

But what of Becky/Jenny? Was she to pine away forever in East Texas? No! Becky went East to college, dated Frank before he went off to war, and in time married him. That would be the author's gift to Jenny: in his imaginary kingdom, she would be the first lady of the land.

When Monday's dreary dawn arrived, the outline was done. Philip reread it nervously. Should it be longer? Should there be more meat on its bones? Would they know he was bluffing, that the story's ending was still a mystery to him? No matter—he couldn't endure another day of this uncertainty. Grim-faced, he pulled on his coat and plunged out into the snow. He was pacing outside Julian Swann's office when the editor arrived for work.

"Goodness, look who's here," Swann cried. "Let's do have

tea. How was your weekend?"

"Here's my outline and first chapter," Philip said and thrust a thick manila envelope into the editor's hand.

"My, that was quick," Swann said and dropped the envelope atop his desk.

"Aren't you going to read it?" Philip demanded.

The editor raised his eyes heavenward but settled down and started to read. Philip watched him like a hawk. He was braced for rejection. What the hell did it matter? Who could live like that anyway, staying up all night? He'd go to work at the White House. Writing fiction was insane.

Julian read slowly, maddeningly so, but at length he dropped the manuscript onto his desk.

"Very nice," he said and began to talk about when a contract would be ready and when Philip could expect the first payment of his advance.

Philip was indifferent to such mundane matters. "Dammit, what did you think of it?" he demanded.

Julian looked surprised. "I told you, I *like* it."

"*What* do you like? What's good about it?"

The editor made a little shrug. "It's quite vivid," he said. "It flows well. The dialogue is especially nice."

"Dialogue is easy," Philip said. "People talk short and they don't talk good."

"Ain't it the truth?" Swann said. "Now, I *do* have someone waiting, so why don't you rush back and write another chapter?"

"Don't you have any criticisms?"

"Nothing that can't wait."

"Dammit, you're my editor. Criticize me!"

"Well . . . I don't *really* agree with your ending, but we can worry about that later."

"What's wrong with my ending?"

"I don't see why Brad has to be convicted of the assassination."

"To punish the son of a bitch, of course!"

"Ah yes, a nice tidy ending. And a happy ending, too. Justice is done. But life isn't like that. Do you think they'll ever prove who killed Kennedy?"

"They might."

"I doubt it. The crime has become too politicized. Even if they had evidence, even if they had a confession, who would believe it? No, I fear that whoever plotted Kennedy's death, if anyone did beyond Oswald, will never be convicted. And, believing as I do that art should imitate life, however sordid or confusing it may be, I tend to think that Brad should also escape punishment."

Philip threw up his hands. "I need to think about it."

"Don't think *too* much," Julian cautioned. "Write!"

The weeks and months ahead were a blur, a waking dream. Philip stayed in his little cell overlooking Central Park and wrote. He slept at odd hours, fitfully, and when he was hungry or restless he walked down to Times Square, stopped in Nathan's for chili or oysters or fried chicken, and all the while studied the people who flowed by, seeking some detail of face or manner, some scrap of dialogue, to steal for his book. His mother wrote that she and Asa were going to Acapulco, that Skip had announced for Congress, and that Alice had won two more tournaments, but their distant adventures were only dim shadows flickering on the walls of his cave; his mother and Jenny were less real to him than the fictional counterparts of them that he shaped and molded each day. He measured time not by the calendar but by the chapters that piled up on his desk and by the decades that passed in the world he was creating, as Brad rose to great wealth and Frank to great power.

One fine April day he deposited the first half of his novel on Julian's desk. He had some money coming then, but what he wanted most was to know if his sprawling, brawling fictional fantasy made any sense to anyone on earth besides himself.

He wondered how long he would have to wait for Julian's response. Eve had told him horror stories of editors who kept writers waiting weeks, even months, before they read their manuscripts. But at nine the next morning his phone rang.

"Well, you kept me up until three," Julian announced.

"And?"

"It's good."

"Just good?"

"Quite good, in spots."

"You don't like it!"

"No, I do, very much."

"What's wrong with it?"

"Philip, *nothing* is wrong with it. It reads like the wind."

"Dammit, tell me what you think!"

"Well, if you insist, I think you could loosen up a bit."

"What the hell does *that* mean?"

"Well, the courtship of Frank and Becky *is* rather chaste, and the fact that they produce children seems nothing short of miraculous. And Brad seems hardly aware of the fair sex at all."

"The book isn't *about* sex," Philip protested.

"No, the book is about power, but power and sex tend to be rather closely associated, don't you think?"

Philip scowled into the phone. As usual, he thought the editor was right. "I guess writing about sex embarrasses me."

"Of course it does," Julian said. "Because we're taught that it may be all right to *do* it, but we must never *talk* about it. But don't you see, in books we can talk about it and pretend it's fiction; I mean, we know more about Molly Bloom's sex life than we do about the women we sleep with. I urge you not to be *too* tasteful."

And so, as spring marched with bright flags through the park beneath his window, Philip stayed in his cell, loosened up a bit, and kept writing.

One day that spring, Eve's two children knocked at his door. Philip had come to feel great affection for Andy and Gillian and to share Eve's pride in them. "Perhaps I've been silly and selfish and amoral," Eve told him one night, "but my children have always come first with me. I stayed with one man for two years who bored me *stiff*, because he was so darn good with the kids. Those children are the justification of an otherwise frivolous life."

Andy and Gillian wanted to talk about Vietnam. Andy had done some research. "It's a civil war, you see," he said solemnly. "The French were driven out. Why would we want to send soldiers there?" Philip could not bring himself to give his honest opinion, which was that Johnson was sending troops to Vietnam because it was an election year and he wasn't about to let Barry Goldwater accuse him of "losing Vietnam." Instead, hating his own cowardice, he promised to call a friend at the White House and have him send up the speeches and policy papers that, in theory, would make sense of U.S. policy. The two teenagers seemed pleased, but Philip was upset by their visit. He resented the outer world's intrusion on the private world he was creating, where he controlled all wars, deaths, and other disasters.

President Frank Morgan's years in politics had convinced him of something that the real-life Wade Kingslea had decided years before: that either government would control oil or oil would control government. Coming to office in a time of fast-rising unemployment, and in the wake of sordid campaign-finance scandals involving the oil industry, Morgan shocked the political world by proposing legislation to nationalize the oil industry.

Morgan's old enemy and political arch-rival, Bradley Wilkes, headed the Petroleum Council, which poured tens of millions of dollars into a media campaign intended not only to defeat Morgan's legislation but to destroy Morgan; impeachment was its final goal. In the face of this opposition, President Morgan crisscrossed America, proclaiming to town meetings and huge outdoor rallies that the Morgan plan would mean more jobs, lower taxes, cheaper fuel, and less political corruption. His eloquence worked wonders: the polls began to show public opinion swinging his way.

Then Brad Wilkes challenged the president to "bring his socialistic road show to Texas and see what honest men think about it."

Morgan's closest adviser, Kevin O'Neal, warned that a trip to Texas would be embarrassing, if not dangerous. Becky Morgan, too, begged her husband not to go. She knew Brad Wilkes and feared for Frank's safety.

Frank Morgan went to Texas.

In city after city, huge, enthusiastic crowds greeted him. David Brinkley, reporting after the Fort Worth rally, declared, "To these eyes, it looks as if President Morgan may bring off the political upset of the century—this crusading David may defeat the Goliath of Big Oil, and in its own backyard of Texas!"

Brad Wilkes watched that report in a rage, for he knew it was true: frightened congressmen were deserting oil's cause in droves, rather than face the wrath of the voters. The president was coming to Brad Wilkes' unnamed hometown the next day for a huge, final rally. Wilkes, facing political defeat and personal humiliation at the hands of a man he had hated for thirty years, grimly gave his old friend and chief of security, Willard Pendleton, the go-ahead for their long-planned Option B, wherein two former CIA assassins had agreed to kill the president for five million dollars each.

That much—the politics, the conspiracy—had been easy. Even the assassination was easy to write, if painful. The hard part came after the murder.

Someone had to pursue Brad and his conspiracy, doggedly, vainly, but with some distant hope of success. But who? One possibility was a fictional Hob Wilkes, a renegade FBI agent who feared that a senile J. Edgar Hoover had sanctioned the conspiracy. Another candidate was Kevin O'Neal, the president's close friend, who in Philip's mind was a mixture of Harry Flynn and Robert Kennedy. A third contender was young Sam Wilkes, Brad Wilkes' estranged son, who had been raised by his mother after Brad deserted them to begin his quest for oil.

Philip wrote draft after draft, only to see each one end as a blizzard of crumpled paper on the floor of his cell. The ending wouldn't come. The author paced, cursed, mumbled, neglected to eat, sleep, shave, or bathe. His life had become quite insane, of course. In his more rational moments he realized that. He had spent four months in a small room agonizing over people who didn't exist but who had become more real to him than the flesh-and-blood figures he could glimpse down in Central Park.

And he loved it. He'd never been so happy. He knew a poem of John Donne's in which the poet said his love "makes one little room an everywhere." That was how Philip felt about his writing; it made his borrowed cell above Central Park an everywhere. He recalled his grandfather's boast that he was a lord of the earth. He understood that now, that fierce, raging pride of self, for there were days when he believed that his overflowing imagination made him, too, as much as Wade Kingslea, as much as any mortal, a lord of the earth.

Julian called one morning with unexpected good news: "I've sold the English rights to your novel for a very respectable sum."

"Sold the English rights? I haven't finished writing the book!"

"That's true. But the editor was in New York and I let him read the first half. He was *most* impressed and offered us ten thousand dollars for your English hardcover and paperback rights. I could have gotten more later, but I wanted a sale now, to start the momentum rolling. This is just the beginning, my boy. Keep working!"

Julian's call left Philip drunk with happiness. Someone actually liked his book, someone besides Julian, who he feared was demented anyway. His book would be published in England! The home of Shakespeare and Chaucer and Andrew Marvell and Christopher Marlowe and George Orwell and Graham Greene and Somerset Maugham—the most civilized damn nation on earth!

God save the Queen!

One day late in June, to Philip's amazement, he finished his book.

For weeks that day had eluded him. There was always one more scene that cried out, "Improve me!" Then, abruptly, there was nothing more he could see to improve. Better writers might have polished this or tightened that, but Philip was finished.

Cradling his bundle in his arms like a baby, grinning inanely at pretty girls on the sidewalk, laughing madly at trees and taxicabs, he raced to Wide World Books and entrusted his offspring to that good and wise man, Julian Swann.

He had never been so glad to be rid of anything in his life.

He spent the rest of the day walking the streets, reestablishing contact with the real world, staring at faces, savoring humanity's bright colors and bizarre ways, reminding himself that people laughed and cried and fornicated and died by the millions without giving one damn about the book he had written.

Of course, once his book was published, all that would change.

One blistering midsummer day Philip met Julian for lunch at "21."

"Good news, my boy," Julian announced when their drinks came. "I've sold your German rights for five thousand dollars."

"German?"

"The Germans feel a strange affinity for Texas," Julian explained. "Also, much more importantly, we have a nibble from Hollywood."

"How serious a nibble?"

"I think we could get ten thousand dollars for an option

right now, against perhaps fifty thousand if the movie is ever made. And if we hold off until publication, and the book is the success we hope, those figures could double or triple."

"Who's the offer from?"

"A man named Feldman. You wouldn't know him, but he's produced a good many successful pictures. He has a reputation for being a bit . . . how shall I put this?"

"Shady?"

"Sensationalistic, let's say."

"Hold off. And I want to do the screenplay."

The editor frowned. "That could be quite a sticking point, you know."

"I don't want some hack screwing up my book."

"Philip, you're a novelist. As novelists go, you're relatively sane. People who make movies are insane. And they can drive people like you insane very quickly. Believe me, I've seen it happen."

Philip shrugged. "Hold off awhile," he said. "What else is new?"

"We really must decide about your title today."

"I keep going back and forth," Philip admitted. "I've thought about 'The Plot' and 'The Conspiracy' and 'The Rivals.'"

"Too vague, too dull," Julian said. "'The Plot' could be a gardening book, couldn't it? We must find something sexy, something eye-catching."

"Maybe something about power," Philip suggested. "How about 'Of Pride and Power'?"

Julian dismissed the idea with a wave of his hand. "What is this book *about?*" he demanded. "What is its *essence?*"

Philip shrugged. "Power. Ambition. Greed. Violence. Love. Hate. Texas. America."

"No, no," Julian said. "That's too vague. *This is a novel about a plot to kill a president!*"

Philip shrugged. That seemed to him self-evident.

"Wait, that may be it!" Julian cried. "'The Plot to Kill the President'! How's *that* for a title?"

Philip was speechless.

"No, no, that's not quite it," Julian declared. "Wait, it's coming." He was gazing upward, a man possessed. "I have it! 'To Kill a President.' That, my boy, is a title that will sell books!" He waved to the maître d'. "Champagne," he demanded.

"Wait a minute," Philip protested. "I'm not sure I like that title."

Julian peered at him in disbelief. "Not like it? Why in the world not?"

"Dammit, it's . . . bald. Blatant."

"Your title, Philip, is no place for subtlety," Julian said. "And it *is* a book about a plot to kill a president, isn't it?"

"Yes, but . . ."

"Of course, it's your book, and you can call it 'The Flowers in Spring, Tra-la,' if you insist. But please consider one thing. We are hoping that a paperback house will pay a great deal of money for your book, and I can assure you there will be far more interest in a novel called 'To Kill a President' than in one called 'The Plot' or those other things you mentioned. That has nothing to do with the quality of your novel and everything to do with the nature of mass-market book sales. People stroll up to the book rack and they aren't saying, 'Well where is that nice young Philip Kingslea's book?' They're simply looking for something to read on the plane, or to take Uncle Charlie in the hospital, and they're confronted with hundreds of books on that rack, all crying out, 'Buy me!' Well, are those good people more likely to reach out and choose a novel called 'To Kill a President' or one called 'The Plot'? The question answers itself, doesn't it?"

Philip nodded unhappily.

"Believe me, Philip, your excellent book has found an excellent title."

The waiter poured their champagne, and Julian proposed a toast.

" 'To Kill a President,' " he said proudly.

Philip grinned. "To sell a book," he said and drank deeply.

The next morning she called, beckoned, and of course he answered her call, joyously, and yet with part of him asking why, with the future so bright, he let himself be drawn back into the past.

They met in the lobby of her hotel, the Pierre, a palace designed to nurture the world's most beautiful women, and amid its galaxy of sleek models and haughty heiresses no star shined more brightly than Jenny Kingslea.

She was eye-catching, heart-stopping, in blue silk and raw pearls. He touched her hand and felt rich.

"We could eat here," she suggested.

"I know a good place."

"I have a car."

"We can walk."

"Let's take the car—I may want it after lunch."

Complications, compromises: his restaurant, her car.

Her car was a Kingslea Oil limousine. Philip settled beside her in its soft leather and wondered if the polite young driver was a Kingslea Oil spy. But that was her problem. He had no problems anymore.

He took her to Clos Normand, a good and unpretentious place. It was sweet to glide past the bar and see men's heads turn with military precision as his Jenny passed by.

They sipped vodka and talked about his book. "P.K. lights up the sky," she said, her face aglow. "You see, you didn't need Princeton."

"That's right," he said. "All I needed was Texas."

"Am I in your book?" she demanded.

He blushed. She grinned. "Will I like me?"

"I loved you."

She touched his hand. "Any other familiar faces?"

"A certain oil tycoon may not be my biggest fan."

"Wade?"

"Who else?"

"Good! I hope you roast him."

"Dear old Gramps?"

"He's an awful man, and getting worse."

Philip was alert, curious. "How so?"

"Oh, God, where to begin? He made a pass at me, a serious pass, not a month after Skip and I were married. He's decided he hates Johnson, and he's pouring millions into the Goldwater campaign. He's keeping some twenty-year-old dancer he found in New Orleans, and when he's not shacked up with her he's out raving about Communists. He fired one of his Mexican gardeners last month because he decided he was a spy for Fidel Castro. I truly think he's insane. Except that by definition, a man with a billion dollars can't be insane, can he?"

"And his dear wife?"

"Just as crazy. He raves about politics and she raves about her museum. Livie's Louvre, we call it. I dread the grand opening. She wants LBJ to speak—Wade's livid about that, of course—and Billy Graham to preach and the UT Marching Band to play. What can I say? Culture comes to Cowtown."

"Skip?"

"Running for Congress and probably going to win."

"Do you campaign?"

"Token appearances."

"If he was smart he'd use you all he could."

"He doesn't want me around. He's sleeping with a girl from his advertising agency."

"The fool."

"It doesn't matter. It's all falling apart."

"You said you might have a baby."

"It was too cynical."

He took her hand. "So what are you going to do?"

Jenny finished her vodka and Philip nodded to the waiter for more.

"I don't want to spoil his campaign. Maybe next year I'll fold my tent and silently slip away. It's so awful—we married for all the wrong reasons. Him out of guilt and me out of fear. And people think we're so glamorous. Jesus!"

He saw a woman staring at them. He guessed he and Jenny looked glamorous, too. He wondered if all the beautiful people you saw in these fine restaurants were as confused, as hopelessly screwed-up, as they were.

She grinned. "I want us to have a happy lunch. I'll tell you all the gossip."

They drank and ate well, while Jenny told tales of scandal and stupidity, avarice and intrigue, the occasional triumphs and endless follies of their generation as it lurched toward thirty. She even reported a scurrilous story about him: word had spread in Fort Worth that he was living in incestuous sin with Eve. He loved that. In fact, he had known Eve as the most generous of friends, the most devoted of mothers, and the most faithful of lovers to Jean-Pierre. But who would believe that?

While they were having coffee, two tall, elegant women, models perhaps, passed their table. One was saying, "So he says to me, 'I bet you never got laid by a guy in argyle socks before.' Jeez, talk about no class! And it wasn't even true."

Philip and Jenny exploded with laughter. Finally, when they were quiet again she said, "I have a fantasy, P.K."

"Tell me."

"You may not like it."

"I'll like it."

"It's about you and me."

"I know. I have it too, sometimes."

"I keep thinking that, after I leave Skip, maybe you and I could . . ."—she lowered her eyes—". . . give it a try."

The moment had come, as he always knew it would, and he variously wanted to hold her, to cry, to laugh, and to race out of the restaurant and out of her life forever. Was that love?

"I don't mean to put you on the spot . . ."

"You're not . . ."

". . . I guess I'm well-worn baggage by now. . ."

"No . . ."

". . . but you know everything about me, and I know everything about you, and I respect you so much, what you've done with your life. And I . . . well, I think that finally I'm going to pull my life together. I tried running away and I tried marrying rich and the next time I'm going to try love."

She blinked back tears and his own eyes burned. "I've known a lot of women," he said. "Some really fine women. But I keep coming back to you."

"See me as I am now," she said. "Not the way I used to be."

The waiter brought the check and Philip paid it.

"What do you think we should do?" Philip asked her when the waiter had gone. They were the last customers.

"I can't do anything until after Skip's election. I'm Caesar's wife until then."

He nodded. "I'll be all tied up in knots until my book comes out."

"I think we'll have to wait a little longer, but please call me. And maybe next year . . ."

Outside, her limousine glowed in the afternoon sun. She touched his face. "Can you stand a tiny criticism?"

"As long as it's not literary."

"That shirt, P.K. That coat. You're going to be a famous author. We really must do something about you."

His garments turned to tatters at her glance. "I haven't thought much about clothes this year," he admitted.

"Come shopping with me. Let me buy you some presents."

He laughed. "Jenny, it happens that I have twenty thousand dollars in the bank and more pouring in every day. In the immortal words of Jett Rink, I am one rich son of a bitch. Lead on—*I'll* buy the presents!"

Her limousine glided as if by magic to the most sumptuous shops on Fifth Avenue, a block that Jenny knew as intimately as they'd once known the five-and-dimes of Camp Bowie

Boulevard. She led him by the hand, from one lavish emporium to another, until she made the afternoon a breakthrough for him, a rite of passage. For years he had feared spending money, unable to escape the time when there had been so little. Now Jenny taught him the joys of profligacy. Under her gentle prodding he bought Sulka ties and Cardin shirts, Bally shoes and Tiffany cuff links, silk pajamas and calfskin luggage, suede jackets and sharkskin belts. When he would protest, "But I don't *need* that," she would say, "That isn't the question—do you *want* it?"

When guilt finally overcame him, she persuaded him to buy gifts for others, so he started again, choosing Godiva chocolates and Steuben glass for his mother, a Swiss watch for Asa, a T. Jones jacket for Alice, an antique chastity belt and a leather-bound set of Proust for Eve, a Caran d'Ache lighter for Jean-Pierre, a jade heart for Gillian, the complete Hank Williams for Andy. The only one he bought nothing for was Jenny; "Not yet," she would say, "not yet." Finally, as the stores closed, she led him out to her waiting limousine. He had spent more money in three hours than he had earned in his three years as a newspaper reporter and loved every minute of it.

They drove back to the Pierre, her limousine piled high with his loot; he thought of his Quaker ancestors, heading west in an overflowing covered wagon, a century before. Jenny took him into the Pierre's small bar for a celebratory drink. Exhausted from their orgy of buying, they drank in silence, until she smiled proudly, brushed his hair back from his brow, and said, "I want my present now." He took her hand and they slipped into an elevator and rose up quickly to her cool, shadowy suite, their sanctuary in the world of the rich, and in the sweet summer twilight her bed was a magic carpet that carried him higher and higher, into a golden sky, into the future, into the unknown.

Just after Labor Day, Philip and Julian met for lunch. Philip was tanned and relaxed after spending a month in Key West while assorted editors, typesetters, and publicists worried about *To Kill a President*.

"Your health, my boy," Julian said, hoisting his Bloody Mary. "I do have a bit of good news."

"What?"

"Well, a few more foreign sales, if those interest you."

Philip shrugged. Foreign sales were small potatoes now, loose change. "What about the movie deal?"

"We now have an offer of fifty thousand dollars for an option, and from a good producer."

"Do they want me to do the screenplay?"

Julian lifted his hands helplessly. "What can I say? You've never written a screenplay."

"I'd never written a novel either."

"Philip, I urge you, as a friend, to take the money and run. Who knows if the movie will be made? You must focus on your next novel."

But Philip was in no hurry to talk about his next novel. He figured his price was going up every day he waited. "What's new on the paperback sale?" he asked.

"We continue to have a great deal of interest. Of course, we'd have more interest if we had a movie sale."

Philip sighed. Was he just being stubborn? Did he really want to write a screenplay? "Okay, okay, I'll think about it," he said.

"Excellent," Julian replied.

A raven-haired young woman stopped at their table and spoke to Julian with great animation and a soft Mississippi accent. Julian introduced her as Elizabeth Ashley. Philip rose, touched her hand, and found himself incapable of speech. She told them about her new movie, and Julian urged her to keep a diary, with an eye toward a future book.

"That's the most beautiful woman I've ever seen," Philip said when the actress went to join three men at a corner table.

"Yes, isn't she lovely?" Julian said. "Now, I'm still dickering with the Literary Guild, but I fear that John O'Hara's latest has edged you out for the main selection and we'll have to settle for a featured alternate."

"I can stand being shot down by O'Hara."

"That's the spirit, my boy. Time is on your side. Now, moving on, our publicity people are anxious to talk to you."

"About what?"

"Your television appearances, for one thing. And also possible items they can plant in the gossip columns."

"What kind of items?"

"Oh, is Becky Morgan based on Jackie Kennedy, that sort of thing."

"Dammit, Becky is based on my sixth-grade sweetheart in Texas. I don't want crap like that in the gossip columns!"

"Philip, advance copies of your book will reach the newspapers any day, and there is going to be a great deal of 'crap like that.' The fact is that you are Wade Kingslea's grandson, and you worked for President Kennedy, and you've written a novel in which an oil millionaire very much like Kingslea plots the murder of a president rather like Kennedy. You shouldn't underestimate the controversy that lies ahead."

"I just don't think we should encourage it. This is a damn good novel. It can stand on its own."

"Yes, it's a good novel. And it is also a *roman à clef*—a quite honorable literary *genre*—involving some very famous people. Let's face it, Philip, we wouldn't be printing a first edition of fifty thousand, or expecting a six-figure paperback sale, if your name was Philip Smith. You really can't have it both ways, you know."

Philip poked at his salad and tried to think. He knew that what Julian said was true. For months, locked in his fantasy world, he had pretended he was writing for himself alone. He thought you couldn't worry about what people would say or you'd never write anything. But now reality was at hand. He was not innocent of newspapers and controversies. There was going to be one hell of a flap.

"Tell your publicity people to call me," he said. "I'll wallow in the mud with them."

"Good lad," Julian said and waved for more drinks.

"My first lover was a black man, you know."

Philip and Eve had met for lunch at the Plaza's Palm Court, and they lingered into the late afternoon as Eve talked about her girlhood. He loved to hear her talk, to hear all women talk. It was incredible the things they would tell you.

"He was Wade's chauffeur at Hillcrest," she continued. "He lived in a room over the garage. Wilson was his name. He'd been a blues guitar player in his youth—he taught Robert Johnson how to play. He was such a gentle man. I used to go up to his room and he taught me some chords on the guitar. Naturally, one thing led to another. I was fourteen and not exactly *shy*. He taught me *everything*. I never had any problem with sex after that. I had problems with *society* but never with sex. Of all the men I've slept with since then, there have only been two—no, three—who could compare with Wilson as lovers. I can't tell you how I cried when he died. I mean, Wade and Livie could be devoured by wild dogs tomorrow and I wouldn't shed one tear, but Wilson's death broke my heart. My God, the things he knew about women!"

Philip tried to place Wilson. He remembered his mother telling him about the first time she'd met Coyle, when he took her to a party at Hillcrest after a football game in 1935. Coyle got drunk and a chauffeur had driven her back to TCU. He guessed that had been Wilson.

Life was like that, a jigsaw puzzle, and if you had time and luck enough you found that all the pieces fit.

One day a New York *Times* reporter made the trek to Philip's suite at the Algonquin. He was about thirty and looked as if he'd been born at Brooks Brothers. He began by saying how much he'd enjoyed *To Kill a President*. With Philip thus disarmed, he proceeded: "But I'm wondering, Mr. Kingslea, if Bradley Wilkes isn't a thinly disguised portrait of your grandfather and if, therefore, you aren't in effect charging Wade Kingslea with complicity in the Kennedy assassination without having any evidence to support such a charge."

Philip swallowed hard and declared that his book was fiction, not fact. The reporter kept pressing him about the similarities between the fictional Wilkes and the real-life Kingslea. Philip hated it, because at one level what the reporter was saying was so clearly true. He was forced to deny the obvious, if only because of the libel laws.

The *Times* reporter was most cordial as he departed, but Philip was left with an unhappy feeling that he was about to be charged with the literary crime of the century.

He spent the day roaming the streets, counting the hours, like a man awaiting his execution. He thought he would rather face a firing squad than be written about in a newspaper, even the *Times*. He had been in the business and he remembered how many times he had savaged some poor fool just for the fun of it.

At eleven that night he was in Times Square, snatching up a copy of the first edition of the *Times* and racing to the neon glare outside Nathan's to see what damage had been done. He groaned when he saw the headline, two columns wide, on the front page, just below the fold:

Fact, Fiction Mingle in Novel
Of Presidential Assassination

The story began by saying that Texas oilman Wade Kingslea's grandson, a former aide to President Kennedy, had written a novel in which an oilman who resembled Kingslea plotted the assassination of a president much like Kennedy. "Although the twenty-eight-year-old author insists his book is pure fiction," the article continued, "his novel contains many parallels with real people and events," and it went on to give a lengthy summary of the book's plot. The story concluded, "Julian Swann, Wide World's flamboyant editor in chief, is betting that *To Kill a President* will soar to best-sellerdom on the wings of widespread public suspicion of the Warren Commission's conclusion that Lee Harvey Oswald acted alone in the Kennedy assassination. A great many book-buyers, Swann believes, will not make fine distinctions between fact and fiction as they read Kingslea's fast-paced, suspenseful *roman à clef*."

Philip read the story over three times before the unexpected truth sank in: it was wonderful, and it would sell thousands of books. He let out a whoop of triumph, one that went quite unnoticed in the mad carnival of Times Square, and hurried to find a telephone to call Julian.

The New York *Times* was delivered to Skip and Jenny Kingslea's home each day, along with the old, reliable *Star-Telegram,* and Jenny therefore was surprised one morning, as she had coffee in her Chinese-red study, to read on the front page of the *Times* about her lover's newfound celebrity.

Reading the story a second time, she thought back to a time when she was a cheerleader, standing on the WHHS stage at a pep rally, berating Philip and his scruffy friends on the back row of the auditorium for not cheering the team. Jenny savored the memory. Who would have thought that one day she'd be reading about Philip on the front page of the *Times?* Or should she have known, even then, that anyone that smart and proud and angry would wind up famous, one way or another?

"The painters are here, Mrs. Kingslea."

The new maid hovered in the doorway.

"Show them to the kitchen," Jenny said curtly.

"More coffee, ma'm?"

"No, nothing."

Jenny turned away. She hated the girl. She'd told Skip a

hundred times she wouldn't have Mexican help but he'd brought this girl home anyway. Jenny thought she was there to spy on her.

She threw down the *Times* in frustration. Philip's success, his freedom, mocked the chaos and captivity of her own life. She had come home and done the things you were supposed to do, the charities and tennis and football games. She had tried to build a new life among her old friends, but it hadn't worked. She was different. She saw that now. Not because of Mexico. In a crazy, terrible way, Mexico had helped her, by showing her she was different. She'd been different all along, like Philip. But all those years she'd been playing cheerleader and homecoming queen, playing the roles they taught you to play, he'd been marching to a different drummer. And he'd succeeded—he'd broken through. She remembered graduation night when he'd raved about them as Scott and Zelda. Well, he'd done his part. Now it was her turn. Not to be Zelda. That was not the best analogy. But to break free of the past, to get to where he was. But could she? Could she just walk away? Her husband was running for Congress. And his grandfather, that rich, dangerous old man who thought he owned them, was already suspicious of her. She was afraid of Wade. She had been so terribly wrong to marry Skip. She saw now that to marry money was a bargain with the devil, one you could only lose. She was alone now, in a mansion that was a prison, and the past was quicksand sucking at her feet.

Jenny screamed.

When she got control of herself, she reached for the telephone. The story said he was staying at the Algonquin. She had to talk to him. She had to break through. She had to escape.

"P.K., you're famous," she said. "I read the *Times*."

Her hands trembled, but her voice was as clear as a bell.

"Where are you?" he asked.

"At home."

"Oh. Yeah, I'm famous. Or infamous. Watch for me in tomorrow's *Star-Telegram*. Their guy just called. It was like he was interviewing a child molester. I seem to have pricked the civic pride."

"When will you come to Fort Worth?"

"In a couple of weeks, I think. We're waiting to hear from the *Today Show*. They don't usually do fiction, but I may be scandalous enough to get on. After that I'll come to Texas for interviews and talk shows. I dread it, but we figure the controversy will sell books."

"I have to talk to you," she said.

"I know. I want to see you."

"Philip, it's *important.*"

Her cry for help began to pierce his self-absorption. "Is something wrong?" he asked.

"Yes. Everything's wrong."

"What is it?"

"I can't talk on the phone. Just come see me. Please. Hurry."

"I will," he promised. "Just as soon as I do the *Today Show.*"

The Manhattan bookstores were selling out of *To Kill a President* as fast as they got copies. Something was happening that Philip had not dreamed of when he wrote his novel. He had written out of his own pain and frustration over the assassination, but he had struck a nerve with thousands of Americans who shared his anger and his suspicions. When he visited bookstores, people pumped his hand and said things like "Keep up the good work!" No one cared if his book was well or ill written—all that mattered was being the right book at the right time.

Julian called on a Friday afternoon to report that the *Today Show* had scheduled him on Monday morning.

Philip had a date that night, with a girl named Jill who worked in Wide World's publicity office. She took him to Elaine's, the uptown literary hangout. They joined some people, and it was all right, but Philip's mind was on Jenny and his book and the *Today Show,* and he drank too much and almost got into a fight with an English writer who made some snotty remark about his novel. Finally he wandered out onto Second Avenue, not sure where he was going, but Jill caught up with him and hailed a cab and got him safely back to the Algonquin. "Get some rest," she urged. "You've got to look good on the tube."

He spent Saturday morning touring Fifth Avenue bookstores, signing books, savoring his tiny share of the world's celebrity. That afternoon he was back in his hotel room, pad and pencil in hand, listing the points he intended to make on the *Today Show,* when the phone rang.

It was Jenny. She was crying.

"What's wrong?"

"Everything! Can't you come home? Right now? Tonight?"

"Jenny, I've got the *Today Show* on Monday morning. I'll fly down there after that. What's *wrong?*"

"I'm going to have a baby," she said. "That's part of it."

He knew what was coming, even before she said it.

"It happened that day at the Pierre. But you don't . . ."

"Jenny, look, I'll . . ."

"It's not your problem. Either way, I'll handle it."

"What do you mean, either way?"

"Either I'll have the baby or I won't, but either way you won't have to worry. I can raise a child. If I leave Skip, I'll have buckets of money. Oh God, I shouldn't say that on the phone. I think they're tapping my phone. The maid is spying on me. Philip, I'm afraid. He's crazy."

"Who? What are you talking about?"

"Wade. He was here this morning. He knows I saw you in New York. He thinks Skip is going to lose his election and he blames me. He threatened me. I'm afraid of him."

"Look, why don't you fly up here? Stay with me for a while."

"I won't run from him. Can't you fly down tonight?"

He thought for a moment. He could fly down that evening, and back the next, and still make the Monday morning television show. But it was crazy. If anything went wrong, he'd blow his biggest interview. Part of him loved her, wanted to fly to her, to comfort her, but another part of him thought her demands were unreasonable. Probably she was upset and imagining things. If she was afraid of Wade, she could call her father instead of asking him to fly halfway across the country.

"Jenny, I can't do it," he told her. "I'll fly down Monday. Just hang on. Monday night we'll work everything out."

"Please hurry," she cried. "I'm so afraid."

For all his certitude, the fear in her voice was real, and it chilled him to the bone.

He was interviewed on the *Today Show* by a woman who'd once played Jane in the Tarzan movies.

The two of them sat in facing chairs on a brightly lit set, as if they were in someone's cozy living room, but in fact they looked out onto a huge dark cavern where burly men in blue jeans pushed big cameras around. And somewhere in that darkness was America.

He could dimly remember Jane, as he thought of her, from the Saturday matinees of his youth, when she was up on the silver screen, being saved from crocodiles by Johnny Weissmuller. She had not read his book, and her questions were so inane that he had a wild desire, midway through the interview, to pound his chest, let out a mighty jungle howl, and declare, "Me Tarzan. You Jane. You shut the fuck up."

But he stuck to selling books.

JANE: Isn't there more fact than fiction in your book?

TARZAN: *To Kill a President* is fiction, but it's based on fact. We did have a president assassinated a year ago. My novel shows one way it could have happened.

JANE: The oilman behind the conspiracy in your novel, Brad Wilkes—wasn't he based on your grandfather, Wade Kingslea?

TARZAN: I invented Brad Wilkes. My grandfather invented himself.

JANE: But haven't you used your grandfather's fame to sell your book?

TARZAN: I don't think that many people care about me or him. I think people do care about the Kennedy assassination and want to know the truth about it, and that's why they're buying my book, because it presents one possible version of the truth.

JANE: Do you consider your President Frank Morgan to be a portrait of President Kennedy?

TARZAN: I don't think I could create a fictional character as eloquent and brave and inspiring as John Kennedy was.

JANE: But haven't you accused your grandfather of conspiring to kill President Kennedy?

TARZAN: I don't know who killed Kennedy. I wish I did. But I don't believe Oswald acted alone. If my book makes people talk and think and demand the whole story, then I'm proud to have written it.

As the interview ended, Philip was staring defiantly into twenty million American homes, a friend of truth, a foe of conspiracy, and he imagined he heard cash registers ringing from sea to shining sea.

A mighty storm swept across North Texas that morning. As Wade Kingslea watched the *Today Show* in his upstairs study, gale winds howled outside his mansion and thunder rattled his windows. No less a storm raged inside the mansion as the interview ended. Kingslea heaved himself up from his chair, flung his coffee mug at the television set, and charged like a wild bull through his home, howling with rage, knocking over lamps and chairs, shattering vases and mirrors, vowing blood-curdling revenge. The servants, fearing their master more than the elements, fled into the storm. Even the mistress of the house locked herself in her bedroom, checked the silver-plated .32 she kept beside her bed, and did not breathe easily until she saw, outside her window, her husband striding out of the house to his waiting Fleetwood. He walked through the storm, head high, oblivious to the driving rain and bolts of lightning, and Livie thought he looked like a king, a mad, doomed king. As his glistening chariot roared away she stood at the window, peering into the blue and silver storm, wondering what she could do to save herself, to save them all, from his terrible wrath.

Julian Swann brimmed with delight as he met Philip outside the studio. "A brilliant performance," he declared.

They went for coffee. The editor was beaming. "My boy, I have one more bit of excitement for you today."

"What?"

"I can't break the news just yet—not until I'm sure—but if you'll come to my office at three this afternoon, I think I will have a very pleasant surprise for you."

Philip didn't press him. He guessed it was something on either the movie deal or a book-club sale. Then, as they were leaving the restaurant, he said, "Oh, damn!"

"Is something *wrong?*" Julian asked.

Philip shook his head. "I was supposed to fly to Texas this morning," he said. "But I can get a later plane."

He went back to his hotel and tried to call Jenny, but there wasn't any answer. He slept for an hour, then went for a walk, up to Central Park. Two things were on his mind: money and Jenny. That made him laugh; the two were not unrelated. If you made enough money you got the prizes, the glittering things, the girl of your dreams. And the money was pouring in. He didn't know how much yet. The Wide World people were starting to hint about a "six-figure" paperback sale. And the movie deal was yet to be made. He was going to make a hell of a lot of money from this book. Not millions, like his grandfather had made, but still a lot. The strange part was, he didn't know what he'd spend it on. There wasn't anything he wanted.

Except Jenny.

It wasn't simple anymore. He'd learned she wasn't the only woman in the world. He'd gotten a letter from Chrissie that week. She was coming home from Peru and wanted to see him. And he wanted to see her. Chrissie was wonderful. But she wasn't Jenny. Jenny had something special for him, a magic, that went back as far as he could remember, to two kids playing in a sandbox. Philip thought of Liz Ashley, the actress Julian had introduced him to one day. She'd haunted him ever since. He'd wanted to see her again. Finally he'd told himself that that was crazy, a fantasy. Jenny was the one he wanted. He loved her in a different way now. In high school she'd been distant, unattainable, a symbol of his dreams of glory. He'd needed her then, if only her friendship. Now she needed him and he was glad. He wanted her to need him and he wanted to love her and protect her and help them both escape the madness of the past.

But what if she *was* pregnant?

That had thrown him at first. He'd fought so hard for his freedom, fought against being tied down. He was only starting to understand that nothing could tie him down now. He had the money to go anywhere, to live anywhere, to be free. All Jenny had to do was get the quickest possible divorce. Then they'd be married, she'd have the baby, and they could settle down anywhere they chose. It abruptly came to him that there could be nothing better in the world than to have a child, his and Jenny's child, and to bring it up the way a child should be brought up. That was the greatest challenge on earth. The thought of raising a child with Jenny electrified him. Philip began to sprint across Central Park, yelling, laughing, waving his arms like a madman. People stopped and stared, but he only laughed louder. Let them think he had gone crazy; he knew he had suddenly gone sane.

At three o'clock he was ushered into Julian's office. He felt impatient. Whatever business the editor had, Philip wanted to get it over with and catch the late plane to Fort Worth. He'd tried again to reach Jenny and this time the line was busy. Several men were waiting in the editor's office. Philip recognized all but one as Wide World executives. Julian introduced the other man as Jay Burton, an independent film producer.

Julian was beaming. "Philip, we and Mr. Burton have just reached tentative agreement on one of the best film sales I've ever seen."

The producer pumped Philip's hand. He was a reasonable-looking fellow. "It's a fine novel," he said. "And it's going to make a fine picture." He and Julian outlined the terms of the agreement: an initial fifty thousand dollars, against a total of one hundred fifty thousand when the picture was completed, plus two percent of the producer's net profits. And Philip was to have the option of writing the first draft of the screenplay. There were more details, but Philip lost interest.

"I'll sign it now," he said.

"You don't *have* to," Julian reminded him.

"You haven't been wrong yet," Philip said and scribbled his name. There were handshakes all around, and Julian said, "Let me just add that today I'm ordering a third printing of an additional twenty thousand copies of *To Kill a President*. I believe we're due a celebration!"

Soon the office was filled with Wide World's editors and publicists. Champagne began flowing and music playing. People pumped Philip's hand and hugged him. His book was headed for the top of the best-seller list, they assured him. Everyone was giddy. Julian brought Wide World's president, a man named Morrison, by for an introduction, and produced a batch of rave reviews. It was all so insane. He might make a half-million dollars off this book. A book that had been conceived in this very office not ten months before. A book he hadn't even wanted to write.

Philip downed a glass of champagne and grabbed another one. A Beatles record was playing, adding to the magic of the moment, and people were dancing.

"Love Me Do."

Oh yeah!

He was rich.

He broke into laughter and went off to call Jenny, but her line was still busy.

Eve appeared and gave him a kiss. Julian whispered that he'd made a dinner reservation for several of them.

Jill, the girl he'd taken out the previous weekend, whispered her congratulations. "I'm sorry about the other night," he said.

She laughed. "You're not the first drunk writer I ever saw."

"Join us for dinner. Julian has a celebration planned."

"I'm not invited."

"I'm the guest of honor, and you're invited."

Enjoying Jill, he thought again of Jenny. He slipped away and tried her number again; it was still busy. He called his mother, but no one answered. *What the hell are they doing down there?*

He drank more champagne. The president of Wide World threw his arm around Philip's shoulders and began to make a speech. Philip broke free and danced with Jill. The afternoon seemed timeless, golden.

A moment came when Philip stepped away from the others and stared out at a distant, flaming sunset. America seemed spread out before him, streets and buildings and cities like toys on a playground.

Jill touched his arm. "Julian says we should be going."

"Are you ready?"

"I have to go to my office."

"I'll go with you."

Her office was about the size of the room where he'd written his novel. Jill fixed her face in a mirror on the back of the door. Philip sat at her desk. His head was spinning from the champagne.

"My well came in today," he said. "My gusher."

"I know."

"Do you want to have dinner with these people?"

"Sure. Don't you?"

"I'd rather go get a pizza with you."

"That would be nice. But this is important to Julian. Besides, you may as well get to know the president of the company. You're an important author now."

"Screw the president of the company," Philip said. "I don't need him. I'm the goose who lays the golden eggs."

She touched his shoulder. "Be sweet," she said.

Be sweet. Such good advice. Don't let it make you hard and arrogant, like Skip, like all those bastards you grew up hating.

He lowered his head to her desk and started to sob.

"I'm scared," he whispered.

"You ought to be," she said.

He washed his face and they went back to Julian's office. Just a few people were left, finishing the champagne, listening to the Beatles.

As they started to leave, Julian's phone rang. "Ah, fame,"

he said and answered it. Then, to Philip, "It's for you."

Philip expected a reporter. Instead, it was one of the two people he wanted to talk to.

"I tried to call you," he said. "Listen . . ."

"Philip? I have to tell you something."

"I just signed a great movie deal. I get fifty thousand dollars up front, and . . ."

"Something terrible has . . ."

"I want to treat you and Asa to a trip to Europe."

"For God's sake listen to me! Something terrible has happened."

His blood ran cold. He thought of Asa, Alice, car wrecks, plane crashes, the world's rough justice. *Beware the sun, my child, its rays are hot and they will melt your wings!*

"What is it, Mother?"

"Jenny. . ." She was crying.

The Beatles were singing a Chuck Berry song, a fifties hymn to bobbysox and drive-ins, to jukeboxes and cheerleaders, to lost innocence and eternal youth. Julian, seeing Philip's face, cut off the music and hustled people out of the office.

"Jenny . . . she's . . ."

"For God's sake, Mother, what's wrong?"

Louise summoned all her strength and forced her message out in one terrible burst:

"Wade killed her. He blew her head off."

CHAPTER THREE

Leroy Thomas (Roy) Sykes, Tarrant County's district attorney, grew up in the part of Fort Worth that was most often called "out in Poly." Poly was the unfashionable east side of town that took its name from Polytechnic High School. If you grew up out in Poly in the Depression, the way Roy Sykes did, the mansions and millionaires that reputedly lurked across town in enclaves like River Crest and Westover Hills were as distant as the moon.

Sports were Roy's passion in those days. In 1941, his senior year, he was a stalwart of the Poly Parrots' football and baseball teams. The day after Pearl Harbor he and all his friends enlisted in the Marine Corps, and four years later he came marching home with a chestful of medals. He had made an easy transition from the combat of sports to the combat of war, and he came home hungry for more combat and not having the slightest idea where to find it.

One day, downtown to buy some shoes at Leonard Brothers, he took refuge from a thunderstorm in the Tarrant County courthouse. He chanced upon the trial of a 90-pound beautician who was accused of shooting her 270-pound husband between the eyes, hacking his body into manageable hunks, placing those hunks in grocery bags, loading those bags into the trunk of her LaSalle, and driving in the middle of the night to Z. Boaz Park, where she was caught redhanded while digging a suspiciously large hole.

The woman's lawyer, a dapper old fellow with a moustache and yellow suspenders, passionately declared that the deceased was a drunken brute who beat his client like a gong, that she had fired only in fear of her life, and that the subsequent dismemberment had resulted from a combination of temporary insanity and a broken heart.

Roy Sykes, watching this performance, was seized by a white-hot Baptist rage such as he had not known since his first encounter with the Japanese. He would have liked nothing better than to throttle both the murderous beautician and her smooth-talking lawyer. When the jury quickly brought back a verdict of guilty, Roy let out a whoop of approval that got him ejected from the courtroom.

No matter. He was back the next day, and every day after that, enraptured by the criminal courtroom's endless tales of greed, violence, and duplicity. He came to view the courtroom as a battlefield in the war between Good and Evil, a conflict not unlike his hand-to-hand combat with the yellow-devil Japs in the South Pacific. A decision quickly followed: he would devote his life to dispensing swift, sure justice to all those sorry sons of bitches who raped, robbed, murdered, swindled, and otherwise inconvenienced the God-fearing, law-abiding people of Texas. He enrolled in night law school, passed the state bar exam with the highest grade ever recorded in Fort Worth, and in 1951 presented himself to the district attorney for employment.

He was turned down flat.

The district attorney, a wily old political fox with a great and much-admired mane of white hair, blithely announced that he had no openings. It was a lie. He hired two young lawyers the next week. The two new men's grades on the bar exam, combined, did not equal Roy Sykes', but they were graduates of the University of Texas law school and they came equipped with rich wives and country club connections. Young nobodies from Poly with night-school diplomas were supposed to chase ambulances, defend brown and black people, and otherwise settle for whatever crumbs were left over.

Roy Sykes had a better idea.

He began seeking out the clients that no one else wanted. The poorest of the poor. The most guilty and least deserving wretches in the jail. A man who chopped off his wife's head and placed it atop his TV set, like a trophy. A woman who had poisoned at least six husbands. Child molesters, thrill killers, car-bombers—Roy Sykes represented them all. He went before juries and he wept, he pleaded, he cajoled, he lied, bullied, and browbeat, he pulled every underhanded trick known to the legal profession, and in the process he won acquittals in eight straight highly publicized capital cases. He also made himself a legend. Mad Dog Sykes, they called him. By the time he won a confessed baby raper's acquittal, several citizen's groups were circulating recall petitions, seeking to have the district attorney ousted for incompetence. Thus it was that the white-maned DA visited the young lawyer's one-room, walk-up office one day.

"Young man, what's your price?" the DA demanded.

Roy took no pleasure in his victory. He hated what he had been doing. He had started drinking, for the first time in his life. The week before, after he'd won an acquittal for a black pimp who had drowned two whores in his bathtub, the happy defendant had tried to shake Roy's hand and he'd gone crazy and beaten his client half to death.

"I want a job," he told the DA.

The white-maned law enforcer, who had twenty thousand dollars cash in the pocket of his frock coat, could not believe his ears.

"Come again?"

"A job on your staff. Like I asked for before. I want to put the bastards in, not keep 'em out."

"You're hired," the DA said.

For several years thereafter, Roy Sykes was a happy man.

His troubles began when his predecessor was indicted for tax evasion. In the confusion that surrounded the scandal the local Democratic political machine faltered, and Roy Sykes, whose honesty was legend, was elected to replace him.

Alas, within months the honest, zealous young DA was under fire from all directions. Local liberals, a small but vocal band, protested that Roy seemed unaware that the Constitution granted certain rights to suspected criminals. The police turned against him when he prosecuted two of their brethren for burglarizing a liquor store. Reporters were outraged because he preferred to try his cases in the courtroom rather than in the newspapers. The city's movers and shakers complained —after he prosecuted a state senator's son and an oilman's wife—that Roy seemed not to understand that different standards must be applied to the misdeeds of the rich and the poor. Finally, there was a general sense among Fort Worth's better people, who were increasingly concerned with museums, high fashion, highbrow music, and *haute cuisine*, that Roy Sykes was just too damn much of a tobacco-chewing, grammar-mangling Poly Parrot to remain a top public official in their increasingly sophisticated city.

At the very moment when the news came of Jenny Kingslea's death, Roy Sykes was thinking about Jenny. He never told anybody that, because it sounded too weird, but it was true. He was sitting with his boots up on his desk drinking coffee and reading a story in the *Star-Telegram* about Skip Kingslea's race for Congress. The gist of the story was that Skip had a shot at losing, despite his money and his looks and his celebrity, because he somewhat lacked the common touch. Roy Sykes devoutly hoped that Skip got his ass whipped. He didn't give a damn for any of the Kingsleas. Except Jenny. Jenny was a pearl. He could remember every time he'd met her. He remembered her straight-ahead smile and the way she made you feel like you were the finest son of a bitch on earth. Why the hell would a girl like that marry a prick like Skip Kingslea? Roy Sykes was pondering that mystery when his secretary raced in screaming that somebody had been murdered at Skip Kingslea's house.

Roy bolted from his office and roared west at eighty miles an hour. He was halfway to Ridglea when he told himself to slow down, to watch his step, because any murder involving the richest family in town could only be a time bomb, begging to go off in his face.

He slid to a stop in front of Skip and Jenny's big, colonial-style house, raced past a horde of howling reporters, and confronted Joe Donner, the chief of detectives.

"What the hell?" Roy demanded.

The detective nodded toward a large, formal living room. The coroner and a police photographer edged back out of the way. Jenny lay on a Persian rug before the marble fireplace. She wore jeans, sneakers, and an old TCU sweatshirt. A pink and jagged hole gaped in what had been the most beautiful face of a generation.

Roy shut his eyes and said a silent prayer. His prayer became a vow: he would make some bastard burn for this.

"Whatta you got?" he demanded of Donner.

"The old man's in the next room."

"What about Skip?"

"He's on his way. Would you believe he was giving a live TV interview when it happened? It's the alibi of the century."

"Yeah, I'd believe it," Roy said. "Anybody else in the house?"

"The maid. A Mexican girl. Says she was upstairs and didn't hear a thing until the gun went off. At eleven, she says, when the news was on the radio. Then she hid in a closet."

"Let's talk to the old man," Roy said, and they crossed the hall to the Chinese-red study.

Wade Kingslea was sitting in a scarlet armchair like a king on a throne. He wore a suede jacket and an open collar. There was blood on his shirt and his right eye was swollen shut.

"Hello, Roy," the old man said.

"Have you had medical attention, sir?" Roy asked.

"Don't worry about me. Just tell me what I can do to help you catch the killer."

"Tell me what happened."

"Gladly. I was at my office this morning when I decided to have a talk with Skip. I drove out around eleven, in the middle of the storm. When I got to the door I heard screams. I ran inside and found Jenny struggling with a man in a dark suit. He was about thirty, with reddish hair and sharp features. Six feet tall, at least. We began to struggle. He drew a gun from his pocket. A .44, I'd say. Jenny seized him from behind and we were all three fighting for the gun. Somehow it went off and Jenny was hit. The man jerked the gun free and clubbed me with it, then ran to the back of the house. I stopped to examine Jenny but she was clearly beyond help. Thinking the man might be lurking in the back of the house, I went out the front door and drove to the Ridglea Country Club to call police. The man must have escaped out the back door. Have you found him yet?"

"No sir, not yet."

Kingslea's face reddened. "Well, by God, you'd better set up roadblocks and patrol the airports and do whatever it takes until you find him!"

"One other question, Mr. Kingslea," Roy Sykes said. "As you left the house, did you see anyone?"

The oilman scowled. "I may have passed a man. What does it matter?"

"Only because we'll be looking for others who might have seen the killer flee," Roy said. "Maybe you'd like to go to the hospital now. We can have someone drive you."

Kingslea rose to his feet. "I'll drive myself," he said. "You boys get cracking and find the killer."

The old man marched out the door. Roy Sykes sighed.

"Any sign of the gun?"

"Nope."

"You got any bright ideas?"

"Maybe we better do like the man said and arrest every red-haired son of a bitch we see."

Amid a new outcry from the reporters on the lawn, Skip Kingslea burst in the front door, ran to the living room, and fell to his knees beside his dead wife. "Oh God, oh God," he moaned.

As a person and as a politician, Skip Kingslea inspired the most violent extremes of emotion. People either loved or hated Skip, either believed his every word or none at all. The district attorney and the chief of detectives, as they studied the young millionaire's show of grief, tended toward the skeptical side.

"Make you a deal," Sykes muttered. "You take him and I'll take them wolves outside."

"Some deal," Donner grumbled.

Roy Sykes marched out to meet the press. It was the only part of his job he hated. There were twenty reporters on the lawn and more arriving every minute.

"Jenny Kingslea, Skip's wife, was killed at approximately eleven o'clock this morning," Roy began. He gave them the facts, without unnecessary gore or speculation. He repeated Wade Kingslea's story of the intruder and the struggle. When he finished, the reporters began shouting questions, demanding the gore and speculation he had denied them. He sparred with them a minute, until they suddenly lost all interest in what he was saying.

The grieving husband was in the doorway, his face pale as death.

"Who did it, Skip?"

"What's this do to your campaign?"

"Are you withdrawing?"

"Did she have any enemies?"

Skip stared at the reporters until they fell silent and the only sounds were the whirr of the television cameras and the distant rumble of thunder. "I can't think about politics now," he said finally. "My heart is in there with Jenny."

Cameras clicked wildly and reporters shouted a score of questions, but Skip stumbled back into his house.

"Slick," Donner muttered to Sykes. "Ten bucks says he wins big."

The reporters hurried away to file their stories. Roy thought he'd better swing by the Ridglea Country Club and check the old man's story from that end. Just as he was entering his Ford, a car stopped across the street and a stocky man of fifty with close-cropped gray hair got out. Roy reached out to the man, feeling emotions he rarely allowed himself.

"Dusty, I'm truly sorry," he said. "If there's anything I can do."

Roy Sykes could remember watching Dusty Rhodes play for the Cats, before the war. He'd been a customer of his gas station for a decade. He could remember Jenny working at the station, as a teenager, and her and Dusty pitching a baseball on slow afternoons.

"There's something you can do, Roy," Dusty Rhodes said bitterly. His dark eyes burned in a ravaged face. "You can arrest Wade Kingslea."

Roy's blood ran cold. "What do you mean?"

"Just what I said. She called me Saturday night and asked me to come get her. She said she was leaving Skip. The old man came in while she was packing. He was ranting and raving, saying she couldn't leave Skip. He called her a whore. I took a swing at him, but she begged me just to get her out of there. She spent Saturday night and Sunday with me. This morning she got up and watched that other Kingslea boy on television, then said she was coming back here to get some of her clothes. He must have found her here and killed her. He was here, wasn't he? That's what the radio said."

"He was here," Roy admitted.

"And you let him go?"

"Dusty, he says he walked in and found a stranger attacking her, and she was shot in a struggle."

The father's body seemed to swell up, as if it could not contain his rage. "Arrest him, Roy," he said quietly. "Arrest him or I'll kill him."

Roy Sykes slumped behind the wheel in despair. How the hell did he get into a mess like this? He was cursing his fate when someone tapped on the car window.

An elderly man in bifocals peered in. Roy rolled down the window. "Mr. Sykes?" The man had a polite, precise, almost timid way about him. "I'm Howard Garfield. I'm afraid I need to talk to you."

Sykes sighed and told the gentleman to climb in.

"I believe we met once," Garfield said. "When you spoke to the Kiwanis last year."

"Of course." He thought the man was an insurance executive, something like that. "What can I do for you?"

"I'm afraid I was a witness today, to something terrible. When I saw you arrive I knew it was time to tell my story to the proper authority."

"What did you see?"

"I'm recently retired, and I had a golf game scheduled this morning, but of course the storm canceled that for me. I puttered around the house and watched television, and then I saw Mr. Kingslea park in the driveway and go into Skip's house. A few minutes later I heard a gunshot from the direction of the Kingslea house. Naturally I went to the window and looked out. Finally I put on my raincoat, thinking I'd better investigate. As I crossed my yard, Mr. Kingslea came out of the house. He walked right up to me. It was pouring rain, and I don't think he noticed me until I said, 'What's wrong, Mr. Kingslea?'"

Howard Garfield slipped off his rain-wet bifocals and stared at Roy Sykes with wide, disbelieving eyes. "He said to me, 'Get out of my way or I'll kill you too!' And I looked down and saw the gun in his hand."

That rips it, Roy thought, but what he said, very calmly, was, "Then what happened, Mr. Garfield?"

"He got in his car and drove away."

Roy started his engine. "Go back home, Mr. Garfield," he said. "I'll have someone pick you up soon. We need to take your statement." The older man climbed unhappily from the car and Roy roared off. He had so much to do now. He had to talk to the people at the country club. He had to find the damn gun. He had to get some men around Wade Kingslea so Dusty Rhodes didn't kill him before the law had its chance.

Roy laughed aloud. His life would be a lot simpler if Dusty did shoot the old bastard. Right now the case he had wasn't worth a damn. It was the kind of case where it's easy to indict and hard to convict, your classic no-win case. Roy thought of an old saying, that if you struck at a king you must kill him. He was about to strike at the richest man in Texas, and he hoped to hell he could kill him, because if he didn't he'd be an ex-DA faster than you could say M-O-N-E-Y.

Philip's plane got him to Fort Worth just in time to confront his grandfather on the courthouse steps and to be knocked down by the old man's bodyguards for his trouble. As Wade Kingslea's several hundred admirers began to drift away, Philip got up, dusted himself off, and went to find the district attorney's office.

The district attorney was not in the best of moods. He was not happy that the judge had so blithely freed Kingslea without bond, nor was he pleased by the spectacle of several hundred citizens gathering to cheer the man accused of a bloody and senseless crime.

When Roy's secretary said there was a Philip Kingslea to see him, he laughed. *What now?*

The young man's first words were, "Do you remember me?"

"Sure, I almost put your ass in jail, ten or eleven years ago, for gettin' too friendly with your English teacher."

"Journalism teacher."

"Beg pardon. Plus, a couple of months later, you broke Skip Kingslea's nose. You still fuckin' and fightin'?"

"I quit fighting."

"Smart boy," Sykes said. "You wrote yourself a book, too, didn't you? Pissed a lot of folks off. Hell, my wife can't hardly read and she bought a copy after she heard how awful it was supposed to be. Me, I'm a Mickey Spillane fan myself. So what's on your mind, young Mr. Kingslea?"

"I've got evidence against my grandfather."

Roy Sykes' eyes narrowed. "Spit it out," he said.

"Jenny and I were friends. She called me Saturday, at my hotel in New York. She said she was afraid of Wade Kingslea. She said he'd threatened her, called her names. She asked me to come down here."

"Did she say why he was mad at her?"

"He thought she was going to leave Skip and that would hurt Skip's political future. She was terrified. She thought the telephone was tapped. She thought the maid was spying on her."

"Damn interesting," the DA said.

"I'll testify to it," Philip said. "If it'll help hang Wade Kingslea."

"Let me ask you a couple of things. You'd known Jenny how long?"

"Since we were kids. All through school. And in Washington, before she married Skip."

"And you'd seen her since her marriage?"

Philip hesitated. "Once or twice."

"And you kept in touch by phone?"

"That's right."

"And she called you at your hotel on Saturday, in New York, to tell you she was afraid."

"That's right."

"Why do you reckon, if she's in Fort Worth and afraid of Wade Kingslea, and her father lives maybe five miles away, she calls you in New York?"

"I told you, we were friends."

"Were you more than friends, maybe?"

Philip reddened. "What kind of a question is that?"

"It's the kind of question you'll get on the witness stand if you testify against Wade Kingslea."

"I won't answer a question like that. It's not relevant."

"The judge decides what's relevant. You're under oath. And I'd advise you to think twice before you perjure yourself."

"Okay, we were . . . more than just friends."

"And her husband and grandfather knew about it?"

Philip remembered the Kingslea Oil chauffeur in New York, the last time he saw her. "They might have."

"So your grandfather hates you, because of that damn book of yours, and he thinks you're gonna run off with Skip's wife and screw up his boy's big plans for the future, and then on Monday morning he sees you on the television and blows his stack and drives over there and has a fight with her and kills her. Is that what you think happened?"

"Yes," Philip said. "But look, what I want to testify to is the threats. What she told me. How she was afraid of him. Not the personal stuff. You're the lawyer—you've got to keep that stuff off the record."

"The law doesn't let you pick and choose what you say on the witness stand."

"You'll try, won't you?"

"I'll try to put Wade Kingslea's ass in the electric chair. Is that what you want?"

"Maybe I could help you. Maybe I could be an unofficial investigator for you."

"Yeah, and maybe you'd turn up dead in a ditch, too. What I want you to do is make yourself scarce. Leave me a phone number. Don't come back unless the other side subpoenas you."

Roy Sykes gave Philip his unlisted number and walked him out to the corridor. Back in his office, he took a chew of tobacco and grinned. Young Mr. Philip Kingslea didn't seem like a bad fellow, as Kingsleas went. He didn't know a thing about the law, of course, and he therefore had one hell of a rude awakening ahead.

Four reporters ambushed Philip in the lobby of his hotel. He fought past them, to the safety of his room, where scores of messages were waiting. He returned a call to Wide World's publicity director, who could barely contain herself. The wire services, she explained, had carried a story and picture of Philip's confrontation with his grandfather on the courthouse steps.

"The networks are all calling," the publicist declared. "The *Today Show* wants you back—and them we owe. That fellow at the *Times*—he's looking for you. Everybody wants you. I think you'd better fly up, then we'll sort it all out."

"Millie, I'm a witness in a murder trial."

"No problem. Our lawyers can coach you. You can talk around it."

"Millie, a friend of mine was killed. I'm not going to use it to sell books. No interviews. Period."

"Philip, it's not just selling books. It's *you* I care about. If you snub the *Times* and the *Today Show,* people who've helped you, they're going to remember it the next time out."

"Don't you understand? Somebody's dead."

"Don't *you* understand? You can have the biggest book of the year, if you quit acting like a Boy Scout. You're a writer, aren't you?"

"I'm a writer but I'm not a damn ghoul!" he yelled and hung up.

The phone kept ringing until he told the switchboard to cut it off. A reporter from some tabloid banged on his door, yelling that he would pay five thousand dollars for the exclusive rights to his story. Philip realized he had to hide out until the trial. He thought of Key West, Nashville, Europe. Then he realized there was a better place to go. He spent the afternoon driving northwest, across the prairie, into the past.

Goodwill, even in its glory days, had been in the middle of nowhere. It was located between Abilene and Amarillo, on those lonesome plains where for centuries Indians hunted buffalo, where for a few years white men hunted oil, and where now few travelers stopped unless, like Philip, their destination was yesteryear.

At three thirty Philip passed a sign that proclaimed: "See the Wade Kingslea Museum of Oil History—Refreshments—Tours—Climb the Oil Rig—Follow Signs to Goodwill!"

Philip half-remembered a clipping his mother had sent. Wade Kingslea had built some kind of memorial to himself up at Goodwill.

By four he had arrived at Norway, the county seat, and entered the county courthouse. He located the county clerk, an elderly woman with bright orange hair, and told her he had come to seek information on a murder in Goodwill in 1920.

The woman broke into laughter.

"Don't you have records?" he asked.

"In the first place, there was too many murders in Goodwill to keep track of," the woman said. "In the second place, we had a fire in 1931. So I reckon you're plumb out of luck. Sorry."

"I'm a reporter," he said. "I'm gathering information about Wade Kingslea, back in those days."

"Well, why didn't you say so?" the woman declared. "Have you been out to the Oil Museum?"

Philip admitted he had not.

"That's the place to start. I reckon Will Clinkscale is the world's number-one expert on the subject of Mr. Wade Kingslea." She peered at the clock over the door. "If you hurry, you can make it before he closes."

After its boomtown days, Goodwill had slowly become a ghost town, then after forty years had been revived by the coming of the Oil Museum. The Excelsior Hotel and Gusher Saloon had been restored and now catered not to wildcatters and roustabouts but to the tourists who flocked to the museum.

Philip followed the signs south out of Goodwill. After a few miles he came over a low hill and suddenly saw an oil derrick looming above the prairie and beside it the handsome, domed museum. The derrick was the old-fashioned, squat, wooden kind, a faithful reproduction of Louella Booker #2, the rig that had produced the original Kingslea-Festus gusher in the fall of 1920. It differed from the original rig only in that wooden stairs had been installed in it, leading up to a platform that circled the rig, some fifty feet above the ground, so that visitors could gaze out at the barren prairie that once had yielded up such awesome wealth to Wade Kingslea and other giants of the past.

A few cars were parked in the museum's lot. Inside the glass doors, Philip encountered a man in his fifties who had the generous belly and florid complexion of a serious drinker. "Only ten minutes till closing time, friend," the man announced.

"I'd like to look around. What's the charge?"

"No charge for ten minutes. Help yourself."

Philip stepped into a large, graceful room filled with photographs and exhibits. There were old photographs of Goodwill in its boomtown days, including one of Wade Kingslea, Uncle Billy Festus, and two young women grinning on the steps of the Gusher Saloon. There were ingenious working models of oil rigs that showed the rotary bits cutting through the various layers of the earth and even simulated the oil gushing to the surface. Philip stopped in an alcove of lifesize pictures of his grandfather. The earliest picture showed Wade in his early twenties, on the steps of a farmhouse with his young sons, Hoyt and Coyle, beside him, squinting into the sun. Other pictures traced his career forward: with Clint Murchison in the twenties, in a tuxedo at his wedding to Livie, and finally with a procession of the famous and powerful, from Will Rogers and Babe Ruth to Roosevelt and Churchill. Philip studied the pictures gravely, trying to understand his grandfather, trying to reconcile the greatness with the madness.

He noticed the fat man beside him. "I guess my ten minutes are up," he said.

"Take your time," the man said. "I'm Will Clinkscale. I reckon you're Philip."

Philip looked at the man again. He had bright, shrewd eyes. "That's right," he said.

"Take your time. I'll be up front. I usually wet my whistle about this time, and I don't mind company."

Philip pressed a button and a recorded voice said, "Howdy, friends, this exhibit will tell you about the fabulous life and times of Wade Kingslea, the tall Texan . . ."

Philip found Will Clinkscale sipping bourbon and listening to the evening news. He waved Philip into a folding chair and poured him a glass.

"Your health, sir," he said. "What brings you to these god-forsaken parts?"

"Curiosity."

"Ha! Curiosity killed the cat. I hear you stopped by the courthouse to see if Wade ever killed anybody."

"News travels fast."

"Not much news up this way. Well, you're barking up the wrong tree. He killed three fellows all right, no doubt about that, but I understand the sheriff gave him a medal, because those three were in bad need of killing. Say, how'd you like to climb the derrick with me? There ought to be a fair-to-middling sunset."

They mounted the stairs slowly, in deference to Clinkscale's bulk, and when they finally reached the platform, Philip was stunned by the beauty of the sunset burning across the ragged Texas plains.

"Nice, ain't it?" Clinkscale said. "Real basic, you might say."

"What're you doing here, Mr. Clinkscale?" Philip asked.

"Call me Will. What I'm doing here is I'm kind of a half-ass historian. Taught for a while, down at West Texas State, and wrote me a couple of little books—nothing like *your* book, of course . . ."

"A book's a book, Will."

"Well, some *do* make more money. Anyway, I proposed this museum to your grandfather, five years ago, and he went for it in a big way and put up the money. There's not a finer museum this size in the country. Means a lot to people up this way, to think there's something more to their lives than just tumbleweed and coyotes. Anyway, he asked me to be the curator here, and in my spare time I'm working on another book."

"About what?"

"What else? Your grandfather. His life story. Of course, there've been some other books, but they were mostly by liberals who hated him for being rich. I never minded him being rich. I'd be rich myself, if I could figure out a way."

"Is he cooperating with you?"

"In a manner of speaking. I'd say your grandfather is more interested in mythology than facts at this point, but he talks to me. I'd like to sit down and talk to you one day. This book of yours is a darn interesting twist."

A red-orange sun floated on the horizon, setting the clouds aflame. "How do you feel about my book?" Philip asked.

"To tell you the truth, it made me mad as hell—but it never bored me."

Philip grinned. "I'll accept that verdict."

"You see," the older man continued, "all you're really doing is adding to the legend. You wanted to hurt Wade by saying he killed Kennedy, and you sure pissed him off, but you didn't really hurt him. Heck, I've been thinking of adding a copy of your book to the exhibit."

"What about the murder charge?"

Will Clinkscale sighed. "What can I say? I *hope* he didn't do it. But he could have. It wouldn't be out of character. I think he's a prisoner of his own mythology now. I don't think he can control all that he does. America treated him like God for forty years. So should we be surprised if he ignores our laws and kills somebody?"

The sun dropped swiftly out of sight, a chill swept through the evening air, and they climbed down from the derrick. "Can you join me for dinner?" Philip asked.

"I appreciate the offer, but I need to work tonight, or this book'll never get written."

"I'll come back tomorrow," Philip said. "Your museum deserves more than ten minutes."

"Your grandfather deserves more than ten minutes," Will said. They went to their cars. "I was thinking, you might want to know more about your family history, and I could help you."

"How do you mean?"

"Well, for example, how much do you know about Christina Pridemore?"

Philip tried to remember. "She was one of the Quakers who came to Texas after the Civil War, wasn't she? His grandmother?"

"And your great-great-grandmother. A fine, brave girl, God rest her. How would you like to read her diary?"

"You've *got* it?"

"I told you, son, I'm a historian."

March 21, 1866
We began our long journey to Texas today. We were up at dawn, saying our last good-byes to dear friends in Goose Creek and soon we were off, our battered old platform-spring wagon stuffed fuller than a Christmas turkey. It is evening now, and we are camped south of Middleburg. Perhaps, Dear Diary, I should begin this narrative by looking back, to the world we are leaving behind.

We are three on this journey. My husband, Ebon, my sister, Sarah, and myself, Christina. We leave behind our beloved, plundered Virginia, our Paradise Lost! Sarah and I grew up as the Wade sisters of Goose Creek. Our Quaker ancestors came down from Pennsylvania a hundred years ago and founded the villages of Goose Creek and Waterford. Growing up, Sarah and I wanted for nothing, unaware that our pastoral paradise was doomed. Our undoing, of course, was the institution of slavery. Our two Quaker villages were tiny islands of Loyalty in a great sea of Rebellion. In the spring of 1861, Virginia voted overwhelmingly to leave our beloved Union. Our young Quaker men were forced to flee, lest they be conscripted into the Rebel Army. Among the departed were two most dear to Sarah and me: my Ebon Pridemore and her Harry Janney. I cannot describe the years that followed. The two armies sweeping back and forth across our poor, ravished valley. Our father carried off to die in a Rebel prison. Our mother following him, victim of a broken heart. Sarry marrying brave, handsome Harry Janney, and he so soon dead in a Georgia swamp.

My only consolation, after four years of loss, was this: my kind, loving Ebon, having spent the war years as a nurse in a Union hospital near Baltimore, finally returned safe to me and brought with him a most unexpected wedding gift. In his hospital, among the countless men he succored with prayers and morphine, was a Texan named Jack Dalton, who in his final delirium whispered of a farm beside a river, of rich soil and high grass, and with his last ounce of strength wrote a will, leaving that farm to Ebon!

I will not detail the debate that followed. Enough to say that I was the timid mouse but that finally, when I saw that light in Ebon's eyes when he spoke of this Texas farm, this dream he had embraced, I put away my fears. And so, at last, we are on the road.

April 27

I have ignored Thee, Dear Diary, but with cause. As we moved down the Carolina Trail, through endless Virginia and into rugged Tennessee, the spring rains have given us a multitude of muddy roads to mire in and swollen creeks to ford. For every good day of twenty or twenty-five miles, there is a hard day of five miles or two or none at all. We sleep with Friends when we can find them, and at the roadside when we cannot. We are slowed not only by the elements but by Ebon's good nature. His years in the military hospital left him with as much medical knowledge (if I may boast) as many doctors, and our wagon spends many hours stationary under a shade tree while Dr. Ebon sews up cuts, sets broken bones, and ministers to assorted bellyaches. Two nights ago, as we crossed into Tennessee, he delivered his first baby! I saw the child rise in the lamplight, heard its first proud howl—a baby! God's Gift! Man's Hope!—and I ached for my own baby, mine and Ebon's.

June 7

The Arkansas roads are primitive, and our going has been slow. Last night, as we sat by our campfire beside a pine forest, two men rode up. They said they were returning from the Indian Country of Montana. Sarah and I retired to the wagon, but Ebon sat by the fire talking to the men. I could not help overhearing. The visitors soon spoke of Indians. Educated men, they hated the Indians with a passion that can scarcely be imagined. They described unbelievable outrages and atrocities they had seen in Montana, Utah, and elsewhere. One of them told of a time when Blackfeet Indians had surrounded his wagon train. He said, "Looked like they was gonna overrun us. All us men took an oath that we'd shoot our women and children before we'd let the Injuns take 'em alive. And believe me, Mr. Pridemore, God in Heaven would have understood!"

Can such horrors exist? Dear and Loving Father, protect us!

July 3

We crossed into Texas on the first day of July. We peered about for Paradise but saw only the dusty road and weeds and wildflowers and scrub pine and an orange sun poised above a horizon that seemed as wide and distant as eternity.

July 6

Three days ago we topped a hill and beheld a miracle: two-score wagons drawn up in a circle beside a small, muddy creek. This proved to be a Fourth of July Celebration. Travellers had gathered from miles around, greeting old friends from the road and making new friends. Food was brought forth and shared, and there followed a joyous evening of fiddle-playing, square-dancing and song-singing.

That night as the moon rose, we heard explosions nearby. I asked Ebon if it was fireworks. Another man replied, "Mr. Colt's fireworks, I'd say." In truth, a second Celebration had begun a quarter-mile down from ours. Ours was a circle of Families; theirs of Drifters and Cowboys. Through the night we heard gunfire, howling, and raucous laughter, some of it feminine.

The Fourth dawned bright and fiercely hot. In the morning the children paraded about and prizes were given for Best

Costume and Most Eloquent Declamation. After lunch came Entertainment! A troupe of players, bound for New Orleans, had chanced upon our campsite, and they performed mime, juggling, feats of magic, and for a grand finale, their version of the final act of Hamlet. *It was, Dear Diary, a* Hamlet *like none other, long on Swordplay and short on Poetry, but Immensely Popular with Old and Young alike.*

Still, our day was to be spoiled. At sunset, as we Travellers were observing a brief, patriotic ceremony, gathered around our Nation's Flag and singing our National Anthem, four men with guns swaggered up, obviously drunk.

"What do you want here?" someone asked them.

"Some of us ain't real fond of that there flag," one of the gunmen said. He was wearing the tattered remains of a Confederate uniform, and a red bandanna at his throat.

I could not contain myself. "It is thy country's flag!" I declared.

"Texas is my country," the man said, and began to tear down our beloved flag. I tried to stop him but he pushed me to the ground. Ebon ran forward but the man slashed his face with his gun.

"Drop it," said one of our men, a farmer from Ohio. He and two others had stepped from behind a wagon with shotguns at the ready. The Confederate spun toward them and the shotguns exploded and inflicted terrible and Fatal wounds. The other troublemakers were swiftly disarmed. They dragged their lifeless companion away, leaving a trail of blood behind.

I wanted to leave, that very minute, but Ebon said we would be safer there with the others. We spent the evening singing beloved old hymns around a campfire while men with shotguns stood guard.

July 28

Dallas was a pleasant place. Its main street boasted two churches, three banks, and a milliner's shop that was Much Admired by Sarah and me. Its owner asked where we were going. We said Fort Worth was our next stop. The man became quite agitated. "What's decent folk like you going there for?" he demanded. "If the Injuns don't get you, the cowboys will. Stay here in Dallas, Folks. We're building us a decent Christian community. Those people in Fort Worth don't care 'bout nothing except guns and cows and barbed-wire whiskey!"

July 30

Fort Worth, although only thirty miles farther west, is very unlike Dallas. Its main street is more inclined toward saloons than churches, and its citizens more often cowboys than clerks or clergymen, but the atmosphere is warm and hospitable. I had to laugh when I saw pigs rooting on the main street, and cowboys sleeping away their Excesses outside the Silver Dollar saloon.

We left Fort Worth early this morning. At the livery stable, Ebon confirmed our directions with an old man who was watering our mules.

"You heading north with them women?" the man asked.

Ebon said that was correct.

"Couldn't get me up thar," the old one declared. "Thar's Injuns up thar."

"We'll trust in the Lord," Ebon said mildly.

"You Baptist?"

"Quaker."

The old man broke into malicious laughter, and declared that we should continue on the road we were on, "and then turn north at the Abolitionist Tree."

"The what?" I asked. I thought I had misunderstood.

"The Abolitionist Tree," the man said with a cackle. "You'll know it when you git thar."

We rode west, beside a good-sized river, until up ahead we saw a crossroads dominated by a huge old oak heavy with summer leaves. We were less than fifty yards from the tree when we noticed something dangling from its limbs. We drew closer, puzzled, peering into the shade of the tree, and when suddenly both Sarah and I comprehended what we were seeing, we broke into cries of horror and disbelief.

Two skeletons swung from the tree, nooses tight about what had been their necks, twisting slowly in the hot Texas wind. There was a hand-painted sign nailed to the trunk of the tree and Ebon, over our protests, drove us forward until we could read its terrible inscription:

Two Abolitionist Preachers
Come to Fort Worth
To Agitate the Niggers
1860
This Here Is Them
God Dam Their Eyes

I cried and cried and cried until I could cry no more. I begged Ebon to turn back, to Dallas, to Nashville, to Virginia, to some more civil place. Ebon comforted me until I was calm, and soon we were moving again, into desolate prairie land, toward our new home.

August 4

We arrived in midmorning at our destination, a place called Liberty, which might generously be called a village. A man who said he was the sheriff greeted us, and when Ebon explained that we had come to claim Jack Dalton's farm he quickly summoned another man. The second man was a cowboy, with blue eyes, a fierce look about him, and a fearful scar on his throat.

"I'm Earl Cantrell," he announced. "What's this about Jack Dalton giving you a farm?"

Sarah and I exchanged a glance—so this was the famous Earl Cantrell! We had heard of him in Fort Worth.

Ebon handed him Dalton's will, which had been notarized by the commander of the hospital where he died. Cantrell glanced at it contemptuously and declared that it could be a forgery.

Ebon said, "Here, Earl Cantrell, this is Jack's diary. He asked me to show it to thee if we should meet."

Cantrell read the diary, while everyone waited in silence. He seemed to be Judge and Jury in this place. When he finished reading his eyes glistened.

"You're Pridemore?" he said. "The one he prayed with?"

"Yes."

"How did he die?"

"At peace with his Maker."

Cantrell turned away. Clearly, beneath his rough exterior, he was a good man. When he had composed himself he said, "His folks were killed by the Comanches. I raised him like my own son."

"He spoke of thee often, with great affection," Ebon told him.

"So he gave you the riverfront farm?"

"He said he had no heirs. If it is thine . . ."

"It ain't mine, it's thine, Mr. Pridemore," Earl Cantrell said. "I own a hundred thousand acres hereabouts, and I don't begrudge you four hundred. Now get them womenfolks of yours inside and we'll have us some dinner."

We had a long and enjoyable meal, in a sort of tavern. Earl advised Ebon to think not only of farming but of the cattle business. There was more talk of Indians, too. Earl said, "Some fellows up in Oklahoma caught two Utes stealing their horses, so they strung 'em up, and now the Utes is on the warpath."

He suggested that we spend the night at his house, but Ebon told him that, like Moses, we yearned to see the Promised Land, and soon we were off on the final few miles of our long journey.

My poor words cannot express the Joy and Thanksgiving we felt as we first laid eyes on our new home. It is a cabin, set amid a grove of cottonwoods, on a hillside overlooking a bend in a small river. The cabin is small but solid, built of logs and mortar, and to us weary travellers, after four months on the road, it seemed a great mansion indeed. We knelt outside its door and thanked the Author of All Magnificence for our safe delivery to this new home, this wild paradise. Then we hurried to the bluff overlooking the river and watched the sunset. As far as we could see, golden sunlight danced on the prairie, on sagebrush and patches of mulberry and mesquites that dot the landscape as it sweeps to the low hills to the northwest. At dusk, a deer slipped out from the trees and drank in the river.

I am overwhelmed by the beauty around us. For so many weeks, as we traveled, Texas seemed to me only hot, barren, a purgatory. Tonight, as I gazed out at the prairie, purple in the dusk, I saw a new Texas. I saw its beauty and, I think, its meaning. There is the beauty of the wildflowers, and possibilities that truly seem infinite. Here there are no boundaries. Here a man can be all that he is, can make his dreams come true. That is my prayer for my dear Ebon, that this land, and my love, can give him all the Happiness he so truly deserves.

Enough. It is late. Sarah has gone to sleep in the wagon, and Ebon and I are to occupy the cabin. I want this to be a special night, a night of the deepest love and celebration, a night we will both remember, to the end of our days.

August 5

It is early afternoon. We awoke early, cleaned the cabin, unloaded the wagon, gathered firewood, set traps for squirrels and rabbits, and went for a long walk around our Paradise Found. Returning, we splashed in the river, caught one small fish, and lunched on dried beef, eggs, tea, and wild berries. We then napped in the shade by the river. I awoke before the others. My happiness with our land, our home, our kingdom, grows with each passing moment. This too: last night, there was such Sacred Intimacy between Ebon and me, that I do believe in my heart we have created the Ultimate Blessing, a child, to make our happiness complete.

The others doze on. Ebon snores, in his gentle way. This afternoon we must

3 Indians

Three weeks after Jenny was murdered, Wade Kingslea called a news conference.

Fort Worth had been flooded with writers, reporters, and photographers from all over the world, and more than a hundred of them crowded into the Kingslea Oil auditorium, grateful for even a glimpse of the accused billionaire.

At the stroke of noon, Wade Kingslea stepped to the microphone and announced, "I've asked you here to meet the man who will be my chief defense counsel."

The reporters perked up. There had been intense speculation as to who would lead the Kingslea defense. Such celebrated names as F. Lee Bailey, Louis Nizer, and Edward Bennett Williams had spun through the rumor mill.

But the young Texan who strode grinning to the microphone was not one of these nationally known legal wizards. The Texas reporters, recognizing him, winked at one another, even as their out-of-state colleagues gaped, frowned, or, in the case of one young woman, let out a frightened cry.

"Hi, I'm Stump Wildeman," said the lawyer, a slender man in his thirties whom the Almighty had blessed with a choirboy's face, jet black hair, a razor-sharp intellect, and a physical deformity that, for some, took a little getting used to.

Hargis Wildeman III was the son and grandson of doctors who practiced in the Central Texas city of Temple. It was his father, delivering the baby, who first glimpsed the imperfection that would shape his son's life: his right arm ended at the elbow in a round, pink nub from which protruded five tiny buttons that would, in a more perfect world, have been four fingers and a thumb.

It was not an uncommon deformity, and the boy's parents vowed that he would enjoy a perfectly normal childhood. That he did not was no fault of theirs but rather was because, when he left his loving home, young Hargis was endlessly tormented by other boys. "Stump, stump, look at him jump," the boys sang, giving him the nickname which he first hated, then embraced.

Stump's torment ended when he was ten and learned to fight more ferociously with one arm than the other boys could with two. He proceeded to become a star athlete in high school, playing baseball, football, basketball, and tennis with remarkable agility, and also a straight-A student and president of his class.

He enrolled in the University of Texas and continued his winning ways: he joined Kappa Sigma, starred in interfraternity athletics, and squired the most beautiful sorority girls on campus. Indeed, his success with the coeds inspired a good deal of sullen speculation along Fraternity Row as to just what sort of unspeakable pleasures Stump Wildeman afforded women with that damned stump of his.

As graduation neared, Stump's father and aged grandfather urged him to continue the family tradition of medicine. For once in his life, young Hargis III disappointed his family, and for reasons they would never fully understand. His father and grandfather were good, Christian men who saw the world as a benign place where they comforted the afflicted and were, in return, universally beloved. Their namesake held a darker view of life, one shaped by taunts and beatings in his earliest years. For Stump Wildeman, life was a war, and his chosen battlefield was the court of law.

He led his class of the University of Texas Law School, married a rich and beautiful woman, and set up practice in Houston, which in the postwar boom was winning recognition as both the richest and most violent of Texas cities. As one dramatic courtroom victory followed another, it became clear to other lawyers that Stump Wildeman, with his choirboy's face and crippled arm, had indeed turned his disability to an advantage.

"He screws up a jury's head with it," an opposition lawyer once complained. "The first time they see it, they're repulsed. You can see 'em squirm. Then, once they get used to the damn thing, they start feeling guilty and want to make it up to the poor cripple."

"It ain't just the juries," another barrister declared. "When he sticks that goddam thing in your witness's face, he forgets everything you told him to say. He'd confess to killing his mama, just to get that ugly damn nub out of his face!"

"I might add," Wade Kingslea continued, "that Mr. Wideman's first advice to me was to make no public comment prior to trial. I am therefore unable to give you my opinion on the district attorney, his case, his motives, or his witnesses, until this matter is concluded—but, by God, I'll say a mouthful then! Hargis, why don't you take over now?"

Stump Wildeman flashed his choirboy's grin. "Any questions?"

"What's your defense, Stump?"

"Mr. Kingslea came upon Jenny struggling with an intruder and almost lost his own life trying to save her. The real question is why the district attorney hasn't arrested the true killer."

"You know who he is?"

"We hope, at the proper time, to identify the killer."

"What about the neighbor who says he saw Mr. Kingslea with a gun?"

"We'll answer that in time. In the meanwhile, you might ask the district attorney what happened to that mysterious gun."

"You want a change of venue?"

"We want this trial right here, right now. Mr. Kingslea asks nothing more than to be judged by the good people of Fort Worth, his home for more than forty years, and as quickly as possible."

"Stump, do you think the DA's got a case?"

"Absolutely. A case of galloping political ambition."

"What's your fee in this case, Stump?"

"Next question."

"They're saying it's a million bucks."

The lawyer grinned. "I won't confirm or deny that. However, just between us, *I'm worth a million.*"

Amid a burst of laughter, Stump Wildeman ended the news conference. The reporters, uncomplaining, headed for telephones and typewriters. They were delighted that Kingslea had hired a colorful, quotable lawyer, one who would provide good copy to send back to their demanding editors and jaded readers.

An NBC News correspondent shadowed Stump back to the Hotel Texas and pressed him hard on the million-dollar fee, which he hoped would get him onto the air that evening. The lawyer, who lusted for national television exposure but recognized certain professional restraints on his self-promotion, winked at the reporter and said, "Friend, nobody's gonna sue you if you say it's a million—but you say it, not me!" With that he hurried up to his suite, where he was met by a sultry blonde who was officially his secretary and unofficially his mistress of the moment. He intended to divide the afternoon between the blonde and some private detectives he was interviewing. All in all, he had concluded, the defense of Wade Kingslea would be a damn sight simpler if he could produce the redheaded burglar for his client to identify.

Philip stayed up most of the night reading Christina Pridemore's diary, and the next morning he was back at the Oil Museum to see Will Clinkscale.

"I can't thank you enough for giving me that diary," he declared. "My God, she was so wonderful! And she could *write*. I had no idea of all that Quaker history and the trip down from Virginia. My great-great-grandmother! I feel like I *know* her. I feel like she's *inside* me. My God, I *hope* she is. But what happens next? Her diary just says 'three Indians' and stops."

"You mean you don't know what happened?"

"If I ever did, Will, I've forgotten."

"You need to read the Court of Inquiry report."

"What's that?"

"The next chapter in Christina's story."

"Can't you just *tell* me?"

"I could. But I won't. It's too fine a story to dribble out secondhand. The report's in the state archives."

"You mean I have to go to Austin?"

"That's right. I'll give you the name of the man to see."

Philip grinned. If he left right away, he could be at the archives that afternoon.

COURT OF INQUIRY

The following is the official report of an interview with Mrs. Christina Pridemore, taken on September 16, 1866, at the home of Mr. Earl Cantrell, rancher, outside Liberty, Texas. Present, in addition to the Witness, were Major Harold Willoughby, USA, Investigating Officer, and Corporal E. S. Jones, Stenographer. The interview was undertaken in accor-

dance with Directive 11-602, issued by General Wayne Tolson, in connection with the deaths of two Ute Indians on August 6, 1866.

Q. *Mrs. Pridemore, will you please relate the events of August 5, relating to your abduction by the Indians.*

A. *We had arrived in Liberty the day before, my husband, Ebon, my sister, Sarah, and myself. We proceeded to our new farm and spent the night there.*

Q. *Were you conscious, ma'm, of any danger from Indians?*

A. *Upon our arrival, Earl Cantrell said something about trouble with the Ute Indians, in Oklahoma, but we felt no danger.*

Q. *Yes ma'm. Now, what happened on the 5th?*

A. *We awoke, explored the farm, had lunch by the riverbank, and then napped. I awoke before the others. I was writing in my diary when I looked up and saw three Indians, on horseback, above us on the riverbank.*

Q. *Can you describe them?*

A. *Their leader, Shavano, was in the middle. The others, whose names I never knew, were on either side. One was huge. The other was small and wore a black derby hat. The small one carried a spear, and the others had rifles. They had paint on their faces.*

Q. *What happened next, Mrs. Pridemore?*

A. *I cried out. The others awoke. Ebon got to his feet and said, "What do you want?" He walked up the riverbank toward them with his hand outstretched. "We come in peace," he said. The largest Indian slipped off his pony and came toward Ebon with his hand, too, outstretched. It seemed, for that instant, as if all would be well. And then . . .*

Q. *Take your time, ma'm.*

A. *The large Indian took Ebon's hand and jerked him forward onto the ground and I saw his knife flash out and blood flow from Ebon's throat. I ran forward, to help, but another of the Indians seized me. Sarah ran but one of them captured her. I was thrown over a pony. As we began to ride away, I fainted.*

Q. *Let me pour you some water, ma'm.*

A. *I thank thee.*

Q. *Can you tell us what happened next?*

A. *I awoke at some point. I was bound and thrown across the large Indian's pony. I could see Sarah, likewise thrown across a pony. We were riding north. I knew Ebon was dead. I wished myself dead. But then I thought,* No, Ebon is gone to God, but his baby lives inside me and I must live for us both. *I began to chew at the collar of my dress and to spit the pieces of it out, onto the ground, hoping thereby to leave a trail that our rescuers might follow. The land was beginning to rise and the ponies were tiring. Ropes were tied to our wrists and we were made to walk behind the ponies. If we stumbled, they dragged us along until we struggled to our feet. Finally, darkness came, and we stopped atop a high plateau. Sarah and I were tied to a tree while the Indians made camp. The Indians drank whiskey, and finally the large and small Indians seized Sarah and dragged her a short distance away. I was left behind with Shavano. I . . . this is the most difficult part.*

Q. *Of course. Please understand, Mrs. Pridemore, that it is central to this Inquiry to establish whether or not you and your sister were outraged by the Indians.*

A. *I understand. Yes, we were outraged by the Indians.*

Q. *Both of you?*

A. *Yes. But in different manners.*

Q. *Could you explain?*

A. *The two Indians threw Sarah onto a blanket, tore off her clothing, and attacked her in a manner that is beyond description. At first I tried not to watch. Then I did watch, calling my love and prayers to Sarah, in the midst of the outrage.*

Q. *And then your sister was slain?*

A. *She did not submit passively to the attack upon her. She bit the smaller Indian in a most painful way. He howled like a wounded animal and seized his spear and in his rage he ran the spear through her helpless body.*

Q. *Let the record note a brief recess in the Inquiry.*

A. *I am ready to continue now.*

Q. *What happened after your sister's death?*

A. *The two Indians staggered down to the creek, perhaps fifty yards away, where they continued to drink and to argue among themselves. Shavano remained with me, smoking his pipe. After a while he untied my wrists and began to talk.*

Q. *Do you remember what he said?*

A. *He spoke of his people, the Utes. He said they had been mighty warriors, masters of a great empire, until the white men came. He said they began to make treaties and that with each treaty the Utes' hunting grounds were smaller and more barren. He said the Colorado Utes fought the U.S. Army and were defeated and sent to the Indian Territory of Oklahoma, where his people were starving. Then, he said, the Texans hanged two Utes for stealing horses and that inflamed his people once more. The young braves danced war dances and were determined to ride to Texas for revenge.*

Q. *Did he say how many braves would ride to Texas?*

A. *I do not think so. He said it was better to die as a warrior, and to join one's ancestors, than to starve like a dog in Oklahoma. I begged him to let me go. But he said, "No, I will soon die. But my spirit will live through you." And that was when he . . .*

Q. *You were outraged by the Indian Shavano?*

A. *Yes. But not like my sister. I was not otherwise harmed. When he had finished, he tied my hands again, but not tightly, and walked off into the night. I pulled at the knot with my teeth and it began to loosen. Soon I was free. Perhaps that was what Shavano intended. I ran through the night, across the prairie. In time, I came upon Earl Cantrell and the other men.*

Q. *And you told them where they could find the three Indians?*

A. *Yes. Later in the morning, Earl Cantrell and the others returned with Shavano and the small Indian and the bodies of my sister and the large Indian.*

Q. *And then what happened?*

A. *An argument broke out among the men. One of the men was the father of a child who had been murdered by the Indians before they came to our farm. He insisted that he be given the right to punish them as he saw fit. One of the soldiers said that the law required that the Indians be brought back for trial. In time, the two Indians were tied to trees and whipped and fires built beneath them.*

Q. *Mrs. Pridemore, as you know, some of the men were civilians, and some were uniformed soldiers. Can you tell me what part, if any, the uniformed soldiers played in the death of the two Indians?*

A. *I cannot. I walked some distance away and averted my eyes.*

Q. *Did you in any way indicate to the men your approval of their treatment of the Indians?*

A. *No. I could not, because I did not know my true feelings. In my mind I knew that punishment and revenge were*

*wrong and that I should protest. But in my heart I felt such
pain and sorrow that I could not speak. The men acted in
anger, as perhaps the Indians had. I cannot judge them. The
All Powerful will judge us all someday.*

Q. *Is there anything you wish to add, Mrs. Pridemore?*
A. *No.*
Q. *I wish to thank you for your cooperation.*
A. *Thou art welcome.*

Philip drove from Austin back to Fort Worth. He spent a
few days there, dodging reporters and trying to get a sense of
how the trial was shaping up. A judge had been picked, Ben
Brownlaw, a combat veteran, opera buff, and Baptist elder,
widely regarded as honest, fair-minded, and unimaginative.
The consensus was that Judge Brownlaw wouldn't tolerate
any fancy tricks by Stump Wildeman. Philip called Roy
Sykes, who said he was too busy to see him. "Just keep out of
sight," the DA advised. Philip took the advice and drove back
to Goodwill, his refuge in the past.

"I went to Austin," he told Will Clinkscale. "I read the
Court of Inquiry report."

They were having coffee at the refurbished Gusher Saloon,
soon after the first of the year.

"It's a sad story," Will said.

"Is there more?"

Will nodded. "A young doctor named George Hopkins
treated Christina after she was rescued from the Indians. A
long time later, when he was an old man, some cousins of hers
in Virginia wrote trying to find out what happened to her. I
don't think he ever answered them, but he wrote the story
down in his journal. I can give it to you."

"She was so damn good and kind and decent," Philip said.
"And against the most incredible odds she left something behind, that beautiful journal of hers, that can still move us a
hundred years later. That's not a bad monument for a life,
Will. It's more than most of us will have. Somehow, she's still
alive, as long as people read her story."

"Indeed she is, son," Will said. "Indeed she is."

*My first meeting with Christina Pridemore was on August
7, 1866, when the soldiers brought her back to Earl Cantrell's
house. That was many years ago, but I remember Christina as
if it were yesterday: a fair, slender girl with intelligent fea-*

tures and gentle eyes. I treated her cuts and abrasions, but her real injuries were not physical. In one day she had lost her husband, her sister, and her dream of a new life. There was little I could offer except friendship, which I gladly did. I saw Christina almost daily in those first weeks after her abduction. She liked to talk of her native Virginia, of her parents and her girlhood, and of her Quaker faith, which somehow enabled her to bear her terrible losses. She was as good and loving a woman as I ever met and entirely undeserving of the misfortunes that befell her.

Two months after her ordeal, I called upon Christina, in Earl Cantrell's parlor, and she fell at my feet. She was in a state such as I had not seen since the day of her abduction.

"Doctor, I am going to have a baby," she cried.

"God be praised," I said.

But Christina was not in a mood of thanksgiving. Tears blurred her gentle blue eyes. "Ebon was the kindest, gentlest of men," she said. "Despite all that has happened, I would count myself blessed to bear Ebon Pridemore's child."

"And so you shall, my dear."

Her face was twisted and torn by the pain inside her. "Can thou not see, doctor? Can thou not understand? A child is growing in my womb and I do not know if its father is Ebon Pridemore or a savage Indian!" She wept hopelessly.

"Your child is Ebon's," I told her.

"Is there a way of knowing?" she cried.

Christina, innocent of biology, knew only that she had been intimate with her husband one night and that she had been outraged by the Indian Shavano the next. She prayed that somehow because Ebon's seed was planted first, the child must be his.

"No scientific way," I told her. "But my faith tells me there are no savages in the womb. Each child is conceived and born as pure as Jesus Christ himself, and it is the sinful world that makes savages of men."

Her look broke my heart. "I cannot stand not knowing."

Christina's spirits brightened in the final months of her pregnancy. She made clothes for her baby, cooked pies and cakes, and filled Cantrell's house with spring flowers—and with her own goodness and love. It had been three years since Earl lost his own wife to the Indians and it was clear that his thoughts were much on this shy Quaker girl whom fate had brought to his home.

Christina went into labor in mid-May. I delivered the baby joyously; to bring a child into the world is always a thrilling, sacred act, but in this case I felt special happiness, for I believed that the arrival of the child would at last end Christina's mourning and begin a new and happy chapter in her life.

The child was a healthy, brown-eyed girl. I called the good news to Earl, who quickly produced a bottle of brandy, with which we toasted the new arrival.

Our celebration was short-lived. Christina was bleeding internally and I was powerless to stop it. She died in the shadows of early evening with her baby in her arms. "Call her Virginia," were her final words.

Earl and I buried her beside her husband and sister on a hill above the river on the farm they had come so far to make their home. He deeded the farm to the orphan, Virginia Pridemore, and found a Christian couple who agreed to raise her in exchange for the use of the farm for their lifetimes. Virginia grew into a tall, dark-haired woman who in no way reminded me of her mother. She was a decent woman but taciturn and without imagination. In time she married a strapping, broad-shouldered farmer named Aaron Kingslea, who was notable only for his fiery Baptist religious fervor. In the spring of 1895 I delivered Virginia and Aaron Kingslea's only child, an eight-pound son they named Wade Aaron Kingslea. I have watched that boy grow to manhood. His parents are common as dirt, but there is something in his eyes that promises greatness, in one form or another.

That ends my knowledge of the Quakers who came to Texas in the summer of 1866 and were greeted with such misfortune. Their sole heir, Wade Kingslea, married young and fathered two sons, and I continue to think he will somehow break out of the obscurity that was his birthright and gain the world's attention. Of course I am an old man and could be wrong.

George Hopkins, M.D.
Liberty, Texas
July 11, 1918

Philip put aside the dusty old journal and stared out the motel window across the empty prairie. Dr. Hopkins had been a good judge of character, but neither he nor anyone could ever answer Christina's anguished question. Was Wade Kingslea's maternal grandfather a gentle Quaker or a rampaging

Indian? Did Indian blood somehow account for Kingslea's life of anger and passion, revenge and success? For that matter, what of himself? What drove him? What made him different? He knew how easily he swung from love to hate; there were moments he imagined himself as decent as Ebon Pridemore and times he felt as violent as the Ute warrior Shavano. Or did those distant bloodlines really matter? Perhaps Dr. Hopkins was right, and it was a sinful world that made savages of men.

CHAPTER FOUR

The judge, gruff, burly Ben Brownlaw, summoned the opposing counsel to the bench in the opening moments of the Wade Kingslea murder trial and laid down the law: "Boys, there's a circus outside, but there won't be one in my courtroom. Remember that and we'll get along fine."

Circus was too kind a word; anarchy would have come closer to describing the scene as several thousand reporters, police, curiosity seekers, and hustlers pushed and shoved in a freezing rain outside the county courthouse. Some had hopes of getting into the courtroom; some were content to mill about, dreaming of a glimpse of Walter Cronkite or Mike Wallace or even Wade Kingslea himself; others were busy selling "WK IS OK" and "KINGSLEA FOR PRESIDENT" T-shirts.

Philip fought through the mob and was seated in the courtroom when Judge Brownlaw gaveled the trial to order. Philip was there for the duration: to testify, to take notes, to do whatever he could do to hasten Wade Kingslea's conviction. He was therefore astounded when Judge Brownlaw said to the lawyers, "Gentlemen, I assume we'll invoke the rule," and announced that all witnesses in the case leave the courtroom but remain on call.

"What the hell's going on?" Philip protested to an assistant district attorney. "I've got to see this trial."

"We can't have witnesses listening to other witnesses' testimony," the lawyer said. "You can wait in our office if you want to."

Philip walked into the corridor, fuming, pondering an appeal to the judge, when a dark-haired, disheveled woman named Zora Gilbert pulled him inside.

Zora was a reporter for *Time;* he'd seen her around Washington. "Don't worry," she told him. "I'll be in the courtroom taking notes all day, and I'll get the daily transcript too. Just come by my hotel room every evening and I'll fill you in."

Her price? The insider's information on the Kingslea family that only he could provide, and that she dreamed would win her a cover story on the trial. He shrugged, and it was a deal.

It could have taken months to pick the jury. Stump Wildeman hoped so, because he had dozens of skilled investigators out gathering data on the politics, drinking habits, sex lives, finances, religious views, and assorted quirks of the first panel of one hundred potential jurors. That wealth of data would be passed on to a committee of high-priced psychiatrists, who would judge whether each potential juror would be more likely to regard Kingslea's vast wealth with awe or resentment. Given that expert opinion, Stump Wildeman would have a clear edge in the jury-selection process, as both sides tried to see in the minds of the men and women who would seal Kingslea's fate.

But that was not to happen. Judge Brownlaw declared that he wanted a jury *muy pronto*, so there would be limited challenges and no open-ended questioning of potential jurors. Stump Wildeman protested bitterly, but the judge had his way and they had their jury in five days flat. Round One for the prosecution.

Opening statements to the jury came next. Roy Sykes was first, and he played several roles in his hour-long oration. He was the Lone Cowboy, in his boots and cheap brown gabardine suit, flattering and studying this twelve-headed monster. He was the Servant of the People, chewing a toothpick, invoking God and the Law, declaring over and over that every man, no matter how rich or powerful, must stand as an equal before the bar of justice. He was, finally, the Grim Reaper, vowing to lay before their eyes a threat to kill, a motive to kill, a murderous rage, a brutal, senseless act of violence, and

finally an actual boast of the bloody deed. This is, Roy concluded, a simple case of murder. Do not be deceived.

Stump Wildeman, pin-striped, unashamedly rich, promised
no simplicity. He lectured at length on the concept of "reasonable doubt" and to no one's surprise found it a more elastic
concept than had the prosecutor. Then, his dark eyes smoldering, jabbing furiously with his nub, Stump warned of mysteries to come, plots, conspiracies, jackals who would feed
upon lions. "Wade Kingslea didn't kill anyone," he declared.
"Someone is trying to destroy Wade Kingslea, to deface the
great monument that is his life, to subvert the sacred values
that all Texans hold dear!" The jurors' eyes widened, and the
next day's headlines demanded:

A PLOT AGAINST WADE?

The prosecution's first witness was a rotund gentleman
named Wiseman, the county coroner, and thanks to him most
of the jurors did not eat their free lunch that day. The man
brought pictures.

The photographs documented in chilling detail what devas-
tation resulted when a .44 magnum was fired point-blank into
a woman's face. Jurors gasped, gagged, turned away, and
slumped in silent prayer. Roy Sykes watched the process
coldly, contentedly. He hoped those ghastly images of Jenny's
shredded flesh and shattered bones would make them wake up
screaming. That was the easy part. The hard part was to convince them that Wade Kingslea had pulled the trigger.

Stump Wildeman, in his cross-examination, was content to
establish that nothing in the coroner's testimony ruled out the
possibility of a third person struggling with Wade and Jenny
for possession of the murder weapon.

The coroner was followed by the two policemen who had
arrived first at the scene, and soon the first day of the trial
ended. Wade Kingslea allowed himself a smile as he left the
courtroom, surrounded by his private security forces, to be
greeted by several hundred Texans, mostly women, who had
waited in freezing rain all afternoon to cheer him as he
marched to his waiting Cadillac.

INTRUDER POSSIBLE, CORONER SAYS;
CROWDS CHEER WADE AT DAY'S END

The courtroom was deathly quiet the next morning as Dusty Rhodes took the stand.

His happy-go-lucky face, famous in Fort Worth for a quarter-century, was permanently altered now, overlaid with a mask of rage and pain.

Roy Sykes savored the moment. You could see the jurors soften, open up their hearts. Here was a hero to match against the legendary oil tycoon.

He led Dusty gently through the familiar facts: he operated a Texaco station on West Seventh Street; previously he had played baseball for the Fort Worth Cats (some jurors smiled, summoning memories of the scrappy second-baseman of yesteryear); he ws the father of Jenny Rhodes, who had been married to Congressman Skip Kingslea. Dusty stiffened at the word Kingslea.

"How well do you know Mr. Wade Kingslea?"

"I met him back in the thirties, when I was playing ball. I went to parties at his house a few times. And he's been coming to my station ever since I opened it. I wouldn't call us friends, but I knew him, the way a lot of people did. And of course I saw more of him after Skip and Jenny got married."

"Did you ever have any conflict with Mr. Kingslea?"

"None at all."

Roy Sykes let that sink in.

"Mr. Rhodes, did you see the defendant, Wade Kingslea, on the evening of Saturday, October 31, 1964?"

"I did."

"Could you tell us what happened?"

"Jenny called me at home on Saturday evening, about seven. She said that she and Skip . . ."

"Objection," Stump Wildeman roared. "That's hearsay."

The judged leaned toward the witness. "Don't tell us what someone else may have told you. Just tell us what you saw and did."

Dusty frowned and started over. "I . . . she called me and I drove over to her and Skip's place to get her. When I got there she was packing her bag. She'd been crying."

"Was her husband, or anyone else, there?"

"No sir."

"And what happened next?"

"Just about the time Jenny was ready to go, Wade Kingslea charged up. He stood in the doorway and said, 'I won't let you do this. Not three days before the election.' Jenny said all she was going to do was to stay with her mother and father for a while, that she couldn't stand Skip and him trying to run her life. He yelled that she damn well better unpack her bag or she'd be in big trouble. I said, 'Wade, you get out of our way, or you'll be the one in trouble.' He said, 'You shut your goddamn mouth.' I pushed him out of the way. He pushed back, and we wrestled for a minute, and he fell down. I grabbed Jenny's arm and took her out to my car. Kingslea yelled, 'You slut, I'll make you pay for this!' I wanted to go back and knock his block off, but Jenny wouldn't let me. So I drove her home."

"Do you know any reason he would call Jenny by that term? Slut?"

Dusty's face reddened. "None in the world."

"All right, Mr. Rhodes. Please tell us what happened on Monday morning."

"Jenny wanted to go back and get some of her things. I said I'd go with her, but she said I didn't need to."

"Why did you offer to go?"

"I was worried about her."

"What happened next?"

"I went to my gas station. Then I heard on the radio that there'd been a shooting at her house. I drove out there and she was dead. Wade Kingslea had killed her."

"Objection!" Stump Wildeman yelled.

"Sustained," the judge said. "The jury will disregard the witness's last remark."

"No further questions," Roy Sykes said.

Stump Wildeman came out swinging.

"Mr. Rhodes, how much had you had to drink when you went to pick up your daughter that evening?"

Dusty Rhodes' face flushed with anger. "A drink or two."

"Or two or three?"

"Objection," Roy Sykes declared. "He's badgering the witness."

"Sustained. Move along, Mr. Wildeman."

"Have you ever been arrested for drunk driving, Mr. Rhodes?"

"Objection," Roy Sykes yelled again. "Mr. Rhodes is not on trial for drunk driving or anything else."

"No," Wildeman said, "but he admits he'd been drinking

before this encounter, and I'd like to know how much and how often he drinks."

"The witness said he'd had a drink or two," said Judge Brownlaw, who liked a drink or two himself most evenings. "Proceed."

"All right, Mr. Rhodes. You went to your daughter's house. You were about to leave when Mr. Kingslea appeared. He was in the doorway and you knocked him down. Is that correct?"

"I asked him to get out of our way."

"Then you knocked him down?"

"After he told me to shut my goddamn mouth."

"Did you use any profanity, Mr. Rhodes?"

"Not that I recall."

"Did you say, 'Get out of my way, you son of a bitch'?"

"I don't remember."

"Don't remember? Are those one or two or three or four drinks the reason you don't remember?"

"Objection!" Roy Sykes cried.

"Sustained," the judge said.

"Did you or did you not call Mr. Kingslea a son of a bitch?"

"I might have."

"You might have. And you've lived in Texas long enough to know those are fighting words, haven't you?"

"I don't care what I called him. No man can insult my little girl and . . ."

Dusty Rhodes lowered his head, fighting back tears.

"How old are you, Mr. Rhodes?"

"Fifty-two."

"Do you happen to know how old Mr. Kingslea is?"

"About seventy."

"So you knocked down this seventy-year-old man . . ."

"He was doing his damnedest to knock me down," Dusty Rhodes shot back, and a burst of laughter eased the tension.

"So you and Jenny proceeded to your car, and Mr. Kingslea called something after you."

"He yelled, 'You slut, I'll make you pay for this!'"

"Mr. Rhodes, might you have misunderstood Mr. Kingslea?"

"I understood him."

"Might he have called, to *you*, not your daughter, 'You nut, I'll make you pay for this'?"

"I understood him."

"But you know no reason why he would call your daughter by such a name, do you?"

"No, I do not."

Stump Wildeman pointed his nub at the witness's face. "One other question, Mr. Rhodes. On the afternoon of your daughter's death, did you tell a *Star-Telegram* reporter, and I quote, 'If the state of Texas doesn't kill Wade Kingslea, I will!'?"

Roy Sykes was up like a shot. "Objection," he roared, furious to see the grieving father pictured as a potential killer.

"The witness may answer the question," the judge ruled.

"Yes, I said that," the old ballplayer confessed.

"And did you mean it?" Stump Wildeman demanded.

Dusty Rhodes' face burned with pain and fury. "You're damned right I did," he shouted, as the judge gaveled the day to a close.

"I'LL KILL HIM!" DUSTY VOWS

That night, Philip and Zora Gilbert went to dinner at The Mexican Inn and discussed the trial in microscopic detail. Zora gave her analysis of what impression the witnesses were making, and Philip briefed her on the history of the Kingslea clan, Dusty and Jenny Rhodes, and other actors in the drama. Sometimes, between bites, Zora would whip out her notebook, for she was always working toward the cover story that she was determined *Time* would carry on the trial. Dinner, of course, was on Time, Inc.

They were both staying at the Hotel Texas, and when they started up in the elevator Zora asked if he'd like to come by her room for a nightcap. Philip gave the matter some thought, for he imagined she had more on her mind than a drink. He was tempted but not really interested. Part of it was Zora herself. She was smart and attractive, but ten years as a reporter, ten years of guile and cynicism, had squeezed all the femininity out of her, had left her as tough as a boot.

And it was more than that. This was Jenny's time, a time to remember her, to avenge her, and somehow sleeping with Zora didn't fit.

"No thanks," he told her. "I'm pretty tired."

"Your name, please?" Roy Sykes asked the nervous witness.

"Maria Huerta."

"Your occupation?"

"I work for Mrs. Wade Kingslea."

"Where were you working last November 2?"

"For Mrs. Jenny Kingslea."

"Tell us what happened that morning, Maria."

The reporters and trial buffs were not paying much attention to Maria. Her slight knowledge of the case had already been in the papers: she'd heard a shot and hidden in an upstairs closet. Most of the trial buffs were far more interested in Philip Kingslea's upcoming testimony, which, rumor had it, held the promise of surprises.

"And so, Maria, what did you do when you came out of the closet?" Roy was leading her gently through her story.

"I went into the bathroom and locked the door. I went to the window. I thought maybe I'd climb out the window. Then I saw him, running across the back yard."

It is a prime rule of the legal profession that lawyers never show surprise when questioning their own witnesses. If your witness abruptly confesses to a mass murder, you smile smugly and pretend it's all part of your plan. Thus, as the first warning bells went off in his head, Roy Sykes hesitated only an instant before plunging ahead.

"Who did you see running across the yard, Maria?"

"The man who killed her. He was tall and had red hair and a big gun in his hand."

Cries of astonishment filled the courtroom. Wade Kingslea allowed himself a faint smile. Roy Sykes demanded a recess, as reporters raced for the phones.

Philip got the word from Zora, minutes later. "She's lying!" he roared.

"Prove it," Zora said, grinning, for every new twist in the case moved her closer to a cover story.

When the trial resumed after lunch, Roy said, "Your honor, this witness has changed her testimony. The state no longer vouches for her credibility. We consider her a hostile witness now."

He turned to Maria. The girl looked fragile, fearful.

"How much are they paying you to tell that cock-and-bull story?" Roy shouted.

"They don't pay me nothing."

"It's not what you told us before, is it?"

"No," the girl said sullenly.

"Who told you to change your story? Who told you to say you saw a man run across the yard?"

"Nobody," the girl said. "I was scared. I was afraid of the police. I think maybe they send me back to Mexico. So I think the best thing is to say I don't see nothing. But it wasn't true. I saw the man, just like I said."

For the next hour, Roy Sykes battered the girl Maria and her story. He challenged, ridiculed, and confused her. He charged that she had spied on Jenny, listened to her telephone calls, betrayed her. He vowed that she would soon be deported to Mexico, if not imprisoned for perjury. The girl sobbed, cringed, trembled, but at the end, she clung to her story.

MAID BACKS WADE'S STORY: SAYS SHE SAW KILLER FLEE

"The jury can't possibly believe her," Philip raged to Zora at dinner that night.

"Juries are like the rest of us," Zora said with a little smile. "They believe what they want to believe."

"Your name, please?" the DA asked.

"Philip Kingslea."

"You are a grandson of the defendant, Wade Kingslea?"

"That's right."

"And where do you make your home?"

Where, indeed? "New York City."

"Where were you originally from?"

"Fort Worth. I was born and raised here."

"What do you do for a living?"

"I'm a writer."

"Are you the author of a current best-seller called *To Kill a President?*"

"Yes."

"Describe your relationship with Jenny Rhodes Kingslea."

"I'd known Jenny all my life. We went all through school together. We were both working in Washington in 1961–63, and I saw her several times there, before she came back here to marry Skip."

It was the truth, but not the whole truth. He hoped it would slide past.

"Philip, where were you on the afternoon of Saturday, October 31, of last year?"

"In my room at the Algonquin Hotel in New York."

"Did you receive a telephone call from Texas?"

Philip leaned forward intently. Now, finally, he had the question he'd been waiting for. "Yes. Jenny called me. She was upset. She said . . ."

"Objection," Stump Wildeman shouted. "Anything she may have said to this witness is hearsay."

"Hearsay?" Philip protested, and Roy Sykes jumped to his feet.

"Your honor, the state believes this testimony is admissible under the 'excited utterance' exception to the hearsay rule."

"Mr. Wildeman?" the judge said.

"Your honor," the defense lawyer said, "no 'excited utterance' has ever been admitted in this state when more than a few minutes passed between the declaration and the crime. This witness claims the victim called him some forty hours before she died. That's chitchat, not an excited utterance."

The judge scowled and sent the jury out. Philip was flabbergasted. Jenny had called him and said she was afraid of Wade Kingslea—how could that not be admissible evidence?

With the jury out, Wildeman declaimed at length on the hearsay rule and insisted that in the history of Texas criminal law no 'excited utterance' had ever been admitted if more than two hours passed before the crime occurred. Roy Sykes maintained that the judge had the power, weighing the probable truth of the testimony, to admit evidence such as Philip's. But precedent was against him and the judge was not taking any chances. "Objection sustained," he said. "The victim's phone call to the witness is hearsay and not admissible."

Philip couldn't keep quiet. "Your honor," he said, "you don't understand. Jenny called me and said she was afraid that Wade Kingslea would . . ."

"Young man, just answer the questions that are put to you," the judge said sharply.

Philip was stunned by this turn of events, but he was even more stunned, a few minutes later, when Roy Sykes resumed his questioning.

"Philip, since Jenny's marriage to your cousin Skip Kingslea, were you and she lovers?"

Philip stared at the district attorney with disbelief, then fury. The son of a bitch had double-crossed him.

Stump Wildeman was furious, too, if for different reasons. "Objection," he cried. "This is a murder trial, not a divorce suit."

The judge summoned the two lawyers to the bench.

"Mr. Sykes, what is the point of this line of questioning?" the judge demanded.

"Philip and Jenny's affair is basic to the defendant's motivation. That's what I intend to prove."

"I say this alleged affair is irrelevant and prejudicial," Wildeman protested.

"I'll allow a few more questions," the judge said.

As the district attorney approached him once more, Philip felt trapped.

"Were you and Jenny lovers, Philip?"

He turned helplessly to the judge. "Do I have to answer that?"

"Yes, you do."

"I'll rephrase the question," Roy said. "Is it true that Jenny went with you to your room at the Hotel Texas at approximately 2 A.M. on the morning of November 22, 1963?"

Philip gave up. He was under oath. To lie was illegal, immoral, and dangerous. "Yes, it's true."

"Is it also true that one day last August you visited Jenny's room at the Hotel Pierre in New York for several hours?"

"Yes."

"Had the two of you discussed the possibility that she might leave her husband and marry you?"

"Yes."

He hated that, yet he felt an awful pride, too, a bitter victory.

"To your knowledge did either Skip or Wade Kingslea know of this affair?"

"No."

"How did you and Jenny get to the Hotel Pierre?"

"In a limousine she was using."

"Do you know whose limousine it was?"

"She said it was a Kingslea Oil limousine."

"Tell me about your relationship with your grandfather, Wade Kingslea."

"We don't have a relationship."

"Your novel, *To Kill a President*, concerns an oilman who plots the murder of a president—is that correct?"

"More or less."

"Did you appear on the *Today Show*, on the morning Jenny was killed?"

"Yes."

"Were you not asked repeatedly, on national television, if the oilman in your book wasn't really your grandfather?"

"I was asked that, yes."

Roy leaned forward, smiling in a friendly, folksy way. "Tell me, how do you think your grandfather likes having you go on television and accuse him of murder?"

Wildeman shot up, sputtering his objections, and Roy Sykes said he had no further questions.

Philip caught up with the district attorney in the doorway to his office.

"You tricked me," he shouted. "You knew I didn't want to testify about my affair with Jenny."

"Look, sonny, you're my motive. You're such a prick that you drove Wade Kingslea to murder."

"You could have told me what you were doing."

"Yeah, and you could have skipped the country, too. Calm down. You want to see Kingslea fry? Okay, that's what I'm trying to do."

The defense attorney idly scratched his earlobe with his pink nub as he contemplated the waiting witness. Philip eyed the lawyer uncertainly, no longer sure who was friend and who was foe.

"Mr. Kingslea, now that Jenny is dead, we have only your unsupported testimony as to this supposed affair between you two, don't we?"

"That's true."

"Does it please you to come in here and tell the world this tale of an affair with a woman who's dead now?"

"No."

"Tell me, do you hate your grandfather?"

"No."

"Do you dislike him?"

"There are things about him I dislike."

"Do you believe he treated your mother badly when she divorced your father?"

"Perhaps. It was a long time ago."

"Do you think your grandfather was involved in a plot to kill John F. Kennedy?"

"I think it's possible."

"Do you have any proof that he did?"

Philip hesitated. What was proof? One man's proof was another man's paranoia. "No," he said.

"Isn't it a fact that after the Kennedy assassination you spent a month in Dallas trying to connect your grandfather to the assassination?"

"I spent a month trying to find out the facts about the assassination."

"And after you failed to uncover any evidence against him, you went to New York and wrote a book that in effect charged him with plotting to kill Kennedy—isn't that true?"

"I wrote a novel about an assassination. There's no one named Kingslea in the book."

Wildeman scowled; he jabbed his nub a foot from Philip's nose. "No, but you don't have to be a genius to figure out who you were accusing, do you?"

"Objection!" the district attorney yelled.

"Sustained."

"How much money will you make off your book?"

"I don't know."

"How much have you made so far, in round numbers?"

"About three hundred thousand dollars."

A whistle echoed through the courtroom. Several of the jurors, who did not expect to earn three hundred thousand dollars in their lifetimes, were openmouthed.

Wildeman leaned in close, jabbing with his stump.

"What's your next book going to be about?" he asked. "Your affair with Jenny?"

"Why don't you go . . ."

"Order in the court!" the judge roared. "Ask your questions, Mr. Wildeman."

"You hate Wade Kingslea, don't you?"

"No."

"You wrote a book slandering his good name, didn't you?"

"I don't think so."

"Now you're here, trying to send him to the electric chair, aren't you?"

The stump jabbed closer and closer. Philip backed away, despite himself.

"I'm here to tell what I know."

"You're determined to make him pay, one way or another, aren't you?" Wildeman demanded.

"Objection!" Roy Sykes cried.

"Sustained."

"No further questions," Wade Kingslea's lawyer said with a contented smile.

A dozen reporters chased Philip out of the courthouse. He ran through the freezing rain until he lost them, then he cut back to his hotel and met Zora in her room. He threw off his soggy coat, wiped his face with a bath towel, and threw himself across her bed.

"The star witness," she jibed.

"How was I?"

"You don't know?"

"I felt like a punching bag."

"It was interesting," Zora said. "You turned the whole case upside down. Sykes wants to use you to give the old man a motive for killing Jenny—but to do that he's got to knock Jenny off her pedestal. Meanwhile, Stump's got to paint you as a liar and an ingrate who's out to get poor old Wade Kingslea."

"What's the bottom line? Who won?"

"Oh, I'd say the DA finally won a round."

"Yeah, he won, and I lost," Philip said bitterly.

"What do you mean, lost? You probably sold fifty thousand books today."

"Go to hell," he snapped.

Zora smiled and poured them both a glass of Scotch. "You'll never guess who I saw at the airport this morning," she said. "Your old pal Harry Flynn."

Philip sipped his drink. "Harry Flynn can go to hell, too," he muttered.

PHILIP ADMITS AFFAIR WITH JENNY

Zora was right: sales of his novel shot up fifty percent that weekend.

On Monday morning the prosecution called a sad-faced Mexican named Porfirio Diaz, who said that on the morning Jenny died he had been employed as a cook at Hillcrest. Roy Sykes asked him if anything unusual happened that morning.

"I took Mr. Wade's breakfast up to his bedroom."

"And what was he doing?"

"Sitting in bed, watching the TV."

"Did you notice what was on the TV?"

"The *Today Show*. When I said good morning, he told me to be quiet. I looked at the TV and saw Mr. Philip Kingslea on it."

"Then what did you do?"

"Gave him his breakfast and went back to the kitchen."

"What happened then, Mr. Diaz?"

"About five minutes after I took him his breakfast, he came out of his room, yelling and breaking things."

"What kind of things?"

"Vases. Lamps. Chairs. Anything he saw."

"Where was Mrs. Kingslea?"

"In her room. She came out and yelled at him to stop, but he kept on."

"What was he yelling?"

"One time he said, 'That little bastard, I'll make him pay.'"

"One last question, Mr. Diaz. Why did you stop working for the Kingsleas?"

"I was fired, right before Christmas."

"Was that before or after I questioned you?"

"Objection," Stump Wildeman cried. "The question is prejudicial."

"Overruled," the judge said. "You may answer, sir."

"You called me to your office on Monday, and Mrs. Kingslea, she fired me that Friday."

"No further questions," Roy Sykes said.

Stump Wildeman went after Porfirio Diaz with hammer and tongs. He got into the record that Diaz had once been jailed on a bad-check charge. He forced Diaz to admit that he had been fired by Livie Kingslea after she claimed he had stolen money from her. But after an hour of relentless interrogation, the cook stuck to his story: Wade Kingslea had watched grandson Philip on the *Today Show*, flown into a violent rage, and then driven off into the storm, about two hours before Jenny was murdered.

After lunch, Roy called Howard Garfield, the retired insurance executive who was Skip and Jenny's next-door neighbor. Garfield fidgeted unhappily in the witness chair, while Roy Sykes carefully led him toward the heart of his testimony:

"I put on my raincoat and hat and walked over to Skip's sidewalk. That was when Wade Kingslea came out the front door. I don't think he saw me at first. There was a great peal of thunder, and I said, 'What's wrong, Mr. Kingslea?' He said to me, 'Get out of my way, or I'll kill you too.' That was when I saw the gun in his hand."

"Was he pointing the gun at you?"

"No, no. It was pointing down."

"What did you do then, Mr. Garfield?"

"I froze. I couldn't believe it. He got in his car and drove away. I went back to my house. I didn't know what to do. I was trembling. I was about to call the police when the first police car arrived. Then Mr. Kingslea came back. I was afraid to go over there while he was there. Finally I saw you, Mr. Sykes, and I came and told you what had happened."

Roy gave the witness a moment to calm down. "Is there the slightest doubt in your mind that the defendant had a gun in his hand and that he said to you, 'Get out of my way, or I'll kill you too'?"

"No sir. No doubt at all."

"No further questions."

The judge glanced at the clock, then at the defense attorney. "Mr. Wildeman, it's almost three. Would you like to hold your cross-examination until morning?"

But Stump Wildeman had no intention of letting the jury go to bed that night with an unchallenged vision of Wade Kingslea, gun in hand, admitting one murder and threatening another. He was on the nervous witness like a tiger on raw meat.

"Mr. Garfield, by your own admission, you let more than an hour pass between the time you saw Mr. Kingslea and the time you went to Mr. Sykes with your story. Why?"

"I . . . it's like I explained . . . I was confused. Frightened."

"Isn't the real reason you cowered in your house for an hour . . ."

"Objection!" Roy barked.

"Sustained. Mind your rhetoric, counselor."

"Isn't the real reason you waited that you didn't know what you'd seen and heard outside the Kingslea house? Your imagination was running wild? You didn't know what story to tell the police?"

"No! I know what I saw. And what I heard."

"Or what you imagined."

"Objection!"

"Sustained. Ask your questions, Mr. Wildeman."

"You said you put on a raincoat before you went outside. Did you put on a hat, too?"

"Yes, I did."

"How far was it from your house to the point where you encountered Mr. Kingslea?"

"I . . . I guess sixty or seventy feet."

"Sixty or seventy feet. And how would you describe the weather that morning?"

"There was a hard rain."

"A hard rain. Any wind?"

"Yes, the wind was blowing, a strong wind."

"Would you say the wind was howling?"

Garfield hesitated. "I suppose so. Yes."

"A hard rain. A howling wind. And thunder and lightning too, did you say?"

"Yes."

"Was this howling wind blowing any rain in your face, Mr. Garfield?"

"I suppose so."

"You suppose so. And were you wearing your glasses?"

"Yes."

"What do you wear them for, precisely?"

"I'm nearsighted."

"You're nearsighted. And with the howling wind and the hard rain in your face, do we assume your glasses were wet?"

"I . . . I suppose so, yes. They must have been wet."

"You didn't stop and take off your glasses and dry them with a handkerchief?"

There were a few snickers in the courtroom. "No sir."

"So, your glasses are covered with water, and the thunder and lightning are crashing around you, and you heard Mr. Kingslea say, 'Get out of my way, or I'll kill you too!' Is that your testimony?"

"Yes sir."

"Is it possible, Mr. Garfield, that what he said was, 'Get out of the way, or *he'll* kill you too'?"

The witness worked his jaw muscles unhappily. "No sir. He said, 'I.' 'I'll kill you too.'"

"Think about it. I'll. He'll. He'll. I'll. They sound alike, right here in this courtroom, much less out there in the howling wind. Are you *sure*? Would you rob a man of his freedom, or his reputation, on the difference between I'll and he'll in a thunderstorm?"

Wildeman stood with his stump pointed at the witness like God's flaming sword. Garfield paled, trembled, drew back. "I . . . I'm sure he said 'he'll.' I mean, 'I'll.' 'Or I'll kill you too.'"

The defense lawyer gazed scornfully at the trembling witness. "Tell us what the gun looked like. What make was it? What caliber?"

"I . . . I can't answer that. I only had a glance. It was . . . dark. Metallic. Long, and dark, and heavy-looking."

"Might you not, in this storm, with rain pouring down your glasses . . ."

"Objection!"

"Sustained," the judge said, but the image of the witness with rain pouring down his face was an enduring one.

"Might you not have mistaken some other long, dark, heavy object for a gun?"

"Objection," Roy protested. "The witness has said repeatedly that he saw a gun."

"Sustained."

"I saw a gun, a gun," the witness whispered, but all the conviction had been battered out of him.

WADE IN A RAGE, COOK CLAIMS
"I SAW A GUN," SAYS NEIGHBOR
PROSECUTION RESTS ITS CASE

Livie Kingslea, clad in royal blue, made the witness stand her throne, and Stump Wildeman gave her the treatment due a queen. She was his first defense witness, and he counted on her to set the proper tone.

"Mrs. Kingslea, did anything unusual occur at your home, Hillcrest, on the morning of November 2?" Stump asked.

"There was a storm, of course."

"Yes, ma'm. But was there anything besides that?"

"One thing. I was in my room. The storm had caused one of the shutters to bang against the window. Wade must have noticed it about the same time I did. About nine o'clock, I heard him go to the top of the stairs and call down that someone should fix the shutter."

"Would you say he yelled downstairs, Mrs. Kingslea?"

"He had to, because of the storm."

"Yes ma'm. And can you recall exactly what he yelled?"

"It was something like, 'Somebody fix that damn thing before it drives us all crazy.'" Livie uncorked a sudden, girlish smile. "Wade *does* talk that way, I'm afraid."

On cue, a wave of respectful laughter swept the courtroom.

"Now, Mrs. Kingslea, what time did you go downstairs that morning?"

"Around ten."

"Was there anything damaged or broken downstairs?"

"Yes. The wind had blown open the front door and a vase in the front hall blew over and was broken."

"Mrs. Kingslea, you are, I believe, in charge of household matters at Hillcrest?"

"I try to be."

"Did you recently have occasion to discharge an employee named Porfirio Diaz?"

"I did, yes."

"Could you explain why?"

"He stole from us. The money was found in his room. Naturally I dismissed him on the spot."

"Did Mr. Diaz admit the theft?"

"No, not at all. He grew quite angry. His parting words were, 'I'll make you regret this, all of you Kingsleas!' "

"Thank you, Mrs. Kingslea."

Roy Sykes sparred with Livie for an hour but didn't shake her story: the only commotion at Hillcrest that morning was caused by the storm, not her husband. Livie speared him with her most gracious smile as she surrendered the witness stand.

The second defense witness was a tall, erect black man with the carriage of an African prince. He was Holman Winslow, the Kingsleas' butler, and he gravely confirmed Livie's report of domestic tranquillity at Hillcrest on the fateful morning. He also, over the district attorney's frenzied objections, was permitted to portray his former colleague, Porfirio Diaz, as a liar, a drunkard, and a thief.

Next came the birdlike Miss Garrett, Wade Kingslea's longtime secretary, who sweetly swore that her employer had been the very soul of good humor on the morning in question. When Roy Sykes demanded, on cross-examination, whether it was not unusual for the oilman to drive off into a raging storm for an unscheduled meeting with his grandson, Miss Garrett declared with a doting smile that for Mr. Kingslea, nothing at all could be called unusual.

Skip Kingslea, pinstriped and solemn, as befitted his status as congressman and widower, was the day's last witness, and under Wildeman's respectful questioning he declared that he loved his wife, that he and Jenny would have worked out their problems, and that it was inconceivable that she would have had an affair with his cousin Philip. "I think he's a damn liar," Skip declared. "She may have seen him now and then, but that was only because she felt sorry for him. He's hated me and my grandfather all his life, and this is his way of getting back."

NO AFFAIR, SKIP SAYS
PHILIP "A DAMN LIAR"

On Wednesday morning the defense called the manager of Ridglea Country Club, who said that at around eleven-fifteen on the morning of the murder Wade Kingslea pulled his Fleetwood under the club's big sandstone porte cochere, staggered into his office with blood pouring from a cut on his face, and declared that there'd been a murder. The manager said he listened in horror as Kingslea reported that a tall, redheaded intruder had killed Jenny and escaped. As they waited for the police to come, the manager said, he summoned a porter who brought Kingslea a towel for his face, then fetched him a glass of bourbon.

"Did you at any time see a gun or other weapon in Mr. Kingslea's possession?" Wildeman demanded.

"No sir. Absolutely not."

The porter, Rufus McGee, came next. He was a bald, fleshy man with quick eyes, an ingratiating grin, and skin as shiny as chocolate syrup. He confirmed that he had brought Kingslea the towel and the drink, then had moved his car lest it impede the police. He, too, insisted he had seen no gun in Kingslea's possession. Roy Sykes, on cross-examination, could not shake this portrait of a grieving, battered, unarmed Wade Kingslea.

"They're lying, all of them," Philip raged that night. He got precious little sympathy from Zora. She and *Time* didn't care whether Wade Kingslea was electrocuted or elected governor, only that the verdict be timely, so her magazine could splash it across the world's newsstands on Monday morning. Zora reported that Las Vegas oddsmakers were saying it was three to one that Kingslea would walk away a free man. Philip kept thinking there must be something he could do. The maid, he told himself, there had to be a way to prove they had bribed her.

But he didn't know what it was.

"Mr. Kingslea, you've heard Mr. Rhodes' testimony concerning an encounter between you and him last October 31. Would you please give your recollection of that meeting?" Stump Wildeman asked.

"Gladly," Wade Kingslea said. He dominated the courtroom. Two hundred onlookers leaned toward him involuntarily, like plants straining toward the sun.

"I drove to Skip and Jenny's house that evening, at the request of Skip, my grandson, who was detained at a political rally. I found Jenny and her father, Mr. Rhodes, about to leave. I knew there'd been some spat between Skip and Jenny, and I urged her to reconsider. She was quite cordial, but her father became abusive."

"Explain what you mean by abusive."

"I believe his words were, 'Get out of my way, you son of a bitch, or I'll knock your goddam head off.'"

"What did you do?"

"I tried to ignore him, but he swung at me. We began to wrestle, there in the doorway, and he pushed me down and pulled Jenny out to his car."

"Mr. Kingslea, did you call anything at them as they departed?"

"I'm afraid I did, Mr. Wildeman. I said something like, 'You nut, I'll make you pay for this.'"

"Did you call Jenny a 'slut'?"

"Certainly not. I loved that girl. She was like a daughter to me."

"The following Monday, the morning Jenny died, did you watch your grandson Philip on television, Mr. Kingslea?"

"Briefly, yes."

"Would you explain?"

"Perhaps I should explain that Philip's mother was divorced from my son Coyle when he was a small child. I gather that the financial arrangements were not satisfactory to his mother or him, because Philip grew up with a grudge against me. I've repeatedly extended the hand of friendship, only to be rebuffed. Recently, Philip wrote a book, which seems to imply that I had something to do with the Kennedy assassination. I confess that when I heard Philip was to be on television

I tuned in, out of curiosity. But the discussion was so outrageous that I quickly turned it off. One of my shutters was banging in the storm, and I decided that fixing it was more important than watching the boy sell his book."

"Did Philip's television appearance throw you into a rage?"

"Of course not."

"Did you shout and break things?"

"Certainly not."

"What did you do next?"

"I drove to my office. I was still upset about Skip and Jenny's quarrel, and I called Skip and arranged to meet him at his home to discuss it. I arrived early, found the front door open, and discovered Jenny struggling with an intruder."

"Describe the intruder."

"He was about six feet tall and solidly built. Perhaps thirty years old. He had reddish hair and a rough complexion, and he was wearing a dark suit, white shirt, and no tie."

"What happened next?"

"I grappled with the man. Jenny tried to help me. He pulled a gun. The three of us were struggling for the gun when it went off. Jenny fell to the floor. The man clubbed me and ran toward the back of the house. I bent over Jenny and saw that she was beyond mortal assistance. I thought the man might return to kill me, since I was a witness to the murder. I seized a candlestick from the mantelpiece, for a weapon, then I realized that my best course of action was to get to safety. I went out the front door, into the storm, passed some neighbor in the yard, warned him away, and drove to the country club to call the police."

"Was the candlestick still in your hand, as you left the house?"

"Yes, it was."

Stump Wildeman walked to the defense table, where a brown box awaited him. Wildeman opened it and, with a flourish, pulled forth a dark, metallic object that drew a gasp from onlookers, and even a cheer or two.

"Your honor, the defense would like to introduce this candlestick in evidence."

The candlestick was duly marked and entered. Stump Wildeman gently rocked it in his good hand.

"Do you know what this is made of, Mr. Kingslea?"

"Wrought iron, I believe. It's quite solid; that's why I seized it, for a weapon."

"Would you please take this candlestick, Mr. Kingslea, and stand up, and show us how you were holding it when you left the house that morning?"

Kingslea took the candlestick and stood, towering over the courtroom. Six inches of the dark metallic candlestick pointed toward the floor.

"Very interesting," Wildeman said. "I wonder, Mr. Kingslea, if during a thunderstorm a man with rain on his glasses might look at that candlestick and think . . ."

"Objection!" the district attorney roared.

"Sustained. The jury can see for itself."

"Indeed it can," Wildeman said with his choirboy grin. "Now, sir, you emerged from the house, confronted Mr. Garfield, holding the candlestick in your hand, and said what to him?"

"I can't be precise. I had just seen Jenny murdered and had been struck in the head myself, but I wanted to warn the man not to go inside. I said something like, 'Get out of here, or he'll kill you too.'"

"You tried to warn the man. Tried to save his life."

"That's correct."

"That will be all," Stump Wildeman said.

Roy Sykes put all he had into his cross-examination of Wade Kingslea. He believed that Kingslea had killed Jenny and bribed witnesses, that he was making a mockery of the legal system, and that he might, in the process, scuttle Roy's own political ambitions, but believing was not proving. For two hours Roy probed every possible hole in Kingslea's story. He employed anger, guile, sarcasm, ridicule, and contempt. He raged and thundered, he dazzled the jury and the courtroom, but when the afternoon ended Kingslea was unruffled, disdainful, untouched. "Old Roy never laid a glove on him," the courthouse crowd chortled at day's end, and the headlines proclaimed:

"GUN" A CANDLESTICK, WADE VOWS
DEFENSE RESTS: ACQUITTAL SEEN

At midnight Philip was driving out on the Mansfield Highway, southeast of Fort Worth. Ever since Zora reported his grandfather's testimony he'd been half-crazy. Zora had dragged him off to dinner at the Cattleman's Cafe, to take his mind off the case, but it hadn't worked. They're lying, he kept raging, and halfway through dinner he bolted from the restaurant, leaving behind the startled Zora, and set off on his desperate journey.

He found the little horse farm without difficulty, stopped in the driveway and was halfway to the porch when a figure emerged from the darkness and beamed a flashlight in his face. "Hold it right there, mister," a man said. "Don't make no fast moves. Who are you?"

"I'm Philip Kingslea. I want to see Roy Sykes. Who are you?"

"Deputy Tomlinson. We ain't lettin' just anybody wander up and knock on his door these days. Let's see your ID."

Philip handed over his driver's license, and the deputy took the light out of his face. "Okay, Mr. Kingslea. Roy ain't here. He might be at his office."

"I tried there."

"Then I reckon he's plumb out of touch. You the one that wrote that book?"

"Yeah."

"You hit the jackpot, buddy. Listen, I got some stories to tell that'd knock your eyes out. Maybe you and me could . . ."

Philip escaped from the deputy and drove south. He had to talk to Roy. They had to prove that the maid was lying. He came to a truck stop and decided to stop for coffee. He'd wait half an hour and try Roy's home again. He sat in his car for a moment, going over the possibilities for the millionth time. Where was the murder weapon? How could they turn the butler around? What about Rufus McGee, the porter?

He was beating his fist against the steering wheel in frustration when two men came out of the diner.

One of them was Roy Sykes, caught for an instant in the light, drawn and nervous.

The other man was stocky and had a porkpie hat pulled low over his eyes. Philip stared at him in disbelief.

The two men walked through the darkness to Roy's pickup truck, talked and nodded a moment longer, then Roy drove away.

The other man lit a cigar and started toward a Chevrolet. Philip raced after him. "Hey, wait a minute," he yelled.

Hob Wilkes spun around and in one sudden motion slammed Philip against the side of a truck. "What the hell do you want?" he demanded.

"I . . . I was looking for Roy," Philip said. "Calm down, will you?"

Hob didn't relax his grip. His narrow eyes burned six inches from Philip's. "Listen, if you want to live and do well, you forget you ever saw me. Understand?"

"Hob, we're on the same side," Philip protested.

"I'm not on anybody's side. You just forget you saw me. Okay?" He relaxed his grip and stepped back.

"Okay, okay. But give me a clue, will you? What the hell's going on?"

Hob Wilkes pulled his porkpie hat low over his eyes and scanned the parking lot before he spoke. "Just remember one thing," he said. "There's more than one damn way to skin a cat."

He climbed into his anonymous-looking Chevrolet and was swallowed up by the blackness of the Mansfield Highway.

Monday was expected to be a quiet day. Stump Wildeman's crew of legal eagles was known to have a slew of motions to introduce, all of them demanding a directed verdict of not guilty. No one expected the judge to buy those motions, but they would prove that the legal eagles were earning their princely fees, and they would assure everyone else of an easy Monday.

That was not how it turned out.

"Your honor," Roy Sykes announced. "The state recalls Rufus McGee."

As the country-club porter with the round bald head and the rich chocolate skin returned to the stand, the legal railbirds exchanged grins. What did old Roy have up his sleeve?

"Mr. McGee, last week you said that you gave Wade Kingslea a towel and a drink, that you moved his car for him, and that you saw no sign of a weapon, either in his possession or in his car. Is that correct?"

"That's what I said, yessir."

"I am going to ask you again, Mr. McGee. On the morning of November 2, when Mr. Kingslea came to Ridglea Country Club, did you see any weapon?"

Rufus McGee was an unhappy man. He squirmed, smacked his lips soundlessly, and grimaced as he struggled to frame a reply.

"Yessir, I seen one."

"Tell us where."

"After I took Mr. Kingslea his drink, he gave me twenty

dollars. I thanked him and he asked me if I wanted to make some more money. I said sure. He said for me to go move his car, and when I did, to look under the front seat and I'd find a gun and . . ."

Wade Kingslea leaped to his feet. *"That man is a goddam liar!"* he roared.

The courtroom was a babel of confusion and disbelief. The judge called for order. Stump Wildeman stood beside his client, shouting his objections. The witness was sweating, trembling, and trying his best to sink into the witness chair and disappear. The only calm person in the courtroom was Roy Sykes, who waited patiently, the most fragile of smiles on his weather-beaten face.

"Order, order, or I'll clear the courtroom," the judge shouted. "The defendant will be seated."

Kingslea dropped reluctantly into his chair. If looks could kill, Rufus McGee would have been the deadest man in Texas.

An unruffled Roy Sykes resumed his questions. The black man gasped for breath. He seemed near coronary disaster. But slowly he continued his story: "He said I'd find a gun under the seat and he wanted me to get rid of it, and he'd take real good care of me."

"What did you do?"

"I went out and moved his car, and like he said there was a gun under the seat. I went and hid it in the trunk of my car."

"Where is the gun now, Mr. McGee?"

"Bottom of Lake Worth."

"And *did* Mr. Kingslea take care of you?" Roy savored the line, as an actor might a favorite passage from Shakespeare. Roy had taken his lumps; now it was the other side's turn to sweat.

"I reckon he did. A man come by my house one night and . . ."

"Objection, objection," Stump Wildeman shouted. "Who is this man? What does he have to do with anything?"

"That's what we're trying to find out," Roy Sykes said.

"I don't believe a word of this," Wildeman declared.

The judge pounded his gavel. "The jury will ignore that exchange. One more outburst and you'll both be in contempt. Proceed, Mr. Sykes."

"So a man came by your house, Mr. McGee?"

"Yessir. He told me to come outside. It was so dark, I never see'd his face. He said, 'Where is it?' I figured I

knowed what he meant, so I said, 'In the bottom of the lake.'
He handed me an envelope and he said, 'You ever speak one
word about this, you're a dead man.' I said, 'Yessir,' and he
went away."

"When was this, Mr. McGee?"

"The day after Thanksgiving."

"And what was in the envelope?"

"Ten thousand dollars."

"And what did you do with that money?"

"Put it in a fruit jar and hid it out back of my house."

"When did you take the money out?"

"Yesterday. When I decided to tell the truth."

The district attorney produced an envelope thick with
hundred-dollar bills, which he dumped onto the defense table
with a flourish. "The state offers this money in evidence," he
announced, as the courtroom stared in wonder at the small
green mountain of bills.

"Mr. McGee, were you telling the truth last week when
you said you saw no weapon?"

"Nossir."

"Have you told the truth today?"

"Yessir."

"And do you have any motive, except to tell the truth?"

"Nossir, so help me God I doesn't."

"No further questions."

Stump Wildeman got up, his choirboy's face pinched in
rage. He paused a moment, studying his notes, letting the
witness sweat. While the porter recanted, Wildeman's staff
had been frantically gathering scraps of information on Rufus
McGee.

"Your honor," Stump began, "obviously I no longer vouch
for this witness's credibility."

"I understand your position, Mr. Wildeman."

The lawyer jabbed his nub at the porter's glistening face.
"How much did they pay you to tell these lies?"

"They didn't pay me nothing."

"Where were you from July 1947 to November 1951?"

The Negro twisted unhappily. "In prison."

"What for?"

"I stole some money."

"You stole some money?" Stump repeated witheringly.
"Did you hide that money in a fruit jar under your house?"

"Objection," Roy protested.

"Just ask your questions, counselor."

"How much money do you make at the country club?"

"Fifty dollars a week, plus tips."

"How much money did you make last year?"

"Four or five thousand dollars."

"How much did you pay for that new Pontiac you drive?"

"Objection," Roy Sykes said. "He's badgering the witness."

"Sustained."

"Isn't it a fact that you make more money bootlegging than you do at your job?"

"Objection!"

"Sustained."

"Mr. McGee, are you or are you not a bootlegger?"

The Negro mopped his brow with a red bandanna. "I sells a little whiskey sometimes," he croaked.

"Have you ever paid income tax on your whiskey money?"

McGee stared at his shoes. "Nossir."

"So you could go to federal prison for tax evasion anytime the U.S. attorney felt like sending you there, couldn't you?"

McGee gulped and nodded grimly. "Yessir."

"Is that how they got to you, Rufus? Did they tell you they'd send you back to prison if you didn't tell lies against Wade . . ."

"Objection," Roy yelled. "The jury can decide when this man was lying and when he was telling the truth. And when some of Mr. Wildeman's other witnesses were lying too!"

The judge cried out for order, reporters raced for their telephones, and when the dust settled court was adjourned.

PORTER: "I HID WADE'S GUN"

A reporter from the Chicago *Tribune* buttonholed Philip in the corridor and told him about McGee's turnabout. Philip broke away and sprinted to the hotel, where he found Zora on the phone to her editor. "Jake, it's the wildest damn trial in American history. He's the richest man ever tried for murder, and he's bought off half the witnesses, and now one of his witnesses has come unbought. Dammit, it has *got* to be your cover!"

She slammed down the phone. "It's gonna be the cover," she said. "I've got to send them five thousand words tonight."

"I'll get out of your way," Philip said.

"Hell no. Sit down. I need your help. Fix us a drink."

Zora began banging out her story. From time to time she yelled a question over her shoulder—What was Jenny's middle name? What year did Wade marry Jenny?—and he shot back an answer.

He thought it a strange charade. Zora had worked on this story for three months and had interviewed more than a hundred participants. She had the awesome resources of Time, Inc., behind her, and she would write a well-documented, vastly detailed story that would, inevitably, be the last word on the Kingslea trial for millions of people.

And she didn't have the slightest idea what was happening.

Philip thought he was starting to understand, and he could never tell her.

He thought Zora had missed the story when she glimpsed Harry Flynn at the airport and dismissed his presence in Texas as a coincidence. Zora was a good reporter, but the great reporters had an extra dimension. The great reporters were most often half-crazy. They saw conspiracies everywhere and usually they were right, even if they couldn't prove it. Philip didn't believe in coincidences anymore. Harry Flynn hadn't come to Texas for the barbecue. Harry may have loved Jenny; he sure as hell hated Wade. He was a tough, formidable enemy, and he had the even more formidable specter of the Kennedys behind him.

Philip figured that Hob Wilkes was allied with Harry, one way or another, that he was an FBI man, or maybe an ex-FBI man, who had given his allegiance to the Kennedys. It was damn sure no coincidence that Hob had met secretly with Roy Sykes on Friday night and then on Monday morning Rufus McGee flip-flopped and stuck the smoking gun in Wade Kingslea's hand. Maybe Wildeman was on to something when he asked McGee about his bootlegging and his fear of federal prosecution. Harry could have devised the plan, and Hob nailed down the deal. Rufus McGee might or might not be telling the truth about the gun, but if the jury bought his story he could send the richest man in Texas to prison, perhaps for the wrong crime, but to prison just the same. Hob Wilkes was right: there were countless ways to skin a cat, even a billionaire cat.

Judge Brownlaw's instructions to the jury took three hours, focused largely on that enigmatic phrase "reasonable doubt," and managed, in the great tradition of American jurisprudence, to leave the jury more confused than ever.

Each side had three hours for its final argument to the jury. Roy Sykes went first.

This is, Roy told the jury, a simple case of murder.

Probably Wade Kingslea did not go to Jenny's house to kill her. Probably he took his gun because he was determined not to be humiliated by her father again. But he went there overflowing with hate and fury, at his grandson Philip for belittling him on television, and at Jenny, whose affair with Philip he feared would wreck Skip's political career.

They argued. Perhaps he pulled the gun to frighten her. Perhaps it went off by accident. But once Jenny was dead, Wade Kingslea set out to avoid the consequences of his deed. He raced out into the storm, confronted a neighbor, and then realized he could not simply flee the crime. He drove to the country club, invented his tale of a redheaded intruder, and bribed the porter Rufus McGee to hide the murder weapon.

Who supported Kingslea's tale of an intruder? Only a frightened maid in his employ, who had first told police she saw no one. Who else backed his story? His wife, his grandson, his butler, his secretary. But what did disinterested witnesses say? Dusty Rhodes heard the threat, "You slut, I'll make you pay for this." The neighbor Howard Garfield reported the doubly damning words, "Get out of my way, or I'll kill you too." Rufus McGee had come forth with the true story of the missing murder weapon.

A single case, Roy repeated, complicated only by the defendant's belief that his wealth put him above the law. The jury's duty, he concluded, was to apply the law equally, to Wade Kingslea as it would to the most humble citizen of Texas.

Stump Wildeman saw the case quite differently.

He saw a vast conspiracy at work. Only you good people, he told the awed jury, stand between this conspiracy, these alien forces, and their goal not only of destroying the great Texan, Wade Kingslea, but of also corrupting the legal system and indeed befouling the good name and dignity of the great state of Texas and all its citizens, high and low.

The jurors listened openmouthed as Wildeman outlined, in bold, brilliant strokes, the scope and nature of this sinister plot against the Lone Star State.

Only a few of the prosecution witnesses were let off

lightly. Howard Garfield, the next-door neighbor, was only a confused frightened man who had misunderstood what he saw and heard in a violent storm. Dusty Rhodes, too, should be forgiven, for he was a father, crazed by drink and grief, who truly did not know what he had done and heard the night he confronted Wade Kingslea.

With Rufus McGee, however, the conspiracy began to surface like an ugly serpent. Who was to be believed? This ex-convict, this bootlegger, or a great Texan who had walked with kings and presidents? And why had Rufus McGee abruptly changed his story? Was it because, as an admitted bootlegger, he feared *federal* prosecution? Stump Wildeman relished that word *federal*, because he knew the jurors had been conditioned by a lifetime of Texas politics to view the federal government as the relentless enemy of individual freedom and states' rights.

From the perfidy of Rufus McGee it was a short step to the mystery of Philip Kingslea. Who was this young man who had fled Texas for Washington, D.C., who had worked for the Kennedys, whose book had blackened his grandfather's good name, and who now claimed to have had an adulterous affair with the martyred Jenny? What were his motives? Hatred? Revenge? Greed? And what sinister forces loomed behind him in that malign conspiracy against Wade Kingslea?

Wildeman's eyes blazed, his voice soared, his stump jabbed hypnotically. His dark tale stroked the paranoia that burns in every mortal breast: there are demons and devils, out there in the darkness, lusting to destroy us. He was playing, moreover, to the resentment many Texans felt, in the aftermath of John Kennedy's assassination, as outsiders had seemed to blame all Texans for the deed of a single madman. And finally, Wildeman was appealing to the local mythology that equated the immense wealth of a few Texans with the pride and self-esteem of all Texans. Why, indeed, were mysterious forces trying to destroy this great man, Wade Kingslea?

Roy Sykes listened grimly as Wildeman spun out his dark saga. He saw the jurors being sucked in, caught up in the defense lawyer's web, almost certainly forgetting the simple case of murder that the state had presented to them. Fortunately for Roy, the law gave him the last word, and when Wildeman sat down he quickly attacked the jury, like a medic slapping an unconscious child, trying to jolt them back to the world of money and blood, murder and reality. This is a simple case, he told them once again. The evidence is clear. A woman is dead. Do not be swayed by wealth or mythology. Remember your oath. Do your duty.

With that, the fate of Wade Kingslea was in the hands of twelve of his fellow Texans, two of whom had attended college, four of whom were women, none of whom were black or brown-skinned, one of whom had glanced at Philip's book in a bookstore, all of whom worshiped the Protestant God, three of them would not eat in restaurants that employed Negroes, one of whom still treasured the day, fourteen years before, when she had sold Wade Kingslea a box of Band-Aids in a Servall Drug Store on West Rosedale, and none of whom had ever owned a Cadillac automobile or ever expected to.

At the end of its first full day of deliberation, the jury had not reached a verdict. With each passing hour, the prospects for an acquittal seemed more bright. Juries usually hang a man fast; more time is needed to bestow innocence.

As the jury deliberated, the crowd outside the courthouse grew larger. Thousands of people overflowed the sidewalks and blocked the streets, lured by the magnets of media and celebrity and the hope of cheering Wade Kingslea when he emerged a free man.

Wade waited confidently for the verdict at Hillcrest; he was busy conferring with the architects and designers of the Wade and Olivia Kingslea Museum of World Art, which was scheduled to open in the spring.

As the jury's deliberations entered a third and then a fourth day, Philip spent most of the time in his hotel room, reading, watching television, and from time to time conferring with Zora, who was more or less permanently on the phone to her editors, insisting that a week's delay would make the Kingslea verdict an even bigger story. "Make up your minds, you sons of bitches," she would rage at the unreachable jurors who were endangering her dreamed-of cover story.

After a week of deliberation, the jurors reported themselves hopelessly deadlocked.

Judge Brownlaw refused to accept that outcome, reminded them of the time and expense that had gone into the trial, and directed them to keep trying.

Two more days passed, and the jury again declared itself permanently and irredeemably deadlocked. Judge Brownlaw angrily declared a mistrial.

As word of the outcome spread like a prairie fire, out of the courtroom, into the streets, across the city and the state, almost no one was satisfied.

Philip Kingslea, hearing the news, burst into tears, because it seemed to him that Wade, with his money and his mouth, could literally commit murder and go unpunished—unless, as he had once vowed, he himself supplied the punishment.

Zora, and other journalists, wanted a clear-cut, win-or-lose verdict to write about, were no less frustrated—Zora, too, burst into bitter tears, because of the possible loss of her cover story.

For Wade Kingslea, too, who had sought total vindication, the hung jury was a bitter disappointment.

But the thousands who filled the streets around the courthouse soon began to chant, "We want Wade! We want Wade!" Stump Wildeman, lusting for a few more precious minutes on national television, persuaded Kingslea he should confront both the crowd and the television cameras that waited outside.

As the oilman emerged from the courthouse, a cheer went up that echoed for miles.

Someone handed Kingslea a bullhorn. "I stand before you a vindicated man," he bellowed, and the multitude roared its approval.

"The forces that tried to destroy me will themselves be destroyed," Kingslea declared, and the crowd cheered again.

Suddenly, a man slipped through the circle of reporters, photographers, and policemen who surrounded the oilman. Kingslea's eyes widened as he recognized Dusty Rhodes and saw the silver-plated .32 in his hand.

Shots, screams, and shouts filled the air. Wade Kingslea tumbled to the sidewalk, a crimson oval spreading across his shirt. Policemen drew their guns. "Get a doctor!" someone cried. Children were trampled as panic engulfed the street.

Somehow, in the confusion, Dusty Rhodes escaped.

Philip spent the evening drinking with some reporters who were as confused as he was. Word came from the hospital that Kingslea was not badly hurt. Two shots had miraculously missed him, and the third had passed through the fatty part of his upper arm, producing a great deal of blood but no great harm.

"The son of a bitch is too mean to die," a reporter grumbled.

Another reporter speculated that the only person ever likely to serve time in the Kingslea case was Dusty Rhodes, the dead woman's father, who was probably the most decent character in the whole rotten mess.

Two days later, Philip was asleep in his hotel room when Zora banged on his door. He awoke reluctantly and let her in.

"He's gone," she cried. "Vanished."

Philip groaned. "Relax. They'll find Dusty. He'll probably turn himself in."

"Not Dusty, dammit! Wade. *He's* gone."

Philip stared at her. "What?"

"Wade Kingslea has flown the coop—and with me on deadline!"

"He's at Hillcrest, isn't he?"

"No, dammit. Livie called the police. She's afraid Dusty has kidnapped him or killed him."

"How could Dusty get near him? He probably flew to Mexico or somewhere."

"He's under court order not to leave Texas. They've got marshals watching his private planes and he hasn't been seen at the airports."

"Then he's shacked up with his girl friend."

"No, I've talked to her. And I've talked to his chief of security, too. They don't know where he is. All they know is that he's gone and his Fleetwood is gone. It's like he just up and headed for the hills."

Philip thought about it for a while and the answer came to him. He started to get dressed. He guessed he owed Zora a break.

"Come on," he told her. "I'll take you to him."

CHAPTER FIVE

He drove northwest all afternoon, across the desolate prairie.

Zora slept most of the way, then awoke as they passed through Goodwill's strip of restored hotels and saloons. "Where are we?" she asked, rubbing her dark eyes in disbelief. "It looks like a movie set."

"We're almost there," he told her.

A gate blocked the road to the Museum of Oil History. Philip left the car and climbed over the gate. Zora got out and saw the old oil derrick looming ahead of them. "Jesus Christ, what's that?" she exclaimed.

"It's the past," he said. "Come on."

She scrambled after him, clutching her camera and notebook, and they hurried toward the museum.

Halfway there, Philip saw his grandfather atop the derrick. He looked like God up there, hunched over the railing, gazing out over the rolling land.

Will Clinkscale rushed out of the museum. His eyes were red and he smelled of whiskey. "Go back, Philip," he cried. He raised one trembling hand, like a guardian angel. "Don't bother him now. Leave him be."

"I have to talk to him."

"He's not in a talking mood. He don't much care if he lives or dies."

"He'll talk to me," Philip insisted.

Zora was quietly snapping photographs of Wade Kingslea silhouetted against the wide, untroubled sky. "I'm going up there with you," she said.

"No you're not," Philip said firmly. "Stay here."

Zora angrily waited with Will Clinkscale while Philip ascended the perfectly restored Louella Booker #2 derrick. He stepped onto the platform, high above the earth.

"I thought you'd be here," Philip said. "It was the only place that made sense."

"I've always been here," Kingslea said. "I was born here. I'll die here."

He did not look around. He was wearing a pearl-gray suit, boots, a string tie, and a white Stetson. His right arm was in a sling.

Philip leaned against the railing, a few feet down from his grandfather. "You'll outlive us all," he said.

"This derrick is on the exact spot of the original, you know," Kingslea said. "I climbed up here one morning, nearly forty-five years ago, to fix a guy wire in a storm, and that's when my gusher came in. I felt the earth tremble and the derrick start to shake. I thought I was going to die. But I leaped for the guy wire and slid down it. It tore my hands to pieces." He opened his big, gnarled hands and stared at the old scars that crisscrossed them.

"The derrick exploded and tossed me up like a leaf. I landed in mud and it saved my life. God saved my life. I believed that then and I believe it now. Despite the atheists and Communists, I still believe in God and his plan, and I know he saved my life for a purpose that day."

"What purpose?" Philip asked.

"That I would do good on this earth. That I would be a leader of men. That I would help this nation stand firm against the forces of evil and anarchy. And I did. When we were threatened by Hitler, Roosevelt called me to Washington, and I went, and we defeated him—it was oil that defeated Hitler, you know. Eisenhower called me too, just before he went to Korea. Settle that damn war, I told him. Who the hell needs Korea? Nixon wanted my advice too. And LBJ now. They all do."

"Ask LBJ who the hell needs South Vietnam," Philip said.

The old oilman scowled. "No, they won't want me in Washington anymore, not after this trial."

"You weren't convicted of anything."

"I didn't have to be. You and your Kennedy friends did your hatchet job well. You put a cloud over my head. Mine and Skip's too."

"I think you'll both survive."

Kingslea pulled out a cigar and lit it with a gold lighter. The sun kissed the western horizon. The old man smiled.

"When we were drilling this well, Fanny used to drive out

and bring me a picnic lunch. Fanny O'Brien she was then. She was young and full of piss and vinegar. A damn fine woman. I should have married her, but I was too bullheaded to know it. So I went to Fort Worth and met Livie, and she was rich and beautiful and haughty, and I thought I had to have her."

Kingslea shook his head. "Livie's a hell of a woman, too, but it's hard living with a queen bee. Sometimes a man just wants to kick off his shoes and tell stories and maybe have his back rubbed—you could be like that with Fanny."

"I liked her," Philip said. "I used to see her sometimes in Dallas. We'd talk about writing and she always encouraged me."

Kingslea chewed his cigar. "I heard you were snooping around, asking if I killed some men in Goodwill."

"That's true."

"You should have asked me. You passed the farmhouse where it happened on your way here. A big place with a windmill beside it. There were three of them. One was a big scar-faced fellow, a killer. I'd had a run-in with him on the train coming up, and my mistake was not killing him then. When he got to Goodwill he hooked up with two drummers out of St. Louis and they tried to cheat me and Billy Festus out of our field. They lured us into that farmhouse and got the drop on us. They'd have killed us, but Billy jerked a Derringer out of his boot and gut-shot the scar-faced one. I finished him off, then I chased down the other two. They begged me not to kill them. Jesus God, what was I supposed to do? Turn them over to the sheriff? It was kill or be killed in those days. I didn't beg for mercy when they had the drop on me, and I didn't dispense mercy when the shoe was on the other foot. The world's a jungle, Philip. Perhaps you've learned that by now. We're wild animals, all of us. We try to love, but we have to kill."

The rim of the sun disappeared below the horizon. A nightingale sang in the distance.

"I read Christina's diary not long ago," Philip said. "Will gave it to me. I was glad to learn about her."

Kingslea's face softened. "She was a fine, brave woman," he said. "If there's a part of us that's gentle and good, it came from her."

"She was a good writer, too. Sometimes I think she's inside me, a muse."

Kingslea nodded. "She's part of us both, and so is Shavano, the Indian who raped her. My grandfather. Your great-great-grandfather. He was a Ute warrior, the son of a chief. The Utes were brave men, fighting back against overwhelming odds."

"She didn't know who was the father of her child," Philip said. "Shavano or her husband, Ebon Pridemore."

"I've never doubted it," his grandfather said. "I've felt Shavano inside me. I've felt his strength and his anger and his courage. He told Christina that he would die but that he would live through her, and he has. He lives in you and me."

Kingslea gave his grandson a sidelong glance. "Have you ever killed a man?"

"No."

"It's not so terrible a thing. It's part of life on this earth. What was it the poet said? 'Each man kills the thing he loves.' There are many ways of killing, he wrote. The coward does it with a kiss, and the brave man with a sword."

"Or perhaps a .44."

The oilman scowled and puffed his cigar.

"Since we're talking about killing, let me ask you something," Philip said.

"Go ahead."

"Were you involved in the Kennedy assassination?"

Kingslea's eyes flashed. "You wrote the book—you tell me."

"I think you had something to do with it. There had to be more than one assassin, and that means a professional job, with plenty of money behind it."

Kingslea tossed his cigar into the twilight. "I'll say this. I wouldn't have been ashamed to have done it. He was turning the country over to the Reds."

Philip had tried to be detached, a reporter, but he felt his anger rising. "What about Jenny? Did you kill her? Was she turning the country over to the Reds too?"

Kingslea's temper flared too. "I'll tell you one damn thing. That black son of a bitch was lying when he said he hid a gun for me. Why would I entrust my freedom to a reprobate like that?"

"Why would he lie?"

"Because your friend Harry Flynn paid him to lie—paid him or scared him. He and his Kennedy friends still control the Justice Department. They probably told him they'd put him in prison for life if he didn't lie about me. The Kennedys are determined to destroy me and everything I stand for."

"You paid the maid to lie, didn't you?" Philip demanded, but the older man ignored his question.

"You were one of my mistakes, young man. I let you get away from me and you turned against me. My own flesh and blood, working with my enemies to destroy me. That's a terrible crime, to turn against your own flesh and blood."

"I never tried to destroy you. You'll destroy yourself. If you helped kill Kennedy, or if you killed Jenny, you deserve to be destroyed."

"You didn't prove a thing," the old man raged. "You bribed a witness and you got your hung jury but you didn't prove it. But you've dragged my good name in the mud. You've put the mark of Cain on me. The world won't remember all that I accomplished, all that I did for America, only the lies in your book and the lies in that courtroom."

"It was a fair trial. It was more than you gave Jenny."

Kingslea turned to face Philip. His eyes were blazing. "I said I'd have it all. I stood here on this derrick and felt the oil blasting up from the earth and I swore I'd have everything I'd ever dreamed of. But now you and your lying, fornicating, race-mixing friends have taken it all from me. You stole my good name, do you hear? I could have made Skip president but you stole that too. You've torn down everything I spent a lifetime building up. Damn you, I hope you're satisfied!"

The old man was raving, sputtering; his white hair blew across his face and his eyes blazed like prairie fire. Philip stared long and deep into his grandfather's face and it was as if he'd never seen him before. He thought, quite suddenly and absolutely, that the old man was mad. Whatever he had been before, he was no longer deserving of fear or anger or hate, only of pity.

"Come on, let's go down," Philip said. "It's getting dark."

"Did you think I'd give up without a fight?" Kingslea thundered. "Did you think I'd sit around and wait for the Kennedys to put me in prison or for Dusty Rhodes to kill me? Did you think Wade Kingslea wouldn't fight back? You can't destroy me! No one can destroy me!"

His good arm shot out and he seized Philip by the throat.

"It's you who'll be destroyed," Kingslea cried, and he pushed Philip back over the railing. Philip struggled to free himself but his grandfather's grip was like steel.

Far below them, Will Clinkscale yelled, "No, no!" and Zora Gilbert snapped photographs as the oilman, silhouetted in the twilight, pushed Philip farther back over the wooden railing.

"You can't destroy me!" Kingslea howled. Philip fought back, flailing with his hands, trying to twist free, and then with a cry he felt the railing start to break loose.

"You can't destroy me—I'll live forever!" Kingslea cried, and the two of them plunged into space.

Zora got it all, frame after frame, and when the two men crashed to the earth she ran forward, with Will Clinkscale trailing behind her, and knelt beside them, there at the foot of Louella Booker #2.

"Oh Lord, are they dead?" Will asked.

Zora wasn't sure. The old man lay motionless, but Philip, whose body had fallen atop his grandfather's, seemed to be breathing. Zora, gripping her pencil and notebook, leaned her face close to his. "What happened?" she demanded. "Why did he do it?"

Philip's eyes opened. He felt a terrible pain in his leg. He saw Zora's anxious face, his grandfather's broken body, the oil derrick looming above them, and high up in the northern sky, a single bright star.

"Mythology," he whispered. "It's all mythology."

CHAPTER SIX

The official opening of the Wade Kingslea Museum of World Art took place on a day of cool breezes and warm sunshine, of wildflowers and soft blue skies, the sort of lush, lazy spring day that Texans claim for theirs alone.

The museum itself, a soaring glass and sandstone building atop a low hill, near the Will Rogers Coliseum grounds, was everywhere hailed as a masterpiece. Coyle Kingslea had seen

to that. His father had given him increasing control over the
Kingslea Foundation, which directed both the museum and a
hundred-million-dollar program of medical research, and
Coyle had employed the finest architects and curators to en-
sure that the Kingslea Museum was second to none in its size
on earth.

Indeed, although this day honored Wade and Livie, and
their museum, it was in large part Coyle's day. He had
planned the ceremony carefully, determined that this would be
a day of reconciliation, an end to mourning, a new start for
their deeply divided family.

The day began, inevitably, with a parade, complete with
floats, brass bands, and mounted horsemen—Coyle made that
bow to Cowtown's past. Next came a barbecue lunch for
thousands, catered by Mr. Walter Jetton himself. By early afternoon, three dozen dignitaries and family members had
gathered on the speaker's platform before the museum, and
thousands of art lovers, schoolchildren, and curiosity seekers
were gathered in front of them, perched on folding chairs or
stretched out on the soft grass.

At precisely two o'clock the nation's most celebrated
preacher, Billy Graham, stepped forward to invoke God's
blessing on the new museum. The Reverend Dr. Graham, in
particular, asked God to bless "Thy departed servant, our beloved Wade Kingslea," and with perfect tact did not enumerate
the details of his servant's departure.

Following the prayer, Livie Kingslea welcomed the public
to the new museum. Livie, regal and magnificent in her mid-
sixties, declared that the museum was a monument to her late
husband's vision, his generosity, and his love of his native
state. She had the good sense to be brief, and she was rewarded
by a heartfelt standing ovation. For the first time in her
life, Livie was beloved, for she was rich, proud, and tough,
and those were qualities her fellow Texans gladly honored.

Skip Kingslea was the next speaker. This appearance was
important to the young, widowed first-term congressman, for
Skip still dreamed of higher office. At first he had feared that
Jenny's murder and his grandfather's trial had destroyed his
political future, but all the polls said that those fears were
premature. Scandal and violence had only endeared him to the
voters of Texas—if the polls could be trusted, Skip might
soon be running hard for senator or governor.

The crowd cheered wildly as Skip proudly introduced the

day's main speaker, the President of the United States, Texas' own Lyndon Johnson.

The spring air exploded with howls and rebel yells as the long-legged, big-eared, grinning Johnson strode forward. He kissed Livie, bear-hugged Skip, and waved his arms delightedly to the roaring crowd, while some of his more frenzied admirers threw their hats in the air and set off fireworks.

Finally the commotion died down, and Lyndon Johnson proceeded to deliver a very fine speech.

Art is vital to a nation, he declared, as vital as farms or banks or factories. The United States stood poised at the brink of a golden age, he vowed, and it would be the artists and poets, the painters of pictures and dreamers of dreams, who would point the way to greatness.

As Philip Kingslea watched Lyndon Johnson deliver the speech, he found himself unexpectedly moved. It was easy to be cynical about Johnson, and yet he did not doubt that some part of the big Texan believed every word he spoke. In little more than a year as president, Johnson had earned the respect of skeptics like Philip. His brilliant, landslide victory over Barry Goldwater had demolished the political right, perhaps for a generation, perhaps forever, and swept in the most progressive Congress since the New Deal. Johnson stood astride the political world like a Colossus, the astounding Texas Populist who already had enacted historic legislation on civil rights, education, and medical care. It seemed there was truth to his rhetoric: the nation might truly be entering a golden era, a time of unity and progress and prosperity. If there was any cloud on the horizon, it was the U.S. involvement in Vietnam, but surely, with the election past, with Congress eating out of his hand, Johnson would soon bring home the troops, so no pointless foreign adventure could endanger his dreamed-of Great Society.

As Johnson spoke on—too long, but forgivably so, before a friendly audience on a glorious day—Philip let his eyes sweep across the men and women who shared the platform with him.

He glanced briefly at Livie, who had no more desire to share a stage with him than he did with her. But he had come to please his father, and because he thought Coyle was right when he said they were all Kingsleas, they had all been actors in the same sordid drama, and they owed it to themselves to salvage some dignity, some show of unity, from the wreckage of two deaths and much heartbreak.

He looked at his father with pride and love. After fifty years in Wade Kingslea's shadow, Coyle had seemed to grow younger and stronger in these past months. He was silver-haired and serene now, a very rich man who did not care about money, a survivor. Coyle had survived his father, and M&I, and a quarter century of alcoholism. He had been broken and torn, scorned, humiliated (fragments of poetry flashed through Philip's mind: *Though they be mad they shall be sane, Though they sink through the sea they shall rise again),* and now, with his father gone, and himself at the helm of one of America's great foundations, he was determined to redeem his life. As Lyndon Johnson waved both arms, furiously proclaiming his devotion to the arts, father and son exchanged a glance. Coyle winked, Philip winked back, and they broke into broad, happy grins.

Philip scanned the crowd, looking for a late arrival, someone who was supposed to meet him here. He didn't see her, but he spotted Dusty Rhodes in the front row of spectators, his face still ravaged by grief but willing to make peace with the survivors of the man he thought had killed his beloved daughter. Perhaps Dusty's presence had been made easier by the fact (and this had been Philip's idea, phoned to Coyle from his hospital bed) that there would be, at the very heart of the new museum, a Jenny Kingslea Memorial Garden. Did it matter? Philip liked to think it did, liked to think that sometimes people would come to that garden, read her name and understand that Jenny, in her day, had been a flower.

Eve Kingslea and her children, Andy and Gillian, were at the far end of the platform. Eve looked mildly amused by all the hoopla, but her children were awed by the president and the Texas-size spectacle around them. Both teenagers wore small blue-and-white Peace buttons. Andy had called Philip the week before and said that he and Gillian didn't think they could share a stage with President Johnson without some expression of protest over the war in Vietnam. At the same time, Andy admitted, they didn't want to disturb a ceremony at which they were guests. Philip had suggested the Peace buttons as a positive way to make their point.

He watched the two teenagers as they watched Johnson, eager to believe his promises of peace and progress, and he thought suddenly of Christina Pridemore, his gentle Quaker great-great-grandmother. He thought her unconquerable spirit still lived in young people like Andy and Gillian, that they were the hope of the world, the ones who might truly build a great society.

Louise was sitting beside Philip, with Alice on the other side of her. Philip had insisted that she be there, as the price of his own appearance, and Coyle had gladly agreed, despite Livie's objections. Philip looked at his mother, a handsome woman of almost fifty now, and thought that she too was a survivor. She had survived Coyle's drinking and Al's misdeeds and found happiness with Asa in middle age. That afternoon, as they walked toward the speaker's platform, Philip and Alice and Louise had found themselves surrounded by people with autograph books and cameras. A few people had wanted Philip's autograph, or for him to sign copies of his novel, but most of the attention had focused on Alice. She had won two golf tournaments already that spring and had her picture on the cover of *Sports Illustrated,* and topped things off by getting engaged to a likable young giant who played end for the Dallas Cowboys. As Louise and her two children mounted the platform, with Alice's teenage fans still cheering behind them, she suddenly burst into tears. "I'm so proud of you both," she sobbed, dabbing at her blue eyes with a Kleenex.

"Mom, we're proud of *you,*" Alice said, and the three of them embraced, alone for a moment in their private celebration.

Lyndon Johnson finished his speech, declaring, "We cherish the arts because we cherish the human spirit!" and stepped back waving as the audience stood and cheered and the TCU band began to play "The Eyes of Texas."

All at once, the crowd of thousands joined in singing their state song, not in the lively tempo of football games but slowly, as an anthem, a hymn. Philip did not sing, but he was moved by the words, words he had heard a thousand times before, words that were a promise to some Texans and a curse to others:

> The eyes of Texas are upon you
> All the livelong day
> The eyes of Texas are upon you
> You cannot get away

The song was right, of course. You could not get away.
You tried to escape the past but it stayed with you, hot on your
heels, until finally you turned and confronted it.

> Do not think you can escape them
> At night or early in the morn
> The eyes of Texas are upon you
> Till Gabriel blows his horn

He gazed out at the city's jagged, glittering skyline, at this
rich, rough, restless city that had shaped him, and if part of
him cursed it, another part of him felt a new, unexpected affection for it.

He had just emerged from Harris Hospital, where he had
slowly recovered from the fall that had killed Wade Kingslea
and would have killed him, too, had he not landed atop his
grandfather.

During his weeks in the hospital he was flooded with cards
and calls and visits from people he'd forgotten, kids he'd
known in school, friends of his mother's, people who said
they were proud of his success and were praying for his recovery. They came out of nowhere, out of the past, people who
seemed genuinely to care about him, and he realized that for
years he'd judged the city by a few people who were rich and
obnoxious, people who were fucked-up by too much money as
surely as others were fucked-up by too little, and forgotten the
greater number who were decent and kind. He even had a
bedside visit from Skip Kingslea, and if it was awkward, if he
suspected Skip's motives, it was still the right thing for him to
have done. He wondered if, someday, he and Skip might try
to understand each other.

A close look at death is not the most joyous of experiences,
but it may not be an entirely negative experience either; there
are lessons to be learned. Philip's left him with a glowing
realization of how precious, and how precarious, life is. He
remembered Chrissie telling him you had to love all of life,
love winos and bag ladies, love stray cats and tax collectors,
and he had laughed and called her a cockeyed optimist. Now
he understood. During his first weeks in the hospital he fell in
love with everyone who entered his room, nurses, doctors,
janitors, whatever. He wanted to touch them, to watch them
smile, to listen to their stories late at night, so he would not be
alone in the darkness knowing he ought to be dead. He still

had his walls, his defenses, he would always have those, but he thought they weren't so impregnable now, he thought he was ready to let the world a little closer to his heart.

When he could walk with crutches, Zora came to visit, all aglow because her exclusive coverage of the death of Wade Kingslea had won her a Pulitzer nomination. Philip had taken her for a night on the town, several nights in fact. He took her to barbecue joints like Sammy's and Angelo's, and to Joe T. Garcia's and his other favorite Mexican restaurants, and out to the Jacksboro Highway to honky-tonks where they still played the old Hank Williams and Lefty Frizzell records, and to cool, dark bars around TCU where you could still bop to the Clovers or snuggle to the Platters. Sometime that week he realized he was home, like it or not, that no fancy French dinner in Manhattan would ever make his mouth water like a plate of Texas barbecue, that no Broadway extravaganza would ever thrill him like Hank singing "Jambalaya," that no Hollywood goddess would be as beautiful as the memory of Jenny twirling in her cheerleader's costume. Those things were part of him, and there was no escape, at night or early in the morn, till Gabriel finally blew his horn.

Lyndon Johnson, one arm draped around Livie and the other around his wife, Lady Bird, was still leading the crowd in chorus after chorus of "The Eyes of Texas."

Philip was restless. There would be a VIP reception next, inside the museum, but he didn't care about that. He kept scanning the crowd.

Then he saw a cab stop, over on West Lancaster. He grinned as he watched her get out, wearing a full skirt and a bright peasant blouse, swinging her bag, and march confidently toward the museum.

Philip whispered good-bye to his mother, mounted his crutches, and eased himself down off the platform.

He hobbled across the grass and she came running to him, arms outstretched, skirt flying. Then Chrissie threw her arms around him, laughing and crying all at once.

"My God, you look so wonderful," she kept saying.

"You too," he said, and it was true. Chrissie's year in Peru had thinned and toughened her; she was a tall, brown, strong, lovely young woman.

"Let's get out of here," he said and they started back toward the street. The crowd kept singing behind them and it was like a final curtain, the end of something, time to be moving on. Since his grandfather's death, the city had changed for Philip. It no longer seemed menacing or hostile; it was an American city, with all the ugliness and violence and inequity that implied, but with its bright spots, too, and more real and vital and fun than most cities. Still, he burned to leave it now. Chrissie had a job with the Peace Corps in Washington, and a new apartment in Georgetown, and they were going to try living together again.

"When do you get off those?" she asked.

"In a couple of weeks. I'll have a limp."

She hugged him. "Like Lord Byron."

He hailed a cab and told the driver to take them to the airport. As they moved east through the city, Chrissie snuggled beside him and his thoughts went again to the past.

"I remember leaving here for the first time, eleven years ago," he told her. "Hitchhiking to college in Tennessee with fifty dollars in my pocket. I told my mother I'd come back someday and show all those rich sons of bitches who'd looked down on me in high school. The crazy thing is, now I'm back and I don't want to show anybody anything."

"Once you can, you don't have to," Chrissie said.

"I just want to get on with my life. Everything stopped last fall, when Jenny died, but now it's time to start up again. I've got a new book I want to write—I can't wait to tell you about it. My God, there's a whole world out there. Cities I want to see and music I want to hear and wine I want to drink and books I want to write and mistakes I want to make and . . ."

"And somewhere there's a nice little house you want to buy," Chrissie said. "Where you can settle down with a good woman and make babies and have a dog and cultivate your garden and do all those dumb things you swore you'd never do."

He squeezed her hand and began to laugh. "Oh sure," he said. "The dumb things too. We'll get around to them, one of these days, won't we?"